NOT CURRENTLY EVIL

CONSORTIUM OF CHAOS: BOOK SIX

Elizabeth Gannon

Books by Elizabeth Gannon

The Consortium of Chaos Series
Yesterday's Heroes
The Son of Sun and Sand
The Guy Your Friends Warned You About
Electrical Hazard
The Only Fish in the Sea
Coming Soon: Not Currently Evil

The Mad Scientist's Guide to Dating
Broke and Famous

Other Books:
Travels with a Fairytale Monster
Nobody Likes Fairytale Pirates
Captive of a Fairytale Barbarian

The Snow Queen

You may also enjoy books by Elizabeth's sister, Cassandra Gannon:

The Elemental Phases Series
Warrior from the Shadowland
Guardian of the Earth House
Exile in the Water Kingdom
Treasure of the Fire Kingdom
Queen of the Magnetland
Magic of the Wood House
Coming Soon: Destiny of the Time House

A Kinda Fairytale Series
Wicked Ugly Bad
Beast in Shining Armor
The Kingpin of Camelot
Best Knight Ever
Coming Soon: Happily Ever Witch

Other Books
Not Another Vampire Book
Vampire Charming
Love in the Time of Zombies
Once Upon a Caveman

While at Disney World once, years back, I was standing in line behind a little girl who was wearing a pink and sparkly princess dress and carrying a Pirates of the Caribbean doll. She was telling her mother about her future, apparently having given the matter some thought. "I won't really have to work when I grow up," she told her mother seriously, "because I'm going to be a famous assassin."

Kid in line in front of me at the Magic Kingdom that day, this book is dedicated to you.

You're awesome.

Don't ever change.

Unless… you know, it's part of your parole or something.

"Now if I do what I do not want to do, it is no longer I who do it, but it is sin living in me that does it."

- Romans 7:20

Prologue

"AS A RULE, WE GO ABOUT WITH MASKS, WE GO ABOUT
LOOKING HONEST, AND WE ARE ABLE TO CONCEAL
OURSELVES ALL THROUGH THE DAY."

- Mark Twain

3 YEARS AGO

Angela R. Ceigh, AKA "Harlot," stared down in total disinterest at the frolicking ducklings in front of her. She had never had anything in particular *against* ducks, but in the current circumstance, they did little to improve her rather foul mood. In fact, the more she stared at them, the more irritated with them she became. She was really starting to *hate them*.

Fucking ducklings.

She let out a long breath and leaned back in the uncomfortable plastic chair, looking up at the water stains which dotted the dirty ceiling.

Her honorary uncle, Hector Hopper, AKA "The Roach," pushed the duck puzzle in question out of the way. "Christ, I *hate* that fucking thing."

"Then why do you *always* have it with you whenever I come to visit?" She asked in confusion.

"Take a guess." The old man gestured to their surroundings. The interior of the visiting room in the Mesa Verde Super-Person Retirement Castle wasn't exactly the most luxurious of accommodations that someone could hope for. In fact, it was basically just a plain white room with a dozen folding tables and rusty metal chairs. "The ducklings are the only thing to do in this goddamn hellhole." He looked around the room suspiciously. "Closest thing we got to currency on the inside." He tapped the box to the puzzle. "There ain't a wrinkled motherfucker in this place that wouldn't *kill* to have The Ducks with them, girly." He pulled the object closer. "But they ain't getting them today." He raised his voice and glared at his fellow residents. "*You hear me, you grasping sons-a-bitches!?! MINE!!!*"

She rolled her eyes and started picking at the scrapes and gouges which marred the surface of the dingy tabletop. "So, what do you think I should do?"

He looked confused. "About what?" His eyes narrowed in suspicion. "If *you're* after The Ducks now, you can just..."

"No," she cut him off before he could finish the paranoid threat, "I don't want your stupid puzzle." She made a face at him. "I mean about the Agletarians. Someone's going to have to do something about them."

"Why don't ya quit your bitching and do it yourself then?" He threw his hands wide in exasperation. "Any villainess worth a damn should be able to handle a half dozen paper pushers, right? I killed enough foreign diplomats in my day to fill the goddamn UN."

"Because I'm not an assassin, for one. I *steal* things, not *kill* things." She let out another sigh. "For *another*, I'd be recognized before I ever got into their embassy. And finally, I have an exam in college that I still need to study for. If I miss it, my whole GPA will crash and burn. And *you know* Syd will never let me hear the end of that, and it'll all end with my professors tied to chairs while he beats better grades out of them."

Hector took on a wizened tone. "I said it before and I'll say it again: education is just another route to the commie infested waters of intellectualism."

She ignored that. "I just don't know what I'm going to do, Uncle Hector. We need someone who can get in there and get the job done, and we just don't have anyone who won't be recognized, and who can also handle themselves against a small army." She ran her hand through her hair. "But if we *don't* do something, they'll send someone else to kill us. Frankly, I'm still not entirely sure why the last assassin they sent is being so cooperative."

"Who'd they send?"

She shrugged. "Big guy. Purple hair. Super strong. I think his name's... Hazard something?"

Hector shook his head. "Never heard of him. Local boy?"

"Brit."

He scoffed in annoyance. "Fucking foreigners coming in and stealing *our* good hired killer jobs." He tapped his finger against the tabletop, obviously believing himself to be making an important point. "Back in the *old days*, that contract would have gone to an *American* psychopath."

"Yes, that was my main complaint about someone sending a killer to murder my father in front of me, as well: the killer's *accent*." She rolled her eyes again, long used to her uncle's insanity. Hector hated *everyone,* which, unsurprisingly, was making his retirement a *nightmare* for everyone. The man was habitually incapable of letting things go, no matter how minor they were or how many decades had gone by since. "Can we just forget about the increasingly multinational nature of costumed crime-for-hire and refocus on my *real* problem, please?"

Hector lit his cigar. "Christ on a pogo stick, do I have to do *everything*?"

She shook her head. "You can't smoke in here."

He ignored her. "What's your daddy paying you for if you can't handle one little suicide mission? Your whole generation is failing in the evil business and it's because you have no follow-through. No wonder all the best evil is now getting outsourced overseas."

At the table across from them, another resident in the retirement home looked up. "Her generation is failing in the evil business because they've finally seen the light and realize that crime doesn't pay."

Hector turned to glare at the eavesdropper, something akin to disgusted horror on his face that the man would even speak to them. "Hey, was I fucking talking to *you*, Gary? Huh?" He sounded annoyed. "Do I hassle you when your grandkids come in here and screech and scream about what a great Cape you were? Do I tell them what a fucking pussy you were in the War? No. So SHUT UP!" He refocused on Harlot. "Where was I? Oh yes. Like I was saying, I know someone who can help you with this. He specializes in… *unorthodox* warfare." Hector's evil smile grew, obviously imagining some horrible scene he had witnessed firsthand and was now just itching to tell her about in extreme and unnecessarily gory detail. "Best I've ever seen at sabotage, demolitions, espionage, infiltration, assassinations… You name it. All that ninja shit I can't spell. Ice water running through his fucking veins, this guy. Can kill a man just by *staring at him hard*. One soulless motherfucker. Evil straight down to the bone." He took a puff from his cigar, completely ignoring the warnings on the oxygen tank which was hooked to his wheelchair. "Sort of an adopted kid of my idiot fucking Cape brother, Roy– may God ensure his loser soul continues burning in Hell– but I try not to hold that against him, because he's family."

"Can you put that out, please?" She pointed at the cigar. "You know it's not good for *either* of us."

Roach made a face, but obediently extinguished his cigar on the warning label affixed to the side of the oxygen tank. "Happy?"

At some point in her life, that type of behavior probably would have surprised Harlot. Sadly, she'd known her uncle too long. "*Ecstatic*, Uncle Hector. Thank you." She let out a weary sigh and tried to get back on topic. "You'd really want to risk your nephew on a suicide mission?"

"Aw, we ain't close." Hector waved a hand in dismissal. "Doesn't even talk to me much; wants to do his own shit. A 'crazed loner' type of deal-y, works alone, only calls when he's drunk or suicidal. But it wouldn't be risking a nephew. Niece, either."

She stared at him in confusion. "Huh? What does that mean?"

"It means I got no fucking clue which the kid is. Never even seen his face. Even when he was young he preferred masks and baggy clothes. Could be a niece, a nephew, a fucking opossum from *Jupiter*, for all I know." He shrugged. "Don't matter much in my book; a badass is a badass and it's none of my business. When you get stabbed in the throat with a goddamned katana, you don't exactly ask the ninja fucker who did it if he's got cunt or cock, now do you?" He laughed at the very idea. "Besides, it won't be a risk. Walk in the park.

12

Kid's earned his villain chops... mostly by chopping people up." He chuckled in amusement again, obviously thinking back on *another* blood-soaked scene of carnage and mayhem he'd witnessed. "Used to worry about him turning to Caping, but he's *more* than proven he's got a pair. Waaaaay tougher than Roy ever was— may his torment never end." He set about searching his pockets for another cigar, forgetting about her constant dire warnings of lung cancer and assurances that smoking near the oxygen would turn the entire building into an explode-y fireball of death. "'Honorable' is just another way of saying 'asshole,' girl. Let me tell you something, if you want to *truly* be at your best, you need to forget all about..."

Harlot cut him off, not needing to hear his latest crazy idea about how she *should* be behaving. "So what's his power?"

"Depends on when you ask him. It changes by the day. He's a stone cold villain though... just crazier than a shithouse rat on bath salts." He made a swirling "insane" motion at his temple. Typically, her uncle described truly delusional people as "a visionary" or "a dude/bitch that makes *sense, for once,*" so for *him* to recognize someone else's insanity was very rare indeed. And terrifying. If *Hector Hopper* said you were nuts, you must be REALLY friggin' nuts. Like more nuts than the Planters factory. Like "squirrels must follow you home from the park," kind of nuts. "You want someone to terrorize your enemies, *he's* your guy." Her uncle assured her. "He'll take care of your little political spat for you... for a *price*. And it won't be cheap. The best never is."

"How much?"

"I'll see if I can get you the family discount." He placed the duck puzzle on his lap and started to wheel himself from the room, eyes scanning the other residents, waiting for them to make a play for his prize. "Goes by... *'Multifarious.'*"

****

Two days later, Multifarious was standing on the street in front of the Agletarian embassy, insane and alone and planning a series of horrible murders.

All in all, it was a fairly ordinary night.

A lesser assassin would have brought a team of mercs, but Mull worked alone now. She wasn't about to let anyone that close, ever again. She'd had her fill of partners. And, honestly, humanity. Which was fine, given her job. Generally speaking, "hired killer" was a bad profession to go into if you were a people person. On the other hand, having "nothing but irritated contempt for everyone" was definitely something that every killer should include on their resume.

Most solo assassins would have gone all ninja on this bitch; sneaking in by zip-lining onto the roof or tunneling in from the sewer, but Mull had never been a fan of unnecessary steps. That was just bullshit mercenaries did to make themselves look cool.

There were quicker and easier ways to get into a building, especially when there was a party going on.

If there was one thing all evil rich people loved, it was parties. There were a *shitload* of galas, masquerades, and charity benefits in this town, all of which provided the perfect cover. Someone really should tell them one day that if they'd only stop having parties, none of their shit would get stolen, killed, kidnapped, or blown up.

But no one had asked Mull for advice on that yet, so she didn't bother to tell them.

Personally, Mull had wanted to simply blow up the entire building. No fuss, no muss. The targets would be eliminated and the explosion would be *awesome*. But her clients had insisted that there be no collateral damage. Which was stupid. Why would you hire someone like Mull if you were *at all* worried about a little bloodshed? It was like hiring Monet and then complaining about all the damn water lilies.

Everyone wanted to stand in the way of her art.

Philistines.

She turned her head to look at the large security gate and the guards which were patrolling the grounds, checking invitations. All in all, they were doing a fairly competent job. Good for them. Hopefully, they wouldn't be blamed for what was about to happen. There weren't enough people in the world who enjoyed their jobs, even if the jobs were in the "evil dictatorship" sector.

Mull was personally *always* looking for a career in the evil dictatorship sector, but she was really holding out for a management position. Generally speaking, you shouldn't ever take a job which put you on the bottom rung of a totalitarian regime. There was little chance for advancement and the company benefits all involved toiling.

These particular guards didn't seem to be letting the situation bother them. They were focused. Professional. Orderly.

Mull didn't trust order. Because it always depended on things *staying* orderly. But that just wasn't the way the world was. Order was only temporary. As soon as you introduced an unknown element into the mix, order crumbled into chaos.

And Multifarious *was* chaos. That's where she lived and thrived.

Order limited your options, it told you what to do and who to be... but *anything* could happen with chaos.

She casually threw several tire spikes into the road, just as one of the limousines made the turn into the driveway of the building. Three tires immediately exploded, the rims causing a shower of sparks and smoke to be thrown into the air as they ground against the pavement. The limo lost traction and crashed into one of the security planters next to the gate.

The guard in the security booth frantically waved at the driver, and the occupants of the limo rushed out, obviously worrying about there being some kind of bomb.

The best part about killing rich assholes was that they either arrived at a party without a date, because they were losers, or they arrived with a dozen skanky women, because they were losers who wanted everyone to think their dick was bigger than it was.

And *that* was Mull's ticket into any party in the world.

Because Natalie Quentin was welcomed pretty much everywhere. She was a complete nonentity.

The partygoers milled around, watching security fuss over the stricken vehicle and try to clear it from the entryway, and Mull figured she had about twenty seconds before the guests got sick of waiting for their chauffeur to settle the matter with the guards, and would just walk through the gate instead. And once that happened, all Mull had to do was nonchalantly walk through the gate with the rich asshole and his entourage. It wasn't like the guy who arrived at a party with a dozen skanks really took the time to learn all of their names anyway. He wouldn't notice one more.

Sure enough, the partygoer and his gang of slutty women got bored and were making their way towards the building itself. The man flashed his invitation and pointed to his dates, and they were ushered forward. Mull smiled flirtatiously at the guard as she strolled by him, taking her "date's" arm and being escorted inside.

All too easy.

Technically speaking, it would have been just as easy to sneak into the party dressed as herself, but Party Line was more at home at parties than Mull was anyway. People were generally suspicious of a guest wearing a full facemask with a Kilroy symbol etched into it. Since casualties had to be kept to a minimum, Multifarious had chosen to wear Party Line's dress and Natalie's face. It had been a group decision, and like *all* group decisions, it left no one particularly happy.

Plus, Mull's way probably would have involved strolling up to the guard booth and putting two into the security guy's head and one in his chest with a silenced .45, which would have gone against the client's instructions.

No unnecessary casualties.

Which meant no fun.

Being forced to listen to the inane demands of idiots completely sucked.

If Monet's clients had told him he couldn't paint what he wanted and instead had to paint something hideously soulless, Mull would have bet he'd paint Impressionistic haystacks and colorful water lilies all over their fucking corpses!

But whatever.

Natalie's wholesome little cherub girl-next-door of a face did put more people at ease than Multifarious' mask and white combat gear, which was good. And Mull *did* like nice things. Particularly if they were *shiny.*

She spun in a small circle, admiring her tight blue sequined evening dress. It set off Natalie's candy apple red hair and sparkling smile quite nicely. On a normal day, it wasn't really something that Natalie would *ever* consider wearing, but Party Line had insisted, so Multifarious was helpless to stop it.

It was all very confusing, but Natalie looked too nice to even care at the moment. Not that Natalie herself would have thought so, but no one listened to her anyway, so who cared. Nat was *ridiculous* and the rest of her knew it. Getting advice from her would be like getting advice from *Hello Kitty*. All rainbows and sunshine and bullshit.

Mull couldn't stand Natalie most of the time. Even when they were both Party Line.

She surreptitiously abandoned her date as soon as they were inside, and made her way towards the buffet area. Mull hated to work on an empty stomach.

She popped some shrimp cocktail into her mouth, hoping that she wasn't allergic to shellfish today. You could never really tell. Some days she might be, some days not. Her whole life was like that and it all depended on the luck of the draw.

She absently looked around the room, noticing with a frown that there were quite a few members of the Freedom Squad in attendance at the Agletarian embassy.

Her client had *not* mentioned that Capes would be involved. Particularly the most powerful Capes around. These weren't the "corner store robbery" kind of superheroes, these assholes were pure "giant asteroid of space dragons is going to collide with the city!" style heroes. They were big league shit.

It was a small matter, since Mull could handle them, but it did complicate things. Party Line's powers were *not* at a level where she could go toe-to-toe with the entire Freedom Squad. Last Tuesday? Mull would have *owned* all those jackbooted little bitches and sent them cryin' home to mama. But today was a brand new day, and the powers she had today weren't going to damage the city's go-to protectors, even though the protectors in question were shady as all fuck.

To her right, Captain Dauntless was talking to someone who was dressed in a military uniform, looking like the champion of freedom that he claimed to be. Personally, Mull had always hated the asshole. He was fully capable of twisting her into a pretzel today though, and not feeling badly about it after.

But he had absolutely no idea who Natalie even was, which meant that Mull was safe as houses at the moment.

No, Natalie wouldn't hurt anyone, asshole. Just look how cute she is.

Sure enough, the man in question paid no attention to her. His superhuman vision passed over her without a second thought.

Mull smiled a devious smile.

Deciding that the shrimp wouldn't kill her, she grabbed another handful and started up the stairs on one side of the ballroom, paying no attention to the guards which surrounded the landing. Guards were *Multifarious'* problem. *Party Line* was running the shots right now, which meant that *Natalie* needed to be an innocent little redhead, who was simply lost. If *Mull* were calling the shots, she'd "gun and run" the whole party, mowing down her targets and leaving. If *Nat* were calling the shots– which was an *absurd* idea– she'd be at home watching some stupid TV drama about the trials and tribulations of a group of handsome veterinarians or some such silly bullshit. But no, *Party Line* was in charge at the moment, which meant that the situation called for a little more... *finesse*.

A dark-haired man with a ponytail was talking to the security guard at the top of the stairs and pointing out the window towards the front gate. He was wearing a military uniform, complete with enough ropes and fringe to make a window treatment at a bordello jealous. He was yelling at the other man about something, his voice tinged with the distinctive Agletarian accent. Mull had always hated it. There were a lot of really cool accents in the world, but that one was a shit one.

"This is *unacceptable!*" He screamed. "My father will have you *hanged for this!*" He tossed what appeared to be a magazine at the guard, apparently upset that the other man might be reading during work hours. On the cover, teen sweetheart Bekki Bartlett posed in swimwear with her Olympic silver medal. "Tell your people outside I want that vehicle *moved and searched,* and until then, *no one* is to be allowed in. Bar the gates!"

"General Ponytail" turned on his heel and stalked back down

the stairs, glaring at her as he went by.

She smiled at him shyly, trying to look charming. Nat couldn't do a lot as far as sex appeal went, but she could manage "flirtatiously innocent" if the situation called for it. It wasn't a lot, but it could be a momentary distraction for some men, since they'd start to imagine what she'd look like doing *not-so*-innocent things.

Predictably, it worked fairly well and she could feel his eyes on her as she continued up the stairs. Technically speaking, it was probably a bad idea to attract attention like that, but Party Line *liked* an audience when she worked. Mull might prefer to move silently and kill quickly, but Party Line enjoyed being watched. It was like... *foreplay*.

For her part, Natalie didn't like strange evil men looking at her, ever. Because Natalie was boring and frigid, which was why no one liked her.

Fuck Natalie.

She wasn't even real.

The ponytail guy stopped on the stairs behind her, either about to question where she was going... or maybe just watching her ass. Either way, if he became an obstacle, Party Line had four different ways she could kill him without the guard seeing and Mull had more than a dozen.

Natalie had none. Because there was no situation in which Nat was useful. And Mull had spent *years* looking for one, so she spoke from personal experience. Party Line had only known Natalie for a day, and she already found her tedious. At a social event, Natalie would be the woman Party Line avoided or made fun of with her other friends. Not that she'd *tell* Natalie that, because it would require actually speaking to her, but Natalie got the message anyway.

"General Ponytail" got called away by someone and he rushed off to handle some new evil related emergency.

That was the other thing Mull disliked about potentially working in the Evil Dictatorship sector: everything had to be such a big damn deal.

Mull reached the top of the stairs and smiled at the guard. "Oh, excuse me." She giggled in feigned embarrassment. "Can you tell me where the ladies room is?"

"Downstairs." The huge man with the automatic weapon pointed to a hallway which branched off the far wall of the rotunda below them. "You're not allowed up here. This is *private*."

"Oh dear." She pressed her hand to her chest, drawing his attention to the low cut of her dress. "I'd *really* rather use this one, if that's okay." She took on a slightly ominous tone and leaned closer to him. "I have," she lowered her voice to a conspiratorial whisper, "...*girl stuff* to do." She warned, meeting the man's eyes seriously and raising both of her eyebrows to drive home the horrific gravity of the unspecified problem. "You *don't* want to know."

The man looked vaguely ill and immediately waved her through.

That was Party Line's favorite excuse for doing something she wasn't supposed to do or being someplace she wasn't supposed to be. It was *perfect*. As long as you were dealing with men, anyway. Women would obviously ask just what kind of "girl stuff" could only be handled in an off-limits area of a foreign embassy, but men were so afraid of learning something new about women's bodies that they avoided the specifics like some horrible mysterious plague.

Party Line smiled at the man in thanks and strolled down the hall for several steps, then stopped, grabbed one of the expensive-looking marble statues which was sitting on a table, and smashed him in the back of the head with it.

He crumpled to the floor and she dragged him over to prop him upright in a nearby chair, then she stooped to grab his weapon.

An UMP40, firing .40 cartridges.

Yep. Multifarious could handle that. And its matte black finish looked *really* good with Party Line's dress. Some women wore handbags, but Mull had *always* preferred a good quality automatic weapon. It just said: "Hey boys! Look at me! ...Or I'll fucking *pump your guts full of lead!*"

She gave a contented sigh, pleased with how well this party was working out now. It had overcome some initial bumps and was now really turning into the highlight of her social season. She'd have to send her host a thank you note.

After she killed him.

"Assassin" didn't have to mean "rude," after all.

She made her way down the hall again, absently dancing with herself to the sound of the orchestra downstairs. They were *wonderful.* She'd asked them to play "*MMMBop*," which they'd been reluctant to attempt, probably because it was such a classic. But $200 and a gruesome death threat had convinced them that they could do the song justice. Repeatedly.

She'd really do her best to remember to try not to shoot any of them tonight. Or at least leave them a tip if she did. Maybe it would help pay for their funerals or whatever. It was the *least* she could do.

The other partygoers looked a little perturbed to finally be hearing *real* music for once, staring at the city's most accomplished classical orchestra in confused bafflement and barely restrained annoyance, as they played the song again and again.

It's Hanson, motherfuckers! The greatest musicians of our time! *Listen to them until you love them!*

She stopped at the end of the hall and made her way into the room on her left. It was a study and it overlooked the back gardens of the embassy. She popped her head out the exterior window and casually tossed her weapon onto the balcony of the room next to it.

She walked into the hallway again, straightened her clothes and tried to look as vapid as possible, then knocked on the large doors at the end of the hall.

A moment later a huge man threw them open and leveled a gun at her. "You ain't supposed to be in here. This is off-limits! *Who sent you?!?*"

The world was *so* paranoid sometimes. What had happened to manners?

"I'm not? You sure?" She made a show of looking down at a slip of paper in her hand, which was actually a receipt for a Mega-Burger she'd eaten an hour ago, but which she was apparently pretending was some kind of reservation slip. "This the... Agnatainian Governing Council?" She deliberately mispronounced the country's name, *possibly* going too far with the "dumb" act, but whatever. Could a girl ever really be *too* dumb for men?

The man cocked his weapon. "What of it?"

Mull shouldered her way inside, secure in the knowledge that there wasn't a man alive who would gun down a pretty lady in an evening gown, unless she did something *really* unacceptable and posed them an immediate threat. And even then, they'd hesitate. Breasts were better than *any* body armor you could buy. Your ticket into any party, social event, or building in the world. A pretty face and a low-cut dress was the *ultimate* superpower in this all-too sexist and objectifying society.

"Then I think I'm in the right place." She spun in a circle to look at the whole room, and made a low whistling sound, as if impressed. "Nice digs, boys."

The room was actually fairly ordinary, but she doubted they wanted to hear that. Generally, people preferred lies to the truth. Masks were always more interesting than the faces they concealed.

The not-so-great room was filled with a large conference table which stretched from one end of the room to the other, and around it were seated a dozen *depressingly* ordinary old guys. She was always hopeful that one of these jobs would involve like... an *octopus* man or something, but they never did. Sadly, most of the world's problems were caused by old dudes just like these, sitting around tables in not-so-great rooms just like this one, and doing worse things to people than even the most *badass* Octo-Badass could ever dream of doing.

It was all *very* disillusioning.

Evil used to be about the show. Now it was too focused on the awards season.

The guard roughly slammed his hand down on her shoulder. His thumb moved along her skin for an instant though, obviously liking the feeling of power and control he got from manhandling her... which would have actually been kind of hot if she were a complete whore. Sadly, she was not. It just made her kind of pissed off and disgusted.

Party Line bordered on the whorish though and had no objections to the action, despite the fact that it made Natalie's skin crawl. Nat really needed to calm down and embrace the often insane elements of life. For all her hippie bullshit though, Nat didn't like being touched by anyone.

Natalie had... issues. Which was another reason why no one liked her.

That and the fact she was a fucking lunatic, obviously.

Mull was more inclined to agree with Natalie on the issue, but to be fair, she *was* about to kill the man, which kind of ruined the potential romance of the evening. True, she'd made a few exceptions to that rule over the years, but she was *really* trying to cut down on killing the people she'd slept with or sleeping with the people she had definite plans to kill. It just made things messy. Not in the literal sense, as she also always tried to avoid shooting them while in the physical act itself, just in the *metaphorical* sense.

Having to figure out a way to get some dead naked guy out of her apartment at 9AM on Christmas morning was a pain in the ass and she wasn't about to make *that* mistake yet again.

Aaaaawkward.

"Who is *this?*" Shouted an important looking bearded man from the end of the table. His silly military uniform was crammed with even more medals and brightly colored sashes than General Ponytail's had been. It was a wonder the weight didn't tip him over. Half of them were probably just bottle caps or some shit. It looked like the dude coated his chest in Elmer's glue and then rolled in glitter and ribbons until he looked like one of the goddamn *My Little Ponies.* "What is she doing here, Bolten?"

Party Line spun around to flash Natalie's most beguiling smile at him. "I'm the *entertainment.*" She prowled towards him, reaching up to the straps of her dress. "Your friends sent me here as a gift." She let the garment drop to the floor. "They thought you'd *like* me."

If the man had half the sense that God gave a rotisserie chicken, he'd realize how truly *stupid* that excuse was. He'd question who these supposed "friends" were, how she'd gotten past the guards in the hallway, and why someone would send a *stripper* to a foreign embassy during a formal gala event.

But the man was an idiot. When you really came down to it, most men were. Once they saw a half-naked woman, they stopped caring about all of the trivial stuff like security and common sense. Generally speaking, no man would *ever* ask too many questions of a woman who was taking off her clothes for him.

She pursed her lips in thought.

Huh.

Evidently, Party Line had issues with men in general. Every other thought in her head was some complaint about them.

Interesting...

The nature of Multifarious' powers meant that she had a new ability and persona each day. Some days, the difference in personality was negligible and she barely noticed. Some days, she was suddenly a raging bitch who not even she could stand. Some days her power was useless, some days it made her a very effective criminal, and some days it basically made her a god on earth. It was all the luck of the draw.

Still, on days like this one, it was kind of exciting to discover something new about herself, even if she'd only *be* "herself" for another fifty minutes before being replaced by some newer version. Not a completely new person or anything, just a new set of powers, beliefs, and ideas about the world. Every 24 hours, she got new little quirks and exciting ticks, which made her *her*. It was the equivalent of putting a few thousand people's personalities, passions, and powers into a blender, then slamming back a fresh glass of "Multifarious" every morning. The *core* of Multifarious remained mostly unchanged, she just sometimes spoke weird languages, could move shit with her mind, or lost the ability to recognize faces.

Once, she'd had a tail.

That had been a weird day.

Today though, she was Party Line, and although being basically powerless, she'd apparently developed a rather hefty amount of distain for the abilities and intelligence of the opposite sex, as well as being *far* more flirtatious and comfortable with her own body than Multifarious and Natalie would ever *dream* of being.

But either way, Multifarious was more than happy to let Party Line use Natalie's face and body to put these guys at ease. Which sounded weird, but made sense if you were as insane as she was. Natalie was the mask which Multifarious wore to look normal, and right now, Mull was letting Party Line use that mask to more easily wipe out the heads of a sovereign nation so that she would get paid, and Multifarious could then afford to pay for Natalie's apartment and her tendency to purchase Steve McQueen movies on Amazon late at night.

It made *perfect* sense.

She sat down on the man's lap and put her hand to her breast. "Oh, there are so *many* of you." She bit her bottom lip nervously. "I've never had so many men at once before."

Mull almost scoffed at Party Line's words. That was probably the most *idiotically* slutty thing to ever pass Natalie's lips. Still, she had little doubt that it wouldn't work.

...Little doubt that it *would* work? Or "wouldn't"? Fuck, Party Line sucked at grammar too. Mull hated it when that happened.

Whatever. Whichever one meant, "men are fucking stupid," that's the one she meant.

Sure enough, the man chuckled and smoothed a strand of hair from her face. "We'll be gentle."

"Oh, that's a relief," Party Line smiled, adding a sinister edge to Natalie's *disgustingly* innocent face, "...because I *won't*." She smashed the back of her head into his nose, pulverizing the cartilage and driving it into the man's brain, causing blood to explode from his face. She pushed off the table with her foot, knocking the chair they were sitting in backwards and crashing through the balcony doors behind them. She continued her roll and came up holding the silenced automatic weapon she'd thrown onto the balcony from the neighboring room moments before.

The guards at the entrance to the room raised their weapons to fire, but she gunned the men down before they got the chance.

The Agletarians at the table stood up in shocked disbelief, drawing their own weapons.

"Gentlemen," she hopped up onto the table, "The Consortium of Chaos says '*payback is a bitch with a machine gun.*'" She opened fire, emptying the clip into the Agletarian assembly, exactly as she'd been hired to do.

For some reason.

To be perfectly frank, even on the best of days, it wasn't Mull's policy to get overly involved in the reasons for doing what she was doing. If she did that, her whole life would collapse. She was like the Coyote in one of those old Looney Tunes shorts: she was fine as long as she didn't look down and see that she wasn't walking on anything. Because the second she took the time to really think about it... well, it wouldn't be too good for the Coyote, that was for damn sure.

Another guard burst into the room and Mull silently cursed Party Line for not paying more attention to the number of people. That fucking girl, man. Her and Natalie. Their inattention to details was going to get Mull killed one day.

She tossed the empty gun at the man, catching him above the right eye. She dashed across the table, leaping off of it and kicking the man in the face before he could recover. He turned and brought his arm up to viciously backhand her.

The force of the blow caused her to stumble in the *stupid* fucking high heels which *stupid* fucking Party Line had chosen for this *stupid* fucking mission, and crash into the table. It was *embarrassing* to be hit by someone so unskilled. Normally, the impact would have been cushioned by her Kilroy etched facemask, which Mull *always* wore, but sadly in her *stupid* fucking brilliance, Party Line had taken that off before ever beginning this job.

Multifarious missed her face. She hated being without it. It was *sooo* much better than Natalie's. Nat's wasn't cool or memorable at all. Everything about that girl was lame.

Party Line licked the blood dripping from her mouth and was oddly turned on by the violence.

...Mull was *really* going to have a heart-to-heart with herself when this was over, and tell herself that she did *phenomenally* stupid things sometimes, and to wizen up before she kicked her own ass.

Also, that she was being *really* creepy at the moment.

Ew.

The guard pulled a knife from his pocket and tried to stab her, but she spun to the side, long used to dodging knives. She'd spent many years living with an *expert* at stabbing things– occasionally her— and the motion was second nature to her now. This dude wasn't *nearly* as skilled with a blade as Ronnie had been, and she'd survived countless spats with *that* asshole.

Her relationship with Mercygiver had been a 'love/ hate' kind thing. In that he loved to hit her, and she hated every fucking bone in his entire body.

This guy, though, was a walk in the park. Like a tropical vacation, only with switchblades instead of little paper umbrella drinks.

The movement caused her hand to slide across the table and she instinctively grabbed a cake server in the process. She twirled the wide bladed utensil around in her hand for a moment, then smiled at her new friend. "Let's have some *fun*."

The man lunged at her with the knife and it was all she could do to keep from laughing at his *appallingly* bad form. She grabbed his wrist to redirect the attack, then plunged the blunt serving utensil downward into the base of his neck. He made a gurgling sound as blood flowed from the devastating wound, and collapsed to the ground.

"Piece of cake."

Mull made a face at Party Line's stupid joke.

She stepped over the body, trying not to get blood on her shoes.

Fucking men.

They were *all* useless.

Mull frowned. And *again* with the men bashing!?! What the hell was *with* Party Line, anyway? Why was she so down on men? It was tiresome and weird. Men were awesome. Well, most of them. Okay... *some* of them, but the ones that were worthwhile more than made up for all the assholes out there. But *apparently* Party Line just wanted to be a bitch.

A bitch who was having *waaay* too much fun being naked and fighting dudes.

Again, she was finding herself *creepy as fuck* today and she needed a good talking to. Frankly, she was beginning to long for midnight, when a new persona would appear and Party Line's oddities and perversions could be forgotten.

At this rate, Party Line would frighten Natalie and *then* there'd be trouble. Nothing on this earth could complicate a situation like Natalie, and Mull went out of her way to keep the girl uninvolved.

Mull often dreamed of there being a day when she'd be... normal. Some new version of herself which wasn't completely insane. Or as boring as insipid-ass Natalie, obviously.

Those days were a rare treat. She relished them the same way others might remember being a happy child on Christmas morning opening the gift they dreamed of, or the sensual embrace of a lover.

Those days... those days were nice. She felt like herself. She felt normal.

But she hadn't had one in years now, and she suspected they were gone for good.

Most of the time, whoever she was on a given day... well, shit got dark.

She casually wiped the blood spatters from her body with the table cloth and her fingerprints from the weapons, and then tossed the fabric into the large fireplace to destroy the DNA. She bent to collect her dress, and slipped it back on. Although she fully intended to still have that conversation with herself about respecting her victims and herself, she did have to hand it to Party Line: stripping first *was* a good idea. In retrospect, it allowed her to kill a room filled with men without getting one drop of blood on her gown. Now, she could stroll out of this room without anyone being the wiser.

Sometimes, you just needed to trust yourself. Even if you'd only be yourself for another fifty-eight minutes, and when "yourself" kinda creeped you out.

Besides, a room filled with dead men was *hardly* something anyone should care about. They were dogs. All men were.

Shut up, Party Line! Go away, you freak!

She walked out of the room and started to make her way down the hallway and back towards the party.

The girl was just *so*...

An arm appeared through a partially opened door ahead of her, carrying a silenced pistol. She grabbed the man's wrist, pulled him forward to slam his face into the back of the door, then threw her weight against it, closing his arm in the jamb. She repeated the process several more times, then wrenched the gun from his hand and absently shot him through the door four times.

A second later, Mull heard the distinctive "whoosh" that Captain Dauntless asshole made whenever he started flying, and she instantly collapsed to the floor, playing dead.

The Cape noticed the bodies in the doorway, including her, but was too preoccupied with the possible fate of the faaaaar more important people in the council room. Generally speaking, the deaths of security guards and bystanders went unnoticed in these kinds of situations. Capes paid attention to the VIPs.

Saving rich people got you on the news. Saving poor people got your costume dirty.

The hero continued down the hallway before disappearing into the room to check on the wealthier victims.

Mull calmly got back to her feet, rolling her eyes.

No one ever checked the bodies. Sloppy.

Given the man's enhanced senses, he probably could have heard her heartbeat on his way by... but not over the sound of the orchestra downstairs, which was continuing to loudly belt out *MMMBop* again and again like their lives depended on it... because in a very real sense, it absolutely did.

Mull killed people for money, but if someone disrespected Hanson, she'd go all *pro bono* on their shit. Pieces of them would rain down from the skies like some kind of Biblical plague.

She stopped next to the unconscious security guard she'd spoken with on the way here, and inspected her makeup in one of the hall mirrors.

Yep. She *still* looked goddamned perfect.

"Perfect?" Mull had never thought of herself as "perfect." Hell, even Natalie could only manage to call herself "kind of pretty" and that girl was *all about* happy sunshine and seeing the best in people. But apparently, in addition to being a tad sexist and a little into BDSM, Party Line was *also* conceited.

Was it really conceited to like what you saw in the mirror though? What, just because she might not be particularly "exotic" or have "bedroom eyes" that meant that she should be ashamed? The hell with that! That was *JUST* the kind of shit that the entrenched masculine patriarchy liked to tell millions of impressionable young women and...

Shut up, Party Line! Jesus Christ, girl! You look like fucking Becky Thatcher and you know it! Now stop being weird and focus on just getting out of here before the world's most powerful Cape figures out there's a victim missing.

Yeah, yeah. She made a face at herself, rolling her eyes.

Some people just didn't want to see the big picture, that was all. She'd accomplished her mission, killed a dozen men and now it was just a matter of getting out of the building... and past security which was now blocking the exit and checking IDs...

Uh-huh. And I bet you've got some incredibly cunning and ingenious method for getting out of this, don't you, Party Line? Something that no one could possibly see coming?

Of course she did.

Party Line *always* had a way to get out of these types of situations. Even when she was Multifarious. Or Natalie.

It was a method which *never* failed.

You just had to plan it carefully...

She beamed at the first man she saw, flashing him Nat's all-too innocent smile. The guy was broad-shouldered and tall, with a shaved head and an *absolutely gorgeous* face. His suit was impeccable and so pristinely white that it looked like bridal fabric.

He was... striking.

Important looking.

There was no question that this was a *man*.

The kind of guy Nat would hide from in nervousness and the kind that Party Line was already having nasty thoughts about. But even Party Line hesitated for a second, recognizing that someone who looked like that would obviously have a date for this event. And high standards of beauty which Natalie couldn't hit on her best day. With a ladder. And a jetpack.

Fucking Natalie was going to ruin this for Party Line. How typical.

"Hi!" She greeted him excitedly. "Can you take me back to your place?" She rubbed up against him and "accidentally" gave him a view down her dress. "I *really* wanna get out of here."

The man swallowed, looking uncomfortable. To Party Line's

surprise however, he ignored the view of her cleavage she was offering. Instead he took a small step back away from her, giving her more space. "Umm... Uhh..." He looked around the room like he was nervous or checking for something. "Okay, miss." He quickly nodded. "Yes, I can escort you home if you need a ride."

"That would be wonderful, lover." She put her arm in his. "This party's dead anyway."

Oh, Jesus.

Party Line liked puns.

There was *no possible way* she could become any more annoying.

It was going to be a loooong night.

The man in question ushered her through security, who completely ignored him for some reason. Like he was above all suspicion.

He cleared his throat. "My name is Oswald, miss."

Chapter 1

EARLIER THIS MORNING

Oswald Cullen Dimico, AKA "OCD," didn't feel well today.

His sinuses ached, probably a warning sign of an unseen infection which was slowly killing him from the inside out.

He found himself breathing too heavily, which could indicate chronic obstructive pulmonary disease.

His skin felt blotchy, which could be an allergic reaction to something he'd touched and which would soon cause his throat to close off, asphyxiating him.

And the air in this bar was filled with cigarette smoke, which he could feel filling up his lungs with carcinogens and tar.

Oz was sitting at a table inside Joe Chester's Bar, in an area of the city which smelled more like urine than most outhouses. The light overhead was lit and sputtering, despite the fact that it was still sunny outside, and the faint electric buzzing sound mixed quite well with the buzzing of flies, which filled the space.

His feet were sticking to the floor, and he hoped it was due to remains of spilled alcohol, rather than blood or semen.

With this city, you could never quite be sure.

All told, this was Oz's absolute nightmare. It was dirty, disorganized, and crawling with bacteria.

He didn't like it.

Oz was the type of person who listened to the flight attendant's safety talk every time he was on a plane. He even read along in the emergency checklist guide from the seat pocket in front of him, just to make sure they covered everything.

Not that he really was on planes a lot, as he didn't like them.

Planes were unsafe, obviously, but they were also *hotbeds* of germ infestation. The recycled air meant that you were basically breathing in a hundred other people with every breath. Their sweat and their skin and their bacteria. Microscopic bits of their last meal and their foulness and the *unspeakable* things they did to each other.

Tiny bits of their excrement were landing on your tongue, filling your nose, and being inhaled into your skull.

Strangers' feces were touching your brain. Right now.

You were tasting it all. Breathing it in. Making it a *part* of you.

It was *revolting*. Like putting a hundred people in a blender and then drinking them all down.

Oz was the kind of person who, after leaving his apartment, would return to check and double-check that he had turned off the oven, despite the obvious fact that his apartment didn't actually have one. And then he'd check and double-check that he had remembered to lock the door, always pushing his body against it in the same way, and attempting to turn the knob three times: first clockwise, then jiggling it counter-clockwise, then a more forceful turn clockwise accompanied by bumping against the door with his shoulder to check to see if it was secure.

It was the only way to be *absolutely certain* that the door would remain closed and the outside world could not infiltrate his one sanctuary.

At the moment though, Oz was really more concerned with work.

Oz was currently taking part in a Consortium of Chaos operation to figure out what the hell was going on. His employers were forced to have missions like that a lot, because they were, for the most part, staggeringly incompetent.

They were morons.

It was a sad fact of his new life.

He worked with idiots who focused more on crime, sex, and talk shows, than they did their jobs of protecting the city. Which wasn't too surprising, given the fact that they had only stopped being super-villains nine months ago.

There were some strange disappearances of late in the city though, and so Oz had been dispatched along with a couple other coworkers to see if he could discover the whereabouts of the citizens, and what was causing them to vanish.

Once upon a time, Oz never would have taken this mission. Once upon a time, Oz had been a part of the Freedom Squad, a superhero group dedicated to protecting the city from the scourge that was the Consortium of Chaos. Then things got weird and his former coworkers went off the rails, and so Oz had been forced to switch sides in order to help save the city from them. And almost died *himself* in the process. So, now Oz was a former hero, joining up with former villains, to be... something. At best, they rarely achieved higher than "anti-hero," but Oz hoped that with his patient help, they could all make it 24 hours without committing some fresh atrocity. But more than likely, his coworkers would get him killed long before that happened. Or kill him themselves, either deliberately or in a "childish prank gone horribly wrong" sort of situation.

It was inevitable, at this point.

He had resigned himself to it.

He shifted in the wooden chair, saying a silent prayer that it wouldn't crack through. He did *not* want to touch the floor of this place. As it was, he was already planning on burning his shoes before he even entered his apartment tonight. It was one of the reasons why he kept several completely sanitary pairs in the lobby, just in case. It was *amazing* the number of people who thoughtlessly walked through all manner of disgusting things, then happily tracked all of it back to their homes without first decontaminating their shoes.

He stared down at his phone, which he cleaned twice a day with disinfectant, and replaced every six months to avoid germs which were resistant to antibacterials.

He was silently debating with himself whether or not he should call her.

On one hand, he wanted very much to hear her voice and make certain that she was okay. But, on the other hand, they weren't really "dating." Or, really, even "friends." She was just a woman who Oz deeply, *deeply* enjoyed.

Would it be creepy to call up the woman you saw at a department store every day, just because you felt like talking to her?

Oz wasn't really the best at judging what was "creepy" though.

Things like that mystified him. And he'd been told more than once in his life that almost everything he said or did was creepy or freaked people out.

So, he simply stared at the illuminated screen, which promised that with a touch of the button, he could be speaking to Natalie Quentin.

The world had thrown Oz away several times in his life. Literally and figuratively.

No one in this world had ever wanted him. His parents had their own dramas. His aunt and uncle viewed him as a scary burden they were saddled with. His jailors had thought he was irritating. The Freedom Squad ignored him. The Consortium still viewed him as an outsider. And there wasn't a person in this city who could identify him in a line-up, no matter how hard he tried to be a hero for them. No matter how much pain he endured or how high a standard he held himself to.

Oz was trash. He would never amount to anything and everyone knew it, including him.

He'd wanted to be someone extraordinary his entire life.

But it wasn't until Natalie looked at him that he really understood what that was.

When he touched that woman, it was like everything clean and fun and pure was washing over him. Cleansing him of all of the trash that had been heaped onto him over the years. Letting him finally breathe.

When Natalie was around, Oz wasn't afraid anymore. He felt like a hero. Like he wasn't just something that everyone threw away or unwillingly endured.

She was beautiful in a way that made him want to sit back and marvel at her. In Oz's mind, she was the epitome of the female form. Every single thing about her was perfect. He could happily spend hours, just looking at her.

Of course, such a thing would be completely against the way Oz lived his life.

It would probably scare her.

But try as he might, he couldn't stop noticing the gentle curve of Natalie's hip. Or the way her breasts moved when she walked. Or the way her breathtakingly perfect lips curved at the corners when she was amused or silently laughing at someone.

Every tiny movement of that woman's body was an erotic daydream.

And Oz treasured each and every one.

But Oz could tell already that he wasn't going to press the button on his phone. Because... because Miss Quentin was a woman who deserved better than trash. And when you came right down to it, that was all Oz was. Deep down, Oz recognized it.

He'd only pull her down too.

As he was sitting there pondering the Miss Quentin matter and waiting for the bar tender to return from a break, Oz was joined by one of his teammates on this particular mission: Multifarious.

Oz had never had an issue with the masked individual.

Yes, he or she was a deranged lunatic, who killed people like someone else might eat breath mints, but at least he/she wasn't a jerk about it.

Oz found Multifarious' brand of crazy... relaxing.

Not that being around someone so unpredictable didn't also drive him completely up the wall, just that Oz was used to thinking of himself as the craziest person in the room. And he didn't really have to worry about that when Mull was around.

More than that though, he worked quite well with Multifarious. They almost always went on missions together, probably because they managed to cover all possible reactions to a given situation. Between the two of them, there really wasn't much they didn't know how to handle.

Generally, Oz's rules of engagement on use of force went something like: speak, shout, show, shove, shoot to warn, shoot to kill. His goal in every situation was to keep it from escalating, while still pursuing his objectives. If he could get what he wanted without a fight, that's what he was going to do.

Multifarious, on the other hand, had rules of engagement which were more like: shoot to entertain yourself, shoot to kill, blow up the entire block while laughing like a demented madman.

While it would be easy to view their drastically different Caping ideologies as a negative, in practice, it usually meant that Oz was the one charged with the talking and Multifarious was the one who took over if things went sideways. They each got to play to their strengths.

All in all, it was a professional relationship which worked quite well.

Truth told, Oz genuinely *liked* Multifarious. A lot.

"How they hangin', Oz?" Mull asked grabbing a chair from another table and pulling it over to sit across from him. He/she arranged it backwards, leaning over the backrest.

"Still waiting for the bartender." Oz informed the masked person. "He should return momentarily."

Mull snorted. "He's probably behind all of this, and is using this time to run away." He/she predicted, the electronic filter in the Kilroy mask somehow managing to convey the comically grim tone. "Your problem is that you trust people."

Oz made a humoring sound. "Yes, I'm sure."

Mull pointed at the drink which was sitting in front of him. "Can I have a sip of that?"

Oz held up his hands. "I would rather die than even touch that beverage glass." He said honestly, trying to keep from retching at the bacteria and germs clinging to its surface and floating in the lukewarm liquid inside.

Mull grabbed the glass and nonchalantly dumped it on his/her facemask... which didn't have a mouth hole. The liquid simply dripped down the plastic and onto the white combat gear uniform he/she was wearing, which was today accented by a Hawaiian shirt and straw hat.

Oz simply stared at his partner, mystified. Then he started to laugh, in spite of himself. "Multifarious..." He began, trying to stifle his amusement.

"I am not Multifarious," the masked person reminded him, "today I am.... *Otium!*"

"I see." Oz was used to random craziness from the person, it was one of the few aspects of Mull's personality which carried over from day to day. "And what can you do today?"

"I haven't the foggiest fucking idea." Otium-née-Multifarious informed him seriously. "But whatever it is, I hope I get to do it soon, because I'm bored as shit."

Oz nodded. "Well... that makes sense, I suppose. Given your code name today."

Otium-née-Multifarious' head tilted to the side, like he/she was confused.

"You're 'Otium.'" He explained. "Historically, as in: the idle wasteless free time of a Roman soldier away at war, but not actually fighting. Like, you can't relax even when you have time off, because you know that you'll soon be called upon again and you'd rather be fighting to the death than waiting for it to happen."

"Huh." Mull finally said. "Interesting. I had no idea what that meant."

"I like history." Oz explained, then frowned at his partner's news. "Wait... you chose a code name without even knowing what it meant?"

"Maybe." Mull shrugged. "Shit, I don't know. It sounds like you pay more attention to this kind of thing than I do." The masked figure looked at him appraisingly. "And who wears a *tie* to fight crime?" Mull gestured to Oz's white suit and sweater vest, which doubled as body armor. The only spot of color on his outfit was the scarlet red double "C" logo of the Consortium of Chaos, which was pinned to his lapel.

Oz made another humoring sound.

"You look like you're about to give someone a fucking audit, or sell them ice cream." Mull advised. "You need to be more *dramatic."*

Given his associate's current attire, he chose to ignore the criticism. "Were you and Poacher able to find out anything from the other patrons of the bar?"

"You want to *work?*" Mull sounded horrified. "Really!?! Here we are, on our own, just the two of us, no supervision... and you want to waste that time actually doing our jobs?"

"There is a young woman missing." Oz reminded him/her. "She hasn't been seen since yesterday afternoon, in front of this bar."

"Your problem is you're too high-strung." Mull flipped a dismissive hand. "You gotta learn to vent, Oz. I mean it. You bottle up all that stress and unvoiced irritation, and sooner or later, you're taking a rifle up to the top of a bell tower and trying to shoot people. I seen it happen." Mull pointed at him meaningfully. "And without proper training, you're not going to hit *shit,* which makes it even worse."

"How does that make it worse?"

"Because everyone deserves to be killed by a professional, Oz. Better to be slaughtered by a professional than wounded by an amateur."

"I'm not sure many would agree with you on that point."

Mull tapped the tabletop. "Which is why the world is in the state it's in."

"I don't even know what that means." As usual, he felt completely confused when conversing with Multifarious. "I get the feeling that you're just thinking up profound sounding replies to my logical statements, without stopping to really consider if your words actually form a coherent viewpoint or not."

"To be perfectly honest, I've already forgotten what we were even talking about, yeah." Mull suddenly snapped his/her fingers. "Oh yeah. Your general stick-in-the-mudness. Got it." Mull turned the chair around so that he/she could rest his/her boots on a chair at the table across from them, paying no attention to how that affected the people who were actually sitting there. "I just don't understand why you pay so much attention to this whole 'Hero' thing."

"I believe in heroism." He said simply. "I believe in helping people. I believe in stopping bad guys. I believe violence is only justified if it's the last resort and there's no other way, but if it's justified then I'll go all out. I don't believe that the world is nothing but death and destruction. And I believe the Consortium can be more than petty, bickering monsters who are always seconds away from trying to kill our friends." He stared into the Kilroy face mask his partner was wearing. "I think we're better than that."

"That's only because you haven't known the Consortium crew that long."

"Possibly." He cleared his throat. "But not everything needs to be handled with a combat mentality. Most street level crimes can be dealt with by understanding the motivations behind it and dealing with them. True, sometimes you get a genuinely bad apple who is unwilling to improve themselves and their community, and in cases like those, more traditional punishment options are available through the justice system." He straightened his suit. "When you come right down to it, most people just want to be heard. If you listen to them and offer them understanding, they'll come around."

Mull was quiet for a beat, then slowly cringed away. "What planet are you living on, Oz?" He/she held out his/her hands. "Damn, and people say *I'm* delusional."

"Violence just breeds more violence." He reiterated.

"Not if you do it right." Mull crossed his/her arms over his/her chest. "Violence done *right* has a very pleasant finality to it."

Oz spent a great deal of time on missions debating Multifarious about the nature of humanity and the world. He wasn't sure why, exactly, but he found it oddly enjoyable.

All told, the masked psychopath was one of the few "friends" he had.

Which probably said more about his life than anything else.

Multifarious gestured to his/her own chest. "Practical reality." Mull's hand moved to point at Oz. "Idealistic fantasy."

Oz almost smiled at that simplified take on their personalities. He found himself tapping his finger against his chest. "Idealistic reality." He pointed at Mull. "Nihilistic fantasy."

"Oh, you're *so* unsupportive of my interests." Multifarious rolled his/her eyes. "Every day I gotta hear how I'm gonna be arrested for this or hanged for that." Multifarious pointed at him again. "That's ethnocentrism, is what that is. You simply have no respect for my culture or my way of doing things."

Oz squinted, trying to follow that logic. "I don't think homicide really classifies as a 'culture'..."

"Who made *you* an ethnographer!?!" Multifarious cut him off and dramatically swung an arm at him, like he/she was announcing his presence to the entire bar. "Jesus fucking Christ, we got Bronislaw Malinowski, over here people." Multifarious lowered his/her voice. "He's an ethnographer, Oz." He/she explained. "I watch the National Geographic Channel, I know my shit."

"Yes, I know who he is."

"See, the thing you don't realize," Multifarious leaned forward in his/her chair, obviously believing the next point was important, "is that *everything* you do in life is going to piss someone off. No matter how careful you are or how out of your way you go, *someone* is going to get pissed off anyway. In fact, just pointing that out is sure to piss someone off. Because people can't help but get angry with things that annoy them and people get annoyed by weird irrational shit. And if there isn't something that pisses them off, they'll invent it."

"You spent three hours the other day, screaming at me for not knowing the difference between a 'clip' and a 'magazine.'" He reminded his masked teammate, rather taken aback by the idea that he/she could ever throw stones about someone getting angry over silly things.

"But at least you understood it in the end."

"Not really. Most of that time was just you ranting about springs." He reminded Mull. "Which I still don't understand either. Why were you ranting about *springs*?"

Mull took on a dark tone. "*They know why.*"

Oz let out a sigh, not even surprised by that answer.

"Chastity belts." Multifarious volunteered as a non sequitur.

The sudden change of topic, especially to something so intimate, made Oz feel uncomfortable for some reason. "I'm… I'm sorry?" He stammered. It made him think things. He wasn't even sure what it was making him think, but there were definite thoughts in there which he shouldn't be having.

"They never actually existed, did you know that?" Multifarious asked. "Someone just thought them up one day in the nineteenth century and told people that women used to wear metal underwear which was padlocked by their husbands, because the person thought it would piss people off. And it does. So now, millions of people all over the world get to imagine that chastity belts once existed, and they can get angry over this strange and entirely fake idea that some random sex-starved Victorian asshole dreamt up one day."

"Okay." Oz had no reply to that. He wasn't entirely certain he was supposed to have a reply to that, actually.

"And that's fine." Multifarious continued. "But you need to understand that none of that matters. Let them get pissed off if that's what they want, but trying to understand other people is a waste of time." Multifarious pointed at Oz's chest. "The next time you do something wrong or someone gets angry with you, instead of apologizing, I want you to look them right in the eye and say 'Fuck you!'"

"I don't think that's really necessary." Oz shook his head. "Getting angry never makes things better. I'd rather just take responsibility for the..."

Multifarious waved off that idea before Oz could finish. "Watch, it's easy." Mull stood up suddenly and deliberately bumped into another one of the people at the bar.

The woman stumbled to the side. "Oh, I'm sorry...." The woman began.

"*Fuck you, lady!*" Multifarious yelled into her face.

****

Ten minutes later, the woman had finally stopped crying and her boyfriend's unconscious form was being dragged from the scene by the bar's bouncer.

But Oz and Multifarious were now sitting at a different table, since Mull had put the boyfriend's head through the last one, shattering the wood.

Oz simply stared at his masked companion, waiting.

Mull cleared his/her throat awkwardly. "Okay... I'm not going to lie: that was an aberrant reaction, which spiraled out of control fairly quickly. But you understand what I mean, right?"

"I understand that you just assaulted a civilian, which is sure to get you called out on the news again."

Mull waved a disinterested hand. "Oh, fuck the news too. You gotta break free of all that shit, Oz. Free your mind."

"Uh-huh. I'll bear that in mind, thank you."

"That shit from *Braveheart,* where landlords get to rape brides on their wedding day? *Primae noctis?*" Multifarious shook his/her head in certainty. "Nope. No evidence of that either. It's complete bullshit designed by later generations to piss people off and give them a fake belief that things are getting better. But things *aren't* getting better: it sucked then and it sucks now. And no matter how many bullshit fake horrors we pretend to triumph over..."

"Well, we stopped smallpox." Oz observed calmly, not bothering to hide the amused sarcasm from his voice. "That was pretty cool."

Mull continued like he/she never even heard him. "...or how many meaningless achievements we celebrate, it'll go right on sucking."

"I think we should just focus on the matter at hand..." Oz began.

"People will *find* shit to be outraged over, man. I'm telling you." Mull reiterated, like a closing argument. "They *like* hating things. If they don't have something, they'll invent it, and then they'll never shut up about it. Trying to appease them is pointless."

"And how does this relate to assaulting that woman?"

"Oh, fuck her too." Mull flipped a disinterested hand. "She overreacted. She really should have tried harder to deescalate the situation."

"How can you 'deescalate' a super-powered stranger randomly assaulting you and then knocking your boyfriend out cold?"

"She shoulda found a way." Mull said simply, sounding put-upon and helpless to alter reality. He/she held up his/her hands, as if blamelessly washing them of the whole situation. "All I'm saying."

He absently went back to surveying the bar, looking for possible threats and making a mental note of everything. Oz was in the habit of gathering as much information about things as he could, even if it was ultimately meaningless. It was another one of his compulsions. He *had* to do it. He didn't want to. It was just something his mind told him *had* to be done.

He looked up at the ceiling, silently counting the acoustic tiles.

Mull followed his line of sight. "...The fuck are you doing?"

"This room has 35 ceiling tiles." He reported, eyes returning to his partner.

Mull was used to his compulsions and didn't bother asking why he would be counting them in the first place. "You sure?" Mull asked, sounding doubtful. "*Completely* sure? What if you missed one...?"

Oz thought about it for a moment, then his eyes cut back to the ceiling, to make *absolutely certain* of the number.

Mull started snickering.

Oz finished his count and went back to staring into the white opaque material of his teammate's etched Kilroy faceplate. "I don't appreciate being mocked."

"I'm not 'mocking' you," Mull assured him, "I'm *teasing* you."

"What's the difference?"

"With one, I'd be laughing at you because you're an idiot, and with the other, I'm laughing at you because I find your collection of little oddities utterly *adorable*."

Oz wasn't sure how to respond to that. But it made him

feel… good, for some reason.

"The thing you don't understand," Oz began, leaning forward, "is that…"

Poacher arrived on the scene, flopping down into the chair next to them. "What's this about a bar fight?" He turned to look at Oz. "You startin' bar fights now, Oz?"

Oz shook his head. "I didn't start any…"

"Leave him alone." Multifarious snapped. "He can start as many fights as he wants."

"I didn't…"

Poacher held up his hands, surrendering the point. "I'm just sayin' that maybe we shouldn't go gettin' into fights in a bar we're supposed to be staking out."

"We do not start fights, we merely respond to fights which happen around us." Multifarious insisted. "I'm 'chaotic neutral' and Oz is 'lawful good,' so…" Mull trailed off, recognizing that Poacher was staring. "What? It's…"

Poacher cut him/her off. "I've lived with Stacy for *six years*, I know what 'The Nine Alignments' used in *Dungeons and Dragons* are." He sounded insulted that Multifarious would even doubt that. "I'm just objecting to you being 'chaotic neutral.' *Arn* is chaotic neutral, you're straight-up 'neutral evil' and you know it."

"'Neutral evil'!?!" Multifarious jumped to his/her feet. "Who the fuck taught *you* how to work up a character sheet!?!" Mull pointed at him. "This is why I hate working with 'Chaotic Good' people!"

Oz just blinked at them in mystification, completely lost. "I don't understand what this argument is even about."

"We're debating what our predominant identity trait is." Mull explained. "You have nine choices, on a spectrum. I'm saying that I'm a morally ambiguous free-spirit who doesn't play by the rules, and Poacher's contention is that I'm a selfish, conscienceless killer, who does bad stuff because I like it."

"Ah." Oz considered that for a beat, then turned to look at his masked companion. "I don't think you're evil."

"Ha!" Multifarious seemed very pleased by that and flipped Poacher off. "Told you, pig-fucker!"

"Well, of course he's going to say that! He's a fucking 'Lawful Good' choirboy!" Poacher protested, sneering at Oz. "And just 'cause Mull isn't currently evil doesn't mean that the classification is wrong."

"I don't consider myself good." Oz told them seriously, considering the matter. "I can try to be, but I'm not. And I feel like I'm getting farther and farther away from it as I go on."

Poacher simply rolled his eyes.

"My family is..." Oz began.

There was a noise from the back of the bar.

"Hold that thought, baby doll," Mull cut him off and stood up, "I've got work to do. You wait here."

Oz swiveled in his chair, watching as the masked person stalked across the bar, followed by Poacher. "What's going on?"

Mull pointed at a man who just walked in through the rear door of the bar. "*That* fucker is wanted on all kinds of kiddy-raping shit."

"How do you know?"

"Because I might hate doing this job, but that doesn't mean I suck at it."

Oz shrugged, accepting that explanation. He stood up to follow Mull and join in the questioning.

Mull waved him off. "Syd and I got this, don't get your hands dirty." He/she pointed towards the bartender, who had finally returned from his break. "You question that guy about the missing lady, leave the pedo to us."

Oz paused in his tracks for a moment. "You and Syd are going to be okay on your own?"

For some reason, he wasn't entirely comfortable with the idea of letting Multifarious go off alone with a wanted sex criminal, even if Poacher would also be there too. Hell, there was a very good chance that Sydney was wanted somewhere for one or two sex crimes himself.

He wasn't entirely sure why he should worry about such a thing though. It made absolutely no sense. There were few people in the Consortium who could handle themselves in a fight as well as Multifarious. But... he still didn't really like the idea.

Mull snorted. "Yeah, I think I can handle one asshole who likes to go to children's playgrounds and play 'One Pocket Pool,' Oz."

Oz paused, his brow furrowing in confusion. "I don't know what that means." He admitted.

Mull let out a sharp bark of laughter and turned to look at him. "Oh, *that's* my Oz." He/she shook her hands in the air. "You're just sooo *OZ!*"

Oz frowned. "Is... is that an insult?" He called after Mull, feeling like it was. "Mull?"

He didn't get an answer.

Fifteen minutes later, Oz had finished his questioning of the bartender and casually exited the bar, searching for his teammates.

Then watched in horror as Multifarious fell from the rooftop of a nearby building, and landed in a dumpster next to him.

Chapter 2

'I CAN'T GO NO LOWER,' SAID THE HATTER: 'I'M ON THE FLOOR, AS IT IS.'

- Alice's Adventures in Wonderland

NOW

Oz didn't feel well tonight.

He'd thrown up an hour ago and the stomach acid was dissolving his teeth. His lips felt dry, probably because he was dehydrated and his organs would soon start shutting down. He had a headache, which was a clear sign of a blood clot in his brain or a stress related aneurysm. His legs hurt, which undoubtedly indicated deep vein thrombosis. He still felt out of breath and the muscles under his eyes hurt, which were symptoms not even his mind could connect to a deadly disease or ailment.

To be honest... Oz just felt tired. Straight down to what remained of his soul.

He was pretty good at self-diagnosing his medical problems though. He always had been. It was an essential element of his day.

But Oz didn't really care about that right now. Despite his obsession with keeping germ-free and following the rules in order to avoid catastrophe, Oz wasn't overly concerned about what might happen to *him*. Sure, he might always buy new socks rather than washing his old ones– because otherwise it was the equivalent of wearing dirty diapers strapped to your feet– but that was just common sense.

No, at the deepest level, Oz's series of obsessions and rituals weren't really to protect *him* at all. Some of them could be used that way, but the *ultimate* goal was about protecting others. Given the choice, Oz would gladly shoulder the burden of tragedy alone.

That was the job.

That was what Oz signed up for. That was why Oz routinely left the safety of his home, which went against *every* instinct in his body. Going out into the world was stressful, dirty, and dangerous. It needlessly exposed him to germs, which would then be tracked back into his apartment. Oz didn't like doing it. But he did.

Because bad things should happen to *Oz*.

No one else.

No, at the moment, Oz didn't care at all about the fact that he was sitting in the waiting room of a *hospital,* of all things. A HOSPITAL! That was where dangerous pathogens lived, for Pete's sake! This *whole building* was so contaminated that it wouldn't be safe to be here, even if you leveled the whole thing and then drowned the area in enough disinfectant to rival the Biblical flood.

He didn't care *at all* about that right now.

He absently looked down at the red curl in the palm of his hand.

It was *her* hair. The paramedics had cut it off of her when they tried to suture the wound to her head and...

No.

She was going to be fine. She had to be. He'd followed all his rituals to the letter, hadn't he?

He was pretty sure he had, anyway. And if he hadn't that would just... well, that would be the end of him. It would have proven that he was a selfish piece of trash, who couldn't even do *one simple thing.* He had failed to do one of his rituals, and someone he cared about had...

He swallowed, as he thought about the end of that sentence.

No. Miss Quentin was going to be fine.

He had watched Multifarious fall from the building into one of the trash receptacles this afternoon, and as he rushed to check on his coworker, he discovered that the masked figure was in fact the woman he'd been rather infatuated with, Natalie Quentin. She was an employee at Oz's favorite store and... well, the truth was that it was his favorite store because *she* worked there, but that was immaterial.

In either case, the sudden realization that the two people were one in the same should have come as a much bigger surprise to him than it actually did. It was like he'd known it all along somehow. Or maybe that was just a coping mechanism.

The woman had been all but dead, whether he knew who she really was or not. The fall had crushed her beautiful body but she was still somehow clinging to life.

And all of this was Oz's fault.

That was the only explanation.

Oz had failed to do something... and that had brought this about. He was being punished by some unseen force, most likely because he hadn't managed to count the number of times the siren sound repeated for the *entire* ambulance ride. He'd tried. He tried so hard, but he just couldn't. And now that lapse had brought about this horrible event.

His life was dying.

The only thing in this world that Oz had ever wanted.

Everything was dying around him. And Oz was forced to watch.

Again.

"I think it's going to rain." Sydney Voldar, AKA "The Poacher," said conversationally from the seat next to him outside the hospital's ICU. "I've got a pain in my left leg." He tapped his *right* knee for some reason, but didn't bother to explain how a random ache was at all indicative of rain, especially when it wasn't afflicting the leg specified.

Oz continued staring at the strand of red hair in his gloved hand, but the other man didn't take the hint that Oz didn't really feel like talking. Sydney was one of those magical people who could have an entire conversation with you, without you ever needing to say a word. He had more than enough thoughts, feelings, and ideas to fill up any pauses.

The man was a child.

A large, murderously violent child.

"Yeah..." Poacher continued, clearing his throat. "Ever since that confounded lion got hold of me, I've..."

"Is your story going somewhere?" Oz croaked out, the first time he could remember speaking for an extended period. "Is the rain or lion somehow material to whether or not Miss Quentin survives?"

The other man appeared to think about that for a moment. "Not to my knowledge, no." Sydney finally decided, shaking his head. "That lion hasn't shown itself in years, so odds are that it won't appear tonight." He took on a determined face. "But don't worry. I'm *ready* if it does. I'm *always* ready."

Oz went back to staring at the hair.

Poacher frowned down at it, then at Oz's shaved head. "Don't think that's your color, New Guy."

"No." Oz agreed, trying not to cry. "I should have known better. It's... it's made for beautiful things. Not trash."

"Riiiiight..." Poacher drew out, sounding uncertain. "And that means...?"

"Nothing." Oz's voice sounded dead, even to his own ears. "Trash means nothing. It can't amount to anything, because of what it is."

"Trash?" Poacher guessed.

"Yes."

"Uh-huh."

Oz continued staring at the red curl in his hand, thinking about the graceful way Natalie's hair moved when she walked. Wanting the opportunity to see that even just once more. Wanting that so much it made him want to cry.

"Oz?" Poacher asked, sounding concerned. "What are you thinking about right now?"

"Lieber Coffee..." Oz whispered, somewhere far away. A place he hated, but a sight which brought him the only comfort he'd ever known.

"You want coffee?" Poacher sounded amazed by that, but got to his feet. "No problem, I'll go get you some, my man."

That got Oz's attention, yanking him out of his memories.

"NO COFFEE!" Oz bellowed. "That pot probably hasn't been washed since the Bicentennial! You'll get sick, then make her sick! Her doctors sick! The maintenance people so sick they miss something! You'll take the entire building down with you! *You'll kill her!*"

"Jesus!" Poacher jumped at the sudden change in volume. "How in the fuck can coffee cause structural failure?"

"It just... it just..." Oz kept staring at the curl of red hair, "...can."

"Huh." Poacher's eyes cut over to the coffee pot in sudden suspicion. "Well, learn something new every day, I suppose." He flopped down into the seat again. "They should put a warning label on those things, man."

"The adhesive used on most warning labels is toxic." Oz all but whispered, still feeling like he was in a daze.

"Huh." Poacher's eyebrows rose. "Didn't know that either. Good to know."

They fell into silence again and Oz lost all concept of time. He was dimly aware of the fact that his clueless companion had gotten a tennis ball from somewhere, and was now casually bouncing it off of the wall across the hall from them.

A large, murderously violent child who was *incapable of sitting still for more than five seconds at a time.*

"...which makes sense, if you really think about it." Sydney finished up a thought Oz had missed the beginning of, but somehow was still *sure* that the man's conclusion was factually incorrect. "And I've often thought you can tell a lot about a person by how they answer that question, you know?" He tossed the ball against the wall again. "You're lost in the mountains. A bear attacks you and you're unable to get away. It rips you half to death. Just before killing you, it walks away. You don't know if it's because it's through with you or if it's just taking a little break and will return. You have one bullet in your rifle. Do you take the shot at the retreating bear and risk angering it? If you miss or fail to kill it, it might come back and finish you off. Or do you hope it is leaving for good and *not* take the opportunity to shoot it while you still can?" He nodded to himself. "Really makes you think about some stuff." He turned to look at Oz. "What's your vote, man?"

Oz wasn't listening.

"I'd shoot." Sydney decided after a moment, as if there had ever been a question as to whether or not he would choose the most violent response to any given situation. "Take your shot and live with the consequences, that's what *I* say." He was silent for a long beat. "Because the bear always comes back. Always."

Oz still wasn't listening, only dimly aware of the man's chatter.

After an unknown period of time, Amy Eden, AKA "Amity," glided over in her usual Pilgrim themed outfit. She gently knelt down in front of him with her characteristic grace. Amy was one of the few members of the team that Oz had no issues with. She was kind, capable, humble and *always* impeccably clean. There was an air of quiet competence around the woman, and when she was nearby, it felt like your mother was tucking you in at night. Or so Oz assumed, anyway, since his own childhood hadn't exactly been idyllic.

He got the sense that hers hadn't either though. There was something almost sad about the woman; a look in her eyes that Oz recognized all too well.

"Oz, honey, how are you doing?" Her voice was soft and filled with genuine concern. "Sydney says you haven't said anything in two hours."

It hadn't been two hours since the "bear" story, had it?

She leaned her head down so that she blocked the red curl in Oz's hand, trying to get him to look at her. "You can't keep things bottled up, Oz honey. Okay?" The woman was gentle and warm. She had *no* business hanging out with the rest of his coworkers, who were *all* degenerate perverts and/or shiftless layabouts. The only people in the organization Oz had *any* respect for were Miss Quentin, Amy, Mack, Ceann, and Lexington. The rest of them were just deadweight and stymied every effort to achieve something worthwhile. It was like asking drunken sea monkeys to research String Theory.

"I got no clue what his problem is. He's broken or something." Poacher shrugged, as if at a loss over why someone wouldn't want to talk to him for hours about hypothetical gruesome bear maulings. "I don't do 'feelings' stuff, so I called over the... you know... the nicest person ever."

"Aw, that's so sweet, Sydney." Amy sounded *truly* moved for some reason. "I'm *touched* that you'd look to me when needing assistance, and so *proud* that you're looking after Oz in this difficult time." She reached out to gently pat the psycho's hand in comfort. "If anyone was ever foolish enough to doubt your *true* worth, your behavior tonight has surely shown them what an *honorable* and *kind* man you are. I am *so* proud of you."

Across the hallway, Amy's twin sister Emily Eden, AKA "Enmity," made retching sounds. She was wearing her "winter" costume, which looked very much like the witch hat and skimpy underwear she wore during the warmer months, only it was now a witch hat and shiny red pleather instead of red satin, and the garters connected to her high heeled thigh-high *boots*, rather than thigh-high *stockings*. She also wore a black overcoat to shield herself from the cold, but since she always wore it open, the effect was probably minimal.

In essence, she was now dressed as a pole dancer or flasher, rather than a hooker.

It was a welcomed change. He hated being seen with co-workers who refused to wear clothes, and at least the overcoat covered the girl to some degree.

Life with the Consortium had showed Oz that he needed to celebrate the little victories.

Amy ignored her twin's sound effects. "Oz, honey, I realize this is a horrible time to ask, but do you know if Multifarious would want to receive last rites or have a clergyman or representative of any particular faith or denomination come in to pray for her? I'm afraid I'm usually in charge of organizing such things, but we never had a chance to discuss her wishes. To be quite honest, I only just learned that she *was* a 'she' today." She paused, like switching to her actual line of interest. "Perhaps you could call your own religious representative at the same time? You could talk to them about what you're feeling while..."

"She's not going to die." Oz choked out for the hundredth time tonight. "She... she can't."

"I'm praying she doesn't, Oswald. I truly am. But she still should have someone here, honey, just in case. And so should you."

She bit her lower lip. "Someone... someone *you* can talk to about this." Amy advised. "Because I'm afraid what will happen if the Lord says it's her time to..."

"*She's not going to die!*" Oz bellowed. "*I don't give a shit what the Lord says!*"

"Hey!" Poacher's eyes narrowed in sudden fury at Oz. "Unless you wanna tell the Lord that *in person* tonight, *you watch how you fucking talk to...*"

"No, it's alright." Amy waved Sydney off, her voice tender and understanding. "Oswald is just upset, that's all."

He opened his mouth to apologize, but she simply patted his hand, cutting him off.

"I know." She smiled in kind reassurance. "I understand. That was my fault. Please don't worry about it, even for a second." She put her arm around him, and Oz didn't move away from the contact. Which even in his current state, he recognized as a bad sign. Oz hated being touched. Even being close to people caused his stress levels to go through the roof. The fact he hadn't moved away from her meant he was having a serious, serious problem with his emotions. And an out-of-control Oz in such a filthy environment was... bad. Very, very bad. "No matter what happens in there, I want you to know that there are people here who *love you*, okay? We're your family. We *need you* in our lives, so you've got to take care of yourself. That's what she'd want. That's what *we all* want. We *need you* to hold yourself together and keep being the brave and strong person we've all come to know and love, okay? It'll be alright. No matter what happens, it'll all be okay because you're with your family now. And so is she." She gave him a gentle smile. "Do you need a hug?"

"No." Poacher shook his head vehemently. "No, he *doesn't* need a hug, Aim."

"Oh, let her hug him if she wants to. His fucking girlfriend splattered all over the pavement." Emily chimed in as she smashed her fist into the front of the Coke machine repeatedly in an attempt to get it to dispense her cherry flavored beverage. "What harm could it do?"

"You stay outta this!" Poacher yelled. "No one asked you!"

"You asked me over here 'cause you asked *her* over here!" Emily pointed at her twin. "Package deal, asshole! You take the bad with the good, and right now the 'Bad' is telling you to let the fucking 'Good' hug Oz if she wants. This is very traumatic for *her too*, you know! You know how upset she gets when..." She slammed her fist into the machine again and screamed several obscenities, which was a rare display of frustration from a woman more commonly seen frustrating others.

"If Amy needs a hug, I will *find* someone for her to hug. Like a nun... or Harl or a fucking *baby lamb* or something, I don't know." Poacher pointed towards the other side of the room. "But right now, if you could just get the hell out of here, that'd be great."

Emily flicked him off and started towards the coffee pot.

"*No coffee!*" Poacher bellowed. "It'll cause the building to collapse!"

Emily spun around to pin him with an incredulous look. "What the fuck does that mean? How can coffee..."

"It just will." Poacher cut her off. "Oz said."

"Oh, Oz is out of his goddamned mind." Emily rolled her eyes and grabbed the entire pot of coffee. "Frankly, I think he's one of the craziest people around." She drank a long swallow of the liquid directly from the pot, then glanced at Oz. "No offense. I mean, I know you're like grieving or whatever right now because you're crazy and the crazy girl you're stalking took a header off a rooftop."

Amy frowned reproachfully at her twin. "Em, perhaps you can..."

"I know, I know." Emily rolled her eyes again and started to leave the room. She finished off the coffee, then absently dropped the empty glass pot into the trash as though it were a disposable cup. "I'm going." She paused in the doorway and glanced back at Amy, apparently waiting for her to catch up.

Amy gave Oz's hand one more reassuring squeeze. "If you need to talk to someone, I'll be right here, okay? Or dear Sydney." She turned to look at the man in question. "I'm sure he'll stay with you through all of this and make sure you don't need anything. He's *such* a good man, as you've undoubtedly noticed. A man who..."

Emily cleared her throat and Amy stopped that thought, hurrying away to catch up with her twin.

And the room fell into silence again.

"What the fuck is this?" Poacher snapped after a moment. "Mull's out of it for like five seconds and you start putting the moves on poor Amy? I mean *Amy!?!*" He pointed a finger at Oz in warning. "You *touch her* again, and I'll..."

"I was merely sitting here." Oz felt compelled to argue, despite feeling dazed and numb. "*She* touched *me.*"

"Just saying." Poacher crossed his arms over his chest and leaned back in the hospital chair, stretching his legs out in front of him. "If any part of *you* touches any part of *her* again, the next people who touch you will be *me* and then the *undertaker*. Get me?"

Oz pinched the bridge of his nose, ignoring the fact that he hadn't washed his hands or changed his gloves, and they were now near his eyes and thus passing all manner of germs directly into his body. It didn't even matter anymore. "I never should have joined up with you people."

"Frankly, that confused all of us." Poacher fished into his breast pocket for some beef jerky, which had probably been made during the Cold War. "What was the deal with that, anyway?"

"It seemed like a good idea at the time."

"Story of my life, little buddy. The story of my life." Poacher chuckled. "Well, for what it's worth, you're not the *most* useless little dipshit we got on the team."

"Thank you."

"You're welcome." Sydney nodded. "Most of the people more useless than you have already been killed though, so if I were you, I wouldn't get too comfortable around here unless you smarten up a little." He clapped him on the back, in an act that was probably meant to be reassuring but was delivered hard enough to cause posterior rib fractures. "See? See how much easier it is to get along with me when you're not acting like a complete douchebag?"

"This has been very illuminating." Oz intoned emotionlessly. "Can you please go somewhere else now?"

"Nope. 'Fraid not. See…"

"I don't care." Oz cut him off. He pointed towards the ICU doors. "Right now, all I care about is *Miss Quentin*."

"That bitch is tough as nails." Poacher informed him with authority. "She'll pull through."

"Are you a doctor now?"

"No, but I've thrown plenty of people off of roofs, so I have some experience in this field." Poacher considered that for a beat. "In fact, I'm kinda an *expert*." He tossed his tennis ball against the wall again. "Believe me, someone throws Mull off a roof, I know *exactly* how…"

"What?" Oz interrupted him again. "What was that?"

"I said: 'I'm an expert on…'"

"No, not that." Oz's mind whirled and the fog which had been clogging his thoughts all night cleared in an instant. "Someone *threw her!?!*"

"Well… yeah." Poacher sounded confused. "Didn't we tell you that? Figured it was kinda obvious. No way would she ever slip or take a header off the roof on her own, man. She's too good at…"

"Who?" Oz bit out, his hands forming fists.

Poacher shrugged. "Dunno him. Rumor is it's some norm crime bigwig. Monty says his name is 'Mercygiver'? They apparently know each other and..."

That was all Oz needed to hear.

He got to his feet and stalked down the hall, growing angrier with each step. All his life he'd had an explosive temper, boiling beneath the surface. He worked hard to keep it in check. Hold back the smoldering darkness which everyone saw in him. But right now, he didn't care.

Let it burn.

"Uh, Oz?" Poacher hurried after him worriedly. "Where are we going? You got the 'badass killer' walk goin' on and if we're gonna go killin' someone, I'd like to know before the shooting starts. It'll help to avoid any *misunderstandings*, ya know?"

Oz ignored him, prowling through the nearly empty hospital in search of his quarry. Most of the Consortium was currently in the field, allegedly "looking for clues," which Oz suspected involved taking naps, playing skeeball, and getting into pointless arguments with each other about game show results.

His coworkers were *idiots*.

He rounded the corner of the hallway and spotted the man he was looking for. Standing near the nurses' station stood the head of the Consortium's Purchasing and Production Department, Montgomery Tarkington Welles, AKA "Robber Baron." The man was dressed as a nineteenth century industrialist, right down to the top hat. ...A hat which good manners would say he had to *remove* once inside this building, but which Monty continued to wear because he was an evil son of a bitch who didn't care *at all* about good manners.

An evil son of a bitch who was apparently friends with the evil son of a bitch who'd thrown Natalie off a roof, and as soon as Oz got his hands on him, *that* motherfucker was *dead!*

Monty turned to look at him as Oz prowled forward. "Ah, Mr. Dimico. Is there any news? Should I tell my workers to begin wearing their black armbands or..."

Oz covered the distance between them in an instant, and the man's smug expression changed to one of utter confusion. He looked downright *shocked* as Oz grabbed the asshole by the front of his *stupid goddamn* coat and slammed him up against the wall.

"Talk!" Oz shouted into his face as the man's feet dangled in the air. *"Where is he!?!"*

Monty's expression returned to its normal smug calmness,

bordering on amusement. "Of whom do we speak?"

"Mercygiver!" Oz spat out. "You're *going* to tell me where he is, *right fucking now!*"

Beside them, the hulking form of Monty's zombie Viking bodyguard, Draugr, reacted instantly. She was several inches taller than Oz and *far* stronger. She grabbed him by the back of his shirt, putting the blade of her large Dane ax under his chin, preparing to behead him.

The woman was mean and strong and already dead.

And Oz ignored her completely, remaining focused on Monty.

The other man pretended not to understand how bad this situation was about to get. "I fail to see what would be in that for me."

"How about this: you *tell me* or I'll kill you right here." He met the man's one good eye. "And you *know* I can do it."

"Yes." A slow smile crossed Monty's scarred face. "Yes, I know *exactly* what you're capable of, Mr. Dimico." He peered at him as if seeing him for the first time. "Hello, Oswald." His smile grew wider. "It's nice to finally meet you. I *knew* you were in there somewhere. I told the others as much when they voted to allow you into our organization, but they didn't believe me."

"Are you going to tell me or am I going to kill you right here?"

"How about a *counteroffer*?" Monty sounded *utterly* unimpressed by Oz's threat. "I will tell you what you want to know, if you do a... small favor for me in the future? Nothing major. Just vote with me on..."

"Fine." Oz agreed immediately. It would be quicker than killing him and digging through his pockets for clues. "I don't care."

"*Splendid.*"

"Hey!" Poacher bellowed, shouldering his way into the scene. "What the fuck is *this!?!*" He pushed at Draugr, trying to knock the woman off of Oz. "Best put your dog on a *leash*, Monty." Poacher growled, pressing the twin barrels of his elephant gun under Draugr's chin. "Unless you want me to *put it down*."

The zombie woman's creepy glowing eyes narrowed in animalistic rage and she bared her teeth in a snarl.

Poacher rolled his eyes. "*Anywhere, anytime, anyhow,* sister. You name it and I'll fucking *be there*." His voice lowered. "But if you don't take your hands off my boy there, you're going to die *right here*."

"How about you, Mr. Voldar?" Came a voice behind them. "Where do *you* want to die?"

They turned to see Monty's *other* constant companion, Higgins. In recent weeks, Monty's ever-faithful lackey had taken to wearing a pearl handled Colt revolver at his waist. Oz wasn't entirely sure why, but he was fairly certain it wasn't good. No longer content to dwell mysteriously in the basement, the Purchasing and Production Department was growing increasingly militant and involved in more and more Consortium activities of late.

Ordinarily, Oz would be concerned about that. He'd be gathering information on what they could be planning and holding conferences with Wyatt on the options the company had to counter Monty's men and their *undoubtedly* evil schemes.

At the moment though, Oz didn't care.

Hate was flowing through his veins like fire, and he certainly wasn't going to back down.

"Kindly back away from my employer and Hildy." Higgins cocked the gun. "Please."

Poacher eyed the man, looking unimpressed. His hand ever so slowly moved towards the knife at his waist.

"Don't." Higgins warned.

"I assure you, Higgins is *quite* good with that weapon." Monty chimed in. "In fact, the way this deck is currently stacked, it looks as though he'll be the only one walking out of this hallway tonight." He glanced at his lackey. "Higgins? I'd prefer donations to the 'Montgomery Welles Memorial Fund' in lieu of flowers at my funeral."

"You have a memorial fund?" Poacher asked.

"Of course." Monty thought about it for a moment. "I'd like it to be granite." He decided. "Perhaps me on horseback, if that's not too clichéd."

Poacher laughed as he inspected the scene and the deadly weapons displayed. "Okay, how about we get this shit *going*. On three…"

Draugr and Higgins didn't seem at all phased by that idea, Monty continued smirking like he'd just won the lottery, and Oz was too far gone to care about the possibility of being decapitated by a zombie.

"One." Poacher readied his weapons. "*Two*…"

"What the hell is going on here!?!" Wyatt's voice boomed through the room. "*Why* is your zombie attacking Oz, *Welles!?!*" He demanded, paying no attention to the fact that Oz had his forearm against Monty's neck, preparing to kill him.

"Dammit." Poacher made a face. "Leave it to Wyatt to spoil

the fun."

J. Wyatt Ferral was in de facto control of the Consortium of Chaos, since the man had married its founder's daughter, Harlot. He was one of the few people in the organization who could maintain even semi-order among the team's *startlingly* violent, entirely unpredictable, and ominously insane work force.

Oz didn't have a huge problem with Wyatt, but that didn't mean they were best friends either. Honestly, Oz thought Wyatt's idea about the group being able to achieve something was basically delusional. He was willing to go along with it, but Oz understood that he'd have to do most of the heavy lifting in the "heroism" department. On a pessimistic level, Oz suspected that the man knew it was all a lost cause, but that Wyatt was too in love with his wife to admit it. Wyatt would get himself killed, trying to bring order to the chaos.

Wyatt was an idiot too, honestly. He just hid it better behind inspirational speeches and lectures.

Monty pushed Oz back and straightened his suit. "Miss Stoneblood and Higgins were just explaining to Mr. Dimico about the importance of *friendship*." He smirked. "The man who has the most friends, wins the fight."

"Fuck you, fuck your friends, and fuck the 'Corpse Bride' over there." Poacher took hold of Oz's shoulder and pulled him away from the scene, careful to keep the barrel of his weapon pointed at Draugr. "That creepy decomposing bitch comes near my boy again, and we're all gonna see how her weird regeneration thing deals with being *cremated*."

The woman watched their retreat with predatory eyes, her entire body tense, waiting for an opening. She took a step forward to follow them.

Monty's hand shot out in front of her to halt her progress. "Now, now… there's no need for *that*, Miss Stoneblood." Monty looked quite pleased over this entire fight, like it had gone exactly as he'd planned. "A deal is a deal. Higgins? Please be so kind as to tell Oklahoma Mike to cooperate fully with Oz's investigation. Whatever he needs. Anything Oz asks, is *me* asking." He straightened his coat. "Nothing moves in this city without one of my Irregulars hearing about it, Mr. Dimico. Take my word for it: you will soon find Mercygiver. Oklahoma Mike has *never* failed me."

"You're sending Oz to talk to a *pimp?*" Poacher asked in amazed disbelief. "*Oz?*"

"I'm sending Oswald to talk to a dear friend and a valued member of my Irregulars." Monty sounded almost insulted. "I'm terribly sorry if the help isn't coming from a source which meets *your* stringent moral standards, Sydney." His voice dripped with sarcasm. "I *know* how offended you are by depravity."

"And the other matter, sir?" Higgins asked seriously. "We just got word of it, and…"

Monty smiled deviously, like he was enjoying knowing something that no one else did. "Oh, I think our teammates can take care of it, don't worry." He said softly. "They'll figure it out in time."

"And if they don't, sir?" Higgins whispered.

Monty shrugged, looking unconcerned.

"What's. Going. *On?*" Wyatt demanded again, spacing the words out because he thought his audience was too stupid to understand. Which, to be fair, more than half of them probably were. "Don't we have enough problems without you morons killing each other in a *very public* hallway? Huh?" Wyatt pointed towards the ICU. "Mull is in there *right now* fighting for her life and…"

Oz looked down at the floor, recognizing that Wyatt was right. He needed to keep his anger under control. He didn't want to hurt anyone…

He was losing it.

He was a good person… Nothing like his aunt had said… He wasn't an evil man and he never would be.

Normally in cases like this, he'd just go shopping at the store and see Miss Quentin, who always calmed him down and brought his obsessions under control, but that obviously was an impossibility this time.

His hands were shaking as he started to silently count to five, again and again, trying desperately to get ahold of himself using one of his rituals.

One-two-three-four-five-One-two-three-four-five…

It wasn't working.

Oz was losing it.

Without Miss Quentin, Oz was losing it.

"Yes, we're all aware of where she is, *thank you*, Ferral." Monty turned to smile innocently at Wyatt. "We're all just *so* overset about this tragedy which has befallen our *dear* teammate, and I think we're all feeling on edge." He held his top hat over his heart, his voice somewhere between taunting mockery and terrible acting. "I hope she knows that *everyone* in the Purchasing and Production Department is praying for her speedy recovery. We are simply *prostrate* with grief over this senseless heartbreak."

Draugr grinned in amusement at her boss' barely concealed

sarcasm.

"I can see you're really broken up about it, Welles." Wyatt pointed at him. "Out. *Now.*"

"Frankly, I wouldn't want help from any god which would listen to *Monty's* prayers, anyway." Poacher informed no one in particular. "'Prolly like that 'Temple of Doom' god, or somethin' with all skulls and chanting and shit."

Oz focused his entire mind on not simply killing Montgomery before the man could say another word.

Ten quadrillion voices started telling him to go for it, pledging their assistance if he did and sharing with him all of the reasons why Monty deserved it. Whispering to him from the floor tiles and the wallpaper and his own contaminated hands...

One-two-three-four-five-One-two-three-four-five...

Wyatt ignored that, remaining focused on Montgomery. "I don't know what you're *really* doing here, but I want you and your little friends to *leave.*" He told the other man again, pointing at the door. "*Now.*"

Monty tipped his top hat theatrically. "And so we shall." He limped towards the elevators. "Still, you'll never know how glad I am that *you're* here, Wyatt. It's *right* where you should be. Trust me on that." The elevator doors started to close and the man smiled again like he was enjoying a private joke. "Good *luuuuck...*" He all but sang before disappearing from view.

Poacher waited until Monty was gone, then slipped his weapon back into its holster strapped to his back. He turned to glare at Oz as he made his way back towards the doors to the ICU. "Not to question your decision-making here New Guy, but maybe you should *chill the fuck out* before deciding to piss off 'Dr. Strangelove' and his undead army, huh?"

"Montgomery doesn't scare me." Oz informed him, taking a deep breath to steady his mind.

"I ain't afraid of rattlesnakes either, but I *sure as hell* wouldn't go out of my way to fuck with one." He paused. "Unless I was hungry. You ever had rattlesnake? Those little bastards are delicious."

Poacher's powers involved being able to exhibit the abilities of any creature whose skin or fur he wore. Which meant that he ate a lot of weird things and had more than a few stories about animal attacks.

The novelty of the tales had long ago worn off for Oz.

Wyatt stood motionless for a long moment, watching the

elevator doors. Something was obviously bothering the man. A lot. "Start evacuating the hospital." He ordered as Lexington Gwinnet walked up behind him, dressed in her usual Revolutionary War patriot uniform.

Lexie looked confused. "Why?"

"Just please do it, Lexie." Wyatt started towards the stairs. "Quick as you can." He looked back at her. "Monty just left. And the rats don't leave unless the ship is sinking."

The woman nodded and immediately dashed to the nurse's station to begin the process.

Oz continued down the hall, intending to go run a quick errand. "The only man I mean to have words with tonight is Mercygiver, but I'll fight *anyone* who stands between me and him." He stormed towards the elevators. "I'm going to go arrest him, so that when Miss Quentin wakes, I can share the good news with her."

"Yeeeeah... that's not gonna happen." Poacher dashed ahead of him, blocking his path. "Oz, you and me ain't really that close. Truth be told, I don't know jack-shit about you and don't really care to learn. I do, however, know a lot about that girl in there, so I hope you listen to me right now because I'm being completely serious with you: Mull is a stone-cold *killer*. Killed more men than old age." He shook his head. "Someone *beat the living shit* outta her and then tossed her off a roof." He pointed back into the room. "And whoever did *that* to someone who could probably take *me* in a fight, is *not* someone you want to meet up with alone." He shook his head again. "Because if that motherfucker could do *that* to her, then– and I'm really sorry if this hurts your feelings, little buddy, but I don't really care—you don't stand a *fucking chance.*" He crossed his arms over his chest. "So, no. No, you're *not* going after him alone. Getting yourself killed won't help her in any way. So, we're going to sit right here until she stabilizes or..." He cleared his throat, because he couldn't bring himself to say: "dies." "...then you and me– and probably a couple other capable badasses– are going to look into this. I'll track him down and then once we've beaten him to within an inch of his life and he's no longer a threat, you can finish him off. Okay? How's that sound?" His tone was one of an adult promising their child an ice cream cone if they behaved themselves at the dentist.

"Stand. Aside." Oz growled, his anger struggling to get free. "I mean it, Sydney. You'll *never* see me more serious than I am right now. I'm *going* to go bring that man to justice, and then..." He stopped, unable to go on. Recognizing for the first time that there really wasn't a point if Miss Quentin died. No point for rituals or justice or Oz himself. "...then..."

For a moment, Oz was a child again, huddling under the table. Feeling the dirty fast food wrappers and cold ketchup under his palms, mixing with the hot blood...

And there was nothing Oz could do. He was as helpless then as he was to save Natalie now.

He was useless. Useless trash.

He'd just make everything worse.

He sank to the floor and put his head in his hands, trying not to sob.

"I know." Poacher sat down in one of the plastic chairs, his voice grim. "Look, man. I ain't gonna lie to ya. You got dealt a real shitty hand today. And I'd like to say it'll get better, but we both know that it probably won't." He leaned closer to him. "But now is not the time to go losing your shit, Oz." He told him seriously. "When that time arrives, I'll let you know. But it isn't now." He met his eyes. "Hold together."

Oz nodded weakly, swallowing the lump in his throat. "...Okay."

"Good. Because you're important. Important to her, important to the rest of 'em." Syd stopped to think the matter over. "You're lucky. I ain't never been important to anyone. That's just not who I..." A song came over the hospital's sound system which caused Poacher's head to snap to attention. He pointed at the ceiling. "Connie Francis?" He instantly brightened, like that meant something. "Oh, shit! This is my *jam,* little buddy!" His head began to bob to the music. "This is a sign, my man. Connie makes *everything* better, doesn't she?" There was an irritatingly cheerful buzzing sound and he reached down to his pocket. "Excuse me for a sec, 'kay?" Poacher answered his cell phone in direct violation of hospital policy. "Hey, what's the...?" There was the sound of panicked shouting from the phone's tiny speaker. "Well, how much blood is there?" The man wondered calmly, then paused to listen to the answer. "Hmm... Well, that's no good then." He began to tap his hand to the beat of his Connie Francis song and mouth along to the words while he listened to the person on the other end of the call. "No, look in the cabinets for bleach." Pause. "No, *bleach.* Fabric softener won't help."

Oz got back to his feet, trying to get ahold of himself again. His anger and hate were fading, replaced with a determination to be here for Miss Quentin, *then* deal with tracking down her attacker. And having an emotional breakdown.

Oz always tried to have careful control over himself.

He had slipped, but he was better now.

And no one had died.

"I can't come right now." Poacher told the person on the phone, but the caller didn't seem to appreciate that news. "'Cause I'm watching the New Guy for Mull, that's why." Poacher explained. "Look, just give me the address and you get out of there quietly, and I'll call up Flannery and she'll take care of it, okay?" The person said something and Poacher scoffed in dismissal. "Oh, that could've happened to *anyone*. Happens to me all the time. Don't worry about it."

Oz was about to ask him what that meant, but trailed off as he caught sight of a doctor walking down the hall. He raced over to her. "Has Miss Quentin's condition improved at all?" He asked anxiously.

The doctor blinked at him in bafflement. "Improved?" She looked confused. "I'm a pathologist."

Oz's eyes narrowed. "Why are you here then?"

"...You called for me?"

"I called for The Mortician." He corrected.

"We don't have a mortician on staff." She shook her head. "You'll have to call one of the local funeral homes."

"Not 'a' mortician, '*The*' Mortician!" He threw his arms out in exasperation. "As in 'OUR' Mortician! He was supposed to come in here and look at her!"

"You guys have your own mortician? Wow." She picked up the paperwork and glanced at it. "Judging from your friend's chart though, my guess is you supply him with a lot of work." She flipped over one of the papers. "*Jesus*... This looks like the sheet of a DOA, not someone who..."

"She's not going to die." Oz told the woman, trying to keep his temper under control.

The pathologist put the chart down. "I think you need to prepare yourselves for this." She advised. "Call her family so that they can come say goodbye, because she doesn't have long."

"We're here already." Poacher corrected.

Oz nodded. "And we're *not* saying goodbye."

Chapter 3

"'WELL!' THOUGHT ALICE TO HERSELF, 'AFTER SUCH A
FALL AS THIS, I SHALL THINK NOTHING OF TUMBLING
DOWN STAIRS! HOW BRAVE THEY'LL ALL THINK ME AT
HOME! WHY, I WOULDN'T SAY ANYTHING ABOUT IT,
EVEN IF I FELL OFF THE TOP OF THE HOUSE!' (WHICH
WAS VERY LIKELY TRUE.)"

- Alice's Adventures in Wonderland

Some days you wake up and there's no cereal.

Some days you wake up and there's no milk.

Mull had woken up this morning and found she was out of both.

And that's how she knew she was going to die.

It was amazing the number of things which could be predicted with breakfast foods. Not that Mull had really heeded her sundries' warning. No, she would have gone to work anyway.

Mull liked her job.

And she wasn't even overly fond of cereal. That was Natalie's deal. Because it was perky and colorful and utterly meaningless. Natalie's entire idiot life was spent in Happy Cartoon Cereal Land.

Still, Mull was actually rather surprised to wake up. The last thing she remembered was fighting her ex, Rondel Stanna, AKA "Mercygiver," on a rooftop, then... Well, she hadn't so much "lost," as it was that the fight was called on account of sudden de-elevation and catastrophic organ damage.

It actually hurt to open her eyes, which was probably a bad sign.

She reached up to pull the oxygen mask from her face, but found that just moving her arm caused her to almost scream in pain and pass out from exhaustion.

Beside her, a shadow moved...

On instinct, Mull blindly grabbed for a knife from the tray of food next to her and stabbed it into the shape.

Sadly, she'd only managed to grab a bendy straw, which immediately bent in half and fell to the floor. Plus, the action had forced her to move her shoulder, which made her gasp in agony. She was bleeding there. And something serious was broken, because it didn't feel right.

But they hadn't fixed it in surgery.

Which Mull knew was also a bad sign. That meant she had bigger problems than a busted shoulder, which she wasn't expected to survive.

She was basically strapped to this bed and she couldn't move! Fear surged through Natalie like a wave, eyes darting around. She was on the verge of a full-fledged panic attack, which would be a *really* bad idea in her present condition.

When Nat got afraid, bad things happened.

Mull recognized that fact, but was unable to stop it. Her breathing tried to quicken, but the pain and busted ribs made that all but impossible. It felt like someone was sitting on her chest, which only made the panic worse.

"Miss Quentin?" Someone asked, his voice breaking. "It is very good to see you. Although I could have done without being stabbed."

Mull blinked her swollen eyes, trying to see through the gauze and tubes which covered most of her vision. "...Oz?" She croaked in uncertainty. Her throat felt like it was almost bleeding it was so sore.

"I'm here." The man assured her with quiet confidence.

Natalie relaxed, the panic falling away. Oz was one of the few people in this world who she trusted completely. If Oz was here then she was fine.

Well... she was still in some kind of hospital, but she wasn't in any immediate danger from anything other than dying from her injuries.

"You're in the hospital." Oz told her softly, apparently thinking she couldn't recognize the space. "How... how are you feeling?"

She blinked at the stupid question, but found it almost charming. "Hospital." She croaked. "How... do you think... I'm doing?"

Oz relaxed slightly and leaned forward. "I supposed that's fair." He cleared his throat. "Can you tell me what happened?"

She absolutely could, yes. But Oz needed to be protected from the darker elements of Mull's world. She would deal with it, once she was out of this place and Oz was safe somewhere. Protected behind locks and bars and expensive security systems. Somewhere far away from Mull's former partner.

She simply stared at him, through swollen eyes.

Oz seemed to view her obstinance as amnesia, and nodded. "Well, don't push things. It might be best not to remember some of it."

Jesus. Nothing was sadder than Oz giving her the victim speech. "I got beat up, not gang raped, Oz. It's not traumatic, it's just painful."

Oz laughed, but there was something off about the sound. She wasn't really used to hearing him laugh at all, but this time he sounded... nervous. No. He sounded scared. And grieved.

Shit...

She looked down at the bandages covering her chest, then met his worried eyes. "Let me see the chart." She said softly, moving her oxygen mask aside.

"...You're going to be fine." He assured her, his voice noticeably strained.

"Let me see the *chart*, Oz." She repeated, more forcefully. "Please."

He picked up the chart and held it for a moment, obviously thinking about his best course of action, then reluctantly handed it to her. Her eyes skimmed the page, cataloging the catastrophic damage to her body.

Damn.

She tried to make a whistling sound, but was unable due to her split lip and general lack of breath. "Jeez." She weakly tossed the chart onto the table. "Guess... guess I won't have to worry about how I'm going to pay my MasterCard bill anymore."

"You'll be fine."

"No. I won't." She told him flatly. "We both know it." She tried to smile, but it had no real emotion behind it. "I appreciate your lies though. Thanks. That's sweet."

He opened his mouth to reply, but obviously struggled for something to say. Finally, he simply nodded.

By his nature, Oz was hopeful. He was one of the only people in the Consortium who had hope for the future. He wasn't dark or gritty or any of that nonsense. Oz was idealistic and he believed in people. He knew that he wasn't the most powerful person in the world, but he was willing to put himself in harm's way, all the same. Because he was a genuinely good person and there wasn't a thing you could do to him which would ever change that.

There was something so comforting about that.

Mull always treasured that about him.

Seeing even *him* be unable to argue with her about her looming death made it extra tragic somehow, and that drove the point home.

"I've imagined how I'd die my entire life." She looked around the hospital room. "I didn't picture it this way." She let out a long wheezing breath. "Fucking *Ronnie*. I really should have killed him before now." She pointed at Oz. "This is a learning opportunity for you: if someone might kill you one day, kill their ass *first*."

"I'll keep that in mind."

They both fell silent.

Rationally, she recognized that there were a hundred thousand different things she should tell this man, while she still had the opportunity. But Natalie was in charge at the moment. And Natalie was a coward.

No one liked Natalie.

Luckily, it was looking like the world wouldn't have to put up with her for too much longer.

Her eyes cut over to the pile of paperwork sitting on the table beside Oz. "And what have you and Shaggy been investigating while I've been out, Scoob?"

He frowned in confusion. "Who?"

She made an annoyed sound. "Jesus, buy a TV."

"I had a TV once, but its magnetic fields were giving me brain cancer and microbes in the ground water were messing up my reception anyway."

"Uh-huh." She absently started pressing random buttons on her IV, just *because*. "You're kinda high-maintenance, anyone ever tell you that, Oz?"

"I can't say as they have, no."

"Well, in any case, you are. You're like one of those exotic butterflies that need their own hothouse to keep alive. Too precious for this world." The IV started to make a frantic beeping sound, which she ignored. Hopefully beeping meant "Okay, okay, I'll start dispensing more morphine, lady." She met his eyes again. "Ready to tell me what you were investigating now?"

"Mercygiver." He spat out.

Mull's blood froze. "Yeah, that's not really a good idea. Just... Just let me deal with him, okay? He's not someone you should really be around."

"So I'm told."

"Yo!" She called as loudly as she could, ending in a weak pained cough. Her mouth started to taste metallic, which she could only assume was from blood. Which was very, *very* bad. "Asshole! Get in here!"

She knew he was out there. It was the most annoying place in the world he could *possibly* be, which meant he was obviously there.

Sure enough, Poacher's head popped into the room a second later. "Yeah? What?"

"You're letting Oz go off to fight Rondel?" Her eyes narrowed in rage. "You are a fucking idiot, anyone ever tell you that?"

"Absolutely." Poacher nodded seriously. "My parents' last words to me."

"What the fuck is your problem!?!" She demanded. "You can't let him go off on his own!"

"He won't be 'alone,' I'll make sure I'm right there to back him up." Poacher promised.

"Then you're *both* fucking idiots."

"And *there's* my last words to my parents as they drove away, yeah." Poacher chuckled to himself at the memory. "'Course, I doubt they heard me over the sirens."

Oz frowned, obviously unaccustomed to being involved in this kind of conversation. "I should point out that the doctor has given you orders to remain calm."

"Believe me, I'll be *perfectly* calm as I slap the shit out of you both and then die."

"Whatever." Poacher rolled his eyes. "I'm gonna go get a sandwich. You want anything?"

She moved, wincing in pain and the unexpected sensation of being unable to feel her legs. "Some new internal organs would be nice. I think mine are shot."

"I doubt they have that at the lunch cart, but I'll ask." Syd pointed down the hall. "They probably have hot dogs, which are mostly organ meat and stuff, that might count."

Natalie held up a finger to Oz, indicating that she needed a moment. "Can I talk to this moron alone for just a sec?"

Oz nodded, but didn't look especially happy about the idea of leaving her side. "I'll go speak with your doctors about their treatment plans."

She tried to keep from rolling her eyes. "Treatment plans." Right. Their treatment plans involved a coffin and then a large bill being sent to her estate.

Oz shuffled from the room, leaving her alone with Poacher.

She held out the medical chart to him, and the man glanced down at it.

"Well..." He obviously tried to come up with some way of sugarcoating it for her.

"No bullshit." She ordered, meeting his eyes. "I'm a professional."

He moved the covers from off of her chest and stared down at the bandaged wound for a long moment, his face unreadable. "You have about an hour." He pronounced, his voice tight. "Thirty minutes, if you talk a lot." He cleared his throat. "I'm sorry."

Receiving sympathy from Syd was pretty much the saddest thing she'd ever experienced. Both in terms of it indicating just how far she'd fallen in life and in terms of his typically blissfully oblivious face being contorted with grief. "Yeah." She nodded somberly. "About what I figured." She let out a long wheezing breath. "I really fucked it up good this time, Syd."

He was silent for a long moment. "Yep." He finally nodded. "Everybody does, sooner or later, girly." He looked down at the floor. "...Everybody does."

She cleared her throat, trying to keep it together. Crying in front of this asshole would be the final humiliation at the end of a *particularly* humiliating day. "Listen... you're basically my only friend besides Oz, Syd. Well, the only friend I even *kinda* trust, anyway." She met his eyes again. "When I'm gone, I'm putting *you* in charge of Oz. Keep him safe from himself, okay? Make sure he doesn't do anything— or *anyone*– stupid."

He made an annoyed sound, like a child refusing to do his chores. "*Ooo-ooh*, I don't want to spend the rest of my life watching out for that little loser, Mull! Come on!"

She just continued staring at him.

He made a face, like she'd misunderstood. "I didn't say I *wouldn't*, just that I won't *like* it." He nodded, sounding sulky. "I'll never understand why you're so interested in him anyway. The guy creeps me out sometimes. He's like the suburban guy who is revealed to be the killer at the end of the Lifetime movie, but yet you knew it all along. And everyone will talk about how, 'It's always the quiet ones.'"

"He's a good person. Better than us."

"Oz is out of his fucking mind and you know it."

"You can be out of your mind and still be a good person." Natalie tried to keep her voice steady, thinking about leaving Oz without anyone to protect him from himself. "Oz is just in his shell right now. The world hurt him and he's hiding from it. We need..."

She swallowed, feeling weaker. "We need to..."

"He...," Poacher cleared his throat, recognizing that she was getting tired and wanting to end the argument, "he won't be alone. Anyone messes with your boy, they'll mess with me. I'll fuck their shit up good, and let them know you sent me. You have my word." He let out a long sigh. "Hell, I don't plan on living much longer anyway. I can watch out for him until then. No big deal."

Natalie stared at the floor with unfocused eyes, trying to comprehend that she was going to die today.

The cereal had warned her, obviously, but it was still a hard concept to accept.

It was one of those things she'd always known, but it something that was going to happen in some far off distant future.

But death was going to find her in the far off distant *now*.

Somehow Captain Crunch had known.

Captain Crunch always knew.

"Well... shit." She finally said softly, coming to terms with the inevitable. "Ain't that a bitch."

"Yep." Poacher nodded. "Did... did you still want me to get you that organ sandwich? Or not? Because if you eat quick, you could probably finish it off." He paused. "Unless there's a line at the cart. Then you'd kinda be fucked. I mean more than you already are, obviously."

"Don't waste your money."

"Oh, I wasn't planning on *paying*." He waved off that insane idea, heading for the door. "Haven't paid for anything but strippers since I was 10."

"You started visiting strip clubs at 10?"

"Hell no." He turned to give her a friendly wink. "Before that they just danced for free."

Oz appeared at the door again. "Are you done with your private conversation? May I return now?"

Mull rolled her eyes. The way Oz said "private conversation" was the same way someone else might have said "are you done fucking like drunk teenagers?"

"Yes, our torrid affair is done." Mull informed him. "He's finished making violent love to me and now I'm in that blissful warm period which follows."

"Oh." Oz nodded, processing that. "Um... good. I don't know why *anyone* would..."

"That was a joke." She told him, not entirely sure if he knew that or not. Sometimes it was hard to tell with Oz. She seriously doubted anyone in his life had ever teased him before.

Which was sad. Because with her gone, there'd be no one to change that. She could *tell* Syd to do it, but he probably wouldn't like being ordered to flirtatiously tease Oz on occasion. That seemed like the kind of thing which might be too big an ask from her.

"Ah." Oz looked vaguely relieved.

She pointed at the pitcher of water on her hospital tray. "You're kind of slow tonight, you know that?"

He immediately poured her a glass and then held it out for her so that she could get a drink. "Well... I've had a bad day."

$Chapter$ 4

"ALICE THOUGHT THE WHOLE THING VERY ABSURD, BUT
THEY ALL LOOKED SO GRAVE THAT SHE DID NOT DARE
TO LAUGH"

- Alice's Adventures in Wonderland

THREE YEARS AGO

Oz didn't feel well today.

He thought his throat glands were swollen. He had a slight headache, which could be a brain tumor. His eyes felt strained, obviously an indication of a stroke. And the lighting in the embassy had made his skin itch. Every second he'd been there, he could feel cancerous melanomas slowly forming in his skin cells, like plants thriving under a glow lamp.

He had been having a bad night.

He hated parties. He hated all of the people, and the noise, and questionable food which *anyone* could have tampered with. He hated awkward small-talk, he hated having to wear dress clothes since there was never enough time to ensure they were properly sanitized, and he hated wasting time which would be better spent on more important Freedom Squad duties than "mingling." Oz had only recently joined the city's largest super-team, but he wasn't finding his new coworkers especially endearing. But Oz was used to that. He never really felt like he fit in anywhere.

The world was preoccupied with nonsense and Oz always felt like the last sane man alive.

Strictly speaking, Oz was against most forms of "fun." Despite what the word implied, fun just… wasn't very fun. It was annoying. And it forced you to be around annoying people, who were most likely intoxicated. There was more to life than listening to the ramblings of crazy people, and hoping to escape their company before they began vomiting their last meal all over the floor.

Oz had warned several partygoers that their drinking was

possibly the sign of a deeper alcohol abuse problem, but they hadn't welcomed his advice or business cards for local chapters of AA, for some reason.

Then his supervisors in the Freedom Squad had forbidden him from trying to help people at the party recognize their own self-destructive addictions. Which, to Oz, made absolutely no sense. Helping people was about more than just rescuing them from villains or burning buildings. Helping people sometimes meant that you needed to rescue them from themselves.

But, then again, that was why he was being punished with this assignment in the first place.

Oz's employers didn't like him; he didn't fit in with the Freedom Squad. They looked down on him because Oz had gone into heroics without the near mandatory years as a sidekick and without graduating from the Horizons Academy, where most prospective heroes matriculated before entering the profession. Oz had found his way directly onto the Freedom Squad team, and the rest of them didn't like it. Particularly since he'd done so directly from his prison cell.

Plus, they found him creepy.

The Freedom Squad recognized his power and allowed him to join, but had still stuck Oz at a flimsy desk in their dimly lit basement. The cold drafts there doomed him to arthritis and the florescent lights overhead slowly poisoned his body with deadly rays, while the constant buzzing drove him mad. His employers gave him all of the jobs that they considered themselves too important to do, which meant that Oz spent most of his time dealing with the police and going out on patrols with the other people the team thought expendable.

Tonight was no exception. The Freedom Squad had sent him to the formal event because everyone on duty was required to go. Even him. So, he just sort of stood in the corner for most of the night, trying to avoid the idiots around him. Oz had gotten good at that over the years. Most people steered clear of him by instinct, recognizing... Well, they were undoubtedly recognizing what his aunt had always called his family's "curse." But Oz didn't believe in curses or "bad blood."

That's what he had told his psychiatrist in prison, anyway, but she hadn't listened. And the other inmates were entirely unwilling to attend his PowerPoint lectures on the issue.

At the moment though, he was driving one of the partygoers home from the event at the Agletarian embassy. And Oz didn't really know why he was doing that. It certainly didn't seem like something he would ordinarily do.

It was very curious.

A complete stranger was sitting inside his vehicle. She was sitting there, a foot away, and Oz could smell her perfume. Oz HATED perfume. It got caught in his throat and made him retch. It was some horrible oily miasma of toxic chemicals, dripping down a stranger's sweaty body, which tried to choke the life from his lungs every time he was around it. Perfume was a nightmare! ...In this case though, he found the soft jasmine scent completely feminine and enjoyable.

It was very, *very* pleasant.

Which *also* didn't seem especially "Oz" to Oz.

What was going on with him?

Was this a symptom of some deeper problem? His mind instantly raced through every disease, condition, and ailment he'd ever studied, searching for a medical explanation for his strange activities tonight.

And he didn't sense any unknown pathogens in the car with him. But that was sometimes like trying to listen for a specific whisper in a stadium crowded with people screaming.

"So... you're with the Freedom Squad, then?" The redhead asked, sounding oddly uncertain about the news. Most people were excited to meet one of the heroes who protected the city. Not that Oz really considered himself in that way, since he spent a large part of his time doing paperwork and trying to mitigate the corruption and idiocy of his bosses. But still... it would have been nice if the woman was impressed with him.

He'd always wanted to be extraordinary.

But no one was ever really impressed with Oz.

It was one of the reasons why he'd never been able to make parole.

Well, that and the fact that he told the woman on the parole board that the mole on her neck could be cancerous.

Which it almost *certainly* was, no matter what she claimed. He had probably saved her life.

But that wasn't the kind of heroics that people appreciated. That was the kind of heroics that left you standing alone at the party, avoiding people.

"Yes."

The redhead nodded and began fiddling with the knobs on the radio, switching off his history lecture and turning on techno club music instead.

Oz stared at the woman's graceful fingers as they twisted the volume higher, amazed both that she would change the station and that he wasn't at all upset that she had turned on such aggressively awful music.

She had such *beautiful* hands.

Which... was probably a creepy thought to have. Oz wasn't sure. He couldn't recall ever having thought that before, so he wasn't sure if it was something that other people thought about or not.

People confused Oz.

He didn't really spend a lot of time around them.

For one thing, people were the primary vectors for any number of deadly diseases, parasites, and germs, all of which were constantly stalking Oz. He had to be on his guard every second of every day. They could ambush him at any moment.

For another... Oz... Oz didn't really trust himself enough to be around people for long. He was too afraid of... Well, he just didn't want to slip, like the other people in his family had. He didn't believe in "bad blood" but he'd certainly seen its alleged effects, and he didn't want that to happen to him.

He was a good person. A hero. He was in no way evil; he was trying his best to live a moral life.

He needed to keep his footing firm.

...For a split-second, he was surrounded by garbage again, feeling cold, rotting blood drip on his face.

As quickly as the memory started, it was gone, and the nightmarish smell of the dump was replaced by the alluring scent of jasmine.

"I haven't seen you around before." She said, sounding vaguely curious. She looked at him with inquisitive eyes. "Where have they been hiding you, huh?"

"Connecticut."

"Is that where you're from?"

He shook his head. "No. You?"

She shrugged. "I'm from all over."

"You don't really like sharing details about yourself, do you?"

"My life is a jigsaw puzzle, Oz. I could show you pieces of it, but neither of us would have any idea what the fuck the bigger picture is." She shrugged, as if helpless to control her own life. "Besides, you're what? Mister open, all of a sudden?"

"Well, at least I'm willing to share my name and occupation." He defended, turning left and trying to ignore the impulse to turn down the radio. The volume was undoubtedly harming his ear drums.

He could feel them dying, their screams mixing with the wails of the so-called "instruments" used in this particular song. "And why I was at a party inside a foreign embassy."

"Maybe I just like being 'mysterious.'" She teased. "I very rarely get the chance. I'm not very exciting."

"I find that hard to believe."

She absently stared out the window, watching the city's nightlife. "Do you like being a hero?"

It was a change of subject and Oz took a second to silently debate whether it was a diversionary tactic to return the topic to him, or if she just really found her own life uninteresting.

"Sometimes." He finally answered.

"I don't really understand how anyone could like the things the Freedom Squad does." She decided, sounding righteously indignant. "The entire purpose of superheroes is to keep people down using intimidation. And you bastards in the Freedom Squad, you're the worst of all."

"I don't know that I'd say '*worst*'," he hedged, recognizing that the woman had a point, "I'd say that we're..."

"You look around this city and you know what I see?"

Oz had no idea. "Buildings?"

"I see a people who are sick to death of the oppressive boot of imperialist super-powered thugs, stepping on their necks!"

"Superheroes consistently rank as some of the city's most popular citizens."

"All of those polls are lies." She announced, as if having received inside information on them.

"Some of them were done by the most respected news sources in the country."

"A country run by those very same super-powered thugs!" She threw her arms wide in the confines of the car, and Oz again noticed how lovely her perfume was. It smelled like dreams and promises. "Of course they agree! Everyone agrees with a system which benefits *them*!"

Oz squinted in confusion, trying to follow along. "So, I'm not just part of a corrupt profession, I'm part of a corrupt government now?"

"You're a victim in all of this too, Oz!"

"Oh. Well, that's nice."

"You're just the poor brainwashed patsy they have out in front, giving their crimes a comforting face!"

He frowned at that, trying to process the idea. "No one has

ever found me 'comforting.'"

"...then The Capes get inside your head when you're young, guiding you to be one of them. To buy into their horrible practices and engage in the rape of this country." She nodded. "Every single hero is a sex offender!"

"I'm not sure statistics support that claim, ma'am." He thought about it for a beat. "I'd say no more than half."

"The problem with the world is laws."

"I thought the problem was the Capes trying to *enforce* those laws?"

"The Capes are just victims, Oz, keep up. Laws are someone else trying to enforce their will on you. Someone else playing god. But think of all the horrible things that laws have given us. Slavery. Wars. Killing people. Taxes. Daylight Savings Time." She shook her head. "Laws are the problem. We can't have them and be free."

"You're suggesting that we... outlaw *laws*?"

She nodded, obviously pleased that he'd been able to understand her argument so well.

Oz had no real reply to that. His entire world was built around routines and rules, which governed everything he did, said, and thought.

Oz had rules about how many times he needed to flip the light switch when he exited or entered a room, and rules on how many steps he needed to take inside each square of concrete he was walking on, and rules on how many times he needed to count to five before turning on the shower nozzle each morning.

Rituals were the only thing which brought order to the chaos of the world and gave him a sense of control.

You follow the rules, bad things won't happen.

So the idea of tossing all of that aside was...

Well, he knew her idea was insane, but at the same time, he found himself half convinced by it. If for no other reason than he liked the sound of her voice and the way she moved around in the small confines of the car.

Oz was rarely this close to someone. His own compulsions usually kept him much further away from people, for fear they'd contaminate him in some way.

But being close to this woman was... exciting.

"When you put it that way," he shook his head, "on second thought, no. I don't like working for the Freedom Squad. I like being a hero, but they're rarely heroic."

"Yes!" She slapped her hand down on the back of his in a

congratulatory way. But Oz almost winced it was so inappropriately erotic.

Oz didn't like it when people touched him, even when he was wearing gloves. Particularly if he didn't know the person. That was how you caught diseases which would kill you in moments. But in this case, he found himself coping quite well. As her slender fingers curved under to touch his gloved palm, Oz closed his eyes and tried to remain professional, for fear he'd do or say something which scared her.

"How about you?" He cleared his throat and moved his hand away, changing the subject and trying to keep his voice level, because her touch having that kind of impact on him was probably another one of those things people would consider creepy. "Do you like whatever mysterious things you do?"

She nodded. "Yes. Most days. Well... *some* days." She paused again. "Did... did you ever feel like you're two people? I mean, like there's a surface you and then there's another you that you don't really always like?"

Oz immediately thought about his aunt screaming at him about his father. A darkness simmering below the surface of his own mind. ...Body bags lined up in the parking lot of the fast-food restaurant. ...The dump filled with things screaming at him to kill everyone. "Yes." He nodded. "I do."

"Why do you think that is?"

"People have layers. People..."

"People are assholes." She finished for him. "Hate-filled assholes."

"That too." He stepped on the brake, avoiding the need to run a yellow light.

"But to return to your puzzle analogy..."

"That was your analogy," he corrected, "I didn't..."

"Everybody out there has pieces which form a single image. And it might be mysterious, but if you spend the time, you can figure out what it shows. Because all of their pieces belong to the same puzzle. And all of their puzzles can be sorted onto the appropriate shelf."

"Okaaaay..." Oz squinted, trying to keep up, since her earlier puzzle metaphor was now being changed to mean something completely different.

She turned in her seat to face him, looking curious. "So, where do you belong, Oz?"

Oz opened his mouth to reply to that, but then realized he

had no answer. His mouth hung open for several beats. He didn't really belong anywhere. And he knew it.

She nodded. "Thought so." She said cryptically, interpreting his silence as a reply. "See, the thing about it is that people just *think* the world has order, but really, everything we do is utterly meaningless."

"That's ridiculous. Every action you take could be your last. The radio is on too loudly, that could distract me and cause us to crash. Your decision to blare this dreadful noise could have a significant meaning. When you left your home this morning, did you take the time necessary to disinfect your doorknob?"

Her brow furrowed in confusion. "Why would I disinfect a doorknob?"

"Because you touch it dozens of times a day, with unclean hands. And it's not just you. Diseased homeless drug addicts, wandering your neighborhood, could have tried that knob while you were away..."

Her eyebrows shot up. "Jesus, where do *you* live!?!"

"...searching for something easy to steal. You come home and even if they *aren't* now lurking in the darkness of your apartment, their germs and the bacteria which was clinging to their soiled woolen gloves is now coating your knob! Then it's on your hand after you open the door!" His voice grew louder and more panicked as he thought about the severity of that issue. "Then it's *inside* your apartment! It's all over your clothes and your food and it finds its way straight into your blood supply! Then it *is* you! *You are someone else's germs and fecal matter, which were smeared on your doorknob because you didn't disinfect it!*"

"Fuck, man!" She looked equal parts amazed and amused. "You are just..."

"Or there's the fact that you didn't lock your door when you entered this vehicle, which could allow a carjacker easy opportunity to drag you from the car at the next stoplight." He pointed at the lock in question. "That decision could have profound consequences. Because everything matters and we are always one second away from catastrophe. *Always*."

The car was silent for a beat.

The redhead hit the "lock doors" button.

He turned his head to briefly look at her and he began to get worried. Oz paid careful attention to his health, because you never knew what information might be important and could save you from certain death. You needed to constantly be aware of your symptoms if you wanted to diagnose the cause.

So it was with a calm clinical mind that he realized that something was very, very wrong with him.

It was probably the perfume. It wasn't right that he wasn't bothered by it. The only reason he wouldn't be bothered by the perfume, or by the woman herself, was if something else was *really* bothering him. Some unseen illness which was only just now manifesting itself, at the worst possible time.

It had probably been metastasizing in his system for years. Slowly growing, poisoning the rest of his body...

"You okay, Oz?" The woman asked him, sounding worried about whatever it was she saw on his face.

Even she was recognizing that he was ill, which meant it was probably terminal.

"I see spots." He got out hoarsely. "My breathing feels labored. I've got some dryness of the mouth." He tried to swallow, but found it impossible. "My heart rate is going up." His eyes darted back and forth in growing panic. "*Why is my heart rate going up!?!* I... I could be having a heart attack right now. These could be the last words I'm ever able to say..." He tried to swallow again, but only managed to get halfway there, making it feel like he was drowning and unable to get air. "...Oh Jesus..." His breath came in short panicked gasps, as he began to hyperventilate, feeling like he was unable to breathe or swallow.

"Huh." The redhead remarked calmly. "You've got yourself a whole *heap* of problems, don't you?"

Oz nodded, unsure if the woman was diagnosing his current ailment or his entire state of mind. But either way, his answer was accurate.

"Interesting." She pointed at him. "Let me tell you something: never trust anything you can't see the flaws in. Because it's either fake or the flaws are just waiting to appear and take you by surprise. The surface of things is a lie." She patted the back of his hand again. "But if you *know* what the problems are, then you're golden."

The sudden attack of Oz's newest mysterious sickness was forgotten for a moment as he considered that, his attention now fixed on her small hand, and how good it felt resting on his.

"You're having a panic attack, baby doll." She said calmly, her voice almost flirty. "Don't worry, it's *adorable*."

Oz frowned, breathing steadying. "I am?"

She nodded. "'Fraid so."

The redhead casually put one of her feet onto the dashboard of the vehicle. The motion was both difficult and foolhardy, since it required her to hike up her skirt a great deal and also place her leg onto the airbag panel. If they got into an accident, she would instantly be broken in half.

Oz didn't warn her of that though, because he was preoccupied with not looking at her legs.

It took every ounce of his incredible willpower not to admire them.

Because they looked really, *really* amazing. They were long, and smooth, and feminine. Strong, like a dancer's. There was just something so clean and appealing about them. Sexy, but in a calming, *wholesome* way. They were... perfect.

Extraordinary.

Oz was obsessed with cleanliness. He found fault with everyone's appearance and could *feel* the germs and grime on them. But the only thing dirty about that woman was the thoughts she inspired.

Which, again, was very off-putting.

If literally *anyone else in the world* had put their feet up on his dashboard, Oz would have had no great difficulty ignoring their shapely legs and would have rightly reminded them of how many germs clung to shoes and people's feet. If they hadn't instantly removed their grimy shoes from his dash, he would have immediately kicked them from the car and driven away. It was the only logical option.

But in this case, he wasn't doing that.

He wasn't at all worried about the interior of his car.

And he didn't know what that meant.

All he knew was that he wanted to look at her legs.

"How would you spend your last day if you knew you were going to die?" She wondered aloud, as if that were the most obvious question to ask someone you just met... who was also *allegedly* in the midst of a panic attack.

"Trying to figure out a way not to die." He answered. "Obviously."

"No. You're missing the point." She shook her head. "See, there's no way to stop it. You're going to die. You only have 24 hours to live. To be you. The only question is how you'd spend that last day."

"I'd spend it trying to figure out just what was going to kill me, and making sure that it didn't."

"But you can't."

"Why?" It was an honest question. "I'm a superhero, it seems like I should have the resources to..."

"The point is to determine what it is you want from your life." She interrupted. "Like, if you suddenly gained reality warping powers and could make your life turn out however you wanted, how would you choose to die? *That's* the question."

Oz considered that for a moment, still confused. "If I had reality warping powers, why wouldn't I use them to cure myself?"

She made an aggravated sound. "Just forget it."

"Fine." Oz nodded, still not really understanding the point of the exercise. "How would *you* spend your last day?"

"Every day *is* my last day."

Oz frowned, uncertain if he heard that right. "Excuse me?"

"You ever see one of those movies where the person is told they're dying and then they start doing crazy things like quitting their jobs and sky diving? Just because they're trying to live their lives to the fullest? My life is already like that every day, even without the faulty diagnosis." She heaved a weary sigh. "I have no idea what I'd do, honestly. Because, in a way, I'm too close to the situation. I guess that's why I ask people." She gestured out the window. "I... I go through every day, feeling like my life is roulette, you know? And I look around, and everyone else has got their shit together. Everyone else is at the party, having fun, and I'm just there to..." She trailed off.

"Stand in a corner." Oz finished for her. "I understand."

"Well, *I* sure don't. How come I'm the only one who..." She got out, then stopped again. "Why am I talking to you about this?" She asked seriously, as if confused herself. "What the fuck?"

"I don't know."

"I don't even *know* you." She sounded amazed with herself, bordering on horror. "You're just some Cape from a group that's..."

"They're idiots." He finished for her. "You can say it, it won't offend me."

"I was going to say 'fascists,' actually."

"Some of them, certainly." He nodded, admitting the point. "Some of them are just trying to make a difference though."

"You a fucking idealist or something?

"That's the job."

"No, it's not." She shook her head. "You're a hero: your job is to kung-fu and look good on magazine covers."

"You have a very limited definition of what constitutes 'heroism,' miss."

"God save me from the rule-followers." The redhead rolled her eyes. "They make the game go on so long."

"My job is to make everyone else's lives better."

"Well, you could take off your shirt."

"Huh?" Again, he was pretty certain he'd heard her wrong.

"Nothing." She cleared her throat, suddenly looking embarrassed. "I've got this... *thing* today. It makes me say stuff I wouldn't ordinarily say. But it should be all cleared up in..." she looked pointedly at the digital clock on the radio, which displayed 11:49, "...eleven minutes."

Oz stopped the car at another stoplight and turned to stare at her in confused amazement.

She stared back.

"You have the whitest teeth I've ever seen." He thought aloud, not even thinking about what he was saying.

"Thank you." She shrugged. "Weird and vaguely creepy thing to say, but said with such genuine sensitivity that it's actually kinda sweet for some reason." She tucked a strand of captivatingly red hair behind her ear, in a subtle little move that was so endearing and sexy that it made Oz hard as a rock. "Anything else about me strike your fancy?"

"I'm afraid it could be misconstrued, and I don't want to make you uncomfortable."

"Oh, it wouldn't make me uncomfortable." She waved a dismissive hand. "Compliment away, baby doll. For the next ten minutes, I'm a gal who *loves* compliments."

"Your perfume doesn't make me retch."

"Awesome. That's always the goal." She deadpanned.

The car fell into silence.

"Really? That's it?" She snorted, sounding almost insulted. "Perfume? Come on! Eyes, hair, legs, tits! Go for the gusto! Surprise me!"

Oz was utterly enraptured by all of those features, actually, but didn't really want to discuss them. He was worried about crossing a line. "I think that would be socially inappropriate."

"So?"

"I... I don't think I'm supposed to."

"So? If people only did what we're *supposed* to do, our ancestors never would have come down out of the trees." She pointed at him. "If you're going to flirt, take the field and hit the line hard!"

A hundred thousand compliments flashed through Oz's mind at once, ranging from friendly to downright pornographic. Things he liked about her that he hadn't even consciously realized that he liked, and things which were the epitome of everything he'd ever wanted.

But Oz's life had just not prepared him with the ability to say any of that. Oz was the most risk adverse person you were ever going to find, and pushing the envelope here was pretty darn risky. He thought things were generally going pretty well with the woman, and he didn't want to ruin that by saying something which would cause him to cringe later. He'd scared a lot of people in his life by being "creepy" and he wasn't about to do that here.

Oz's eyes slid down to admire her legs again. "Your... your dress matches your shoes quite well."

"That's really the best you have?" She groaned in annoyance. "This is the problem with men. They..." She trailed off, then softly swore to herself. "Fuck. I'll be so glad when today's over."

Oz frowned in disappointment.

"Oh, not you." She waved a hand at him, rolling her eyes. "I mean me."

"I don't understand."

"Me either." She stared at him silently for another long moment. "You're like... one of those 'nice guys,' aren't you? A goddamn rule-follower. I heard about you, but only met one other before." She nodded in certainty. "Out there saving puppies from machine gunners."

"Most people inform me that I 'creep them out,' actually." Oz corrected, as the light turned green again.

"Really?" She sounded hopeful for some reason.

"Apparently, I'm in constant danger of becoming evil. I'm told it's in my blood."

"Well then... maybe there's hope for you yet." The woman sounded amused and impressed. "Some days I'm evil too."

"This is an odd car trip conversation." He thought aloud.

"I wouldn't know."

"Don't take many car trips?"

"Not with someone else." She paused. "Well... not someone else inside the *cab* of the car, anyway."

The digital clock switched to 12:00.

The woman made a face at the radio, which was still blaring dance club music. "Why are you listening to this shit, Oz?"

"I didn't turn it on."

"Well, I hate this, so I know it wasn't me."

Oz opened his mouth to respond to that, but found himself at a complete lack of words.

"Where was I?" She asked, sounding confused.

"You were espousing on what is wrong with the world and complaining that I failed to compliment you correctly."

"Ah, yes." She snapped her fingers. "The problem with the world is that everyone is selfish and flagrantly breaks the law without ramifications."

"Yes, I know that's what..." He paused, just processing her words. "Wait... what!?! That's the exact opposite of the argument that you were making, not two min..."

"That's why heroes like the Freedom Squad are so important." She nodded. "People need role models to show them the greatness they can aspire to."

Oz was very confused now. "*Huh!?!*"

"What the world *really* needs is to focus on the love of Jorva."

Oz was almost afraid to ask, but recognized that he had to. "Who or what is 'Jorva'?"

"The Goddess of Freedom and the Hunt."

"Okaaay..."

"I'm a strict adherent to her wise teachings."

Oz felt completely lost by the sudden change of direction this conversation just had. "...Which are?" He asked, feeling helpless.

"I'm not sure yet." She admitted. "But it's still early in the day. Sometimes it takes a few minutes."

"Huh." Oz had no response to that. "Well, I fully support all faiths, obviously. Even the spontaneous ones which don't yet have actual tenets."

"That's nice. You're not as totalitarian-y Nazi as some of your Cape friends."

"Thank you." He nodded, accepting the praise. "I thought you *liked* the Freedom Squad though?"

She considered that for a minute. "I've got a lot of thoughts about them today, I haven't figured them all out yet." She shrugged disinterestedly. "How did you get mixed up with them, anyway?"

"If you want to do good work, you have to go where the resources are."

"And that's what you were doing at the Agletarian embassy then?" She arched a perfect red eyebrow. "'Good work'?"

"I was... I was doing my job." He decided, recognizing that it was a weak explanation even to him. "And just what were *you* doing there, anyway?"

"'My job.'" She snarked, repeating his words.

"Your job is to go to parties at foreign embassies?"

"Maybe I'm a hero. That's apparently their main activity. And they can't..." She trailed off. "Dammit. I think I'm a vegetarian."

"You are?"

"No!" She paused. "Well, today. Maybe. Unless I can convince myself not to be."

"I... I find conversing with you to be a very confusing experience."

"Me too."

Oz spent most of his life trying to walk a narrow line he'd charted for himself. Trying to keep his life orderly and his mind free of... darkness.

But at the moment, his mind was firing on all cylinders, trying to keep up with his passenger. She couldn't possibly be as weird as she seemed. She had to be making sense, he just needed to figure out either how to understand her mind, or how to reason with her.

He didn't seem to be having much luck with either of those things though.

So, instead, his often underutilized imagination began to daydream about this woman, while he continued to not look at her legs.

In his head, the woman was smiling at him as she stepped out of the shower in the morning. Not a seductive smile, but... something so warm and pleasant. A perfect smile flashed just for him, because she was happy to see him.

No one was happy to see Oz.

It was the single most erotic thing Oz's mind had ever imagined. And he wasn't even focusing on her body, he was focusing on the comfortable intimacy of her smile. This wasn't a sex fantasy, this was... a *life* fantasy. He wanted the life that image promised, not merely the body it featured. He wanted to be the kind of man who could deserve that smile from someone so beautiful. To be someone that could inspire that kind of trust and happiness. Someone... someone who wasn't trash.

Someone who was the woman's hero.

Oz was very rarely comfortable anywhere. With anyone. Even himself.

And at that moment, Oz just didn't care about the rules he'd created for himself anymore.

He wanted that smile. He wanted someone so beautiful to smile at him in complete adoration.

And, yes. If he was being honest, he wanted to see that

woman stepping from the shower, beads of water dripping down her clean perfect body...

He had no idea who this woman even was, so this wasn't love at first sight. He simply wanted what she *represented.* He wanted the crazy mixed up reality she seemed to live in. This woman was... freedom. She was everything he'd ever both dreamed and feared his life to be. All of the things which his aunt had warned him about and all of the things his rituals urged him to avoid.

She was mysterious and weird and chaotic and pure and...

She needed his help. The bruise to her face told him that, even if she'd refused to tell him the truth about how she'd gotten it. She was some kind of damsel in distress, and Oz was a superhero! He'd gone his whole life wanting a chance to rescue such a beautiful woman from an unseen danger.

She was a break from everything which made him tired. And afraid. She was... She was some kind of deliverance. Or some kind of siren, here to drag him into the abyss.

And he would look forward to either of those options, just so long as it was different from the monotony that Oz lived with on a daily basis.

But then reality set back in. And Oz started to think about all of the things which could go wrong and all of the many, *many* reasons why ogling some random redhead was a bad idea. It would get him into trouble. He wasn't entirely sure what Freedom Squad rule it would be breaking, but they must have had something about that in their bylaws. There was doubtlessly mountains of red tape to keep someone like Oz away from someone as perfect as this woman. Besides, even if it wasn't against his employer's standards and practices, it was certainly against Oz's rituals. And when rituals were broken, when patterns of behavior weren't followed, bad things happened. Things fell into chaos.

Plus, she was in need of his assistance, which meant that he couldn't exactly abuse that aspect of their relationship. Just *being* a Cape was enough to have power over someone, which was a whole other issue. From a public relations standpoint as well as a moral one, hitting on this woman was a terrible idea.

He started staring at his passenger with something akin to sad longing. If he were a different kind of man, he could have had someone like that. He would be saying something charming right now, or impress her with some grand accomplishment he'd made.

But that just wasn't Oz.

Oz was trash.

And trash didn't impress treasure. All it could do was look on with sadness at something which it could never have.

"You know, I had you pegged for a rule follower, Oz," the woman observed calmly, "but I respect the fact you just did 90 through a stop sign."

Oz looked down in alarm at the speedometer, then turned the wheel sharply to avoid a parked cab. *"Cheese and crackers!"*

The car was silent for a beat.

"You did *not* just fucking say that." She finally got out, sounding amused.

"Um…"

"I'm just going to pretend you said something profane and manly."

"Me too."

She snorted in laughter. "Forget it, we all have bad days." She pointed out the window at a seemingly empty street. "This is me anyway."

Oz pulled the car up to the curb, then peered out at the neighborhood. "You sure? It doesn't look residential…"

But the woman was already out of the car and walking away.

Oz couldn't remember ever feeling so dispirited. It was like Oz's chance at… *something*, was walking away from him. Leaving him to wallow in his…

A second later, the woman was stalking back to the car. She tapped one glittery red fingernail on the glass, and Oz lowered the passenger side window. "Okay, look. I don't…" She trailed off, then swore to herself. "I mean, *fuck* this is weird." She started to wring her hands, obviously uneasy about something. "Okay, see, today is a *really* bad day to do this, because the myself I am today isn't really a 'myself' that…" She let out an annoyed groan and stamped one of her feet. "Know what? The hell with it." She extended her hand. "Natalie Quentin. I work at the Department store at Van Cleef Square." In her hand was a business card. "Come find me, Oz." She swallowed, like the words left her feeling exposed. "If… if you want." She made an odd hand gesture. "May Jorva's love go with you, always." She paused for a beat. "Fuck, that's going to get annoying." She whispered to herself. "Fuck today and everyone responsible."

Oz looked down at the object that she'd given him. The business card was completely blank except for the information she'd written down on it in pen. Which was certainly odd. Oz couldn't figure out why anyone would carry around blank business cards, but when he looked back up to question the woman about it, she'd disappeared.

Oz lived a normal, predictable life.
And Natalie Quentin could completely destroy it.
He couldn't wait.

Chapter 5

"'I CAN'T EXPLAIN MYSELF, I'M AFRAID, SIR' SAID ALICE, 'BECAUSE I'M NOT MYSELF, YOU SEE.'"

- Alice's Adventures in Wonderland

PRESENT DAY

Mull's last meal consisted of what was allegedly some sort of creamed beef, on what appeared to be a soggy waffle.

Her looming death looked like a relief compared to taking so much as a single bite of that.

For his part, Oz looked equally willing to face the grim reaper rather than go within half-a-mile of the meal. He looked positively relieved as she pushed the tray away.

"I still don't understand why they would even bring me a meal." She wondered aloud. "It's the middle of the night and I've got half-an-hour to live, tops. Do they really think that I'm peckish?"

"Maybe they think it will give you strength and calm you?" Oz guessed, eager to dismiss the idiocy of others, because he was a positive person.

"It's just making me want to go all 'Gordon Ramsey' on the kitchen staff, Oz."

"I've seen that show." Oz declared with an obvious amount of pride, apparently happy to understand one of her pop culture references. "I respect his dedication to cleanliness in his kitchens."

"I meant the swearing and insults he screams at people."

"Oh." Oz nodded, looking down at the floor, his pride in his TV knowledge fading. "Yes, he does seem to do that a lot too, doesn't he."

They sat in silence for a long moment.

Oz cleared his throat, trying to find a way to phrase something. "What... what is..." He paused. "...I mean, how can..." He trailed off again.

"I think what you want to ask is: 'what the fuck is *wrong* with you, Mull?'" She offered. "That about sum it up?"

"No, I would never make light of your…" He trailed off again.

"'Psychosis.'" She finished for him. "It's a nice way of saying: 'completely fucking insane.'"

"Yes, I'm familiar with the term." He shifted in his seat. "What I'm most interested in is…"

"Whether I'm really Natalie or Multifarious?" She guessed.

"Something like that, yes. And it would be nice to be able to complete a sentence of my own, incidentally. You are putting words into my mouth and I feel they are giving you a less than kind opinion of me."

"Relax." She closed her eyes again. "You're golden."

"So, who am I talking to now?"

"You're talking to me, of course." She tried to snort in amusement, but only ended up in almost choking to death. "Who… who else would be in my room?"

"And who is 'me'?" He tried again.

She took on a pitying tone. "You're *Oz*. Remember? Your name is Oswald D…"

"That isn't what I meant." He shook his head. "If you don't want to talk about this, I will abide by your wishes, but I really feel like this is a discussion that we will need to have at some point."

"My life is an open book. It's nothing but gibberish and crayon doodles, but still open." She told him, weakly trying to rearrange herself on the pillow. "You got a question, fire away while I'm still here to answer them. I'm told you have about twenty minutes though, FYI. So you'd better hurry."

"Who are you *really?*"

"If I knew that, Oz, my life would be a whole lot simpler than it is." She told him seriously. "Suffice to say that I'm always who I say I am."

"So, you haven't been…," he shifted in his chair again, "…laughing at me, then? Because I didn't recognize you at the store even though I see you almost daily?"

"I don't recognize myself half the damn time, Oz. Can't hold that against you. Besides, you're always a bright spot in the day." She opened her eyes to look at him, remembering something. "I tell you I finally got them to agree to retile the second floor of the store?"

"Excellent." He nodded, looking pleased. "The disorderly variation of tiles has bothered me for some time."

"Yes, I know it does." In actuality, that was the entire reason why she'd pushed so hard for the change. No one else in the entire world gave a fuck about the size of tile used on the floor of a department store, except Oz. And if it bothered Oz, then it bothered Natalie. And bad things happened to people and things who bothered Natalie.

He frowned. "If someone had told me that I'd be having a conversation with you about tile choices while you lay in bed covered in blood from your fight with a hired killer, I would have doubted their sanity."

"Hired killers aren't so tough. It's the crazy bastards that do it for *free* that you gotta watch out for."

"I'll keep that in mind." He reached for one of the containers of apple juice on the table, then glanced over at her again. "May I please have one of these, Miss Quentin?"

"Dude, you can mix it with tequila and inject it into your veins, for all I care. I won't need it where I'm headed."

"Just drinking it should be sufficient, thank you."

"Although, now that I think about it, 'where I'm headed' probably has nothing *but* hospital food..." She shook her head, an act made especially painful because of her neck injuries. "I haven't really done anything to endear myself to any higher powers."

"Well, except Jorva."

"Who the fuck is 'Jorva'?" She snorted.

He shrugged helplessly, looking crestfallen again. "I... I don't know." He carefully opened the sealed container, then used a sanitary plastic straw to take a sip. "I'm still trying to understand your dissociative identity disorder, that's all."

"I don't have multiple personality disorder, Oz." She rolled her eyes in dismissal. "I just have... you know... a secret identity or whatever."

"A secret identity who has an entirely separate life and who refers to herself in the third person." He continued for her.

"Yep."

"I'm afraid that's called another personality."

"Oh, it is not, you drama queen. You've read too many self-help books."

"Yes, I'm afraid that it is." He finished off his drink and carefully placed it in the trash, going through extreme precautionary measures to ensure that his hand came nowhere near the receptacle itself.

"Well, I don't think I'm going to have time to explain it, because things aren't looking so hot for the kid right now."

Oz frowned. "Who is 'The Kid'?"

"Apparently, I am today." She tried to shrug but it hurt too much. "Never called myself that before, because it's obviously asinine, but whatever. Can't help a shitty day, can you." She cleared her throat, which still felt raw and bloody. "Anyway, rumor has it that I'm a dead psycho walking."

"You... you will be fine."

"Very convincing, Oz." She cleared her throat again, this time using the sound to hide an involuntary cry of pain, as something in her chest began to hurt worse than ever. "You're a terrible liar. I bet you've never done anything wrong in your entire white bread little life, so it's a new experience for you." She teased, hoping to change the topic and get him talking about something so that she didn't have to. She was circling the drain at this point. She could feel it. It wouldn't be long.

"I did a prison term once."

"For?"

He was silent for a beat. "Sixteen counts of first degree murder, sixty-seven counts of robbery, nineteen counts of grand theft auto, thirty-three counts of arson, forty carjackings and ten counts of... something not pleasant."

Her eyebrows rose in surprise. "You go upstate?"

"Yes."

"Huh." She nodded in approval. "Good for you."

"I am pleased that you are pleased."

"Anything else?"

"And... and I killed my cousin."

"He deserve it?"

He was quiet for a long moment. "I don't know."

"Little secret you learn about life when you see it from as many angles as I have, Oz? *Everyone* deserves it." She nodded in certainty. "You killed him, ya probably had a reason. And your reasons are nobody's fucking business, because: *anarchy*."

"There is an order to..."

"Fuck 'order.' I order at a restaurant or when I'm taking hostages." She rolled her eyes. "Life doesn't have order, it's just some shit that happens. Because: *anarchy*." She tapped her finger on the rail of her bed, then winced because the finger was broken. "Dwelling on shit that's happened distracts you from the shit that's *happening*."

"Live for the moment."

"Well, in my case, a moment is all I've got left."

"You told me that before."

"I did?"

"Yes." He leaned closer to her, his voice softer. "You said that your life was like one of those people in comedies who are misdiagnosed with a terminal disease, and then do insane things as a result because they no longer feared the consequences of their actions."

"I hate those fucking movies."

"I've never seen one." He gently smoothed a hair from her forehead, which was an exceptionally rare physical contact from him. Oz didn't like touching other people. She knew that. Which meant either that he knew she was close to death or that the disorderly tangle of her hair was sending his OCD into overdrive and he simply *had* to straighten it.

"That's sad." She frowned, genuinely feeling bad for him. She met his eyes, getting lost in the beautiful and unknowable depths of darkness they offered. "I got stabbed to death today and thrown off a roof, but glimpses of your depressing little life still make me sad."

Oz smiled humorlessly, and looked down at the floor.

It was a small movement, but Natalie recognized it. Oz wasn't going to argue with her about her chances of survival anymore.

"I'm so sorry, Oz." She whispered, recognizing that he seemed to care more about her life than she did.

She was really going to die today.

But, on the bright side, at least she wouldn't have to work on the store's parade anymore. Every year, Natalie spent waaaaay too many hours trying to help out with that stupid Thanksgiving parade. She'd finally found a way to avoid it. Of course, if she could have chosen, she probably would have found a method which didn't involve her gruesome death, but at least it was sure to work.

She found herself unable to look at Oz anymore, it was too absolutely heartbreaking. Both because she wouldn't get to see the man again and because he... he'd close himself off even further after this. Oz wasn't really a "people" person. He kept to himself and did his job. As far as she knew, it was all he had. And she was the only non-coworker he seemed to talk to, despite the fact that she was *also* a coworker.

But either way, dying now felt like a failure. A betrayal of her friendship with this man.

She knew she never should have gotten involved with him. It put him in too much danger.

Fucking Ronnie. Her ex had somehow managed to hurt Oz through her.

She stared in silent contemplation at the turkey drawings

that someone's kid had made using their hand and a crayon. The bottom read "Happy Tanksgiving!" in a childish scrawl.

Jesus. Learn to spell, kid.

Thanksgiving was shit.

But if there were tanks involved, she could probably get behind it.

Thanksgiving decorations in an ICU were also the height of cruel irony. "Aren't you glad for everything you have? Oh… wait. That's being taken away from you, isn't it? All well. Piss off, then."

Mull wasn't a fan of Thanksgiving, in general. It was just a reminder that she didn't have any friends, her family didn't know who she was, and she was completely insane. Thanksgiving was the one day a year when she was supposed to sit around and reflect on all she had been given. But her life was basically shit. Which wasn't exactly something that Norman Rockwell painted on magazine covers.

The whole basis of the holiday was an artificial thankfulness, masking one of the most commercial holidays around. Christmas got all of the attention, but at least it had a veneer of religion. But Thanksgiving was an entirely made up holiday, its commercialism was worn on its sleeve. A few hundred years ago, a bunch of white people decided to take one day off from killing Native Americans and eat all of their food instead, then a couple hundred years later, some states decided to take a day off from slaughtering each other in the Civil War, and bingo. A joyous holiday. Where families took one day off from hating each other, and planned to gorge themselves on slaughtered turkeys, then on cheaply priced personal electronics.

But everything about Thanksgiving was fake. Turkeys, parades, the family get-togethers. Those were all designed by marketing people and artists, in order to sell specific kinds of foods and encourage certain kinds of behaviors. The only reason why turkey was the unquestioned Thanksgiving food was undoubtedly that the people at Butterball had paid more for that privilege than the people at Fruit Roll'ups, back in the day.

None of it meant a damn thing.

Mull tried to rearrange herself on the bed.

Oz continued to stare at the floor.

"You okay?" She finally asked him, recognizing what a stupid question it was.

He nodded tiredly, wiping at his eyes. "I'm… I'm just not ready to lose 'The Kid,' Miss Quentin."

That was the single saddest thing she'd ever heard, and all she could do was nod in understanding. "Hey, imagine how I feel."

She finally got out, voice breaking, not for her but for Oz.

The fact that Oz was so handsome just made this all the sadder. His normally polished and pristine appearance was all rumpled and messy, which only made him look better. Or, at least like he needed a hug. *God*, she wanted to hug him. To be in his arms and have him tell her that everything was going to be alright. Because, she'd believe him if he told her that. There was something about Oz that made it seem like he could do *anything*. From the second she'd first seen him, she'd felt it.

But not even Oz could save her from this.

Mull was going to die tonight.

And she'd never even gotten to hold that man's hand.

A deep sense of failure filled her. Roy had been right about the problems with being a Cape and trying to have a personal life. It inevitably led to pain.

What a shitty, *shitty* day.

She went back to silently critiquing the artistic merit of the child's drawing on the wall, doing anything she could to avoid the things she didn't want to say.

It wasn't like she and Oz were in a *relationship,* relationship. But it was always something that Mull cherished and thought would someday go somewhere. It was one thing in her life that made her feel normal. And... wanted. She liked whatever it was she had with Oz. She liked it more than anything else she had in her life.

But in a few minutes, it would be over. And she'd been too much of a coward to ever take it anywhere. For all of her bullshit about living each day to the fullest, Natalie had completely failed in that regard.

Fuck Natalie.

A moment later, Holly Claus wandered into the room, smiling widely. "Hey, girlfriend!" She paused in the doorway. "Sweet baby Jesus, you look terrible." She frowned slightly. "Or so I assume anyway. I've never actually seen your face before." She walked closer to the bed, squinting at her. "Do you normally look like this or is today just a bad day?"

Holly was a perky, perfect Christmas-themed blonde villainess, who had more friends and more family than Mull could ever possibly hope to have. Holly was the kind of person Mull would ordinarily detest on general principles, but who was so damn happy and badass that she ended up liking her anyway.

"Bad day."

"Damn." Holly made a low whistling sound. "Must be a

really bad day. I'd be so pissed if someone dyed my hair that color."

Mull snorted in amusement, careful not to move too much. "No, my general fastfood mascot appearance is the result of shitty genetics."

"I think your hair is the most beautiful thing I've ever seen." Oz assured her softly.

Mull was taken aback by that and turned to look at him in amazement.

Now?

The bastard picked *now* to start complimenting her!?!

Poacher walked in a second later and distracted her, focusing on the handprint turkey on the wall like it was somehow baffling. "The fuck is *that*?" He wondered aloud, looking at it like it was some ancient alien god he didn't yet recognize.

Mull's squinted her bruised eyes at what was in Holly's arms. "Whose baby is that?"

Holly beamed down at the child in question. "Harlot's."

"Is she downstairs?"

"No, she's overseeing the investigation."

"Then why do you have her baby?"

"Are you kidding? Look at this little fella!" Holly held the child up as if to prove a point. "Every time she turns her back I snatch little Petey and run away. I have to! He's so impossibly cute! He's saying," Holly bounced the baby up and down, waggling him like a puppet and taking on a high-pitched baby voice, "'I want to go on an adventure with my Aunty Holly. She's my best-est friend!'"

"Uh-huh." Oz turned to look at the child in Poacher's hands. "And whose baby is *that*?"

Poacher shrugged. "Beats me." He pointed over his shoulder towards the nursery down the hall. "They got a whole mess of them in that little room over there." He gestured at the baby in question. "This one was the best I could find. I think it's The Cheerleader's or something. You know, that pregnant bitch from The Roustabouts?" He shook his head. "She ain't pregnant no more."

"Why is there a room of babies in the ICU?" Mull asked, feeling confused.

"I had you moved to the Maternity Ward." Oz informed her calmly.

"I'm in the Maternity Ward?" Mull looked around. "I'm not *actually* pregnant though, am I? Because if I am, one of you has *a lot* of explaining to do."

Oz cleared his throat. "Given the attack on your life, I

thought it best to place you in another area of the hospital, just in case."

"That's so paranoid." She pursed her lips, then immediately regretted it as they split open even worse. "I respect that."

Holly waggled the baby in her hands as if it were a puppet again. "'What about me, Uncie Poacher? Don't you think I'm the cutest?'"

"Right now, your voice is kinda pissing me off." Sydney shook his head. "So, no."

"He can hear you!" Holly gasped, clutching the baby closer as though to sooth its hurt feelings. "It's best not to anger the future leader of our team! One day, this little heartbreaker is going to be in charge!"

"Hell, I say we put him in charge *now*." Poacher snorted sarcastically. "Couldn't do any worse than his father does."

Holly waggled the child at him, taking on a baby voice again. "'Don't make me ang-gwee, Uncie Poacher, or I'll kick your ass with my tiny tiny little baby feet.'" She started playing with one of the instruments of death in question, then looked up at Poacher excitedly. "Shit! *He's got little toes and everything!* Oh my God! Aren't they just the *cutest* things you've ever seen!?!" She nodded her head in growing certainty. "Yep, I'm totally keeping him. Harl can just have another one. This is 'Petey *Claus*' now."

Sydney looked down at the baby in his arms, then at Petey, then back at his baby again. He frowned. "I think this one's defective." He turned the infant over, as if searching for some kind of switch which would turn it on and make it more entertaining. "I wanna trade."

"No!" Holly pulled her honorary nephew and newly stolen first-born away. "This one's mine! I found him first!"

Mull was getting a headache. "Where's my sandwich?" She asked Poacher, hoping she could make her visitors leave so she could get back to talking with Oz about all the things she didn't want to say.

"The lunch cart was closed. But here, take this." Poacher handed her the infant.

Mull held up her hands, refusing to touch the thing. "I don't want a fucking baby!"

"Do you have any idea the kinds of germs and bacteria which thrive on infants?" Oz asked, sounding vaguely horrified by the idea. "It shouldn't even be in here while Miss Quentin is convalescing."

"Mothers are the backbone of this nation, Mull." Poacher informed her seriously, ignoring Oz. "Don't listen to the media: it's possible to have both a family *and* a career. The modern woman is..."

"Just shut up." Mull stared up at the ceiling, feeling more annoyed with this world than ever. "I can't believe my last words are probably going to be telling Syd what an asshole he is."

"To be fair, I think those are a lot of people's last words." Holly offered.

"More than I'd like, but less than I'd expect." Poacher informed them seriously.

Oz cleared his throat. "Perhaps the two of you could go somewhere else."

Holly made a face. "But I just got here."

"And I'm sure Miss Quentin appreciates your visit." Oz stood up, obviously intending to shoo them both from the room. "But I think right now what she needs is..."

There was a strange sound coming from the floor above them, which caused Oz to stop in his tracks.

Everyone stared at the ceiling.

"What was that?" Oz frowned as the sound happened again, louder this time.

"Thaaaat sounded like an energy pulse weapon of some kind." Holly informed them casually, continuing to play with her best friend's infant son. "Unshielded. Probably putting out... a buck ten of plasma, maybe? But with a tinge of something else in there, which I didn't quite..."

Oz stalked to the door and popped his head out into the hall to gage the situation. "How many men we talking here?"

Poacher tilted his head to the side, listening. "Sounds like one."

Oz turned to look at Mull for a ruling.

"Nah. It's not Ronnie's style to kill me in a hospital." She shook her head. "Besides, I messed him up pretty good too. Even *he'd* take more time to heal than this."

"Two." Poacher updated. "One two floors below, one two floors above. Heavy boots. Closing."

"He could have sent someone..." Oz thought aloud.

"Oz? Do I really look like the kind of girl you only send *two guys* to kill?" She snorted in amusement, then winced at the pain. "Give me a *little* credit, will you? Ronnie would have sent *at least* a dozen guys to off me."

"Who *else* wants you dead?"

"Well, my landlord isn't my biggest fan. But we're still at the 'angry letter' stage, she hasn't resorted to hired assassins. Yet."

"They're still closing in on this floor." Poacher updated.

Oz was silent for a beat, obviously deciding on the best course of action. "They're here for Miss Quentin."

"How do you know?"

"I just *do*."

Poacher thought that over for a second, then nodded. "Okay."

"We are not ready for a fight." Oz shook his head, recognizing the vulnerable position they were in.

Poacher handed the baby to Holly, then checked his weapon. He closed the breach of his elephant gun with a snap. "I was *born* ready for a fight. As an infant, the obstetrician slapped me on the ass to make me cry, and I hit him back."

Holly pointed at the gun. "Lucky no one took that on your way into the hospital."

Poacher gave a dismissive snort. "I'd like to see them try."

There was muffled shouting from the floor above them.

Oz stepped backwards from the door. "Syd, you know that little room with all the babies?"

The other man nodded. "Yeah..."

Something on the floor above them exploded, shaking the building.

"Grab as many as you can." Oz dashed for Mull's bed, wrenching it away from the wall and towards the door. "We're pulling out."

Holly passed both of the infants to Mull, and Poacher took off towards the door. He turned back to look at Mull for an instant. "See you soon, girly." Syd all but knocked one of the doctors to the floor as he ran from the room.

The woman steadied herself on the door jamb, frowning in confusion as Oz wheeled Mull's bed and IV towards it.

The doctor moved to block his path. "You can't leave with her." She shook her head. "Where do you think you're going?"

"There is an emergency situation and I am evacuating with my teammate." Oz didn't bother to stop the bed, instead using it to literally push the woman out of the way. "Please stand aside."

The doctor stumbled back, but continued to try to halt their progress. "Security will deal with whatever is going on, there's no need to immediately jump to the worst case scenario."

"I'm a superhero, ma'am." Oz shook his head. "I'm in the 'worst case scenario' business."

"Look at this!" The doctor picked up Mull's chart and waved

it at Oz. "Shattered pelvis, broken legs, dislocated shoulder, broken collarbone, orbital fracture, a detached retina, broken nose, three-quarters of her ribs are fractured, her lung is punctured, her heart is perforated, her spine is fractured in three places, she's got skull..." She trailed off. "You know what? I'm just going to summarize this and tell you that I'm *amazed* she even made it to the hospital. She shouldn't even be *conscious* right now, she *should* be in some kind of coma. Because the only thing holding your friend's body together is the fabric of her hospital gown at this point. Everything in her is broken, punctured or bleeding. She'll never walk again and her organs are shutting down." She stepped into the bed's path again. "You move her and she's dead."

Oz paused in his tracks to consider that for a moment, then looked down at her. "Are you mobile, Miss Quentin?"

She smiled at him, the blood from her split lip staining her teeth. "Baby doll, I'm in my *prime.*" She informed him weakly.

Oz started forward again.

"She is the victim of a very serious crime." The doctor called after them. "*She won't make it five minutes if you move her!*"

Mull absently began feeling around her bedding for a weapon, careful not to jostle the infants that her teammates had saddled her with. "Lady, I'm not a victim, I'm a *professional*. Do you have any idea the damage I can do to someone in five minutes?"

Ahead of them, one of the walls exploded in a fireball of orange sparks.

Oz blinked at it in astonishment. "What the heck was *that?*"

Holly grabbed the other end of the hospital bed, helping Oz to maneuver it in the corridor. "I don't know, but I'm asking my dad for one for Christmas."

They cut to the left, hoping to make it to the elevator banks.

Oz tapped the earpiece in his ear. "Floor 7 of the hospital is under attack by an unknown force. We are evacuating Multifarious and the infants in the maternity ward, but we need everyone to get here. NOW!" He shouted over the radio.

"Copy, Oz." Wyatt's voice came over the line. "You heard the man, people. Floor 7. Let's go to work!"

Mull tried to refrain from an eye roll.

Several more explosions sounded, deafening even over the fire alarm.

Mull could think of at least five different ways out of this current situation. Unfortunately, all of them involved being able to move. Which, sadly, she wasn't able to at the moment. And certainly never would be again.

They rounded the last turn and the elevators were in sight. Standing in front of them, Wyatt frantically waved an arm. "The other way!" He shouted, racing towards them. "*Go the other way!*" He reached an intersection and glanced to his left. He had just enough time to try to form a telekinetic shield, when an energy blast knocked him straight off his feet and through the wall of one of the hospital rooms, and then straight through the opposite wall in the room, and into the next, leaving a series of jagged holes.

Into the corridor walked a man wearing some kind of body armor, which had glowing orange sections, interspaced with an unknown black metal. He looked like a mix of a SWAT team member and an alien bug.

Oz stopped in his tracks, trying to wheel Mull's hospital bed in a new direction.

Holly shook her head in amazement, staring at the unknown attacker. "Ooooh... we are so *fucked.*"

Oz was obviously putting everything he had into moving the heavy hospital bed in a new direction, which was hopefully towards another exit.

"I'll hold the line. You get her clear." Holly informed them, then nodded her head at Mull. "Girl... you take care of him, understand?" She let out a long breath, obviously realizing that Mull would be dead in moments, either way. "I don't like goodbyes. They go against my jolly nature and make my naturally twinkling eyes all red and puffy."

"I know." She met her eyes again meaningfully, acknowledging the unsaid farewells to a friend. "I *know.*" She repeated, then swallowed. "So... I guess I'll see you when I see you. If we end up the same place, that is."

"I don't die. It's a whole thing." Holly shrugged. "Sorry."

"Oh. Then... I guess we won't."

"Well, I *probably* would if the world imploded or you shot me with some kind of..."

"Consortium: form on me! Everything we have!" Oz shouted over her, keeping the team up to date. "Floor 7 is hot! Wyatt is down! *Danger is close!*"

Holly raced towards the unknown attacker.

"What do you mean 'Wyatt is down'?" McCallister MacReady, AKA "OverDriver," asked over the radio, sounding confused. "What happened to Wyatt?"

"*I MEAN HE'S FUCKING DOWN!*" Oz shouted at Mack,

temper snapping.

Beside them, Holly pin-wheeled through the air from another energy blast, crashing through the glass window of one of the offices.

Mull swore.

Oz ignored it, remaining focused on his goal.

"Just go!" She waved him away. "I'm dead anyway, you need to..."

"*We leave this hospital together or not at all.*" Oz snapped, showing a remarkable team spirit despite his complete dismissal of his two other newly critically injured teammates.

Ahead of them, the last bank of elevators finally appeared. Oz slammed his fist repeatedly into the button, apparently trying to get the elevator to somehow arrive faster.

To their right, one of the weird super-suited people rounded the corner, holding some kind of weapon.

Mull opened her mouth to scream a warning at Oz, but in that moment, Natalie's panic crashed into her, leaving her gasping for breath and unable to make any sound but a small squeak of fear.

Fucking Natalie.

Oz moved to stand in front of her, as the other man prepared to fire.

And for the briefest of moments, Mull felt completely safe. Like Oz could somehow stop all of this and protect her.

No one ever tried to protect her from anything. She found the idea deeply, deeply appealing.

Then that emotion was overshadowed by the realization that Oz was about to be killed in front of her, and sheer terror filled Natalie's mind.

Before the attacker got the chance to fire at Oz though, there was the sound of a gunshot and something struck the soldier in the head. He stumbled to the side.

Mack barreled down the hallway towards them, shooting the man several times with a .38 special, causing their assailant to stumble backwards a step as each round from the revolver impacted him, but he stayed on his feet. "Oh, give me a fucking break!" Mack shot him one more time, with similar effect. His gun clicked empty. Mack swore viciously and finally simply tossed the empty handgun at the man's helmeted head, not slowing down his charge. He used his powers over machines to open up the door behind the man. "*Just go down you son of a biiiiiiiitch!*" He crashed into him, knocking them both down the open elevator shaft and out of sight.

Mull could tell she was just about reaching the end. Natalie's panic had raised her heartrate and now she was bleeding out from a hundred wounds.

That fucking bitch.

It wouldn't be long now.

"Just… go…" She breathed softly, hoping that Oz heard her.

He didn't appear to, or if he did, he was ignoring her order. His gaze slid around the corridor, obviously trying to plan an escape.

To their right, Holly smashed the glass cabinet on the wall with her elbow and grabbed the fire ax inside. She paused at the open elevator shaft and turned to face them. "I'd take the stairs if I were you. Because this won't end well." She took a deep breath, looking tired and uncharacteristically bruised. "YOLO, right?" She stepped backwards into the darkness and plummeted down.

Oz started pushing the bed again… And Mull lost consciousness.

****

Surprisingly, she came to an unknown number of minutes later, in what appeared to be the lobby of the building.

It wasn't a gentle wake up call.

She was tumbling onto the cold tile floor. The entirely *different* hospital bed she'd apparently been lying in, having been knocked over by a blast from one of the unknown attackers. She could only assume that Oz had simply lifted her from the heavier bed and physically carried her down the seven stories, then found her a replacement bed and made a break for the exit.

Instantly she started to feel around for the infants who had shared the bed with her, but she saw no sign of them. Which meant that someone else must have rescued them from the scene while she was out cold.

In the waiting area of the lobby, it looked like a bomb had gone off. The attacker was leveling his energy gun at Lexie. He pulled the trigger… and nothing happened.

Mack held out his hand, controlling the weapon with his powers. "Yeah, you're not going to shoot any more of my friends today, asshole." He wheezed, doubled-over in pain from earlier rounds of a fight Mull had missed.

Lexie smiled, unsteady on her feet from the battle. "Not so tough without your…"

The man smashed the butt of his weapon into her face and Lexie went down.

Mack straightened, bracing his feet. "Poll?"

The digital form of Polybius, the Consortium's artificial intelligence appeared beside him. "His suit is not accessible by any conventional electronic means which I can find. The signal it is receiving is randomized and I am unable to break into it at this time."

"Fine. I can't get a handle on the suit either, powers can't nail it down. So we'll have to do it the *ol' fashioned way* then." Mack slipped on a pair of brass knuckles and looked over at Mull, face somber. He knew what was about to happen. "Might want to git while the gettings good, sweetheart." He warned. "I can give you... *maybe* thirty seconds." He glanced at his digital partner, voice tight. "Ready to do somethin' really stupid, darlin'?"

Polly shook her head, looking concerned. "McCallister..." She began worriedly.

But Mack wasn't listening.

And Mull wasn't going anywhere. Not in thirty seconds, not in thirty days. Every single movement was an agony she had never before known, and she'd been hurt a *lot* in her life. It took everything she had not to just start screaming in hysterical pain, just sitting perfectly still, there was no way she was going to drag herself to the door before she died.

Below her, the tiles of the floor began to feel warm and slick, as she bled out.

But that didn't stop her. She didn't know where Oz was, but she knew where he'd been headed when she last saw him. And she knew that wherever he was, he'd be better off if she was there to protect him.

She started clawing at the floor with her broken fingers, trying to draw her bleeding body towards the automatic doors.

To her left, Mack moved to cover her escape, marching straight at the unknown man. The attacker swung at him with a heavy fist, but Mack dodged to the side, and the blow instead hit one of the support pillars of the building and knocked a huge chunk of concrete free. Mack punched the unknown man hard enough to crack the clear faceplate of the power-suit he wore... but it wasn't enough. He grabbed Mack by the neck...

Mull was on the verge of losing consciousness again, she could feel it. From her position on the floor though, she had a good view of the large clock above the entrance to the building.

It showed 11:59.

And for the first time in as long as she could remember, Mull spoke to God.

"Come on... come on... gimme something..." She watched the digital numbers count up, heartrate increasing in terror and anticipation, which was just quickening her imminent death. "Gimme something I can use... *Please*, God... *Please*..."

The clock showed 12:00:01.

Her entire existence shifted into a new version of herself, like the spinning rolls of a slot machine clicking into place and stopping on...

A brick.

A fucking *brick*.

Yeah, that would do...

Mack weakly hit the man again, but the attacker's robotically enhanced grip wasn't going to budge.

The fight was over. Mack would be dead in a few more seconds and he knew it.

But even on death's door, the man looked rather surprised as Mull calmly got back to her feet. She twisted her neck to the side, popping newly healed bones and tendons back into place. She put her fingers to her now healed lips and whistled loudly to get the attacker's attention too.

The man turned to look at her, then frowned behind his broken transparent facemask.

"You wanna brawl? That it?" Mull asked him, stalking forward. "You look at me and you see a little girl in a paper hospital gown, all broken and bloody. Easy pickins' for a big tough man like you, yeah?" She yanked out her IV and absently tossed the tube aside. "Well, mister, I don't know who you are or what you want, but you haven't *seen* angry until you've seen a clinically insane, trained assassin, super-villainess, with PMS and a missing boyfriend!" She slapped her palm against her chest. "You wanna see angry? *I will SHOW YOU fucking angry!*"

The man pulled his energy weapon again and fired at her.

She simply turned to the side, meeting the blast with her shoulder and tearing through it with her newly invulnerable body. "Ehn-ah-ah." She shook her head. "Now you wanna start shit with ME!?! With *my* friends!?! And you think I won't stop you because you're a big scary man in a metal suit!?!" She pointed at the clock, which showed that it was 12:02. "Sorry, pal. You're *two goddamn minutes too late.*" She closed the distance between them and the man dropped Mack to the floor, preparing to fight her. "You wanna step in the ring with me?" She challenged, then absolutely leveled the attacker with a right straight punch, just about breaking him in half and sending him flying down the hall like a leaf in a breeze. "Ding-ding, motherfucker!"

The man slammed into the far wall, dislodging his helmet and making it skid away. He lay still for a moment, obviously hurt.

Good.

Mull calmly stalked after him, her healing powers now working on returning her hair to its normal length, after her doctors had shaved it to suture her wounds. "My powers sucked yesterday, but today I'm a goddamn *Brick House*." She growled at the man. "Hazard level of strength and durability, with some useful accelerated healing to take care of the rest. Which means *no one* pushes me around today!" She planted her foot on the center of the man's neck, pinning him to the ground. "For the next 23 hours, fifty-seven minutes and nineteen seconds, I CAN PUNCH A WHOLE IN *THE FUCKING SKY!*" She smiled cruelly, pressing downward on him with her newfound tremendous strength. "And guess what that means for *your* skinny ass?"

The man's neck snapped.

Mull stared down at him in silence, trying to decide if she had any idea who the hell this guy even was.

She didn't hear the second attacker as he came up behind her, the sirens and fire alarm were too loud. She did, however, hear the man's screams.

She spun around to face him, only to see the man withering away to nothing inside his armor, like an ant under a magnifying glass. It was like… something was eating the man away. Making him decay in fastforward. The man's body… melted, like something from *Raiders of the Lost Ark*. His mostly empty armor landed by her feet, and Mull looked around the interior of the lobby, searching for a cause.

She didn't have to look hard.

Laying on the ground a short distance away, Oz was glaring at the man with creepy black eyes. His whole body was shuddering, then he stopped. His eyes cleared, then he pulled his legs up to his chest and started shaking again.

Which was… odd.

Mack got back to his feet and staggered towards the door. "Have… to… get out…" He whispered through bruised vocal chords, bending to grab Lexi's leg and start pulling her towards the door.

Mull didn't need to be told twice. She missed the middle part of this particular fight, but was willing to accept her teammate's warning without asking too many questions. She grabbed Oz, who was still shuddering, and ushered him towards the exit.

They reached the parking lot, where an assortment of other broken and battered Consortium members were scattered in the rain.

Above them, Poacher dove from a third story window, just as the building rocked from an explosion.

Mull reached up to shield Oz from the falling debris, as half of the hospital looked like it came down in front of them.

Poacher held one of the newborns from the maternity ward in his arms, then held it aloft like a football player in the end zone, showing everyone that he'd managed to rescue them all. For one terrifying moment, Mull thought he might actually spike the baby in a celebratory dance. But, thankfully, he refrained.

She looked back at the burning rubble of the building where she'd just almost died.

Mull hated hospitals.

Chapter 6

"'IF THERE'S NO MEANING IN IT,' SAID THE KING, 'THAT
SAVES A WORLD OF TROUBLE, YOU KNOW, AS WE
NEEDN'T TRY TO FIND ANY."

-Alice's Adventures in Wonderland

Two hours later, Mull was ducking under the crime scene tape and re-entering the crumbling structure of the hospital's north wing. Whatever had exploded inside had done a number on the surroundings.

She stepped over the burned wreckage of what appeared to be an office chair, searching for Oz. The man had refused medical attention and was still in here somewhere. Mull wasn't a mental health professional, but she knew a lot about what crazy looked like. And Oz wasn't doing too well.

After the building exploded, it took her fifteen full minutes to even get him to look at her. Instead, the man just huddled in a ball with his eyes closed, slowly rocking back and forth. Whatever the man had done to the mystery assassin, it had pushed Oz to the edge of something bad.

Mull wasn't sure what the exact nature of Oz's powers even were, but she was seriously worried about him now.

She wasn't used to Oz being delicate or in danger. Oz was... *Oz*. He was the most responsible and with-it person she'd ever met. Oz was the man who helped you with your problems, he wasn't someone who had serious problems of his own. Yes, he was often distracted with compulsions and rituals and tirades about cleanliness, but that was understandable and kind of cute. This was something different. And she didn't like it.

Oz was the most ordered and... *safe* person in the world.
He was *extraordinary*.

There was something wrong with Oz. Deeply wrong. Something she'd never noticed before. The foundations of the man weren't as rock solid as he liked to pretend, and whatever had happened tonight, it had shaken him. Shaken him *bad*.

The thought of that scared her more than she would have anticipated.

It didn't take her long to find her wayward partner. He was standing in the area where one of the nurse's stations had once been located. He was wearing a decontamination suit that would have made Darth Vader jealous, carefully placing all of the brochures for blood pressure medication back onto their scorched display. The action was a complete waste of time, since this wing of the building itself was a total loss, but Oz's mind wouldn't let him escape it. Instead, he was using a ruler to meticulously arrange the pamphlets into orderly stacks, using the level to make sure they were straight.

Mull didn't claim to be an expert on whatever-the-fuck was wrong with Oz, but she understood generic crazy. If Oz's condition was going nuts and making him waste his time like this, something deeper was going on with him.

"Hey," she stopped a few steps from him, feeling like she wandered in on something personal, "you okay?"

He moved one of the stacks an infinitesimally small amount to the left, his entire concentration on ensuring that it was the proper distance from its neighbor. "Where were you?" He asked, avoiding the question. "You shouldn't be alone right now."

"I was looking into something." She leaned against one of the columns, then thought better of it as a piece of the ceiling fell down at her feet. "How are you doing, Oz?"

"I'm fine." He assured her, sounding distant. "Why?"

Mull shrugged. "Oh, no reason. Just the fact that you've been screwing around in here for two hours."

"I'm investigating."

Mull looked around at the circle of order he'd made in the midst of the chaos of the rest of the lobby. "How is this helping?" She took a step towards him. "Oz, you're kinda freaking me out here, which is really hard to..."

"How is Wyatt?" Oz asked abruptly, cutting her off. "Did he make it?" His tone implied that Oz was pretty sure that the other man was dead.

"He got banged up, but he'll pull through." Mull leaned against the counter next to him. "Tyrant's not lucky enough for Wyatt to die in the field."

Oz let out a long breath. "It's my fault."

"I don't see how. Unless you were one of the guys in the super-suits."

112

"I was on-duty, I knew there was a problem, I should have stopped them."

"You don't even know who they are."

"It doesn't matter."

"Your problem is that you take on too much responsibility." She informed him softly. "You need to learn to say 'fuck it, shit happens' more."

"It doesn't happen if you're careful."

"It happens whether you're careful or not. This is a messy business."

Oz ignored her logical observations about the nature of superheroing in the city, and continued to mess around with his stack of pamphlets. The process of getting them exactly right was made more difficult by the fact that his hands were shaking.

Mull's frown deepened, growing increasingly worried.

Oz's patience snapped and he swept all of the brochures off of the counter in frustration, then kicked the singed supports of the desk several times until they broke in half.

He watched the cascade of leaflets as they floated back down to the floor, then silently began to pick them all up again.

Mull had never seen anything like it before. Something was triggering him though, she just wasn't sure what.

She stepped closer to him, taking his hand to stop him from fussing with the pamphlets for a moment. "Oz, seriously…" she met his eyes, "are you alright?"

"You almost died." He said softly, looking away.

"But I got better. That happens."

Oz was an intelligent, kind man. But something was broken in his head at the moment. And there wasn't anything she could do to help him with that.

She wasn't used to thinking of Oz as weak, but at the moment, her first impulse was to wrap her arms around him as tightly as she could, and tell him that everything was going to be okay.

But she didn't. Because she wasn't that kind of person today. And because she was fairly certain the man would be freaked out by physical contact anyway.

A man didn't wear a decontamination suit if he was looking for hugs from random people.

Oz was strictly the kind of man you admired from afar. Because he didn't want you any closer. And even if he did, you'd only get him killed anyway. Oz was a man of perfect order, and Mull was sheer chaos.

He was better on his own, like the hero in a western. He wandered the city, righting wrongs. He didn't get involved with the local riff-raff.

"I killed a man tonight." He calmly observed to no one in particular, like the idea amazed him.

"Meh. He seemed like an asshole anyway." Mull snorted, expecting her companion to share in the joke. But instead, he continued to simply stare at the floor. "Oz?"

"I'm fine." He assured her, picking up more of the fallen papers. "I... I've just had a long night, Miss Quentin."

"Cops kill people in the field all the time." She tried, wanting to make him feel better. "He left you no choice."

"Are you sure you're okay?" Oz asked suddenly, turning to look at her. "Because just because you're okay today doesn't mean that your wounds won't return tomorrow when you no longer have these powers."

"Oz, you're changing the subject." She took another step closer to him, softening her voice. "Are you going to be all weird about this now? Because of some piece of shit that was trying to kill us all?"

"I do not regret my actions. I regret his." Oz cleared his throat. "But I would kill him a million times over to keep you safe. Without a second thought."

"Thanks, Oz. But... I don't really need protecting today."

He met her eyes again. "I think you need to be protected more than anyone I've ever met in my life, Miss Quentin."

"I run into a few problems..."

"Like getting thrown off a roof, stabbed, shot with a shotgun a couple weeks ago..."

"...but I can take care of myself, there's no need for you to worry. Or to get all bent out of shape about some dirtbag you had to take out. Besides, it's not like this is the first person you've ever killed."

He was silent for a beat. "You shouldn't go anywhere without someone else with you. It's too dangerous." He pointed at her. "From now on, if you're going somewhere, I'm going too."

Mull had no objections to that. It would allow her to keep a better eye on him, both to protect him from whoever was trying to kill them and to make sure he was taking care of himself. Oz's problem was that he cared more about other people than he did about himself. Mull didn't give two shits about other people, so she was the perfect person to ensure that Oz didn't "selfless" himself to death.

"Do you have any idea who could have attacked us like this?"

He asked, placing his pile of brochures onto the remains of a table, then squatting down to retrieve some more.

She reached into her pocket and pulled out her phone. "I tracked the registration of every car in the parking lot."

"You think the assassins *drove* here?"

"I don't think they rode in on *elephants*, Oz. Had to get here somehow." She flipped through the pictures on her phone. "Every car in the lot belongs to someone who has business at the hospital or in the area... except *one*." She held up the image of the vehicle in question. "A 1971 Buick 'Boat tail' Riviera. Tags come back to one 'Willis Gibson,' a man who doesn't seem to have existed until Halloween, when he rented an apartment uptown."

Oz looked at the photo, his sharp eyes memorizing the man's features. "Do you recognize him? Was he one of the attackers?"

"Nope."

"Was the car stolen?"

"Doesn't appear to be, no. Or if it was, he didn't report it. He bought it at a dealership last week. Paid cash." She put her phone away. "Why would this random no-account asshole send men to kill us?"

"I don't know." Oz got to his feet, voice filled with hard determination. "*Let's go ask him.*"

****

Half an hour later, they were pulling up to the nondescript building where their chief suspect lived. The neighborhood was utterly ordinary. Personally, Mull disliked ordinary. She didn't trust it. Ordinary was how evil hid. Everyone knew that.

Oz pulled the car into one of the reserved "Hero" parking spots, which were scattered around the city, designated with a sign featuring the familiar symbol of a man in a cape.

"On one hand, I like the fact we won't have to walk far. But on the other hand, parking here kind of ruins the low-profile we should probably be going for." She observed.

Oz shrugged. "I don't hide. If he wants a fight with me, he knows where to find me."

Mull smiled, pleased to see that Oz had recovered some of his characteristic balls-to-the-wall boy-scout-iness. "Yeah, fuck him. This is *our* parking spot."

"Enjoy them while they last because the city is in the process of removing them."

Mull shook her head. "Ain't no more heroes anymore."

"A real hero doesn't care about free parking."

"But a real hero should be *given* free parking, all the same." She shook her head. "I don't know about you, but I'm not circling the block looking for a spot if there's a bank robbery going on, I'm just going to keep driving."

Oz unbuckled his seatbelt, then carefully checked and double-checked to make certain the emergency brake was engaged. "They've done studies and determined that 72% of Capes would choose another profession if they had their lives to do over again."

Mull snorted. "Not me. I love low pay, spandex, and vigilantism."

Oz started to chuckle, and the sound made Mull uncommonly happy for some reason. Oz so rarely laughed about things, the man was almost always deadly serious. And... sad. There was something so lonely and small behind Oz's facade of unflappable (though obsessive compulsive) protector. Mull didn't know why that was, but it always made her want to try to help him find some joy in life.

She closed the door to Oz's Prius and made a face at the boring brownstone buildings which surrounded them. "Jesus. I feel like a stickball game could erupt around us at any moment. If I try to open a lemonade stand, I want you to shoot me."

Oz looked up at the building, then started towards the front steps. "I still think we should consider calling for backup."

"You really want to deal with our coworkers?"

"No."

"Exactly. They'll just screw everything up and you know it." She swatted him in the chest with the back of her hand in a show of comradery, then immediately regretted it, instantly recognizing the fact that Oz didn't really like other people touching him. Germs and all. He was delicate. "Sorry."

He frowned at her. "About what?"

"I prefer to work alone too, that's one of the reasons why we work so well together."

He squinted slightly, trying to process that. "I'm... not sure I follow that logic."

She ignored that. "I'm a dying breed, Oz. My life is one of those awesome 90s action movies that they don't make anymore because everyone in Hollywood is a pansy now. You know the kind of movie I mean. Where a cynical, chain-smoking, foulmouthed, self-loathing, drunken loser anti-hero, shoots bad guys and blows random shit up, while his bosses yell at him for breaking every rule in the book. There's gratuitous amounts of nudity and imaginative profanity, it's always nighttime, everyone is an immoral piece of shit, and everyone is drowning in cheap alcohol. There's graphic torture and brutal home invasions. It's bloody, and fast-paced, and features an uneasy mix of comedy, violence, and genuine human anguish. That's my life." She started up the front stairs, stopping halfway up to scan the street behind her for possible threats.

"And you don't think I fit into that?" He asked.

"Well, at first I was thinking you were my mismatched buddy cop..."

"Uh-huh..."

She continued up the stairs. "But now I'm thinking you might be the pretty and innocent friend, who dies for my sins and to give me a greater motivation to kill my enemies and blow shit up in the climax of the film."

"It's nice that you've got this all figured out. Just imagine if you couldn't use terrible movies to explain complicated elements of our real lives."

"I don't even want to *imagine* living like that, Oz." She was horrified by the mere idea. "You just need to face the fact that the world is *Death Wish*. I'm Charlie Bronson, the last sane man in a world gone mad... you're his catatonic daughter who gets raped by Jeff Goldblum."

"I... I don't think I'm his daughter." Oz defended, as if having given the matter some thought.

"Well, you could be Denzel Washington, if you want. But Charlie Bronson shoots him too." She paused to squint at him. "You *do* have a certain 'Denzel' quality about you..."

"Does Bronson kill *everyone* in this movie?"

"Yeah." She nodded immediately. "'Cause he's Charlie Bronson. If he wasn't shooting punks and whooping ass, he wouldn't be Charlie motherfuckin' *Bronson*."

"Isn't there anyone who isn't a sociopath in the film? Aren't there any normal people?"

"Nope." She shook her head. "It's the most realistic film you'll ever see. Practically a documentary."

Arriving at the front door of the apartment building, Mull squinted down at the nameplates, looking for their guy. None of them seemed to be his name, but one of the apartments was lacking any kind of identification. Which meant it was more than likely their suspect.

"So... should we buzz him?" Oz wondered aloud, looking down at the doorknob, obviously debating whether or not it would be destroying evidence to spray its surface with antibacterial solution. "Or should I call the police to get a warrant first?"

Mull had far more experience than Oz did with getting into places she wasn't wanted. She couldn't imagine *anyone* not wanting Oz somewhere. "We buzz him and he'll rabbit on us." She reminded him, scanning the nameplates again. "And I don't deal with cops. They keep trying to arrest me over every little thing." One of the plaques identified the occupant as "Kristi Skye," the name spelled out in pink glitter ink, followed by her Instagram username and an inspirational hashtag. Mull tried to avoid the impulse to vomit. But the woman in question was perfect for her current requirements. Anyone that silly was sure to have a lot of friends stopping by unexpectedly. And anyone with a lot of friends undoubtedly had trouble identifying them all. ...Or so Mull assumed anyway. She'd personally never had a lot of friends, but she couldn't imagine them being easy to tell apart. She took on an utterly insipid voice and pressed the call button.

"Yes?" The woman asked, sounding even more irritatingly vapid than Mull imagined.

"Happy Thanksgiving, girl!" Mull called into the microphone cheerily. "It's me! Let me up!"

Sure enough, the door buzzed a moment later, as Kristi unlocked it for them.

Mull opened it and ushered Oz through. "See how easy that is, Oz?"

"Wouldn't it have been just as easy to obtain entrance legally?"

"I haven't broken any laws." She defended. "I didn't lie to dear Kristi, it *was* me. She's the one who decided that I was a 'me' she knew."

Oz squinted, trying to follow the logic of all of those pronouns. "I always find conversing with you to be confusing, Miss Quentin." Oz looked up the stairwell, obviously expecting gunmen to be waiting for them.

Mull rolled her eyes at the man's paranoia. But then thought about the situation for a moment, and shouldered him out of the way. "Stay behind me, Oz." She ordered, starting up the stairs. "I'm bullet-proof today."

Oz made a face at the idea, but didn't voice his obvious unhappiness about her being the one who would take the brunt of any attack.

"I think I should be in front." He decided after a moment, still sulking.

"You have super-strength and invulnerability today?"

"Well, no, but..."

"Don't be sexist, Oz." She turned to pat him on the shoulder. "I got this, baby doll. Don't you worry your pretty little head about it."

To her surprise, Oz snorted in amusement. "I'll try not to, Miss Quentin."

Mull was standing on the stair in front of him, their height difference lessened. From her position, she once again noted that the man smelled really good. Clean and strong and... wholesome. Mull had no experience with wholesome. But she found it so exotic and intriguing.

Oz was the kind of man that the world wouldn't let someone like Mull anywhere near, for fear she'd corrupt him. And that idea was *genuinely* exciting.

Oz was genuinely exciting.

Every time he looked at her, Mull got excited. Oz had the strange ability to make his mere glance feel like a soft and hot caress, making her body sing. It was one of the most enjoyable parts of her day, truth told. She *loved* that Oz looked at her like that. She woke up every day afraid that she'd somehow do something bad enough that he'd see the truth about her and stop. That he'd recognize that she was a terrible person, who had no business being around him. Thankfully, he hadn't yet.

She met his eyes, feeling the familiar feeling of desire shoot through her, heightened by the shared desire she told herself she saw in his eyes. "I have told you many, many times to call me 'Brick House' today." She breathed, trying to keep her voice steady and not tinged with the throaty tone of lust she felt at the moment.

Oz shook his head. "I'd rather not, thank you."

"Why?"

"Because it's ridiculous."

"It's a codename! *All* codenames are ridiculous! They're supposed to be!" She defended. "Besides, I usually go to Wyatt for help with them but he's still in the hospital at the moment, so I have to make due."

"That must be very hard for you." Oz observed unemotionally, for some reason, seeming oddly unhappy about the mention of her talking to Wyatt about personal things.

"It is, Oz, it really is." She swallowed, unexpectedly feeling a kind of intimacy in the moment. "You could... you could call me

'Natalie,' if you wanted." She offered, shifting on her feet like an awkward fucking sixth grader talking to a cute boy. "Or 'Nat.'"

"I would prefer that, yes."

Mull beamed, feeling like she'd just made an important step. But then the smile faded, recognizing that she had said "Natalie" and not "Mull." Which was odd. Natalie didn't really deal with coworkers. Well, not the ones from the Consortium, anyway. Natalie usually kept to herself.

Mull wasn't sure what the deal was with that. But she wasn't going to complain. Oz needed help coming out of his shell more. And... and she liked the way her name sounded coming from him. Not that it was technically *her* name, it was Natalie's, but it was pretty close and would do in a pinch.

She cleared her throat, trying to break the sudden odd feeling which filled her and hung in the air. "I... I guess we should get back to work, huh?"

Oz nodded, continuing up the stairs, surreptitiously taking the lead so that he was once again the one most in the line of fire from potential attackers on the floors above them.

The action didn't make Mull happy. Oz was being careless with his life. And if one of them was going to get shot today, it sure wasn't going to be him.

She raced to catch up with him, but to her surprise, the man sped up, trying to outpace her. For two flights they battled back and forth, until Mull hopped up onto the railing of the stairwell and vaulted up a flight, to pull herself over the bannister, skipping the last flight of stairs.

Oz arrived at the door a moment later, frowning, but she could tell he was actually having a good time.

She pointed at the door. "I win."

"That was incredibly dangerous and you just needlessly risked your life to win a childish race." He lectured.

She rolled her eyes. "Don't be a sore loser, Oz. I won and..." She trailed off, noticing that the door to their suspect's apartment was ajar. She met Oz's eyes meaningfully.

He nodded and tactically arranged himself at her side, backing up her next move. "How durable are you again?" He whispered, still concerned.

"Pretty durable."

"Define 'pretty.'"

"It would take... about 150 quintillion megatons to kill me."

"Ah. Hopefully our guy doesn't have access to

150,000,000,000,000,000,000,000,000 sticks of dynamite in there then."

"Well, in this town, you can never tell." She paused. "Did you do that math in your head?"

"I like math." He explained. "It's orderly."

"Ah."

She pushed the door open with her foot, then moved to the side in case someone took a shot at them. When there was no sound from inside the room, she leaned around the doorjamb again, peering into the darkness.

"It's clear." Oz announced with complete confidence, starting into the room. "But I think we should call the police."

Mull snorted at the idea, shouldering her way past him. "Why? We got this, Oz."

"We are destroying evidence, just by being here. Altering trace fibers, moving things around, contaminating the scene with touch DNA…"

"What are you 'touching'?" She laughed, amused to no end by the way the man's mind worked. "You planning on fondling all this guy's shit, Oz?"

"Microscopically, we already are."

She made her way towards the apartment's kitchen. "I don't care about microscopes, Oz. Had one when I was a kid, broke it trying to miniaturize a hamster."

The kitchen was clean in that way that told you that no one really lived there. The sole evidence of the resident was a takeout menu stuck to the fridge with a magnet. Mull looked at the appliance for a long moment. "We should check that…" She decided, feeling the stirrings of fear inside her.

Oz's eyebrows went up. "For what?"

"Sometimes people stuff bodies into refrigerators." She said softly. "As a message."

Oz frowned, his conception of world not allowing for something so obvious. "You want to check the refrigerator…. for bodies?" He said slowly, like he was trying to decipher a foreign language.

"I *always* check my refrigerators for bodies." She defended, trying to keep her voice low so that anyone in the apartment wouldn't hear her. "Because I live in the *real* world!" She opened the door of the appliance… to find it empty, except for a can of Diet Coke.

Oz turned to look at her, silently gloating.

"Shut up, Oz." She made a face at him, then opened up the

beverage to take a sip.

He gestured to the other side of the kitchen with his thumb. "Wanna check the oven next?"

She swatted at him in annoyance, then started silently towards the door to the bedroom. Which was closed. And people rarely closed the door to their bedroom when they were leaving for the day. Which meant that, chances were, the guy was still lurking inside.

She pointed at the door and Oz nodded again, taking up a position on the opposite side of the frame from her.

She had to hand it to the man, he had good instincts on how to be a killer. He might be a rule-follower, but he understood how to move through a dangerous situation. Which was pretty cool.

It had been a long, long time since Mull had worked with a real partner. And that had never been nearly as enjoyable as this. Working with Rondel had been... an absolute nightmare.

Oz prepared to breach the door, looking over at her to make sure she was set.

She nodded.

Oz kicked the door open, immediately stepping aside to get out of her way, so that Mull could make entry and engage any attackers they found inside.

But no attack came.

Instead, the suspect was simply sitting behind a desk inside, silhouetted in the darkness by the dim morning light filtering in through the dirty curtains behind him.

Oz started forward, utterly unintimidated by a mysterious suspect lying in wait for them. He was such a confident and fearless man when he was working.

He was an aspirational hero... who no one aspired to be, for some reason. He was a trustworthy, moral person. Innately good. One of the few remaining examples of that personality type left in the Caping industry in the city. But his personal issues turned people off and not many tried to see the deeper perfection hidden within.

But Mull always had. She could see beneath the mask he wore.

He was... stalwart. Like a heroic knight or brave lawman.

"Willis Gibson." Oz announced the man's name like a school administrator calling a misbehaving student to his office.

Her mouth curved, enjoying the commanding tone he took on when he was dealing with people he believed to be criminals. There was a composed power to Oz, despite his often neurotic behavior. And she'd always found it so oddly erotic.

"We are with the Consortium of Chaos, here on official business, and we…" He trailed off when he saw the blood.

Both of the man's hands had been pinned to his desk with butcher knives, and a third blade was stabbed straight through his forehead. The knife was used to pin a note in place.

And Mull's blood ran cold, immediately recognizing the handwriting before she even processed the words.

"Sorry Kitten, he wouldn't fit in the fridge."

Rondel.

Her psycho ex had killed this guy for some reason.

And a surge of fear went through Mull as she considered that, immediately spinning around, half expecting the man himself to be lunging from the darkness in an attempt to kill Oz.

"We… we need to get out of here, Oz." She decided, backing away from the body in growing terror. *"Now."*

For his part, Oz seemed far less disturbed by the body then she would have expected. Probably because he seemed to find living people disgusting already, it wasn't like them being dead was really going to somehow make that worse.

He looked down at the body with a cold clinical eye. "Why?"

"Because Rondel killed this guy and he could still be here!" She wanted Oz as far away from this place as possible. There was nothing Rondel would love more than hurting Oz. He'd kill Oz, and he'd force her to watch.

"Mercygiver?" That seemed to interest Oz. "You sure?"

"Pretty damn sure, yeah." She motioned towards the door. "We need to go."

Oz pursed his lips. "Why would he kill this man?" He wondered aloud, then started to open up the desk drawers, obviously looking for clues. "It makes no sense."

Mull shifted on her feet impatiently, but then recognized that there was no way she was going to get Oz out of this apartment. The man could be the most stubborn person in the world when he wanted to be. He always thought he knew best. "This is a really bad idea, Oz." She warned.

"He's not in the apartment at the moment. Which means that if this is a trap, he's already waiting outside for us." He started sifting through paperwork. "Which means the more we know about how he figures into this, the better."

"There is no possible way Rondel didn't sweep this apartment clean of anything we could use to track him, Oz." She shook her head. "He's way too careful to leave anything behind. I *guarantee* you, he went through every single inch of this place. Whatever it is you think you're going to find, if it was in this apartment, it's long gone now."

Oz nodded, recognizing that she was probably right but too caught up in his rule-following to listen. And instant later he straightened. "So... we need evidence that wasn't in the apartment *yet*..." He cryptically decided.

She frowned at him. "Huh?"

Oz grabbed a set of keys from off of the desk and started from the apartment. A moment later, they were both standing in front of the residents' mailboxes. "That man was murdered at least an hour ago. But the mail only just arrived. Which means..."

"...Ronnie couldn't have taken it." She nodded, impressed with that thinking. That was one of the reasons why she always enjoyed working with Oz: he was the best Cape she'd ever seen in her life. Well, that and the fact that the man was fucking *gorgeous,* which also had a lot to do with it.

That man was *absurdly* hot, and Mull got a genuine thrill just watching him.

Oz squinted at the lock on the mailbox, then put on a second pair of gloves. "Do you know the kinds of horrible things that get sent through the mail?" He explained, defending himself against her unspoken criticism.

She leaned against the wall next to him. "I got a box of dead swans in the mail once."

"Who sent them?" He sounded puzzled by that. "Why?"

She shrugged. "Once you become a super-villainess, you learn to stop asking questions like that, Oz."

Oz opened the mailbox and pulled out the mail, which was almost entirely junk. Ads from local stores and whatnot. But Oz stopped shuffling through it when he came to the last letter in the stack. It had no return address.

He looked at her meaningfully, then tore it open.

Inside was a single sheet of paper, with seemingly meaningless letters printed on it. He held it up to her.

"What the fuck does 'xvwzh sompt lmtna fuuqf jpwgg fjge' mean?" She wondered aloud.

"I have no idea." Oz shook his head. "But a man doesn't typically get mail with nothing but random letters on it."

"A code?"

Oz shrugged. "That would be my guess."

"I'm shit at codes today, Oz." She warned. "I had a day two months ago when I was really good at them, but today, that's just meaningless to me."

Oz pursed his lips, then placed the letter flat against the mailboxes to take a picture of it with his phone. He pressed several buttons, then was silent for a beat.

"Yes?" Came the voice on the other end of the speakerphone.

"Marian?" Oz asked. "Did you get the image I sent you?"

"Yes." Marian Willson, AKA "The Librarian" said in her eternal calm. "That is an exceedingly complicated substitution cypher. There are approximately 15,000,000,000,000,000,000 possible combinations. It would take a supercomputer decades to crack that."

Oz frowned. "That's what I..." He began, but Mull cut him off.

"Cut the shit, Marian. You're smarter than any computer. *What's it say?*"

"Your letter reads: 'Train leaves the station in 7 days. Be ready.'" Marian announced.

They both stared down at the letter, trying to decide what that meant.

"Anything else you can tell us about it?" Oz asked.

"It is written in a more complicated variation of the Agletarian diplomatic code." Marian informed them calmly. "I do not know what you two are up to, but I would advise extreme caution."

Mull made a face.

"We'll be careful. Thank you, Marian." He hit the disconnect button on the phone, looking up at Mull. "Did you and Mercygiver ever work with the Agletarians?"

"Just once."

"What happened?"

"They hired us to kill someone. Rondel ended up killing our contact and leaving their source, one of our partners, stuffed in a mailbox with postage stamps on his forehead."

Oz's eyebrows rose.

"Oh yeah." She nodded. "Ronnie is a prankster."

Oz carefully put the letter back in its envelope, then sealed it in an evidence bag he produced from his pocket. Because *of course* the man would carry evidence bags with him everywhere he went. This was *Oz* they were talking about. "Doesn't sound like the Agletarians would be open to working with him again."

"I wouldn't think so, no."

"So, Rondel hires those men to attack the hospital..."

She shook her head. "That's not Ronnie's style."

"But let's just say it, for argument's sake. He hires the men to attack the hospital, because he wants to get to you."

"Okay." She shrugged. "For what reason? He usually does all of his killing in person."

"Then, he comes here and kills Mr. Gibson to eliminate the witness..."

"But he just tried to kill me yesterday. That kind of limits the suspects. So what would it matter if this guy implicated him? Especially since he literally *left a note* identifying himself as the killer."

Oz shook his head. "It doesn't make any sense."

"Nope."

"So, perhaps the Agletarians hired the men to kill you, because..."

"They try to kill us all the time."

"But why you *specifically*?"

"I haven't killed any of them in years. Except for the ones a few weeks ago, during that whole Super-Person Resistance Movement mess." She rolled her eyes. "But we all killed a bunch of them, so I don't know why they'd be stuck on me. Or what Rondel would possibly have to do with that."

"Maybe it has to do with the people you were supposed to kill, years back."

"Doubtful. Since it was the Consortium."

Oz's eyebrows soared. "The Agletarians tried to hire you to kill the *Consortium*?"

"Yeah."

"But then you took a job to kill *them*."

"Yeah."

"Which..."

"...doesn't help us explain any of this."

Oz silently considered that. "So, what's going on then?"

She shook her head. "I honestly have no idea."

They were both silent for a long moment, recognizing that this was far more serious than they'd first thought.

Oz's voice sounded concerned. "Something else is going on and we're only seeing pieces of it." He looked up towards the apartment where the dead man was still waiting, then out towards the street. "We've stumbled into something here..."

He didn't need to tell that to Mull. She'd always had a sixth sense about such things. And whatever this was, it was going to be very, very bad.

She didn't like the idea of Oz being involved in it.

"This is going to get loud, Oz." She warned seriously. "Louder than anything you've been around before. Blood in the streets kind of shit." She met his eyes. "Can you handle that?"

He started towards the exit. "I think you'd be surprised at what I've been around before, Natalie."

Chapter 7

"'SERPENT!' SCREAMED THE PIGEON. 'I'M NOT A
SERPENT!' SAID ALICE INDIGNANTLY. 'LET ME ALONE!'"

-Alice's Adventures in Wonderland

22 YEARS AGO

The redhead's smile was dazzling, and looking at it impacted straight down to his soul.

It was innocent and teasing and completely charming. It seemed to promise something exquisite and pure. Something which would make the person on the receiving end of that smile complete. Something which would just wash everything clean and make everything alright forever. Something that offered *life*.

Something... which apparently had to do with coffee.

Oz sat on the tree limb, looking out at the decaying billboard which featured the image in question. A redheaded woman in an elegant blue housedress was serving something called 'Lieber Coffee' to some unseen individual. The red cup sat on an outstretched tray in the woman's elegant hands, like some sacred Holy Grail, offered to an unseen man by an angel. She was looking at him like he was the most amazing person she'd ever known. Like he was... extraordinary.

Oz had never actually heard of the defunct brand, and the tagline under the image simply provided the words "At the end..." and the rest of this cryptic message was long gone. The ad appeared to be from the midcentury, its colors now sun-faded and stained. Just how it came to be here and how it had survived this long was anyone's guess, but Oz spent a great part of his days staring at it. Not because it had extraordinary artistic merit, just because he found it relaxing for some reason, and it was one of the only things visible from the tree.

Everywhere else he looked, there were only mountains of trash.

Oz's aunt and uncle owned the local dump, and the cramped

ramshackle trailer which served as their home was positioned right in the middle of it.

Oz hated it. It was like drowning. Drowning in a sea of other people's trash and mistakes.

The sights and smells were overwhelmingly awful.

He escaped the home whenever he had the opportunity, climbing the property's only tree and looking in the one direction which wasn't just a pile of garbage.

That tree was Oz's window on the world. The one place where he could feel safe and alone.

But the day was drawing to a close, which meant that Oz would have to return to reality and abandon his imaginary world.

Not that Oz really had much of an imagination, but even 25% of one was better than 100% reality. *Anything* was better than reality, really.

Oz was the only ten year old in the world already trying to get a full-time job so he'd have enough money to move out, while simultaneously researching "Is it possible to put *yourself* up for adoption?" at the library.

He dropped his book to the ground and started climbing down from his perch. It took a few minutes, but then his feet were once again planted on the soft, vaguely damp soil, which was peppered with bits and pieces of a thousand different types of trash.

He tried to keep the area around the tree relatively clear of debris, but the ground itself contained the garbage. It ran too deep in it. The litter was always right below the surface, no matter how much you raked or how hard you tried to hide it. A month ago, he'd spent three full days carefully trying to remove all traces of trash. And it had looked so clean and orderly when he was done. But the garbage had returned within a week. Uncovered by the wind and rain, the shame once more exposed. It was impossible to get rid of it and Oz was getting to the point that he was sick of even trying to.

It might be clean at the moment, but it wouldn't be for long. You could tell. His aunt was right about that.

Filth would out itself in the end.

Oz took an almost clinical fascination with the idea, because it confirmed what he already knew to be true: things which looked clean were always dirty. As such, he had long ago self-diagnosed himself as a serial killer, still in his formative years. He was well-acquainted with the warning signs, watching for them in himself the way other boys might await a holiday or a meteorologist might observe the weather.

He didn't recall an abnormal amount of bedwetting as a child, but he wasn't really sure how one defined a "normal" amount of something so horrible. He didn't start fires, as a rule, but he wasn't afraid of them either, which was probably a bad sign. And he saw no point in hurting small animals. So, as of yet, he hadn't reached the stage of exhibiting the three biggest warning signs of burgeoning serial killers. Still, he was a loner and he did feel a disconnect between himself and other people. He wasn't on the same page as they were, he'd always seen that. And he had violent thoughts sometimes, which he hid from people.

He could feel it, even if there was no evidence of it yet. Which meant, honestly, it didn't really matter if he was showing the classic serial killer telltales or not. He would *eventually*. There was no doubt.

One day, Oz's life was destined to be featured on one of those crime shows, talking about what a quiet, odd boy he was, and how the warning signs had all arrived later in life than they normally did, but were ignored, just the same. He'd gone so far as to think about the exact photos they'd use for the program, probably something where he looked haunted, gaunt, and angry. He didn't think those photos actually existed, but they'd probably be taken once he completed his metamorphosis into a madman.

It was inevitable.

Oz was a serial killer, even if he never actually killed anyone. He could feel it. And everyone told him so. Repeatedly.

It kept him up at nights. It was yet one more reason why he preferred to be alone.

He brushed off his book, one of the *Hardy Boys* mysteries, which he'd bought for 10 cents at the library's book sale. Generally, Oz would have vastly preferred to buy the book new and wrapped in sterile plastic, but his aunt and uncle weren't really readers, so there was no way they would have given him money for that.

Oz liked mysteries. There was an order to them which he appreciated. There was good and there was evil, and evil could be defeated if you just followed the clues. And there were *always* clues to solve any seemingly impossible mystery life threw at you. Everything made sense, if you looked at it long enough. Everything had a place and nothing was messy.

And Oz liked the Hardy Boys especially. He liked the idea of having someone to solve mysteries with. Someone you could trust. Because Oz couldn't even imagine such a thing. Oz wasn't really a people person and he didn't have any friends. He'd *never* had any friends and he was utterly okay with that. He honestly didn't want any. People were silly and dirty and irritating. But he liked reading about the Hardy Boys and imagining having a partner and a friend. Someone who *didn't* irritate and disgust him.

One day, some very noble men and women would probably need to stop Oz, once he truly lost his mind and started doing bad things. They'd need to work together to do it.

He had nothing but respect for them. Hopefully, they'd manage to do it before he killed too many people. It wasn't that Oz *wanted* to hurt people, at all, but he predicted that he one day would. That was how these things went.

Trash couldn't hide for long.

He switched off his small radio, and James Taylor instantly stopped singing about fire and rain. Oz had hung the radio from a red reflector nailed to the tree, which was there to keep the trucks from crashing into the tree at night, but this area of the dump hadn't really been used in years. Which was why Oz liked hanging out here.

His uncle's dump had existed since the 1930s, providing local communities the perfect place to discard the things they didn't want anymore. The things which were too disgusting or too dangerous to keep around.

Like Oz himself.

His uncle made ends meet by occasionally allowing people to dump toxic chemicals here. Or charging the criminal element a fee to turn a blind eye to the fact they were using his land to dispose of... problems. Bloody, dismembered problems.

Oz had little doubt there were dozens of people buried forever in the mounds of garbage which circled the site. Slowly decomposing in the filth. Gradually being eaten away by the rats and the mangy seagulls which were forever moving around in the horror.

Living at the dump was an absolute nightmare. One which Oz couldn't wake from, no matter how hard he tried.

Oz made his way down the path and ran smack into one of the principle reasons *why* living here was so horrible: his cousin.

The older boy towered over him, cigarette dangling from his lip. The boy stood up, pushing his friends out of the way. "Hey there, Creepy." He advanced on him, face contorting with sudden rage. "Been meaning to have a talk with you..."

"Kick his ass, Hooch!" The skinny girl standing next to his cousin encouraged.

His cousin always went by "Hooch." It was one of those nicknames which caught on because his cousin kept trying to make it a

132

thing. Probably because his given name was "Meryl." The other kids in the neighborhood quickly realized that if they ever wanted to survive past high school, they'd better start embracing the nickname he'd chosen for himself. Personally, Oz thought it sounded stupid. He saw no sense in going by anything other than your actual name.

"I don't want to fight." Oz told him, backing away.

Hooch pushed him. "Did I ask what you wanted?"

Oz stumbled backwards.

"What'chu got here, huh?" Hooch grabbed the book and looked down at it. *The Hardy Boys.*" He sneered out the title and then batted the red cover against Oz's forehead. "Boys make you hard, Creepy? That it? That why you're so weird all the time?"

Oz tried to grab the title, but Hooch hit him in the face with it.

Hooch's friends laughed.

"Yeah, I gotta keep you from reading shit like this, don't I? Isn't that what a good cousin should do?" Hooch threw the book as hard as he could, out into the dump.

Oz watched it pinwheel through the sky and then disappear into the mass of garbage, never to be seen again. The mystery contained within would never be solved. The villains it featured would forever escape the Hardy Boy's justice.

The order the book promised was now replaced with chaos.

Messy, messy chaos...

Oz felt his anger stirring, sick to death of being bullied and even more furious about the mess.

Hooch's father hit Hooch. So Hooch hit Oz. And any other kid he could get his hands on. Hooch was one of those people who didn't feel happy unless he was hurting something.

And his usual target was Oz.

"I want you out of my life, Creepy." Hooch reminded him seriously, as if Oz had somehow forgotten it. "You're just another piece of fucking trash that Mom and Dad decided to stuff into our house!"

Oz had been taken in by his aunt and uncle when his parents had... Well, when his *mother* had died, anyway. And he wasn't exactly adjusting well to the change.

"His old man, he goes crazy and carves those people up, and now I got to put up with him." Hooch thought aloud, then turned to look at his small gang of idiots. "That sound fair to you?"

Hooch's friends shook their heads, laughing in slack-jawed acquiescence.

"Way I see it... I'd only be getting justice if I were to end you right here...." Hooch met his eyes. "A little revenge for what your psycho father did..."

Oz's father, Henry Arthur Dimico, had calmly walked into a Mega-Burger and killed his wife and sixteen other patrons halfway through his meal, before turning the gun on himself. His last words were reportedly: "*I told them NO fucking pickles!!!*"

He was not a well man.

He had somehow survived his suicide attempt, but had not spoken since. Not even at his trial.

Oz only had the vaguest memories of his father. They were all entirely ordinary, involving fishing, and laughing at comedians on TV, and tying Oz's shoes. Nothing at all which would evidence the man's troubled psyche. But then one day... whatever levee there had been in the man's mind finally broke. And the nice guy was suddenly evil.

That idea frightened Oz. He didn't like its implications. He didn't like the thought of waking up and being a completely new person, who could be capable of something so horrible.

This concern was reinforced by what had happened to Oz's brother.

His brother's girlfriend had broken up with him right before a dance at school, so he had strangled the girl. Then drove to her family's house and strangled them too. The next morning, he had been shot to death on the street in front of Oz's elementary school, during recess.

Oz had watched the whole thing, from the base of one of the slides.

But he didn't like talking about that.

It scared Oz too much. It was like looking into a crystal ball and seeing what he was sure would be his own future.

Evil was a latent personality trait in the Dimicos, it seemed. And Oz was terrified of catching the mysterious and peculiar insanity which seemed to afflict men in his family. There was no escaping it, but Oz was scared of it all the same. He had structured his entire life around that fear, readying himself for sudden madness or all-consuming hate which he'd be compelled to take out on the world.

But Hooch didn't actually care about that, the death of Oz's mother, or any notion of personal responsibility. Hooch just didn't like the fact that Oz had invaded his life, or that his parents had given Oz half of Hooch's room. The beatings were so frequent now that Oz's aunt had literally drawn a line done the center of the dirty floor using masking tape, showing each boy their territory. But the line noticeably moved closer and closer to Oz's bed each morning, as if by magic.

Oz would have gladly given Hooch the *entire* room, just so long as he didn't have to be there to see it. Oz just wanted to be somewhere else. *Anywhere*, really. He didn't want to be in Hooch's room any more than Hooch wanted him there.

Oz missed his parents. He missed his brother. He missed his old life. He missed the people he thought he knew, and the things they once did. He missed the masks they had apparently been wearing. He missed... he missed himself. Again, Oz was not a part of the world. Half the time, it felt like either his old life or his new one were fake. Just delusions of a diseased mind, finally cracking under its own weight.

The foundations of Oz's world were crumbling and broken. The more things shook, the more danger there was that Oz would collapse. And whatever new structure was revealed under the debris... it scared Oz.

Bad blood would out. And no matter how much dirt you piled on top of it or how many air fresheners you used, you could always smell the dump. *Always*.

Whatever Oz was... was what Oz was doomed to become, whether he wanted to or not.

"How about it, Creepy?" Hooch pushed him again. "What have you got to say for yourself, huh? Mom says that you're just as crazy as your old man and your psycho ass-wipe of a brother. That true? Huh? That why you spend all your time out here with the rest of the trash!?!" He pushed him harder, causing Oz to stumble.

The radio in his hands tumbled free, and as Oz bent to pick it up, Hooch smashed it to bits with the heel of his boot.

"Oops." The boy's evil sneer grew, relishing the destruction of one of Oz's only remaining possessions.

His mother had given him that radio the Christmas before she was killed. Oz carried the red plastic case everywhere, unwilling to let it out of his sight, for fear of Hooch getting his hands on it.

But now it was gone.

Just like his book of mysteries which would never be solved.

Just like his mother.

Sometimes, the memories Oz didn't think he had, stirred to life again. And he was suddenly younger, lying on the dirty tile floor of the restaurant, feeling cold french fries and ketchup on his palms... mixing with the slick, hot blood... looking at his mother's face as she died.

The screams...

Hooch punched him in the stomach and Oz doubled over, falling to the filthy ground. Hooch kicked him as he tried to get up, causing Oz to collapse again.

He pressed Oz's face into the muddy ground. "See, what we got here is a problem. I don't want you in my life. I don't want you reading your creepy books and listening to your lame-ass music in *my* room." He leaned closer to growl into Oz's ear, pressing Oz's face further into the slimy mud, which smelled of chemicals and garbage. "Which means... you're going to leave or I'm going to *make your life hell,* do you understand me!?!"

Oz's mouth and nose disappeared into the filthy water which quickly filled the hole Hooch was pressing him into. The icy runoff from the garbage was now covering his face and Oz couldn't breathe.

When he couldn't hold his breath anymore, he inhaled a gasping mouthful of garbage water. The noxious fluid rushed into his straining lungs, offering only death.

And his eyes popped open, like he'd been hit with a cattle prod.

Oz could see the world. Not the world that people usually saw... he could see the *REAL* world. Watched as it came to life before him.

Trillions of microscopic organisms and lifeforms, all snapping to attention and waiting for their orders. There were more organisms in a teaspoon of dirt than there were people on the planet. 10,000,000,000 bacteria per square centimeter of your mouth alone. Eight-legged, worm-like spider creatures, forever swimming in the grease which filled the pours of your face. And microanimals which couldn't be killed with heat or cold or the vacuum of space. You couldn't suffocate them, dehydrate them, or starve them. You could freeze them in ice for millennia and irradiate them, and they wouldn't even notice.

They were everywhere. They were eternal. They were unstoppable. And they covered everything you owned and everything you touched and everything you ate. Moving and eating and screwing and having little microbe wars.

A hundred thousand tiny mites were shitting on your face, right now.

Life on this planet, in a very real sense, was microscopic. People and the world they inhabited were just walking petri dishes. Huge moving vessels, which carried around the *real* possessors of this disgusting earth. God had given the world to the microbes and the viruses and the bacteria. The little things that people overlooked and stepped on.

The trash.

But they could be very angry, if you let them.

They were as willing to destroy their environment as man was willing to destroy his.

Poison it. Consume it. Sicken it. *Burn it down*.

All they were waiting for was an order.

And sometimes... Oz felt like they were all waiting for him to issue it. Swore he could hear them in the darkness of the dump... urging him to do it. Telling him things about the objects they were clinging to and the kinds of worlds they moved through...

As he looked at his own blood as it began to swirl within the garbage water his cousin was drowning him in, Oz felt that anger grow. Could feel it moving through his veins like liquid evil, spoiling the flesh it touched. Could hear the trillions upon trillions of unseen microorganisms and germs around him, stopping to watch the commotion.

Waiting...

Whispering...

And Oz knew, in that instant, that if he asked them... they could devour Hooch like he'd never even existed. Five hundred *centillion* tiny lifeforms, suddenly focusing their anger and their hunger and their hatred on his enemy. Each taking tiny bites at a microscopic scale, but together, they could consume him in minutes. *Seconds*. If they had the proper motivation and instruction. They could wither Hooch away to nothing... Make his body decompose, while he was still alive...

Yes... Oz knew what they could do.

He recognized the power of trash and forgotten things.

But Oz was not his father. He wasn't his older brother. He wasn't a killer yet. And it would take something a heck of a lot more important than defending his own life to ever make him one.

He unclenched his fists, trying to calm down before he lost control. Before he did something that Hooch would regret. His uncle hurt Hooch, Hooch hurt Oz, but Oz was determined to end it there. He didn't want to hurt anyone. He just wanted to be left alone.

Oz struggled free, gasping for breath and vomiting up the indescribably horrible water. He doubled-over, retching.

Hooch took the opportunity to club him in the back of the head with a piece of debris, knocking Oz out.

When he came to, forty-five minutes later, it was dark out

and his shoes were missing.

Oz let out an annoyed sound.

He was really, *really* getting sick of his cousin.

He picked his way along the uneven path through the dump, cursing Hooch for every sharp stone and chunk of glass which cut Oz's feet.

He eventually made it back to the shabby cabin which served as his home now, and shoved his way inside. The latch on the front door didn't work and when you opened it, there was a sliding sound as it pushed aside the pile of junk on the floor behind it.

Oz's aunt was a hoarder. She didn't throw anything away, no matter how useless, which was probably why Oz was here.

Personally, he would have preferred it if they'd just let the state take him away. Or if they let Hooch finally kill him. *Anything* would be better than this.

The woman looked up from her microwave pizza, which she was eating out of a salvaged plastic Cool-Whip container. Like most things in the house, all of the bowls had started out as something else. "You've been fighting again." She observed, with no real concern about the blood stains or bruises which now covered Oz.

His aunt's dark brown hair hung in greasy strands across her forehead, because the shower in the trailer no longer worked. The plumbers could not be called to fix the problem, because they would need access to the pipes, which was impossible because of all of the trash the home contained. And they couldn't clean the house to allow the workmen access to the problem, because... Oz wasn't sure, actually. But there must have been a reason which made sense to his aunt, even if Oz couldn't fathom what it could possibly be.

"No, ma'am." He shook his head, trying to get through the room without a lecture. "I..."

"Can't just live and let live, can you? Always have to fight people. Thinkin' you're the big man." She rolled her eyes and pointed at him with the doughy crust of her soggy meal. "Bad blood outs, that's what I say. Your father was a killer, boy. Took your mother from us. I told her not to marry that soulless devil, but she didn't listen to me. Insisted that we were wrong about him and that he wasn't evil. But he was. He surely was, as any man God himself ever damned." She gestured to him again, the gelatinous burned cheese dripping down into the repurposed plastic bowl, which was yellowing and stained from age. "Brother too. We tried to look after him for your mother, give him a good life. But what did he do, huh? How did he end up?" She snorted in derision. "Just like his waste of a father. And just like you're gonna. Because *bad blood outs.*"

Oz's brother... Oz's brother was a lunatic. There was really no argument there. Not that his aunt and uncle had really helped matters, but they also weren't entirely to blame.

Ellen refocused on her meal. "That's the way things are, Oswald. You can't change what you are, and sooner or later..."

"I'm not evil, Ellen." Oz told her flatly, hoping he sounded more definite than he felt.

"Not yet." She took another mouthful of food. "But you will be. If you stay on this road, you will be. Because it's in your blood." Her tone implied her beliefs were backed up by the umpteen hours of televangelists the woman watched every day on KNNR Channel 10, after the *Farmer Frank* show was over. Whatever money didn't get spent on box loads of trash, got sent to the pastors on the TV, in exchange for supposed rewards in the afterlife.

Personally, Oz thought the woman should probably be giving this speech to her son– since the boy was already a sadist and was working hard to become a sexual predator, the way other boys might take on a summer job– but he'd never heard her say anything against her dear precious Meryl. Which was a shame. Because his live TV exorcism might be good ratings for his aunt's TV religious advisors.

Still, Oz sometimes thought about smothering the woman with a pillow. He wasn't prepared to act on that, obviously, it was just a mental image that popped into his head every few weeks, but it probably wasn't a normal kind of thought to have about someone who annoyed you.

Which meant... that his aunt was right about him.

He *was* evil.

Which terrified Oz. And made him even angrier.

She pointed towards the kitchen. "I waited for you as long as I could, but if you're not gonna come home in time for dinner, that's not my fault." The woman shook her head, viewing his fifteen minute absence as a personal attack. "I've missed too many meals because of your nonsense already."

"That must have been very hard for you." Oz told her unemotionally, not pointing out that the woman's weight struggles indicated that she was by no means skipping meals or the fact that he was responsible for *cooking* most of said meals, because she always claimed to be too exhausted to do it. "Happy Thanksgiving, Aunt Ellen."

She made a noncommittal sound, too focused on her tabloid to pay attention to him.

Oz began to leave the room, limping on his bruised feet and trying to ignore the various types of unknown sticky debris and dirt which his bare skin and open wounds were picking up from the matted tangle of the filthy carpet.

"Your father named you after the Kennedy assassin," Ellen called after him distractedly, sounding almost bored, "you know that, right?"

He tried not to roll his eyes. He didn't know why his aunt loved to remind him of that little factoid about his life, but she did at least once a week. It had long ago ceased to be effective in belittling him, and now his only real thought about it was that it was probably a warning sign that his aunt was going senile. She'd just told him the Kennedy thing this morning, and she typically waited at least a few days before mentioning it again.

Oz made his way into the small house's living room area, using his foot to clean trash on the floor out of the way, so that he could sit down. The couch was a lost cause, as it was currently crowded with old plastic juice containers, which his uncle had salvaged and would (supposedly) one day recycle for money. But that had been six months ago, and the containers were still there. At this point, the smell of putrid fruit juice was filling the house and it was breeding small flies. Oz had tried to throw the bottles away or recycle them himself, but his aunt and uncle had been horrified about the mere thought of that. So the containers had returned, multiplied, and Oz had gotten screamed at for two hours about why he shouldn't touch other people's things. And, obviously, reminded about his supposed Lee Harvey Oswald connection again.

In front of Oz, sat a pile of three TVs from various eras. When one TV stopped working, a slightly newer model was simply stacked on top of it. His aunt and uncle claimed that at some point, they would have enough money to fix all of the TVs, but in the meantime, it was just a tower to electronic impermanence.

Oz used needle-nose pliers to turn the old dial on the TV— since it was missing the plastic knob—and the picture came to life with an odd reddish glow, due to an unknown malfunction with the tube. That was the problem with old electronics you fished out of the trash. If his aunt and uncle noticed anything wrong with the signal, they never mentioned it. Oz himself was in charge of keeping the electronics operational, but he could already see that his uncle would soon force him to go out looking for a new one, which would mean more dangerous and disgusting searching of dumpsters. If it were up to Oz, he wouldn't have a TV at all, but very little of Oz's life was up to

Oz.

Oz used the pliers to turn the dial to channel 40, because *The Lone Ranger* was coming on.

And he was instantly transported to a world of right and wrong. Where things were clean and bullies always got what was coming to them.

Oz didn't really like TV, he thought it was mostly a waste of time. Plus, it meant that you had to be inside the house, which was torture.

But he liked *The Lone Ranger*.

He liked the purity of it.

Oz liked purity. He liked perfect heroes and scandalous villains. He liked always knowing right from wrong. He liked the idea of the hero in the pristine White Hat riding after the train robbers to save the beautiful damsel in distress.

He liked *order.*

For the briefest of moments... Oz w*as* that hero, and the squalor which surrounded him was forgotten. He was more than trash. He was someone important. Someone... special. Extraordinary.

Someone *alive.*

A moment later, Oz's uncle nonchalantly switched the channel, and the real world once more returned.

Oz's uncle set up a metal folding chair— the couch still occupied by the precious plastic containers which his uncle seemingly had no intention of ever moving— and sat down in it to watch the static-y news, without even acknowledging that Oz was currently watching another program.

For the briefest of instants, Oz imagined himself grabbing the channel-switching pliers from his uncle and using them to stab the man in the throat, while screaming obscenities at the top of his lungs and crying hysterically.

But as quick as the horrifying image appeared, it vanished.

Oz was pretty sure that normal people didn't think such things though, even if only in an idle way.

Because Oz was evil. Everyone said. And one day soon, he'd become a monster.

Bad blood would out and there seemed little chance that Oz wouldn't follow in his father and brother's footsteps.

On the screen, the reporter was looking at the camera with a serious expression. "...for comment." She finished, then the angle switched, showing a little icon of a prison next to her head. "Officials at Sutherland Prison said the execution was carried out at 5:30 today, with no difficulties. This marks the third execution in the last four years." The image switched again, this time showing a booking photo of the inmate in question. "Henry Arthur Dimico was convicted of the murder of seventeen people inside a Mega-Burger in…"

The rest of the story was interrupted by Oz's uncle's applause. "'Bout time they gassed that asshole." He took a celebratory drink of beer from his broken ceramic mug, which appeared to have been a desk accessory in its previous life. "Too bad they couldn't do it more than once." He let out a hacking laugh of sheer delight. "They killed him on Thanksgiving! HA!"

Oz's aunt came into the room to watch the broadcast, casually tossing aside the bowl she'd used in eating her pizza. "Wish I could have been there to see him piss himself in fear as they pulled the switch."

Oz's attention was stuck on the bowl, as the burned yellow cheese slowly oozed out onto a pile of newspaper ads from the 4th of July.

But like the plastic jugs, the newspapers would one day supposedly be recycled for wealth unimagined. As soon as his aunt and uncle had "read all of the articles they'd missed," anyway.

His silent observations of the oily horror which was cheese and shag carpeting, were interrupted by his aunt, who seemed to want to make this a learning opportunity for him. "You see?" She pointed at the screen. "See what happens when you live the kind of life you're living?" She put her hands on her hips, her fingertips leaving greasy smudges on her lilac stretch pants, which were at least fifteen years old and had been rescued from a stranger's trash. "Do you have anything to say for yourself?"

Oz turned back to the screen, where an image of his parents was just disappearing, to be replaced by a weather forecast.

He tried to conceive of a thought, if not something he actually felt, then at the very least some feigned emotion which would make his aunt happy. But… but he just didn't feel anything.

The Oz who had known those people was long gone now. He barely remembered them. And in the abstract, he missed the life they represented. He missed the version of Oz they knew and the people that Oz thought they were. But at the moment… he was really more concerned about what would happen once the pizza cheese fully melted into the carpet and the rats in the wall discovered it.

"May I just go to bed?" He finally asked, not really caring about the answer.

His aunt rolled her eyes and heaved a disgusted sigh,

interpreting his retreat from the room as his being obstinate and refusing to leave his evil lifestyle behind.

"Soulless little freak." His uncle mumbled under his breath to his aunt. "Gonna kill his-self before he's a teenager, you can tell."

Oz didn't wait for a further reply, and made his way down the narrow hallway to his room. The walk was made more difficult by the piles of "perfectly good shoeboxes" which his uncle had brought home two years ago, and which he still hadn't found the *perfect* use for. One day though, the tattered cardboard was certain to bring hope to mankind and the inconveniences they caused Oz each and every day would be worth it.

Inside his room, Oz noted with no real surprise that the dividing line on the floor had been moved again, so that now Hooch had about 80% of the space and Oz no longer even had enough room to sit on the bed with his feet on the floor.

But Oz didn't care.

He flopped down into the bedsheets, which his aunt and uncle had bought at a garage sale. They were emblazoned with dancing images of *Strawberry Shortcake*. But Oz didn't care about that either. He routinely used a good portion of his meager savings to take the old sheets to the laundromat five blocks away.

They were Strawberry Shortcake and they were so old they had holes in them, but they were clean. They were the one thing in the house that was. There wasn't a speck of dirt marring Strawberry Shortcake's fading red hair. And Oz took an inordinate amount of pride in that.

He fell asleep, brushing the occasional roach from his exposed arms and listening to the rats move around in the thin walls.

In his dreams, the world had a perfect order...

Chapter 8

"I DON'T THINK THEY PLAY AT ALL FAIRLY,' ALICE BEGAN, IN RATHER A COMPLAINING TONE, 'AND THEY ALL QUARREL SO DREADFULLY ONE CAN'T HEAR ONESELF SPEAK -- AND THEY DON'T SEEM TO HAVE ANY RULES IN PARTICULAR; AT LEAST, IF THERE ARE, NOBODY ATTENDS TO THEM.'"

- Alice's Adventures in Wonderland

Oz didn't feel well today.

He felt congested. He noticed some struggle to breathe, which could be an indication of lung cancer. His heart felt like it was skipping beats. His thoughts felt foggy, which could be early-onset dementia or perhaps some kind of poison. And his equilibrium felt off.

To be fair though, it could be his companions making him feel that way.

To borrow from Stevenson, it was frequently Oz's fortune to be the last reputable acquaintance and the last good influence in the lives of downgoing men.

He didn't set out to live his life that way, it just sort of happened.

And life on the Consortium of Chaos team wasn't any different, sadly.

It wasn't that Oz hated his teammates. They were the closest things he'd ever had to friends. It was just that sometimes he believed that they *deserved* to be hated. Intensely.

Some days, there was a part of Oz's mind which loathed them all. But there was a part of Oz's mind which secretly hated a lot of things, so that probably didn't mean much. And either way, there was a bigger part of his mind which recognized the fact that he... needed them. Oz didn't have anyone else in his life. Just these people. Which meant that they were his cross to bear, whether he was happy with it or not.

The thing was, no matter what Amity had to say on the

subject, Oz was still very much an outsider here. He was the "New Guy," a former adversary they allowed to attend their meetings and go into the field with them... but Oz wasn't family. Oz would *never* be family here. He was an immigrant to their shores. And most of them made sure to regularly remind him of that.

Which was fine with Oz, honestly. He was used to living with people who didn't like him. No one did, really. He'd grown up with his aunt and uncle, then he'd lived with the other prisoners, then he'd lived with the Freedom Squad.

Oz had been an outsider his entire life.

He didn't mind, as he didn't really want to be around people anyway, since they were hotbeds of disease, but that didn't make it any less true.

Still, there were some days when he felt like he'd like to be closer to the people here. Luckily, those thoughts were usually done away with by meetings. Anytime he was stuck in a room with a group of Consortium members for a long period of time, he was glad they didn't like him, because it meant they wouldn't talk to him a lot.

Oz had always wanted to be the hero. Always wanted to be the man in the White Hat, rescuing damsels. But his life just hadn't worked out that way. He had been a complete nobody at the Freedom Squad. He had never really gotten to do anything other than the mundanities of superheroics that no one else wanted to do. But he'd... felt like he was dead. Buried alive in the horrible people who surrounded him and the ghastly things they did to people when the cameras weren't on.

Generally, he thought the Capes in this city were petulant and whiney, alternating between getting into useless pissing contests with each other and unexpectedly trying to doom the entire world. Add in some unnecessary costume changes and some inevitable returns from the dead, and that was basically the industry.

He'd never once felt like a hero. It was soulless work.

Then he met Miss Quentin.

And he recognized that he no longer cared if he was the hero or the villain. Just so long as she was there too.

Within a week of meeting her, Oz had doubled the number of hours he spent going on missions with the Freedom Squad. Started taking on his own projects, without their approval. Dedicated himself to doing genuine *good* in the world. Moved out of the Freedom Squad's housing and had gotten his own apartment, which he tried to leave on a semi-regular basis. Oz had begun to feel better about himself and the work, which was one of the reasons why he had sided against the Freedom Squad and had helped the Consortium defeat them.

As if to prove a point, the Consortium's resident liaison with the city and government, Laura McPherson, shook her head. "Listen, we're all sorry that Wyatt was injured, but I'd really like to know what the hell happened last night and why I've got the mayor screaming at me for blowing up a hospital!?!"

With Wyatt injured, leadership at the Consortium meeting was kind of up in the air. Harlot and the Commodore were both at Wyatt's bedside, so the control structure of the Consortium was basically all MIA. Technically speaking, it should have fallen to Julian Sargassum, who was fourth in command because he had just been with the organization longer than almost anyone else here. But Julian was deeply apathetic about such things—to say nothing of the fact that most of the room would ignore him anyway—so he passed off his responsibilities to his... girlfriend? Fiancée? Queen? Oz wasn't sure how to refer to the woman, but in any case, the Consortium's press agent, Bridget Hanniver, was leading the meeting at the moment. She and Julian had gotten very involved with each other while the rest of the Consortium was busy in Agletaria, and were for all intents and purposes now a formal "couple."

Oz had no real issues with Bridget. She was fairly normal. She hadn't been around the others long enough to go mad yet.

"We did not 'blow up the hospital,' the hospital blew up." Bridget reiterated, already used to calling the Consortium team "we," despite the fact that she was nowhere near the hospital last night. She seemed to have no difficulty finding her place here and instantly being accepted by the others. In the space of a couple of weeks, the woman had gotten further on that front than Oz had in months of living here. "That's an important distinction that you're failing to grasp." She ran a hand through her hair. "If you have questions about that, perhaps you should ask the Agletarians about it." She pointed to Oz. "Oz and Multifarious have uncovered some compelling evidence linking them to this."

"I am not Multifarious." Natalie informed them seriously. "Today I am..." she gave her characteristic dramatic pause, "*Brick House!*"

The room fell into silence as everyone took that in. They were all used to Natalie switching between personas every day, but it just invited them to rate her choice of codename. And, obviously, it rarely was a main topic of conversation on a day when the Consortium was in genuine peril. In the instant case though, it was probably just the unexpected novelty of having Natalie sitting at the table without her Kilroy face mask and computerized voice box.

Not that Oz could blame them for that. He also found looking at Natalie... distracting.

The mask had been damaged in her fall from the roof, and it hadn't been repaired yet. Oz was perfectly happy with it being gone.

"Well, at least Mull's finally off the pogo stick." Mack thought aloud, looking for good news in all of this. "I hated that day."

"And it's better than the time she claimed to have the 'power of apples.'" Cory Henderson Henries, AKA "Vaudeville," agreed. "I still don't know what that means."

"Remember 'Jive Turkey'?" Amy asked the room. "That one was remarkably festive, since it was the holidays."

Marian didn't look up from whatever it was she was doing. "It took me forever to deal with the legal fallout of that time she was claiming to be 'Boba Fett' though."

Cynic nodded, agreeing with his wife. "Murder and kidnapping are one thing, but trademark infringement is *not* cool."

"The Lucasfilm/Disney people were *not* amused." Marian agreed.

"Those fuckers are *mean*." Cynic made a face. "I've been evil for centuries, but *those* motherfuckers are scary."

"Speaking of which," Bridget looked utterly thrilled to be at the meeting, "when do *I* get a codename?"

Emily didn't look up from her nails, her tone sounding bored. "All in favor of making Bridget's codename 'Bridget'?"

Hands shot up disinterestedly, eager to end the issue and move on.

Bridget's smile faded. "But... but that's not fair." She protested disappointedly.

"Fear not. They lack that power, my love." Julian soothed, patting her hand in comfort. "You decide whatever you would like your codename to be and I shall make it so."

"I don't care about codenames, I don't really care about the Agletarians, I care about *Mercygiver*." Oz crossed his arms over his chest. "I want to know what we intend to do about him?"

Cory frowned in confusion. "Who?"

"They *both* tried to kill her last night, so I don't know why you're so focused on one over the other." Bridget argued.

"Because one of them almost succeeded." Oz snapped.

McPherson didn't look impressed. "The Agletarians almost succeeded too. And unlike Multifarious' other attacker, the

Agletarians killed a dozen people... who you *failed to save*."

"We got everyone we could. That wasn't our fault." Lexington defended. "Personally, I'm amazed we did as well as we did."

"They *were* in the hospital, in all fairness, some of them were probably half dead to begin with." Arnold Benedix, AKA "Traitor," added seriously, like it was the height of logic. "If they were *completely* healthy, they wouldn't have been there at all, right?"

The room stared at him in silent amazement.

"What?" Arnold looked confused. "What'd I say?" He rolled his eyes, obviously feeling picked upon. "Oh, like *I'm* somehow the asshole now, is that it?"

"You're *always* the asshole, Arn." Mack assured him.

"The TV is saying that this is what happens when they let Capes into the same hospitals as the Norms." Emily shook her head. "Can you believe that shit?"

"Yes. I can. And I think this is a warning that you people should be sent *elsewhere* from now on. We are instituting a new rule: no more going to *regular* hospitals." McPherson announced, like she was somehow in charge. "Your job is to protect people. Going to civilian hospitals endangers people, so if leaving the city before seeking medical treatment saves *even one life*, I'd like to think you'd be all for it."

"I will state this for the record once and *only* once: my people love this city..." Bridget began.

Poacher and Emily looked at one another and silently mouthed "*my* people?" in surprised but dismissive uncertainty, apparently confused by Bridget's unannounced power grab.

"We protect this city." Bridget continued. "And if any of my people are injured while doing their job, this city *will* treat those injuries or we will stop protecting this city. That is *not* open for debate."

"Well... I've decided that I like her more than I like Julian..." Natalie announced.

Julian nodded, beaming with pride that his betrothed was putting her foot down. "Me too." He agreed.

"...which, granted, is a low bar." Natalie finished her thought, then flashed her duel thumbs up. "But happy to be part of your team, Bridge."

Cory looked amazed by the argument. "Even when we were villains, we could still go to the hospitals. This idea is fucking crazy."

"It's just something that's being discussed." McPherson

defended. "If you have objections to the new policy, you are free to voice them."

Emily cupped her hands over her mouth. "FUCK YOU!" She flipped the woman off. "How's that for giving it voice?"

Holly shrugged. "Hell, if I'm going to be treated terribly either way, I'm going back to villainy. Now I know where all the cool expensive shit is stored around town, so it'll be really easy." She nodded persuasively. "I got a map and everything."

"Wyatt's got that key to the city." Poacher volunteered. "I bet that thing opens up all kinds of safes and stuff."

"Pretty ballsy to suggest to my face that I should let you risk my wife's life for people I don't even know." Steven O'Probrian, AKA "The Cynic," leaned back in his chair, passively looking at McPherson in bored disinterest, like she was an aquarium. "You remind me of this one girl I used to know back in the old country…"

"'The old country?'" Marian repeated, looking utterly amused and charmed by her husband. "Really? That is what you are going with? Are you from *Brigadoon* all of a sudden, Steven? Because as far as I know, your knowledge of Irish culture seems to consist entirely of Guinness, the opening two and a half lines of *Danny Boy*, and repeated viewings of *Far and Away* on basic cable."

"Nicole Kidman is hot as fuck in that." Poacher thought aloud.

"She is a remarkable talent, yes." Amity agreed.

Emily shrugged. "She's overrated."

Poacher glared at her in sudden theatrical fury. *"Fuck your lies, whore!"*

Emily started laughing.

"You people are children." McPherson put her face in her hands. "I don't know if I should be afraid or just sit here and pray that God takes mercy on your idiot souls."

"My fiancé *is* a god, you bitch." Bridget snapped. "You don't pray *for* him. You pray *to* him."

"Do you see why I chose to be alone all those years, my heart?" Julian looked around the room in distaste. "These people are *horrible*."

Bridget shrugged, accepting that as a given. "Well, they're surface-dwellers. What can you really expect?"

"Very wise." Julian nodded in appreciation of that sentiment, then leaned down to kiss the top of her head. "Very wise, my love."

Oz didn't care about any of this. His only concern at the

moment was finding the man who tossed Natalie off a roof. In Oz's mind, that was the key to everything.

"If you people insist on wasting my time like this, I will go find Mercygiver on my own." He told them flatly.

Natalie made a face. "I'd really prefer that you stayed out of this one, Oz."

"I can take care of myself."

She didn't look convinced. "All I'm saying is that you should stay here with everyone else and let me handle it." She flashed him a persuasive smile. "I'll deal with Ronnie and then we both can deal with whatever the hell the Agletarians are up to. Okay?"

That was not okay with Oz.

Oz was not a possessive man. But there was a small part of his mind that was always in shadow. The little bit of himself that his aunt always warned him would grow bigger and bigger until it consumed everything good inside him. And at the moment, that little piece of darkness was *furious* that another man would touch Natalie like that.

The woman had a way of fanning the flames of his worst impulses, and Oz wasn't exactly struggling to stop her.

Oz believed that you needed to understand what an enemy wanted in order to remove the problem he or she represented. If you found out the root of the problem, you could end it. In this case though, he *knew* what Mercygiver wanted. He wanted what *any* man who looked at Natalie would want: he wanted *Natalie*. The man wanted her, and since he wasn't going to get her, Mercygiver was intent on making sure no one else did either.

Oz fully intended on killing Mercygiver when he got the opportunity.

It was against everything that Oz had ever believed, but... He'd killed once for Natalie today already. He was fairly certain he could do so again without trouble.

Which... probably should have worried him more than it did.

But it didn't. At all. Because he'd gladly toss aside everything he'd ever believed and everyone currently alive in this city, if it meant Natalie was safe.

Natalie recognized the angry determination on his face. "I really don't need to be protected, Oz. You're just going to get hurt in this. Trust me: this is going to go bad in ways your orderly brain can't even conceive of." She sounded almost worried. "*Please* just let me handle it."

Oz squinted in sudden realization.

She was worried. About him.

In his entire life, Oz couldn't remember anyone worrying about his safety before.

It was... nice. He almost smiled at the very idea.

Oz wasn't someone people worried about. Oz was the kind of person who worried people. It was entirely different. But for the first time ever, his death would actually mean something to someone. Unfortunately, that someone in question was in very real and very serious danger at the moment, so Oz was more than willing to risk himself to save her.

"I spent last night watching you die, Miss Quentin." He shook his head, looking into the stunning blue depths of her eyes. She had the most beautiful eyes he'd ever seen in his life and it felt like his heart skipped a beat every time he met her gaze. They were sparkling and intelligent and teasing... "That *won't* happen again." He vowed.

Bridget nodded. "We will solve this, Mull, don't worry about it."

Natalie snorted. "Do I look worried?"

Poacher wagged his hand in the air. "Kinda."

"Well, I'm not." Natalie defended. "If Oz wants to get himself killed over this, that's his prerogative." She sniffed indignantly. "I just think he should be a little more careful with his life, that's all."

"Well, *someone* here has to state the obvious," Clarice Thompkins, AKA "Pastiche," announced, "why don't we just let Multifarious and the government work this out with the Agletarians? She doesn't even technically work here and if they're allegedly willing to go to this much effort to kill her, they probably have good reason."

"That's not going to happen." Oz told her flatly.

"They are here to discuss a peace treaty." McPherson reminded them. "Seeing as how the last time you attempted such an agreement it ended up with you killing their leader..."

Poacher shook his head. "That wasn't us."

"They are trying to avoid a war," McPherson continued, "so I think we should do everything we can to hear them out."

"The only thing I want to hear out of my enemies is screams of pain." Emily told the room.

Poacher nodded in agreement, like she was the height of logic. "I think we should kill them before they kill us."

"You do not command the government or our military." McPherson shook her head. "You will *not* interfere with foreign relations again."

Poacher arched a challenging eyebrow. "*Or*?"

Cory sat up straighter in his chair. "And what happens if 'foreign relations' wants to interfere with us?"

"The government's policy on this is going to be 'Wait and See.'" McPherson smoothed her suit. "At this point, we should focus on covert information gathering without doing anything which could be interpreted as an escalation. Thus far, the Agletarians haven't done anything to indicate that they mean us harm."

Holly snorted. "Aside from blowing up a hospital and trying to kill Mull?"

"There's *no* proof it was them, and..." McPherson began.

Emily rolled her eyes, talking right over the woman. "I guess they were just visiting sick kids while dressed in their evil techno death-suits, and we overreacted."

Poacher chuckled in amusement. "Maybe one of them *Make-a-Wish* kids asked for a foreign assassin to show up and kill Mull."

"And you stood in the way of that final dream, you selfish bitch." Emily's eyes narrowed at Natalie in mock anger. "That poor dying child."

"To be fair," Bridget interrupted, "I can think of at least *three* people in this room who would use their final wish to do something very similar."

"I'd want to go to Paris." Poacher announced. "I'd much rather watch a foreign assassin kill Mull in Paris. It'd be all cultural and shit."

McPherson continued as if the others hadn't spoken. "We are going to allow them to remain here as long as their diplomats want to speak to authorities. We're trying desperately to smooth over the crisis in their country that *you* created and our government wishes to avoid any further unfortunate episodes. They don't want to risk a war, no matter how much you people seem to *want* one."

Bridget icily straightened the pile of papers in front of her. "I see." She steepled her fingers. "So a hostile force has invaded and tried to kill several hundred people, including us, and the government's response is 'wait and see'?"

"How come the government's policy is never 'wait and see' when *I* blow shit up?" Holly pouted. "Whenever I so much as *touch* a stick of dynamite everyone's like," she took on an exaggerated tone of voice and waggled her hands in the air, "'it's the end of the world! Burn that monster! *Burn her!*'"

"We have no evidence that the Agletarians were behind the accident at the hospital." McPherson shook her head. "We can't base policy off of unproven rumor and bias."

"I got your 'bias' right here, you fucking bitch." Emily flipped her off. "Eat. My. Ass."

"Even if your paranoia is correct, fighting them will only make this worse." McPherson explained. "The best way to minimize damage and needless casualties is to let diplomacy take its course. I recognize that you think that's a terrible thing to suggest, but we're all adults here. And this is the real world. And in the real world, heroes make sacrifices for the greater good."

"There is no good greater than me." Monty announced simply.

"They're actively trying to kill us." Holly gestured around the table and then at McPherson. "While you're talking to them, they're killing us and you're telling us to take it? What, better that *we* all die than *you*."

"That's the job." McPherson said flatly.

Holly made a face in dismissive astonishment. "Oh, fuck you, lady."

"So... it's sounding like we're on our own." Poacher summarized. "Again."

"Yeah, *there's* a big surprise." Cory rolled his eyes. "Jesus, the fucking *A-Team* got more help from the authorities than we do."

"We kill more people though." Natalie added, like that detail more than made up for it.

"But *they* had Mr. T." Emily shook her head. "I'd join *any* team that has Mr. T on it."

"No question. He's hardcore." Poacher nodded. "T don't fuck around."

"A remarkable entertainer, yes." Amy added.

"Do we have any leads on this Mercygiver guy?" Bridget asked, finally focused on the matter at hand.

"No." Oz shook his head. "Not yet."

"But I have graciously offered the assistance of my Irregulars in that." Montgomery volunteered.

Bridget looked confused and suspicious. "...*Why*?"

"See, I asked that too." Natalie nodded, obviously pleased that Bridget agreed with her assessment of the situation.

"I care deeply about this team." Montgomery defended, his voice flat and unconvincing to the point of being mocking.

Bridget rolled her eyes, but let the matter drop. "Okay, so what about the Agletarians?"

"I just got finished telling you, there's *no proof it's them*."

McPherson chimed in. "You're jumping to conclusions."

Bridget ignored that. "We've got one of their super-suit things, right?"

Oz nodded. "One of the suits exploded and was too far gone to salvage, that's what brought the building down, but I was able to recover the other one from the wreckage of the building, yes."

"Probably should hose it off before anyone tries it on or anything though." Poacher suggested. "Word is that Oz liquefied the asshole who was wearing it last."

Emily made a face. "Ew."

"Pretty fucking awesome, little buddy." Poacher praised, holding out a fist to Oz in a ceremonial fist bump.

But Oz saw nothing praiseworthy about being forced to kill someone. It had to be done, but it certainly wasn't a celebratory event.

Some of Oz's earliest memories were watching people die. Bodies contorting as the bullets ripped through them.

Oz didn't like it when *anyone* died.

It meant he had failed.

If he'd been a better hero, he could have found a way to talk down that man last night or disarm him in a non-lethal way. He could have turned the man and gotten him to tell him who had hired him and why they wanted Natalie dead. If Oz were a *true* White Hat, he could have used that man to solve this entire mystery, right there. This could have all been over.

But Natalie was endangered and there simply wasn't a question about what needed to be done.

Oz still didn't like it though.

It made him think of his aunt's constant warnings about his family's curse.

Bridget pivoted in her chair. "Machines Department, you want to explain that armor?"

"Oh, McCallister changed the name back to 'Engineering Department.'" Polly informed the other woman. "But we're also the Motor Pool, so it doesn't make much sense."

"That armor ain't technically a 'machine,' it's a weapon." Mack announced. "That's why I haven't figured out how to control it with my powers yet. I'll get it eventually, it'll just take some time and a little practice. Sometimes it's like tryin' to pick a lock." He turned to look at his digital companion. "And the name makes perfect sense, Poll, I don't know why you keep sayin' that."

Bridget looked at the woman to her left. "Weapons

Department, do *you* want to explain this?"

"That's not a weapon, that's *armor."* Holly shook her head. "I understand the energy blasts, but I'm not paid to figure out the suit." She pointed down the table. "I kicked it over to the Production Department to reverse engineer it."

"Which, obviously isn't a job for the *Engineering Department.* For some reason." Bridget pinched the bridge of her nose.

Natalie let out a sharp bark of laughter. "Jesus! I am so screwed if *this* is the crack team that's trying to rescue me." She looked over at Oz. "See why I want to handle this on my own?"

Bridget continued trying to find someone in the conference room who could be *at all* helpful. *"Production Department* do *you* have a report on how we can stop these armored madmen from slaughtering us?"

Oz wasn't happy about the idea of Monty doing anything.

"Not currently, no." The man shook his head, but took on a determined look. "But I've got my *best* people working on it as we speak."

All eyes cut to Higgins, who was sitting in the corner, staring at the body armor their attacker had been wearing. Higgin's was leaning forward in his chair, his chin in his hands, eyes focused on the vest intently. Just staring at the object as if waiting for it to break into song.

"Well, does that ever make *me* feel confident." Natalie crossed her arms over her chest.

"Is there are particular reason why we've got *Oliver Twist* over there examining it instead of Marian?" Cynic wondered aloud, unhappy about trusting anyone but his wife with something.

"Because a new variety of techno-armor is not an Accounting, Legal, or Research issue." Marian informed him.

"Can we please make it one?" Cynic all but begged. "Because that guy's kinda creeping me out and I distrust *the shit* outta him."

"He has a system." Marian defended.

Cynic snorted. "His 'system' has been going on for an hour now, and frankly, I think he's just asleep."

"Monty is evil and an insufferable SOB, but Higgins is legit." Mack added. "He might be misled, but he's the real deal. You wanna talk about understandin' how somethin' is manufactured, Higgins is the O.G. in that regard."

"He won gold in the Henchmen Olympics two years ago." Amy chimed in, obviously still proud that someone in her "family" had achieved such an accomplishment.

Monty nodded. "I only hire the best people."

Bridget didn't look convinced, asking for a go-ahead from the Weapons Department. "Holly?"

Holly waved a disinterested hand. "Let the man do his job."

Bridget decided to let the matter drop. "So, the men at the hospital arrived there in a car registered to someone else, who Oz and Mull then found dead in his apartment." She looked at Oz. "Were you able to find anything else at the scene?"

Oz thought about the coded letter from the Agletarians and the note from Mercygiver.

"No." He shook his head.

It wasn't that he didn't trust everyone on his team. But he didn't trust everyone on his team. As soon as there was a definite link between this event and Natalie, the city would place the blame for it on her.

And he'd rather risk the city than Natalie.

Which wasn't something a true White Hat should *ever* think, let alone act on. But Oz didn't really care.

Natalie looked surprised by the idea that he'd withhold such sensitive information from the team, her head whipping around to squint at him.

Marian also looked up, as she tried to determine his motives for the lie.

"What *I* want to know, is how Monty *once again* managed to avoid a catastrophe." Mack turned in his chair to address the other man. "You got anything you want to tell us?"

Monty shrugged like it was a nonevent. "Wyatt started to evacuate the hospital two minutes after Higgins first informed me of the possible but non-specific threat of attack."

"You're saying you... what?" Mack looked baffled and dubious. "*Warned* Wyatt?"

Monty was silent for a beat. "In my own way." His head tilted to the side. "So, from a certain point of view... *I* saved hundreds of people."

Mack didn't look convinced. "Why should we believe that?"

"Because I'm telling you that."

"You're an opportunist and a liar." Mack reminded him.

"But I'm also very capable." Monty shook his head. "If I planned to kill you last night, you *all* would have been in the building when it blew."

The room silently considered that.

To be honest, that was a pretty fair defense.

Poacher cleared his throat. "Personally, *I'm* just wondering why everyone was so surprised that Mull was a chick, and how in the hell no one else noticed that her breasts are fantastic. I noticed it day one, no matter the cheap costume she wears." He pointed at her. "Look at 'em! How could you not see them all this time?"

The entire room turned in unison to judge the woman's body.

Oz's eyes stayed there.

They were... *remarkable*, yes.

They were utterly perfect in his opinion. Full, but soft and delicate. They added deeply feminine curves to her body, and Oz had spent more time than he cared to admit daydreaming about them. And they weren't even her *best* feature!

The thing about Natalie Quentin was that each aspect of her was made better by the others. So, her breasts were amazing on their own, but paired with her stunning legs, sparkling eyes and entrancingly shiny hair? They were made even better, something which he wouldn't have assumed was possible.

"Ya think?" Natalie looked oddly interested in the topic, looking down at her body as well. "I've never been in love with them."

"Nah, you're good. Perfect size and shape." Poacher waved off that concern and it was possibly the first time Oz had ever agreed with the maniac. He was now contemplating killing him right here for admiring Natalie's body, true, but Oz still agreed with him. "How do you do so much running and flipping around? Do your costumes have support?"

"Sports bra, then body armor, and you're all strapped down and ready to rock." Natalie gave the man a thumbs up.

Oz's mind imagined the soft-looking globes of flesh being pressed against the rough fabric of a Kevlar vest...

The pencil he was holding snapped in his hand.

"Really?" Poacher nodded, like this was information he'd one day need. "Huh."

"Wow." Bridget shook her head sadly. "I'm *so* glad we had this conversation about Multifarious' *décolletage*."

Cynic frowned in confusion. "Like paper glued down onto shit?" He snorted dismissively. "Fuck crafts."

Poacher shook his head. "Amy made me a décolletaged serving tray once that was pretty epic."

"Not 'decoupage,' you moron," Emily swatted at him, "*décolletage!* It means breasts!"

"To be fair," Cory defended, "maybe it was a serving tray decoupaged with pictures of..."

"Enough." Bridget announced firmly. "Moving on."

Higgins suddenly stood up and stalked over to his boss. He leaned down and whispered something into Monty's ear.

"Interesting." Monty's brow compressed in thought. "You sure?"

Higgins nodded.

Monty frowned slightly. "Well, I don't see how that could *possibly* help us to..." He paused and a slow smile crept across his scarred face. "Oh. Wait... I've had an *epiphany*. Yes, I think we can engineer something like that." He began to write something down. "We need to get to work. When the meeting is over, gather the Executive Staff, I'll start setting things up."

Higgins nodded eagerly.

Bridget crossed her arms over her chest. "Care to share this stunning discovery?"

Monty pretended not to hear them, focusing on his paperwork.

Bridget cleared her throat loudly. "*Montgomery?*"

Monty looked up. "I'm sorry, did you say something to me?"

"What did he say?" Bridget pressed. "What's the story on the armor?"

Monty made a show of looking into the crystal globe on top of his cane. "Among other things, Higgins says he has never seen anything like it before."

"And?"

"And if *Higgins* hasn't seen it, it doesn't exist." Monty leaned back in his chair. "At least not *here*."

"Meaning what?" Bridget's eyebrows rose. "You are seriously telling me that you believe that aliens or an interdimensional being blew up the hospital?"

"No, don't be ridiculous." Monty shook his head. "I'm telling you that the Agletarians blew up the hospital using alien and/or interdimensional technology."

Bridget snorted. "Bullshit."

"Okay." Montgomery made a show of pulling out his phone. "You're right, I'm sure. This is technology which can be found anywhere, I mean, I'm just in charge of purchasing, so what would I know. You say it's readily available, so I guess I'll just have to find this armor for sale somewhere." He typed something in. "I suppose I'll start with 'Etsy'..."

Emily snickered.

Bridget didn't bother replying, and spun in her chair. "Cynic? This is *your* department. You want to tell me why we have to listen to *Monty* for an Intelligence report now?" She stared at the man for a long moment, just noticing his bizarre attire. "What fresh hell is this?"

"Libs and me have switched places today." Cynic explained, straightening his tweed suitcoat. "It's part of this…"

"Contraction." Librarian interrupted, putting her sandaled feet up on the conference table.

"Fuck!" Cynic pounded the table in anger and pointed at Bridget. *"She made me do it!"* He took a calming breath, his eyes traveling up and down his wife's legs which were currently exposed, thanks to the cargo shorts she was wearing. "It's part of this thing where we're trying to better understand each other… or something. Honestly, I don't really remember why we're doing it anymore. But it's sexy as fuck."

Librarian shook her head. "That does not sound like something I would say."

"Oh yeah, well I think *I* would have pointed out how hot you look in my style of clothes by now." His eyes ran down the front of his wife's T-shirt, which advertised that it was from Mars, Arizona. The tagline read, "Get Your Ass to Mars" and featured a prospector trying to shove a smiling cartoon donkey down a dirt road towards the town.

Marian moved under his gaze, her breathing visibly quickening. "I'm just waiting for the right time."

Cynic shook his head. "I never wait for the right time!"

"Seems like you did last night." His wife arched an eyebrow flirtatiously. "And twice this morning."

"See?" Cynic snapped is fingers. "Inappropriate discussions of private sexual matters in front of a room full of our coworkers? Now *that* sounds like me." He pulled his wife onto his lap. "It's uncanny."

"Contraction." She whispered in his ear.

Cynic pounded the table in frustration again. *"Fuck!"*

"As fascinating as this is, I'd still like a report on why all of this is happening, Cynic." Bridget pressed. "I recognize that this is how you usually do things, but Wyatt is in the hospital and innocent people are dead."

Cynic cleared his throat, slightly more serious now. "Word is, the Agletarians are hell-bent on getting us this time. We've culled their crazy herd for years and now we're left with the most diehard homicidal sons-a-bitches they got and they *literally* have nothing left to lose. Thus, in my *professional* opinion: we're *fucked*."

Bridget ran a hand through her hair. "Marian?"

Cynic's wife nodded in agreement. "I concur with Steven's profane but entirely accurate assessment of this situation. In fact, if anything, he has understated the matter."

Bridget pinched the bridge of her nose. "Well, then I'd say we have a very serious security issue on our hands."

All eyes turned to the empty Security Department chair where Miles Gloriosus, AKA "Keystone," typically sat. Since his return from Agletaria, the Consortium's aging tough guy hadn't been seen much and today was no exception. The assembly turned to look at the stoic face of Barbara Frith, AKA "Bobbi," standing behind the vacant chair. She cleared her throat. "The Captain is…" She paused as if searching for the right word to describe her commanding officer, "…on sabbatical."

Poacher rolled his eyes. "Translation: 'he's off the wagon.'"

Bobbi's eyes narrowed dangerously, obviously taking offense. "He is taking some *well-deserved* personal time."

"…at the liquor store." Poacher finished for her.

Bridget let out a long breath. "Fine. Well, tell Miles we wish him the best in whatever he chooses to do."

"…whether that be booze or blow." Poacher added under his breath.

"*Enough*, Sydney." Bridget snapped, like a babysitter scolding a child.

"Fine." He shrugged and held up his hands in surrender. "Sorry I pointed out he's *always* been a drunken loser."

"He's *not*." Bobbi's face flashed with uncharacteristic anger at Poacher. "Miles is the…"

Bridget cut her off. "So, are you in charge of the Excessive Force then? Could you give us a rundown of how your security detail plans on stopping the Agletarians?"

Bobbi's face fell and she looked down at the floor. "I'm afraid I can't do that. For all intents and purposes, the Excessive Force has been wiped out as a fighting unit."

"So who's going to handle security?"

"I could get my girls in here to do it." Poacher offered. "They've been asking to spend more time with me anyway, and I been teaching them *all kinds* of useful shit."

"Girls?" Holly asked in confusion.

"He means his fan club members." Cory clarified. "The little girls who have joined the 'Poacher Pals.'"

Bridget shook her head. "We are *not* arming preteens and sending them into harm's way."

Tyrant looked pointedly at Stacy. "*Anymore*."

The girl made a face at him.

Monty leaned forward. "Until this staffing crisis can be dealt with, my Irregulars are only too *happy* to assume the responsibility of protecting the Crater Lair as well. ...Under *my* supervision, obviously." His smile grew. "It would be our genuine *pleasure*."

Bridget didn't look happy over that idea and glanced down the table at Oz. "How about any of our newer members? Do they want to...'help', Monty's men?" She stressed the word, emphasizing that their responsibilities would be to watch for threats from the Purchasing and Production Department itself.

Oz shifted in his chair. "I doubt it. Generally, they're not so much interested in..." He trailed off. "Umm..."

"Caring about whether we live or die." Natalie finished for him.

"Yes. But I was looking for a nicer way of phrasing that." Oz shifted again. "You scare them."

"It's 'cause we're so badass." Quinn Aguta, AKA "Tupilak" chimed in. "Some people can't deal with our levels of awesome."

Bridget heaved another weary sigh. "Well, our 'awesomeness' notwithstanding, just tell them to help out Bobbi."

"I can't do that." Oz shook his head.

"Why not?"

"Because I need them to aid me in tracking down Mercygiver." He straightened in his chair. "Miss Quentin is still in danger, and I can't spare any manpower at the moment."

"I'm not really asking here, Oz." Bridget told him flatly. "We need someone to guard the base. Your department is the only one with the people right now."

"I'm glad you're not asking, because if you *did,* I'd be forced to *refuse* your request." Oz's voice took on a hard edge. "They are *my* staff. *I* need them."

Poacher heaved a theatrical sigh. "If only Miles wasn't busy inducting himself into the 'Alcohol of Fame' right now."

"Fuck you, Poacher!" Bobbi snapped. "Miles is *twice* the man you are!"

"Only if you go by his blood-alcohol level, honey." Poacher rolled his eyes, then looked around the table at the others, who were staring at him like he'd crossed a line. "What? Oh, I'm so *terribly* sorry for pointing out that that coked-out bastard is MIA again. Silly me."

"This bickering is pointless." Marian looked down the table at Natalie. "Multifarious, do you *want* or *need* the Consortium's help in tracking down your attacker?"

Natalie snorted. "Hell no. This is *nemesis* territory, which means that all of you should stay out of it. Besides, anyone who tags along is destined to just get kidnapped and used as a hostage against me anyway. You're going to be hogtied and used as bait to lure me to one of those big 'sky beam' things in the last act, as the city is destroyed around me. Jesus, haven't you people ever *seen* an action movie?" She pounded a fist on the table. "This is *my* epic quest which I need to do alone! 'Hero's journey,' not '*Heroes'* Journey!'"

"Thus, we have *two* entirely interrelated problems to solve, both of which involve putting the Agletarian troops currently hunting us into early graves." Marian began ticking them off on her fingers. "Multifarious does not require the assistance of Oswald's men, thus freeing them up to assist us in protecting the Lair and ensuring that Montgomery respects Mile's department and the Irregulars respect Bobbi's position." She stood up. "There. It took me three seconds to solve this idiotic problem you people have been arguing about for an hour. Crisis adverted, bloodbath postponed. Now I can finally leave and go have audaciously loud sex with my husband." She pointed at Cynic. "You. Now. We're going."

"But I haven't saved the city yet." Cynic protested weakly as he was pulled from his chair.

"Fuck heroics."

Cynic grinned in amusement and let himself get dragged towards the door, his hand reaching down to rest in the back pocket of Marian's shorts. "Later, losers."

Before they got there though, Harlot burst in. The woman had dark circles under her eyes, no doubt from worrying about Wyatt, who was still in the Consortium's infirmary. The man had been in pretty bad shape.

Cynic and Marian stopped in their tracks, like being confronted with the undead.

Even in her frazzled and overwrought state, she still squinted at their reversed attire, but didn't bother to ask about it.

Bridget quickly vacated the chair at the head of the table, so that the woman could sit down. To be honest, it looked like if she didn't sit down, she was in definite danger of *falling* down.

Bridget retreated to her usual chair, which was next to Julian. The man immediately pulled her close and began to tell her what an amazing job she had done dealing with the "idiot surface-dwellers."

"What do we got?" Harlot asked the room weakly, unconsciously echoing what her husband often asked in an emergency.

"Aliens." Poacher said simply. "Working with an evil dictatorship and/or Mull's crazy ex. Or something, it's still being debated. And Marian and Cynic are about to go get their fuck on again. I predict they'll do some weird shit to each other today."

Marian nodded. "I concur, yes."

Poacher pointed at Oz. "Oz is going to head up the Mercygiver part of this."

Harlot processed that. "And the Agletarian part?" She asked, her voice sounding raw.

"Dunno. But it's going to be bad." Holly shook her head. "Two of those guys held off six of us for twenty minutes and destroyed a building in the process."

Harlot tucked a strand of hair behind her ear. "Well, how many more of these soldiers do we think there are?"

Everyone looked at Cynic, now trusting the Intelligence Department for something other than his never-ending supply of crude limericks.

Harlot being here meant everyone was suddenly playing with their head in the game.

The Consortium had different factions and petty squabbles, but *everyone* loved Harlot. She was one of the few people here who could unite them. She needed them to be their best selves right now, so that's what they'd give her.

It was one of the only things about this group that Oz genuinely respected.

They were a family. A bickering, horrible, dysfunctional family, which frequently tried to kill each other. But a family none-the-less.

Oz had never been part of a family. It was interesting to see how one operated, even if he was an outsider.

"About a thousand." Cynic got out hoarsely, answering Harlot. "And they've all got those suits."

The room was silent for a long moment.

"Can we win this?" Harlot asked seriously. "If... if things go bad and we gotta throw down with these guys in the streets again, as things currently stand, can we take them?"

Marian was quiet as her brain quickly worked out every possible eventuality. "No." She finally declared. "There are simply too many of them and they have access to technology we can't match. I am familiar with our tactics and abilities, and I predict a 75% likelihood

164

of everyone in this room who is not immortal or invulnerable dying if we engage the Agletarians within the city. And even if we did manage to emerge the victors in the battle against them, the civilian losses would be in the tens of thousands, if not higher."

"Okay." Harlot let out a long, shaky breath, rubbing her palms against her eyes, accepting a hard truth. "If we can't beat them... we'll just have to *cheat*." Harlot turned to look down the table at Montgomery. "Monty, a thousand very dangerous men are here to kill my husband and infant son. Consider yourself *off the chain*." She met the other man's eyes, her voice suddenly rock hard. "*Win*."

The room was deathly silent, recognizing that something major and terrifying had just happened.

Oz was the first to speak. "You can't do that without a vote, Harlot." He said. "That's..."

"I will take care of this, Harlot." Monty cut him off, his voice softer than it normally was. "I do not pretend to like Wyatt, at all, but I will make them sorry for hurting him. In the end, they will recognize their mistake." He nodded at the woman in certainty. "You have my word on it."

"Agreed." Poacher nodded. "No one fucks with Wyatt while I'm around. We're going scorched earth, wrath of fucking god kind of shit." He raised his hand. "I'm in. Whatever sick, demented shit Monty wants to do to them, I'm *in*."

Oz shook his head. "I doubt that's what Wyatt would want."

"Are you an expert on my husband now, Oz?" Harlot rounded on him. "Did you and he spend all night talking in the ICU? Because I seem to be having difficulty asking what he'd want, since he's still unconscious and hooked up to fucking machines!" She waved a dismissive hand. "You don't like my plan, *get out*. Just quit and go back to the Freedom Squad."

Oz calmly met the woman's eyes. "I understand that you're angry and afraid. But I don't deserve that, Harlot."

"If Oz is leaving, so am I." Natalie told Harlot flatly, anger evident. "He's the reason why most of us are still alive."

"You don't technically work here *now*, Mull." Emily snorted. "You're not on staff, you just hang out here sometimes and we pay you to kill random people who piss us off."

Harlot turned away from Oz, looking tired.

"I'm... sorry." Harlot whispered to Oz. "I know you're one of us, I just..."

"I know." Oz nodded. "I know *exactly* what you're feeling and I understand it. I merely disagree with your solution. That doesn't mean I don't care about Wyatt or that I don't want to see the Agletarians stopped."

"Oz is right though, this should have a vote." Mack interjected. "You don't put Monty in charge of..."

"No, no, I'm done screwing around." Harlot shook her head, cutting him off. "They put my husband in the hospital and tried to kill my friends. The gloves come *off*. We tried to make peace at that stupid conference in Agletaria. We tried it Wyatt's way. Now we'll do it *mine*." She stood up. "They want a fight? Well, now they've fucking *got one*. We're going to take away their ability to *ever* make war on us again. And *anyone* who gets in our way on this will be treated the same, Mull's ex and space aliens included. *Fuck'em all*." She tapped the tabletop. "This is what we're doing. All other projects are on hold. All members are called in. The Agletarians are going to get everything we've got, understand? We hit them as hard as we fucking can and we *show them* why this world was afraid of us for so long. They... they almost killed my husband." She looked down the table again, her voice cracking. "You fucking *destroy them*, Monty! Do you understand me!?! *Salt the fucking earth!* You send a message about what happens to people who go after my husband and son. Make the goddamn angels *weep* over the pain you inflict on those bastards!" She stormed from the room to return to her husband's bedside, yelling back over her shoulder. "*BURY THEM!!!*"

"As always." Monty bowed his head to her slightly in appreciation, obviously liking the order. He turned back to the table, looking at the team with his eerily soulless eyes. "I will win this war if I have the assistance of nine members here, one delivery truck, full command of our security forces, fifteen pounds of Weald Forged metal from Princess Rayn's kingdom... and a dragon."

Poacher frowned. "Where are we supposed to get a delivery truck?"

"My Queen's lands are *off-limits* to your schemes, Welles." Tyrant roared.

"If I give you the metal and a dragon, can you win without me having to do anything?" Rayn asked, obviously barely paying attention to any of this. "Because I'm busy this week picking out paint colors for the baby's room and don't feel like wasting time killing people in another of this dimension's *endless* wars."

"*Most assuredly*."

"Take it." She shrugged, looking disinterested. "What do *I* need it for?"

"You can't just *give* Monty stuff he wants!" Mack sounded

shocked. "*Never* give him what he wants!"

"Why?" Rayn sounded genuinely confused.

"Because he can't be trusted." Bridget argued. "He's the most immoral person I've ever met!"

"Morality is the last refuge of the unimaginative." Monty informed them calmly.

"SEE!?!" Mack pointed at Monty as if the other man had just proved his point for him. "No one sane would say somethin' like that!"

"Oh, Mack. You know I love you like a brother, but I think you exaggerate in this instance." Amy laughed pleasantly. "Montgomery may struggle with chronic unpleasantness, but we are his family and we should support him."

"He *killed* his last family." Bridget reminded her flatly.

"There's never been any proof of that!" Higgins yelled at her. "Those charges were an *insult!*"

Monty took on an inspirational tone and placed a hand over his heart, as if feeling the weight of his struggles. "To be great, is to be misunderstood." He intoned wisely.

Higgins nodded, as if hearing some profound insight about the world and the nature of man.

"He's a fuckin' madman." Mack reiterated. "I've known him since I was a boy, and I'm tellin' you, he's gonna get folks killed."

"They blew up Wyatt!" Poacher shouted. "I don't give a shit about their feelings!"

"I mean innocent folks!" Mack retorted. "Folks that don't got nothin' to do with this!"

"Possibly." Monty agreed, voice dead. "But that's not my department."

"So that's it then?" Mack asked the room at large, sounding disappointed. "Just fuck the whole hero thing now?"

They all silently considered that.

"That's just how the world works." Monty decided after a moment. "It's no coincidence that Hallmark doesn't make a 'You tried to kill my friend but I still wuv you' card." Monty gazed into the crystal globe on the top of his cane again. "Sometimes things happen. And once they do, you can't ever go back."

Bridget sank back into the chair at the head of the table. "So, now Monty is going to handle the Agletarians, which terrifies me to even contemplate, let alone *say*, and Mull is..." She looked over at Natalie. "Do you want to stay in the Crater Lair as protection?"

"I'll go with Oz." Natalie announced.

"I think you're making a mistake." Bridget shook her head.

"It'd be much safer if..."

"I'll go with Oz." Natalie repeated, her voice certain.

Chapter 9

"'I'VE HAD NOTHING YET,' ALICE REPLIED IN AN
OFFENDED TONE, 'SO I CAN'T TAKE MORE.'

'YOU MEAN YOU CAN'T TAKE LESS,' SAID THE HATTER:
'IT'S VERY EASY TO TAKE MORE THAN NOTHING.'"

- Alice's Adventures in Wonderland

Rondel Stanna, AKA "Mercygiver," wasn't a man who typically cared about destiny or fate. Truth told, he viewed most of that kind of thing as the ridiculous ramblings of crazy people. Rondel preferred to believe that a man's success or failure depended entirely on him and not the stars.

He had started out with absolutely nothing. Alone, impoverished, and treated like the lowest filth which ever walked or crawled. He had no home, or family, or friends. But he had taken that as a challenge. The world might have told him, repeatedly, that he was some worthless piece of shit, but that had only served to make him *angry.* He welcomed that hate. Used it as a reason to continue excelling. Hated the world right back.

He didn't need the help of any god or destiny for that. It wasn't the spirits who pulled the strings, it was *him.*

But sometimes, it seemed like things were simply destined to be. Like the gods were arranging the foolish humans the way they wanted.

Such was the case with Rondel and his former partner.

Rondel had spent his entire life alone. He'd assumed he always would be. The only people he'd ever known had all been horrible, and they didn't understand him. They had just wanted to use him.

But that crazy redhead had arrived in his life and completely turned it on its head. Changed everything he thought he knew. Showed him such *amazing* things...

For the first time, Rondel *had* someone. He knew where he belonged and he knew that there was someone in the world who he could count on. Yes, sometimes they disagreed and quarreled, but they were a *team*. That girl was the only family that he'd ever had. She was a piece of him.

Rondel loved her.

Completely.

He'd loved her from the second he'd first seen her, lost in the way the girl saw the world and the way she made him feel. His entire life had been empty, painful, and alone. But when she was around... he felt like he was... loved. Like he could safely be himself, and not have to worry about anyone hurting him or using him for their own ends.

Some of the happiest days of his life were spent lost with that girl.

All he wanted on this earth was to be with her again. Even if only for a moment...

He was still going to brutally kill her, obviously, but that didn't mean he loved her any less.

Rondel had desperately tried to fill the void she'd left in his life. Tried it with women. Tried it with men. But... it always felt so empty and meaningless. She'd taken away the parts of him which were capable of ever being content again. Her betrayal had ripped it from him.

That bitch had used him. Made him think she cared about him. But she'd just been playing him for a fool, the whole time. And *then* she'd tried to kill him.

But Rondel was *not* an easy man to kill. He'd grown up in a hell she couldn't possibly *imagine,* and it would take more than her to get rid of him.

He was going to get her back. Whether she liked it or not.

Rondel's underling, Mr. Jack, looked up from his workbench. "Boss?" His eyebrows soared. "Damn, I figured you were dead."

Two days ago, Rondel had gotten into a fight with the woman and it hadn't gone exactly to plan. He'd tossed her off a roof, true, but she'd just about killed him too.

Theirs had always been a very physical relationship. This time, it just got a little out of hand. Which was perfectly understandable. She'd betrayed him and left him to die alone. That would have made *anyone* angry. And although Rondel considered himself one of the last *truly* reasonable men alive, even he had his limits.

Rondel rolled his eyes. "The woman stabbed me, but I have endured far worse from her over the years." He ran his hand over the area where the blade had entered his chest. "She's getting sloppy."

"Uh-huh." Mr. Jack scrambled to his feet, trying desperately to look like he was doing something vital for Rondel's business, rather than undoubtedly just watching online pornography featuring ballerinas. "So… what's the plan then?" He swallowed. "Because it looks like there are parts of this plan that you aren't sharing with me." He pointed at the TV, where the newscaster was standing in front of the wreckage of a building. "We're blowing up hospitals now?"

"You have a problem with my actions?" Rondel arched an eyebrow.

Jack shook his head. "No, no, just…"

"Good. Because that attack wasn't my doing. That was the Agletarians."

Jack pointed back and forth between them. "And… are *we* involved with them? Are we with them or against them?"

Rondel continued staring at him.

Jack took that as an answer.

Rondel absently watched the newscast, which showed the woman standing next to her perfect, shining knight. The man was *grotesquely* heroic-looking. It made Rondel's skin crawl.

Those two were trying to be happy? She thought she could, what? Just replace him? Start over with someone new and leave him out in the cold? No. Hell, no! You *didn't* leave Rondel. You didn't treat him like some piece of shit you were glad to be rid of.

Not after all he had done for her. Not at all.

He'd kill her. He'd make certain that no one else on earth would ever touch her again.

She would belong to him forever.

And then… Rondel wouldn't be alone anymore.

His eyes narrowed at the screen, continuing to watch the man who she thought could replace him. "Do you think he's better looking than I am?" He wondered aloud.

"Huh!?!" Jack looked confused and appalled by the question. "What!?!"

He pointed at the man on the TV. "Do you think she loves him?"

Jack looked uncertain. "No?" He said hesitantly, obviously trying to gage what answer Rondel wanted him to give. "…Yes?" He sounded even more uncertain, worrying that the wrong choice would get him killed on the spot.

Rondel continued watching the newsfeed, hating the woman. Hating her happiness. Wanting her to *know his pain.*

She'd made him feel alive. And then she'd abandoned him. And for that... she was fucking *dead*.

"Listen, you want to play all mysterious and creepy mastermind, that's your business, Boss, just trying to figure out what we're doing here." Mr. Jack finally announced. "Because it seems like there's..."

"I'm going to humiliate her body in every way I can," Rondel interrupted, "...and then I'm going to kill her."

Jack considered that for a long moment, looking taken aback by the news. "Umm... Boss?"

"Stop being so squeamish. I'm perfectly capable of killing her, Mister Jack." Rondel snapped, hating being doubted by someone so weak and useless. "I recognize that the roof fight didn't go as I planned and that she's on a team of super-powered people, but I assure you, I *can* kill her."

"Okaaaay..." Jack was unwilling to argue the point further.

"Yes, I realize that I will die in the attempt." Rondel sank into his chair. "But I don't care, just so long as I *take that bitch with me*."

"If you're dead? How am I getting paid?"

"That's a good point." Rondel started towards him threateningly. "Perhaps we should just *settle up right now*."

Jack put his hands up and retreated. "No, no." He shook his head. "Not necessary. I'll figure something out. No need to worry."

Rondel started towards the door again. "We will wait until the moment is right and all of my plans are in place, and then we will wipe that girl off the face of the earth." He let out a deep sigh, trying to hide the pleasure that idea gave him, but recognizing that it was apparent. "It will feel *so* good to finally kill that bitch."

"That's... super." Jack nodded to himself. "I'm glad we had this talk. Let's please not talk about our feelings again? Yes? Because yours are weird and terrifying. Some creepy Freudian shit, Boss."

Rondel stopped to glare at him.

Jack instantly backed down, taking a cautious step away. "Which, I *of course* mean as a compliment."

Rondel exited the room and went back to his plans.

Chapter 10

*"'I WANT A CLEAN CUP,' INTERRUPTED THE HATTER:
'LET'S ALL MOVE ONE PLACE ON.'"*

- Alice's Adventures in Wonderland

Oz didn't feel well today.

His balance felt off.

There was mold somewhere in this building, which was causing his lungs to become inflamed and his eyes to water.

This neighborhood was in an industrial zone, and he could practically *feel* the chemicals and fumes which had soaked into the concrete and the buildings. Most of the chemicals were probably illegal. They were probably carcinogens and poisons, filling his lungs with every breath. It was like walking into a gas chamber. Every second he was here was one second closer to death.

That was why he didn't feel well.

He knocked on the door and it was opened an instant later.

Natalie smiled at him broadly and ushered him inside.

That woman's smile always just about stopped his heart. He found it so appealing that it took everything in him not to grab her and pull her against him, confessing everything he felt about her.

But that would be inappropriate.

It hadn't been his idea to leave her alone, even for an instant, but she had insisted. Something about him making her nervous with his pacing around. She was still coming down from 30+ sleepless hours, so Oz had decided to give her a few minutes to rest, remaining in the Crater Lair until she'd had a chance to sleep. In patented Natalie fashion though, the woman had taken that break from being watched at every moment to return to her apartment and continue with her life.

Oz was not a fan of that plan.

People were trying to kill her, so it made no sense to stay at the most obvious location anyone searching for her would look. He was not at all pleased that she was ignoring her own safety like this.

While on the car ride over to her place though, he had managed to convince her to stay with him until the matter was settled. All in all, he had expected more of an argument about it. But she had agreed almost immediately.

Which was... odd.

Oz was used to being confused by Natalie's actions though, so it wasn't exactly surprising either.

As he stepped into her apartment, he wondered why the sight didn't horrify him as much as it obviously should have. The space was... crazy. Like a dozen different houses were shuffled together and then arranged around a single apartment in a jumble. But it was a chaos that had a deliberate order to it. It was the product of an eccentric mind, not a lazy housekeeper.

The space wasn't dirty or disgusting like his aunt and uncle's house had been, it was just... crazy.

Piles of things around that obviously were placed there for a reason, but Oz couldn't begin to guess what it was.

Multicolored walls.

Posters of boybands from the 1990s and concerts from the 1890s and velvet paintings of sci-fi robots.

It was like walking around in Natalie's mind, and he found himself grotesquely fascinated by it. Yes, being here was causing his compulsion for order to go nuclear, but he couldn't look away from it.

Natalie made her way further into the apartment, while Oz bolted the door behind them. They were only going to be here for a few minutes while she collected some things, but it never hurt to be cautious.

The door was secured with nothing but a simple deadbolt and a chain lock.

Oz automatically put "installing a good quality lock on the door" on his internal list of things he needed to do. For a professional assassin, he really would have thought the woman would have more than two locks on the door. Heck, Oz himself had seven. One of which had a reversed mechanism and was always kept *unlocked,* so that anyone picking the other six would inadvertently lock the seventh.

He followed behind Natalie, through the foyer and into the main living area. There was an opening in the wall which formed a breakfast nook, although the counter was currently filled with an overflowing mass of paperwork.

"What's that?" He gestured to the large pile of envelopes on the counter.

Natalie shrugged, apparently unconcerned. "That's the mail I don't open because it's going to be bad news."

He blinked at her in confusion. "Okaaaaaay. Um... why not just throw it out then?"

"Because it might be important."

"Then shouldn't you open it?"

"I just *said* I didn't *want* to open it because it's going to be bills and letters yelling at me for doing or not doing something." She looked at him like he was insane. "If I *opened* the mail I don't want to open, then it would completely eliminate the need for the pile of mail I don't open."

"Ah." For the first time in his life, Oz was confronted with something that both made complete sense yet was also entirely insane.

So he simply stared at the mail, vainly trying to come to terms with that contradiction.

Natalie noticed his confusion. "You okay?"

"I don't feel good."

"You don't look good." She tilted her head to the side. "You dying or something?"

"Possibly. I haven't had a physical in two weeks, so something could have come up in that time."

"I'm not used to you not looking perfect, Oz." She sounded concerned.

"I'm tired."

"Did you sleep at all last night?"

"No."

"Or the night before?"

"No."

"I was the one dying, how is it that *you're* the one who looks like shit?"

Oz knew perfectly well why he hadn't slept. Because she had been dying and he spent most of the night vacillating between crushing grief, boiling anger, and near catatonia. And he'd spent last night once again looking over all of the information they'd thus far managed to collect about their enemies.

But she didn't need to hear that.

"I don't know." He finally said simply, carefully turning one of the pink ceramic cats on a shelf so that it was more in line with its companions.

Of course, the action was entirely pointless, since the shelf *itself* seemed to have been nailed to the wall at a slight angle, but it was the only thing Oz could do at the moment.

This apartment was... He'd never been to a haunted house of any kind, but he very much guessed that the experience was a lot like this. Not in the sense that there were ghosts, just in the sense that this apartment represented his own personal nightmare. But one which was somehow presented in a safe way, so that his terror was rendered fun. Or at least like an adventure you knew you could survive.

It was very strange.

He must have been staring at the off-kilter shelving for too long, as Miss Quentin finally snapped at him. "What's *wrong* with you?"

"A lot." He admitted, taking the question large-scale.

"Such as?"

"I don't feel well."

"You're always like this." She reminded him.

He shrugged, making his way towards the living room to continue the security sweep. "I always don't feel well."

"I've never met anyone in my life who *never* feels good."

"I just..." He shrugged helplessly again. "I don't feel well."

She cautiously approached the refrigerator and threw open the door, again obviously expecting a body to tumble out, but only finding sugary and unhealthy foods. Personally, Oz found them scarier and more horrifying than a dead body would have been. "You know what I think your real problem is?"

"Some kind of unknown form of leukemia?" He guessed, making a serious self-diagnosis.

"You don't have any fun."

"Not feeling well is not fun."

"If you started having fun, you'd start feeling better."

"I don't think that's necessarily true. Lots of people have fun which ends up killing them. They..." He trailed off, distracted by the living room. "What's that?" He pointed towards a mannequin in the corner.

Natalie started to pull a "Hello Kitty" suitcase from a hall closet, and Oz unconsciously tilted his head to the side to get a better look at her rear. It was the kind of thing he would be completely horrified by seeing someone else do, but which he still felt compelled to do when it was Miss Quentin. There was something about the woman which seemed to inspire him to admire her. It was wrong and juvenile and a complete betrayal of her trust. He knew he should feel guilty and ashamed for it. Knew it was a sign that his "bad blood" was winning out... But Oz didn't care.

That woman had an *amazing* body. It made him happy to look at her. And there were precious few things in this world which could make Oz happy.

She turned to look at the object he indicated. "That's a robot from the Pirates of the Caribbean ride."

"Really?" He turned to look at it again. "Huh. Where did you pick something like that up?"

"The Pirates of the Caribbean ride. Duh." She started past him, but then stopped when she saw he was staring at her in amazement. "What? They had a ton of them in there. They'll never miss one redhead."

"Why is it that everyone in the Consortium thinks that's somehow a complete legal defense?" He threw his arms out in exasperation. "According to them, the world is completely blind and uncaring about its own property going missing."

Natalie made a humoring, dismissive sound and tossed her suitcase onto her bed.

Oz paused in the doorway, recognizing that he shouldn't go into the room. This was her private space and he hadn't been invited. It was crossing a line.

On the other hand, he was in charge of her security at the moment and her bedroom hadn't yet been swept for dangers.

Plus… he'd sworn to himself that he was going to be forward in showing Miss Quentin how important she was to him. He wasn't about to ever get into a position of her dying without knowing how he felt again.

Oz's only goal in life was that woman.

As he stood in the doorway, silently debating, he noticed a creepy looking doll on the shelf across from him. There was something hypnotic about it and he couldn't look away.

"That's a ventriloquist dummy." Natalie informed him, like a tour guide.

"Why do you have it?"

She snorted. "Why does *anyone* have a ventriloquist dummy?"

"Ventriloquism?" He guessed.

"Do I *look* like a stage performer, Oz?" She rolled her eyes.
"Then why?"

"I just told you!" She threw her arms out in exasperation. "Jesus, are you going to make me *repeatedly* explain why I own everything I own?" She tossed an armload of miscellaneous clothes into the suitcase, then stuffed the remainder back into the drawer without thought to order.

Oz kept staring at the dummy. "It isn't one of those dolls from a few years ago that hypnotizes people, is it?"

"Not if you don't look at it, no."

Oz snapped out of his trance and turned away from the doll. "Why on earth would you keep something like that in your living room? A madman creates a dummy that hypnotizes people into doing the doll's bidding, and you keep that around?"

"I like it. I think it's cute." Natalie tossed some more clothes into the suitcase. "I traded a stuffed iguana and three left boots for it."

"Why did you have three left boots?"

"Because I still wear the right ones sometimes."

Oz had no response to that.

"I wish you'd take your life a little more seriously, Miss Quentin." He told her instead.

"You know, if my biggest problem in life was that I never felt good, I'd spend my time seriously trying to change that, rather than lecturing other people on how to fix theirs. But you don't. Your solution is to close yourself off further from the world."

"The world is most of the reason I don't feel well."

"*You* are the reason you don't feel well." She sounded annoyed with him. "You're unhappy. And that unhappiness is manifesting into imagined physical ailments."

"My physical ailments are making me unhappy, mostly because I see more with my powers than other people do. I can *see* the filth and the germs that they overlook. That's what my powers do. I can feel them everywhere around us..."

"So?" She snapped, like none of that mattered. "Just tell the filth and the germs to leave you alone then! You control them, they don't control you! Tell them to fuck off!"

"It... it doesn't work like that."

"*Make it* work like that!" She stuffed a toothbrush into her suitcase without first securing it in a sterile housing. The brush was currently touching her clothes, collecting all manner of contaminants. It would be like brushing your teeth with socks and underwear. She didn't appear to even notice the nightmare she'd just created. "Believe me, Oz, I've had some crazy fucking powers in my life. And every single one of them can be made to toe the line and not fuck with your day. Take charge of your own life, Oz. For God's sake. Stop trying to save other people and recognize that *you're* the one dying! Living like this is killing your soul!"

"Let me ask you something, Natalie: how's *your* life going?"

He crossed his arms over his chest, unsure how this had become an argument, but suspecting it had to do with his own defensiveness.

"It's going fine," she sniffed indignantly, "if people would butt out of it!"

"No, I mean your *real* life. Because I look at you and I don't see someone who has got everything together. Roach is probably the person you're closest to in the world, and he didn't even know you were a woman until this week. You have closed yourself off from people too, don't you pretend that you haven't."

"I'm doing it for the safety of others though, and..."

"The safety of others?" His eyebrow soared at that obvious lie. "Please. You know half a dozen people who are impervious to all harm, at least two who can bend reality at a whim, several who claim to be completely *immortal,* and dozens of others who would *gladly* lay down their lives for you if it meant that you were in it. Myself included." He shook his head. "You're not protecting anyone. You're protecting *you.*"

"Yes. Yes, I am!" She pointed at him, now angry. "Let's get one thing straight: I like the Consortium crew. They're funny. They're entertaining to spend time with. But I do *not* trust them. At all. I am an independent contractor, I have serious trust issues. Most of our coworkers are either idiots, evil, or an unknown." She went back to packing. "I steer clear of them if I can manage it. Because when the shit hits the fan, I don't know what they're going to do. And I don't like the unknown."

"Neither do I."

"That's why this whole 'Monty is in charge of the proverbial launch codes' thing is crazy. That asshole is like If Jack the Ripper and Ayn Rand had a baby. I don't get what the hell Harlot is thinking on this one, and is the *perfect* example of why I don't get involved with the Consortium's internal politics."

"I understand it." He leaned against the doorframe, getting an odd enjoyment from watching the woman haphazardly toss stuff into the messy bag. It was everything in the world that usually freaked him out, but when she did it, it was somehow adorable. "They tried to kill her father. They hurt Harlot's husband. She hates them now."

She nodded. "Touching Wyatt is like killing John Wick's fucking dog, yeah. You don't do that and live."

"...So, she's playing her most evil and hateful card." He continued. "And she doesn't care what Monty does to them, just so long as she doesn't have to be afraid of them anymore. I understand that. It's a perfectly natural reaction for anyone to have. But Harlot isn't anyone, Harlot is supposed to be a superhero. Whether it's her husband or a perfect stranger, she needs to consider what will happen if she does this. Montgomery is not Poacher. He's not a terrier she's trained to do tricks for her, because it loves her. Montgomery is a wolf. Wolves don't *do* tricks. All they do is eat things, and the more you feed them, the stronger they become. And this is putting him in a position to hurt a lot of people. Us included. Because Montgomery hates everyone. That's who he is. Someone hurt him and now he hates the world. So, if you want my honest opinion, I agree, it's a very bad idea to involve him. She should have come up with a better plan. I don't agree with it. But I don't make the decisions in this organization, all I can do is try to minimize the damage he inevitably causes."

She stopped her packing and turned to look at him. "What would you do if someone was trying to kill someone you cared about?"

"I'd kill him myself." He reminded her. "And I'd work with Montgomery to find the other men responsible, if that were the only option." He shrugged. "I didn't say I wouldn't do exactly the same as Harlot, just that I don't think it's the right choice."

"Well, I guess the best offense is a strong defense." She paused. "Wait, or is it 'best *defense* is a strong *offense*'?" She thought about it for a moment, then shrugged. "I'm going to say both."

"The best offense and defense is to have a strong offense and defense?" He summarized. "That doesn't make any sense."

"It makes perfect sense!"

"No, it doesn't."

"Oh, shut up." She pulled something else out of the crowded closet and handed it to him. "Here, check this out. It's one of the Eimin Blades, forged by the ancient sensei of the Neru Clan thousands of years ago, deep in the mountains of Hokkaido. The blades are stronger than any metal known to man and will kill anything; body and spirit. They say the soul of a demonic killer was forged into the metal of the blades and his monstrous screams can still be heard howling in the wind when they are used for evil." She took on a haunted, ghostly tone. "To even see the blades... is to see death."

"Uh-huh." He glanced down at it, then back up at her. "It says 'Made in China' on your antique Japanese sword."

She squinted down at the engraving. "So? Maybe the ancient swordsmith was Chinese."

"Don't you think it's more likely that someone just bought a cheap decorative samurai sword at the mall? Maybe someone looking for a way to culturally appropriate a ninja backstory in a hurry because she needs a new identity every day?"

"Possibly." She looked over her shoulder in confusion, as if trying to spot something in the chaotic closet. "Shit... I wonder where the Eimin Blades went then? I've got two of the damn things. Huh. I'm pretty sure I have them around here *somewhere*." She gave up searching and shrugged. "All well, I got a lot of swords and they're one of them. If you see any little sword-y dagger things that look like they're capable of killing the dead, try not to stab yourself with them. Death blows, Oz. Trust me, I been dead a few times and everyone on the other side is a dick."

"Why have you been dead a few times? What happened?"

"Umm... you don't want to hear about that."

"Meaning, Mercygiver did it to you."

"Yes. We were together for a long time." She paused in her packing. "And it was always bad. Sometimes it got *really* bad."

"I don't understand why you would ever let him treat you like that?"

"I... I don't know either. I ask myself that all the time." She paused for a long moment, voice breaking. "Do you have any idea what it's like to take a backseat in your own life, Oz?" She looked down at the floor. "To give someone control and watch yourself doing things... Things that you don't want to do, but you do them anyway because, in that moment... you *think* you do? Because you were *told* to want them? Like a madness in your blood that you can't get rid of?"

Oz flashed to his aunt's dire warnings about his innate evil. "I've had some experience with the concept, yes."

"I joined up with him when I was a girl. And he told me that I was special and that together we would do great things. But we didn't. At the end of it, all I got were broken bones and scars. And... and the nightmares." She swallowed. "He hurt me, Oz. He... he hurt me bad." She smoothed a strand of her hair behind her ear, still not meeting his gaze. "Turned me into someone I didn't want to be. It took me years to work up the nerve to try to kill him. And I'd thought I'd done it. But..."

"Sometimes garbage doesn't stay buried." Oz observed, making a silent vow to kill that man himself, when the opportunity first presented. Oz was a man who lived his life by a lot of rules and guidelines, but the first entry on that list was: if you hurt Natalie, you die.

"Exactly." She nodded. "That's why I don't work with partners anymore. They... they die. And they can hurt you. And he can't hurt them to get to me..." She paused, squinting at him like he distracted her from her thoughts. "Why the fuck are you hovering?" She gestured to him. "Are you just standing there because the thought of entering someone else's bedroom disgusts you or are you standing there because of some obscure bit of gentlemanly manners I've never learned?"

"The latter."

"Whatever." She rolled her eyes. "Come in if you want, stand in the hallway alone if you want. Whatever floats your boat, Oz." She dumped a package of bullets into her bag, next to her toothbrush. "Jesus. You're so high maintenance. Pretty soon I'm going to have to remind you that it's okay to blink, it won't offend me."

"I'm not worried about offending you, I'm worried about scaring you." He admitted. "People... people have told me that I'm always on the verge of being evil. That I creep them out. Men in my family are cursed with insanity."

She snorted, tossing a handgun into the bag. "I'm out of my goddamn mind, Oz. Full-blown batshit balls-to-the-wall gonzo crazy. And not in the 'Cynic's so socially unacceptable, isn't he funny!?!' way, but in the 'Holy shit, hide the cutlery before that loony bitch kills us in our sleep' way." She threw several knives and a domino mask into the bag. "I have the leftover shit from ten thousand different personalities rattling around in my head. It's... it's a mess in there."

"Well... sounds like neither of us feels good then."

"So it would appear." She sighed.

He looked at her for a long moment.

The moment turned into two.

And Oz noticed that his pulse was now racing.

He was pretty sure it had nothing to do with his ailments now, it was entirely due to the woman standing across from him.

The pulse alarm on his watch went off, warning him of his elevated heart rate, just in case he needed medical attention. He'd set it to a very low level, because he wanted an early warning if something was wrong.

Natalie tore her eyes from his, glaring at the object on his wrist. "You know what? I'm sick of this shit." She started towards him angrily. "If you think you're dying, I can help you along with that. Or you're going to start living right fucking now." To his surprise, she slapped him across the face. Oz stumbled backwards into the hall, bumping one of the tables and almost sending its varied contents spilling across the floor. She prowled after him. "What do you want? Huh?" She slapped him again, more surprising him than causing actual pain. "You wanna die or do you want to start living? What will make you fucking happy!?!"

"Ow!" Oz backed away. "Can you stop..."

"What. Do. You. Want!?!" She demanded, raising her hand to hit him again.

He caught her wrist. "You. Alright? *You'd* make me happy." He admitted, her wrist feeling delicate and soft in his gloved hand.

The answer seemed to take her aback. "I... I can't even make *myself* happy, Oz. You don't want me." Her voice broke. "Trust me, you *don't* want me."

"I think I do." He assured her softly.

He leaned closer and their lips touched. Due to Oz's difficulties dealing with the outside world, this was technically the first time he'd ever kissed anyone. The entire idea had always seemed gross to him. The exchange of trillions of horrible viruses and pathogens.

In practice though, Oz found it pleasant.

An instant later and the dark parts of Oz's mind took over, slamming his lips into hers more forcefully, staking a claim to them.

He'd almost let his stupid brain get in the way of being with her.

She'd almost died. She'd almost died and he'd almost let his fear over his powers and his preoccupation with germs stop him from taking what he wanted while she was actually here. She could have died and Oz would have regretted not trying this for every second of his life.

Natalie made no effort to escape him, instead wrapping her arms around his neck, returning the kiss.

Oz took that as an invitation to continue, running his hands down her back, touching her body places he'd never touched before.

She let out a small sound of pleasure, raising her leg to wrap around him.

Oz ran his hand down her thigh as she held it against him, fulfilling a dream he'd had for three solid years. Unsurprisingly, her legs felt as amazing as they looked. Soft skin over strong, elegant muscles. He wanted them wrapped around him. He wanted to feel them pulling him close, offering her body to him.

...But then Oz considered the matter, his brain once more getting in the way of the fun he was having.

He hadn't washed his hands since he'd arrived in the building. And even though he was wearing gloves, he'd touched the elevator buttons, the doorknobs, the table in the hall, and the pile of mail! *Mail!* Mail was some of the dirtiest things in the world, and now he was smearing all of those germs and microbes all over the perfection of Natalie's body.

And he hadn't showered in almost three hours.

He was filthy and disgusting.

She was just out of the hospital, the *last* thing she needed was for someone to infect her with a super-virus simply because he didn't wash his hands before touching her.

Oz had spent his entire life obsessively cleaning his own hands, because he knew the filth was always there. He could feel it, no matter how much soap he used.

Oz was trash.

And trash had no business being anywhere near someone as amazing as Natalie.

He tried to push the idea from his mind, but it refused to go away. It somehow fused itself with his own guilt over her almost dying. She'd almost died once, and now was he really willing to risk her life? Because of something so simple? When you came right down to it, that was selfish. He should just go wash his hands, and then everything would be fine.

Unfortunately, the internal conflict was causing his other OCD tendencies to come to the surface. And the entire room now felt like chaos which needed to be organized if this moment could ever hope to be completely perfect.

His sudden distraction did not go unnoticed.

Natalie stopped the kiss and lowered her leg, simply staring at him with an odd look on her face. Oz wasn't entirely sure what it meant, but he knew it wasn't good.

"Can you please not look so disgusted while we're making out, Oz?" She said softly, sounding hurt. "It kinda kills the mood."

Oz swore to himself, something he very rarely actually did. "Sorry, I know. It's not you, it's just..."

"I know." She nodded in understanding, looking tired. She sat down on the bed. "It's my fault. I should have known better." She gestured to the left with her head. "The bathroom is that way, if you want to compulsively wash your hands and mouth or whatever."

Oz stood still for a beat. "It's... it's *really* not about you." He assured her again.

She nodded. "I know."

"I just... I touched the elevator buttons on the way in, without thinking, and now I just can't..."

"I know." She nodded again, not willing to argue with him about it, because she was already resolved to the conclusion about

184

him she'd reached. "It's okay."

But Oz could tell it most certainly wasn't. He just wasn't sure how to go about changing that. Because the compulsions sometimes seemed to hold Oz hostage. He couldn't control them. He tried, it was just...

They scared him. They were the part of him which terrified him, and he knew he couldn't beat them.

"I'm sorry." He told her softly. "I just... I can't..."

"You don't want to be with me, Oz." She told him simply, tilting her head to the side. "You just *think* you do." She stood up and closed her suitcase. "I'm... I'm a Manic Pixie Dreamgirl, Oz."

"Is that your name today?"

"No... well, yeah. I guess. But do you know what that is?"

"Should I?"

"A Manic Pixie Dreamgirl is the kooky love interest in a movie who is psychotically chipper and acts as a ray of sunshine to the brooding hero of the film. She dances in the rain and collects crystals and seashells and all that bullshit. Teaches him how he should celebrate his failures and live every day to the fullest." She started towards the door of the bedroom. "But the Manic Pixie Dreamgirl doesn't have an actual storyline of her own. She's just... a prop. Because if you really start to think about her... what kind of life would she have to have had in order to come out being like that? A bad one. But no one wants to see that. Her problems are not so easily solved. It's better if the movie just focuses on her as some shallow, ethereal creature who spreads sunshine and warmth. And probably dies young, a symbol of the lost innocence and the joy of unspoiled childhood." She stopped in front of him to meet his eyes for a moment. "The Manic Pixie Dreamgirl doesn't get a happy ending. She's just *someone else's* happy ending." She pushed past him into the hallway.

"*I'm* someone else." He reminded her, sounding almost desperate.

"Are you saying you think you can make me happy, Oz?"

Oz didn't reply to that. There was no way in the world that Oz could ever make *anyone* happy. His life was a mess and his mind ensured that he was almost always miserable. He couldn't even kiss a girl without it somehow ending up as an insult and embarrassment.

He recognized the fact that he was destined to die alone, probably in some kind of antiseptic-smelling hospital room somewhere, hiding from the outside world.

That was all the future held for Oz. That was the happiest ending he could expect for himself. And although he recognized it, as surely as he recognized his aunt's warnings about his darkness, he was helpless to change it.

Oz was either going to turn into a monster or a hermit. And either way, his compulsions would be there. They were going to torture him until they finally killed him. His own mind would hold him hostage until he died.

No matter where he went or what he did. That was how Oz would end up.

He knew that.

And there wasn't room in that kind of life for anyone special. It would be selfish to involve them in it, let alone suffer from any kind of delusion that they could somehow be happy. His compulsions would just ruin their lives too. Trap them in his insanity. Rob them of their light and their freedom.

She grabbed a hat from off of the hook on the wall. "You can't even kiss me without being grossed out by it."

"I've never been 'grossed out' by you." He shook his head seriously, completely truthful on that point. At no time in his life had he ever looked at Natalie as anything but an absolute wonder. "I told you that had *nothing* to do with..."

"Oh, come off it, Oz." She snapped. "I can't blame you. I mean, me? Fuck, I kill everything sooner or later. Or they leave on their own once they get sick of me. Even my fucking goldfish."

"You're comparing me to dead goldfish?"

"The goldfish didn't die, they just ran away."

He squinted in confusion, trying to follow that. "How do gold..."

"The point is that is you are fucking depressed and I can't help your life not suck." She interrupted. "That's not my job."

"I'm not depressed." He retorted. "*I'm* not the one taking antidepressants."

She glared at him for a moment, looking less surprised that he would know her medical history than he would have expected. But she probably recognized that he was paranoid and obsessive enough to be following a lot of people, so it didn't appear to worry her. "I don't take antidepressants." She snapped, correcting him. "*Natalie* takes antidepressants."

"Why does she take antidepressants?"

"Because she's depressing?" Natalie guessed, looking mystified by the actions of her own supposed secret identity. "I don't know. That bitch is nuts. Everyone knows it."

"You can talk to me, you know." He said softly. "I know he

scares you."

"He *doesn't* scare me." She shook her head emphatically. "Ronnie has nothing to do with this."

"Yes. He does." He said simply.

"*He should scare you too!*" She snapped. "He's going to kill us, Oz! He's going to find us and he's going to kill you and..."

"I don't die easy, Natalie." He shook his head, standing taller. "If he comes to my door looking for trouble, he's going to find it."

She watched him silently for several breaths.

"I am a Manic Pixie Dream Girl, Oz." She reiterated softly. "I can't be responsible for both protecting your life *and* giving you a reason to live it. You can't be with me. That's..."

"I thought you were my 'cynical foulmouthed private detective partner' in our hypothetical movie?" Oz pressed, interrupting her. "Now you're saying you're the innocent ethereal maiden?"

"I can be both."

"I don't see how."

"Don't limit me, Oz!" She pointed an angry finger at him. "I fucking hate that!"

"You can't be both my kooky inspiration to embrace the wonder which is life *and* my anti-hero buddy cop." He crossed his arms over his chest. "I refuse to accept that bizarre narrative and seriously doubt any screenplay like that would ever be greenlit by a studio."

"That's just the way it is, whether you accept it or not." She pointed back and forth between them rapidly. "*This* is what happens when a psychotic spends the day with a psychopath. We're from *two different worlds*, Oz. You're sitting over there Howard Hughes-ing about germs in dimly lit rooms or whatever, and I'm just wondering why the number four smells like apples and is plotting against me." She met his eyes and shook her head again. "We can never be. And you know it."

The apartment fell into silence for an extended period, as they both stood there and reflected on their argument.

Personally, Oz was using the time to dwell on the memory of the feel of her thigh against him. He found it *remarkably* pleasant.

His new goal in life was to have her grinding against him again, making that soft, breathy sound. He liked it. It was a little cooing hum of need and desire, surrendering herself to him, which was utterly going against her usual confident and strong façade.

Oz wanted to hear nothing in his life but that sound. He'd make it his fucking ringtone, if he could.

It made him feel like a hero. Like *her* hero.

Oz might have mental problems, but he'd have to be completely *out of his mind* to not want that.

He just needed to figure out how to circumvent his own brain first. And possibly hers as well. There were complications, true, but he was sure he could figure them out.

She cleared her throat, sounding awkward. "I... I think I'm the world's foremost expert on tea today, by the way." She informed him, her beautiful voice once more sounding soft.

"Oh. That's... nice." He stood straighter, getting ahold of his emotions again. "We should have some."

She scoffed at that suggestion. "Do I look like the kind of person who has a lot of tea sitting around, Oz?"

"You're the foremost authority on something you don't enjoy?" He deadpanned.

"I'll only be the foremost authority on it for *today*. Tomorrow, I'll probably go back to hating it. I usually do. It tastes like someone simply gave you water in a glass they didn't bother to wash first." She dropped her bags and started towards the kitchen. "We'll have hot chocolate before we leave instead. But we'll need to use forks to stir it, because all the spoons are dirty."

He frowned. "Why don't we just wash the spoons?"

"Because we still have forks." Her tone sounded genuinely confused, as if mystified by his insanity. "*Duh*."

Oz blinked after her in amazement.

On the other hand, trying to bring order to *some* chaos was completely futile.

Oz watched the woman open one of her cupboards, feeling like she was farther away from him than ever. None of this had gone the way he'd wanted.

There was still a distance between them. Like she was on earth, while he was staring at her from the surface of the moon or something.

Chapter 11

'I WISH I HADN'T CRIED SO MUCH!' SAID ALICE, AS SHE
SWAM ABOUT, TRYING TO FIND HER WAY OUT. 'I SHALL
BE PUNISHED FOR IT NOW, I SUPPOSE, BY BEING
DROWNED IN MY OWN TEARS!

- Alice's Adventures in Wonderland

16 YEARS AGO

He had walked on the moon.

Watched the sun rise from the summits of all the tallest mountains on earth.

He'd stood alone against the worst humanity had to offer.

Shaken hands with seven Presidents and ten kings.

Been thanked by teary-eyed victims and cursed by fiendish inhuman evil.

And now, Roy Hopper, AKA "Kilroy," was a security guard at a department store, because that was the only place that would hire him. Sadly, the downside of having a secret identity was that you couldn't exactly list "Masked Superhero: 1937 to Present" on your resume.

But he had no regrets.

He hadn't gone into the field for acclaim or riches. That was one of the reasons why he wore the mask. If you weren't careful, it all went to your head. You forgot who you really were and lost yourself in the process. You forgot *why* you were doing it.

Of course, the inverse of that was also true.

There was a constant danger that if you wore a mask long enough, you forgot what the face beneath looked like. You started to think you were the person you dressed up as.

Which was one of the reasons why Roy didn't get involved with other superheroes. He'd never joined any of the super-teams or done interviews. Roy wasn't in the game for all of that. He didn't fight crime to make himself feel better or because he was even necessarily the best suited for the job, just because... someone had to.

Because the world was the way it was.

Because no one cared.

And if he didn't try to help people, no one else would.

The only sign that Kilroy had ever been there were a hundred thousand messages he'd scrawled on things, all over the world.

He might have shunned the spotlight, but *no one* could ever doubt that Killroy was here.

He continued making his rounds, checking the deserted sales floor of Drews department store. It was one of those buildings that hadn't been remodeled much over the years, which meant that it had a large open atrium that rose up five stories. From that central area, the different departments branched out in four directions, displaying all of the consumer treasures that money could buy.

Roy had grown to love this store. It meant something to him now. It felt like... home.

There was a noise above him, and his eyes instantly snapped to trace its source. After spending so many decades as a hero, it was second nature to him now.

A second later, Roy saw both the source of the noise *and* the reason why he'd come to love this stupid store so much.

The 10 year old redhead in question arrived on the scene, standing up backwards on the handlebars of one of the store's bikes, riding it down the stairs.

Roy winced, wondering how much his young companion's attempts at daredevilry would cost him tonight.

To be fair, the girl was very, *very* good at things like this. Anything that required a superhuman balance and nerves of steel. Roy himself had always been blessed with enhanced agility and balance, but the little girl could pull off stunts and flips that Roy couldn't have pulled off on his best day.

But that wasn't surprising.

The girl was powerful. More powerful than he hoped she ever had cause to realize.

The girl moved her feet, using her weight to turn the bike in a lazy circle when it reached the bottom of the stairs, then ran it straight into a display cabinet. The action had been deliberate though, and she used the impact to backflip over the glass display and land directly in front of him like a circus acrobat.

She held out her arms. "Applause, applause!" She cupped her hands to her mouth and made the sound of a roaring crowd.

"We've talked about this, Red." Roy shook his head. "There's no room for showing off when you're on the job."

The girl rolled her eyes. "I'm not *on* the job, Roy." She rearranged her red ponytail. "I don't work here, I just break in." She smiled up at him. "Unless, of course, you want to take me on as a sidekick?" It was a job pitch she frequently made, and she sounded hopeful and eager. "Please? I think I'd be *really* good at crime-fighting."

"I don't believe in sidekicks." He told her honestly. "This is a lonely business, Red. You're on your own. Everyone else is a hostage, a victim, or a distraction. You do your job and you go home. You don't take your work home with you, because you'll never find anyone who would understand it and it'd be too dangerous for them."

"Why?" She sounded baffled by that idea. "It makes more sense to take them along if they're in danger. Loving someone capable of defending themselves would mean that you didn't really have to worry about them as much. They'd be a partner. Someone... you could have fun with."

But Roy was far beyond the days of ever being able to go into the field again. And even if he wasn't, there was no way in the world that he'd work with her.

He'd grown to love that crazy little girl. But... she scared him sometimes.

The things she could do...

The things she sometimes said...

"Red..." He began.

"Nah, that's not who I am today." She assured him, casually reaching over to begin juggling a half dozen glass paperweights, like the dexterity and concentration it took were nothing. "Today, I'm someone else."

"Uh-huh." Roy's hand snapped out to grab each one of the very expensive glass orbs from the air in succession. "I'm used to it."

"I don't really feel like I need to limit myself to stuff like that, Roy." She shook her head, the very picture of mischievous youth and enthusiasm. "When I become a hero, I'm going to do so much amazing shi..." she paused before using the profanity, then quickly chose a more acceptable word so that he didn't reprimand her language again, "...stuff."

Roy carefully arranged the paperweights on the shelf again. "I don't see how, since you refuse to go to the Horizons Academy." He turned to look at her, launching into his standard lecture. "I still think you should get *professional* training if you intend to go into this field."

"Hanging out with those rich pukes?" The girl rolled her eyes. "Fuck that, Roy."

He decided to let her language slide for the moment. "You'd get to march in the store's Thanksgiving Parade if you were a student..." He teased, hoping the thought of the attention and the pageantry would appeal to her.

"Do I seem like a girl who enjoys *walking*? For any reason?" She arched an eyebrow. "Now, if we could take your *motorcycle*..."

The girl loved the old Indian cycle he'd sometimes driven during the war. She seemed to view all of that chrome and white metal as some kind of magic, calling her to the business.

But Roy didn't ride it anymore. It had been parked in his warehouse apartment behind the store for years.

"I've spoken with your foster parents and they say they'd have no problem with you enrolling."

The girl looked almost amused. "Roy? They wouldn't have a problem if I decided to take up crack cocaine and cliff-diving into active volcanoes." She shook her head. "They don't care what I do, I'm just a tax write-off for them. Which is why it's," she looked down at her plastic GI Joe wristwatch, "...4AM and I'm in an empty department store with you and they have nothing to say about it."

"They love you very much." He tried, feeling more like it needed to be said, whether or not it was true.

The girl continued to stare at him. "No, they don't." She countered, sounding accepting of that fact. "But it's sweet of you to lie, Roy. Thank you."

Roy had known the girl for a few years now. And in his opinion, she was amazing. Terrifying at times, but still amazing. He'd always been a loner. He'd never had a family, except his idiot brother. But hanging out with the girl had really shown him what he'd been missing all these years.

He loved that little girl. She was the daughter he'd always wanted.

"I love you too, Roy." She smiled at him, looking touched.

Roy's eyes cut over to her, a sudden twinge of fear slicing through him again. Was she...

"Yeah, I'm psychic today." She bobbed her head, hearing the unspoken question and answering it before he could even finish it. "It's pretty cool, huh?"

Roy didn't think it was cool. The girl's powers seemed limitless and varied. He always hoped that eventually they'd reach some kind of equilibrium and she'd better understand how to use

192

them, but they were constantly shifting and growing in intensity.

Some days, the abilities were broken and didn't work in their intended ways.

Some days, they were limited to agility and endurance.

Some days, they were truly staggering in their sheer power. Stronger than anything he'd ever seen. Stronger than anything he'd ever *hoped* to see. ...Nightmarishly powerful.

And Roy suspected that sooner or later, she'd develop a power which would endanger her, if not the entire world. Some powers *couldn't* be controlled.

The girl waved away his unvoiced concern. "Relax. I got a handle on this, Roy." She held up her hands to her forehead. "Just... whatever you do... don't think of anything gross or perverted."

Roy's mind immediately followed her suggestion, against his will.

The girl burst out in taunting laughter, utterly enjoying the embarrassing images which she'd caused to unwillingly pop into his head.

Roy made a face at her. "You're not funny, Red." He started off to continue his rounds. "Telepaths shouldn't *ever* read people's minds without permission, unless there's no other choice. There isn't a telepath Cape around who would *dare* to read someone's thoughts on a whim. Having powers is a burden and should be treated with responsibility, even if you only have them for 24 hours."

"I'm *10*, Roy." She reminded him, following along behind him as he walked through the store. "*Recharging my phone* is too big a responsibility for me."

"If you want to be a heroine, that's something you're going to have to work on." He carefully instructed, not for the first time. "It means that you have to put others ahead of yourself. Protect people from each other and themselves. And, most importantly, from you. It's an honor and a heavy burden. It is not a life many people can live. It is often not a happy one."

"Why wouldn't it be happy?" The freckles on her tiny nose moved as her face scrunched up in confusion. "Everyone loves a hero."

"Not so much." Roy shook his head. "Best to do the job and go home. That's the only way you can be a hero and be happy. When you start internalizing the things you see and the mistakes you make... nothing good comes from that. Just madness, hate, and misery."

"So is that what you do?"

Roy's mind thought back on his life, recognizing that a lot of it was horrible.

He'd been engaged once. A beautiful woman named Melissa, who brought joy with her everywhere she went. It was impossible to see that woman and not fall in love with her. She ran a charming bed and breakfast out of an old Victorian house on the outskirts of Washington DC. And Roy had loved that woman with *everything* in him. Everything he had was her.

He'd come home from one of his missions, to find Melissa missing. He had searched the entire house and hadn't found a sign of her. Talked to her family and all of her friends, and no one knew where she was.

Hours later, he'd gone into the kitchen... and found that a villain named "8-Pints" Potts, had broken into that same B&B... and murdered Melissa. He'd stripped her body and stuffed it into Roy's refrigerator as a message to him. It had...

"Holy shit!" The girl's eyebrows soared in amazement. "*In the fridge!?!* How does that even work!?! What did he do with the food to make room!?!"

Roy looked down at the ground. "Please stay out of my head, kid."

She nodded, looking shell-shocked. "Sorry, Roy. It's just..." She trailed off. "I'm sorry about your girlfriend. I didn't mean to make you sad."

He patted her on the head reassuringly. "It's okay. Sometimes it's okay to be sad, if you're thinking about people you loved that aren't there anymore. Because there are good memories of them too. Life can't ever be one thing or the other. Life has *layers*." He cleared the lump in his throat. "You can't dwell on things though. It's not healthy."

Of course, Roy had spent most of his life dwelling on that event.

He'd never gotten involved with anyone else after that.

The girl arched an eyebrow at him, silently calling him on his unspoken contradiction.

"It's my advice, Red, that doesn't mean I personally follow it." He heaved a sigh, wishing he didn't have to have this talk with her. "Some things... they're hard to walk away from. And once they happen, there's no going back. You live in those moments forever, never able to just move past them. Because some horrors... they'll follow you." He met her eyes again, tone serious. "Don't. Look. Back."

The girl swallowed, processing whatever new terrible imagery she saw in Roy's mind. "Do... do you think I could be a hero one day?"

"I think you can be a hero right now, if you want."

She instantly brightened. "Really?"

"Yes. By being the kind of person you'd want a hero to be. Helping people who need help. Donating your time to worthy causes. Trying to understand, rather than…"

The girl made an impatient sound, like she was bored with his lecture. "I mean a *real* hero."

"Let me tell you something: it's easy to throw your weight around when you've got powers. And yeah, the fighters get the headlines. The guys duking it out with trans-dimensional threats and blowing apart asteroids with one punch. But there is nothing on earth more heroic or challenging than helping people at a community level. Going out there and interacting with them on days when the world *isn't* ending. Sometimes a person's having the worst day of their lives, but the city goes on without noticing because that crisis isn't related to a world-destroying emergency. A hero is someone who listens to their fears and helps them overcome them, even if they have nothing to do with giant robots or the 'Demonic Comet.'"

"I think I want to be the 'fighting giant robots' kind." She broke the news to him. "Sorry."

"As I said, it's not a life for everyone." He admitted. "People love the ego boost of knowing that they're the toughest. But you should only ever fight to *save* people. That's the only reason to do it. You shouldn't fight to prove that you're the best at fighting. And if you can get by without fighting at all, then that's what you should do. But some people, they just want to see the adulation on the children's faces and stand in the spotlight, after some brutal battle. But the one in the spotlight is often blinded. It's the man in the shadows who can get the most done. He's the one who can see the best. See what's hidden."

"Is that why you were all 'super-secret government stuff'? I don't think I'd like that." She waved a dismissive hand. "You weren't even in the Lovers of Liberty. No one in the city even knows who you are now. But if you had fought a five-hundred foot squid on Ellis Island or a giant robot thing? With the whole city watching? No one would *ever* forget that."

Roy tested the lock on the front door, using his flashlight to ensure that the outer lobby was still empty. "I've seen a lot of fights. Watched a lot of powerful people kill things because they could. Because they wanted to. It made them feel good. Honestly, I don't even remember half of their names now." He paused in his tracks.

"...But during the war, I watched a private run out into a mine field and carry back the mangiest dog you've ever seen. Gave it the last swallow of water in his canteen. I *know* that man's name. All these years later." He nodded, silently saying a prayer for the man's soul. "Most heroic thing I've ever seen. *That* was something worthy of remembering."

"What happened to him?"

Roy looked down at the floor. "He got shot on the way back with the dog, fifty feet from safety. He died the next day."

"And that doesn't tell you something about that particular brand of heroism?"

"I know he helped something weaker than himself and was willing to put his own life on the line. He did what was right, no matter the consequences. To me, that's heroism. It's about the act, not about the outcome. God is in the process, not the result. It's not the kind of heroism that gets headlines or wins medals, but it's heroism all the same." He nodded at the truth of his own words. "Helping people to your own detriment. Following the rules of your own conscience, no matter the result. Being willing to listen, rather than hating." He met her eyes. "Do good deeds because they're the right thing to do. If they're not the right thing to do, don't do them, no matter the outcome."

"I think that's crazy. And stupid." She snorted at the idea. "Why would I want to be a heroine who followed *rules*? I'm never doing anything like that."

"If you're after glory, there are better careers. This one is usually thankless. And painful. You have to earn it. You have to struggle for it. You don't know what it is to hit someone unless you've been hit yourself. If it's just handed to you or if you're just so spectacularly powerful that you can do it all, that's a very dangerous thing. If it's all easy, then nothing means anything. And if you're capable of anything, then you could be capable of *anything*. There are a lot of very easy to cross moral lines in this business and not all of them are marked."

"The job description is 'fighting evil,' it's not that hard."

"Yes, it is." He nodded his head. "Evil is not always readily apparent. Sometimes it looks just like everyone else, hiding in plain sight. Silently hating the world." He met her eyes again. "Hate is one of the untamable elements of life. No hero or heroine can stop it forever. You can fight evil. But you can't beat it all. This job is Wack-A-Mole, you can only try to stop it when it next appears. We have no more hope of stopping hate completely than a fireman has of stopping the element of fire from ever appearing again." He swallowed, remembering a thousand battles and a million scars. "It wears you down, over time. But being a hero means never letting it *keep* you down."

The girl rolled her eyes again. "Whatever, Roy. Everything with you is always so complicated. You're always looking for reasons why things can't be simple." She started off towards the rear of the store and the kitchenette in the small apartment he used. "What'd you cook for dinner today? Hopefully something good."

"There's no such thing as 'simple,' Red." He called after her. "The world's problems are multifarious; they can't ever be solved entirely, no matter who you beat up or what powers you have."

She turned around to walk backwards, spreading her arms wide. "If the world's problems are so varied, maybe the world just needs a heroine with a different power set each day." She pointed at him, smiling. "But I'm *still* not going to the Horizons Academy, old man. Forget it."

Roy watched her walk away, shaking his head in amused resignation.

That girl was already so headstrong, and she still watched cartoons. He was genuinely afraid of what would happen once she grew up.

One of his joys in life was watching that little girl interact with the world. And his greatest fear was that she'd...

He cut the thought off in his head before it fully formed, just in case she could read his mind from the break room.

Roy had lost his brother Hector to darkness. His brother had long ago become a super-villain, dedicating himself to being "The Roach," a madman who kept trying to destroy the world.

Roy was constantly afraid that he'd lose the girl to that kind of life too. And he knew all too well that if the girl ever *really* wanted to cause destruction and death... she'd be faaaaar more effective at it than Hector had ever been.

Roy made his way to the back of the store, checking the rear doors.

He loved his brother and the girl, but...

The door he was checking unexpectedly swung open when he pressed against it, the lock having been broken. Roy stared down at it in confusion, his nightly routine interrupted and his brain not yet caught up to that fact.

He walked through the door and out into the alleyway beyond, fully expecting to find another teenage addict searching for something easy to steal in the store. He found them out here all the time and it wasn't a big deal. It usually cost him a few bucks to buy them a meal and get them into treatment, but...

"Hello, Killroy."

Roy recognized the Agletarian accent immediately. He spoke three dozen languages. Agletarian was one of the shit ones. And it was the only one he *always* listened for, because he knew that he'd one day hear it again.

The bullet struck him before he even saw the men in the rain-drenched alley, slamming into his chest and knocking the breath out of him.

Sadly, Roy had long ago ceased wearing the body armor he'd incorporated into his white uniform. He stumbled forward, hand sliding along the rough brick wall to his left.

In front of him, two men appeared from the shadows. They were dressed in suits and Roy didn't need to be told who they were or what they wanted.

"*Where'd you hide it, Killroy?*" The man on the left asked, gun still leveled at him.

The men had miscalculated though. They obviously assumed that Roy possessed some kind of invulnerability or enhanced durability. Sadly, that was not the case. The only real powers Roy had ever possessed related to strength and agility. The rest of it was just a costume and memorable mask.

They'd just shot an old man in the chest, and the results would be the same as shooting anyone else.

He staggered forward, tripping on weakening legs, and fell into the icy puddle which filled the center of the alley.

The men swore, recognizing their mistake. They'd just killed the hero they'd been sent here to interrogate.

Part of Roy thought that was pretty funny. If it hadn't ended up with his death, it would have almost been worth it to see their faces.

He coughed, flecks of warm blood spattering his face and then being washed away by the cold rain.

It wasn't fear that he was feeling. He was an old man and he wasn't afraid of death. No, he just felt... sad.

He had failed.

He'd worked his whole life to prevent bad things from happening to good people. To try to make the world a better place and keep people from killing each other over senseless things. To give them a symbol, seemingly everywhere, letting them know that they

198

were not alone in their struggles and pain. That other people cared about them and were their brothers.

He'd tried to make the world a better place.

But in the end... he had failed. He had failed in the worst way possible.

And there was no one left to prevent bad things from happening to him. Or to others.

And it would get so much worse.

The door to the store swung open again. "Roy?" The girl called into the night. "Are you..." She stopped in her tracks, meeting his eyes and instantly recognizing what was happening.

The alley was entirely silent except for the sound of the rain pouring down and Roy's labored gasps for breath.

He gave the girl a small nod of his head, as a sign of respect for who she was and what he knew she could do. And as a goodbye to a big part of his life. Certainly the thing he was most proud of, anyway. The part he loved, more than anything.

"It'll be alright..." He whispered softly to her, feeling himself already going home to Melissa. "It'll... be... alr..." He slumped over onto the wet concrete, the pain now gone. He met the girl's eyes from his position, as his vision grew dimmer. "Don't..." He mumbled to her weakly, trying not to cry. "Please don't..."

He had walked on the moon...

****

She stared for a long moment at the still body of the man she considered her real father, then stumbled back to huddle next to one of the dumpsters. The action caused the metal to creak and groan though, a noise the killers would certainly hear, if they hadn't already seen her exit the store.

Whoever the men were, they'd killed Roy and they would certainly come for her next.

She had no idea what to do. But for the first time in as long as she could remember, she was terrified.

Something moved in front of her and she looked up to see a darkened figure standing over her. The young man stepped into the flickering light of the overhead lamp mounted on the exterior of the building, casting shadows on his dark face. He was older than she was. And he was holding a gun.

Unfortunately, she recognized him. Even without her powers today, she would have been able to identify the man.

He tilted his head to the side upon seeing her again. "Hello, child."

She blinked up at him. "Hello, Rondel." She choked out, trying to sound more confident than she was. "I should have known you'd show up. But I thought I was finally *rid of you*."

"I'm rather hard to kill, child." He told her flatly. "Run all you like, but I'll find you eventually. I'll *always* be back."

"So I've noticed." She nodded, hot tears still streaming down her face, unnoticed. "Evil never dies."

A sinister smile crossed his face. "Too bad the same couldn't be said for the old man."

She bit her lower lip to keep from sobbing again. Rondel was so mean! He didn't have to be that mean!

Her hands balled into fists, preparing to hit him.

Rondel rolled his eyes. "Oh, come now. We can't have that, now can we? You need to make your peace with this now, because you're not really going to have too many more opportunities again." He gestured with the gun. "Sadly, you'll be leaving us shortly."

She met his harsh gaze defiantly. "I'm not afraid of you."

"Do you think the dinosaurs looked into the night skies with fear as they beheld the tiny spot of light on the horizon which heralded the comet which destroyed them?" He asked her calmly. "If 200 million Europeans had watched as a single flea was carried to their shores on the back of a rodent, do you believe they would have had even a *glimmer* of fear that it would bring with it the Black Death and the destruction of their lives?" He shook his head. "No. The weak and stupid never know enough to fear the small things which bring their deaths. Because they're weak and stupid."

"Maybe." She stood up, her legs feeling like jelly. Roy had taught her to stand up to bullies though, even ones as scary as Rondel. "But I'm *still* not afraid of you." She crossed her arms over her chest to show her determination on this issue. "So you know what? You go ahead and do your *worst*."

"You're going to die tonight, child." He sounded almost amused. "You know that, right?"

"Yes. And I don't care anymore."

"That is a very mature attitude." He nodded. "It usually takes people many more decades to understand that life is shit and everything is a lie."

"That's not what Roy says." She defended quickly. "Roy says that..."

"The old man is dead." He interrupted. "He's dead and he's

not coming back."

"*Because of you!*" Her hands balled into fists again, her teeth gritting in fury.

"Yes." Rondel nodded. "He is not the first, and he won't be the last. So, you have a choice to make: you can die here with him or you can come with me."

She pointed at the other men, who were making their way towards them. "What about them? I can't just…"

"I can handle it." He told her with utter confidence. "If you agree to come with me, I will kill them both right here and we'll walk away. We will walk away and we will never come back."

"You're *with* them!" She shouted in indignation.

"I'm with no one but me. Ever." Rondel lowered the gun. "And I can take you far away from here, where I'll show you everything I know about protecting what's yours." He knelt down in front of her so that they were eye to eye. "This life is nothing but a competition to be the killer or the victim. That's all it is. Capes, and villains, and soldiers, and death rays… All of that is a distraction. Fuck the rules, I can show you how to *get* what you want. *Do* what you want. *Kill* who you want. I can show you how to master chaos and use it to *rise*." He pressed the gun to her forehead. "Or I can kill you right here and you'll never have to deal with this pain, girl. I'll give you a choice."

She turned to look at Roy's fallen form, then at the gunmen who were still walking towards her.

Hate, and fear, and an unbridled rage filled her. She wanted these men punished. She wanted someone to teach them a lesson. Even if that someone was just as bad as they were. Even if it was someone *worse*.

"If… if you kill them, I'll go with you." She promised softly. "They… they killed my father. If you make them bleed, I'll do whatever you want."

"Once you do this… I'll *own you*, kitten. Do you understand?" He met her eyes. "You will be *mine*. Body and soul. Simply an extension of my will. I won't be letting you go. And there will be no escape."

She was silent for a beat, then firmed her jaw again. "As long as they're dead and you made them suffer for what they did… I don't care what happens to me."

"Excellent." Rondel started towards the men, preparing to *slaughter them*. "You know, I think this is going to be the beginning of a beautiful partnership, Kitten."

Chapter 12

"ALICE HAD GOT SO MUCH INTO THE WAY OF EXPECTING NOTHING BUT OUT-OF-THE-WAY THINGS TO HAPPEN, THAT IT SEEMED QUITE DULL AND STUPID FOR LIFE TO GO ON IN THE COMMON WAY."

- Alice's Adventures in Wonderland

PRESENT DAY

It wasn't that Oz's apartment was uncomfortable, it was more like it wasn't really there at all. She'd seen model homes that looked more lived in. The entire space was so... empty.

Everything was glossy white plastic and steel. It was like an Apple iPhone had thrown up everywhere.

Mull had no experience with such an empty and vaguely uncomfortable space. It wasn't that it made *her* uncomfortable, it reminded her of Oz so that would have been impossible, just that it was the space's primary feeling. It was like the apartment *itself* was telling you that it was uncomfortable, asking for your help. Begging for it.

This apartment was like walking through Oz's mind. It was pristine and weird and looked expensive. You knew instantly that it was someplace you weren't supposed to be. There were doormen and locks and rigid social structures which kept someone like Mull out of somewhere like this.

Mull... kinda liked it.

It was weird and like walking through an alien landscape, but she liked it all the same.

Sadly, the man himself had gone to check in on Wyatt an hour ago, which meant that Mull was currently in the apartment with what she definitely considered her B-team of bodyguards and undoubtedly soon-to-be-kidnapped friends.

Holly watched Mull suspiciously, like she wasn't entirely sure who she even was.

"Why are you staring at me?" Mull finally asked, trying not to roll her eyes.

"I just realize that I know nothing about you."

"You never know anything about me." Mull reminded her. "Fuck, *I* don't know anything about me. That's kinda the nature of my powers. 'Me' changes every day."

"Coke or Pepsi?" Holly demanded, quizzing her.

"Black Pony Scotch."

"Han or Luke?"

"Vader." Mull made a face. "But not the prick-y Hayden version."

"Blaine or Duckie?"

"James Spader."

"Fuck yeah!" Holly nodded in agreement, obviously pleased that someone else understood the intricacies of *Pretty in Pink*. "Now I remember why I like you."

"How could anyone forget why they liked *me?*" She was mystified by the mere idea. "I'm amazing. I'm like the fucking *messiah* of cool bitches and awesome shit. Little girls everywhere should be cosplaying as me while attending 'Cool Bitch Con' each year."

"You *are* the only person I know who's ever had a swordfight while snowboarding." Holly admitted, beginning to casually flip through a mail-order catalog of mysterious European antiseptics, which Oz had laminated for some reason, undoubtedly to keep away horrible germs he claimed covered everything.

"...In Florida." Mull added, pleased with the way that whole job had worked out.

"Although, I still don't understand why you're here." Holly thought aloud. "I mean, I get that some people are trying to kill you, so you're lying low and all, but why *Oz*?" She sounded mystified. "Why not stay at someone else's place? Hell, you could come stay with my family. We're much stronger than *Oz*," Holly said the name with bewilderment bordering on distaste, "and we're not so weird."

"Because I don't trust them." Mull said flatly.

"Ouch." Holly took on a feigned insulted tone. "That hurts, Mull."

"I trust Oz." Mull continued. "I am absolutely sure of who Oz is. And I am equally sure that he will do whatever he has to do to keep me safe."

"Do you *need* him to keep you safe?"

"Hell, no." Mull snorted at the idea. "But I like it, all the same. And it keeps him in my sight at all times." She was silent for a moment, a million nightmarish images whirling through her head. "Do you have any idea what Ronnie would do to Oz if he got his hands on him?"

"I think Oz could hold his own." Holly announced after a moment. "It's always the quiet ones that are the most evil, you ever notice that?" She turned the page in her book. "Oz is unstable. I mean, I know you like him for some strange reason, but he's got this sheen of twitchy, awkward... *niceness* which is perpetually on the verge of falling away. The guy is always like ten seconds away from going completely nuts. Even just standing there, he's... unsettling."

Mull nodded. "I find that so compelling."

"Yeah." Holly pursed her lips. "I kinda do too. Huh. Well, the point remains the same. He's... damaged."

"Name me one person we know who isn't."

Holly's eyes cut to Lexie, who was giggling like a schoolgirl over something one of the cartoon pandas on the laptop screen was saying.

"Lexie doesn't count." Mull flipped her hand dismissively. "I don't think she's even human. She's like Amy, she comes from the distant and alien planet called 'Nice.'"

"Amy is my favorite Disney princess." Holly agreed. "But I'd want her doll to have a sparkly-ier dress, obviously."

Mull calmly continued to survey her surroundings. She'd arrived last night and had fallen right to sleep. Oz had insisted that she take the apartment's lone bedroom, so she didn't really get a chance to look around until the morning.

Now, she was standing in the middle of the most Oz-ian space she'd ever seen, holding onto one of his bed pillows. She'd accidentally drooled on it in her sleep and now she was in search of a washing machine, because she didn't want to watch the man's horror at seeing that she'd despoiled something so clean and ironed.

Sadly, she'd yet to find one in the apartment or the hall outside. She was guessing that Oz simply bought new things rather than washing things once they'd been used. Which was so incredibly wasteful and crazy that as soon as she thought up that idea, she knew it had to be true.

There were only two things on the walls of the entire apartment: a poster of a mid-century advertisement for coffee, and a movie poster of The Lone Ranger on horseback, speeding after a runaway train. On the caboose, a damsel was reaching out for the masked hero, pleading for rescue.

"Oz doesn't even drink coffee." Mull thought aloud, looking

at the smiling ginger-haired woman in the ad in confusion. "I don't get it."

Holly looked up from her magazine. "You know what he drinks?"

"Everyone knows." Mull shrugged. "The man drinks hot water. No flavoring, just plain water. That's so insane the entire world would take notice of it." She shook her head in amazement. "Just thinking about it... hot water!?! *What the actual fuck!?!*"

Holly tossed the magazine away and pulled a book out of her bag. "That's nuts, yeah."

Mull watched the magazine pinwheel through the air and almost let out a gasp, afraid that the magazine would break something Oz loved. But then she remembered that you could play a round of fucking Rollerball in here, complete with the motorbikes, and not hit anything. Still, Oz would freak out about the magazine on the floor, and he was already upset enough.

She hurried over to pick it up and return it to its overly complicated storage container, before Oz saw it.

Holly silently watched her for a moment, looking disgusted. "Is this who you are now? Someone who cleans her man's apartment while he's away?"

"I don't think it'd be possible for a steam cleaning service to make this apartment any more spotless than it already is, Holl, the man literally vacuums *four times a day*. I'm just trying to be a good houseguest." Mull defended. "And... and he's not 'my man.'"

"He's chasing after you like he's Cookie Monster and you've got chocolate chips in your panties." Holly arched an eyebrow. "That makes him your man, assuming you want him."

"Oh, he is not!" Mull rolled her eyes. "He's a perfect gentlemen."

Holly made a disappointed sound. "How boring."

Mull turned in a circle again. "Where does he keep his stuff?" She gestured to their surroundings. "You know? Like his supply of shirts that don't quite fit right and his broken DVD players that he might need one day for some reason." She spun in a circle again, looking for hidden closets or shelves. "His *stuff*?"

"Maybe he doesn't have any."

"That's so sad." She considered that for a moment. "We should buy him some."

Holly looked up at her in amazement. "You want to buy junk to put in his closet while he's gone?"

"I'm not saying that. I don't think 'things' equal happiness,

206

just that people usually have them anyway."

Holly snorted at that idea. "Sweetie, if things don't make you happy, you're buying the wrong things."

Mull pointed at the end table. "The man has a rotary phone." She gestured to it more emphatically, just in case Holly had overlooked its presence in the room. "How is that still a thing? *Why* is that a thing!?! They don't even make those anymore! I don't think they even *work* anymore!"

Holly opened her mouth to reply to that, but then paused, looking confused and uncertain about the object.

"He's got like a dozen different kinds of lettuce in his refrigerator." Mull gestured to the kitchen, continuing to list all of the many reasons why Oz was crazy. "What the hell is up with that?"

Holly frowned in confusion. "How many kinds of lettuce does one man need?"

"I know!" Mull spread her arms wide. "They all taste the same! *Like lettuce!*" She gestured to the apartment's only other room. "And he's got a whole little area over there filled with nothing but wrapped presents!"

That got Holly's attention. She vaulted over the modern-looking couch and ran for the gifts in question, reappearing with several of them.

Mull opened her mouth to object, but Holly had already ripped the first one open.

Holly stared down at the object in confusion. "A Darci doll." She looked up at Mull. "Does Oz collect toys? Because... he doesn't seem cool enough for that."

Mull shrugged helplessly, unable to explain the man's mind.

The next box was a "Happy Retirement" picture frame, and the final one contained a woman's feather hat.

They both stared at the objects, completely mystified.

Mull shrugged again. "I have no idea why he has all of this." She set about cleaning up the wrapping paper. "We sell this shit at the store, but I don't know why Oz would buy it."

"Maybe he's so unloved and alone that he buys things for himself? But then... doesn't open them?" Holly guessed. "That's so sad and creepy. And displays a really shitty gift-giving ability, you'll need to watch out for that if you want to continue this relationship with him." Holly gave up opening the gifts, which was *really* saying something about their quality, since Holly *LOVED* opening presents more than basically anything else in the world. "Oz is one of the weirdest people I've ever met." She flopped back down onto the couch. "You should introduce him to my brother E.N., I bet they'd get along *famously.* He's creepy and obsessive too."

"Oz... he has a few quirks, but I think he's really coming out of his shell lately."

"The only time I've ever seen him have any fun is when he's with you, I'll give you that." Holly went back to her book. "He was almost normal in Tijuana with us."

"What a delightful trip that was." Lexington added, turning away from the TV show she was watching on the laptop. "Such a beautiful country."

Mull flopped down into one of the chairs, which was covered in a disposable and undoubtedly sterile plastic covering.

They could perform fucking brain surgery in this room. Using nothing for the scalpel but the sharpness of the hospital corners on Oz's bed sheets. He'd somehow managed to fold those things to the width of one electron!

It was so clean that in his spare time, Oz could assemble microprocessors on the toilet seats.

They could eat off of Oz's floor and it'd literally be cleaner than any dish in Natalie's apartment.

"What am I supposed to do, Holl?" She asked, feeling lost. She didn't know how her situation with Oz could possibly come to a satisfactory conclusion. The man was just... so very, very different than she was.

Holly turned the page in her book, looking more interested in it than in Natalie. The piece of literature was titled "*Sexual Tyrannosaurus,*" and its cover showed the aforementioned dinosaur looming over a bound cavegirl, who was wearing the remains of a tattered cheetah skin and appeared to be on the verge of orgasm just from looking at the vicious creature about to mount her. The tagline promised "When Beauty met Beast, the result was Jurassic *Sparks.*"

Personally, Natalie had no idea how such a relationship could possibly work on a physical level, let alone emotional, since it involved a large extinct lizard, but she wasn't one to judge others for their insanity.

"Forget him." Holl shrugged. "Personally, I think you just need someone to," Holly turned the page in her book, reading aloud a passage, "'*make your womanhood quiver in anticipation of his pulsating carnivorous masculinity.*'" She pondered that for a moment, as if giving the issue serious thought. "That's never happened to me. Maybe I should start dating other species..."

"I've never really thought of dinosaurs as being especially

masculine. Or of them being sex symbols before." Mull pointed to the cover. "To say nothing of the fact that they weren't even *around* when people were. Or that the entire concept is just... gross."

"You're *just* like the other small-minded cave people, girl." Holl looked aghast at Mull's judgmental attitude. "Trying to stand in the way of their love because their timeless reptilian passion threatens your narrow little world." She pointed at the back of the book. "It's right here: '*Passion Knows No Epoch*.'"

Mull ran a hand through her hair. "If it's a narrow worldview to not dream about fucking *Barney,* then I guess I'm narrow-minded."

She paused, now wondering if Oz would freak out that she'd just touched her hair and then one of the sterile and antiseptic surfaces in his apartment. Should she wash her *hands* first? Or the surface of the chair, *then* her hands? Was there some kind of industrial solvent she'd need to clean *everything* with?

"All I'm saying is that 'Tyrannox, the Lizard King' wouldn't be so weird about his girlfriend." Holly turned her page. "And he sure wouldn't live in such a creepy apartment."

"Maybe his cave-girlfriend is fine with it, because she recognizes that it's a complicated pre-historic world, and that he needs her." Mull pointed at the cover. "Maybe she doesn't want to push."

"What the fuck do I care about *her*?" Holly snorted. "I don't give a shit what her story is, I want to read about the lizard." She made a face. "No one reads the book for the girl. Hell, I barely know her name. She's just there to be my generic stand-in and not do anything that pisses me off too much."

"Why don't you read something with an interesting heroine?"

"Because I don't give a shit about the heroine, I just want a possessive and dangerous hero."

"You know what? I was with a 'possessive and dangerous' man for a while. As it turns out, it's not so much fun. I'll take a strong and gentle guy who treats me like his treasure, thanks." Mull decided. "Besides, you would kick the shit out of any 'possessive' man, Holl."

"Well, I also wouldn't want to fight the Predator, but that doesn't mean that I can't enjoy the movie. What I enjoy reading isn't what I enjoy living. If it was, I'd just live it and save myself the four bucks."

Mull considered that for a beat. "I would *love* to fight a Predator. Fuck, that would be cool."

"And I don't deny you that." Holly turned another page, obviously bored with Mull's personal drama. "But wouldn't you rather read about him fucking some innocent little village girl first?"

"Dammit. I probably would." Mull admitted. "I just don't understand the point of your book, that's all. He's a lizard! He doesn't fucking bathe! What would that smell like after he's been feasting on a dead brachiosaur!?!"

Holly eyed her over the top of her book. "You're one of those women who votes for her to choose *Raoul* over the Phantom of the Opera, aren't you?" She shook her head in condemnation. "Sweet baby Jesus, how can you live when you're that boring? Why not just overdose on sleeping pills. I don't read books to see people make good decisions. I want the road less traveled. I want *spectacularly* inappropriate pairings, that make me equal parts uncomfortable and turned-on. I pay my $4 to see a virgin cavegirl get fucked into unconsciousness by a goddamned horny T-rex!" She shook the book at her. "Your problem is that you don't know what awesome is, that's all. None of that boring 'Chick Lit' holding hands bullshit. Nope. This is just the *good stuff*." She tapped one gloved finger on the cover. "Right here. If you wrote your Christmas list, asking for 'awesome shit that's guaranteed to brighten your day,' *this* is what the workshop would deliver. I know that for a fact."

"Your dad leaves people porn under the tree?"

"Only if they've been very good or very naughty." She sounded completely dismissive of Mull's criticisms. "And I'll have you know that this is one of my niece's *favorite* books. I read it to her every time I see her."

"How old is the niece?"

"Seven."

"You should never be around children." Mull deadpanned.

"You sound like my idiot brother now." She turned another page. "Again, Oz and he would really get along."

"I just..." Mull trailed off. "I just don't know what to do."

"Well, what was the last serious conversation about this you had with him?"

"...We talked about my ex, and my crippling mental problems, and I told him we could never be together."

Holly nodded sarcastically. "Smooth. That's the way to win the boy's heart."

Mull made a face, recognizing that was probably true. "How am I supposed to reach Oz?"

"Sex." Holly answered immediately.

"He freaks out about kissing, you really think I can get him into bed without him melting down?"

Holly glanced at her over the top of the book again, looking more interested. "You kissed him?"

"Well... he kissed me."

"Uh-huh."

"And there was some petting going on..."

"Uh-huh, uh-huh..."

"And... then he got all weird and decided he needed to wash his hands."

Holly burst out laughing.

Mull's face darkened. "This is the kind of shit I'd mention in my *13 Reasons Why.*" She deadpanned. "You'd be tape number *one*, bitch."

Holly wiped a tear of mirth from her eye. "He touched you, then went to wash his hands." She burst out laughing again. "Oh, *that's* a move you won't find in any one of these books." She shook the novel at her, then went back to reading. "Oz, Oz, Oz... you're a *treasure*."

"He said it had nothing to do with me, it had to do with the buttons in my elevator." Mull defended, feeling oddly offended on his behalf.

"The oldest excuse in the book." Holly replied sarcastically.

"It's... it's actually kinda sweet, if you think about it."

"You're reaching. It's not sweet, it's creepy and insulting."

"No, he just didn't want me to get dirty."

"See, I'd prefer a man who *likes it* when things get dirty."

"That's not who Oz is." Mull looked down at the floor for a moment, her voice softening. "He's... delicate. He thinks he's very strong, but he needs to be protected. He's fragile, in some ways."

"And boring."

"But he's not."

Holly turned the page. "Your boyfriend is like expensive olive oil, girl: extra virgin."

Mull rolled her eyes. "Oh, he is not."

Holl nodded in certainty. "You can smell it on him." She looked around the apartment. "No sign any woman has ever been here, and he's not *nearly* cool enough to be gay. Which means: virgin. And it makes sense if you think about it. He doesn't like touching buttons in an elevator, I can't imagine he'd like touching too many women."

"Even if that's true, it doesn't make him boring." Mull shook her head. "He's the *farthest* thing from boring you're going to find." She leaned forward in her chair. "He's like... 'Spicy Vanilla.'"

"I don't think that's a thing."

"Well, that's what he is." She nodded. "He seems boring and kinda ordinary on the outside, but he's actually one of the most exciting people you're going to find. He's weird and mysterious and has all of these little quirks that are fun to discover. Oz is special. And I don't mean in an 'everyone is a special gift' bullshit way, I mean he's *genuinely* special. He's better than us."

"Pft. I could take him."

"You know what I mean. He needs someone to protect him. From the world and from himself. Because assholes keep trying to change the little things about him that are unique and cool. They keep trying to make him feel bad about himself."

"I've never noticed Oz to be one particularly interested in changing to be more popular." She turned her page. "In fact, he's one of the most stubborn people I know."

"Good." Mull nodded. "I like him the way he is."

Holly rolled her eyes. "His insanity and pathological fear of germs are definitely swoon-worthy, yeah."

"He killed a man to keep me safe." Mull snapped. "When I was dying in a bed, he was fucking *there*, all night. And he treats me better than anyone in my life has ever treated me. And that's both me *and* Natalie."

Holly made a "Hmm" sound, unable to argue with those points. "I will say that I'd put up with a lot of weird shit if someone looked at me the way he looks at you." She turned the page. "Hell, I'd sleep with *you* if you looked at me that way."

Oz was one of those perfect, conventional, straight-laced guys who seemed to exist only to tell his boring and frigid wife how extraordinary she really was, and to constantly save her from her own stupidity. Oz was going to spend his whole life doing mind-numbingly safe things, without ever really *living*.

He was destined for a lifetime of grotesque suburban normalcy or else living all alone in some kind of germ-free super-fortress.

And Mull wasn't happy with either of those options. She wanted something better for him. She thought he deserved that.

She liked Oz. She liked talking to him. She like being around him. She liked looking at him. She *loved* kissing him.

She found the man incredibly appealing. He was handsome and strong and kind. She found the innocent way he looked at the world so very cute. He was... extraordinary. Paradoxically, someone who she both felt the need to protect and someone who made her feel

212

like stepping behind him and allowing him to save her from herself.

But...

But there was something so sad about Oz, sometimes. He was a man constantly disappointed with himself. Mull looked in the mirror and had no idea who she was. But Oz looked in the mirror and *knew* who he was, he just didn't like what he saw. It was a different and much scarier situation. Mull had never really considered it before.

Mull was a different person every day. If she didn't like herself, she could just wait 24 hours and she'd have another shot at it.

But Oz was stuck with himself. Stuck trying to make do with what he saw as his own weaknesses and failings. There was something very sad about it.

Not that it made him any less attractive, mind you, it just added another flavor to him. A salty nougat center which really set off the otherwise sweet and impossibly appealing treat he represented.

Which... was a rather disturbing and yucky way of phrasing that.

And since when did she use the word "Yucky"?

The fuck was *that* about?

God, she'd be glad to be done with the day and once again become a woman who wouldn't dream of using the word "yucky" in any context.

In any case, she... wanted Oz.

Which meant that she needed to be careful with him. Because not only did it open Oz up to all kinds of horrors her enemies could inflict on him, but... but it also exposed him to her wild shifts in personality.

She could hurt him.

If they got too close, Mull was entirely capable of breaking Oz. He was an ordinary little machine, moving along the track he planned for himself. And Mull could wreck all of that for him.

Mull was chaos.

"Sex... sex complicates things anyway." Mull decided, shaking her head. "And to be honest, I'm pretty sure trying it would just scare him. And I'm not ready for the ego devastation of that. I mean, you're right, the guy can't even operate a light switch without gloves and antibacterial shit. I really can't imagine him confronted with sex. I think that would be awkward for him. And the last thing I need is for him to be skeeved out by me. At the moment... let's just go with 'holding hands' and go from there."

"Wait... so *you're* looking to get involved here?" Holly glanced up at her again. "Or are we just talking what *he* wants?"

"I don't get involved. Ever. It's a point of pride." She said a little too quickly. "Getting involved requires trust, and I don't trust anyone."

"Wasn't I giving you advice on how to win him?" Holly asked, mystified. "I thought I was telling you how to break through his frigid and virginal façade, and get at the lunatic beneath? I'm lost here."

"I'm a complicated woman." Mull shifted in her chair nervously. "We're... we're just having a conversation."

Holly processed that. "And is this a conversation where I'm supposed to tell you what you should do, or a conversation where I'm supposed to support whatever decision you've obviously already made but are pretending like you haven't?"

Mull paused for a beat. "The second one."

Holly nodded. "In that case: I think you're making the right decision, obviously." She pointed at her. "You be you." She took on an inspirational tone. "True love finds a way."

Mull rolled her eyes. "You can dial your fake support back a bit. Keep it believable. I'm 'complicated,' not a moron."

"Ah. Sorry." Holly turned the page in her book. "Misread the room." She crossed her legs, getting back to business. "So you're just looking to hold hands with Oz, like a second grader on the playground because..." She trailed off, inviting Mull to finish.

"Because I like Oz." Mull said flatly. "I really do. And I'll be happy with as much of him as his limitations will allow."

"I just don't understand you sometimes." Holly snorted at the idea. "You need a psychiatrist who likes a challenge, girl."

She ignored that. "I don't want to get involved with Oz in a serious way. Ronnie will kill him." She looked down at the floor. "Ronnie is like a psycho in a slasher film."

"*You're* the one who's a weirdo in a mask." Holly pointed at the calendar on the wall. "And we're approaching a national holiday. Generally speaking, in slasher movies, it's never a good idea to piss off weirdos in masks when a themed holiday is approaching."

"He's... soulless." Mull continued, ignoring Holly's nonsense. "He's going to kill everyone, for absolutely no reason other than hate."

"Well, it's a good thing you're dating a virgin then." Holly decided calmly. "They always live through horror movies."

"Oz is *not* a virgin." Mull made a face at her, then paused, considering the matter. "Okay... he *probably* is, but that's okay. It's kinda sweet, actually."

Holly snorted at that. "It *would* be 'kinda sweet' if he was

214

saving himself for someone special or was merely shy. It's not 'kinda sweet' when it's only because he's too disgusted by women to even look at them."

"I don't care if he's disgusted by other women." Mull shrugged. "Awesome. Thanks for the good news. I don't want him looking at them anyway. I just want him to not be disgusted by *me*."

"Oz is the nicest person I've ever met." Lexie announced, paying attention to the conversation during the commercial break. "He was the only one in the Freedom Squad who ever believed in me."

"He smells like a laundry detergent commercial." Mull thought out loud, dreamily thinking about being so close to him. "Like the good kind, you know? The one that smells like summertime and home?"

"Oh, that's hot." Holly rolled her eyes again. "Shit. I might want him now. I just need to find a full-body condom that'll cover me from head-to-toe, so he won't get terrified by actually touching me."

"Fuck you, Holl." Mull flipped her off. "This is why I don't tell people things and why I wear a mask all the time."

"Sounds like you've got it all worked out now though." Holly turned another page. "Perhaps you two can make gentle and respectful love, then fall asleep watching the 8 o'clock news."

Mull crossed her arms over her chest, feeling pouty and annoyed. "Oh, shut up."

"Personally, you can keep that nonsense." Holly waved the book again. "I want to be *fucked*; completely and thoroughly. Plowed like a snowy road on Christmas Eve. If I haven't passed out from ecstasy, the guy has failed." She snorted in derision. "But with Oz, I think it's more likely that you'll just get bored and fall asleep during the act."

"Out of curiosity, when *was* the last time you had a boyfriend, Holly?" Lexie asked innocently.

The room fell into silence.

Mull held out her hand and then opened it, like she was dropping an invisible mic. "Lexie gets the square on that one."

"I might not be currently dating anyone, but I still understand the male mind." Holly defended.

"Oz already likes me, it's just a matter of the whole physical part." Mull explained.

"Uh-huh." Holly turned the page of her book. "You know what's sexy?"

Mull crossed her fingers theatrically. "Please don't say 'dinosaurs'... please don't say 'dinosaurs'..."

"Not 'dinosaurs' plural, no. That's just ridiculous." Holly scoffed at the idea. "Dinosaurs are utterly monogamous once they find their fated 'Lizard Mate.' Everyone knows that."

"*That doesn't even make sense!*" Mull shouted, pointing at the book. "And even if it did, it still couldn't be a human, because dinosaurs laid fucking eggs! How would that even work if they married a human woman!?!"

"I read one about the Loch Ness Monster and a captive Druid girl once, who was a virgin sacrifice to him. Not to overstate, but I believe it brought meaning to life and made all subsequent works of man and god superfluous. Pretty fucking hot, you know? I'd plug that into my veins if it were possible. Made my insides feel like one of those vintage bubble-lights on a Christmas tree." Holly rearranged her head. "*Totally* holly jolly."

"Have you noticed that all of your books seem to have the same setup?"

"Who are you now? A book critic? Is that your fucking power today?" Holly casually flipped her off. "Sweet baby Jesus, just shut up about all the cool stuff you're too lame to understand, okay? You just sit there and work on how to keep your ex from killing you and how to keep your current boyfriend from vomiting on you during sex because he's a virgin and you disgust him, and let me get back to my story, okay?"

"You're failing the Bechdel Test right now." Mull deadpanned. "I want you to know that."

"The Bechdel Test can blow me." Holly rolled her eyes. "In the real world, I'm free to badmouth or lust after any man I want, and you get to listen to every goddamn word of it. That's a law. What's the point of having girlfriends if you can't complain to them about the idiot guys you know?"

"Companionship?"

Holly waved the book. "That's why I've got *this*, thanks. No offense, but the romantic dramas of 'Danyalayla and Tyrannox, the Dino King' are more entertaining than you. I tolerate you, but this is my *real* friend." She settled down with her book again. "In the sequel, his brother the Carnatorus shows up and there's a threesome. But don't spoil it for me, I'm working up to it. I think the brother is going to be my favorite character." She made a low hum of pleasure. "Ooooh... he's so forbidden and *dangerous*..."

"In all seriousness, Natalie, I think if you like Oz, you two can work things out." Lexie assured her earnestly. "Yes, he sometimes gets weird with his compulsions, but... it's not like he can control them right now. He's sick and we can't blame him for that. He needs treatment. Exposure therapy, an environment of pure safety, that kind of thing." She paused. "I believe that he cares for you a great deal too. And that's something that you two need to work on, whether or not it's hard."

"Like the fact that your psychotic ex will get a sexual thrill out of gutting him in front of you, or the fact that there seems to be an entire country trying to kill you now." Holly added.

Mull spread her arms out in exasperation. "Why are you even here, Holly? Huh!?!"

"I'm reading my book." She reminded them. "I'm thinking about joining the Consortium's Book Club and this is last week's reading. Say what you will about him, but Sydney can recommend one *hell* of a good erotica novel."

They sat in silence for several moments, as Mull considered her situation and felt that it was more and more helpless.

"I just..." Mull heaved another sigh. "I'm wondering if Oz even wants me."

"It's a confusing time for you right now." Lexie said softly. "But I genuinely believe that Oz can help you through that."

"Men aren't confusing." Holly agreed. "I mean, every villainess claims to have the magical ability to 'control men's minds,' but really, the only thing you need in order to have control over men's minds is the ability to make doughnuts while naked." She shrugged. "They're a simple gender."

Lexie frowned over at her. "You make doughnuts while naked?"

"I can do *a lot* of things naked." Holly announced, with obvious pride.

Mull squinted at her. "Are you being serious right now?"

"Not even *I* know." Holly shrugged. "It's all very post-ironic."

"Well, I'm not domestic." Mull said flatly. "So your point is moot."

"Well, then you need to slut yourself up some." Holly suggested. "Show more skin."

Mull shook her head again. "My standard costume is designed to be tactical and as a consequence, it covers my entire body. But when I wear it around, people think I'm hiding who I am or something."

"Generally speaking, most people think that, when you wear a mask at all times and refuse to tell them who you are." Holly took on an exaggerated mystified face, like she sarcastically couldn't understand that reasoning. "Go figure."

"Just because I don't like to put everything I got on display in *my* costume," she gestured at Holly's dress, which accentuated her sexbomb-y build, "doesn't mean that I'm hiding or that it's a safety blanket. It just means that I prefer more utilitarian things."

"Hey!" Holly looked insulted. "My outfit is *very* utilitarian!"

"Low-cut red velvet Santa dresses aren't 'utilitarian' in a fight."

"I'm basically bullet-proof." Holly shook her head. "Not really seeing a need for scratchy body armor." She took on a wizened tone. "Freedom of movement is the most important thing in a fight, to say nothing about my everyday comfort."

"You live at the North Pole, Holl." She argued. "As in: 'subzero temperatures.' Generally speaking, that's also not proper polar attire unless you want to have breast reduction surgery with a little help from *frostbite*."

"Oh, I only live up there sometimes. Hardly at all anymore. I split my time between here and the *South* Pole. And I'll have you know my dress is *lined*."

"That makes all the difference then." She agreed sarcastically. "According to Paige King, that yell-y TV bitch that's not that *other* TV bitch, you're setting a bad example for all the little girls and aspiring heroines out there."

"Yes, because there's nothing more empowering than listening to other people when they tell you what to wear." Holly snorted at that idea. "They're just jealous that I can whoop their asses in heels, that's all. But really, I'm only trying to make it fairer for my victims. If I wore flats all the time, I'd just embarrass them before they died."

"My point is that my costume is plenty sexy on its own." Mull insisted. "I don't have to show skin."

"Up until a few days ago, none of us knew you were a woman, because you're wearing basically the same outfit that an old guy wore during World War II." Holly deadpanned. "That's not really sending out the 'Tell me about it, Stud' vibe you're looking for right now." She shrugged, like the truth was self-evident. "You want to get a present, you gotta leave out the cookies and milk."

"That's possibly your most disgusting and yet somehow confusing Christmas-themed sex metaphor ever." Mull decided. "Wow."

"Yeah, I'm proud of that one too." Holly agreed, looking

pleased. "It really came together, didn't it?" She started eating a candy cane she produced from somewhere. "Besides, since when are you interested in this kind of thing?"

"I think it's part of my personality today."

"Well, that sucks. I'd just stay in bed all day if my mind kept telling me to dress like deceased male veterans from the Greatest Generation, and be unhappy with my body."

"I am perfectly happy with my body," Mull began, "and I don't think..."

The key hit the lock and both Lexie and Mull were instantly on their feet, ready for a fight.

Holly took another sip of alcohol from her gingerbread man shaped flask, and didn't bother to look up from her book.

Oz opened the door. "Is everyone okay?"

"Nothing stirring here, Oz." Holly called. "Just hanging out in the empty warehouse you call a home, trying to find something to do. As it turns out, some days are fit for nothing but sitting around and mentally undressing coworkers." She glanced over at Lexie and frowned. "Of course, it's usually more interesting than this." She shook her head in disgust. "You need a *makeover*, girl."

Oz hurried into the apartment, looking upset about something. "So you haven't been watching this then?"

"Watching what?" Mull frowned.

"You don't own a TV, Romeo." Holly reminded him. "We all tried staring at the place on the wall where one normally would be, but it didn't seem to do the trick. Your wall color is boring too and we quickly tired of the 'Semi-gloss Hospital White' show."

Mull glared at Holly, her temper on the verge of snapping.

Holly winked at her. "Relax. I know what I'm doing."

Oz tapped several buttons on the computer and the screen switched to show a news conference.

Connie Storms, that bitch from the news who wasn't Paige King, was summarizing what appeared to be a press conference with the Agletarians.

And a tall man with mottled orange skin, who appeared to be...

"Uh-oh." Lexie shook her head. "Mack's not going to like that Monty was right about the 'aliens' thing."

"General Skrlj," Connie continued, "the city wants to..."

"Are you fucking kidding me!?!" Mull gasped, staring at the letters on screen. "That's not a name, that's a bad hand at Scrabble."

"We need to hear this." Oz reminded her. "These are the

men who are trying to kill you."

"Well… some of them, anyway." Holly added. "These are just the ones she *didn't* sleep with first."

On screen, the Agletarian general was espousing his crazy ideology, mixed with denials of responsibility for… anything, really.

Apparently, the small assembly was in town for a meeting with the government and was now leaving again. They were going back home. Supposedly.

"I don't understand why Skrlj…" Oz began.

"It's like, Christ, man. Buy a fucking vowel." Mull interrupted, unable to get over that.

"If he's here to kill you, we need to know *why* and how that connects to Mercygiver." Oz continued.

Mull continued watching the screen. "Shiiit… I hope that other guy's not really an alien. I do *not* have a space themed power set today. I'd be utterly useless in space."

"I don't think that's the most important part of this situation, Natalie." Oz shook his head. "The important part is that now your enemy has a name and a face."

Mull snorted at that idea. "He's *not* my villain. He's just some asshole." She waved a hand in dismissal. "My nemesis would be way cooler than that, I'm just saying. He'd somehow be tied into my origin story, not some underling from a country I've never even visited. And his name would be one I could actually pronounce without sounding like a sneeze." She shook her head vehemently. "No, no… fuck him. I refuse to be involved with his idiocy. Let someone else handle it. He can be *their* nemesis, I don't want to be associated with him. I'll wait for the *next* evil power-hungry general guy, thanks." She rolled her eyes. "And why am I watching an info dump about space aliens, anyway? I don't care. I'm changing the channel."

"But they're here to kill *you*!" Oz insisted.

"No, they're not." She shook her head again. "They're just here to…"

General Skrlj turned his head, and Mull's words died on her lips.

"Oooooh, shit." She winced. "On second thought… we might have a problem, yeah."

On the screen, Skrlj flipped his ponytail back over his shoulder.

"That's 'General Ponytail,'" she ran her hand through her hair, "I kinda killed his father and uncles this one time."

"Why?"

"Because the Consortium paid me to."

Chapter 13

"DEAR, DEAR! HOW QUEER EVERYTHING IS TO-DAY! AND
YESTERDAY THINGS WENT ON JUST AS USUAL. I
WONDER IF I'VE BEEN CHANGED IN THE NIGHT? LET ME
THINK: WAS I THE SAME WHEN I GOT UP THIS
MORNING? I ALMOST THINK I CAN REMEMBER
FEELING A LITTLE DIFFERENT. BUT IF I'M NOT THE
SAME, THE NEXT QUESTION IS, WHO IN THE WORLD AM
I? AH, THAT'S THE GREAT PUZZLE!"'

- Alice's Adventures in Wonderland

Oz didn't feel well today.

His skin looked blotchy, probably the result of some sort of cancer. His whole face felt puffy, which could indicate either an allergy to radio waves, or perhaps encephalitis. He had a sore throat. The big toe on his right foot felt like it was going numb. And his vision felt foggy.

But above and beyond all of that, he felt bad because of the Natalie situation.

Oz was standing at the elevator in his building, waiting for Natalie to appear from his apartment.

He'd messed up the day before yesterday. He'd seriously, *seriously* messed up.

Oz was generally used to ending up with nothing, but that didn't mean he liked hurting Natalie.

He had *never* intended her to...

He let out a long sigh.

The problem was his own mind, and he knew it. No matter if he was thinking about her or not when he became preoccupied with washing his hands, it wasn't something he should have been thinking about while kissing her.

That was completely unacceptable.

He should have been focused on kissing the literal *woman of his dreams*. But instead, thanks to his own innumerable mental problems, she was now insulted and angry. And rightly so.

Oz had no idea how to go about fixing that, because the root cause of the problem remained the same. He was still morbidly aware of how many horrible microscopic monsters were clinging to every surface of the world.

There was no turning that off.

And as long as he was aware of it, it was very difficult to subject Natalie to it.

If she could see the germs and bacteria which clung to his hands, she'd be as disgusted by him as he was. There was no way she would *ever* let him touch her. But that didn't exactly help his case any.

To be honest, he preferred her being angry with him, to her being repulsed by him.

He leaned against the wall, which he cleaned three times a day with bleach, recognizing that for the first time, his life was going to be destroyed by his own inability to do what needed to be done. He needed to stop with his obsessions and rituals. It was the only possible solution.

But recognizing the solution was a far cry from completing it.

And Oz wasn't sure he was strong enough for that. He'd tried before, but... It always ended in total failure, and then the rituals and obsessions ended up getting worse as a result. He had them semi-under control at the moment. Trying to change that, in any way, was very dangerous. It could lead to him being unable to leave his apartment at all. Again. Or something even worse.

Oz's mind scared him. He wasn't sure what kinds of things it was capable of doing to his life if he pissed it off.

It was, after all, evil.

A moment later, the door to his apartment opened and Natalie exited.

Oz's mouth hung open in shock, and suddenly his own obsessions and self-diagnosed ailments were the *furthest* things from his mind.

"I am not Multifarious. Today I am," Natalie paused dramatically, "*Jungle Lass*."

Oz was really too taken aback by her attire to respond to that in any way other than an awkward nod.

Her costume today consisted of a bikini made of scraps of leopard skin. Attached to her waist was a flint dagger, and she wore a necklace and anklet of Dentalium shell and crocodile teeth. She didn't bother wearing shoes. Just where she'd gotten her outfit and the accessories was anyone's guess. Oz had long since stopped asking how Natalie was able to do the things she did. She was absolutely amazing, so it only made sense that she'd be able to put together a cohesive and detailed costume every day, no matter how many supplies she had access to.

Either way, the costume showed FAR more skin than any he'd ever seen her wear before, and he was having a difficult time concentrating. She was basically wearing a bra and loincloth, for God's sake. The Kilroy emblem was drawn in red pigment along the curve of her breasts.

He fought a losing battle to keep from staring at the design and the soft skin it was displayed on.

All in all, Poacher had been right: the woman's breasts *were* spectacular. Not that he couldn't also detest the man for noticing them and commenting on it, just that Oz was completely unable to disagree with him.

He wasn't a man given to sexual fantasy, but they were the stuff of every dream he'd ever had.

Oz wasn't entirely sure how the woman's powers worked, but he couldn't help think this was all an effort to torture him by showing him the glorious body his own weakness had robbed him of.

It was a torture he richly, richly deserved... and was rather enjoying. It made him harder than he could ever remember being in his life, and he knew there was absolutely nothing he could do to alleviate that, but he was still enjoying her costume *immensely*.

"So... what can you do today, Nat?" He finally mumbled, once he'd regained the power of speech.

"I have enhanced agility and strength today, and I can talk to animals in their secret language." She pressed the elevator button and stepped inside when the doors opened. "And wrestle alligators."

"If you can talk to them, why are you wrestling them?"

She pursed her lips. "Good question." She exited the elevator when it reached the ground floor. "I'll have to ask them."

Oz's gaze slid down her body to settle on her rear, which was *barely* covered by the animal skins she was wearing. The fabric swayed back and forth with each movement of her hips, and Oz found it captivating. Her flesh looked firm and soft and challenged everything he knew in his orderly mind. It made him have dark impulses, things he'd never thought before about anyone. He wanted to feel that woman's ass against him, while she made that soft breathy sound again, his body inside her...

He cleared his throat, trying to regain his composure, and then realized how absurd her costume was. "You realize it's 38 degrees today, right?"

"Cheetah fur is very warm." She told him simply. "It's no red velvet Santa dress, but still warm."

"Uh-huh." He seriously doubted that, but didn't really care. If she said she was comfortable, he certainly wasn't going to tell her what she could and couldn't wear. It was her body. Oz's only concern was her health and whether or not he'd actually be able to concentrate on anything except staring longingly at her amazing curves today.

He seriously doubted that too. He'd only been in her presence for five minutes so far, and it was already physically painful.

It was kinda fun, actually.

Normally, the things which tortured Oz were horrible and disgusting. It was an odd novelty to be tortured by something he actually *wanted.*

Oz had never really... well... gotten to ogle someone before. Granted, it was still inappropriate, given the fact that Natalie was undoubtedly still mad at him, and the fact that they were in a very serious life and death situation, and the obvious fact that she was a co-worker, but Oz had simply stopped caring about that.

He was going to thoroughly enjoy looking at Natalie's body. Because a few days ago, he'd almost lost the ability to ever see her again. And because he *wanted* to look at her. He almost never got to do what he wanted to do.

Thus, Oz fully intended to admire the woman's curves until his eyes bled. Or she asked him to stop. And since neither of those things had happened yet, he was going to drink her in, every single time he thought he could get away with it.

That woman was... Well, it was like Oz had lived his entire life in darkness, and Natalie Quentin was the sun. He just wanted to *bask* in her.

She was strong and smart and opinionated... She was beautiful in a way that made him change the way he looked at the world. She did things he would *never* do and dealt with situations in ways that he would never even consider...

But... but Oz's entire life was trash. And she was an absolute treasure. He would happily spend the day just looking at her, even if he knew he could never touch.

"So, what's on the schedule today?" She asked conversationally.

Oz would have preferred to keep her safe in his apartment, with several brick walls between her and everyone who could possibly try to hurt her. But Natalie had informed him that his apartment was the most boring place she'd ever been.

Which, to be fair, was probably true.

She was exciting and dynamic and fun.

Oz was boring.

Even he knew it.

It was one more reason why he recognized he didn't deserve her. And never would.

In either case though, she had demanded to come with him when Oz got a call asking for assistance this morning.

That didn't mean that Oz had to like it though. In his mind, all of this was a needless risk. He *knew* better than this. But he also knew that no one won an argument with Natalie. His partner was obstinate and absolutely unstoppable once she got going.

"There might be a lead." He ushered her down the street, trying not to get angry at the men who also took conspicuous notice of her attire. That would be ridiculous and petty and possessive, none of which Oz was.

Still, whatever the men saw in his eyes when he glared at them, they quickly fled the scene.

Oz should have felt bad about that. It wasn't in the least bit heroic. He recognized that. But he didn't feel bad. At all.

Those men should have *known better*. Especially since Oz was obsessive enough about the neighborhood to know where each and every one of the men lived.

As far as he was concerned, Natalie Quentin was *his*. He'd been the one who fought to keep her alive in that hospital, and now that he had her in hand, there was no way in hell he was going to let some stranger on the street enjoy her.

Which... sounded *dangerously* possessive and was in no way how Oz considered himself. But still seemed to be how he felt.

That was possibly his own innate evil once more rearing its head.

Or perhaps it was the fact that the woman was *fucking amazing!*

He frowned, unused to using profanity, even in his own mind.

As he pondered the bizarre situation, his eyes lazily settled on her rear again. And he instantly felt much calmer. There was something about Natalie that simply made him feel better, and always had. As it turned out, her wearing next to nothing simply made him feel better, faster.

It was like science. But with legs that went on for miles.

Which, again, was something he should feel bad about dwelling on, but didn't. Being evil had its advantages.

"A lead on Mercygiver or a lead on the Agletarians?" She asked.

"I'm not sure yet." He admitted. "Some of the other Consortium members are there now."

"Ah." She nodded.

Then they fell into awkward silence.

And when even *Oz* recognized that it was awkward, you *knew* it was awkward.

"I'm trying, Natalie." He said softly. "I'm not a well man, and I do things sometimes that I wish I didn't. But..."

"Hey, did you see the pics of the new Vasnetsov D-38?" She cut him off, blatantly changing the subject. She made a low whistle. "That rifle is *dreamy*. Like, 'I want to find that behind my door in *Mystery Date*' kind of dreamy."

"No, I didn't see it." He cleared his throat. "What is it?"

She made a face. "I need more chick friends." She snapped her fingers. "Holly." She decided. "If *Holly* were here, *she'd* understand lusting after a sexy piece of deadly artillery like that. Because she's *normal*. Or Poacher."

"You want Poacher to be one of your 'chick friends?'"

"He kinda already is, actually. Dude likes more girly shit than *I* do. And I carry a friggin' *Hello Kitty* umbrella."

They fell into silence again.

Oz's attention was drawn to a young couple sitting inside a coffee shop. They were draped all over each other, casually holding hands and giggling, obviously in love. The woman brought their clasped hands to her lips and kissed the back of the man's hand, smiling like he was her every dream brought to life.

And Oz instantly hated them.

They were intimate and casual in a way that Oz recognized he would never be with anyone. They weren't concerned about their own mental health or whether or not they were evil or whether they'd be able to save the woman from a team of assassins.

All they cared about was each other and their love.

They were everything that Oz had never had and never would.

And he hated them for that.

"Did you know that there is a layer of our atmosphere which is entirely made up of viruses?" He asked Natalie, trying to sound casual. "The virosphere. They are pulled up there by weather patterns, or formed in the atmosphere itself, and some might even be extraterrestrial in origin. An estimated 800 million of them fall to each square meter of the planet, each day, sometimes after traveling thousands of miles. It's like a rainstorm of pestilence, which never ends." He held out his arms. "And it's falling onto ground that is covered with tens of millions of bacteria, and countless other micro-organisms. A lot of which don't even have names. Scientists did a study and found that 48% of the genetic material collected in the subway system was unidentifiable." He met her eyes. "It's so bizarre and crazy and plentiful, that they've never even seen it before." He tapped his chest. "But I have. I can *feel it.* I can tell you where each and every one of those tiny organisms came from and what they want."

"Does this have a point, or is it just a science lecture?"

"What I'm telling you is that if I'm occasionally distracted or I do things that seem completely crazy, it's not always my fault." He shook his head. "Don't get me wrong, my behavior the day before yesterday was unquestionably out of line and insulting, and I've already apologized and asked for your forgiveness. But I'm trying to help you understand that I'm dealing with a world that you've never even seen. A world that sometimes impacts how I deal with the *actual* world. And I tell you one final time that it isn't you I'm disgusted by touching, but the idea of spreading those kind of repulsive organisms to your perfect skin. It distracts me. But it has absolutely nothing to do with you or how I feel about you." He met her eyes. "To put it another way: if you *knew* your hands were covered in manure, you wouldn't want to start touching my face before you washed them? Because I think that would be the natural impulse. I'd *hope*, anyway."

She paused in the street to process that for a moment, then nodded. "Okay." She started forward again. "Apology accepted, Oz. Don't worry about it."

Oz followed after her, undecided if the matter was truly dropped or if he'd merely been forgiven for a single incident. But either way, he was glad.

As they approached the next corner, the crossing signal started to blink red, indicating that if he was in the midst of crossing that he needed to hurry, but that he shouldn't *begin* to cross. Oz paused to wait out the light, while several people behind him simply hurried across the street despite the warning.

Natalie processed the situation and Oz's refusal to break the law, then nodded sarcastically at him. "Thug life." She teased.

Oz snorted in laughter. "There were 10,437 pedestrian

accidents in the city last year." He reported. "It makes no sense to risk death for a matter of seconds. We can just wait here and play it safe."

"Good morning, OCD!" The man next to them on the corner greeted him cheerily. "Always happy to have a superhero around!"

Natalie arched an amused eyebrow at Oz, obviously unused to dealing with the public in a positive way.

The man looked confused as to why Oz was simply standing on the sidewalk rather than following the crowd across the street though.

Oz pointed at the crossing signal.

The man looked at it, questioningly.

"I'm not wagering my life on the vagaries of New York City traffic." He informed the man. "And there is urine from seventeen different people on the asphalt, which would undoubtedly cause an infection in an open wound from even the slightest injury."

The man stopped in the street, dumbfounded, then glanced at Natalie to see if Oz was serious.

Natalie nodded at the man, sharing his confusion and amazement at Oz's aversion to risk. "He's really fun at parties too." She deadpanned.

Oz waved goodbye to the man, then leaned closer to Natalie, just in case the other man suddenly reversed directions and sprang at her. You couldn't be too careful. He took special care to avoid using his vantage point to look at the woman's cleavage... which was *perhaps* a feat too great to ask from any mortal man. He failed completely at it, his eyes settling hungrily on the globes of flesh hidden behind the tattered fur top, suddenly wanting to bury his face in them.

"Mack and I started a project last month, where we began doing more small-scale heroics in specific neighborhoods, to get to know the people and build stronger relationships." He said to distract himself, gesturing to the surroundings. "I took the blocks around my apartment."

"Which would also include the area around the store." She looked up at him. "Is that a coincidence?"

Oz shrugged innocently, pretending like he'd decided to start a regular patrol around her place of work for reasons *other* than keeping her safe and possibly seeing her more often.

"I know community heroics would go against your antihero methodology, but..." He began.

"I'm not an anti-hero." She corrected, cutting him off. "I'm more like a posi-villain." She paused, frowning slightly. "Wait, what would the antonym of 'anti' be?"

"The original word itself." He informed her. "The opposite of 'anti-hero' would be 'hero.'"

"No, I don't think so. I think the opposite would be 'posi-villain.'" She started off down the street again. "One is a hero who does bad things and the other is a villain who does good things."

"I don't think it works that way."

"I do."

"Okay."

"Oh, you just think you're soooo smart, don't you?"

"I got my GED in prison." He made an uncertain face. "Generally speaking, prison is not somewhere one goes for a quality education."

Natalie opened her mouth to reply to that, but was cut off by the sudden arrival of Traitor. Arn was obviously excited about something, which was rarely good. In fact, it was *never* good. Arn was a horrible, *horrible* person.

"Hey guys." He waved at them, casually pushing people out of the way so that he could get closer to them on the crowded street, paying no attention to the fact that the pedestrians he pushed from the sidewalk were now in the flow of traffic and were desperately trying to scramble back to safety before they were hit. "Quick question..."

"I'm pretty sure the answer is going to be 'no,' Arnold." Oz warned.

"It'll be a 'hard no' from me, almost certainly." Natalie agreed.

Arn looked taken aback by their suspicions. "You don't even know what I was going to ask!" He protested.

"I find that it rarely matters." Natalie rolled her eyes. "In the jungle, you're the kind of monster we'd feed to the crocs."

"You're more fun when you're wearing the mask." Arn made a face at her. "And all I'm saying is that I worked up a whole pitch for the Consumer Products Division the other night, but then you put the kibosh on that by not dying. I was wondering what the chances are that things might change again." He nodded persuasively. "Because a special line of memorial Multifarious merchandise could be a *real* shot in the arm for sales, especially coming as it does at the start of the Christmas shopping season. Black Friday is in a few days, and..."

They both stared at the man in silent amazement.

Arn looked confused. "What?"

"It's just..." Natalie shrugged helplessly. "It's just not even worth it."

Oz opened his mouth to tell the man off, but Natalie pulled him away. "Don't engage, Oz. It won't help. He won't understand."

"What'd I say!?!" Arn called after them. "I'm just trying to sell some T-shirts! If you're going to die *anyway,* you might as well help out the team while you're at it!"

They reached the intersection, where a crowd was gathered, looking across the street to where crime scene tape was set up.

To their left, Julian appeared from one of the Consortium's vehicles and was *instantly* booed by every man, woman and child in the crowd.

"Julian remains as popular as ever." Natalie observed.

"Well, there *is* the fact that he killed Mary Sue, the brightest of stars who shined against the darkness of this world." He paused, making a disgusted face as he recognized that the dead woman's brainwashing was still partially in effect. "Damn. I *hate* that."

"I'm told it'll stop in time." Natalie assured him, patting his arm in comfort. "I'm *still* glad I killed that bitch." Her eyes narrowed in fury. "She should have known better than to use her freaky powers on you." She paused for a beat. "And, you know, everyone else."

Oz looked down at her hand as it remained on his arm, and he felt... good. Like he'd managed to overcome his unforgivable actions the other day, and had recovered.

Natalie was standing next to him, her hand on his arm, and she wasn't wearing very much. All in all, the morning was going better than he ever could have hoped.

Julian reacted to the universal hatred by putting his arms over his head and looking overjoyed, like they were cheering him.

Bridget appeared beside him, laughing at her lover's overblown enthusiasm to being hated so *vehemently.*

He was now, unquestionably, the least popular member of the Consortium of Chaos. And Julian obviously LOVED that fact.

Julian strolled along behind the police crowd control cordon, pointing at people in the crowd like he recognized them or was calling attention to particularly vicious protest signs against him. He was obviously drinking in their hate like it was the sweetest liqueur, and grinning like the star quarterback arriving at prom or wrestling heel entering the ring. Oz had never in his life seen anyone more pleased with himself and the world.

He didn't understand that man sometimes. But he guessed that Julian had felt irrelevant for so long, he was basking in the hatred directed at him by the people Julian had always despised.

It was nice that some people got what they always wanted.

232

Oz was happy for them. Despite the fact he knew he never would.

Bridget gestured to Natalie, and she started towards the other woman.

Oz started to follow her.

"Hey, playboy!" Someone called to him. "Haven't seen you in ages."

Oz turned to his right to spot one of his former teammates from the Freedom Squad, Rembrandt, leaning against the hood of a car, looking bored.

The man had never been one of Oz's favorite people. Which was one of the reasons why he hadn't invited him to join up with the C of C when he'd recruited several of the other not-so-evil members of the Freedom Squad.

Rembrandt hadn't so much sided with the Freedom Squad in its final fight with the Consortium, as it was that he simply called in sick for work that day. He either didn't care enough about the city to fight for it, or else he simply wanted to see which team won before he formally picked a side.

Either way, Oz had never particularly liked him. But Oz liked very few people, so he was used to it.

"Rembrandt." Oz inclined his head at him in stiff greeting, and started to lean against the car next to him, then recognized the fact that the car was filthy. There was no way Oz was going to touch it. "You on the job?"

Rembrandt nodded. "I'm working with The Overlords now."

Oz frowned at the news.

"I know, I know." Rembrandt rolled his eyes. "But beggars can't be choosers about such things, I'm afraid. The Consortium took out the Freedom Squad and there aren't exactly a whole lot of Cape organizations left in town to choose from. So, I have to settle for small-timers with less than stellar track records." He glanced over at Oz. "You guys wouldn't have room on your team for one more, would you? Maybe?"

Yes, the Consortium absolutely did.

But not for Rembrandt.

"No." Oz shook his head. "You wouldn't fit in on our team."

The *last* thing the C of C needed was another morally questionable and incredibly powerful psycho walking around its headquarters. Oz was in charge of the former Freedom Squad heroes, and there wasn't a place there for Rembrandt. Ever.

He'd seen the kinds of things that man had done for the Freedom Squad. Willingly. And there were some sins which didn't wash clean.

The man seemed to instantly understand the reasons behind Oz's complete dismissal of his informal application. To Oz's surprise though, Rembrandt seemed to find it amusing. "That's what I've always liked about you, playboy. You don't fuck around. There are a lot of people in this world who would front, and tell someone a line of bullshit in order to save face or feelings." He shook his head. "But not you." He nodded in appreciation of that. "You're not a bitch about things. You man up and always tell it like it is. I'd shake your hand for that, but then you'd get all weird about it." He reached down to his pad of paper and quickly drew an image of a pack of bubble gum, then reached through the surface of the paper and pulled out the object and popped one of the sticks into his mouth. "You change your mind though, let me know." He pointed across the street where a few other of The Overlords were working crowd control. "These Triple A assholes are driving me nuts." He made a face. "The other night, they were chasing a bank robber headed to Queens and one of them freaked the fuck out and ended up *blowing up the F train*." He swore under his breath at the Cape in question. "Jagoff." He shook his head sadly. "People in Jamaica are going to be pulling bits of $100 bills and gunmen out of their hair for days." He was silent for a beat. "They told the news that the guys had some kind of bomb. But they didn't. It was just their own inexperience and fear. Fucking newbs."

"You tell anyone about this?"

"No one to tell." Rembrandt shrugged. "The city doesn't want to hear it, they're helping the team cover it up. It's like the fucking Freedom Squad all over again. The team views the whole thing as a victory." He hopped up to sit on the car's hood. "No matter how fucked up the Consortium is, they're still probably saner than the rest of the Capes in this town."

A new idea occurred to Oz. "You're still pretty tied into the other Cape groups though, right?"

"Somewhat. Why?"

Oz leaned closer, lowering his voice. "I'm interested in anyone talking about a train that's going to be leaving on Wednesday."

"A lot of trains are leaving on Wednesday. It's the day before Thanksgiving."

"I know that, but I'm talking about one in particular which might be important to the Capes or villains in town."

Rembrandt let out a long breath as he thought about it, then shrugged. "Not that I can think of, no. Most of the chatter around town is just soap opera bullshit, and bets about who's going to die

234

next." He pointed to the crime scene. "Now they're saying that *this* could be Cape-on-Cape." He looked down at the street for a long moment, sounding tired. "Hell of a war we're in, playboy, huh?"

Oz continued to watch Natalie's red hair dance in the cold wind as she discussed something amusing with Bridget. She'd tied feathers into it today, and the bright colors made her hair even more entrancing. Oz could literally watch it all day and be perfectly happy. "Have you ever heard of someone named 'Mercygiver'?"

"Yeah," Rembrandt nodded, "back during the 'Super-Person Resistance Movement' mess, I ran into the second-in-command of that crew. Dude named 'Mr. Jack.'" Rembrandt shook his head. "My advice would be to steer clear of that mess, playboy. They're baaaaad fucking mojo."

That got Oz's attention. "Do you know where I can find either of them?"

"Since Alectryon got cooked, a lot of the Norms have started treating Mercygiver like the *new* 'Keyser Söze' in town. A legend that's got a small crew and demands a piece of the action, and if you don't pay tribute, you get *crushed*." Rembrandt blew a bubble with his gum. "What's your problem with Mercygiver? Seems like Norm crime ain't your scene."

"Rondel threw my partner off a roof." Oz told him flatly. "*We're going to have words.*"

Rembrandt pointed at Natalie. "The jungle babe over there? *She's* your partner?"

Oz nodded.

"Daaaaaamn..." Rembrandt let out a long whistle. "How in the fuck did you get that going? I *really* need to join up with the Consortium." He crossed his arms over his chest, joining Oz in silently watching Natalie. "*That* is a beautiful woman, Oz. I've never had a partner or a friend who looked like that. Even when I was with the Freedom Squad." He made a face. "And on The Overlords, I currently work with a 45 year old fat guy named 'Shitstorm.' And I assure you, no artistic liberties were taken in naming him that, the fucking chode."

"That must be very hard for you." Oz didn't care at all about the man's employment troubles.

"You got no fucking idea." Rembrandt looked disgusted. "The smell alone is enough to make me long for the days when you and I used to go out on missions together with Mr. Fahrenheit and Mystery Lad. At least you guys were clean and didn't smell like an outhouse." He pointed at Natalie. "Do I know the girl? Because I don't think I do, which is odd, because I thought I knew every piece of

Cape tail in town."

Oz's eyes narrowed at him.

Rembrandt recognized the unspoken warning and put up his hands. "No offense meant, just admiring something beautiful from afar." He paused. "*Way* afar. Like 'Hubble telescope' territory, not *at all* a threat or a disrespect."

"Multifarious is..."

"*That's* Multifarious!?!" Rembrandt choked on his gum, cutting Oz off. "The crazy acrobat dude in the white suit and mask!?! The Killroy symbol guy!?!"

Oz nodded. "Yes. Although, I'm told her name is 'Jungle Lass' today."

"And you're okay with working with someone who the entire town knows is *absolutely insane*?"

"I work with a lot of people who the entire town knows are insane." Oz deadpanned.

"*And* evil?"

"Lots of people are evil too." He paused, thinking about his aunt's warnings again. "Or will be some day."

"Yeah, but she..."

"She's perfect." It was a flat statement of fact. And Oz believed it. Natalie had some quirks, true, but they were *delightful.* Oz wasn't going to let anyone change them. Ever. And anyone who had problems with Natalie would have problems with Oz *first*.

Rembrandt's eyebrows rose, but recognized this was not something he should comment on. "It's good, playboy. Don't go getting all angry." Rembrandt went back to watching her. "You're right. If she wasn't a murderous psychopath, she would be the *perfect* girl."

"She's extraordinary the way she is." Oz reminded him, just in case there was any doubt on that.

Rembrandt didn't reply to that, still watching Natalie. "Fuck, I would straight-up *murder* anyone who came near that girl if she was mine."

Oz stepped into his line of vision, cutting off his view of Natalie. "She is entirely capable of taking care of herself." Oz flashed him a meaningful glare, just in case the man still had any ideas. "And she's *not* yours." He did his best to hide the unspoken threat attached to the simple words, but it was apparently delivered all the same.

Oz wasn't someone who ever threw his weight or his powers around. But in Freedom Squad sparring sessions, he had absolutely destroyed the other man. And he was perfectly willing to do it again, should the need or desire arise.

Rembrandt held up his hands again, surrendering the point. "Speaking of ridiculously hot women you somehow are lucky enough to work with," Rembrandt popped another stick of gum into his mouth, "word on the street is that Harlot has unleashed her dogs and put Poacher and Robber Baron on eating the Agletarians' lunch."

"They're a foreign army with unknown weapons, who are here to kill us." Oz reminded him bluntly.

"So Harlot's decided to burn down the house to kill a few spiders?" Rembrandt shook his head. "Nah, nah, you don't have to go that hard. Poacher beasting on his own would have been more than enough. But this? I ain't a queasy man about such things, I did jobs with *Badger* back in the day, but this seems like something you should stop."

"My investigation is limited to the Mercygiver side of the matter." Oz informed him. "But it's a situation we're dealing with."

Rembrandt pointed at him, his face serious. "You'd *better* fucking deal with it, because your boy Welles is gonna dissect those guys like a frog in a goddamn science class, with the world watching. You know he don't got a 'stop,' everything is a green light when he gets going. He's gonna make this *whole town* a crime scene. And this city is already on edge, it doesn't need that madman freestyling."

"It's a situation we're dealing with."

"Uh-huh." The man didn't seem convinced. "Hope she's worth it, playboy."

On the other side of the crime scene tape, Oz saw his police contact emerge from the building. He stood straighter. "I'll see you around, Rembrandt."

The other man nodded at him in goodbye. "Have fun hunting Moby Dick, Oz." He paused for a moment. "It's good to see you living, by the way. To be honest, most of us had a pool that you weren't going to make it. We figured you'd be institutionalized or scragged by now." He nodded. "But it seems like you're doing pretty well for yourself, even if your partner is certifiable. Word of warning: you need to be careful of her."

Oz made a humoring sound, but didn't bother to point out the fact that of the two of them, Rembrandt had been the one who aided people in attacking the city. Natalie had tried to save it.

Oz started across the street, feeling oddly good about his life. He'd managed to smooth things over with Natalie, and even a complete dirtbag like Rembrandt was noticing his personal growth.

All in all, Oz was feeling better today.

Chapter 14

"SHE DID NOT LIKE THE LOOK OF THINGS AT ALL, AS THE GAME WAS IN SUCH CONFUSION THAT SHE NEVER KNEW WHETHER IT WAS HER TURN OR NOT."

- *Alice's Adventures in Wonderland*

Oz ducked under the crime scene tape and held it up for Natalie, who followed behind him. One of the officers immediately moved to intercept them, but Oz's contact shooed the man away.

"No, no, OCD is okay." Officer Verity Vasquez assured the other man. "He's got clearance."

The other officer didn't look convinced by that, but let the matter drop.

Oz had known Verity for a few years, ever since he'd worked as a liaison between the cops and the Freedom Squad. As far as he knew, he was the only Cape in town still authorized to make *formal* arrests. Not that he ever really did that—with the memorable exception of the time he'd used that power to place Cynic and Librarian under arrest for damaging Natalie's place of work—just that it was nice to work with police, rather than being like most of the other Capes in town who seemed to view them as an obstacle. Personally, Oz had nothing but respect and admiration for the police. He went out of his way to assist them whenever possible.

Verity hustled him towards the building, as if afraid of something.

Oz frowned at the side of the convenience store, where a group of officers were standing, all wearing more complicated tactical uniforms than the standard patrolman uniform Verity was wearing.

Verity followed his gaze. "Yeah," she nodded, "they're here for you." She lowered her voice. "The city is on the verge of exploding, OCD. Your friends have pushed things too far, and now there's a new unit forming to deal with you all, when it comes to that." She shook her head. "These people *don't* play."

"Why are they after the Consortium?"

"You blew up a hospital this week!"

"That wasn't us, that was the Agletarians."

She pointed at the task force in question. "Tell that to *them*."

A tough looking woman with short dark hair exited the convenience store and turned to face them, looking somehow both unemotional and furious. Her uniform showed her as being in charge of the new task force.

Officer Vasquez stood straighter and inclined her head in greeting. "Commander Legateaux."

The woman stared at them silently for another beat, then spat on the ground by Oz's feet. "Fucking Capes." She growled out, then stalked away.

Oz had no words for how disgusting he found it when people spat on the sidewalk. It was supposed to be disrespectful to him, but really it just made him want to throw up.

"Great." His contact winced and was obviously second-guessing the whole arrangement. "This could get me in a lot of trouble, you know that, right?"

"I recognize that. Thank you, Officer Vasquez." He watched the task force for a moment longer, trying to figure things out. "They wouldn't happen to have power suits, do they?"

"Like Armani?"

"No, like armor that gives them more power." He clarified. "Perhaps ones which glow orange?"

Verity scoffed at the idea. "OCD, we're the *NYPD*. We barely have the funding to buy officer's vests, you think we're going to get super-suits?"

"Just making sure."

"No," she shook her head, "they're not the Agletarians, they're just pissed at you guys. They want to stop you from wrecking shit and they're willing to do whatever it takes to accomplish that." She pointed at the convenience store. "And stuff like *this* isn't helping matters."

Oz refocused on the crime scene. "What's going on here? A super-powered disturbance?"

Verity nodded. "That's what..." She trailed off as Natalie arrived on the scene and joined the conversation. Verity stared at her silently for a moment, then gestured to her in disbelief, looking to Oz for an explanation. "Oh, good lord. Who is *this* now?"

"Today, I am..." Natalie paused dramatically, "...*Jungle Lass!*"

"Jungle Lass." Verity repeated in a deadpan, she pointed at

Natalie's top and the Killroy symbol painted on her exposed skin. "Because your *breasts* are telling me you're Multifarious."

Oz put up his hands to end the looming argument. "We're working the case together, she's involved in the Agletarian / Mercygiver matter and is of great value here."

"'Great value.'" Verity repeated, looking dubious. "Because *I* remember the time she robbed the bank on High street, then we had to chase her for four miles on foot. Remember that?"

Natalie laughed good-naturedly at the memory, and sighed, like she was reminiscing with friends. "Yeah... good times."

"I cannot do my job without my partner's help." Oz assured the officer seriously.

Verity didn't look convinced, but backed down. "Your partner there messes up, and this is over, you understand? You here at a crime scene, Capes working an investigation, my entire career... it's all *over*."

"We will be on our best behavior, I assure you." Oz nodded. "Our only goal is to find the people responsible for whatever this is, and to stop them. You are not equipped to face this kind of super-powered threat on your own, so we will assist you. Trust me, all we want to do is help."

"I trust *you*." Verity pointed at Natalie and started walking towards the entrance of the store. "*She's* a lunatic."

Oz and Natalie followed along behind.

Natalie pointed at the other woman and leaned closer to Oz. "What a bitch. In the jungle, that's the kind of woman we *don't* rescue from the quicksand." She paused, her voice tensing. "You and she aren't... *involved*, are you?"

Oz squinted at her in confusion. "No, of course not. Why?"

Natalie didn't bother to answer, but seemed to relax some.

Verity opened the door to the convenience store. "Okay, here's the situation," she gestured to the back of the store where a woman's body was sprawled, resting against the wall of glass doors which housed the iced beverages, "our vic is one..."

"Kailee Kennedy." Oz finished for her, recognizing the woman because he was obsessive about things sometimes. "She used to run a crew of Capes out of Long Island." He walked closer to the body. "She retired a few years ago though."

Verity shrugged. "Well, it seems like she picked a bad day to get back into the game." She gestured to the damage to the shelving displays in front of her. "Our perp blasted her with some kinda space-age shit that..." She spread her arms out, indicating the huge amount of blood splatter which was dripping down the glass behind the body. "Splash."

Natalie helped herself to a bag of Doritos from the shelf and started munching on them. "What'd the clerk say?"

"The clerk said that..." Verity trailed off, making a confused face, like she was amazed she was even speaking to Natalie at all. "Are you *eating the fucking crime scene*?" She asked in disbelief. "Just what qualifies you for this, anyway?"

Natalie swallowed her chip. "Well, I'm unhealthily competitive, have trust issues, poor impulse control, drink too much, and I don't like dealing with things that I don't want to deal with."

"And you think that somehow qualifies you for police work?"

Natalie arched her eyebrow in challenge. "Have you ever *met* a cop?"

Verity's face darkened. "Oh, fuck you!"

"She didn't mean that," Oz stepped between them, trying to preserve the crime scene, "it's just her personality today."

Verity shook her head. "She's a fucking bitch every day, OCD, you can tell!"

"Not *every* day." Natalie took another chip out of her bag. "Probably three out of five, max."

Oz reached into his pocket and removed two pairs of gloves, shoe covers, and a surgical mask. Better safe than sorry.

Natalie rolled her eyes, having not even bothered to put on shoes this morning. Her feet were bare, decorated only with a shark tooth anklet. For some reason, Oz found himself strangely fascinated by that delicate little accessory. Possibly because it highlighted the bare skin of her legs and possibly because it was... no it was entirely about her naked legs. And little strappy things being wrapped around them.

That anklet was his new favorite thing.

But thinking about that would have to wait for the moment, because he had work to do.

Oz got closer to the body, his eyes following the trajectory of the blast. "What *did* the clerk say, Officer Vasquez?"

Verity pulled out her notebook and flipped through it. "Oh, our man is a real gem. He said that a guy in a mask tried to hold up the store with a shotgun, then our vic..."

"Kailee Kennedy." Oz reminded her, not liking the fact the woman wasn't given the honor of a name. She had protected the city for years. Selflessly. She deserved better.

"Ms. *Kennedy*," Verity corrected, rolling her eyes at Oz's

human decency, "was already in the store, apparently shopping, and tried to stop the robbery. Then..." She shrugged. "I have no idea. Like I said, the clerk was high on god-knows-what at the time."

Natalie looked at the wound, then shook her head. "That's not a shotgun." She ate another chip.

"She was already *in* the store?" Oz asked, standing back up.

Verity nodded.

"So," Natalie fished another chip out of the bag, "our girl the ex-hero is here buying groceries, tries to stop a normal robbery, and somehow ends up getting blasted outta nowhere by a plasma rifle?"

Verity nodded again. "So it would seem."

"That's a hell of a coincidence." Natalie decided, looking over at Oz. "Think this is related to the other thing?"

Verity frowned. "Other thing?"

Oz took off one of his pairs of gloves and promptly replaced it with a second. "We've been investigating the disappearance of some people in the city."

Verity crossed her arms over her chest. "Do superheroes typically do a lot of 'investigating'?"

"Not really, no." Oz shook his head. "We usually just..."

"Beat the shit out of poor people?" Verity guessed, cutting him off.

"Exactly." Natalie nodded, pointing at her and looking at Oz, as if proving a point. "See, *she* gets it. I've been telling him that this is ridiculous, but he won't listen."

"And you're not even a hero, *you're* a villain." Verity reminded her.

"But one who mainly beats the shit out of rich people. So... all the bases are covered." Natalie ate another Dorito, then made a hashtag symbol with her fingers. "Hashtag 'Winning!'"

"Why is she here again?" Verity asked Oz. "Does 'Ariel' here have any qualifications for this new role?"

"I'm the world's greatest detective." Natalie declared seriously.

"No, you're not." Verity deadpanned.

"I most assuredly am."

"Today." Oz clarified.

"Rondel is the world's most diabolical criminal." Natalie chewed on her snack thoughtfully. "I have been taught investigative techniques and criminal justice by all the beasts of the jungle, and have come to this city because it's my mission to take him down."

Verity gaped at her. "...The fuck?" She breathed in horrified confusion, obviously hoping she'd heard that wrong.

Oz shook his head. "There's no proof he's behind this."

"I don't need proof, I just *know*."

Verity rolled her eyes. "That doesn't *sound* like something 'the world's greatest detective' should be saying."

"Did I ask you?" Natalie crumpled up her empty bag, then moved to put it into her pocket, only to remember that she was wearing a loincloth. The movement did allow Oz the pleasure of watching her graceful fingers glide over her hips though, which was a *wonder*. He had no idea that such a tiny, unconscious little motion like that could have such a staggering effect on him, even in this gruesome location. "Who the fuck *are* you anyway?"

"Also not something the 'world's greatest detective' should be saying, since I *just* introduced myself." Verity tapped her chest. "*And* I'm wearing a nametag."

Natalie glanced at Oz. "Can I kill this bitch, please?"

"Um..." Oz swallowed, "I think murdering a police officer would irrevocably move you from the 'anti-hero' role into the 'villain' category."

"And I care about that?"

"Hopefully, yes."

"Listen," Verity ran her hand through her hair, "I'm starting to think this was a mistake. It's obvious that you're not even taking this seriously and..."

"Where's her daughter?" Natalie interrupted.

Verity stopped. "Excuse me?"

"Look at the shit this skinny bitch is buying," Natalie squatted down to the basket of groceries on the floor, "candy bars, snacks, sugary fruit juice..." She shook her head. "You don't buy that if you've got to squeeze into a spandex unitard every morning."

"She's retired." Verity reminded her.

Natalie snorted. "There's '*retired*' and there's 'I don't even give a fuck.'" She pointed at a bottle which was wedged under the shelf. "Children's vitamins. In Darci fashion doll shapes." Natalie stood back up. "Thus: 'Where is her *daughter*?'"

They were all silent for a moment.

"Shit." Verity sighed. "She *is* a good detective today."

Natalie smirked. "Told you."

Oz thought about it for a minute, wondering how he could quickly figure out the personal details of a Cape's life. His eyes flashed to the dead woman's pocket, recognizing that she'd probably have pictures of any children she had in there. But... that would mean

244

touching her bloody clothes and reaching into her pocket, without knowing what he'd find. There could be needles, glass, metal shards... Things which could cut through his gloves, getting her blood on his hands, and possibly even cutting his own skin. Then, her blood would be mixing with his and that was out of the question.

Luckily, Oz had a plan B.

He removed his gloves, put on two fresh pairs, and fished his phone out of his pocket. He pressed several buttons. "Harlot?" He asked into the phone and the other woman's voice came over the line.

"Oz?"

"Yes. How's Wyatt?"

"Much better, actually." Harlot sounded significantly stronger than the last time he'd spoken to her, much more like herself. Wyatt must have gotten a clean bill of health from his doctors.

"Excellent. Please give him my best." Oz cleared his throat. "Listen, I'm working his case and without going into too many details, I'm wondering if you can tell me if Kailee Kennedy has a daughter?"

Harlot had spent her entire life being a super-fan of the Cape set in town, and she ran one of the biggest blogs dedicated to the topic. Oz had complete faith in her ability to give him an answer.

"Yes." Harlot thought about it for a beat. "Her name is... uh... 'Ember.' She turned six in October."

Oz nodded. "Okay, thanks. I'll let you get back to your husband now."

"Bye, Oz. Be careful, please." Harlot hung up.

Oz looked at the others. "She's got a daughter, yes."

"Well, she isn't here now." Verity announced.

Natalie leaned against the shelf. "So when was the last time anyone saw Amber?"

"Her name is 'Ember.'" Oz corrected.

Natalie scoffed at the news. "What the fuck kind of name is 'Ember'?"

"Hers."

"Does she at least have fire powers or something?"

"She's six."

Natalie rolled her eyes. "Fucking hipsters can kiss my ass. Who names their kids something like that? No wonder this generation is so fucked up. Everyone is named like a goddamned video game character."

Oz put his phone away. "Perhaps this isn't the best time to criticize parental naming choices."

"I think her parent has bigger problems right now than me

hurting her feelings, Oz." Natalie gestured to the corpse.

"Jesus!" Verity gasped in astonishment at that. "What the fuck is *wrong* with you!?!"

Natalie waved a dismissive hand. "I was raised by a family of leopards in the jungle, lady, I don't have time to coddle people as they learn about the circle of life."

"She's not herself today." Oz explained, holding up his hands to calm the other woman. "Well, she *is*, but it's not a 'herself' that she'll be tomorrow. And it's not a 'herself' that is an accurate representation of the 'herself' she *normally* is."

"This was such a mistake..." Verity decided again.

"Fine." Natalie rolled her eyes. "When was the last time anyone saw '*Ember*'?"

Verity began to massage her temples. "I can't believe my name is actually associated with this..."

"Your name is stupid too, so don't even start with me, '*Verity*.'"

"Speaking of 'stupid,' what the fuck are you wearing right now!?!" Verity gestured to Natalie's outfit. "Jesus! I'm a gay woman and not even *I* want to see that much of your body, lady! Christ! And it's *fucking winter!*"

Oz ignored them, remaining focused on the case. "So, Ms. Kennedy comes into the store, someone tries to rob the store, she tries to stop it, then a *second* person arrives and attacks her." He considered that. "Which means that either he or she was following her, or else Ms. Kennedy was just *spectacularly* unlucky." He looked down at the floor tiles, absently counting them again and again while he considered the matter. "There's no point to this." He decided. "Killing this woman got them nothing..." He paused, a new thought occurring to him. "...Unless it wasn't about *her* at all. Maybe our unknown individual was after *Ember*. Maybe the girl was *here*, and they grabbed her..."

Natalie casually walked over to the counter to stare at the owner's parrot, which was continuing to squawk wildly.

"If our unknown attacker was using the robbery to get the drop on our vic, so that he could steal her daughter, that's going to be tough to track down." Verity shook her head. "Security camera footage is melted and the clerk was no help. The only other person in here was the original robber, who was wearing a mask, so we have no idea who that..."

"The bird says the robber was in here before." Natalie informed them seriously. "Drives a piece of shit blue van. Only thing

246

he took in today's robbery was some scratch-off tickets."

"How in the hell can you *possibly…*" Verity began, then changed topics. "Wait, the fucking bird told you!?! *It's a bird!*"

"I can talk to animals today." Natalie reminded them. "The bird told me."

"Bullshit!" Verity snapped.

"Okay, that's it." Natalie shook her head angrily. "You're getting on my *last goddamn nerve*, lady. Yesterday, I would have taken it. But today? Today I'm gonna go Rambo on your ass!"

"Rambo loses in *First Blood*." Verity reminded her. "The cops take him to prison at the end."

Natalie was silent for a beat. "…Did we just become best friends?"

"God, I hope not." Verity looked appalled. "Because I fucking hate you."

Oz ignored the by-play, then let out a disappointed sigh. "I know who our robber is."

****

Twenty minutes later, Mull was walking down the hall of an apartment building, apparently going to confront the robber.

This was not the most exciting morning she'd ever had.

Truth told, she wasn't overly thrilled with her personality today. She didn't like being so… *cold*. Mull had often been accused of being an unfeeling maniac, but it felt different now. Part of that could be the loss of her mask, which still hadn't been completely repaired, but it most likely had more to do with being around Oz.

She'd been feeling… vulnerable lately, and this was probably just her powers' way of dealing with that. Turning her into an uncaring bitch.

It felt wrong to be so callous about things.

There really wasn't anything funny about a dead mother and a missing kid. Mull didn't take a lot seriously, but that was something that even *she* recognized as a solemn occasion.

No, she'd be glad when Jungle Lass went away.

To say nothing of the fact that her current outfit left very little to the imagination. Mull wasn't really a shy person, but she was used to wearing body armor and a baggy white outfit. She w*asn't* used to her current attire. She felt naked.

She let out a sigh, climbing the stairs ahead of Oz, because the man disliked "unknown elevators."

What the fuck did that even *mean,* anyway?

Apparently, he personally inspected the elevator in his own building every week, but in cases like this, he chose to take the stairs.

If it had been anyone else on the team, she would have suspected that he was just making them take the stairs so he could watch her ass as she climbed up the four flights in front of him. But that didn't seem especially "Oz" to her.

She'd gladly do it, if that was his reason, but she doubted it.

Oz was a man ruled by his brain, not his libido.

Unfortunately.

She let out another sigh. "So this is what you really do all day?" She asked him, unsure if this was what being a "hero" was all about. "While the rest of us on the team are having fun and setting off cool explosions, you're really doing boring shit like *this?*"

He didn't answer.

"Oz?" She called back to him again.

"...Huh?" He sounded distracted by something. "I'm sorry, what?"

"I asked if this is what being a real Cape is about?" She ran her hand through her hair. "Because this *sucks*. This isn't Caping. This is like... a job." She made a face. "In fact, I've got a job and it's a lot more fun than this one."

"Yeeeah..." Oz trailed off, still focused on something else. "This... is fun..."

Natalie held out her arms questioningly, without turning around, wondering what his deal was. "I just don't get you sometimes, Oz." She let out an annoyed sound. "And this is the worst fucking mystery in the world. We know that Rondel is behind all of this, I don't know why we're wasting our time on this."

That got Oz's attention and he refocused on the conversation. "Why would Rondel kidnap a child?"

"I have no idea. We can ask him when we find him." She pursed her lips in thought. "And *this* is going about it all wrong. We need to do it in the only *logical* way."

"Which is?"

"You and I are going to fly to Thailand, where we will assume new identities as kickboxers and make names for ourselves in the street-fighting ring and as local enforcers." She started counting off the points on her fingers, warming to the plan. "*Then*, when Ronnie asks the local martial arts dojos for any potential henchmen he could hire on, they will suggest us. And *then* we'll get our foot in the door, work our way up the ranks of his organization, and know *right where he is!*"

"That's the only 'logical' way?" He deadpanned. "'Professional Taiwanese street-fighting leagues'?'

"Absolutely."

He stared at her silently for a beat. "I don't know how to kickbox."

"I'll teach you on the plane, don't worry."

"I think there are probably better ways to find someone."

"You just don't understand how these things are done, that's all." She slapped her fist into her palm. "I'm telling you, I know how the man thinks! *This will work!*"

"Uh-huh."

"Oh, you're not even listening right now."

They arrived at the correct floor and started towards apartment 4D.

"Vadik and Ilik Bespalov." Oz informed her, once more getting back to business. "They're brothers. Ilik is convinced that scratch-off lotto tickets are the way to get rich. *And* he drives a blue van."

"How do you know this?"

"Their uncle, Andrusha, was that guy who was shoplifting inside Drews awhile back. Remember?"

"I remember knocking a shelf of shoes on you." She glanced at him. "Sorry about that, by the way."

He shrugged. "I lived." They turned the corner in the hallway. "In any event, I tracked him down after, assuming that *he* was Multifarious. But no. Just a shoplifter. Then he died in the SPRM riot."

"So do you just keep track of everyone's life in this city?"

"When they live in *this* neighborhood I do." He looked at her meaningfully. "Like I said, the blocks around the store are mine. Nothing goes down here that I won't find out about."

"No, you said that about the blocks around your a*partment.*"

"Same thing."

"No," Mull couldn't help but smile, "not really."

He was patrolling the neighborhood where she worked. *Because* she worked there. He had been spending his free hours quietly ensuring that she was safe, without making a big deal of it.

And Natalie decided she *really* liked that idea.

Mull thought it was cute, but Natalie was *completely* charmed. To the point that she was actually glad Mull had let Jungle Lass wear this *ridiculous* outfit today. It wasn't that Natalie was especially proud of her body or anything, but she had no issues with giving Oz a look at it every now and then.

She turned to simply look at Oz, recognizing—not for the first time—that Oz was a *tremendously* handsome man.

And her body was always very, very aware of him.

She loved watching that man move. He was methodical, but so smooth. For a man who questioned himself about absolutely everything, he could do some things with a confidence which was astonishing.

An elderly woman walked past them, and Oz took a step forward to stand aside for her. Because that's the kind of person that Oz was. The small movement put Mull closer to Oz than she usually stood though, and the effect was like a physical blow. Close enough that her breasts moved against his chest, and the sensation was a torture. She drew in a quick, uneven breath, not used to the feeling of being close to someone. Especially not someone she was almost *pathetically* attracted to.

For his part, Oz was probably even less used to it, but seemed to be coping quite well. He mumbled what *could* have been an apology, but he didn't move away from her.

The air in the building suddenly seemed still and warm, despite her minimal wardrobe.

Natalie swallowed, meeting his eyes and feeling like her entire body was growing hot and tight.

Jungle Lass was *not* someone who was at all shy about acting on her natural instincts.

She moved her leg forward, feeling Oz's arousal press against her thigh. He was already hard. For her.

The discovery made her smirk with satisfaction, and it added to her own desire, like tossing a can of gasoline onto a fire.

He didn't shy away from her or try to hide his attraction, he simply stood there, looking into her eyes, with confidence and longing. Letting her feel him.

Oz wanted her.

She felt it at the deepest core of her rapidly warming body.

Whatever his issues were, and whatever else happened... Oz *wanted* her. Judging from the steely feel of his massive body as she rubbed against him, he wanted her a *lot*.

And even Jungle Lass was surprised by how much Natalie wanted *him* in return. And, truth told, how much Jungle Lass wanted him too.

One of the doors at the end of the hallway slammed, and Oz

immediately turned to face the potential threat.

The movement caused him to move against her stiffened nipples though, and it made her breath catch in her throat.

Oz took a step away, assuming that she was sick or something. "I'm... sorry." He said softly. "I shouldn't have done that."

Mull panted for breath for a moment longer, trying to keep her cool. She'd never encountered anyone who could make her feel what Oz could make her feel.

He took a step towards the door, then paused when he saw she wasn't following. "Are you coming?" He asked.

"Just about, yeah." She admitted sheepishly.

Since it was Oz, he missed the double entendre. Which, for some reason, Mull decided was really, really adorable.

He was so innocent and pure and strong.

And she *loved* the fact that he made her feel all kinds of hot and wet and throbbing thoughts, whenever she looked at him.

Yes, there were obstacles in their relationship... but Holly was right: Mull would *deeply* enjoy being dirty with that man. She wanted to do things with him which he hadn't even dreamed were possible.

Sadly, the sexy moment was now broken and that left her in a bad mood. She kind of wanted to beat the shit out of someone now, just to release some of her tension.

She stepped in front of the door to the apartment, preparing to kick it down.

Oz shook his head. "We don't have a 'no knock' warrant, we're just here to talk to him."

Mull scoffed at that idea. "Um... just a reminder: I'm currently evil. I don't really care so much about laws and shit."

Oz gently tried to get in front of her. "And he's also armed." He reminded her, sounding worried about her.

"Relax, I'm bulletproof."

"That was Thursday." He shook his head. "Today, you just talk to alligators and solve mysteries, remember?"

"Shit." She made a face. "Forgot about that."

"Want to come back tomorrow?"

"Nah, it'll be fine." She flipped her hand. "Tomorrow might be an even worse power."

"What's the worst power you've ever had?"

"Use your imagination."

He turned to look at her, still looking genuinely interested.

"You *really* don't want to know." She assured him. "Trust

me."

He didn't turn away.

"Fine." Mull cleared her throat, feeling embarrassed but excited. "I... I was sexually attracted to myself one day. It was... weird. I didn't even make it out of the shower that morning. It was a very long and tiring day."

Oz's expression didn't change at all, he continued staring straight at her.

One moment stretched into two.

Then three.

"Told you that you didn't want to know." She finally told him, clearing her throat and absently straightening her fur top, wishing it covered more of her exposed skin. Oz being so close to her made her breasts so tight, it was distracting.

Natalie was all but screaming at Jungle Lass to... something. It was a strange emotion, involving both feeling naked and kinda liking Oz seeing her that way.

Mull wasn't sure what to make of that. Jungle Lass had some crazy ideas about animals and natural desires, but Mull had stopped listening to that psycho. If it were up to Jungle Lass, they'd be eating raw meat and having sweaty sex by a bonfire somewhere, while mastodons wandered by. Which was an idea that Mull seemed more bothered by than Natalie, which was also very, very odd. Natalie almost never agreed with her other persona on a given day, but in this case, she and Jungle Lass were *completely* on the same page. She seemed...

Without warning, the door to the apartment opened and a young man with dark hair appeared in the entry, looking surprised to find people standing on his doorstep. His eyes cut up and down Mull's minimal wardrobe, staying pinned on her breasts. "*Please* tell me you're here to see me." He said simply.

Oz moved forward. "Can we come in, Vadik?"

The man immediately stepped aside. "As long as you're with her, you can fucking *move in*, mister." His eyes stayed on Mull as she walked into the room to stand beside Oz. "Are you with the CIA or something?" He asked her seriously.

"Yes, I'm with the CIA." She deadpanned. "We all dress this way, it's policy. Langley is designed to look like Tarzan's Treehouse, for security."

"Really?"

Mull rolled her eyes. "You're a fucking moron, you're forbidden from talking."

"We're with the Consortium of Chaos." Oz informed the man.

"You're heroes?" Vadik asked.

Mull shrugged. "More or less."

Vadik shifted on his feet awkwardly. "Are you guys like... hiring at all? Because I got powers and I'm totally ready to throw them around town."

Mull looked at Oz. "Is being an asshole a superpower now?"

"Judging by the Capes in *this* town?" Vadik nodded. "Yeah."

"Don't call us, we'll call you." Mull pointed at the floor. "Wait right by that phone though, okay? Don't even leave for a second."

"We're looking for your brother." Oz's eyes continued scanning the apartment. "Have you seen him?"

"Ilik!" The man yelled into the other room. "A sexy red-haired jungle lady is here to see you!"

There was the sound of scrambling feet as the other man hurried to see the sight his brother promised. He popped into the room, saw Oz, and took off. He ducked back into his room, went through the window, and started to run down the fire escape.

Mull swore, pushing Vadik to the floor as she chased after his brother. "I'll get him, you get the car, Oz!" She called over her shoulder. "Meet me down there!"

She didn't give Oz a chance to object to the plan, following straight after the suspect.

He reached the bottom of the fire escape ladder before she did, immediately racing down the alley away from her.

Sadly for him, no matter the power, Mull was very, very fast, even in her bare feet and running on icy pavement. She closed the distance between them almost immediately.

She grabbed him by the shoulder and spun him around. "Where do you think *you're* going?"

He swung wildly at her, but she leaned back to dodge the strike. It was more an amusement than an actual threat to her. "What the fuck was *that*?"

He swung at her again, but she simply caught his fist in her hand and pushed him back, off balance. "You suck at fighting." She tried not to roll her eyes, but it was very difficult. "I'm trying to impress my sorta boyfriend with how heroic I can be, but you're making it really difficult."

"Leave me alone!" Ilik cried, backing away from her. He held his arms up, flexing like a toddler trying to show you he was angry.

"What the fuck is that?" Mull asked, feeling annoyed now. "No one fights like that! What are you even doing! Put your arms down, you look like an asshole!"

Jungle Lass' instinct immediately told her to jump onto his back and go caveman on him. Ground and pound him into the icy concrete. But... Oz probably wouldn't like that so much. Plus, it would make questioning him hard, unless they wanted to wait for a day when she would possibly develop powers which allowed her to speak to the dead.

This guy was just being difficult.

Things were so much more complicated when you had to talk to people rather than just killing them.

How did people do this all day?

He grabbed a piece of broken shipping pallet and tried to club her with it, shrieking like an enraged elephant.

Mull let out a put-upon sigh, and leaned to the side to avoid the strike. Then she hit him in the throat with her open hand, causing him to gasp for breath and stagger backwards, dropping his weapon.

He turned to try to flee down the side alley, but Oz parked the car at the other end, blocking his escape. He stepped from the vehicle, his clothes somehow still pristine. "We're with the Consortium of Chaos." He told the man with authority. "Please cooperate."

The man made a break for it anyway, betting he could slip past Oz. Unfortunately for him, Oz was a master of the "Jailhouse Rock" fighting style, developed in prison cells and yards all over the country, and the confined space of the alley was perfectly suited for the obscure boxing form.

The fight lasted about three seconds.

Mull found herself oddly turned on by how quickly her partner had decimated the guy. It was less a "fight" and more a "sacrifice." Like some loser had volunteered to be thrown into the ring, just to give Oz a chance to show off.

Again, Mull found Oz very, very sexy.

There was something so oddly appealing about a man who could fight crime without even needing to unbutton his coat.

"What..." the man gasped, still struggling to catch his breath after Oz had punched him in the stomach, "...do you want?"

Oz straightened his suit. "This morning, you robbed a convenience store."

The man tried to look innocent.

"You did." Mull confirmed. "The parrot ratted you out."

He looked confused by that.

"I don't care about the robbery," Oz met the man's eyes, "I care about the murder."

"That wasn't me!" Ilik protested. "That was the other guys!"

"Other guys?" Oz pressed. "Tell me about 'the other guys.'"

"There were... umm..." Ilik thought about it for a second, "there were four or five of them. A couple guys in suits, a guy with a ponytail, and a couple of cats in hats."

"'Cats in hats'?" Mull glanced at Oz. "Shit, let's put out an APB for Dr Suess, Oz."

"Nah, nah," Ilik waved his hand, "I mean like dudes in stupid hats! Tough looking guys! They were there too! Guy with the laser gun shot that Cape, man. And that's when I got the fuck out of there!"

"What about the kid?" Oz's voice was serious. "You see them with a kid?"

The man nodded. "Yeah, little girl. The guy with the ponytail grabbed her."

"These guys with the hats," Oz's eyes squinted, obviously thinking he was on to something, "what *kind* of hats?"

'Like... like that cowboy guy." Ilik raised his hands to show a rounded shape. "You know the guy?"

"The Lone Ranger?" Oz guessed.

"No, like..." Ilik snapped his fingers. "Bat Masterson. That's the guy."

"Dr Seuss and the Sherriff of Dodge City." She sarcastically patted Oz on the chest with the back of her hand, drawing his attention to their achievement. "*We got the bastards now, Baby Doll!*"

Whatever that meant, Oz seemed to recognize it. His voice became even more serious. "Two men in bowler hats were helping the men wearing the power-armor?"

Ilik nodded.

She looked up at Oz. "That mean something?"

He nodded. "Oh, yeah. It means something."

At the other end of the alley, a patrol car rolled into view, here to pick up their suspect.

"These officers are going to arrest you now, Ilik." Oz told the man calmly. "I called them from the car. I think it would be best if you cooperated. Possibly get some drug treatment. Ultimately, it's your choice, but I think it would really help you turn your life around."

"I got this, don't worry about it." She assured Oz, ushering Ilik forward to make the hand off.

"You're not going to threaten him, are you?" Oz asked her

quietly. "Because I don't think that'll do anything but scare him. This needs to be his choice, you can't force him."

She shook her head. "Of course not, don't worry about it." She smiled at him in reassurance. "Hey, it's me! It'll be fine."

She pushed the other man halfway to their destination, then deliberately shoved him to the right so that he'd fall to the ground. "Oops! Sorry about that." She bent down to help him to his feet, then looked over her shoulder to make sure Oz couldn't see. "Alright, you little asshole, you and me are gonna do this *old school*, feel me? None of that 'community policing' namby-pamby bullshit."

Ilik looked scared now.

"See that man over there?" Mull pointed back towards Oz. "The good-looking one dressed like the sexy offspring of a Good Humor Man and Mr. Rogers? Well, he seems to think that you're capable of something *other* than being the asshole we both *know* you are. He thinks there's still hope for you. And he wants you to get on the right road. Which means that you're *going* to turn your little life around. Right now." She pulled an obsidian skinning blade from her belt, making sure that Oz couldn't see it. "Or I swear to Christ and all the angels, I will take this knife and I will cut off your *goddamned face and wipe my ass with it*, do you understand me?"

Ilik frantically nodded. "Yes… yes ma'am…" He stammered.

"Good. I know I kinda look like someone's bratty little sister on Halloween, but *I assure you,* Jungle Lass is *not* a bitch with whom to fuck, understand? I will *destroy you*. I will gut you like a gazelle I'm cleaning for my meal, opening you up, so that everything that you are spills out onto your cheap knock-off Jordans. Right here. And then I will go home and have lusty impure thoughts while watching a goddamn *Idris Elba* movie, understand? And then never think about you again." She lowered her voice into a growl. "Look at me and tell me if you have any doubts that I'm entirely capable of doing that?"

He shook his head frantically.

"*Look at me and answer.*"

"No! No, ma'am, I heard you: 'Idris Elba'!" He started crying, his voice panicked. "*I heard you! 'Idris Elba'! 'Idris Elba,' I heard you!*"

"Good. Now smile and thank me for helping you to your feet, and you'd *better* make it convincing."

Ilik jumped to his feet, doing a less than stellar job of selling it.

"Now, you're going to cooperate with your prosecutors." Mull leaned closer to him. "I'll make you eat your own testicles if you fuck me over on this and drop out of rehab. Get me? You clean up your life or I will make it end in a *smorgasbord* of fucking pain." She tapped the blade beneath her own eye, indicating that she'd be watching. "*Don't* disappoint me."

Ilik literally *ran* to surrender himself to authorities. Mull had never seen anyone so glad to be placed under arrest.

Oz walked up to stand beside her. "Good to see you were able to convince him to get the help he needs and hopefully help others in return sometime down the road."

She nodded seriously. "It was really hard to forgo my violent tendencies and do it your way, but you're right, it is *much* more rewarding to leave the decision up to him and not just threaten him."

They both watched the squad car drive away.

"You threatened him, didn't you." He said simply. It wasn't really a question.

"Oh yeah." She nodded, still watching the car, her fake smile never wavering. "Very much so."

To her surprise, Oz chuckled in laughter.

"So, you know our hat guys?" She asked, turning to face him.

He nodded, echoing her word choice. "Oh yeah."

"Why should we trust this guy?" She gestured to the departing police car. "He's a criminal."

"*You're* a criminal." He reminded her.

"True, but I'm at least good at it." She snorted. "That asshole makes the Hamburglar look like the fucking Zodiac killer."

Oz's brow furrowed in confusion. "What's a 'Hamburglar'?"

She made a face at him. "You don't get to talk again until you get a TV, okay?" She leaned against the wall. "So what's the deal with the hat guys then?"

"August and Anton Masterson. They used to do work with the Freedom Squad's security force sometimes." He shook his head. "*Not* good people."

"Do you know where we can find them?"

He shook his head again. "They're ghosts. I didn't know how to find them even back when we were both working for the same team. And since then, it seems they've become terrorists for hire. They did things on Sandy Island, in the South Pacific, that were horrific in a way that defies all explanation. They didn't just kill innocent people, they made sure they were degraded and tortured first."

"So..." She began, recognizing the hopelessness of this now.

"Dead-end." He summarized. "We still don't know where Mercygiver is or what he has to do with this. We can't track the

Agletarians, and our only lead at the moment are two hired guns who hide from people professionally."

"We could call Marian and see if she can examine the crime scene for us?" Mull tried, grasping at straws. "Maybe break down what kind of space-age weapon was used in the convenience store and where it could be purchased?"

Oz fished his phone out of his pocket and typed something into it. "It's OCD. I hope you're doing well today."

Cynic's voice came over the speaker, sounding thrilled. "Dude, my wife has an IQ higher than Einstein's, is built like a Playmate of the Year, and could literally write a doctoral thesis on proper fellatio technique." You could hear Cynic's grin. "I have *no* problems with the way my day and life have turned out so far." He paused. "If you're calling to be all depressed or dwell on gloomy bullshit today, that's your problem, not mine. Don't ruin my glow."

"I need a crime scene examined." Oz reported calmly. "A full analysis of an unknown weapon, which was probably alien in origin."

"Yeah, sounds like my wife could totally science the shit outta that." Cynic agreed.

"Can you do anything?"

"Fuck, no." Cynic laughed at that very idea. "You shoulda called her."

"I *did* call her." Oz snapped. "You answered her phone."

There was a long pause on the other end.

"Why do you have my wife's phone number, Oswald?" Cynic asked, voice eerily calm.

Oz let out a sigh. "Can you just put her on the phone, please?"

"Do you call her a lot?" Cynic pressed, seriously. "What do you two talk about when I'm not around, Oz?" There was another pause, and when Cynic spoke again, his tone sounded noticeably darker. "What do you say to my wife when I'm gone, I wonder...?"

Mull grabbed the phone. "Cynic, and I mean this as a friend, I don't give a shit about you. I don't give a shit about your wife. Please stop talking about how happy you both are and just *put her on the goddamn phone*."

"Umm... she's tied up right now." Cynic replied, once more sounding normal.

Mull's grip on the phone tightened. "Oz and I don't give a shit, *put her on the phone*. NOW!"

Cynic heaved a longsuffering sigh. "Fine, I'll untie her. But she's gonna be pissed. It took me all morning for her to teach me those knots."

She squinted, trying to trace the meaning of that odd and glaringly incorrect phrasing.

A moment later, Marian's voice came over the line. "Hello?"

"Marian? It's Mull..."

There was a long pause on the other end of the line.

"Why are you calling my husband?" The other woman asked, sounding suspicious and vaguely threatening.

Mull let out an irritated groan, trying to restrain herself from screaming obscenities at the top of her lungs, then hung up the phone without bothering to answer. "You know what? Fuck them. They're crazy. We can handle this ourselves."

"Why do we even work with them?" Oz wondered aloud.

"I have no idea." She ran a hand through her hair, considering the situation for a long moment. "We *do* have one card we can still play..." She began.

Oz winced. "No, I don't..."

"There's a little girl missing now, Oz." She reminded him. "I say we at least *try* to see if Monty's friend can help this lead pan out."

"It's probably a trap."

"So, let's set off the trap and see where it's pointing. Maybe he's after bigger game than us."

Oz was silent, looking deeply unhappy over the idea. "Pimps are bad enough, but a pimp who works for *Monty?* I can't even *imagine* what that kind of man is like."

Chapter 15

"I'M NOT LOOKING FOR EGGS, AS IT HAPPENS; AND IF I WAS, I SHOULDN'T WANT YOURS: I DON'T LIKE THEM RAW.'"-

- Alice's Adventures in Wonderland

The next day, Mull was sitting in the Decomposing Turtle, which was a favorite establishment for the villainous set in town. In fact, it was *the* establishment where the villains went to drink. The colorful moniker kept the Norms away, and the questionable company scared off everyone else.

It was like the *Cheers* bar, only you hoped the people here *didn't* "know your name," because if they did, it would mean they were either plotting against you or casting some kind of dark curse.

The Turtle was the ground floor of the Bluebeard Hotel, which burned down in the 1940s, the deadliest hotel fire the city ever had. 211 people died. But they only found 170 of the bodies. The others were either burned up, or were still lost somewhere in the building.

In 1982, someone went door to door and killed every single person on floor twenty-one. Thirty people died. It was boarded off ever since and the elevators didn't stop there now.

In 1995, four college students disappeared from their room on floor nine. The security footage from the hall showed them entering the room. No one else came in and no one left. They simply weren't there anymore and no one had seen them since.

Three years ago, a dimensional vortex opened up in the ladies room in the lobby, sucking two stalls into the "Dimension of Screams." The doorway now had a "caution: wet floor" sign set up in front of the limitless trans-dimensional murky blackness which loomed beyond.

It was consistently voted one of the top 3 haunted places in the United States. Certain areas of the building *still* smelled like smoke. It was said that you could hear sirens and crying in some rooms late at night. Over a hundred people had killed themselves in the hotel since, some of which hadn't been discovered for months or even years later, due to the hotel's policy of collecting the money in advance and asking no questions. On at least one occasion, someone leapt from the window of their room, but when their friends ran to the edge to see where they had landed on the sidewalk, the body was nowhere to be found. They had simply disappeared in midair.

Villains *loved* the place.

It was like their church, their clubhouse, and Disneyland, all mixed into one. And the basement, colorfully referred to as "The Crawlspace," was an all-purpose hideout/headquarters or event venue, available for rent to any group who couldn't afford to buy a permanent one.

The Consortium had never really hung out here much, since they had their own secret headquarters, but for the unattached villain looking to have a pint with friends, the Decomposing Turtle and The Bluebeard Hotel were their #1 choice.

It took Mull three seconds to recognize that it probably wasn't the best idea to bring Oz here though. You could say a lot of things about the Turtle, but it wasn't the kind of place which was spotlessly clean. Oz was going to freak. And more importantly, the place was filled with villains. And Oz was the most shining hero in town.

Half the room turned to glare at him, obviously planning his brutal death. They generally allowed the other Consortium members to hang out, despite their recent turn to heroics, because they were used to them. Oz, however, was another matter. He was a Cape and everyone knew it. He had *always* been a Cape. He would always *be* a Cape. Because Oz was moral and strong and perfect. And there wasn't a single thing the villains in this bar could do to change that.

Oz didn't look at all intimidated by them.

Oz was one of those rare individuals who couldn't *be* intimidated. At all. By anyone. Despite his often strange and bizarre actions, the central pillars of his actual mind were supported by logic. He wouldn't back down from that, no matter what you threatened or how loudly you screamed. To Oz, every small decision was important. And he didn't compromise himself for anyone. Ever.

There was something deeply comforting and kinda hot about that.

Oz could stand as resolute as a mountain against an army of foes... just so long as none of them were covered in fucking dust mites.

Oz would die before he ever stepped aside.

Mull had spent her entire life in a world of grey, but Oz was as blindingly White Hat as they came.

She could count on Oz. Which... was a strange feeling. Mull didn't count on anyone. In her experience, everyone was selfish, evil, and would let you down. But Oz wouldn't. The only person he ever let down was himself. Oz was constantly disappointed with himself. And there was still something very sad about that.

She wanted Oz to feel like the person she *knew* he was. But it was very difficult to break through to the man sometimes. He was as stubborn and resolute about his opinion of himself, as he was about everything else. And she was starting to think that there was nothing she could do to change that.

Mull stepped in front of him, sending a silent warning to the patrons that Oz was *off-limits.*

Several people ran for the exit, guessing how far Mull was willing to take this if anyone fucked with Oz.

"Surprised to see *you*," the bartender carefully put a glass back onto the shelf, "you're not terribly popular here."

"I'm not terribly popular anywhere, ma'am." Oz assured her, looking at the wooden bar the way someone else might look at an autopsy table covered in crimson gore. "I'm used to it."

"Wasn't talking to you." The woman replied, casually leaning on the bar and looking at Mull. "Figured you'd had enough after last time."

Mull had no idea what that was referring to, but she'd had so many fights over the years, it was difficult to keep them all straight, especially when alcohol was involved. Whoever she'd wrecked, they'd undoubtedly deserved it. Mull sat down at the bar. "I'm not really a hero, don't worry, I'm still evil."

Hedy Marcus, AKA "The Operator," had been the bartender here since forever. The woman still always seemed young though, indicating that she either never aged or simply had good genes. With super-powered people, it was often difficult to tell for sure. "There was never any question what you were, lady." The woman assured her, straightening the elevator operator's cap she was wearing. "You're a *monster.* A hateful killer, who should be run out of town. You are proof that God doesn't exist, because if he did, he'd strike you down where you stood." She brightened, sounding impressed and friendly. "Welcome back to The Decomposing Turtle. What can I get you?"

"We're waiting for someone." Mull tapped the bar. "I'll

have a shot of Black Pony." She pushed Oz into the stool beside her. "And my friend will have whatever you have that's closest to being germ-free."

Hedy delivered the drinks a moment later, sliding the glass of water in front of Oz.

Mull slammed back her drink and tapped the bar again, indicating that she wanted another.

Hedy poured another shot.

Mull absently looked around the bar, scanning it for possible threats.

Along one wall was a banner advertising the Turtle's special dining opportunity: "The Thanksgiving Feast," which seemed to be a folding card table offering a loaf of white bread, an open tin of Spam, and five different kinds of little mustard packets.

In the other corner, a drop-dead gorgeous woman was serenading the room with a husky and sensual rendition of "Never Enough" from *The Greatest Showman* soundtrack. She had a shockingly good voice, and was using it to basically make love to the ears of everyone in the room. Her attitude on stage told everyone that she knew she was going to kick the song's ass.

This wasn't really a karaoke kind of place, particularly when they were basically showtunes, so just why the woman was allowed to sing was anyone's guess.

The music swelled as the song switched keys, and the woman's voice snapped from low and sexy to belting it out like an opera star, reverberating through the bar; clear and strong. Seemingly telling everyone, "Listen to what *I* can do, you failures."

Mull herself could not sing a note. She'd lost four different neighbors to her tendency to sing *Pocketful of Sunshine* in the shower.

She finished her survey and returned to looking at her companion.

Oz looked *completely* out of place here. Which wasn't too surprising, since the man seemed out of place pretty much everywhere. Like he was cursed to be an actor from some other movie, forever walking through this one.

Oz was basically a live-action hero, sitting in a room filled with cartoon villains.

It was an odd mix. But it somehow made him seem even more important.

As he sat there though, a six inch tall giraffe wandered over across the bar to stare at him in curiosity. Oz stared back at the tiny animal expressionlessly... then cautiously slid his water away from it, like he was afraid it would become contaminated. The miniature animal watched the glass slowly moving away, then looked back up at Oz and wagged its tail.

A moment later, a spacy woman in her early 20s hurried over to scoop the little animal up. "No, no, Zoe. That man doesn't want to play with you." She turned to Oz and laughed good-naturedly. "I'm so sorry, you know how curious giraffes are about things." The woman sounded soft and dreamy, like she was talking low, for fear of waking up a sleeping child. Mull got the sense the girl always talked that way.

Oz nodded, humoring the girl. "They... they do all go through that phase, don't they." He got out, awkwardly.

Mull tried to hide her snort of laughter.

Hedy pinched the bridge of her nose, obviously feeling like she was mistreated by the world. "Colby, does Thraex know you're here again, sweetie?"

The girl wandered away without answering, not because she was avoiding the question, just because she was distracted by something.

The woman on stage chased a high note that Mull would have bet no one could have ever possibly hit on their best day, but the woman smashed straight through it effortlessly, apparently still nowhere near the edge of her vocal range.

Bitch.

Mull leaned across the bar so that the bartender could hear her over the music. "We're looking for Oklahoma Mike."

Hedy gestured to one of the booths, which was currently empty.

Mull and Oz made their way over to it and sat down, under some original pencil sketches by the sinister architect, "Frank Lloyd Wrong."

Mull tapped her finger on the table, getting bored. She was used to doing more than this. On the average day, she would have killed like... a *dozen* people by now. This whole "investigation" thing was really hurting her game.

On the other hand, she *was* having drinks with Oz at the moment, so this *technically* counted as their second date. Well... if you counted her almost dying in the hospital as their *first* date, anyway.

The thought made her smile, realizing that it was entirely true.

Mull was on a *date*.

She beamed at Oz, feeling like this was really the start of a beautiful afternoon.

"I think this fork was used in a murder." Oz remarked as he examined the tableware, his face drawn up in horror and disgust.

Mull's smile faded.

Dating was probably easier for some women than it was for her.

The song ended, and the crowd of killers and villains silently parted before the singer as she made her way from the small stage, like she was completely untouchable and everyone in the room knew it.

Mull finished off her scotch and absently watched the woman. She had dark hair and large intense greyish-green eyes. She was wearing a tuxedo jacket and a matching fedora cocked at a jaunty angle.

She cut a striking figure.

She was breasts and legs and shiny neon sex.

Nat thought there were two kinds of pretty: there was "pretty" and then there was "mean girl pretty."

This woman was "mean girl pretty." If she were an actress, it would be impossible for her to ever be anything other than the beautiful rich girl who picked on the overly plain heroine at high school parties, or the villainess who seduced the hero. She would play strippers and femme fatales and rich ex-girlfriends. She vamped it up with James Bond. She was the naked woman in the scene added to liven up a dull section of the film. When Vin Diesel walked into a bar in Moscow, *this* was the bitch you cast to be the incredibly hot and slutty woman sitting next to the mobbed-up Russian gangster Vin was there to kill.

She didn't even say anything in the scenes, because her perfect tits did all her talking for her.

She'd look ridiculous and out of place in any other part, because she always came off as mysterious, seductive, and cruel. No matter what she was doing, every movement seemed sexual and vindictive. Like she wasn't even a real person, she was a masturbatory fantasy brought to life. She had no emotions other than lust, sex appeal, and the desire to take your man.

Natalie herself was "nice pretty." Or more accurately, "cute." She could never be taken seriously as a villain. Or hero. Or adult, really. She wasn't even the kind of pretty which could ever realistically be a main love interest. She was... she was the "nice girl" who dated the heroine's brother. Hers was a simple kind of romance. Her clothes would stay on through the entire film. If you were "Nice Girl Pretty," you were mainly playing flighty kindergarten teachers and the giggling woman who worked at the pet store. You couldn't intimidate anyone and it would be utterly wrong to pair you with the hero of the film. No one would go see that movie. No one cared about you, unless you died horribly from some wasting disease, to show the loss of innocence. Thinking of someone Nice Girl Pretty as a sexual object was just... It would be like thinking of *Shirley Temple* as having hot nasty sex. It was just weird and wrong, no matter her age.

Holly was right: *no one* like Natalie would *ever* have kinky sexual adventures. It just wasn't in the cards for her.

Mull had detested Nat's Nice Girl Prettiness her entire life. It was a constant struggle.

But *this* woman looked like an evil temptress, waiting to pull men into her erotic web of deceit. It seemed inconceivable that there'd ever be a time when she w*asn't* having incredible sex.

This was the girl you would never be and the one you could never have. The unobtainable.

Yep.

Natalie was very jealous of that.

That fucking bitch.

The woman nodded at them in greeting as she slid into the booth. "Oklahoma Mike." Her voice was a smoky purr, like Lauren Bacall's even sexier and more exotic great-granddaughter.

"That's an interesting name for a woman." Oz remarked, looking entirely un-excited by the fact he was meeting a woman who looked like she routinely drove cartoon wolves mad with lust. "Were you born in Oklahoma?"

The woman arched one perfectly shaped eyebrow. "Were you born in 'Oswald'?"

"Well, is 'Mike' short for something?"

"Yes."

They both waited for the woman to elaborate. Good manners would have said not to pry into the woman's affairs, but Mull had never been accused by *anyone* of having good manners. "What?" She didn't particularly care, but if the woman didn't want her to know, then Mull *really* wanted to know. It was the principle of the thing. Again, Mull wasn't really a rule-follower. "Michela? Michelle?"

"Carlene."

"That doesn't make any sense."

"It's an illogical world."

The table fell into silence.

"*Fine*." The woman rolled her eyes in irritation. "I was born in Wellesburg, Pennsylvania. My birthday is Feb 19th. My middle name is Jude. I'm 5'9", 117 pounds. My measurements are 34C-24-35. I prefer the mountains to the beach, white wine to red. I'm *terrified* of airplane travel and piranhas. I have no pets. My favorite book is *The Half Giraffe Telegraph.* I dislike bad hygiene and people who are mean to me. I *love* strong men who keep their promises, and snowy nights cuddled up by the fire with a trashy book. I enjoy model railroading, and as a little girl, I dreamed of working at a zoo because I love animals." She folded her hands on the table in front of her, arching an eyebrow again. "Was that it? Just a recap of my centerfold bio? Is that why I had to come down here and talk to you?"

She exuded a calm businesslike power. There was no question she thought she was in control of the conversation or that she knew exactly what she was doing at all times. In fact, she seemed like one of the most confident people Mull had ever met, smugly so.

She regarded them silently with her almost hypnotically pale green gaze, looking equal parts bored and calculating.

Of course she'd have sexy bedroom eyes which seemed to glow from within like moonstones.

What else would she *possibly* have?

Mull might have just discovered her nemesis. Ronnie was evil and trying to kill her, but *this* bitch she *really* hated.

She wanted to get Oz away from her as quickly as possible. There was no telling what kinds of seductive things she could do to him which would catch his eye. And Mull had *not* invested years in carefully grooming Oz to be her boyfriend to lose him to some other woman.

Oklahoma seemed to be barely restraining an eye roll. "I know your names, but I'm still confused as to just who you people are?"

"I'm Riggs, he's Murtaugh." Mull explained matter-of-factly.

"Okay." Oklahoma nodded, as if that explained everything. "And the purpose of this delightfully mismatched partnership is...?" She trailed off, inviting them to finish.

"We're on a case."

"Do super-types really have 'cases'?" Oklahoma raised one perfectly manicured red fingernail to the bartender, ordering something. "Isn't that usually the domain of private detectives?"

Mull shrugged. "When you have super-powers, you can have anything you want."

Oz obviously wasn't in the mood to beat around the bush with this woman, and got right down to business. "Do you know anything about missing empowered people in the city of late?"

Oklahoma's expression remained unaffected. "Why?" She asked immediately, like her answer might change, depending on the motive behind the question. She suspected that most conversations with the woman involved those kinds of answers.

"You're a hard person to talk to." Mull observed.

Oklahoma shrugged again. "I charge by the hour."

"A few days ago," Oz reached into his coat pocket and pulled out several photos, "Poacher, Multifarious, and I got called to the scene of a missing teenage girl..."

Mull picked up the story from there. "...we found a random psycho pervert there, with a gunshot to the leg."

Oklahoma's brow furrowed. "Who shot him?"

"You a cop?" Mull challenged.

"No."

Mull waggled her hand in the air. "Let's say he fell on the bullet."

"Okay, we can say that." Oklahoma didn't appear to care about the lie. "But what did *he* say?"

"He didn't survive questioning."

Oklahoma didn't appear surprised by that either. "Falls are the second most common deadly accident, particularly when they're onto a bullet in midflight."

"Evil is delicate and I don't pull punches." Mull explained casually.

"But since then, five more people have gone missing." Oz continued. "The most recent was a little girl taken from a convenience store yesterday."

"Oz wants them back." Mull finished for him.

Oklahoma looked at Mull. "And you?"

"I don't really care." Mull made a face. "I'm just coming with, because there's nothing good on TV."

"I believe they're trying to kill Natalie as well, for some reason." Oz added.

"Why would kidnappers want to kill you?"

Mull shrugged. "People are assholes."

"But why kidnap everyone else, but murder *you*?"

Mull scoffed. "Do I seem like the type of girl who gets kidnapped? I'm strictly in the 'potential *kidnapper*' bracket on that."

"Do you have any idea who could be behind this?" Oklahoma inquired, more from politeness than from any apparent interest.

"We're looking for these two men." Oz laid two more photos

on the table. "August and Anton Masterson. They did wetwork for the Freedom Squad security forces, and have been underground since."

"Okay." Oklahoma's expression remained the same. "Anyone else?"

"Well, your boss is at the top of our suspect list." Oz told her flatly, watching to see what her reaction would be.

Whatever he was expecting to find there, he didn't see it. The woman's excruciatingly perfect cover model face didn't so much as twitch. "Mister Welles' name comes pre-printed at the top of *all* suspect lists. He's rarely responsible though."

"How do you know?"

"Because if he were responsible, *I* would have been the one to hire these men." Oklahoma picked up the photos, then shook her head. "And I've never seen them before in my life." She dropped the photos back to the table. "Plus, if he wanted you dead, you'd be dead."

Oz carefully moved the photos so that they were in an even line on the table, unable to stand the disorderly pile Oklahoma had left them in. "I believe it's somehow related to Mercygiver and the Agletarians."

"Uh-huh." Oklahoma smiled as the waiter brought her a strawberry malt. She took a careful sip from the straw, somehow not smudging her vampy blood red lipstick, but impossibly *still* leaving a perfect sexy little lip smudge on the plastic. "And have you told Mr. Montgomery of your suspicions?"

Mull snorted at the idea. "Why would I tell Montgomery *anything*?"

Oklahoma took another sip of her treat. "I'm just wondering what he'd like me to do here."

"He wants you to help us." Oz reminded her.

"I think you'll find that when a Welles is involved, things aren't always what they appear to be." She made a circular motion using her fingers. "'Gears within gears,' and all that."

Mull heaved a sigh, sick of the runaround. "Do you know anything or not?"

Oklahoma thought that over, obviously debating the matter and whether or not she should say something. "As it happens, yes, I am missing one of my clients. An aspiring heroine who is striped like a zebra."

Mull squinted at her in confusion. "If she's a Cape, why is she a client of yours?"

"Because, as surprising as it seems, having stripes has limited crime-fighting applications." Oklahoma ate the cherry from her dessert. "But can you even *imagine* how much men would pay to see her spread eagle and glorious? Just out of mere curiosity, if nothing else. All those interesting lines tracing her flawless curves? She's a work of art. Hell, even *I* kind of want to see her naked." She took another long sip from her straw. "Cape erotica provides so many opportunities like that, to see the unique forms which the human body can take, and marvel at the wonder that is life. God has an incredible imagination and we can best admire His work by looking at it unadorned by clothes, seeing us as He intended." She brightened. "Incidentally, if you're curious, she will have a starring role in a pornographic *Lion King* parody movie that I'm producing. I'm calling it: '*The Loin King*.'"

Mull chuckled in spite of herself.

"She hasn't called in a week and her apartment is now vacant." Oklahoma continued.

Mull was entirely unconcerned. "Maybe she thought twice about becoming a prostitute for Montgomery Welles."

"She is a nude model and aspiring actress, *not* a prostitute." Oklahoma corrected, sounding insulted on the other woman's behalf. "Whether she decides to expand her repertoire or not is entirely up to *her*, not Mr. Welles, you, me, or anyone else. I'm a manager and producer, I simply help people in whatever career decisions they make. But I *can* tell you that if you're only using your superpowers to save the world, you lack imagination."

"So...," Mull summarized, "she was a *prospective* whore for Montgomery Welles."

"She worked with *me*, not Mister Welles."

"But *you* work for Mister Welles." Mull pressed.

Oklahoma shrugged. "Sometimes."

"And the other times?"

The woman's perfect green eyes narrowed. "Are *my* business."

"And you're happy with this relationship?" Mull leaned back in her seat. "Letting someone like *Monty* do this to you?"

"To be clear," Oklahoma's voice took on a harder edge, "this is *my* business. It's a side enterprise I occupy myself with when I'm not needed at home. Mr. Welles provides me free manpower and support when I need it, but *I* make the decisions in my company." She took another sip of her beverage, talking around the mouthful of strawberry malt. "He disapproves of it. Intensely. Finds it '*unseemly*,' if you can imagine that." She nodded in approval, obviously pleased with that.

"When a *supervillain* tells you you've gone too far, that's how you know you're good at your job."

"Technically, he's just a 'villain,' not '*super*villain.'" Oz corrected. "He has no powers, he's just a particularly evil Mystery Man."

"I've always considered the 'super' to mean more that the villain in question is exceptionally dangerous," Oklahoma thought aloud, "not that they possess any sort of super-power."

"Well, you'd be wrong." Mull deadpanned.

"Nice argument." Oklahoma stirred her dessert. "You have real skills in debate, has anyone told you that?"

"Just a bunch of people who are now dead but still wrong."

Oz got the talk back on topic once more. "I think Montgomery has sent us to you because he thinks the disappearance of your friend is part of our investigation, and he wants us to help you."

The other woman considered that while stirring her malt. "If he did, then he must have a lot of faith in you."

"So it would seem."

"Okay." Oklahoma nodded, the situation apparently settled in her mind now. "As it happens, I have a lot of faith in *him*."

"Why?" Mull asked, genuinely both confused and horrified by the mere idea. "He's the most selfish person I've ever met."

"You just say that because you didn't know his little sisters." The woman winked at her. "I think what you seem to be misunderstanding about Mr. Welles is..." The woman's phone unexpectedly rang to the "Heigh-Ho!" song that the dwarfs sing in *Snow White* while working in the mine. She held up one graceful finger again, asking for a pause. "Would you excuse me for a moment, please? Irregulars business." She pressed a button on the phone. "*Speak*." She was silent for a moment. "Why hasn't he been released from custody?" She listened to something, then rolled her eyes, making an exasperated sound, as if she were the most mistreated person in the world. "Oh, fuck the law, I work for *Montgomery Welles!*" She reminded the person on the phone, like that excused her from such trivialities. Her voice became hard as she started shouting. "And if my friend isn't released *within the hour*, I will send a dozen Irregulars to your house and I will put your entire family into a *fucking blender, one tiny bloody chunk at a time*, then use their liquefied remains to *water board* you! *Do you understand me!?!*" She held the phone away from her face to scream into the microphone. *"I will drown you in your wife and kids!!!"* She was quiet for another beat.

"No. No, shut your goddamned mouth! NOW! I *don't* want excuses or a lesson in legalities which *don't* apply to Mister Welles, I'll have my associate *released* or I'll have *your blood*. *Pick one!*" She listened for a moment, then her voice became flirty and calm again. "Mister Welles thanks you for seeing reason, Judge Elliot. Always a pleasure. And have a *wonderful* Thanksgiving." She jabbed one perfectly manicured fingernail into the display, hanging up the phone. "People think that just because you're a hero now, that they can push you around."

Mull nodded. "Word."

Oz frowned at her in amused disbelief. "'Word'?" He repeated.

"I got a lot of shit going on in my head, Oz." She gestured to her temple and made a vague swirly gesture. "I have to go with what I got and sometimes weird stuff comes out. Gimme a break."

"Word." He nodded in agreement.

Natalie snorted in amusement, swatting at him playfully. Then she paused, hoping that touching him didn't cause him to freak out because she'd be spreading her germs or whatever.

She had to remember not to touch him, no matter how much she loved it or how hard it was for her to keep away.

She didn't want to trigger him or make him uncomfortable.

"Sorry." She said softly.

Oz simply frowned at her in confusion. "For?"

Oklahoma refocused on the conversation. "Where was I?"

"I believe you were about to defend your boss, the megalomaniacal madman." Mull reminded her. "We were in the process of thinking you're brainwashed and crazy, while trying not to pity you, because you kinda seem like a slutty bitch anyway."

"Ah, yes. Thank you." Oklahoma nodded, like that reminded her of what she wanted to say. "Let's get one thing straight: I'm an *Irregular*." She moved the lapel of her tuxedo jacket to reveal a double "P" Purchasing and Production pendant, which was dangling along with two other charms between her obnoxiously perfect breasts in a *deliberately* sexual way. Her particular version of the symbol was gold though, signifying that not only was she an Irregular, but she was also a member of Monty's inner circle, the "Executive Staff." She shook her head. "I'm not a drone and I'm not brainwashed. Mister Welles isn't my boss; he's my *family.* I don't have super-powers, I'm just a whore with people skills and an ear to the ground. But I owe that man. I can *never* repay him for all he's done for me." She tapped her fingernail on the table meaningfully. "He has earned my unconditional loyalty. Forever. I don't need pity. This isn't a story where I learn the error of my ways and escape him with your help. I don't need or want that. This is a story where I will gladly do whatever he needs me to do, because I want to do it. I *believe* in Montgomery Welles. I truly do. And there isn't a single Irregular who wouldn't tell you the same." She looked as confused and horrified by Mull and Oz as they were with her. "But for some reason, you people can just never understand what it means to belong to a *family*."

"And what does it mean?" Oz asked.

"It means that if he wanted you dead or if I thought you meant him harm, I'd kill you with my bare hands right here." The woman casually threatened. "Happily. No questions asked, no regrets felt."

Mull gave a long slow "Dammit, you're *crazy*, girl" kind of whistle.

"If you have no one you'd die for and no one who would die for you, then that says more about *your* life than it does about *mine*." Oklahoma reminded them. "But whether you think I'm crazy and brainwashed or not, I would quite literally do *anything* for him, and you are his friends and he wants me to help you, so I extend to *you* that same undying loyalty." Her voice became completely sincere, issuing a solemn vow. "I am not the most powerful person in this city. Far from it. But my organization and its assets are now *yours*. Tell me what you want and I will *get it done*, even if it kills me and costs me every goddamned thing I have in this world. I will do it, I swear to God and Montgomery Welles, I will. It'll get done. You have my absolute *word on it*."

The words hung in the air for a long moment, as they processed the almost religious zeal of the woman's vow.

"We need August and Anton Masterson." Oz finally informed her again. "Quick as you can."

"Okay. How would you like them killed?" Oklahoma asked flatly, like a clerk at a fastfood place asking you if you wanted fries with your order. "Do you want them to disappear or would you like it to be public and bloody as a warning to others?"

Mull brightened, instantly more interested in the conversation. "Oh, public and...!"

"We don't want them dead," Oz interrupted, "we're just looking for them. We need to follow them to get to the Agletarians."

"I understand." Oklahoma pulled out her phone again and pressed several buttons rapidly, then put it to her ear. "Put the word out: Montgomery Welles is looking for August and Anton Masterson. We want their current location, *immediately*. Put everyone on it, tell everyone who owes us a favor that it's time to make good. *Hunt the bastards down*." She pressed the disconnect button, and casually continued the conversation. "Was there anything else?"

"So this is really what you do then?" Mull wondered aloud, feeling like she was watching sausage get made. The Purchasing and Production Department was a bit of an unknown, and Mull was grotesquely fascinated to watch from the inside as one of its wheels turned.

"Yes." Oklahoma nodded. "I oversee Mr. Welles' less tangible assets, such as law enforcement personnel, legislators, prominent citizens, low-level criminals, informants... that kind of thing. Anyone in the world outside of the Irregulars, Wellesburg, and 'Special Projects.' I manage the people we control or who owe us a favor. I relay messages and information between them and Mr. Welles. I issue his orders and make sure they're carried out." She finished off her malt. "Do you know what a political whip is? They don't chart the course or shout orders to the men. They simply make sure everyone on the team is... rowing in the right direction. And I can be *very* persuasive." The next words seemed so obvious to Oklahoma, that they came out sounding like a given. "But it's very easy work. Mister Welles is a man of unborrowed vision." Monty's Girl Friday informed them seriously, something close to pride or wonder in her voice.

"He's a power hungry madman." Oz deadpanned.

Oklahoma shrugged, unconcernedly. "Name me one great visionary in history who *wasn't*."

"He's gotten a lot of people killed."

Oklahoma held up a finger, believing she was about to impart on them great wisdom. "As Helena Welles, Montgomery's grandmother, used to tell me: 'Eggs have no business dancing with stones.'"

"You love him." Oz decided, reading between the lines. "Don't you?" It wasn't really a question.

"Jesus." To Mull's surprise, Oklahoma laughed in delighted mirth, as if that idea were charmingly amusing. "You people have seen *Pretty Woman* too many times." She slid her empty strawberry malt glass out of the way. "It *is* possible to work with someone of the opposite sex without falling in love with them, you know."

"Particularly when they're an asshole." Mull observed.

Oklahoma's eyes narrowed, obviously taking offense on her boss' behalf. "He's just misunderstood."

"I understand him real well." Mull challenged. "He's essentially Ratigan from *The Great Mouse Detective*. But with less singing. And without the inherent charm of Vincent Price."

The woman stared at her for a moment, then snorted in laughter. "Ha! I can see that." She pulled out her phone to type something into it. "Hold on a sec, let me text that to Higgins, he'll *love* it…"

"Maybe we *do* understand him real well because we've known him longer than you have."

"Possibly." Oklahoma was busy sending her text, not even looking at them. "I haven't known him as long as some people. Just since I was 4. Higgins has known him since he was born." She arched an eyebrow. "How about you?"

"I've known him about 3 years."

"207 days." Oz reported, apparently *literally* counting.

"I bow to your greater experience with him then, obviously." Oklahoma pressed send on her phone.

"I don't get it." Mull let out a long, confused breath. "I'm so sick of listening to the Irregulars talk about how amazing Monty is. They treat him like he's God and I just don't understand it."

"Neither do I, to tell you the truth." Oklahoma agreed. "I mean, he's good and all, don't get me wrong, but he's no Montgomery Welles."

Mull and Oz simply stared at the woman, not reacting to the joke at all.

At least, Mull *assumed* it was a joke, anyway.

Oklahoma didn't appear to notice the pause in the conversation. "But that's okay. I'll still help you with your little 'investigation.'"

"We're also looking into the Agletarian matter." Oz informed her. "Can you tell us anything about that? Why they're after Natalie?"

The question seemed to give Oklahoma pause, and her eternally confident façade dropped for the briefest of seconds.

She was hiding something. Something she knew about it. But she wasn't sure if she could tell them or not.

Before they could press her, the phone was already up to her ear again. "It's me, Champ. Question: do you want me to tell them everything or just the stuff they want to know?" She listened to the reply. "Alright, understood." She pressed the disconnect button on the phone. "They're from the research and development branch of the Agletarian military."

Oz's eyebrows soared. "How do you know this?"

"I am surprisingly good at some things. This is one of the ones which doesn't require me to take off my clothes first." She put her phone away. "They call themselves 'Unit 691.' They are, to put it simply, the worst people you can *possibly* imagine. They get their rocks off doing experiments on prisoners and civilians. Cutting them up in the name of science. Giving them diseases to test infection rates. Mowing down political dissidents to test new weapons. They once had a super-person breeding program, in hopes of creating an interesting combination of powers. If you name an atrocity, these guys have the merit badge for it. They've done it to their enemies and their friends and to their own children. All in the service of their fanatical state and their own loony ideals. They are evil, in the truest and least hyperbolic sense of the word. If you believe in Hell, those people *genuinely* belong there." She looked at Mull. "And now they're here in the city. Apparently trying to kill you."

"Why?"

"You're not a popular person, in case it's escaped your attention." Oklahoma seemed to take that as a given. "I barely know you and I already have plenty of reasons to want you dead."

"Do you and Monty know the *specific* reasons why they're here to kill her?" Oz pressed, losing his patience with the woman.

Oklahoma continued staring at him, avoiding the question.

"But you're not going to tell us." Mull guessed.

"I'm with Welles." She reminded them.

"He's a monster, Oklahoma." Oz said softly, trying to reach the woman with reason.

Mull waggled her hand in the air, unhappy with that term. "I'd go with 'malignant narcissist.'"

"Yes." Oklahoma agreed, sounding almost sad about that. Mull wasn't sure whether the woman was agreeing with him being a monster or him being a narcissist. Or both. "He is." She made a circle motion with her fingers, turning them around one another again. "But 'gears within gears.'" She leaned forward. "You're a part of the machine now. Walking Mister Welles' crooked mile, like the rest of us. Just where that road is going and what role you're playing is beyond my pay grade. But I can tell you this: I *will* help you in any way that I can. I am on your side."

Oz let out a tired sigh, seeing where this would end. "...Until Monty tells you not to be." He finished for her.

"Obviously." The woman shrugged again. "I'm an Irregular." Her phone rang and she answered it on the second ring. "Speak." Pause. "Excellent. Yes, I'll tell him. I'm sure he'll appreciate that. Cherry is his favorite." Pause. *"Yes, I'll tell him, I'll tell him..."* She hung up, then pulled a gold pen from her pocket and wrote something down on a napkin for them. "August and Anton Masterson can be found at this address." She slid the paper across the table to them. "They're there now. If you change your mind and *would* like them dead, I can have it done in…" she casually checked her watch, "…8 minutes."

"I think the address will be sufficient." Oz looked down at the napkin, obviously debating with himself about whether or not it was clean enough to touch.

Mull made the decision for him, and stuffed it into her pocket.

"I can get you a search warrant for the apartment, if that would be helpful." Oklahoma volunteered.

Oz shook his head. "We're not the police."

"Mister Welles knows several judges who won't get distracted by that technicality." Oklahoma promised. "Did you need anything else from my organization?"

"I'm looking for Mercygiver." Oz's voice was hard, filled with hate.

That seemed to genuinely rattle the woman. She leaned back in her seat. "Rondel has killed friends of every person in this establishment. Many of the people on that wall over there?" She pointed to a display of dozens of framed photos, apparently honoring deceased villains. "*Butchered them.* You won't find a more unpopular or feared person in the industry at the moment."

"That's why I'm going to kill him." Mull promised.

"I'm sorry?" Oklahoma's impossibly perfect face scrunched up in confusion. "Is that a joke?" She looked at Mull in amazement, evidently questioning how someone so innocent looking could ever stand up to a monster. "*You* are trying to kill Mercygiver? *That's* what this is about?"

Mull nodded.

The woman blinked at her for a second. Then two. Then burst out laughing. She put her head back and roared. "Oh, Champ, you always have the most *interesting* problems, don't you?" She pounded the table in mirth. "My mama warned me. 'It's never easy when a Welles is involved. They are lords of steam and steel, they aren't our kind,' she said, 'They have empires on the brain.' But I didn't listen." She rearranged the hat on her head. "Sometimes I wish I could trade jobs with Higgins and let *him* deal with the crazy for a few days. I tell him stories, but I don't think he believes them."

They continued silently staring at the woman, waiting for her to finish with her mocking laughter.

278

Oklahoma remembered that she was supposed to be working for them at the moment, and cleared her throat to return to her job. "I'm sorry. You're going to kill Mercygiver." She repeated. "Of course you are."

"We don't work together anymore." Mull shook her head. "I hate him as much as *any of you*. He ruined my life and I'm going to make the bastard *bleed*."

Oklahoma's eyes narrowed, silently reminding Mull of all of the horrors she'd helped that man commit over the years. "Frankly, I'm having difficulty believing that."

"I might not look it right now because my face is currently at the shop getting repaired," Mull lowered her voice to a hard edge, "but I *guarantee you*, I am *very* good at my job and I *will* kill that bastard."

"Again, you'll have to forgive me if I remain skeptical." Oklahoma leaned further across the table, her voice low and vaguely threatening. "Listen, you can put on your little show for this *beautiful* gentleman here," she turned to look at Oz, "incidentally, *please* call me and I can find you *lots* of work in my industry," she refocused on Mull, "but I *know* who you are and I *know* what you've done. You are *not* an innocent and you will *never* be on the side of the angels. You haven't stopped. You'll *never* stop. Because you are fucking evil." Her eyes narrowed. "And if this meeting wasn't for Mister Welles, I would spit in your goddamn face right here."

Oz's voice took on a hard edge to match the woman's. "Whatever Miss Quentin did or didn't do in her past is *no one's* business but her own. She's moved on from her dealings with Mercygiver and has made a new life for herself. All of that is behind her. And to be honest, are *you* really in any position to throw stones about making illegal business decisions in order to survive?"

"Touché." Oklahoma seemed to accept that. "No matter. As I said, I would gladly lay down my life for Mister Welles and the other Irregulars. If he wants me to help you, no matter how *distasteful* I may find it, I will help you."

"Where does Rondel hide out these days?" Oz pressed, expecting it to be that easy.

"Mercygiver is obviously *not* a client." Oklahoma shook her head. "I would *never* do business with someone like *that*. So I honestly have no idea. But if you find the Agletarians, Mercygiver will find *you*. My advice would be to be ready." She smiled at them again, once more the helpful waitress asking for their order. Or, more accurately, the evil genie who was waiting for you to wish yourself into oblivion. "Is that all you wanted or did Mister Welles need me to assist you in some other manner?" She paused for a beat. "Anything at all?"

Mull wasn't entirely sure, but it kind of sounded like the woman had just asked them if Monty wanted her to sleep with them or not.

Oz seemed to come to a similar conclusion, and immediately shook his head. "No, I think we're good, thanks."

Oklahoma stared at them silently for a beat, recognizing their inference. She took on a serious, but slightly amused tone. "Sir, with all due respect, if you *really* think Mister Welles would whore me out to you, then you have *vastly* overestimated your importance to him." She stood and started to leave, but then leaned down to whisper in Mull's ear so that Oz didn't hear. "A piece of free advice? If I were you, I'd try to forget all about Mercygiver and just leave things as they are. Trust me when I say this: you've got a nice thing here. He's a beautiful man. He doesn't deserve what I think we both *know* is going to happen to him if you push this."

"I can keep Oz safe." Mull told her flatly, trying to sound surer than she felt.

"Not from you." Oklahoma stood up straight again. "But, as I said, it's none of my concern." She tipped her hat to them. "The happiest of Thanksgivings to you both."

"Well, we'll be sure to tell Monty you helped us like he asked." Oz told her, apparently trying to be nice, because Oz's dominant personality traits were rule-following, obsessive compulsions, and overt niceness to horrible people. It was sickening sometimes.

"Don't bother. I'm an Irregular, Oswald." Oklahoma Mike started towards the door. "He already knows I'll help him."

Chapter 16

Mercygiver stared at the man sitting across from him, debating whether or not to kill him.

On one hand, humanity would probably throw him some sort of parade if he did. It was, perhaps, the only thing Mercygiver could ever do which would secure him a permanent place among the angels.

But on the other... it seemed like it would be such a tremendous bother.

Mercygiver leaned back in his chair. "I think the problem here is that you seem to be under the mistaken belief that I'm still somehow open to being hired." Mercygiver shook his head. "I'm the one who *gives* the orders now."

"I'm not giving you orders, I'm merely informing you that I'm in the need of your services again." The man replied, looking as bored as Mercygiver. "And you need my assistance in achieving your goals."

"How so?"

"Because I'm the only man in town who knows where Multifarious is hiding, and who is also morally flexible enough to sell her out to you." The man casually looked out the window, like this was a bother.

"So," Mercygiver squinted at this unexpected offer, "I help you with your project, and you'll help me with mine." He summarized.

"Indeed." The man nodded. "We have a long history of mutual cooperation. We're both in the business of using non-powered people to take on our super-powered enemies. The way I see it, there's no reason at all why we should have an issue between us."

"Uh... Boss?" Mr. Jack didn't seem at all excited about this business opportunity. "Not to tell you how to do your whole 'crime syndicate' thing, but..."

Mercygiver held up his hand, stopping Mr. Jack's nonsense cold. "Very well." He nodded. "I am open to such an arrangement. But what assurances do I have that this isn't some kind of trap?"

The man looked amused by that. "There is no benefit to me in doing such a thing. Your personal difficulties serve as a nice distraction to my other efforts. No matter which of you comes out on top, it really doesn't affect my business at all." He steepled his fingers. "I typically let associates settle their own internal conflicts, particularly if I can't use it to gain any real advantage. You and I have worked together in the past, but I generally avoid her. I find that she lacks imagination. And OCD is even worse."

"I'm going to kill her, you know." Mercygiver told him bluntly, angered by his words for some reason.

The man shrugged disinterestedly. "A lot of people die in this city. Better her than someone I *do* care about. To be honest, I like you more anyway."

"*You* care about someone?" Mercygiver challenged. "Since when?"

"*I* count as someone." The man crossed his legs. "And I would be so terribly disappointed in myself if you killed me. I really expect better from myself than that."

Mercygiver approached the window and looked out on the snowy street below him. "You a history fan, my friend?"

"Not really."

"Do you know where the term "baker's dozen" originates?"

His guest all but rolled his eyes at that, looking bored. "I typically have bigger issues on my plate than obscure historical trivia, sadly."

Rondel's eyes narrowed, feeling like that was an insult. He immediately considered stabbing the man to death, right then and there. But didn't.

For some reason, the words made him sad, but he didn't know why.

Why did *no one* appreciate history anymore? Why was it so difficult to talk to people about these kinds of things? Was there *no one* who shared his interests?

It was very disheartening.

The world simply didn't understand.

And Mercygiver had grown so tired of trying to make himself understood, that he recognized it was simply easier to make himself *obeyed*.

Christ... he was lonely.

Things were never *perfect* with her, obviously. But... but she had been there. To tease him and laugh at his jokes and...

He could at least *talk* to her. She'd been there to notice his little quirks and share his passions.

But all of that had been a lie.

She'd left him and he was all alone and he didn't know how to deal with that. She had given him a home and a friend and someone who he thought loved him... and then she'd *torn that away from him.*

His new plan was to keep the woman around for a while, before finally killing her, just so he had someone to talk to. Granted, most of that "talking" would involve insults and brutal threats of sexual violence, but the basic idea was the same.

Mercygiver was a broken wreck of a man without her.

He'd make her pay dearly for that.

He stared down at the street, hating everyone. Hating the snow, and the cars, and the trees, and the fucking birds in those trees. He hated the cheerful Thanksgiving themed decorations, and the street signs, and all of the couples in love.

He hated every fucking thing he saw.

He wanted it all to die. To know the isolation and pain that he dealt with every fucking day, and then to die.

Miserable and alone.

He cleared the lump in his throat. "From the 13th century." Mercygiver informed the man, recognizing that the man didn't care and wouldn't understand the metaphor he was trying to make, but he was going to tell him anyway. Because there was simply no one else around to listen. "When a statute was instituted in England, which said that bakers who were found to have cheated customers by not giving them what was paid for or by selling bread with too many air pockets, could be subject to severe punishment, including having their hand cut off with an ax. Unsurprisingly, bakers decided that the best way to guard against this was to give people *more* than they paid for, just to make certain that no one could ever accuse them of not giving their customers the right amount of breadstuffs." He paused. "So, you order a dozen of something and they gave you the 12 you ordered, plus an extra one as insurance against you being unhappy and complaining to authorities, and then the baker losing his or her hands. A 'baker's dozen.'" He turned around to face the man, making his point. "Think of that: unscrupulous bakers tried to rip someone off, and they got mutilated so horribly, that 800 years later, you *still* get an extra bagel, just so that it never happens again."

They were both silent for a moment.

"People can't let bad things go, especially when it gives them power." The man summarized, deliberately missing the threat. "But that's why *our* relationship is so magical: because we *already* dislike each other."

"Very well." Mercygiver nodded, seeing no real downside to the arrangement. "I think we can work together." And if they couldn't, he'd just kill him. Which would also be a benefit to Mercygiver, so win-win. "Where is she?"

"I still need her for one more part of my project." The man assured him. "But as soon as the pieces are in place, I'll let you spring the trap and you can do whatever you want to her, with my compliments."

Mercygiver wasn't happy about the delay, but saw no need to press the matter here. There were other ways to get the information the man possessed. Easier ways. Mercygiver wasn't terribly good at waiting. He'd work his way through the man's underlings one by one until he got the woman's whereabouts.

"And the job you need my assistance for?" Mercygiver asked, rather curious.

Montgomery Welles put his top hat back on his head, a slight smile forming on his twisted face. "I want you to blow up the Consortium's base for me."

Chapter 17

"'WOULD YOU TELL ME, PLEASE, WHICH WAY I OUGHT
TO GO FROM HERE?'

'THAT DEPENDS A GOOD DEAL ON WHERE YOU WANT
TO GET TO,' SAID THE CAT.

'I DON'T MUCH CARE WHERE--' SAID ALICE.

'THEN IT DOESN'T MATTER WHICH WAY YOU GO,' SAID
THE CAT.

'--SO LONG AS I GET SOMEWHERE,' ALICE ADDED AS
AN EXPLANATION.

'OH, YOU'RE SURE TO DO THAT,' SAID THE CAT, 'IF YOU
ONLY WALK LONG ENOUGH.'"

- Alice's Adventures in Wonderland

By the time Mull arrived back at Oz's house, her absence had already been noted. Which wasn't really something she wanted to deal with right now.

As soon as she walked in, Holly glanced up and frowned at her. "Oz said you're not supposed to leave without one of us going with you." She reminded her. "He was quite adamant about that."

Natalie rolled her eyes, putting her coat back on the hook. "I have a job, Holl." She retorted. "The store has a $14,000,000 Thanksgiving parade in a few days, and Mr. Martinez needs all hands on deck."

"Are they paying you extra for that?"

Natalie shook her head. "No, it's a volunteer thing."

Holly snorted at that idea.

"I've spent all morning talking to the administrators of the Horizons Academy, coordinating with them so all of their empowered students can march in the parade. And dealing with the musical acts, which is a whole other set of problems. As it turns out, *The Lusty Carnies* had a scheduling conflict, and the only group I can get is *Half-*

Priced Sex Acts, but then I have an issue with the TV networks not using the name. And, ironically enough, their price is double that of *The Lusty Carnies*."

"It's all pre-recorded anyway," Traitor reminded them, "just use the audio from the real group and hire some random people to pretend to be the singers. Hell, I'll do it. No one will know the difference. Trust me."

Natalie ignored Traitor's suggestion, because as usual, it was preaching the benefits of weaving an elaborate tapestry of lies. "I'm wondering if that bitch from the *Adventure Academy* films wants to try her hand at singing instead..." She tapped her finger against her bottom lip, thinking.

Holly made a humoring sound. "Obviously an issue worth you dying over."

Natalie made a face. "I refuse to lose my job at the store because of Oz's paranoia."

"How is he being paranoid?" Holly squinted in confusion. "You've almost died like... three times this week. So far."

"They tried to kill you too," Natalie rolled her eyes again, "but he doesn't demand that *you* have a bodyguard."

"They only tried to kill me because I was standing next to you. And he doesn't care if I live or die, because he's not trying to screw *me*."

The phrasing got Traitor's attention, and his head whipped around to watch the goings-on. "Wait, what? Who's screwing Holly?"

"No one." Nat rolled her eyes for the third time in as many minutes, wondering if that was somehow one of her powers today.

"Unfortunately." Holly added, heaving a dramatic sigh. "In any event, he got home half an hour ago, then went out looking for you again."

"Where else would I possibly go?" Nat wondered aloud. "I have a job, an apartment, and almost all of my friends are in the room right now." She flopped down into one of Oz's stiff, ultra-modern looking armchairs, wishing the man didn't have crazy issues with fabrics and comfort. It was like sitting on a park bench, but one covered in sandpaper. She glanced over at the man sitting next to her. Apparently, Oz had gotten so concerned about her disappearance that he'd called in one of the Consortium's strongest and most invulnerable members, Hazard Granger.

Hazard was over seven feet of muscle and apathy, tied around the finger of his petite and perky wife.

"Hey Hazz." She greeted him friendlily. "So you got drafted

into this too, huh?"

The man nodded. "Uh-huh." He continued flipping through what appeared to be a back issue of *Nintendo Power* from the 1990s, obviously doing homework for future conversations with his wife. Hazard studied his wife's interests the way other men might study for the Bar exam. Keeping her happy with him was his one all-consuming passion and it typically filled his entire day.

"Where's Stacy?"

"My wife is visiting her nemesis in prison at the moment." Hazard replied, not looking up from his magazine, which featured a cover story on a then new *Metroid* video game.

"Ah, that's nice."

"Why?" Traitor asked, confused by the idea.

"To gloat, look at pictures of our wedding, and discuss the new *Star Wars* movie." Hazz turned the page. "It's a complicated relationship."

"And you didn't go?"

"She made me promise to stay here and watch out for you this afternoon, because you almost died the other day and that was 'such a bummer' and she doesn't want it to happen again." Hazz reported, nonchalantly. "And that Bekki is 'the kind of evil my gentle soul needs to be protected from,' so Stacy wanted to go alone and made me promise not to follow her, 'for my own sake.'" Hazz unfolded a map of a game level, studying it the way someone lost in the woods would look at his only lifeline to rescue. "Which means it's just her... and Kass, obviously."

Before Natalie could reply to that, the bell rang.

Traitor jumped to his feet, looking down at his watch. "Dammit." He raced to the door and leaned against the jamb. "Who is it?"

"Take one goddamn guess." Poacher's voice answered gruffly.

Traitor made a face and opened the door for him.

Sydney stumbled in, an unconscious man slung over his shoulder. "Relax, *I got the bastard!*" He announced with no small amount of pride. "He was lurking around and then put up a fight when I confronted him, but I fucked him up *and good*."

Mull stared at the unconscious man in question. "That's the doorman."

"The Doorman!" Poacher repeated in an "A-HA!" kind of way, like it was a criminal moniker of insidious renown and cracked the whole mystery. "What can he do?"

"Open doors for people?" She looked up at Syd. "You just beat up a perfectly innocent guy."

"Oh, bullshit!" He pointed at the man. "Why is he in costume then!?!"

"That's a uniform." She corrected. "A doorman's uniform which he wears. For his job. As a doorman."

He let out a long sigh and dropped the man to the ground like a ton of bricks. "Well, shit. Wyatt's going to be pissed."

"Meh. Just douse the guy in whiskey and dump him in the alley. Everyone will assume he's a drunk and imagining things." Holly suggested. "That's what I always do."

Everyone looked at her.

"Or don't." She continued, quickly covering. "Because that would be wrong." She returned to her book. "...Obviously."

Poacher nodded, subtly shifting his feet so that he was closer to the door. "I'm fanatically against lying to the public, because Harlot always freaks out about it, but I think what the..." He bolted from the room without finishing the thought, fleeing the situation and the unconscious man, like the coward he was.

Mull let out a sigh.

How typical.

She frowned down at Oz's doorman, wondering exactly what she should do about this. She wasn't really used to there being *consequences* for actions. Usually, she would have been first in line to laugh her ass off over the fact that Poacher had beat this guy up. But this wasn't just some random doorman. This was *Oz's doorman!* That connection to Oz made this guy important. Well, *kind of* important, anyway.

She bent down to check the man's pulse.

The bell rang again.

Traitor jumped to his feet, looking at his watch. "Dammit." He raced to the door, glancing down at her on his way. "If you're looking for his wallet, I think Syd already stole it." He informed her sadly, obviously disappointed that he had missed that windfall. Then he arrived next to the door and leaned against the jamb. "Who is it?"

"Pizza, sir." The man on the other side informed him. "Somebody order three pies?"

Traitor was silent for a long moment. "Pizza?" He asked again, like he'd never heard the word before.

"Yeah," the delivery guy responded, "from Tony's?"

"Do I know a 'Tony'?" Traitor wondered aloud. "The name doesn't ring a bell."

"It's the name of the restaurant, sir." The delivery guy was clearly getting irritated now. "Listen, do you want them or not?"

Traitor looked down at his watch again. "Yeah... I... think... I... ordered... those..."

"*Today*, sir!" The delivery guy's temper snapped. "I have other deliveries to make!"

"In a minute..." Traitor stalled, then opened the door with a friendly smile on his face. "Thanks so much! I'm starved!"

The man on the other side of the door pulled out the receipt. "That'll be $61.38."

Traitor took on a disappointed face. "Oh, I'm afraid you didn't *quite* make it here within your thirty minute guarantee." He held up his watch to show the man. "One minute late." He shrugged helplessly, like it was beyond his control and wasn't the result of making the man wait on the other side of the door. He grabbed the pizzas. "Happy Thanksgiving, though!" He slammed the door and turned around. "Pizza is here! You guys owe me $60."

Natalie watched as the little slices of grease and cheese were handed out, trying not to cringe at the thought of anything staining Oz's immaculate apartment.

"Do we not have plates?" She asked the room, hurrying off to Oz's kitchen to grab them. She threw open several cupboards to find that... no. No, they didn't. They appeared to have one set of dishes and silverware, along with a dishwasher that looked powerful enough to sanitize surgical instruments.

She quickly improvised, grabbing some apparently sterile paper towels and passing them out to the assembly, hoping to head off the worst of the stains and spills.

"If it was anyone but Oz, you'd be the first one to dump the pizza on the floor, just to send a message." Holly critiqued, sounding disapproving of Natalie's common courtesy.

"If it were anyone else but Oz, I wouldn't even be here to have the pizza." Nat retorted, returning to her seat and *carefully* eating her slice. "I want Oz to be happy, that's all."

"Still trying to seduce him?"

Nat didn't bother responding.

"Yep." Holly answered her own question. "And how's that going, girlfriend?"

"...Not well." Nat made a face. "He's hard to impress. I jumped out a window and beat up a guy the other day, and he didn't care. I've never tried to get the attention of someone... *nice* before. It's hard. I don't understand what he wants me to do."

"Be nice?" Holly guessed.

Mull snorted at the idea. "Oh, fuck *that*." She took a bite of her pizza. "I think the problem is Natalie. *Fuck* Natalie. She can't get the job done." She took another bite of her slice, gesturing to her face with her other hand. "It's like trying to be sexy when you look like a goddamn *Precious Moments* figurine."

"Some men go for 'wholesome.'" Holly thought aloud.

"I'd take 'sex goddess' any day." She crossed her legs, then uncrossed them again because the chair was too stiff and uncomfortable to attempt to sit like that without resulting in debilitating spinal injury. "We spoke with this woman this morning who was like... *wow*. You look at her and are positive that somewhere in the world there's a horny teenage boy with only two wishes left. A woman like *that* would have no trouble convincing Oz to overlook the billions of bacteria and viruses crawling all over her skin."

Holly made a disgusted face and slowly put down her food. "Ew."

Mull waved a dismissive hand at her. "Oh, I'm told everyone has them. Don't act like it's just me. You're crawling with microbes and viruses too." Mull angrily took another bite, still dwelling on the woman. "Fucking evil bitch. Oz played it all cool, but I know he was thinking it."

"It's really difficult for me to imagine Oz thinking about *any* woman sexually." Holly sounded equal parts amazed and disturbed by the thought. "I always kinda figured that if he ever got an erection, he'd cry and then go pray about it."

"And you just *know* she was all over him too. Telling him how handsome he was and asking to represent him..."

"Represent him in what?"

"Porn." Mull paused for a beat. "I should kill her." Her voice grew harsher. "Teach her a lesson about trying to keep me from what's *mine*..."

"Wait, wait, wait..." Holly sat up straighter in her chair, "you're talking about *Oklahoma Mike*? Monty's whore?"

"Yeah."

"Oooh, girlfriend," Holly let out a low sympathetic whistle, "you'd better *hope* she doesn't want your man. Because you know I love you and all, so no offense, but 9 out of 10 men would pick her over you. And the last guy would probably pick the 9 other men." She grabbed another slice of pizza. "Sorry."

"Oz wouldn't *touch* that woman."

"I think you'd be surprised at what men will touch if it has breasts."

"His problem is his obsessions and rituals." Mull thought aloud, ignoring Holly. "But I've been reading this book about it, and..."

"You're reading self-help books to fix your creepy virgin almost-boyfriend?" Holly summarized. "*Silent Night*, you used to be cooler than this. What the hell happened to you, Mull?"

"I am not Multifarious," Mull corrected, "today I am... *Tamponade*!"

Holly silently processed that for a beat. "Your codename has got 'tampon' in it? Wow. That is *not* a choice I would have made."

"It's completely different!" Mull protested. "It means to shove something into a wound on a battlefield, in order to hold in blood and..." She trailed off, frowning. "Shit. You're right. That's a *terrible* name. And I have to put up with it all day."

Holly nodded in commiseration. "Sucks to be you sometimes, girl."

Mull opened her mouth to reply to that, but she moved her arm too suddenly and one single pepperoni slipped off of her pizza. It all happened in slow-motion, the greasy circle of meat gradually tumbling towards the carpet and there was nothing Mull could do. It impacted the white berber carpet, *juuuust* missing the sanitary plastic cover which protected the other 99.9% of its surface, and leaving behind a nasty spot.

Oz undoubtedly had the carpet steam-cleaned every few days, but there was no way that stain was going *anywhere*. Ever.

She glanced over at Holly and met the woman's eyes for a long moment, sharing the horror.

Then Mull stood up and quickly moved the chair so that the foot was on that exact spot, hiding the stain.

Holly nodded mockingly. "Honesty is very important in a relationship."

"You rat me out and I'll tell him you did it." Mull warned seriously.

Holly held up her hands, disavowing the argument. Somehow the woman had managed to eat her entire meal and not get a single crumb on her hands or Santa suit. Mull HATED people who could do that. Personally, she'd always been unable to eat or drink *anything* and not leave behind some debris or evidence.

It was one more reason why she and Oz were doomed to failure.

But... she *really* liked Oz.

Trying to start dating him was doomed to catastrophe and

humiliation, but Mull thought it was worth the risk.

And Natalie was completely *certain* of that fact.

"It'll be fine." Holly assured her, sensing the problem. "He won't care."

"He cares about a lot of things we'd both assume he wouldn't, Holl."

"He's so smitten with you, you could dump the entire contents of the trash on his head and he'd just praise your aim."

Mull wasn't so sure. Oz's mind sometimes held him prisoner. Mull could relate to that. But either way, it was entirely possible that Oz would absolutely *freak out* over the carpet. It could send him into some kind of meltdown, triggering every single one of his worst rituals at once.

She considered that silently, wondering what her reaction to that would be.

While she was debating it with herself, she noticed for the first time that Oz's walls had a new addition. At some point today, someone had moved the Lone Ranger poster and had replaced it with a flatscreen TV.

She pursed her lips in thought... no, wait. That had been *her*, hadn't it? She'd bought the TV. Because Oz needed to be open to more things and stop worrying so much. And, also, she obviously didn't want to miss her shows just because she was in protective custody in his apartment.

The screen currently displayed what appeared to be a cheap teen soap opera from the 90s. On the couch in front of it, Vaudeville and Traitor watched the screen intently.

The show's title came up, showing that it was *The World of No*. On screen, a pretty high school age girl with black hair and shining blue eyes was sitting in an ice cream parlor, glaring at the blonde cheerleader sitting at another table. The girl's eyes were so blue they looked computer generated.

"Who's that?" Traitor asked.

"That's Veronica. She's the villainess of the show." Cory informed him, obviously an expert on the intricacies of the series. "She was on my show as well. My best friend."

"Your *actual* friend or her character on your show was the friend of the character you played?" Holly inquired, turning to look at the screen.

Cory shrugged. "Same thing."

"Wait, wait..." Traitor began, "I know her, don't I? She went on to star in that terrible movie where the director was high as balls

292

and started replacing the cast with those creepy puppets, right?" He nodded, having identified the girl. "Yeah, I remember her. Whatever happened to her?"

"She starred in that terrible movie with the creepy puppets, directed by a dude who was high as balls." Cory repeated in a deadpan.

"Ah." Traitor nodded. "Yeah. I guess it is hard to come back from that. Shame."

"Well, she did that one *Murder at Stabbington Lake* sequel." Cory added, apparently familiar with the girl's entire filmography. "The fourth one."

"'The Re-Sex-ening'?" Holly asked.

Cory nodded. "I've always felt her performance as Tina the camp counselor was overlooked during awards season." He decided, like a film critic. "While I prefer the narrative flow of television, she brought an understated gravitas to the character. Sometimes the right actress can turn a small part into a memorable role and steal the entire film. She's a very talented woman. An artist."

Traitor turned to watch the old TV show again. "I remember the shower scene of that movie, but not much else."

"Shut up." Cory bit out.

"Dude, I mean, not to sound weird, but it makes me view that stupid puppet movie in a whooooole new light." Traitor clapped his hands together. "Holy fuck! Just thinking about..."

"*Shut up!*" Cory snapped, fury in his tone.

Discussing TV shows with Cory was often dramatic. Cory had the ability to travel in and out of any television screen, so bashing his favorite TV shows was like criticizing someone's family; you just didn't do it. Unless you were a complete asshole, like Arn. In which case, you did it all the time. Because you didn't care about anyone else.

A lot of people claimed it, but Arn was thus far the only person Mull had ever met who *literally* didn't care about anyone else's feelings or what anyone else thought. Like those cutaways in reality shows where the person tells the camera what they *really* think, but Arn lived every day like that. He just floated through life, being Arn. If life were one of Cory's beloved TV sitcoms, then Arn would be Eddie Haskell, vacillating between being an insincere sycophant and a smiling conman, stealing everyone blind. And people accepted it. Because that's who he'd always been. Hell, people *liked* him. He could be very charming when he wanted to be and more than a few people on the team suspected that was one of his lesser known powers. Most people trusted him, despite themselves. Like he could somehow *make you* trust him. But it didn't mean you couldn't still be confused by his presence in your life. Not in an angry way, just in the way that made you think twice about ever introducing Arn to any of your *other* friends.

Arn was unreliable, irresponsible, and untrustworthy. But he was slick as Tom Sawyer, forever getting those around him to whitewash his proverbial fences for him. No one *ever* got the best of Arn. Not once.

Still, Mull had absolutely no idea what he was doing here.

"I don't understand why Oz invited you here." Mull thought aloud. "Are you *really* the best person to take a bullet for me?"

"Nope." Arn agreed immediately. "I might steal bullets *from* you, but certainly not take one *for* you."

"Then why are you here?" She pressed.

"You're part of the Undercover Department." He reminded her. "The Undercover Department isn't really so much *about* the loyalty, but we have a reputation to preserve. And *no one* fucks with us."

"Uh-huh." Mull barely restrained from rolling her eyes. "What's the real reason?"

"Cut him some slack, at least he's here." Holly defended. "We know worse people than him."

"I don't know if you know this or not," Mull pointed at him, "but Arn doesn't give two shits about us."

"Nope." Arn agreed again, admitting the point without argument.

"He's just here because we pay him and let him do evil shit."
"Yep."

"His *real* super-power is the ability to lie without remorse." Mull continued.

"The clinical term is 'pseudologia fantastica.'" Arn corrected, sounding like an authority on the issue. "I'm in treatment though."

"No, you're not." Mull deadpanned.

"No, I'm not." Arn agreed good-naturedly. "Mainly I just use it to entertain myself and hit on women."

Mull made a face. "I don't think 'Arnold Benedix' is even his real name."

"Nope." Arn laughed at the absurdity of the idea that he'd tell his friends his *actual* name. "Not even close."

"He's a liar."

"You say 'liar,' I say '*imaginative*.'"

"And if one day he gets bored or someone else offers him

more, he'd sell us all out in a heartbeat."

"But I'd feel bad about it." Arn assured them, still focused on Cory's teen soap opera.

"No, you wouldn't." Mull deadpanned again.

"Not really, no." Arn agreed, shaking his head.

Mull pointed at him again. "He doesn't even care enough to lie."

"I believe that honesty is important if there's any hope of trust being built."

"This is just another job to him." Mull made a face.

"Actually, I also have no work ethic." Arn corrected. "I don't want a *job*." He sounded vaguely disgusted by that insinuation. "I'm just here because stealing from you is easier if we're on the same team."

She had no reply to that. It was brutally honest. And... Holly did have a point. Arn might be an asshole, but he was generally a benign one. She didn't have a real issue with the man, she was just confused as to why *he*, of all people, was on her protective detail.

Mull slouched down into her uncomfortable chair, watching the terribly cheesy teen drama on the screen.

A moment later, the front door swung open and Oz stalked in. "Did Natalie call?" He demanded from the doorway.

"Uh-oh, Dad's home." Holly called to everyone sarcastically. "Look busy."

Although it was a joke, there genuinely was that sense whenever Oz was around.

Oswald Dimico was the adult in the room. Always.

"Did any of you even do anything today!?!" He snapped, sounding more irritated than she'd ever heard. "You seriously have *nothing else* you could be doing to help her, *than sitting around my fucking apartment* and...!" He trailed off, as Mull sat up straighter and he saw her over the top of the chair. "Ah." He cleared his throat and straightened his suit, although it was always perfectly orderly. "Good." He stood awkwardly there for a moment, looking relieved and like he wanted to say something, but ultimately just walked towards his bedroom. "You shouldn't leave unless someone goes with you. It's not safe." He advised seriously, stepping over the prone form of his unconscious doorman without comment, most likely because he was long used to the Consortium members inexplicably beating people up, then frowned slightly at seeing the TV. "Why..." He began.

"I bought you a TV." She explained. "I used the store's Black Friday discount code."

"Okay." He nodded, processing that. "Why?"

"Because it made it 40% off. It really makes no sense to have to wait until…"

"No, I mean why buy a TV at all?" He interrupted.

"You needed one."

"Why does anyone 'need' a TV?"

"To watch shit?" She guessed. "I don't know."

"So, you left the apartment, risking your life, so that you could watch… television programs?" He started from the room again. "That doesn't sound especially smart."

When he said it that way, it *did* sound kinda stupid.

Huh.

Mull started after him. "I'm sorry I do a piss-poor job of hiding, Oz. I'm not used to it." She didn't let the bedroom door stop her at all, following right after him. "That's Natalie's thing. I don't hide."

He smiled and shook his head in amused irritation. "You *are* Natalie!" He reminded her in exasperation.

Mull scoffed. "Only sometimes. And even then, not really."

He made a humoring sound. "I'm in no position to tell anyone what to do about their mental health, obviously, but I would suggest that you acknowledge that Natalie and 'you' at least share common interests."

"She does her thing and I do mine."

"We've had this discussion before." He reminded her. "I don't agree with your take on it, I think you always try to have it both ways, but you know more about your own life than I do." He paused. "Or you're *supposed* to, anyway. Frankly, I think you make terrible, *terrible* decisions sometimes." He pointed towards the door. "You just go waltzing out there, God knows where, while there are innumerable psychopaths looking for you!?!"

"It's perfectly safe."

"Safe? Last year, there were 190 unsolved murders in this city."

"Yeah, but I'm probably responsible for 20% of them, easy, so I like my odds."

He didn't look convinced, continuing to glare at her.

She stared at him expressionlessly for a moment. "Oz, I'm not afraid of them."

He looked down at the floor, then his eyes snapped back to hers. "What about Natalie?"

She scoffed. "Natalie's afraid of everything."

"No, no," Oz shook his head, "that's not what I meant. I mean: why are *you* afraid of Natalie?"

Mull snorted at the idea. "I'm not afraid of Natalie. That's..." She shifted on her feet. "That's insane. No one is afraid of Natalie. She's a loser."

"I'm not telling you how to live your life." He stood straighter. "But I know that mine is made better by having you in it, so *please* be more careful with it. And one of these days, you really need to decide where 'you' stop and 'Natalie' begins."

"How about you, Oz? If I'm so desperately needed in your life, why do you look disgusted every time I'm within ten feet of you!?!"

"Oh, I do not!"

"Yes, you do!"

"We've talked about that." He still didn't look convinced. "I have some problems, but I can assure you, they..."

"Yeah, yeah..." she rolled her eyes, "'they don't concern me at all,' I heard that already." Her jaw tightened. "But it kinda feels like it's fucking personal sometimes, Oz."

"Well, apparently, *you* don't even exist. I spent *years* being your friend, only to learn that you were someone entirely different, and according to you, the person I thought I knew was just make-believe." He held out his hands. "Kinda feels personal too, Nat."

"The whole reason I agreed to stay here with you, was so that I could keep *YOU* safe, you ignorant jackass!" She gestured to herself. "*Because* you're my fucking friend! No matter who I am or what I do, *you're the one goddamn constant!* If anything happened to you, because I got you involved in this..." She trailed off. "I'm not the person you're looking for, Oz." She whispered. "Not anymore. She was here last Monday and she might be back tomorrow, but she's not me. Today, I'm a woman neither of us has ever met before. I could be anyone today. I could *hurt you* today, I don't know." She made a tired, helpless sound. "And because I can't even be sure of how I'm going to react to something, my advice would be to keep your distance from me."

Oz stalked forward, casually ripping off one of his impeccable white gloves and absently tossing it aside, then used his other hand to raise her arm and clasped her hand to his.

His eyes burned into hers, determined. "*You* are the woman I'm looking for. Today. Tomorrow. The indefinite future."

Their fingers intertwined, both of them breathing hard.

And Natalie simply stared into the dark pools of that man's

stunning eyes, drowning in them. They were shadowy and mysterious, reflecting both utter security and a hidden danger. There was pain in that man's chocolate colored eyes, but also a deep seated fear. He was afraid. For her. And of himself.

She saw herself reflected in them, and for the first time ever, Natalie saw the problems with both of their lives.

And there were certainly a lot of them.

Her own issues were beyond her abilities to fix, she'd been trying her whole life without success. But Oz was perfect. Damaged, but perfect. And she was reasonably certain that she could help him fix the problems which were holding him back from what he wanted. All he needed was help.

"I'm okay." She assured him earnestly. "I won't leave again without telling someone." She kissed his fingers, still entwined with hers. "I'm just not used to someone caring whether I live or die, that's all. I self-sabotage."

"I think you are afraid and alone and you spend most of your time feeling like your brain *wants* you to be afraid and alone. Like it wants you to be unhappy and away from the people and things that might bring you joy."

She just kept staring at him, recognizing that it was the truth.

"I know this," he continued, "because I spend most of my time thinking the exact same things. I feel like I'm a hostage of the parts of myself that I'm too afraid of to try to change. I'm not strong enough, so I let them control me." He swallowed. "Then I blame them for it, get depressed, and give them even more power."

"That about sums it up, yeah." She cleared her throat. "But I believe that we can get through any of our various insanities, so long as we work on them together. As frustrating as they may be, I believe in us."

She looked down at their clasped hands, and was taken aback by the scars on his skin.

They were chemical burns.

Oz followed her line of sight and tried to pull his hand away, but she locked her fingers around his. He got the message and stopped trying to escape her clutches. "I…" He began, then stopped. "I got thrown away once." He explained. "In a dump. And I can still smell it." He swallowed. "The bodies. Mired in garbage. Rotting in the sun." He looked away. "No matter how much I try to wash it off, it's always there." He cleared his throat. "I used straight bleach once. Scrubbed them until they bled. Added lye. Gave my hands chemical burns trying to get rid of that smell… but it's always there." He shook his head, sounding haunted and like he was about to cry. "...It's always there."

She had no idea what to say to that, so she simply raised their clasped hands to her face, smelling his skin. "All I smell is soap and the laundry detergent you use on your gloves." She kissed his hand, lips lingering on the warmth of his rough skin and getting far more pleasure from the act than she would have expected. "It smells like sunshine. I've always loved it."

Oz let go of her hand and sank down on his bed. "I... I know I'm a project, Natalie." He said softly. "Please don't give up on me."

"I'm not." She promised. "And I won't." She crossed her arms over her chest, feeling her breasts tighten in response to touching the man and now seeing him on the bed. "Besides, if you're a 'project,' I'm a damned 'thesis.'"

"You're not..." He began.

She cut him off. "Yes, I am. You don't need to spare my feelings."

He looked down at the floor. "I like who you are. Even if it changes from day to day. I think you're truly exceptional."

"Thank you." She was genuinely touched by that. "That means a lot." She cleared the lump in her throat. "And I've been reading this book about obsessive impulses..."

"You don't have any obsessions." He reminded her. "Besides your bizarre addiction to breakfast foods."

"Yeah!" Natalie immediately brightened. "Most of the stuff I'm proudest about in my life have to do with my continuing experimentation with different waffle toppings." She nodded happily, pleased he'd noticed. "Peanut butter and jelly on a waffle is a winner. Try it. Seriously. You'll thank me."

His brow furrowed in thought and barely controlled disgust as he considered that culinary marvel.

"In any case, no, I'm not reading it for me." She sat down on the bed next to him. "I'm reading it for you. See, I think what you need is 'exposure therapy.'"

He looked slightly uncomfortable about that suggestion. "Who... is being 'exposed'?"

Nat tried not to smile at the idea of exposing herself to him. Right here. Just to see his shocked and horrified little expression.

The idea had genuine promise, to say nothing of the erotic thrills it would provide her. Again, Natalie was Nice Girl Pretty, and those types of girls never got to have kinky erotic fun. Even if they *really* wanted to try.

"No, it's where you deliberately do things that trigger you, just to show you that it's really not so bad." She explained.

He made a face. "I've tried that. Usually bad things happen anyway. And then get much worse."

"Yeah, but this time, I'm here to make sure they *don't.*" She promised. "I... I can keep you safe, Oz." She held up her hand. "I mean, a week ago, would you have been able to hold my hand like that?"

"*Your* hand?" He asked, like that made a difference.

"No, of course not." She answered for him. "But now you did it, and we're moving on." She paused for a moment, then a new thought occurred to her. "And if you need to go wash it or something, that will *absolutely* not insult me, I completely understand."

Oz shook his head. "I'm fine."

"I... I just washed my hands anyway." She explained, feeling the need to defend herself for some reason.

"Oh," Oz seemed confused as to why the line of conversation was continuing, "...good?"

They sat on the edge of the bed together, both silently staring at nothing and considering their own lives.

"I'm sorry." She finally said softly. "All of this is because of me. If it wasn't for me, you wouldn't have all of these people messing up your house, those people in the hospital would still be alive... and we wouldn't be fighting."

"We aren't fighting." Oz said softly. "We're just both uncomfortable with who we are sometimes, and it upsets us." He didn't speak for a moment, considering something. "And I'm still not convinced the hospital had anything to do with you."

"Meaning?"

"They took that little girl at the convenience store, the teenager last week, and the young woman who was working with Oklahoma." He ticked off the points on his fingers. "They are taking young, vulnerable, super-powered targets..."

"And I'm what?" She arched an amused eyebrow. "Old?"

"You are not an easy target." He clarified. "It's possible you had nothing to do with the attack on the hospital, they might have simply been after someone else."

"Who?"

"Poacher took The Cheerleader's baby from the maternity ward right before the attack, and you were carrying it through the entire fight... And Holly gave you Harlot and Wyatt's son to hold. The Agletarians might have been after the children and we were just caught in the crossfire."

She waggled her hand in the air, dubiously. "Be a hell of a coincidence…"

"We're superheroes, our whole lives are a hell of a coincidence."

"Where does Ronnie fit into that then?"

Oz shook his head. "I have no idea."

"I doubt it. I think this one is on me." She let out a sigh. "I'm sorry I'm not normal, Oz." She whispered. "I'd love to be normal. Just for a day."

"I sincerely doubt it's all it's cracked up to be." He assured her. "And I'm pretty sure if you were normal, you would have been dead a dozen times over, this week alone." He was silent for another moment. "My whole life, all I wanted to be was exceptional. Extraordinary. Someone… someone heroic."

Mull nodded and reached out to put her arm around him, but then thought better of it. Best not to go too far with the whole "exposure" thing and scare him. "Well, mission accomplished then."

He shook his head. "Nah. I'm forced to make decisions which compromise my morals."

"That's life, Oz."

"But it *shouldn't* be."

"Says who?"

He sat up straighter. "I used to watch *The Lone Ranger* every day."

"The shitty Johnny Depp movie?"

"No, reruns of the old TV show." Oz's head tilted to the side, sounding like a holy man describing Heaven. "He inhabited a simple world of right and wrong. The bad guys all wore black hats and were beaten within 23 minutes. And he never had to compromise his ethics or morals to do it. Honestly, I don't think he ever killed anyone. There wasn't even any blood. He found a way to uphold justice so that everyone lived. Everything was fair. Everyone got what they wanted. And he kept his white clothes *spotless*."

"And do you know what happened to him?" She asked. "His TV show got cancelled and his movies bomb. Because that's just not going to get the job done. Not anymore. That's not how the real world works." She shrugged. "You have to get your hands dirty sometimes."

"You can't clean anything if your hands are dirty."

"The only time a mop is clean is when it's never been used." She countered.

"My mop is clean." He argued. "I make sure of it."

Her mouth quirked at the corner. "Out of context, that sounds kinda dirty, Oz."

He didn't appear to have a mind filthy enough to somehow make the statement into something sexual, so he utterly missed her joke.

"I'm worried." He finally confided in her, his voice tight. "When I was younger, I worried about not being able to be The Lone Ranger. But now, I am worried I'm turning into one of the people the Lone Ranger is there to fight."

"Oz, there's simply no way that's going to happen. I *know* evil. And you're White Hat is completely spotless." She squeezed his hand in comfort, utterly forgetting about his issues with touching. "Trust me."

He nodded, still obviously not believing her, but not willing to argue.

She absently looked around the room. "And something I've been wondering about: why do you have so many giftwrapped presents around?"

Before he could answer that, his rotary phone rang.

Mull stared at it in utter amazement. It was like the 1950s were calling and asking for their technology back.

Oz picked up the receiver. "Dimico residence, Oswald speaking."

Mull rolled her eyes at his utterly humorless and straightforward greeting.

He listened for a long moment, then nodded. "Okay. We'll be right there." He hung up the phone and looked over at her. "Our suspects are on the move."

Chapter 18

"'THEN YOU KEEP MOVING ROUND, I SUPPOSE?' SAID ALICE.

'EXACTLY SO,' SAID THE HATTER: 'AS THE THINGS GET USED UP.'

'BUT WHAT HAPPENS WHEN YOU COME TO THE BEGINNING AGAIN?' ALICE VENTURED TO ASK."

- Alice's Adventures in Wonderland

13 YEARS AGO

Oz was murdered on a rainy Monday morning.

He had been visiting his aunt and uncle to discuss his new employment at a medical supply factory, and his cousin had taken that moment to finally snap.

It really shouldn't have come to any great shock to anyone who knew the man.

He'd always been a sadist, and time had only made that tendency more pronounced. As such, when he burst through the doors of the trailer, Oz wasn't terribly surprised. Hooch was one of those people who *always* seemed on the verge of killing everyone in the room. People had said the same thing about Oz, so he was pretty good at recognizing it.

As it turned out, Hooch was upset with his parents over... something. To be honest, Oz couldn't really follow that part of it. There was too much screaming, and Oz had deliberately avoided speaking to the rest of his family, for obvious reasons. They hadn't talked in months. Hooch was so emotional though, so the issue was undoubtedly something minor.

But as soon as Hooch burst through the door, Oz had known what he was there to do. It was written all over the man's face. Whatever tiny bits of a soul had held the man back all those years had finally snapped, and Hooch was there for blood.

He had continued screaming at his parents, then turned to Oz, obviously expecting Oz to back him in this endeavor.

"They made our lives a living fucking hell, Oz," Hooch had spat out, voice slurred with alcohol, "they deserve this!"

And that presented Oz with a very definite choice: he could do what was right or he could get his revenge.

There was no choice there.

Oz had stepped between Hooch and his aunt and uncle, trying to talk the man down and get the knife. Oz had no intention of killing anyone, no matter how awful they had made his childhood years or how much he might have hated them.

And that's how Oz had gotten murdered.

Hooch stabbed Oz, then proceeded to kill everyone else in the trailer.

Oz's body had been tossed into the dump, where it remained for two days. No one found it. His head had been stuffed inside a plastic bag, his hands and legs secured by duct tape. His corpse had been a terrible sight; covered in blood, flies, and filth.

To make matters worse, he wasn't exactly dead.

Depending on how you chose to look at the situation, Oz was either lucky or unlucky, and his cousin had botched the job of finishing him off. Which wasn't terribly surprising, since Hooch had never been especially good at *anything*. He had stabbed Oz several times in the chest, but missed the vital organs. He did a similarly half-assed job with the plastic bag, and didn't bother to make sure it was airtight. The man had always been terribly sloppy when he was off his meds. And when he was drunk. And when he hadn't been getting enough sleep. And really anytime, really.

So, Oz hadn't died.

He was a hard man to kill.

Unfortunately.

Oz had come to in the dump an unknown amount of time later, gasping for air. The bag had been punctured by something in the pile of trash he was stuck in, and he frantically tried to get oxygen into his lungs. Sadly, he managed only to inhale what felt and tasted like used coffee grounds. He shook his head desperately trying to dislodge the bag. He was finally able to tear the hole wider on something, and tried to return his breathing to normal.

That had been at least two days ago, judging by the number of times he'd seen pinpricks of light make their way into his cocoon of garbage. He continued trying to saw through the bindings on a shard of broken glass... or *something* which was sharp, anyway. He wasn't sure.

He tried to ignore the body next to him. His aunt's cold dead eyes were inches from his and had been staring at him accusingly for the past two days. Her cold, stinking, congealing blood continued to slowly drip from her neck wound onto his bare chest, as her body exsanguinated. Apparently, his cousin had decided to dispose of her at the same time he had dumped Oz in this pit, and tossed her body on top of his. His aunt had been lucky though, and the wound put her out of her misery immediately. Oz, on the other hand, had the fun of dying slowly of thirst or hunger, buried alive. Or if he was really lucky, being asphyxiated with mouthfuls of trash or his aunt's blood.

Really, he would welcome either death though, as they both promised a break from the smell. The stench of the dump and his aunt's decaying body and Oz's sweat and fear, all mixed together until it seemed to be a living thing. Some moist, heavy, *thing*, sitting on top of Oz and filling his nose with a smell worse than any nightmare. It was... it was the kind of reeking, putrid dreadfulness that had Oz simply trying to move his head enough to see the wounds to his own chest and guess how much longer it would be until he bled to death. How much longer he'd have to endure this.

Oz had spent the first few hours doing nothing but screaming in shocked horror, trying to wake himself from the horrible nightmare he found himself in.

He'd spent the next day or so crying, begging any kind of god that would listen to take pity on him.

At some point this afternoon, his prayers had switched from begging to be saved to just begging to die. He'd rather be nothing than stay in this hole any longer. It was obvious he was going to die either way, so it might as well be sooner rather than later.

But now, he'd turned all of that off. He wasn't praying or crying or screaming.

He simply stared through the tiny break in the garbage heaped on top of him, babbling nonsense to himself. He wasn't even sure what he was saying, really.

As the sun was setting on his second day in his trash filled grave, he actually recognized *where* in the dump his cousin had disposed of him.

Above him, he could see the faint outline of the familiar coffee ad, the 1950s redhead serving her unseen lover coffee and looking at him like he was her perfect shining hero. The billboard had been buried over the years, now entombed along with him. But he recognized it in the shadows all the same.

Oz's mind snapped back to reality, like flicking on a light switch.

He had wanted to be a hero.

He'd always wanted to prove to himself and the world that he didn't belong in this dump. That he wasn't trash.

But that's what he was now.

Trash.

Literal trash.

Discarded like all of the other unwanted, dirty things which were piled up and forgotten out here in this toxic hellhole.

Oz was going to die here. And there wasn't a single person in the world who would give a shit about that. There was no one to save him.

The redhead with the coffee seemed to find that idea funny, the decaying remnants of her perfect smile challenging him to do something about it.

His meaningless babbling gradually shifted to the opening bars of the *William Tell Overture*.

There was no fucking way he was going to die down here. He'd lived his entire life in this dump, and he'd be damned if he was going to die in it too.

Oz might not be a hero... He might be evil, deep down... But Oz still had *power*. He could still do things his cousin couldn't and he wasn't about to die without giving this his all, no matter how distasteful the idea was.

Oz was trash. It was in his blood now. It was a part of him and always would be.

But trash obeyed its own.

His hands formed fists in the cramped cavern, as he got angrier.

His aunt seemed to beg him not to do it, the roaches and worms crawling over her dead foggy eyes making it look like she was blinking at him in disbelief.

But Oz didn't care.

He controlled germs and bacteria and microbes...

And his cousin had tried to bury him in a fucking *dump!?!*

Oz was going to make him pay dearly for that.

He was going to rip his way through the garbage and then go and show Hooch *what nightmares really were!*

Above him, the redhead on the billboard seemed to be silently daring him to do it, her perfect smile now sly and expectant.

As if she were saying, "Okay... let's see what you can *really* do, Oz?"

Oz's vision blacked over, leaving the human scaled world and accessing his powers.

Nine hundred *centillion* creatures stood at attention, preparing themselves for Oz's orders.

He let out a bellow of sheer rage, using the last of his energy reserves.

A millisecond later, the trash above him dissolved, decomposed, and rotted so fast that it was like it exploded, sending stray bits of paper and plastic shooting into the air. His aunt's body was illuminated in the fading light of day for a brief moment, then it too vanished, consumed by things so tiny and horrible that there weren't even names for them.

The redhead on the billboard's smile was now smug, apparently unsurprised. The ancient paper crinkled before being eaten away to nothing, that smile never wavering.

It was a testament to his "bad blood" that he felt worse about the loss of the billboard than he did about the loss of his aunt and uncle's bodies. Or, for that matter, the people themselves.

Oz really was trash.

The plastic bindings on his wrist vanished too, the microbes tearing through them like they weren't even there.

Oz was too far gone to even care though, rising on his unsteady legs and stalking from the hole.

He needed to get to a hospital.

And then he was going to go have fucking words with Hooch.

****

FOUR YEARS AGO

Oz sat down behind the glass in the visitation room and had absolutely no idea who this man was. Not that it really mattered, but it was rather odd that someone would come see a prisoner they didn't actually know.

Oz had been here for seven years.

He'd seen a lot of weird things in that time, so it didn't really bother him anymore.

The fact that he'd have to touch the little phone attached to the wall of the visitation booth *did* though. Those things were almost certainly never cleaned. Oz didn't even need his powers to recognize that they were crawling with bacteria and disease.

He looked at the phone like it was a rattlesnake, waiting to strike him dead.

And in that instant, he very much would have preferred that it kill him than him having to touch it.

The man on the other side of the glass removed his straw hat and straightened his white linen suit. He picked up the receiver.

Oz continued staring at the phone, still unwilling to touch it.

The man pointed at the phone.

Oz didn't move.

The man on the other side of the glass heaved an annoyed sigh, then summoned one of the guards over to him. He explained something to the woman, pointed at Oz, then handed her three $100 bills. The guard immediately reached for her radio, and a moment later, a guard on Oz's side of the glass arrived and tossed Oz an antibacterial wipe.

Oz looked down at the package, wondering where it had been. When you really stopped to think about it, the packaging of an antibacterial product must be among the dirtiest things around, because no one needed them unless their hands or immediate area where contaminated.

The man on the other side of the window pointed at it, obviously getting annoyed with the delay now.

Oz didn't sense any life-threatening germs clinging to the packet and he finally relented to touch it. He ripped it open, and then spent the next five minutes cleaning the phone and the desk area in front of him.

It still wasn't what one might call "clean," but at least it didn't make him want to vomit anymore.

He picked up the phone, holding it away from his head because he still didn't want the earpiece to touch him. The little speaking holes were undoubtedly *overflowing* with the accumulated earwax and body hair of a thousand diseased criminals.

"Mr. Dimico?" The man on the other end of the phone said in greeting. "My..."

Oz hung up the phone.

Then picked it up again.

Then hung it up.

He repeated the process four times, because he was afraid if he didn't, something bad would happen.

His compulsions had gotten much, much worse since the incident at the dump. And they'd been getting even more extreme in the last few months.

He was falling apart and he knew it.

Oz seemed to spend half of his day now, just doing useless rituals to avoid unspecified disasters which would befall him and the world around him.

It was stupid and annoying, but Oz was helpless to stop it. If he didn't do it, it occupied his every thought. He wasn't able to sleep. He obsessed about it until he threw up, then obsessed about that.

Oz's life *was* his obsessions and rituals now. They owned him.

The ritual fulfilled, Oz once again put the receiver to his ear.

"Really?" The man on the other end of the phone asked, sounding exasperated. "You couldn't have just picked up the damn phone?"

Oz opened his mouth to explain the situation, but the man cut him off.

"I don't care." The man said simply. "I know what your problem is and I know what triggered it." He shook his head. "It still cost me $300 and wasted five minutes as you did your little phone dance."

Oz simply stared at him.

"What are you in for, kid?" The man asked, sounding amused to be able to use the clichéd line. "I've always wanted to say that." He confided a moment later.

Oz watched him with emotionless eyes. "Sixteen counts of first degree murder, sixty-seven counts of robbery, nineteen counts of grand theft auto, thirty-three counts of arson, forty carjackings and ten counts of sexual assault." He paused. "And I killed my cousin."

"Shiiiiiiit," the man let out a low whistle, "you weren't kidding around, were you!?! When you go bad, you go fucking *dark!*"

Oz didn't reply to that.

"You do it?" The man asked calmly.

"The DNA matched." Oz told him simply.

"Ah." The man nodded, then smiled at him. "My name is Prometheus."

Oz simply stared at him, not meeting his eyes. He'd never been a great conversationalist and prison hadn't helped that much. To be honest, Oz would have very much preferred to be left in his cell today.

"So... your cousin."

"He was a troubled man."

"I have no doubt." Prometheus nodded. "And I saw his trial, obviously." He smiled knowingly at Oz. "And your testimony." The man shook his head. "You didn't kill him."

"He got death." Oz argued rationally. "He wouldn't have gotten death without my testimony. Ergo, I killed him."

"You feel bad about getting your cousin lethal injection?"

"We weren't close. He stabbed me in the chest and left me to die under fifty feet of garbage. I'd say we're even." Oz shifted in his chair, suddenly smelling that awful stink again and wishing that he could wash his hands and face. With something very, very strong. Anything to cover up the memory of that smell. "And wrong is wrong, I don't care if you're my cousin who is killing my enemies or not. You kill people, I'm going to stop you."

The man leaned back in his chair. "Your issue is that you view the world in terms of black and white. Things are good or evil, clean or dirty. But that kind of thinking isn't ever going to see the world as a cohesive, realistic whole. It's just a defense mechanism. Your cousin let you down, so your cousin was thus evil and he needed to be reported."

"Or my cousin was a sadistic madman, who deserved to be brought to justice."

"Oh, I'm not arguing that. The man was utterly worthy of getting the death sentence, no doubt. I just mean in general, this is your problem. This is why I always have difficulty talking to you, you're the only one on the team that refuses to compromise your own view of morality."

Oz frowned. "Why would I want to compromise my morals?"

"They're situational. Sometimes you need to."

"No, you don't. Things are as they are. They're good or they're evil, they're clean or they're dirty. Compromising with evil doesn't make the world less evil, it makes the world less good."

"See, the other thing I've never understood about you: you try to correct my understanding of morality, rather than asking just what 'team' I'm referring to." The man shook his head in amused confusion. "You're the only person I've ever met who would do that. Hell, you haven't even asked me *why* I'm here yet." He tapped the desk in front of him, paying absolutely no attention to the trillions of bacteria the action no doubt deposited on his fingertip, like sprinkles on a cupcake. "This road you're on? The world of moral absolutes and panicking about germs? Nothing good lies down that road, Oz. You won't like what you find there."

"I know exactly where it leads, sir. I'm in prison." Oz argued rationally. "It either leads to death or more prison. I am fine with either of those eventualities."

They were both silent for a long moment.

"Most of the human genome is simply viruses which have written themselves into the DNA," he pointed at Oz, "which means that you are mostly made up of leftover protein sequences from stuff that isn't you. It was *never* you. Humanity is just the garbage that a disease shit out, millennia ago. Everyone is quite literally... trash." He opened up his hands, point made. "They make all life possible, even yours."

"I want them gone." Oz looked down at his hands, hating the unseen universe he knew they had clinging to them.

"That's not going to happen. You can't ever clean your hands completely. They'll always be dirty, to some degree." The man shook his head again. "So you can either let it go and learn to deal with it in constructive ways, or you can go crazy obsessively trying to stop it and possibly end up killing yourself in the process. Those are your options."

"I can feel them moving all over me..." Oz whispered. "All over you..."

"At some point, you have to realize there's no such thing as 'clean,' which means everything is dirty. And if everything is dirty, then nothing is. Morality is the same way. There are very few absolutes, because people are imperfect creatures. Because they're literally made up of trash." The man shrugged. "I am telling you that you will drive yourself crazy with this. And to be completely candid with you, I don't need you." The man sounded either sad that Oz wasn't important or annoyed that he needed him at all. "You aren't a huge part of the fight that's coming. But I have to take you in order to get the help of the person I'm *really* after, and I can't get her if you're dead or crazy. So congratulations, Oswald. Fate is here to give you a pep-talk and get you out of jail. I'm going to..."

"I can't be out of jail." Oz replied unemotionally, still tracking the microbes crawling all over his hands. "I'm evil."

"Not yet, you're not." The man corrected. "But if you don't learn to overcome your fear of that, it's going to happen."

"I've been in solitary for 6 months." Oz reported. "But I had twenty-eight quindecillion cellmates."

"Super." The man replied, humoring him. "You're a charmer, I'll give you that." He cleared his throat, returning to his topic. "Like I was saying, the sad fact of the matter is this: you have no great destiny, Oswald. You aren't the linchpin to anything. You are not extraordinary and you never will be."

For some reason, that got Oz's full attention. "I don't accept that." He retorted, feeling insulted.

"Reality doesn't care if you accept it or not." The man shrugged again. "I have seen every contribution you can make to this world. Almost all of them are bad, some are *nightmarishly* horrible, many of the rest are meaningless, but only one or two are positive. If it were up to me, I wouldn't involve you at all. I would leave you here, because I find you surprisingly difficult to manage. You second-guess everyone, you're unstable, and I genuinely find you unnerving. Your only use to me is that you play a significant role in being someone else's destiny, however. I need you only because I need them." He arched an eyebrow. "Are you going to be okay with that, Oz?"

Oz considered the matter for a beat.

Would he be willing to sacrifice his own destiny for someone else's? If that someone else was important to him?

"Yes." Oz nodded. "Yes, but I don't believe you anyway."

"No, I know you don't." The man laughed, looking amused by that answer. "That's one of the reasons why I find you so difficult to work with. The others, they'll cooperate out of vanity or pride or a desperate need for family. All of them are looking for something. But you're a difficult man to understand. I have no idea what it is you actually *want*, even after all this time." He squinted at Oz, as if examining him under a microscope. "We've had this conversation many times, and yet I have absolutely no idea what makes you tick. You're honestly the most inscrutable man in the Consortium." The man gestured offhandedly. "Take a man like your friend Traitor..."

"Who?"

The man went right on talking, like Oz hadn't even spoken. "...every time I have this talk with him, it goes a little differently, because he's difficult to predict. He's a liar, obviously, so he's sometimes hard to pin down. His core goals and desires are usually the same though. I understand what it is he *wants* and I know how to use that to get him where I need him." The man squinted at him in curiosity, like he was a bug in a jar. "But you're something else entirely, aren't you? You're painfully blunt. But paradoxically, that bluntness keeps you almost mysterious. And you don't compromise. You don't do what you don't want to do, even after I carefully explain to you why you need to do it. Because you're always certain there's another way, usually *your* way." The man shook his hands in the air. "I don't understand you. And by this point, I basically understand everything." He paused for a beat. "Door close." Behind Oz, there was the sound of a slamming door. "Scream." Someone in the hallway

312

screamed. "Siren." The alarm in the building started going off, exactly as the man predicted, but he ignored it. "But I don't understand *you*." The man finished. "So, I'm going to try a different track with you today, and I'm just going to come right out and ask you," he leaned forward like a businessman trying to close a deal, "what do you *want*, Oz? Let's say…. Let's say it's your last day on earth and I can grant any wish to make you happy. What do you want?"

"I would…"

"You can't wish for health." The man shook his head, cutting off Oz's obvious answer. "You *never* change, you know that? You even answer the same innocuous random questions the same, even when they're asked years apart." He tapped his finger on the counter. "So, I'll ask again: at the end, what is it you would want from life?"

Oz considered the matter silently, trying to come up with anything in his life he'd want.

"Lieber Coffee." He said simply.

The words hung in the air for several moments.

The man looked confused and astonished by that. "Of all the possible answers you could have given, that was probably the last one I was expecting." He ran a hand through his hair, completely ignoring the fact that the germs his fingers had picked up from the counter were now being smeared onto his scalp, where they would undoubtedly reproduce and grow. "You really like coffee that much?"

Oz shook his head. "Can't stand it."

"See?" Prometheus pounded the table in annoyance. "*This* is what I'm talking about. *I don't understand you*." He snapped. "To be perfectly honest, I'd be happier finding someone else. But she won't have that. I know. I've tried."

"I have no idea what you're talking about. But I'm used to not being wanted." Oz went back to looking at the trillions of bacteria infesting his surroundings, feeling sick to his stomach. "If I were you, I'd get someone else too."

"I'm afraid I *literally* can't. I've tried it many, many times. She keeps killing my other candidates for her heart before they even get to the hospital fight. Hell, before the C of C even fights the Freedom Squad. The sad fact is, she will back *you*. No matter how terrible you are, no matter the ghoulish crimes you commit, or the better men I steer her towards in hopes romance will bloom, she wants *you*. Every time. It doesn't make a difference which side she's on at the start, she's *always* on your side at the end. Which means, if I want her on *my* side, I need to keep *you* from turning into the nightmarish man I've seen you become. Many times." He pointed at

Oz. "When the shit happens, I don't want to fight her. She's a dangerous enemy to have, and always singlehandedly takes out half of my team, sometimes more, and it's not even close. She tears through all of them like a fucking *wrecking ball*. ...Yes, usually singing along to that very song while it's blasting out on her iPhone at the same time she's eviscerating scores of people I need. Because she's backing you. So, I have to have you. If you're not evil, then neither is she. I'm going to use you like bait, to tempt a powerful enemy into becoming my friend. ...But I have no idea how to keep you sane."

Oz didn't bother answering that, too sickened and horrified by how filthy this room was.

He started to hold his breath to minimize his exposure. It would probably save his life.

The man on the other side of the glass busied himself with typing something into his phone. Whatever it was he found there, it made him start to laugh. "Ah, that makes more sense. Sometimes you get so used to failing that you forget that things occasionally fit together without needing to even arrange them." He held up the phone, which displayed an old ad for the coffee brand in question. "This? You want *this*?"

Oz looked at the smiling redhead in the old advertisement, who was looking at the viewer like he was her absolute perfect, shining hero.

He nodded.

"Okay." The man seemed very, very pleased with that news, now grinning from ear to ear. "I understand you better now. You're still weird and kinda creepy, but you're at least a kind of weird that I can work with." He reached down under his chair and pulled out his briefcase. "Congratulations, Oz. You want to be a hero? I'm going to pull some strings and call in a *ton* of favors and get you a position with the Freedom Squad."

"What, like an intern?"

"Oh, no." The man shook his head. "Full Cape position."

"You can't do that. I didn't go to the Horizons Academy. I wasn't even a sidekick." He paused for a beat. "Plus, I'm in super-max."

"I think you'd be surprised at what *I* can do, Oz. I'm older than the gods, I'm motivated, and I'm *very* bored." He met Oz's gaze. "I can *get* you a position there. If you can keep it, I can get you in the door."

"Will that help me be a hero?"

"Quite the opposite, actually. But that's okay. Like I said, sometimes the world is more complicated than merely 'good' and 'evil.'" He flipped a disinterested hand. "The Freedom Squad is monotonous. Depressing. Grey. It's a really, really terrible job. With really, really terrible people. The worst you can imagine. And as long as you work there, every single day, you'll feel like your life is worth less and less. That place is going to eat your soul and kill you slowly."

"Why would I ever want to work there then?"

"Do you want to be extraordinary?" He waved the phone, which still displayed the advertisement. "Redheaded damsels on runaway trains aren't going to catch themselves, Oz. You can sit around, waiting to be evil..."

"I already am, I know it."

"Whatever, I don't even care." The man conceded. "*Or* you can do something with your life." He shrugged helplessly. "But, like I said, I don't actually care about you at all. I need someone that only you can bring to the table. You're just bait, essentially, to remove a very powerful enemy from the field."

Oz leaned back in his chair, recognizing that this strange man was entirely serious

"Sir, I can recommend you a good therapist." Oz told him sincerely. "There's no shame in needing help."

"No, there's not." The man pulled a file from his briefcase. "Don't worry, I'm about to get you some."

Chapter 19

"'IN THAT DIRECTION,' THE CAT SAID, WAVING ITS
RIGHT PAW ROUND, 'LIVES A HATTER: AND IN THAT
DIRECTION,' WAVING THE OTHER PAW, 'LIVES A MARCH
HARE. VISIT EITHER YOU LIKE: THEY'RE BOTH MAD.'

'BUT I DON'T WANT TO GO AMONG MAD PEOPLE,'
ALICE REMARKED.

'OH, YOU CAN'T HELP THAT,' SAID THE CAT: 'WE'RE ALL
MAD HERE. I'M MAD. YOU'RE MAD.'"

- Alice's Adventures in Wonderland

PRESENT DAY

Oz was feeling slightly better today.

Not great, mind you. There were still some problems. The rooftop he was lying on was probably covered in asbestos, despite his best efforts to cover the surface up with a sterile biohazard tarp. The air in this area was certain to be among the most polluted, and all of that stale, contaminated sludge was doubtlessly filling his lungs up like mud coating the inside of a water bottle. The cold was probably going to give him early arthritis, its frozen grip slowly tightening on his joints like the icy hand of death. He could feel it. Every second he remained here, it was one second closer to his horrible demise.

And, obviously, his partner was still MIA. Which was his biggest concern at the moment.

It wasn't that Natalie wasn't trustworthy, it was just that she always thought she knew better than anyone. So, she wasn't someone who took advice well and she *certainly* wasn't someone who ever thought she needed to be protected.

He didn't necessarily disagree with that. Natalie was the strongest, most capable woman that Oz had ever known. But her own fractured mind and her piece-of-crap ex had damaged her. She was strong... but she was also delicate. Far more than she thought she was. If Oz did something wrong... she'd break.

She'd break, and there'd be no coming back from that for either of them.

So Oz spent most conversations with her willing himself not to do something to screw things up. He needed to keep himself under control and calm. He needed to keep *her* calm.

She'd undoubtedly spent too many years with someone telling her what to do. Putting their hands on her without consent...

The idea made Oz's fists close tight enough to cause the material of his gloves to strain under the pressure, popping the stitches.

He made a face and promptly replaced them with another pair from his pocket.

It wasn't that she was weak, it was that she was *important*.

At the moment, she was literally the hero of his life-story. And Oz knew, on a deep elemental level, that *he* could easily become the villain of it, if the circumstances were right.

In either case, his partner had pled for "five more minutes" of sleep this morning and to go on without him, and Oz was so utterly charmed by her sleepy and disheveled expression, that he'd agreed.

He found it very difficult to ever say no to that woman, particularly when she looked so adorable.

That was three hours ago though. And Natalie still hadn't shown up.

He wasn't worried, he knew she was fine. He hadn't heard any sirens or explosions. And she *wasn't* a woman who could be taken in a fight without at least one or two things blowing up first. Plus, he'd stationed Traitor and Flimflam in the apartment, ensuring that she didn't go anywhere. Not that he trusted Traitor, obviously, because that would be *nightmarishly* stupid, but Flannery was usually dependable in regards to such things.

Still, he was getting worried.

If she wasn't here in the next ten minutes, he'd have to leave.

He had traced their leading suspects, the Mastersons, around the city for most of the morning. They were paranoid and tried all sorts of techniques designed to ditch any suspected tails, but Oz was a very observant man. They might have been professionals, but Oz was a *superhero*. He'd managed to follow the men just fine. They had eventually made their way to this otherwise nondescript and fairly isolated seven story building far across the river. There were several open blocks between the building and anything else, and everything about it was utterly ordinary. Everything, that is, but the guard booth and thinly disguised Agletarian military patrols which circled the complex.

Oz was fairly sure that whoever was in charge of the Agletarian side of the attack was in that building, which was one of the reasons why he was so hesitant to leave. In his mind, solving this situation *immediately* was the best course of action. He'd take out the Agletarians and then use them to track down Mercygiver, and then Natalie would be safe.

It was a good plan. But it was messy.

Oz hated messy.

He shouldn't have left her alone. Even with five other members of the Consortium guarding her, in a location that no one outside of their organization knew.

That had been a mistake. He'd known it when he'd done it, but he'd been working under the assumption that "five minutes" actually *meant* five minutes, and that keeping an eye on the assailants would be keeping her safe, since he'd know exactly where the men were and if they moved against her, he'd be the first to know.

But it had been a mistake.

Oz's breathing quickened, panic building.

He became even more aware of the trillions of horrible microbes which surrounded him, like someone slowly turning up a spotlight on them, overshadowing the world of humans. And then the fact that the roof under him was undoubtedly both toxic *and* on the verge of collapse. He'd soon plummet through it as the supports gave way, then the cloud of asbestos would choke his lungs with cancer, and he'd be forced to watch, bleary-eyed and retching up bloody globules of cancerous lung tissue, as assassins sped from this hideout to go kill Natalie!

It was happening. He could feel it. It was happening right now...!

One-two-three-four-five-one-two-three-four-five...

A moment later, he heard someone vault up onto the roof behind him and he instantly turned over to face the attack.

"Fuck mornings and everyone involved." Natalie intoned darkly, making her way across the roof towards him.

He opened his mouth to point out that it was three in the afternoon and could in *no way* be considered "morning," but was struck silent by Natalie's outfit today.

She was costumed as a Playboy Club bunny, complete with heels, bow tie, and ears, carrying a large case of some kind. Her eyes were covered with goggles, each of which featured the Killroy symbol etched into the opaque white plastic.

The outfit was... surprising. Technically, it probably covered more skin than her "Jungle Lass" attire, but the addition of fishnet stockings and overtly low-cut bodice made it far more... sexual.

It was attractive in a way that made professional thought impossible. It invited nothing but distraction, and the need to dwell on the intricacies of her curves.

Oz was fine with that.

As it happened, dwelling on her curves had long been one of his favorite pastimes.

His eyes traced their way up and down her, marveling at the steady way she was able to walk across the roof in high-heeled boots so quickly. Her legs were muscular but slim, and he imagined them spreading open to...

"What?" She asked, noticing that he was staring.

"I didn't say anything." He defended, looking away and feeling embarrassed.

"No, but you were thinking it." She frowned, her expression darkening. "You have a problem with me?"

"No, I'm..."

"*Because I'm getting really sick of your attitude today, Oz.*" She snapped.

Oz squinted in confusion, trying to determine which of the precisely fifteen words he'd said to her today had been so over-the-line.

She gestured to her sexy rabbit attire and held up a machine pistol. "Today I am...." she paused, "*Hare Trigger!*"

Oz snorted in amusement, despite himself. "Okay. Good to meet you."

"Just a warning: I'm *not* a morning person, Oz. Just don't even talk to me until I get a couple of cups of coffee in me, or I can't be held responsible for what I do to you."

He shook his head. "I don't have a coffee maker up here. Or coffee."

Her beautiful mouth turned down at the corners, forming an angry but oddly sexy frown. "I've killed men for less than that, Oz." She flopped down onto the roof next to him, as he went back to observing the activities at the base. "I still don't understand why I had to come all the way out here on a frozen morning, just to deal with this."

"It's the afternoon." He felt the need to remind her.

She simply stared at him, continuing to frown. Apparently,

"Hare Trigger" *didn't* like to be corrected.

"I thought Monty was in charge of the Agletarian side of things?" She finally asked.

"He is." Oz agreed.

"So why are we here?"

"Do you trust him with your life?"

She snorted at that idea.

"Exactly." He carefully recorded the guard's movements in his logbook, pleased that it was keeping to the exact schedule he'd anticipated. "Did you bring Hazard and Tyrant with you?"

She shook her head, absently tossing pebbles across the roof. "Nah, Stacy got back from visiting that ice skating zombies bitch, and she wanted them to go play some stupid card game." She paused. "Tyrant and Hazz, not the zombies, obviously." She heaved an elaborate sigh. "This mission requires a certain level of finesse and down-to-the-bone badassery which they lack anyway, so I think we'll be fine." She absently looked back at him rather than at the soldiers trying to kill her, as if she trusted him completely to deal with that for her. "Plus, the book club is reading that stupid book about the fucking rabbits again and they're both so over-emotional. They'd probably just start bawling if they were here. Fucking babies."

"*Watership Down*?" Oz guessed.

"How the fuck should I know?" She shrugged. "I'm not in the book club. Except when I am, which isn't today." She made a face. "Fuck rabbits."

Oz looked up from his binoculars. "Aren't you *dressed* as a rabbit today?"

"Hell no! I'm a hare! *You got something against hares, now?*" She straightened, like she was preparing for a fight. "Huh?" She pointed at him angrily. "*I've already warned you about your fucking attitude, Oz!*"

"No, no..." he went back to looking through his binoculars to avoid the nonsensical argument, "hares are fine."

"Fine?" She challenged, sounding angrier. "*Fine!?!*"

"*Exemplary.*" He corrected.

She nodded her head, causing her bunny ears to bob in a way that should have been far less attractive than it was. "Damn straight." She took a step to her left so that she was leaning against the edge of the roof, with her back to the evil army assembled below, like they still didn't even matter. "So, what's the plan here? We gonna wait until they have some kind of charity gala, fake an invitation, and then sneak away once we're inside?"

Oz squinted in confusion. "Why would a secret army installation have a charity gala?"

"I don't know." She shrugged. "There are a *shitload* of charity galas and evil parties in this town, have you ever noticed that? $20 says that within the month they'll have some kind of black tie event to showcase a huge diamond, meteorite, or deadly new variety of hypno-velociraptor. I'll lay odds."

"'Hypno-velociraptor'?"

"Oh, aren't you sweet." She sounded charmed by his innocence. "You've led such a sheltered little life, haven't you?" She went back to watching the Agletarians. "So we're just going to storm the building and get some answers? Because I'm cold and I haven't had my coffee and I want to hurt someone over that. I want to hurt someone *baaaaaad*..."

"We aren't going to go in, we'd be hopelessly outgunned."

She flipped a hand unconcernedly. "What you call 'outgunned,' I call an 'economy of force.'"

"We need to be more subtle."

"I can be very subtle."

He looked up and down her costume. "I doubt that."

She turned around to look down at the building several hundred yards away, blocking most of Oz's view. Luckily, it did provide him a much *nicer* view, and Oz overcame his reasonable hesitation to ogle an imperiled coworker and friend, and drank her in.

His eyes traveled up her legs, memorizing every line. His gaze lingered on her rear, tilting his head to the side to get a better look at the fishnet stockings which traveled under her costume. The netting was tightest over her skin there, pressing against the soft but undoubtedly firm flesh.

He wondered what it would feel like in his hands...

The costume had a little puffball of a tail, and for some reason, it simply made Oz's day.

She leaned forward slightly, and Oz must have made a sound or his breathing changed, because she became aware he was watching her. "Stop looking at my tail, Oz."

Oz tore his eyes away. "Sorry."

"Nah, I'm just kidding, I don't give a shit." She laughed.

"Okay." He wasn't sure what to say to that. His mind raced, once again returning to her legs. "The seam in your stockings is crooked." He heard himself saying, like it was someone else talking.

The seam which ran up the back of her leg was indeed crooked though. For some reason, it wasn't sending his need for things to be orderly into overdrive. It was just... something to say, because otherwise he was pretty certain all he'd be able to get out was a groan of desire and lust.

She snorted in laughter. "Is it?" Her surprise sounded entirely fake, for some reason. Like she'd expected him to see that. "Well, I'm glad you were looking closely enough to notice, Oz." She turned around and put her leg up on the crate Oz was using to support his binoculars. The movement opened her legs and allowed him to see her inner thigh, with him between them. "Why don't you go ahead and straighten it for me?" She arched an eyebrow over her Hare Trigger goggles. "Please?" The word came out breathy and deeper.

Oz watched her, debating with himself. It was cold enough at the moment that he could see her breath, watching as it grew faster. The swell of her incredible breasts rising and falling, forming a little cloud around her beautiful face with each breath. There was something deeply erotic and intimate about watching her breathe.

It took Oz's own breath away to watch her. It felt like she'd reached into his chest and wrapped her fingers around his heart.

"I can't straighten it from this angle." He said softly, otherwise at a loss for words. His desire scared him. It was unlike anything else he'd ever felt in his life, and he wasn't certain how that would affect his powers.

If he lost control of them, they'd both be liquefied in seconds by trillions of tiny germs and microanimals.

For a moment, Oz was rendered still, imagining nightmarish scenarios where he accidentally hurt Natalie...

"Try." She demanded.

Oz swallowed, eyes moving to her exposed flesh and the fishnets which covered it. And his control snapped. He moved his hand to her ankle.

"Lose the glove." She shook her head. "You touch me, *you* touch me."

He tossed it aside like the damn thing was on fire, closing his fingers over her skin and tracing them upwards. Enraptured.

She was warm, despite the cold. Downright hot.

He noticed with a small bit of disappointment that she wasn't wearing an anklet today, his finger tracing over the spot on her skin where it had been the day before, without him even recognizing he was doing it.

He had wanted very much to touch that.

He got to his feet, the action putting him uncomfortably close to... areas of her body he most wanted to explore.

She seemed to recognize that awkward closeness too, shifting her hips back, like she was shocked by the feelings it brought. "Fuck…" She said under her breath.

Oz stepped closer, his hand on her thigh, feeling like he was being allowed to touch something sacred. His eyes flicked up to her, making sure he still had permission.

She nodded. "It's still crooked." She breathed, looking away because her face looked flushed now. "It makes me feel too tight, Oz. Please help me with that…"

He gently moved her chin so that she was looking up at him again, and Natalie's breathing was even quicker now. On some level, he recognized that he was surely scaring her, but he was too far gone to let that bother him.

He could hurt her. His powers were too dangerous to mess with. To say nothing of the fact that his scarred, contaminated hands had no business being anywhere near her perfect, smooth body.

He was trash. He shouldn't be doing this…

She put her hands flat against his chest, looking up at him, mouth parting.

His hand slid around to caress her inner thigh, while his other hand moved along the outside, still marveling at how smooth her skin was. And it was growing even hotter. She was soft, delicate skin, over the strong muscles of a dancer. He moved her fishnets so that the seam would be even, and in the process, the back of his fingers accidentally brushed against the fabric which covered the apex of her thighs.

He hadn't meant to touch her there, but even as it happened he realized that it was a sensation he'd be reliving for the rest of his life. It was absolutely heavenly.

Natalie stumbled away like she'd been shot, swearing to herself. "*Holy fuck!*" She almost fell over, and Oz's hand shot out to steady her. She leaned over, panting and looking weak.

"Are you okay?" He finally asked, feeling like he'd overstepped and scared her. "Did I…?"

"I'm fine." She announced, straightening to her full height and trying to act nonchalant. "Everything's fine. Just…" She swallowed, her skin flushed. "Didn't really expect that to… you know… *feel* like…"

Oz nodded. She had been in an abusive relationship. He needed to be more careful about touching her.

She let out a long breath. "Christ… *What a way to start a morning*."

"It's 3 in the after..." He began, then stopped, recognizing that it would only make her angry. Hare Trigger seemed to live up to her name, always on the verge of getting angry over meaningless things.

Natalie straightened the bodice of her costume, then yanked at the bow tie collar around her neck, like she felt it was choking her.

The action caused her breasts to move, drawing Oz's eyes to the spectacular view they presented. Her stiffened nipples pressed against the white satin, unashamedly. Oz found the sight captivating and it hit him harder than any punch he'd ever received in his 1,278 consecutive days as a hero.

His hands fisted at his sides, trying to keep himself away from her through sheer force of will. Trying to keep himself from grabbing her and losing himself in her. It was a fight he wasn't going to win, but it was a fight he respected Natalie enough to have.

She apparently followed his line of sight, and frowned in embarrassment. She started to turn away from him, then stopped. She started to cross her arms over her chest, then stopped. Finally, she just stood there, hard points of her nipples still visible, looking awkward. "It's... cold." She said softly.

Oz's gaze remained fixed on her breasts, completely uncaring about the fact it was *tremendously* inappropriate to do so. At the moment, he didn't care at all about that. Or the fact that it embarrassed her. All Oz wanted in the world was to watch her breasts. To feel them clutched in his hands. And in about 5 seconds, he was seriously scared he'd move to do just that.

If her breasts were cold, the only gentlemanly thing to do would be to warm them with his palms, right? That would be downright heroic...

"Oz?" She asked softly, like she was seeing someone entirely different. "You okay?"

Oz couldn't answer. He was afraid it would be incomprehensible. His erection pressed against the front of his pants hard enough that he was becoming increasingly concerned about permanent physical injury. The pain merely added to the lust though, making him angry and eager to be rid of his clothes.

"...Oz?" She all but whispered.

And that snapped him out of his momentary lapse of control. No matter how much he might want that woman, there was no excuse for scaring her. Oz scared a lot of people with his behavior, but he'd never actually scared *her* before. And it made him feel ashamed.

"I'm fine." He cleared his throat, trying to return his voice to normal. "Just... tired."

It was a lie. And they both knew it.

"I'm sorry." He told her honestly. "You don't need to be afraid of me. Ever."

"I'm not afraid of you. I just..." She swallowed, looking uncomfortable. "At least my stocking is straight now."

Neither one of them wanted to deal with what had just happened, so the topic was dropped without further comment.

It did nothing to really sooth Oz's desire though, if anything, conversing with her just made it grow stronger. He'd always found her way of looking at the world and the carefree tone of her voice to be so entirely attractive. Even when she was Multifarious. And *those* erections had been even odder and more inappropriate for him than this one was. Because he had never even seen Mull's face. Or knew whether or not she was a woman. At the time, he'd been a little disturbed about it. But he just... liked her. Mull was sexy and fun. Thankfully, it had turned out that the woman he was lusting after and the masked sexless coworker he... sometimes had inappropriate thoughts about, where one and the same. It really made things simpler.

But Oz had been alone his entire life. He could deal with unfulfilled desire.

She didn't seem to notice the trauma she was doing to his nether regions, absently leaning over to pick up the case she was carrying.

The stunning sight of her body at a new angle, was physical agony for him.

Oz turned away, wincing in pain and trying to somehow rearrange his body so that the pressure against his fly was lessened. The action was useless. He simply wanted her too much.

Natalie opened the case. "I brought supplies, by the way."

He looked down at the pieces of a very large weapon which were secured in place by straps. "I don't think we'll need a rifle. This is simply going to be observation, and then Arn and Flannery are going in undercover."

She shook her head and began assembling the weapon. "Technically, it's too big to be a 'rifle,' this is a *'cannon.'*" She patted the side of the ridiculously long 20mm weapon. "It's five times more powerful than Syd's silly little elephant gun. Over *three* times as powerful as a fifty cal. *This* is what you use when you want to kill Robocop, as he's standing behind a tank and a cinderblock wall and *another* Robocop. It's like hitting someone with a *lead brick* which is

326

traveling at twice the speed of sound. This is my baby." She beamed in obvious pride, running her finger over the small image of a pink sleeping smiley face, which was wearing a princess hat, with a line of green Zs over its head. "I call her: 'The Dreamland Express.'"

"Don't you think that's a bit of an overkill?"

"If something's worth killing, it's worth overkilling, Oz." She set up the sniper weapon on the edge of the roof. "Very rarely in life will you ever find yourself saying: 'Damn, I wish I'd brought a smaller caliber weapon.'"

"I just think perhaps and anti-tank gun isn't the best choice for our current circumstances." He continued.

"Do the Agletarians have tanks in there, Oz?"

"Not to my knowledge."

"But you don't know that they *don't* have tanks either." She exclaimed, like it was the height of logical thought. "So I'm going to go with the biggest gun I got, and then if the situation calls for it, we'll work our way down from there." She snapped the sniper scope into place and secured the gigantic weapon's heavy bi-pod mount. "I modified it to be full auto once, but the chain of rounds weighed over two hundred pounds, and firing it melted down the barrel and dislocated my retina."

Oz wasn't sure how to respond to that. "That... that must have been very hard for you."

"Well, the next day I didn't have eyes at all, so it worked out."

Once again, Oz was at a complete loss. "Okay..." He finally got out, constantly amazed by the world Natalie lived in and unsure how he could function in it.

"Got something for you too." She reached into the bag. "Things could get loud, and you'll need to be strapped."

"I don't really like guns." He shook his head. "I can do just fine without them."

"Yeah, but your powers are weird and they freak you out. You'll hesitate to use them, and hesitation gets you killed in a fight." She pulled the silver weapon from the case. "A custom Colt M1917 revolver." She jammed the magazine into place. "It's a .45, double-action. Six shots. Super simple. Point it at what you want to die." She stared at it silently for a moment, lost in thought. "Roy carried this through the war..." She cleared her throat self-consciously. "It... it's my father's gun." She clarified. "He shot Nazis with it. So, if you're looking for the weapon that stands for something good, this is your buddy. It's never done anything but stop genuinely evil men. Roy was

a hero. In the truest sense. You... you would have liked him." She
held the weapon out for him. "I've never used his gun for any job. It
shouldn't be used for the things I do. It's meant for White Hats."

Oz recognized that it would be an insult not to take the
weapon, so he did. He looked down at the Kilroy symbol etched in the
side, then slid the pistol into his waistband.

"Do *not* lose that and *don't* die." She ordered harshly, then
paused. "Please."

"I won't lose it." He assured her. "I'll keep it safe."

"It's meant to keep *you* safe, moron." She sounded
exasperated as she reached for his radio and pressed the transmit
button. "This is The Mad Hatter. Alice and I are in position at the Tea
Party, over."

Oz frowned. "Does that have to be my codename?"

"Hush, Alice." She waved off his concern. "Stop distracting
me."

"Well, couldn't I be one of the other characters from the
book?"

"What book?"

"*Alice in Wonderland,* obviously."

"What the hell does *that* have to do with anything?" She
sounded completely baffled. "Why would you bring up some random
book right now?" She spread her arms out questioningly. "You're so
weird sometimes, Alice." She pressed the transmit button again.
"Cheshire Cat, you copy?"

"This is Cat, I read you, Hatter." Traitor's voice came over
the radio. "The Doormouse and I are about to serve the tea. Two
minutes out."

"Copy." She put the radio down and turned to look at the
building across from them. "So, we've got 50+ hostiles by my count,
spread out over the grounds and bottom floor. An unknown number
of hostiles inside, along with our target. No signs of the kidnapped
people though." She paused, thinking it over. "My suggestion: blow
up the building."

"But Traitor and Flannery are about to make their way
inside!" He argued. "And we're here looking for innocent kidnapped
people."

"Meh." She shrugged. "Fuck'em all."

Oz shook his head. "I don't think that's a good idea." He
picked up his binoculars, watching as Traitor drove their stolen guard
jeep back towards the entrance, stopping at the guard booth so that
the man could somehow talk his way inside. "Door guards, metal

detectors, an elevator which only operates if a special coded key is inserted, a separate keycard is needed on the seventh floor landing, and finally there is a lock on the door to the main office which can only be opened with an iris match." Oz informed her, updating her on the research he'd been doing all morning.

"Gotcha." Natalie nodded at the news.

"Now, Flannery and Arnold are disguised as soldiers and will lie their way inside. They will carefully make their way to the back of the base, where they'll cut the power at exactly 3:45. The backup power will kick in 2 minutes later, and we will use that time to loop the video playback on all of the security cameras so that we can approach undetected. We will infiltrate the base and hook up with Arnold and Flannery, and we will enter the ventilation system and then lower ourselves down into the commander's office. Information suggests that he will return to his office between 4:00 and 4:30, at which point we will take him. Our extraction will be covered from the back fence by Flannery. If the situation goes dynamic and he makes a run for it, we will pursue but not engage in the city itself. If we are discovered, we will evacuate three blocks east, where I have placed a clean getaway vehicle." He firmed his jaw, recognizing that the plan needed to be executed flawlessly, as this might well be their only chance to catch the Agletarians sleeping. "We need to move quickly but deliberately. We need to get in there silently and then get out again without..."

"Yeah, uh-huh. Sounds good, Oz." Natalie interrupted, sounding distracted for some reason. "Hey, can you do me a favor and cover your ears real quick? Cool." There was a series of LOUD explosions next to him, rocking the rooftop and sending up a cloud of dirty snow, despite the tarp he'd laid out. "Or we could skip it all and just do *that*."

Oz stumbled to the side and hit the ground, crawling closer to the edge to watch as the heavy rounds from Natalie's huge weapon continued to tear the Agletarian base apart.

Natalie's hand flew over the bolt, loading rounds and firing them into their targets faster than Oz would have expected anyone to be capable of doing.

An explosive round crashed into the guard house, tearing a hole in it the size of a dinner table and shooting a plume of fire out the back. Unfortunately, Traitor and Flannery were currently standing in front of the building, and they both dove out of the way as burning debris rained down on them.

Natalie started laughing, like it was the most hysterical and fun thing she'd ever done.

Oz pressed his hands over his ears harder, the noise from the weapon deafening.

Rounds began impacting the building below them and Oz moved closer, fully intending to shield Natalie.

"Relax, Oz. At this distance, they might as well be attacking us with a stapler." She assured him over the sounds of battle.

A car tore down the street, firing at the roofline around them.

"An MP-5?" Natalie snorted in dismissal. "Bitch, please." She put a round straight through the car's roof and into the driver, splattering him all over his companions and causing the car to crash into one of the security fences. A moment later, she sent an incendiary round into the vehicle's gas tank, making it explode, burning the surviving occupants.

The sound of an attack chopper still could somehow be heard over the din though, as the Agletarian craft lifted off from a hidden pad and hovered in the air for a moment, bristling with weapons.

"And *you* said that I wouldn't need a cannon, Oz!" Natalie reminded him, shouting over the noise. "Don't you ever get tired of being wrong!?!"

"*It's a complicated issue!*" He yelled back, unsure if he could even be heard.

"Is it? Huh. Well, I find a good quality anti-materiel cannon makes things real simple for you." She winked at him. "Someone once asked the Red Baron how he was able to shoot down so many other planes and what his secret was. Do you know what he said?" She asked calmly, looking through the scope.

Oz nodded. "'*Aim for the man...*'"

She moved the bolt, loading another round.

"'*...Don't miss him.*'" Oz finished.

She fired and a moment later, the front of the helicopter exploded as Natalie shot the pilot. The helicopter started to spin out of control, smoke trailing from its flaming cockpit.

Natalie loaded another round. "Wait for it... wait for it... *Bingo*." She fired again, and the huge round tore through the base of the rotors, causing the entire assembly to break free of the fuselage and then come crashing down like a spinning scythe, directly into the soldiers who were assembling in front of the building. They were instantly cut to pieces. The body of the helicopter, along with all of its unfired ordinance, crashed through the front of the building and

330

exploded, turning the lobby into a fireball and blowing out every window in the structure.

The noise echoed through the silence for a moment.

Oz just blinked in complete shock, trying to comprehend how his carefully planned covert mission could have ended in 60 seconds of gunfire and explosions.

Natalie jumped to her feet and pumped her fist in the air. "*Yeah!* What'd I say, huh? What'd I say? Wrecked it. R-E-K-T." She swatted her hand against his chest. "'Loop the security tape,'" she repeated, sounding deeply contemptuous of the idea, "what were *you* thinking?" She reached down to her bag, pulled out her machine pistols, then attached a couple of wicked looking swords to her back, letting out another excited laugh. "Come on, let's go finish off the survivors, Oz!"

To his surprise, she simply leapt off the roof, jumping almost all the way to the building across from them. Apparently that was one of her powers today, in addition to her tendency to take offense at things.

Oz continued staring at her in disbelief, his ears still ringing. He...

He'd never really met anyone in his life like Natalie Quentin before.

It was quite possible that she was insane. Or evil.

But he thought she was *amazing*.

Absolutely amazing.

And he was completely in love with her.

He hurried after her, taking the fire escape stairs three at a time and sprinting towards the Agletarian headquarters, which now looked like a war zone. By the time he pushed his way through the wreckage of the security fence, Natalie was already in a shouting match with Traitor and Flimflam, who were covered in ash and looked shell-shocked.

Flannery was so angry about the plan spontaneously changing and her almost being shot with a cannon, that she looked on the verge of stroke. "Are you pure mental!?!" She challenged, pushing Natalie back. "Ye coulda killed us!!!" She pointed at her and glared at Traitor and Oz. "I will *never* work with this radge again, do ye understand me?"

"About every third word." Natalie squinted in confusion as if trying to understand her. "I don't know what a 'radge' is, but I don't think it means anything." She turned to Oz. "Oz, is that a word?"

"Umm..." Oz began. Flannery was second-in-command of

the Public Relations Department, and also worked with the Undercover Department. On an ordinary day, the woman was calm enough, and spoke without any trace of an accent. But if you got her angry enough, it was sometimes difficult to decipher what she was saying.

"Don't ye start with me!" Flannery shouted at him, cutting him off. "*She's* off her head, pure skyrocket, man, but yer supposed to know better!" She threw the cap of her military disguise uniform at Natalie, then went back to glaring at Oz. "But no, you're just willing to let her do whatever crazy shite she wants, 'cause you're pure gantin' fur sex."

"I understood the words 'sex' and 'shite.'" Natalie updated seriously. "The rest is in another language."

Flannery let out a bellow of rage and charged at her.

Traitor caught her before she could reach Natalie, and had to physically carry the other woman away. And when even *Arnold* recognized that he needed to do something, you *knew* there was an issue.

"I'm sorry you were almost hurt." Oz told Flannery calmly. "That must have been very hard for you."

"*Go take a running fuck at a rolling doughnut, Oz!*" Flannery shouted back, still struggling to get free of Arnold's grasp and attack Natalie. "Ya bastard!"

"'Doughtnuts'? What the fuck?" Natalie spread her arms out in mystification, like the other woman's accent made her meaning indecipherable. "Are you trying to say something else and I just can't *understand it* because you sound like 'Groundskeeper Willie,' or is that a slang w..."

Oz put his hand up to stop the argument. "I think we understand what she meant, Nat." He shook his head. "She's probably upset because you fired a 20mm explosive anti-tank round into a building she was two feet from." Given her personality today, he was trying to keep things as non-confrontational as possible. "Without... you know... even a warning."

Natalie paused to consider that for a moment. "Jesus. I can't believe people are ruining a perfectly good day with negativity. I mean, all I want to do is go shoot some people, but *noo-ooooo*. I just... oh, hold on..." She bent down to pull a knife out of her high-heeled boot and pushed Oz out of the way. In the distance, one of the soldiers was running towards the entrance of the building, somehow having survived her ambush. "*From downtown...!*" Natalie threw the knife in an arc, the blade spinning round and round, high through the air, until it finally came back down to stick directly through the back of the man's neck, one hundred feet away. He collapsed, dead before he hit the ground. Natalie threw her arms out in celebration. "Yeah! Nuthin' but net, motherfuckers!" She looked over at Oz and nodded in satisfaction, obviously expecting him to join her in rejoicing in the carnage. "Somebody set this shit to 'Easy Mode' difficulty, Oz!"

Oz simply stared at her. He'd been with the Consortium for months now, but he still wasn't quite used to this kind of thing.

Oz lived a very orderly life. He didn't typically take part in wars. Particularly ones where women dressed like Natalie. Or, for that matter, *looked* like Natalie. Or *talked* like Natalie.

Shocking violence, overt sexuality, explosions, death…

It was all very overstimulating.

It was messy. And loud. And there was blood and fire everywhere.

And Natalie was grinning from ear to ear, like some kind of demon, relishing the pain she was inflicting on her enemies.

Oz wanted her more than he ever had.

She was everything he'd always avoided in his life, wrapped up in one insane and messy package.

Sex and violence and a bouncing red ponytail.

She smiled at him… and she owned his soul.

Oz's mouth quirked at the corner, utterly enchanted by his unstoppable partner. He found her so amazing. And completely charming. And sexy as all hell.

Flannery was right: Oz *was* wrapped around that woman's finger.

"Watch this, Oz." She threw a lighter into the street, and when it hit the ground, fire raced out in several directions. "If you were looking at this from above, it would look like the Kilroy symbol." She casually explained. "And it'd be *fucking awesome.*"

Oz watched the fire for a beat, then turned back to her. "Don't you think there could have possibly been better uses of your time than painting your own symbol on the concrete with gasoline this morning?"

"Who cares?" She gestured to it. "It looks cool!"

"Only from above."

"So?"

He looked up into the sky. "So no one *is* above us right now."

"You have no sense of theatricality, Oz." She shook her head in disapproval. "That's your problem. You need to have some drama in your life, not to mention the power of branding. You don't even *have* a logo."

Oz went back to watching the flames. "So how long did that take you to plan out?"

"About an hour. Maybe a little more. Used graph paper."

"Ah." He watched the fire spread for a moment longer. "Did you bring a fire extinguisher?"

She snorted at the question. "Why would I start a fire in the shape of my symbol and then want to put it out?"

"Because it could spread and burn the whole city down?"

"I'm a superhero, not a fireman." She crossed her arms over her chest. "Not my problem."

"People could be in danger." He pointed out logically.

"Luckily, I'm a hero. If the fire spreads, I can rescue them from it, right? That's what heroes do. Especially since I'm already in the neighborhood blowing up other shit anyway. So, no problem."

He frowned slightly. "I really think this company needs a refresher course on heroism." He paused for a beat. "And fire safety." He gestured towards the building with the side of his head. "Let's go ask the people in charge why they wanted to kill you." He hoped his voice was level and didn't sound as impressed and turned-on as he felt.

She beamed, obviously liking the go-ahead from him. Then she started through the debris, towards the broken and smoldering remains of the buildings entrance. "I'll clear the road, just bask in my awesome, Baby Doll."

Oz's eyes once more settled on her rear, deeply enjoying watching the way it moved when she walked. "Okay."

Natalie kicked aside the shattered security glass, which might have been bomb-proof, but did little to stop an exploding helicopter from crashing through it. She looked around the lobby, which featured a central atrium all the way to the top. She gestured to the smoldering decorations, which had been arranged around the space, for some reason. "Ya know, they might be evil pieces of shit, but at least they remembered the holidays. And I bet they get a lot of presents this year... provided they asked Santa for gruesome deaths." She casually leaned against the security desk in the lobby, pressing the button for the building's intercom, which surprisingly still worked. "*Attention Agletarians!*" She yelled into the microphone. "My name is Hare Trigger today, and you tried to kill me last week. I took it personal. So now I'm here to *WRECK YOUR SHIT!!!*" She took on a friendly tone. "Please report to the lobby and form an orderly line to be shot dead.

334

Thank you and Happy Thanksgiving!" She placed her phone next to the microphone and blasted out an irritatingly cheerful pop song over the building's speakers, as loud as they would go. The only discernible lyrics seemed to be the nonsense word "*MMMBop*," which the women singing the song used way too frequently.

The song instantly made Oz angry, for some reason.

Soldiers on the floor above them started shooting down at them from the exposed balcony, and Natalie pushed him to the side, before returning fire with her machine pistols. "You done pissed off the wrooooong bitch this time!" She shouted at them. Several of the men went down in the hail of automatic weapons fire, while the rest dove for cover. Natalie looked back at him. "Race ya to the top, Baby Doll!" Then she leapt away, covering the entire distance to the second floor in a single bound, landing among the completely surprised men and cutting them down before they even knew what was happening.

Oz could have handled this in a responsible and methodical way. He could have carefully secured his point-of-entry and waited for Traitor and Flimflam to join the fight. Use the cover to his advantage and ensure complete safety for himself and bystanders.

That's what he normally would have done. It's what he always did.

But in the current circumstances, that wasn't what he was doing. Instead, he was sprinting up the stairs, trying to keep from laughing. For some reason, he was finding this whole thing surprisingly fun. Natalie's enthusiasm for the work was rather infectious. And she looked really, really good in fishnet stockings, which probably had something to do with it.

Whatever the reason, Oz was determined to take Natalie's dare and beat her to the top.

He rounded the corner of the flight of stairs, taking the next flight two at a time. A soldier moved to shoot him, but Oz simply slammed his palm into the man's chest, sending him backwards over the railing to the floor below, knocking him out.

Natalie's annoying pop song continued to blare over the speakers, loud enough to even be heard over the gunfire.

He went up four more flights in a similar way, arriving on the sixth floor to find that soldiers were stationed along an elevated skywalk, shooting down at him. On the other side of the open atrium, Natalie was duel-wielding falchion swords, to hack and slash her way through several guards. She ducked under their gunfire, then slammed one of the swords through the side of one man's head and straight through another, pinning them both to the wall. She used the remaining sword to cut the last guard across his body, clean through from his waist to the base of his neck, then caught the guard's gun before it hit the ground, using it to return fire on the men shooting at her from the skywalk.

And for the first time in his life, Oz wasn't afraid to use his powers. It was probably just to show off, but he didn't even think about it. The bolts holding the skywalk to the structural support of the building were as contaminated and covered with microbes as everything else in this world. And they were only too happy to rust away and eat the metal for him at a microscopic scale. The skywalk hung in place for half a second, then collapsed down through the building, taking the men with it. It crashed onto the floor of the lobby, sending up a cloud of no-doubt toxic debris and smoke.

The men would live, but they'd probably need extended hospital stays. At the moment, they weren't in much of a condition to do anything more than writhe.

Natalie stood up, retrieved her swords, then looked over the railing to see what had happened to the skywalk.

Then her eyes met his. They stared at each other for a timeless moment.

Natalie grinned and her eyebrows shot up, in flirtatious challenge.

Then they both raced to get to the seventh floor first. Oz sprinting up the stairs, while Natalie jumped onto the crumbling remains of the skywalk supports and ran to beat him to the landing.

It was basically a tie, although both claimed victory.

The whole thing was childish, dangerous, and needlessly messy. To say nothing of the deaths which resulted from it. But... Oz didn't seem to care at the moment. Which was certainly odd. He would have expected to. He just... didn't.

In fact, his only real emotion was continuing to dwell on how nice Natalie looked and how her face was brightened by the exercise.

All in all, he was having a good time. Which was terrifying. It undoubtedly indicated that more and more his 'bad blood' was taking him over. But right now, he didn't care about that either.

They made their way towards the only office on the floor, with Oz's eyes scanning every shadow for a possible attack and Natalie dancing with herself, completely ignoring the peril. Her head and hips gracefully swayed to the beat of the song, lost in the music. She grabbed his hand and used it to raise his arm, then twirled herself.

"Do you know 'The Pony,' Oz?" She asked playfully, moving out in front of him to do the dance from the 1960s, prancing from foot to foot and spinning in a circle, arms outstretched. It was a wholly silly and completely joyful little dance. "Come on, dance with me!"

Oz started laughing, utterly *amazed* by the woman.

Two more guards rounded the corner and Oz charged the one on the left, driving his knee up into the man's chest, breaking his sternum and sending him to the ground, then slammed his fist into the man's face as he landed on him, knocking him out cold.

Natalie continued her dancing spin and pulled her gun and one of her swords in the same movement, decapitating the other guard as he opened fire. The rounds impacted the floor, as his head tumbled down by Natalie's feet, at which point she bounced it from foot to foot, then kicked it hard enough to send the head sailing out over the railing of the atrium and through the large Christmas wreath hanging from the ceiling.

She put both her arms straight over her head to signal a field goal in football. "It's up, *it's good!*" She shouted, then went back to dancing, not missing a beat.

Oz started laughing, despite how gruesome it was. "Maybe you should *try* to concentrate, Nat."

She started mouthing along with the lyrics, pumping her arms in the air and occasionally firing off her weapon to accentuate the beat.

The entryway to the main area of this floor was guarded by a thick security door and a complicated computerized lock. Oz's initial plan had been to secretly bypass it via the ductwork and come down on the other side, but given the events of the afternoon, it was safe to say that "subtle" was now off the table.

Instead, Oz simply used his powers on the wall which supported the door, crumbling it to bits.

Natalie danced through the opening, like she didn't have a care in the world.

As they arrived at the office door, Oz stepped in front of her and kicked it down, fully expecting there to be a fight on the other side. "Consortium of Chaos, throw up your hands!" He yelled, bringing his still fully loaded .45 to bear, preparing to kill anyone stupid enough to take a shot at Natalie.

To his surprise though, the room on the other side of the door was simply a waiting room, which held only one occupant.

Oz frowned in amazement at seeing the solitary man though. He knew him.

Natalie did too, stopping her dance and straightening. "Hey, I know you!" She snapped her fingers. "You're that little fake intern fuck-wit!" She snapped her fingers several more times in rapid succession. "What's your name? Wally? Winston?"

"Wendell." Oz supplied, not taking his eyes off the man.

The man had recently appeared in the Consortium's ranks, claiming to have been hired as an intern by Librarian, who was on her honeymoon at the time. The man had hung out with the Consortium, and gone on a couple of missions while Julian was in charge of things. He had somehow gotten credit for stopping the Super-Person Resistance Movement, and had then disappeared. When Marian had returned from her honeymoon, she had informed the group that she had never hired any such person.

So, his identity and motivations were one of the mysteries which most concerned the ranks of the team at the moment. Or, at least the ranks of the team who were sober and sane enough to recognize that it was a problem. The rest of the team had almost certainly forgotten the man even existed.

"Sure, I remember my good buddy Wendell." Natalie moved away from Oz, flanking the man, just in case he attacked or tried to make a run for it. The woman instinctively positioned herself to coordinate with Oz and back him up, without needing to plan it. It was very impressive. "So you were working for the Agletarians?" She made a tsk-ing sound with her tongue. "Say it ain't so, Wendy."

To Oz's surprise, the man started laughing like he found that idea genuinely amusing. "You think this is about *Agletaria?*" He let out another sharp bark of laughter. "Some stupid country that no one has ever heard of and their *idiotic* vendetta against you?" His voice became more serious, his tone darkening. "You really have no idea what's coming, do you? What you're up against? It's so much bigger than anything you and your friends can *possibly* imagine, little girl."

"'Little girl'?" Natalie repeated, then turned to look at Oz. "Why do evil assholes always have to be kinda sexist too? Why can't they ever just...?"

"But you're all too preoccupied to see it. But *I've* seen it." The man continued, sounding haunted. "You can't fight it. Stronger people than you and your friends have tried. But you can't escape evolution. You can only serve it. And if you fail?" His hand moved to quickly pull a gun out of his pocket, then pressed it to his own head. "Your world is dark but I am a herald of Dawn." He met her eyes. "*It's coming.*"

BANG.

Wendell's body slumped to the side.

"Huh." Natalie said unemotionally. "Kinda takes all the fun

338

out of it when they shoot themselves, doesn't it?"

Oz stared at the man for a moment longer, then cautiously approached the body. He put two of his gloved fingers to the man's neck.

"What the hell are you doing?" Natalie asked.

"I'm checking his pulse." Oz informed her, before discarding his gloves and replacing them with another pair. "I'm making certain he's really dead."

"Wow..." Natalie breathed, sounding impressed. "You are so good at this."

He wasn't sure if that was sarcastic or not.

"I don't take chances, and since we know nothing about..."

"No, no," she cut him off, "completely agree with you. One of the first rules of being a hired lunatic with a gun is that you *have* to check the bodies." She paused for a beat. "He really dead?"

Oz shined his pen-light into the man's eyes, looking for a reaction and finding none. He let the man's head slump back down. "Yes." He walked back to stand next to her, changing his gloves again along the way.

"Damn." Natalie sounded disappointed. "I feel so cheated." She casually put an extra bullet into Wendell's corpse. "Okay, I feel a little better now."

Oz gave her a reproachful frown. "Is that really necessary?"

"Probably not, no." She shot the man's body again. "But it's more entertaining than you'd think." She did it again.

"Please stop that."

"Yeah, it's not as fun unless they're running away." She took two steps, then fired into him one more time. "Okay, let's see what's behind door number 2..."

She kicked the door down, not even bothering to identify herself before opening fire on the men assembled inside. Two guards were killed before the remains of the door even hit the floor.

Behind the room's only desk, sat a young man with dark hair. He looked bored, glancing up from his desk like they were bothersome children. "Yes?"

"We're with the Consortium of Chaos." Oz informed him, moving so that he could have a clearer line of sight on the man's hands, just in case he made a move for a weapon. "We've come to ask you a few questions."

Oz glanced around the room, looking for hidden dangers. His eyes fell on the light switch, and he was compelled to flip it on and off eleven times, then turn in a circle.

When he had finished, both Natalie and the man at the desk were staring at him in amazed confusion.

"I have some personal issues." Oz reminded them, clearing his throat. "But that doesn't make my questions any less important."

"Do you always use explosions and..." the man paused to listen to the music now playing through his building's intercom, "*Hanson* to question foreign heads of state?"

"You got a problem with Hanson, motherfucker?" Natalie leveled the gun at his head. "Cause I got no problems with killing you right now, if I hear an answer to that I don't like. There is only *one* acceptable response when someone asks you if you like Hanson..."

"Your men tried to kill us the other day." Oz said simply, ignoring the byplay. "I think this is a proportionate reply."

Natalie nodded. "You sent your people to kill my people, you had to expect that there'd be a reckoning." She paused, her face contorting in a grimace of distaste. "'A reckoning'?" She repeated. "Christ. I really just said that." She looked at the man apologetically. "Sorry, I'm overly dramatic today. Please don't judge. I'm usually cooler than this."

"To be fair," the man corrected, "you sent *your* people to kill *our* people first..."

"You know what?" Natalie spread her arms wide. "I just don't care. I don't care who started it, I'm here to *end it*. And then, just for shits and giggles, end *you*." She paused for a beat. "Although, now I realize that I have no idea who the fuck you even are."

The man straightened his uniform. "I am Deputy Minister Vlk."

"Why does everyone from your country have a name that sounds like the fucking cat walked across the keyboard?"

"*You're* one to talk." The man rolled his eyes.

Oz frowned, not understanding what that meant.

"My father and General Skrlj make up the new governing council of Agletaria." The man paused meaningfully. "After you killed the original one. And then their replacements."

"Wait," she squinted in theatrical confusion, "those would be the guys who hired people to kill my friends first, right?"

"Yes." The man nodded nonchalantly. "And killed Killroy, after he killed our scientists. So again, not to sound childish, but you started it." He rolled his eyes. "I think what..."

"What'd you say?" Natalie straightened, suddenly serious. "What was that about Roy?"

"Don't look at *me*," the man defended, "I didn't do it

340

personally, I was ten at the time."

"Why would a foreign country send assassins to eliminate a retired Cape?" Oz asked, recognizing that this was a deeply personal issue for Natalie and she was within seconds of simply shooting the man. He wanted to ensure they got their answers before that could happen.

"He took something from us." Vlk answered unemotionally.

"What?" Oz pressed.

The man simply continued glaring at Natalie.

"*What did he take?*" Oz repeated, on the verge of losing his temper.

"A prototype of a very powerful weapon." Vlk finally answered. "Something we never should have developed."

Oz took a moment to process that. "Did you recover it from him?"

"No." Vlk shook his head. "The men we sent were killed before they could."

He glanced at Natalie for an explanation on that. She leaned closer to him, lowering her voice. "Ronnie killed them."

Oz nodded, disliking the fact that she'd even had to say Mercygiver's name. He gestured to the lobby area with his head, not taking his eyes off of the man. "Is that why Wendell was here? Is that what he wanted to talk to you about?"

"I'm afraid I can't tell you." The man shook his head.

"Is this a diplomatic immunity thing?" Natalie asked, prowling towards his desk. "Or is it a thing where you're under the mistaken impression I won't get *untold* amounts of joy from beating it out of you?"

"No, it's a 'time' thing." Vlk answered flatly, pointing out towards the lobby of his office. "That was my 4 o'clock appointment."

They both stared at him blankly.

"It's only 3:45, you dumb bitch!" Vlk pointed at the clock. "I don't *know* what he wanted, *because I hadn't heard yet!*"

Natalie processed that for a beat, then broke out laughing. She continued to chuckle for several moments more, then the laughter stopped unexpectedly and she slammed Vlk's face into the top of his desk hard enough to crack its glass surface, knocking him out. Then she did it again, just because she was frustrated.

She let out an aggravated groan, as the other man's body slumped to the floor.

Oz shook his head sadly, making a mental checklist of all of the paperwork and digital files they'd need to take with them when they left.

Things would have been so much simpler if they'd been able to quietly infiltrate this headquarters and investigate the problem, rather than blowing it up.

Not as fun, granted, but definitely easier.

All told, it really had been a messy, *messy* afternoon.

...And this song was *really* beginning to irritate him.

Chapter 20

"IT SOUNDED AN EXCELLENT PLAN, NO DOUBT, AND VERY NEATLY AND SIMPLY ARRANGED; THE ONLY DIFFICULTY WAS, THAT SHE HAD NOT THE SMALLEST IDEA HOW TO SET ABOUT IT."

- Alice's Adventures in Wonderland

"No, no, you're missing the point," Oz insisted, "see, I think the central question is whether or not you should shoot the bear, not whether or not you'd go hiking in the first place."

Mull waggled her hand in the air. "I think I could hit that fucker." She decided matter-of-factly. "Unless it's really cute or something, I'm going to light it up and then mount its head on my wall."

Oz paused to consider that for a minute. "I still think I'd let it go. I have the bullet if it comes back, but if it doesn't, then there's no sense in starting the fight again. I think we can both live."

"Excuse me!" McPherson shouted, trying to get their attention again. "You two aren't off the hook here!"

At the moment, Mull was lounging next to Oz in the Consortium's command room, getting chewed out by their government liaison, for… something. Mull wasn't really paying any attention, to be honest.

"Crap, are you *still* talking?" Mull gasped in astonishment, genuinely amazed that the woman was still in the room. "Sorry, I thought you were done like twenty minutes ago and I stopped listening." She straightened in her chair. "Did I miss anything important? Something which you can hopefully boil down into one or two short sentences to catch me up?"

To her surprise, Oz snorted in laughter.

She turned to look at him, still not used to hearing the man laugh at anything. Things in Oz's world always seemed to be so joyless and maudlin. The man was "on the job" at all times of the day and night. He didn't seem to have any hobbies, outside friends, or pleasures. So she genuinely enjoyed the few moments where it seemed like Oz let his serious mask slip and expose the more light-hearted man beneath.

McPherson apparently took it another way. She pointed at Oz, glaring at Mull with a fiery intensity. "You are a *terrible* influence on him!"

Mull glanced at Oz for a ruling on that.

He shrugged, as if admitting the point.

Mull started laughing and playfully smacked at his arm.

"You turned a city block into a fucking warzone! You killed a couple dozen representatives of a foreign nation..." McPherson continued, sounding furious and horrified.

"Are you here to tell me that the police commissioner is breathing down your neck and that I've broken every regulation in the books?" Mull asked hopefully. "Because, I'm not going to lie, I've kinda always wanted someone to yell that at me. It's really what our buddy team-up is missing at this point."

McPherson's temper exploded. *"Who the fuck do you two idiots think you are?"*

Mull pointed at Oz. "NPR." She pointed at herself. "NWA."

"That's about the size of it." Oz agreed calmly. "Today, at least."

"You assassinated citizens of a sovereign nation," McPherson continued, "then kidnapped one of their diplomats..."

"It was a fun day, yeah." Mull agreed.

"Why did you do this!?!"

Mull considered that. "Well, it might sound clichéd, but sometimes I think God puts things like this in my path just so that I have another opportunity to make everyone an awestruck cheerleader when they see how fucking *amazing* I am."

"You *are* very good at what you do." Oz agreed seriously. "I'm constantly amazed."

"We're *all* amazed by her," McPherson yelled, "because the only thing she's good at is killing people and causing wanton destruction to the city!"

Mull shook her head seriously. "Oh, I don't know. I'm also pretty good at alcohol."

Oz snorted in laughter again, then tried to hide it by coughing.

"He used to be one of the normal ones here!" McPherson pointed at Oz again, obviously blaming Mull for something. *"Look at what you did to him!"*

Mull was suddenly serious, not liking *anyone* insulting Oz in her presence. "I'd do more than that if he'd let me."

That appeared to confuse Oz more than anything. The man just didn't understand flirtation. He was a gentle, chaste soul.

McPherson could tell that Mull was a lost cause, so she focused on Oz instead. "The greatest good for the greatest number means cutting that bitch loose. And you know it. People have already died over this and it's got to stop. Sooner or later, you people will have to stop making other people pay for your mistakes." Her voice lowered. "Your partner is stacking bodies like cordwood and it's got to end now."

Mull turned to look at Oz. "You ever think about how weird it is that that doesn't make sense anymore?" She asked conversationally. "What is 'cordwood,' anyway? I mean, the phrase was invented to give people an idea about the scope of the body problem, but now the only time you ever hear the word at all is when it's *referring* to bodies."

"I think about that constantly." Oz deadpanned.

Her eyebrows shot up in surprise. "Really?"

"No."

McPherson continued glaring at her, obviously not liking the fact that Mull noticed things like that about popular sayings. And, also, probably objected to the many people Mull killed in an average day.

"Listen, I don't solve mysteries, I'm an assassin." Mull reminded the woman. "What the fuck did you *think* was going to happen? They're trying to kill me, I got to them first. End of story."

"You're really not going to stop her?" McPherson remained focused on Oz, expecting him to be the voice of what she considered "reason." "You're going to let her completely destroy our opportunity to look for a compromise here?"

"They tried to kill my friend while she was in the hospital, then brutally murdered a mother in front of her 6 year old child." Oz replied calmly. "Just what kind of 'compromise' would you suggest that I try to make with people like that, Agent McPherson?"

"I'd start with: 'How's about you only kill innocent people every *other* day.'" Mull suggested sarcastically.

McPherson threw her arms out in exasperation. "Even if you kill them all, what makes you any different than them?"

"Well... there's the fact that I'll still be alive." Mull guessed.

Oz tried to cover his smile with his hand, but he still made a soft snorting sound of laughter.

"And you're still okay with this?" McPherson asked, sounding deeply disappointed in him. "*You're one of the sane ones!*"

"*I* make the decisions in my life. I decide who I want to be and what I want to do." Oz calmly rearranged his gloves. "Earlier this year, I looked at my life and voted for the Consortium of Chaos to become my employer. I backed a team of supervillains over the world's foremost superheroes. Because I don't believe in labels like 'hero' and 'villain.' I believe in people. I believe in actions over words. I believe in 'right' and 'wrong.' I believe that most people will make the right choice if they're given the opportunity..."

"*The 'right choice' like blowing up a building!?!*" McPherson interrupted.

Oz ignored her and kept right on talking. "...I believe in second chances but I also believe in personal responsibility and making people pay for their actions." He met the woman's eyes. "I believe in this world. Which is why I'll fight for it. Even if no one else does. I don't believe that violence solves things, to me, process is more important than results. No end is justified by unconscionable means. Had it been my choice, we would have gone a different way on our mission today." His tone grew hard. "But we were attacked. Multifarious decided her best course of action was to strike their headquarters, and in that situation, I will support a teammate over an army of kidnappers and murderers. Any day. Yes, there were casualties as a result. But I don't compromise with bugs and I don't cry when they get stepped on." He let that sink in for a moment, then his tone was once more its usual calm. "Was there anything else you wanted to speak to us about, Agent McPherson?"

Mull nodded to herself, utterly impressed with that man.

Yes, okay, she was *probably* corrupting his lifelong White Hat-ness, but... it was so much *fun* to corrupt him! And he was so good at it!

"You make tolerance sound badass, Oz." She breathed.

He looked confused by that. "You consider equating my enemies to bugs which need to be stepped on... tolerant?"

"Compared to me?" She nodded. "Yeah. That's like fucking Gandhi."

As they were sitting there, the Commodore marched into the room. The Consortium's patriarch wasn't seen in meetings as much over the last few months, preferring instead to play online military strategy video games in the TV room, and hand off the day-to-day matters to his son-in-law.

Today was no exception. The man appeared to be looking for a recharger to one of his laptops, which was still plugged into the wall.

"Commodore Cruel!" McPherson called the man over, obviously believing that he would side with her. "Can you please tell these two that they can't just indiscriminately gun down foreign nationals?"

The Commodore glanced at them, looking bored. "These the crummy creatures that caused the casualties at the clinic and came close to crippling my child's chosen one?"

"Some of them." Mull reported. "Monty's going to take care of the rest in a few minutes, using the information that Oz found in the building we hit."

The Commodore considered that silently for a moment, then nodded. "Capital. Be so cordial as to cheerily continue. I commend you on your contributions to the cause." His voice hardened. "*Crush them*. Leave them cinders and cracked cartilage."

The Commodore swept from the room.

"Does *nothing* matter anymore!?!" McPherson let out an aggravated groan. "This whole team is fucking insane!"

"You're just catching onto that fact now?" Oz deadpanned.

She whirled back to face them. "You're both psychopaths!"

"No, *I'm* the psychopath," Mull corrected, then pointed at Oz, "he's a psychotic."

"I don't like labels." Oz informed them seriously.

Mull grinned, point proven. "See?"

McPherson looked around the room helplessly, as it filled with more members of the team, as if one of them would agree with her.

"Don't look at me, I'm the sociopath." Arnold shrugged disinterestedly, taking his seat at the table. "None of this involves me, so I don't give a shit."

The woman ignored that, glaring at Oz again and looking disappointed. "You pretend to care. Which makes you the worse of all of them."

Mull waved a hand at her sarcastically. "Buh-bye, Laura."

McPherson stormed away.

And that's when Mull started to feel... bad about it. Not the whole "killing inhuman monsters who kidnapped little girls" thing, just the fact that she had involved Oz in the fight.

Oz was... pure. He was an innocent. Stronger than anyone else she knew, but surprisingly innocent about the world. It wasn't right to take that away from him, or put him in situations which would make him compromise his morality.

The Lone Ranger didn't kill every bad guy, even if he had

good reason to do it.

The Lone Ranger found another way.

And... and it was hard for her to imagine Roy gunning down the Agletarians with quite so much zeal either.

Mull was used to doing things in a certain way. A violent and loud way, which was dangerous and exciting. But that wasn't the way Oz was used to doing things. She needed to remember that. She'd acted without thinking and Oz had been forced to follow her.

But... Oz could have been hurt today.

The thought caught her off-guard. She wasn't used to really caring about people. The only people she really worked with on any regularity were Ronnie—and if that bastard had ever gotten hurt on a job, it would have been cause for her to celebrate—and Poacher, who typically was just as loud and violent as she was.

She hadn't really *worried* about anyone in a long time.

To say nothing of the fact that she was guessing that Oz would be pretty sad if she had gotten killed today. She remembered his bedraggled and devastated appearance at the hospital, trying to come to terms with the fact she was dying. She never wanted to see that look on his face again.

Maybe... just *maybe*... there was something to be said for being a little adverse to needless risk and casual murder.

She needed to be more careful.

"I've never liked that woman." Oz decided calmly, somehow managing to dismiss McPherson's entire existence in five simple words.

"I'm sorry." She said softly.

He shrugged. "I dislike a lot of people. I'm used to it."

"No, no," she shook her head, "I mean, I'm sorry that I got you involved in a firefight with an evil army."

"We survived."

"Yeah, but..." She trailed off. "I'll try to think before I do things from now on."

"It worked out." He reminded her. "I probably would have gone a different way, but my way might not have ended so well for us." He was quiet for a breath. "Some men can't be redeemed. Trying to just ends badly."

There was something sad in his tone, like he was talking about a personal experience.

He was talking about himself. For some reason, in that instant, she knew it.

Oz was a man who always seemed like he had more sad

348

stories than happy ones. In their entire relationship, she'd never once heard him mention any funny memories of his childhood or his past or his parents. Hell, Mull's entire life was a shifting kaleidoscope of crazy, and even *she* had some funny anecdotes about her life.

But Oz didn't.

And there was something very, very sad about that.

She moved her hand slightly, so that it brushed against his as they both rested on their respective armrests.

A sense of victory filled her, as Oz's fingers intertwined with hers.

All told, that was a lot easier than she had thought it would be. She was really good at the whole "seduction" thing.

"You don't need to be redeemed," she assured him softly, "you will never be anything other than an honorable and heroic man."

He didn't reply to that, he just continued to look at the tabletop, deep in thought.

As they sat there holding hands, the rest of the team began to file into the room, ready to watch the start of the assault on the Agletarian's main base. Oz had been able to track down its location by pouring over each and every file they had seized this afternoon.

The main part of the Agletarian military was holed up far north of the city, in an otherwise quiet area. There didn't seem to be anything else around, which was probably why they had chosen it. From the looks of the fortified building, the Agletarians had been there for quite some time though, doing God new what.

"Wyatt is going to be *pissed* when he gets back and finds out about this." Traitor predicted ominously.

Emily shrugged disinterestedly. "On the other hand, it's going to be an exciting event in my continuing 'Wyatt and Monty' slash-fiction romance story."

"They bicker because they love." Amy put her hands over her heart, utterly charmed. "It's adorable."

Stacy nodded. "I ship 'WyMon' so hard."

Vaudeville leaned back in his chair. "Is the new chapter done yet?"

"I'm working on it but don't have an exact ETA yet." Emily started to paint her nails. "It's a work in progress."

Vaudeville made a face. "You've been saying that for *months*..."

Emily pointed the brush at him. "Don't rush my genius!"

Mack flopped down into his chair, looking upset. "I still can't believe we're doin' this."

"What's wrong with this?" Traitor sounded confused. "It's not like we really have an option."

"We *always* have options other than trustin' Welles." Mack sounded appalled. "The man is fuckin' evil. And I don't mean that in a charmin' way, I mean that in a 'he's the fucking Lord of Darkness' way. We need to stop him. The man's a fuckin' demon and we all know it!"

Monty strode into the room. "*Woe to the inhabitants of the earth and of the sea! for the devil has come down unto you, having great wrath, because he knows that he has but a short time*."

The man's usual great coat was replaced by a fancier one with a grey fur collar.

Mull had no idea why he would get dressed up for this though.

"Revelation 12:12." Amy glanced up at him, looking surprised. "I didn't take you for someone who reads the Bible, Montgomery."

"He's probably just trying to learn as much as he can about the opposition." Bridget snapped.

"Indeed, indeed." Monty smiled his soulless grin. "My mother was the only daughter of the town's reverend, did I ever tell you that? A *deeply* religious woman." He nodded to himself as if that had meaning.

"And the point is?" Bridget asked.

"Higgins?" Monty turned to look at his assistant. "Do you remember what my mother always used to say?"

The toady was silent for a moment. "'Do the best you can.'" The man repeated, his normally nervous voice filled with both confidence and emotion, as if inspired by the thought, but saddened at the memories it brought up. "'Always do the best you can.'"

"Exactly." Monty smiled in cruel anticipation. "And I believe the Agletarians *deserve* my best."

"Don't worry, that's not creepy at all." Bridget rolled her eyes, looking amazed that she was really in the situation of letting Monty run wild. It *wasn't* going to end well and everyone in the room knew it.

"How do you plan to win this?"

"Hate." Monty replied simply. "They hate us. More than anything else. That's their weakness." Monty sank into his chair stiffly, favoring his bad leg. "Hate is a biography. A roadmap. It can tell you more about someone than anything else. When someone hates you... they are in essence telling you who they are. How they think. What they feel. What they're afraid of. They're telling you how

350

to *beat them*." He calmly checked his gold pocket watch, as the little automaton workmen inside chimed out their happy tune. "People confess their weaknesses, Bridget. All one has to do is *listen*." He was silent for a beat. "Show me what someone hates, and I will show you who they are."

Bridget gestured to the screen, which showed a satellite view of a vehicle traveling down an isolated road. "So your plan is…?" She trailed off, inviting Monty to finish.

"I am going to present where I am strongest and make them think it is where I'm the weakest. I am going to hit them where they think they're the strongest, but they've failed to fully understand why it makes them terribly weak." Monty smiled again, like a hungry animal. "I'm going to show them *the future*."

"And 'The Future,'" Bridget made little sarcastic quotation marks in the air, "involves some new plan which no one could *possibly* prepare for?"

"It's the oldest military strategy in the book, actually." Monty gestured towards the screen. "Behold: our Trojan horse. The stolen Agletarian military truck will be let through security, our operatives inside will unleash the dragon from Rayn's kingdom and…"

"The magic happens." Clarice finished.

"Yes, we sit back and watch natural selection play out." Monty smiled in smug satisfaction. "It will be *beautiful*."

"And if the Agletarians *aren't* complete imbeciles?" Oz asked. "This plan is *stupid.*"

"Agreed." Bridget nodded, pointing at the screen. "I was really expecting something more *imaginative* from you, Welles. You built yourself up as some kind of master tactician, but really 'your best' plan would be at home on any Saturday morning *cartoon show*."

"Cartoons are outlawed in Agletaria. Its rulers believe they weaken the mind." Monty shook his head sadly. "You have no faith in the machine, that's your problem. Wyatt is like that too. You simply can't conceive of anything *bigger* than yourselves." He smirked slightly, as if amused by Bridget's stupidity and conceit. "Gears within gears, Miss Haniver." He took a sip of his tea. "Gears within gears."

Mack crossed his arms over his chest. "I have no faith in 'the machine' because 'the machine' is going to get *innocent people killed*."

"Quite possibly." Monty agreed casually, like it was a small matter. "But, again, that's not my department."

"Do we even know who's inside this base?" Mull asked, feeling uncharacteristically concerned about human life at the moment. She wasn't sure if that was a result of Oz or an aspect of today's personality, but it was now a gnawing doubt in the face of a looming massacre. Ordinarily, she'd be the loudest supporter of this plan, so it felt odd. "There could be... like... *families* in there for all we know, which is probably something we should figure out *before* letting a dragon loose inside."

"Yes, I *too* wish that I could hug all the little children of the world." Monty's mocking tone was as dry as the Sahara.

Emily snorted in laughter.

Monty turned to look at Mull. "Multifarious— and I hope you recognize how *sincerely* I mean this— I give less than a shit about the suffering of the Agletarian people."

"I just think we could try to take out the people trying to kill us without massacring innocent people too." She thought aloud. "That's how I'd want this done."

"Brace yourself for disappointment." Monty advised.

"I prolly could have made a bionic eye for Monty." Mack announced to the room, seriously. "Take a few hours. When I was done, he'd see perfect. Better than ever. But I *didn't* make him one. And I have no intention of ever trying." He gave a meaningful pause. "What does that tell you about my opinion of the man?"

Monty opened his mouth to reply to that, but his phone unexpectedly rang to the opening bars of *Oklahoma!* by Rogers and Hammerstein. He pressed the answer button. "I'm listening." He was silent for a moment. "Understood. If it gets bad, I'll involve 'Special Projects' and play my hold card." He hung up and pressed several buttons on the phone. "Get ready. You might need to fill in until Hildy gets back." Then he hung up again.

Mull glanced at Oz. "I'm starting to think it was a *bad* idea to trust our defense to a megalomaniacal madman." She thought aloud.

"I never thought it was a good idea." Oz reminded her.

"Should we... *do* something?" She wondered, honestly unsure what people were supposed to do when they cared about stuff like this.

"What would you suggest?"

She shrugged. "I have no idea."

Oz considered that for a long moment, then turned to face Monty. "Welles?" Monty turned to look at him and Oz's voice grew cold. "Combatants only. There are missing people who could be in that building, to say nothing of non-combatants living with the Agletarians. Your team touches an innocent in that building, and I will be very upset."

He somehow managed to turn "very upset" into a threat

which brought to mind pools of Monty's blood and entrails.

It was pretty cool, actually. Mull always had to be much more graphic and loud with her threats, but Oz could be downright terrifying without even raising his voice. And the fact that he could do it and *still* retain his role as moral authority, was something special indeed.

Wow.

Monty simply watched him for a long moment, recognizing the seriousness of the warning. Higgins recognized it too, slowly moving so that he'd have a clearer shot at Oz, should the situation fall apart.

To Mull's surprise though, Monty simply smiled. "I know what I'm doing, Oswald." He assured him, turning back to look at the screen. "They've come to take everything I've built." He said softly to himself. "Let's see which of us deserves to have it." He raised his hand and then pointed at the screen. "Higgins... *start the machine*."

Higgins said something into the radio, and the truck on the monitor exited the woods and approached the exterior fence of the Agletarian's base. It halted at the guard booth and the Consortium team inside began to talk their way in.

Everyone in the room watched the unfolding drama with varying degrees of apprehension.

Then the guard waved the truck through the gates and onto the grounds of the base itself.

Monty clapped his hands together and then spread his arms wide, like he was calling their attention to his success.

The sense of relief was short-lived though.

On the screen, Mull noticed a group of soldiers pouring out onto the roof of the building, as if an alarm had been tripped.

She got to her feet, opening her mouth to shout a warning, but it was too late. The men on the roof opened fire and the back of the truck exploded in a fireball, sending debris flying in all directions.

The people in the Consortium's war room gasped in horror as twisted and bloody pieces of their friends rained down from the sky onto the base.

A moment later, the guards were dragging a burned and gravely injured Poacher from the fiery cab of the truck, somehow having survived the initial explosion. He was kicking and cursing at them, trying to struggle free and reach safety.

He took down five of them before they clubbed him over the head and dragged him away.

The fires continued to burn.

The body parts continued to pile up.

And the room was deathly still, too shocked and terrified to speak.

Monty watched the failure of his plan play out for a moment in stony silence, the fiery wreckage reflected in his monocle.

Then he began to laugh.

A demented cackling sound of pure egotism and pitiless disregard for human life. He didn't care at all about the people who had just been incinerated on his command. Or the fact that he had doomed the Consortium and the world along with it. Or the realization that many in the room had just lost friends. He didn't care about *any of it*, because his twisted heart simply thought the horrible scene of death and destruction was amusing.

He rose to his feet, still chuckling, and limped from the room.

"That wasn't exactly 'magic,' Monty." Clarice shouted after him, sounding angry.

Mack turned to the smoking wreckage shown on the screen, as the feed blinked to static. His mouth hung open in horror. "My gawd..." He turned to look at Oz, his eyes wide. "Don't you see what he just did?" He turned back to the screen. "Don't you understand!?! He just wiped out half the people who were standin' in his way here! He took out... oh God..."

Bridget had her face in her hands, staring at the screen like she was going to cry. Julian put his arms around her, trying to calm her down.

Oz let out a tired sigh. "I will deal with the Agletarian side of the investigation too." He announced, like it was a matter which was already settled. "I will handle this incident, and then I will handle *Welles*."

Julian nodded. "I will take my queen, Wyatt, Harlot, and all other vulnerable personnel to the Undersea Base." His hand tightened on his trident. "Then I will return and *help you* deal with Montgomery."

"We need to get Syd back." Mull stressed. "*That's* our priority at the moment."

"Sydney knows the security codes to the Crater Layer." Marian reminded them in her usual calmness. "And the tunnels to get in here."

"He's not gonna say shit." Emily announced. "He's a fucking *beast,* man. Like some kind of 'roided up monster." She shook her head in certainty. "You don't wanna fuck with that. I don't care how many goons or guns you have. Throwing down with Syd is the

354

stupidest– and likely the *last*– thing you do on the planet. That motherfucker is jacked! It'd be like... suicide by badass."

"...but his powers are not steroid induced." Amy felt the need to add, as if defending the man's dignity. "He obviously adheres to the requirements of our drug free workplace."

"Wait... our *what?*" Traitor paled. "Oh, shit." He looked around the room. "Listen, I didn't know that those brownies were..."

"Mack, how long will it take you to change the codes and seal off the secret tunnels?" Bridget interrupted, her voice breaking.

"If we want them to hold against a determined and super-powered foe?" The man did the math in his head. "Longer than we have." He decided. "Syd's tough, but..."

"Oh, grow a fucking pair." Emily rolled her eyes. "He can take it. When push comes to shove, and shove comes to savage beating with a tire iron, that there is the toughest person I've ever known." She shook her head again, looking certain. "Hardest motherfucker walking, no doubt. That son-of-a-bitch won't break, no matter *what* they do to him. Not *ever*. I'd bet my life on it."

"How about your *sister's*?" Bridget asked. "You willing to bet *her* life on it?"

Emily turned to glance at her twin for a long moment and Amy did the same.

They turned back to Bridget. "Yes." The girls said in unison.

"Sydney is a man who'll jump on grenades." Mull reminded them. "He's not afraid of dying for us. But we owe it to him to get him back. This is *not* up for debate. Syd. Comes. *Home.*" She jammed her finger against the table to accentuate the point. "If it destroys the entire city and launches the country into war, *Syd comes home.*"

Oz nodded. "I agree."

Traitor put his feet up on the table. "My dad always said that there were two different kinds of fighter in this world: there's the guy that's going to win because he's stronger than the other guy, and there's the guy who's going to win because he's *tougher* than the other guy. See, they're two different things. The strong guy is going to beat you into submission. He wins because he's more powerful than you. The tough guy, on the other hand, is going to stand there and take everything you can throw at him, and he'll stay on his feet. He won't go down no matter how severe the punishment you're able to dish out, or how long the fight lasts. You can cut him. You can burn him. You can take away everything he's got and heap shit on him that *no man* could bear. But as long as he's alive, he'll just keep right on coming back. Always. You simply can't *stop him,* and sooner or later, you'll get tired of trying and he'll find the opening he was waiting for. If you could get the right shot in, you could take the strong guy down. He doesn't know anything about pain. He's never tasted his own blood or heard his own screams." He shook his head. "But you can't *ever* beat the tough one. He's had too much hurt to ever hurt again." Traitor crossed his arms over his chest. "Anyone trying to beat information out of Syd is going to be *sorely* disappointed. And have very sore fists at the end of it. My money is on Syd. He's got this, us getting involved in it is just going to hurt his game."

"He will break." Marian announced with conviction. "We have a day and a half."

"*A day and a half!?!*" Emily repeated, sounding incredulous. "Oh, that's *bullshit*! That's complete and utter bullshit! I am *genuinely* insulted on Syd's behalf now. It'll take them longer than thirty-six hours just to tie him to the fucking torture table!"

"While I obviously *greatly* respect your opinion, Marian," Amy said softly, "I'm afraid I'm going to have to agree with my sister in this matter. Sydney is *far* too stubborn to break so easily. And he's much too strong to *ever* betray or endanger us. He will protect our family, no matter the personal cost. That is who he is."

"We have thirty-five hours, fifty-nine minutes." Marian affirmed emotionlessly. "After that, the Agletarians will be upon us."

"Oh, fuck you." Emily flipped her off. "You got no idea what the hell you're talking about right now, Marian." She was silent for a moment, and when she spoke again, her voice broke. "Just... just fuck you."

Oz clasped his fingers tighter around Mull's and it made her feel so much better for some reason. "Looks like we took a shot at the bear and missed it." He thought aloud.

"Yep." She nodded, squeezing his hand back. "Guess we'll have to kill the fucker hand-to-hand instead."

Chapter 21

"'I THINK YOU MIGHT DO SOMETHING BETTER WITH THE TIME,' SHE SAID, 'THAN WASTE IT IN ASKING RIDDLES THAT HAVE NO ANSWERS.'"

- *Alice's Adventures in Wonderland*

YEARS AGO

She sat cross-legged on the bar of the unimaginatively named "The Bar" in Flagstone, Agletaria, wishing that she could afford a drink. She was currently in disguise, and thus, her physical face was shown to the world and she felt naked. It was useful at times, but her nauseatingly wholesome and friendly features sure didn't exactly scare people. She often thought of taking a straight razor to the face or something, just to give it some character. An eyepatch, a tattoo, some claw marks, *ANYTHING*. She'd put up with that innocent expression, freckles, and button nose for too long already.

Something drastic needed to be done.

Plus, the bar was a dump. The kind of place that had sawdust on the floor and bloodstains on the walls. But it was as far away from civilization as a person could get, which was always a plus. And it had the finest watered down drinks to be found anywhere in these mountains. Which... when you considered the isolated locale, wasn't saying much.

In the corner, a broken radio emitted intermittent static, while the half dozen drunk and perspiring patrons inside the sweltering, dimly lit room watched each other suspiciously and kept to themselves. Sunlight shown through several large holes in the roof, illuminating random areas around the interior of the space in spotlights of dusty light, but did nothing to chase away the darkness which seemed to loom over the chamber.

Agletaria was a cold country most of the time, but at the moment, it was hot and still inside the bar. Summers here were the *worst*. And it always smelled of stale sweat and mold, no matter where in the country you were.

She had always hated it here. From the depth of her soul, she hated it. There was just something about it that made her angry and... anxious.

Seated at the creaking table in front of her, Rondel busied himself with a game of solitaire. "I do wish you would stop that, Kitten. It begins to grate."

She ignored him and kept playing her harmonica.

"Good *Lord*, but you are difficult." He rolled his eyes behind the designer sunglasses he hadn't bothered to take off, despite the gloom. "You always need to complicate things." He used his foot to kick out the chair across from him so that it skidded closer to her. "*Sit*."

She ignored him, continuing to play the haunting and repetitive tune.

He heaved another longsuffering sigh. "Sometimes I wonder why I don't simply just kill you."

"You want me." She told him casually, gesturing to her body with her free hand. "And I don't blame you."

"My, my," he smiled humorlessly, "aren't we just feeling *extra* confident in ourselves today?" He looked up at her. "Let me explain something to you: I already *have* you, if you recall. And as delightful as I find your company, the reason I don't kill you, is that I'm your *friend*, Kitten. That is the only thing keeping you alive."

"You're my friend now?" She blinked at him. "Being my friend has a high mortality rate, you know."

"Yes, so I've noticed." He placed the queen of hearts down on the king of spades. "You do seem to accumulate bodies at a fairly rapid pace, don't you?" He pulled three more cards from his deck. "But *I'm* still here. Frankly, I'm beginning to think that you and I are *made* for each other."

"Oh god, not this again." She rolled her eyes. "You know I hate it when you do this."

"Do what? Point out the obvious?"

"What we have isn't serious, Rondel. We're not friends, we're not soulmates, we don't 'belong together.' This is simply a beneficial working relationship, focused on a mutual goal. You *know* this doesn't mean anything. Not really. Stop pretending that it does."

"I understand." He nodded sharply, his fingers almost imperceptibly tightening on his deck of cards. "You are merely *using* me. Again."

"Something like that, yes." She flashed him a teasing smile, trying to defuse the situation before it spiraled out of control. The man had a quick temper and once triggered, violence usually followed. "We *do* have some fun together, don't we?"

Her plan to calm him didn't work, and he was up out of his chair in the blink of an eye. He backhanded her and she toppled backwards off the bar. She hit the dirty floor in a heap, holding her jaw and hoping he hadn't broken it again.

The other patrons in the bar were momentarily interested, but then decided it best to ignore the entire matter.

She got back to her feet, once again debating with herself whether she should fight him or back down. She spent most of her days asking herself that, truth told. Ultimately, it didn't really much matter. He was going to win either way.

Deciding that if he hit her again, she'd probably black out, she slunk over to sit in the chair across from him, exactly as he'd ordered.

He watched her expressionlessly. "Where was I, Kitten? Before your rudeness."

"You were explaining to me how we're the best of friends." She reminded him. "Then you hit me. Again."

"Ah, yes." He nodded. "You and I have a history together, don't we? That's important in any relationship."

She opened her mouth to reply to that, second-guessed herself, then decided to say it anyway. "Oh, hell yeah. The way you got Roy killed, then dragged me around the world with you. That's sure the basis of a healthy relationship."

He slowly put his cards down. "I saved you." He reminded her, sounding almost hurt by her accusation. "Where would you be without me?"

"I would still be in New York. With Hector. I'd still be someone I could stand to look at in the mirror! I wouldn't be someone who did the things you've made me do." She shot back. "This?" She pointed at herself. "This is someone I don't even know! *You did this to me!*"

"You don't recognize yourself, because you're not that girl anymore." He shook his head. "Everyone is only temporary. The human body is 72% water. That water is lost and replenished regularly. Cells are damaged and repaired over the years... Hair grows out and is cut..." He met her eyes, his tone almost pitying. "The 'you' you remember being isn't *you* anymore. You're a completely different person now, made up of new pieces and parts. The original 'you' was lost down the drain or on the floor of the hair salon or in the 57 million skin cells you lose in the average day. The you you are now never did any of those things you remember doing. Never loved any of the people you remember, because you weren't really there. You're now something else entirely. Something which merely remembers what another you did, with a different body, continuing on as a new actor in an ongoing play." He picked up his cards again. "You aren't real. You're a re-cast, Kitten. And I, for one, think you're much stronger now."

"I don't..." She got out, still working up the nerve to have this conversation with him. It would lead to badness. And a lot of pain for herself. But it still needed to be said. "I don't want to do this anymore, Ronnie." She whispered. "Please just let me go."

The words had their expected result, and the man's expression darkened. His grip on the cards grew so tight that the entire deck began to bend in half. "You are who I *tell you* you are." His eyes burned into hers threateningly. "Do you understand me? You are *MINE.*" He slammed his palm on his chest. "I don't give a shit about any powers you think you have or any desires you think you feel, unless they're *mine*. You are simply an extension of MY will. That was our deal when you came on this journey with me. You will do what I tell you to do, and think what I tell you to think. If you want to have some kind of identity crisis, you're out of luck. I am uninterested in humoring your ridiculous attempts at personal growth." He refocused on his game. "Shut your damn mouth and do as you're told."

She watched him, her rage building until it seemed like a living thing. She'd lived far too many years under his thumb as it was. Been hurt by him too many times. "*I hate you so fucking much.*" She spat out through gritted teeth, mind racing through a million different ways she could kill him dead, all of them looking so wonderful, that she wasn't able to choose any of them. "I pray every night that you die screaming."

He snorted in amusement at that. "Praying is the equivalent of the audience clapping in *Peter Pan* to bring Tinkerbelle back to life. 'If you only just believe!' It's bullshit." He rolled his eyes. "I prayed *plenty* and what did it ever get me, huh? As they..." He trailed off.

"Maybe God doesn't answer your prayers because you're a monster." She challenged.

"Like he's one to talk." Mercygiver made an unconcerned face. "He's killed as many people as I have. Almost." He pointed at her. "And *don't* start with me." He warned. "You try to leave me or kill yourself again... and I'll make you *sorry*, understand?"

"I've been sorry my whole life." She leaned back in her chair. "One day... you're going to fall asleep while I'm in the room, and you're never going to wake up, Ronnie." She spat out. "Count on that."

"You're not going to touch me. I can't be killed."

An evil smirk crossed her face, filled with suicidal glee. "Wanna wager on it?"

She had taken all she was willing to take from that man.

One way or the other, she was ending it today.

Before he could reply to that, the man they were here to meet walked in. Brendan Simpson was currently the second-in-command of Rondel's organization. Ronnie didn't trust Mull with the position, obviously, so he had Brendan around to take care of all of the stuff that he didn't have time to do, because he was too busy making Mull's life a living hell.

Brendan was a prick. And not in an endearing way. He was that perfect point on the graph where you could be a prick, but not be so big a prick that it was funny or worthy of respect. He was the kind of prick who just made you hate him.

Ronnie was evil, but at least he was intelligent. Brendan was greedy and stupid. What he lacked in brains, he made up for in brawn and an eagerness to do whatever monstrous things Ronnie thought up.

Ronnie liked the guy, for some reason. Was always nicer to him than he *ever* was with her.

She wasn't sure why.

"Hey," Brendan nodded at them as he sat down at the table, "how you doing?"

Ronnie didn't bother looking up at the man. "Still insane, but with long fits of horrible sanity."

Brendan didn't appear to have any idea how to respond to that. "Okaaaaaay," he cleared his throat nervously, "the Agletarians will be here in a minute. You ready?"

Ronnie just watched him, like that was a tremendously stupid question. "Have you ever known me not to be?"

"No, but..." Brendan began.

"Then stop wasting my time." Ronnie snapped. "I don't pay you for your conversation."

Brendan looked furious, but didn't have the balls to object to that.

"I still don't understand what this meeting is even about." Mull protested.

Brendan looked up at her in surprise, then casually helped himself to a drink from the table. "They want us to kill some piece of shit villain group in the States." He gave a helpless, disinterested shrug. "'The Consortium of Corruption,' or some shit? I don't know."

Mercygiver placed more cards on the table. "Don't I *pay* you to know?"

Brendan nodded and grew quiet, recognizing that he'd overstepped.

Mull's eyes squinted, trying to figure this job out. "Why?"

"Why do you pay me?" Brendan frowned, his idiot mind visibly racing. "Because I'm…"

"No, why are they looking to wipe out the C of C?" She pressed.

Brendan shrugged. "How should I know. The Agletarians rarely need a reason to do what they do. Who gives a shit? As long as their money is good, we're for hire, right?"

"I cannot be bought." Mercygiver shook his head. "I do jobs because I want to do them and because I enjoy the work."

"Well, I do them because I need the money." Brendan decided, shifting in his seat. "That's why most people go to work."

Several people in suits arrived at the bar, and Brendan rushed to meet them at the door.

She watched the man silently for another moment.

He was… twitchy. Sweating.

Brendan appeared very nervous today. More than usual.

Her gaze flicked over to look at Ronnie out of the corner of her eye, to find that he had done the same.

Ronnie's head nodded ever so slightly, indicating that he recognized the man's change in attitude as well.

She leaned back in her chair, preparing to jump to her feet if the situation went south. "What would you do if you knew you were going to die?" She asked Ronnie. "If you had one day to live?"

"Kill my enemies." Ronnie announced.

"No, no," she shook her head, "I mean, how would you want to spend your final moments on this Earth?"

"…Killing my enemies."

"That's it?"

"That's it."

"That's sad." She frowned at him, oddly pitying the monster. "There's a lot of hate there. Seems like life should be about more than that."

"Murder is an important thing." He placed the last of his cards on the table, finishing his game. "If you care enough to do it, then it's probably the most important thing you're doing that day."

"I don't know how I'd spend mine." She looked down at the table. "I guess none of us really know. Until we do."

"You'll spend your last day however I *tell you* to spend it."

Her hands clenched into fists under the table, trying to keep herself from hitting him. Now wasn't the time. But soon.

At the door, Brendan continued to chat with the assembly of men who arrived for the meeting.

"Well… they certainly seem chummy." She remarked, returning to the matter at hand.

Ronnie turned to watch the meeting. "Yes, indeed they do." He agreed. "Brendan is loyal." He insisted, like he was trying to cut off her looming statement to the contrary, and to convince himself.

She shook her head. "No, he's not. And you know it."

They watched the drama playing out for another moment.

"We're in a crowded bar right now," she warned, "you could destroy a lot of things if you fight here."

"You say that like it's a *bad* thing." He set to work reshuffling his cards. "You only exist because a beautiful star was destroyed, and scattered into billions of microscopic pieces, perhaps taking a thousand inhabited worlds with it when it blew…"

She put her fingertips up to her temple in irritation and boredom.

Jesus. She was going to kill him for the abuse alone, but his weird little monologues were just the icing on the cake. She was going to kill him *slowly* for making her listen to years of his boring historical little life lessons, which he wrongly believed were somehow making a coherent philosophical point.

He pointed at her. "…You are destruction, on the deepest of levels. Every piece of you is rubble of something better. Something made of fire and gold and cosmic power, which shined for billions of years. You, Kitten, are just a tiny piece of shit that was left behind when it died. We all are. And every day of your life is spent destroying things. Everything you eat, breathe and do. Every movement you make is destroying something else. Destruction *is* creation. It breeds change. Change breeds evolution. And evolution breeds betterment." He paused, taking on a contemplative tone. "I… I would not be who I am today if not for evil men who wanted to destroy things. 'Good' people who let their hate get the better of them…" He snapped back to reality. "I'm sorry, Kitten. Where was I?"

"Brendan." She pointed at his underling. "The meeting with the Agletarians."

He nodded. "Ah, yes."

Brendan and the Agletarians started to walk over to them.

The leader of the men extended his hand to Ronnie... then stopped. He frowned in confusion for a moment, then retreated to talk to his companions.

Several of the men at the bar turned to look at the goings-on, and Mull noticed that they were wearing hidden earpieces.

Brendan hurried over to the men to discuss what had just happened.

Mull turned to look at Ronnie out of the corner of her eye again.

He nodded, understanding what she'd silently told him. "Well Kitten," he heaved a sigh, "I would say that either we've become *irresistibly* popular since we left... or they're planning on killing us." He put his cards down slowly. "We've been sold out."

She didn't say anything because she couldn't argue with that. The men were obviously here to kill them. And Brendan was the only possible suspect on who could have set them up.

Mercygiver looked at Brendan, silently coming to terms with his betrayal. The man's jaw tightened almost imperceptibly, his usual mask of calm menace cracking for the briefest of moments to reveal someone who was... hurt.

She smiled, getting the oddest joy out of watching the man's anger and pain at being betrayed.

Good.

No one in their right mind would be loyal to Ronnie. If he wanted people to feel loyal to him, he should have stopped being a *fucking nightmare* who tried to kill them all the damn time. Ronnie *deserved* this. And even though it was about to end in her death, she was genuinely glad she got to see it.

Fuck Ronnie.

Mercygiver nodded to himself, coming to terms with the situation. "So," he leaned forward in his chair, "I suppose the only question then is: what are we going to *do about it?*"

"I'm not dying today." She announced. "I refuse to die until I've killed *you.*"

He nodded. "My feelings exactly."

The Agletarians and Brendan finished their talk and turned to look at them, friendly smiles gone. They were about to make their move against them.

Ronnie flipped the table over, sending the playing cards up in a cloud, then they both went to work killing the men...

Chapter 22

PRESENT DAY

The next day was not a particularly good one. Generally speaking, Harlot was in charge of freeing people from captivity, but she was away at the moment, so there was no one specifically assigned to that role in the Consortium's roster. Which meant that if she wanted it done, Mull would have to do it herself.

She and Sydney had a gentleman's agreement about such things, since both viewed "rescue" as deeply humiliating. They'd rather free themselves on their own, so there was a 36 hour grace period to accomplish it. After that, if they hadn't escaped, it was open to anyone to do it.

That didn't mean that Mull particularly liked the idea in the current circumstances though, so she'd intended to just free him and deal with his yelling afterwards. Unfortunately, when she'd woken up this morning, she'd discovered that her powers were very, very broken. Whatever unseen force controlled superpowers in this world sometimes screwed up and got its wires crossed, and if she used the powers, unintended things would happen. Bad, possibly fatal things. Like a glitch in the code of superpowered life. It wasn't fun. People in the empowered community were always afraid of broken powers, because they were unpredictable. Having them was always: "You use the power to do X, but Y happens" or "Your powers give you control over Y, but using them is actually killing Z" or "For the love of God, that power over TV remotes you think you have, will also cause the totality of existence to pop like a soap bubble! Don't ever use it! EVER!"

Broken powers absolutely *sucked* and Mull was the only

Cape alive who got them all the damn time. For most people, you were born with broken powers or you weren't. For Mull, it was a constant issue.

Oz looked concerned and curious at the news, trying to gage how effective she could be today and how much danger the powers placed her in. "How broken?" He asked worriedly.

She ran a hand through her hair. "I can cause my bones to vanish."

"Why would you want to do that?"

"I wouldn't, because it would result in all of my insides kind of sloshing together, and I'd collapse like a fleshy bag of skin and blood. Without my skull, my brain would leak out through my ears and eye sockets." She held up a finger to draw attention to her point. "But I *could* do it. And that's what's important."

Oz seemed less than impressed with that argument, making an unconvinced sound. "Well, those definitely sound broken, yeah. I'm glad you haven't been using them today." He casually walked into the bedroom to access his closet.

They had just gotten back after observing the Agletarian base for most of the day, trying to find a way in. Sadly, security had been tightened a great deal and there didn't appear to be any easy ways past it. Mull was willing to risk her own life, but not Oz's. Plus, the Agletarians would most likely kill Poacher at the first sign of an attack, which meant it called for subtlety.

So, Mull was forced to delay and see if she could come up with a better power set tomorrow, which would be better adapted to the needs of this specific circumstance.

Oz being Oz, he'd immediately disposed of the clothes he'd been wearing all day, and took another shower. At the moment, he was dressed in an undershirt and long white flannel pants.

Did men even *wear* undershirts anymore? It seemed so old-fashioned, for some reason.

And who in God's name had flannel which was different shades of white?

There was something kind of charming about the sartorial monotony which was Oswald Dimico.

Still... the man did *incredible* things for sleeveless white tank tops. It really accentuated his broad shoulders and strong muscles.

She tilted her head to the side, casually mentally undressing the man.

The thoughts improved her day tremendously, making her want to curl up in his bed, all warm and safe, and think about him.

Scheme ways to get him into the bed *with* her.

"Natalie?" Oz asked, looking into his closet.

The sound of her name on his lips fanned the flame of lust even higher in her. Her powers might be broken today, but the rest of her body was functioning normally. It was eager to demonstrate that for him, at the slightest encouragement. "Yes, Oz?" Her voice sounded husky, even to her.

He pointed into his closet. "Where are all of my clothes?"

Oh.

"Umm..." Mull tried to get past her lust and focus on more important things. Like, oh, for example, thinking up a quick and convenient lie, "Oh, I... I mean *Holly* she threw those out." The other woman would forgive her. Or she wouldn't, but either way, it was worth it. Upsetting Oz on a normal day was bad, but upsetting Oz on a day when he was dressed in a sexy little tank top and his biceps were putting on a show every time he moved? That was simply too big a disaster to contemplate. Holly needed to be sacrificed for the greater good. She would have done the same. "They were depressing."

Oz didn't seem at all convinced by the lie. "Yesterday, you said you loved the monochromatic look."

"But that was yesterday, Oz." She shrugged. "Today, I realize that the clothes were dragging you down. Color. You need more color in your life. Bright yellow, sky blue, neon green. Scarlet red. Color."

"I'm perfectly happy with white." He started to look through the closet, searching for something her 'slash and burn' style wardrobe de-cluttering might have overlooked. "*Your* standard outfit is white." He reminded her.

"No, Multifarious' standard outfit is white." She corrected. "*My* outfits are very colorful."

"Fine." He seemed to give up on that issue, possibly just thankful that she was Natalie at the moment. "What clothes did you get me as replacements?"

She pursed her lips in thought, admitting the point. "Oh... yeah, that would have been a good idea."

Oz turned to look at her in the horrified, exasperated, and grotesquely fascinated way he usually did when he thought she'd just done something crazy. "You threw away all of my clothes without getting me *new ones?*"

"Just put on the clothes you've been wearing all day, no problem."

"They're dirty." He reminded her.

"So?"

"So I already threw them into the building's incinerator."

"You throw away your clothes after wearing them? Once?"

"Not always." He shifted on his feet. "Just on days when I'm outside a lot." He looked towards the windows suspiciously. "There are a lot of germs out there…"

She tried to refrain from rolling her eyes, then pointed towards the other room. "Well, there's probably some clothes in all of those giftwrapped packages in the hall closet. Just take some of those."

Oz let out a sigh. "No, there's not."

"Well, this will be good for you too then." She brightened, getting to her feet. "I'm still reading that book on exposure therapy, and being forced into something new is good."

"Therapy rarely relies on 'force.'" He deadpanned.

"Oh, you know what I mean." She made a face at him. "Look, you've cut yourself off from the world. You're getting more and more isolated and weird. Pretty soon, your whole life is going to be nothing but obsessions and rituals and also paradoxically hating them, and I'm sorry, I won't allow that." She shook her head defiantly at that idea. She was *determined* to help Oz, whether he liked it or not. "Things are going to get healthier for you, starting now."

"So…" he held out his arms helplessly, "what exactly am I supposed to wear for the rest of the day then?"

Natalie gestured to his current attire. "Just go with that." She was completely fine with that idea. That sounded like a *hell of a day* to her.

"I don't think so." Oz shook his head, his own orderly little mind shocked and appalled at the idea of wearing pants and a shirt out of the house, because someone at some point decided that they were the *wrong* design of pants and shirt, and even though they covered the exact same areas as actual clothes, these would be socially inappropriate to wear outside.

The whole thing was ridiculous.

Still… Natalie was pretty sure she cared about such things today too. As the day wore on, she seemed to be paying more and more attention to proper behavior and etiquette. Although her powers were broken, her personality was pretty conservative. Which was interesting.

A new idea occurred to her. "Don't worry, dear. I know what to do."

****

Fifteen minutes later, Natalie was idly swinging her feet off the edge of the bed, waiting for Oz to emerge from the bathroom.

"Why do you have these clothes?" He asked again, still behind the door.

"I keep some outfits in different sizes on hand, just in case I have grow-y powers." She explained. "It's very important to look your best, even if you aren't quite sure what you'll look like on any given day." She smiled sweetly at the door. "You only get one chance to make a first impression, after all."

Her smile faded, recognizing that this was going to be a long day.

She was like... some kind of *nice* person today. Ick.

As personalities went, "Mrs. Cleaver" wasn't one of her favorites. She casually cleaned the titular cleaver knife on the skirt of her 1950s era party hostess dress, which was black and had little chalk outlines of bodies embroidered on it. The look was emphasized by a demure necklace of interlocking grenade pins, with matching earrings, and completed with several other knives which dangled from the conservative belt of her waistline.

It was, perhaps, the stupidest outfit she'd worn in a long time. But there were probably worse things to be than a "murderous 1950s housewife" kind of woman right now, especially since she was having people over.

Generally speaking, Mull hated entertaining. She had no idea how to cook and she didn't do small talk. So she was *more* than happy to let Natalie and Mrs. Cleaver handle all of that bullshit.

"I feel like an idiot." Oz announced from the bathroom, apparently having finished getting ready.

"Nonsense, dear, I'm sure you look impeccably presentable." She soothed, her tone the one of perfect sit-com mothers everywhere. She held up her meat cleaver, running her finger down the edge and making sure it was the sharpest the blade was capable of being.

"...Why are you talking like that?" He wondered aloud.

"Oh, don't trouble yourself with me, dear. It's just a little touch of..." She began.

Oz opened the door and she trailed off. He revealed that the only thing he'd been able to find which fit him was a fox hunting outfit, complete with the scarlet red coat. Sadly, he'd been unable to find a shirt which would fit, so his bare chest was exposed by the plunging black lapels of the jacket.

Oz being Oz, he'd apparently been unwilling to even *consider* wearing his undershirt for longer than a night. In his mind, it was no doubt contaminated and would need to be bleached several times before it could ever be considered clean, if it wasn't a complete loss already.

For that matter, it was a bit of a miracle that he'd even consented to wear these extra clothes at all. She had expected him to refuse them, since there was no telling where they'd been and what she could have done with them in her apartment, but he hadn't even brought up the issue.

She wasn't entirely sure why he would be more willing to wear her clothes than his own, but either way, it was unexpected.

She looked at him a moment longer, then clasped her hands together in delight. "Oh, don't you look like the cat's meow!"

"I don't know what that means." He grumbled, looking dejected and unhappy. "And I feel like an idiot."

"Well, you don't look like one." She assured him, standing up to straighten his lapels for him. "I think you look quite *spiffy*, dear."

"Why are you talking like that?" He asked again. "And why are you dressed like…"

"Hush now," she put her finger to his lips, "there's no need to have unpleasant conversation before dinner. It's bad for digestion."

"Natalie…" Oz began, her finger against his mouth slurring his words.

She shook her head, not moving her finger. Truth told, it was actually kind of pleasant. The man's lips were soft and warm and promised her so much more than she'd ever asked of them.

Clean, hot lust.

She'd never really considered that such a thing was possible before, especially while having an otherwise perfectly normal conversation, but she recognized it now.

She looked into that man's perfect chocolate eyes and she felt like just throwing herself at his feet like some kind of bimbo on a movie poster. Clutching at his body, trying to feel him against her.

And they stayed that way, both recognizing what the other was thinking.

Natalie's body grew hotter and tighter, eyes locked with his.

Mrs. Cleaver was a conservative, presentable sort of personality… but she could *absolutely* party when the lights went down. Especially with a man as perfect as Oz. Mull could feel that.

370

She might be a 1950s sitcom sort of person, but hers was definitely a sitcom world where the couples *didn't* have double-beds. Mrs. Cleaver's sitcom world involved beds made for two intertwined, sweaty, freaky people.

Oz started to breathe faster, his breath flowing around her finger.

She finally broke their eye contact, to look down at the wide expanse of his chest, which was partially exposed in the ridiculous outfit he was wearing at the moment. It *should* have been stupid, but the man was just so damn handsome and dignified that he somehow managed to make it work.

"Red is your color." She decided breathily, taking an unconscious step towards him. "*Definitely* your color."

His own attention was fixed on the bodice of her dress, then cut back to her face. "I'm trash." He warned her, his voice ragged. "It's in me, you shouldn't…"

She met his eyes again. "Have you seen my apartment?" She shook her head, pressing her finger all the way into his mouth. "I *love* trash, baby doll. I can find so many *fun* things to do with it."

No.

No, that was Mrs. Cleaver's weird G-rated flirty nonsense. It wasn't dealing with the deeper issue here, and Natalie recognized that she'd need to do it herself.

"You're not trash, Oz." She assured him, her voice completely certain. "You're the purest, truest man I've ever met." She finally removed her finger from off of his lips, feeling oddly bad about losing the strangely intimate contact. "You're spending your life doing nothing but trying to prove you're worthy of something. But you're worthy of anything." She paused. "…Well, anything *positive,* anyway, because there are a lot of *negative* things that you wouldn't…" She trailed off, recognizing that she was babbling. "There is no one in this world who I trust more or who I would rather help me. I know you think you're an evil person, but I legitimately *am* an evil person," her voice broke, "so please believe me when I tell you that with one exception, you're possibly the only other genuinely *good* person I've ever known." She swallowed, feeling like the answers to all of her problems could be found in Oz's eyes, if she just looked deep enough. "I…" She trailed off again, only getting out a breathy sound.

Oz continued watching her, his jaw tight.

The door buzzed, startling her from her momentary lusty distraction.

She pointed towards it. "I… I should get that." She

explained, like she needed a reason to do something as stupid as step away from him. Because that's how it felt. It felt deeply, deeply wrong to be doing anything but throwing herself into his arms. "'Cause… 'cause Poacher caused your doorman to… you know… quit." She stepped backwards towards the door, somehow managing to bump into some of the only furniture in the room. The white ceramic lamp which was sitting on the white plastic and steel end table, toppled to the smooth white floor and white carpet. It shattered into a million pieces and Mull winced. Fucking Natalie. *This* was why the girl was trouble. "I'm so sorry, I just…" She started to explain.

Oz didn't even appear to notice the mess, his eyes still focused on hers with longing and a desperate hunger. It looked almost dangerous.

He always looked like a perfect hero. But right now, he was looking at *her* like someone who would delight in doing evil, evil things to her vulnerable body.

She cleared her throat, feeling like his intense gaze was going to make her clothes burst into flames. She found she really, *desperately*, liked the thought. "I'll just…" She continued awkwardly walking backwards, like she was backing away from a tiger about to pounce on her. "…I'll just get the door?" It came out sounding like a question. If he objected to that, she was perfectly willing to make whoever was on the other side wait until morning for her to answer it.

Oz didn't reply, continuing to look at her the way a man lost in the desert looked at a bottle of water.

It was longing, sure, but there was a certainty to it.

He wanted her.

That look silently told her that he was going to have her. It was confident and sure. He was going to use her to make himself feel good. He was planning it all out in his mind. Meticulously.

She knew it. She could read it on his face and in his eyes, boiling beneath his calm surface, like lava. And that knowledge was deeply, deeply exciting.

She bumped into the door, then laughed nervously. "It was just…" She cleared her throat, trying to get ahold of herself again. Natalie's twitchy weirdness around him wasn't going to get the job done either, Mull was fairly certain. It was just embarrassing for everyone.

She opened the door.

"Took ya fucking long enough!" Roach shouted at her. "What, did you need to put your fucking clothes back on first!?!"

Mull looked down at her adopted uncle as he was wheeled

into Oz's apartment. "Hello, Uncle Hector. Lovely to see you, as always." She was really going to need all of Mrs. Cleaver's hostess charms tonight, just to keep herself from killing the man. Or perhaps her mastery of meat cleavers could be put to use instead...

Roach turned to look at her, his face drawing up in horrified confusion. "Christ in a sombrero, what *are* you wearing?"

She straightened her dress. "My face is being repaired, I broke it when I fell off the roof."

"Thrown." Roach corrected, already not letting her live that down. "Which was *sloppy*."

"*Fell*." She snapped. "So I seem to be getting powers which ordinarily wouldn't be used." She gestured to Natalie's face. "Like... girly powers, the ones which don't require masks."

Roach looked up and down her sitcom ensemble. "How *is* 'The Beaver' doing?"

Oz started forward, temper igniting in a flash, hands clenched into fists.

She could tell what was about to happen and immediately stepped in front of him before he was forced to beat the shit out of a disabled elderly man. "He means the TV character." She quickly explained, holding up her hands and pressing them against her partner's chest to keep him from continuing forward. "He's mocking my outfit today, not being gross."

Oz didn't seem convinced by that, but let the matter drop.

"Why do you know *The Lone Ranger*, but not *Leave it to Beaver*?" She asked rhetorically in confused amazement, always trying to figure out the man's twisty and weird mind. "The hell?"

For some reason, the whole exchange made Mull kind of sad. On one hand, she liked that Oz was the type of man who could always be counted on to defend her, but on the other hand, it really indicated that Oz had no idea how to deal with family. Which wasn't surprising. His family had apparently treated him like shit. They were monsters. So of course Oz would automatically assume her family were as well.

She watched him for a beat, suddenly feeling like crying over the fact that no one had ever made Oz feel safe.

Roach's wheelchair was being operated by May, his daughter. The girl's short dark hair was partially hidden by a turkey themed hat, which didn't match her usual "Mayfly" costume, but she didn't appear to care. Truth told, May never really seemed to care about much.

"Now PaPa, there's no reason to tease Mull like that. You know it will just upset her." The girl in question gently chided. Her eyes cut to Oz and she looked rather amused by his fox hunting outfit. "Well... that's certainly a bold fashion choice, Mister Dimico."

"I think Oz looks cute as pie in everything." Mull snapped, inadvertently using Mrs. Cleaver's phraseology for some reason. Which... was weird. "If you don't like it, you can head right on back out the door, May."

May made a pouty sniffing sound. "Well, *someone* is sure snippy today."

"*I* didn't want to fucking come here in the first place." Hector reminded her flatly. "*I* wanted to have a nice Thanksgiving with my family somewhere *normal,* not in this fucking freakshow!" He made a face. "What the fuck kind of name is 'Oz' anyway?" He mused, obviously returning to an issue he'd undoubtedly been grumping about with May all day.

"I was named after the Kennedy assassin." Oz informed them, sounding almost embarrassed about that fact for some reason.

"No shit?" Natalie was genuinely impressed by that, instantly brightening. "That's fucking *awesome*."

Hector looked more confused than anything. "Your name is 'Hector' too?" He guessed.

May wheeled her father further away. "Papa, please don't cryptically confess to presidential assassinations while at Thanksgiving dinner with Multifarious and her boyfriend."

Roach gestured to the largely empty apartment. "Was the rest of the furniture repossessed?"

"Thanksgiving isn't until tomorrow." Oz reminded them simply, ignoring the insult to his home, because he seemed to always assume that people would automatically hate everything he was and everything he did and everything he enjoyed.

"Yeah, I can read a fucking calendar." Roach rolled his eyes. "I don't celebrate Thanksgiving. I don't believe in it. Got my own holiday, the night before. Call it: 'RageGiving Day.' It's a time when you get together with family and bitch about all the bullshit you're *not* thankful for and all the shit they do that pisses you off. All the middling, petty shit that ruins everything and makes you want to shoot some annoying motherfuckers in the face." He pointed around the room. "*And I got a long fucking list this year!*" He explained. "You got a problem with that, New Guy?"

"*You* might have a problem." Oz shook his head calmly. "Because I don't have an oven."

Mull winced, suddenly hating herself. If it wasn't for her, she could use that as an excuse to kick her uncle and cousin out and get

374

back to having eye sex with Oz. Which sounded like a *lovely* way to spend an evening.

She wasn't entirely sure where his boundaries were, but she was genuinely excited to test them.

"Yes... about that..." she began, "I kinda bought you one of those on Black Friday sale too."

Oz watched in amazed stupefaction as a delivery man wheeled the appliance through the door. "You bought me an oven?"

She held up her fingers in a pinching gesture. "Little bit, yeah."

Roach made an annoyed sound. "Oh, stop acting like it's a big deal. She owns the fucking store, she could have bought you a warehouse filled with the fucking things, and it still wouldn't mean shit."

Oz's eyebrows soared and he turned to look at her. "You *own* the store?" He pressed, looking for clarification. "You *own* Drews department store?"

"No!" She shook her head. "My asshole foster parents did."

"Well, where are they?"

She shrugged. "I don't know. Somewhere." She made a disinterested face. "Who cares?"

"She's got control of it." Roach casually peered behind the frame of the coffee advertisement on the wall, probably looking for listening devices or hidden safes. "I made sure of it. It's all hers."

Great.

She'd *deliberately* been keeping that little fact from Oz. Because if he knew that she owned the store, then he wouldn't have to stop by it as much. She'd always used management as a way to keep him dropping by. Telling him that she was trying to get her manager to switch out the floor tile or find stockboys who could organize the sock department, etc. It took her *hours* to mess up her store each morning, just so Oz could come by to straighten it and then she could talk to him about how her incompetent bosses needed to be convinced to listen to his suggestions!

But now he'd know what was going on and he wouldn't have to spend *nearly* the same amount of time in the store anymore. He could just tell her what needed to be changed and he'd know she'd do it, because he *had* to know that she was wrapped around his little finger. She'd burn the fucking store down if he asked her to!

The man was gorgeous and sweet and went through life like a little puppy that had been kicked too many times! He was adorable! And sexy as all fuck!

She spun around to glare at her uncle. "I'm so *glad* you're here, Uncle Hector." She spat out through gritted teeth, even Mrs. Cleaver's eternal dinner party-goddess calm wearing thin. "And for sharing so many things about me."

"Oh, was that a secret?" Roach asked in feigned embarrassment. "Gee whiz, cue the laugh track, I guess."

"Papa, you can see that Multifarious is feeling sensitive about her outfit today, there's no reason to tease her." She paused for a beat. "And you need to take your pill before you eat."

"I don't have to do *shit*." The man insisted.

The workman finished installing the appliance and started back through the room.

Oz, Mull, and Roach stopped their conversation to all watch him suspiciously.

The guy looked vaguely unnerved by that, hurrying from the room and slamming the door behind him.

Oz quickly set six out of the seven locks, then turned to face them. "Did you investigate that man's identity before you invited him into my home?" He looked down at the floor. "Do you have any idea the kinds of places his work boots could have been before they walked on my floor?"

Roach looked at Oz thoughtfully. "You're a paranoid little fucker, aren't you?" He inquired appraisingly. "Huh." He nodded, looking pleased. "That's good. Too many blind assholes in this world, refusing to recognize that everyone else is a piece of shit."

"Leave. Oz. *Alone*." Mull warned, exasperated with her uncle's characteristic behavior. "We are going to have a nice meal together and then you two are *leaving*. I have to get up early to work on the parade."

Roach snorted. "The 'parade,'" he made sarcastic little air quotes with his fingers, "is nothing but terribly lip-synched songs and marching bands from piss-ant towns no one has ever heard of or cares to visit. The parade isn't really a parade anymore. It's just corporate shilling."

"It's a free parade sponsored by a department store." Oz deadpanned, making Roach's entire criticism sound ridiculous.

"The parade is going to be the best ever." She pointed a finger at her uncle again. "Take my word for it. In the meantime, you're not going to be disgusting tonight, you hear me?"

"Yeah, yeah," Roach rolled his eyes, "I'm on my best behavior." He shooed her away. "You go deal with dinner, Oz and I will do some male bonding out here."

Great.

Hector was going to kill him.

****

Oz was pretty sure Hector was going to kill him.

Of course, he went through most conversations with the man thinking that, so he was used to it.

He sat in his living room, watching the elderly man and waiting for him to strike.

Hector sat in his wheelchair silently glowering at him, obviously unhappy about the fact that Oz was spending so much time with his adopted niece.

Roach was one of the last of the old-time villains. "Tie your girlfriend to the railroad tracks, steal Christmas, blot out the sun" style villainy.

Oz respected that. There was order to it. A predictability which could be categorized and anticipated.

But that didn't mean he was really looking forward to spending an evening with the man. Oz wasn't a people person on the best of days, and today was certainly no exception. He still had to stop the Agletarians, track down Mercygiver, rescue Poacher, and most importantly, finish his conversation with Natalie.

And, obviously, find something else to wear.

He started to get to his feet, wanting to escape this room. "I'd better go see if Natalie needs help in the kitchen."

"*Sit.*" Roach commanded, pointing back to the couch Oz had just vacated. "The women will handle the food. It's fine."

Oz found himself immediately sitting back down. "That's rather sexist, sir. Don't you think?"

"Yes." Roach deadpanned. "You know anything about cooking, boy?"

"Well... no."

"Then just shut up about it. There's no shame in assuming a woman is better than you at something. You say it's sexist to make them do it, *I* say it's sexist to assume they can't." He gestured to the door. "If fucking vampires burst in, I'd recommend that the women handle that too." His voice went up an octave in righteous indignation. "They go through *childbirth*, motherfucker. Can you even imagine that? I had kidney stones once and damn near killed myself to end it. I can't imagine passing something the size of a *Christmas ham*. They don't *feel* pain like we do. They're like fucking *machines*..."

"I'm pretty sure they do, sir." Oz shifted in his seat, uncomfortable with this topic. "The human body is..."

"You ever need something tough done, that's *gotta* be done, that'll hurt like all fuck as it's *being* done, you hand it off to a woman and get outta her way." He pointed at Oz to make sure he understood that. "You *don't* fuck with women." He paused for a beat. "Unless you're *literally* fucking women, then it's a necessity. Unless you can find *another* woman to do it instead, which is even better, obviously." He pursed his lips, deep in thought. "You ever fuck two women at once?"

Oz just stared at him.

The corner of Roach's mouth curved in a knowing smile. "You've never even fucked *one* woman at once, have you." It wasn't a question. "You're one of them 'nice guy, rule followers,' I can smell it on you."

"I really don't want to discuss this with you, sir." Oz told him flatly. "Not here, not tonight, not ever."

Roach didn't like that answer. "You're dating my daughter, boy, you'll discuss interplanetary trade or the most watery and smelly shit I've ever taken, if that's what I *tell you* we're discussing." He leaned forward, his tone darkening until it was a threat. "You really think I'd *ever* let you have her? *You?*"

Oz simply stared at him, trying to control his temper. And failing.

Whatever Roach saw in his face, the man recognized it immediately.

"Theeeere it is..." Roach nodded in admiration. "I see it now." He pointed at him again. "I'd never give Mull to someone who wouldn't kill one old man to have her." He smiled. "There's some capital 'E' evil in you after all, isn't there." He readjusted the mix of the oxygen on the tank attached to his chair. "Nothing to be ashamed of."

"Being evil?"

"No." Roach snorted, then paused. "...Well, yeah, that's not something to be ashamed of either." He flipped his hand. "Virgin, I mean. No shame in waiting for the best, I say." He sighed wistfully. "I waited too. A long time. I didn't lose my virginity until I was... 16? No, 15. Jodie. And her little sister Kathy. It meant more because I waited." He looked at Oz, brow furrowed in thought beneath his rubber Roach headpiece. "How old are you, anyway? 24? 25?"

"32."

Roach made a gasping sound. "Christ in a cannon! 32!?!"

He started coughing. "You're not some kind of freak, are you?"

"Define 'freak.'"

"Like some kind of weird-ass communist nutball!"

"No." Oz frowned. "And I vehemently object to Ace people being characterized as 'nutballs,' sir."

Hector ignored that plea for basic decency. "So you've been what? Saving yourself for the priesthood?"

Oz wasn't sure how to reply to that. "Can we please talk about something else?"

"I'm trying to help you not feel like a eunuch and this is the thanks I get?"

Oz shook his head. "I don't feel like a eunuch, sir."

"*You're welcome.*" Roach took that as an admission that he had saved Oz's gentle self-confidence. "Christ in a hot tub, your whole generation is insane."

"My prison psychiatrist said that I don't deal well with human interaction." Oz shared. "I don't like getting close to people, emotionally or physically."

Hector pointed towards the kitchen. "Except Roy's girl."

"Except Natalie, yes."

"Fair enough." Hector considered that while readjusting the oxygen lines so that they didn't get tangled in his plastic roach antenna. "What is your motivation, son? What drives you to do this?" He asked simply. "Because it's got to be something. No one just goes into this work without some need they're trying to fill. Something powerful. Something that won't wear down over time." He held up an open hand. "For most people, it's love. Love never dies." He clenched his other hand into a fist. "But neither does hate. And hate can be just as powerful, if you use it right." He was silent for several breaths. "Spent my whole life hating my brother. I mean, I dedicated every waking hour to discovering new ways to fuck up his life. That was how I defined myself and all I wanted. That was what drove me. I was 'Kilroy's arch-nemesis.' And then that little useless motherfucker went and died. He left me alone. And I realized that... Who the fuck was I now? You can't be the nemesis of a dead man."

Oz squinted in confusion, trying to follow the man's logic. "Are you trying to tell me not to devote my life to hate?"

"Fuck no." Roach snorted at that idea like it was sheer insanity. "Without hate, I never would have become a villain. I never would have followed that asshole's life and kept track of what he was doing. I never would have gone the places I've gone or seen the things I've seen. Hate gave me a family. A reason. Daughters. Friends. ...My

Pamela." He leaned forward in his chair. "What I'm telling you is that hate needs a purpose. Hate is a tool... a motivation, not an end goal. Hate can build great things. And the second it stops getting you where you need to go and starts to *keep you* from getting where you need to go, it's time to move on and let shit drop. Find something else to hate. Or something to love." He nodded at the truth of his own words. "Roy was an absolute asshole. But I forgive him for that. I don't hate him anymore. Because if nothing else, he had an amazing daughter. And I'd blow the fucking Devil if it brought that little girl into my life. My hate ended with love." He pointed at Oz. "So, I'll ask you again: what drives *you*?"

Oz considered that. "People think I'm evil."

Roach arched an eyebrow. "Are you?"

"I... I don't know." Oz admitted.

"Good answer." Roach looked pleased by that. "Never trust anybody who tells you they're entirely good or entirely bad. They're all lying shit-birds." He set about trying to clean something from his tooth using his tongue. "Is that why you're here?"

"No." Oz shook his head. "I joined the Freedom Squad because a man in a hat told me I needed to, because I had a part to play."

That seemed to interest him. "Straw hat? All *Music Man* looking?"

"Yeah..."

"Meddling fucker." Roach spat out. "*Don't* trust him either. He's got an agenda and always did. He'll fuck you over without a second thought if it gets him what he wants."

Oz didn't even bother replying to that. "And I became a better Cape because... honestly? Equal parts wanting to help people and wanting to impress your daughter."

Roach didn't look happy now. "'Equal parts'?"

"70-30 wanting Natalie." Oz corrected.

Roach stared at him silently.

"85-15, wanting Natalie." He admitted, looking down at his floor.

"I'll accept that." Roach nodded, like it was sufficient to pass some kind of test. "Far as I'm concerned, I've got four daughters. Two of them I chose, two of them I didn't. But they're *all* mine, understand?" His eyes burned into Oz's. "That girl was Roy's daughter, which makes her *my* daughter now. I bought her her first sniper rifle. I'm the one who taught her about the birds and the bees by showing her *Hooker-Mania 7*. And if you hurt her, there are no words for what I'll do to you."

Oz shifted in his chair. "I think she's fully capable of killing me herself, sir."

"Nah. She's got too much of Roy in her." Roach made a dismissive face. "That girl is softer than she lets on. There's darkness in her, unquestionably, but she doesn't have it in her to hurt you. Hurt herself, sure. But not you." He met Oz's gaze again. "I have no such limitation though, fair warning. You are trying to fuck 1/4 of my universe." He glanced up and down Oz, looking almost disgusted. "And I don't know you. The girl says you're okay, but she's as crazy as Roy. Trusting. An optimist. Gentle, in her way. So, you got one night to convince me not to simply kill you and blame the Spaniards."

Oz squinted at him in confusion again, feeling like he was missing something. "I'm sorry? ...Why would Spanish people want to kill me?"

"*Everyone* would want to kill you!" Roach reminded him. "You're crazy! And evil!"

"Yes, but I'm confused as to if this is a *specific* group of Hispanic people we're talking about or if you are just racially insensitive and..."

"Dinner!" Natalie called cheerily from the dining room like a sitcom mom, cutting off his question. "Wash your hands and come get it, boys!"

May casually wheeled her father away and Oz followed behind, feeling shell-shocked by the way that conversation had gone.

Oz went to wash his hands and by the time he returned, everyone was staring at him.

Roach gestured to Oz's clean hands. "Trust me on this, I know what I'm talking about: being old is fucking *horrible*. Live your life now, don't try to hold onto it for later. Do what you want, don't just try to squeeze in a few extra unhappy days at the end of it. Better to live than survive."

That actually seemed to upset Natalie. "You're unhappy?"

"No, I'm perfectly happy." Roach gestured to Oz. "But *he's* sure as hell not going to be. Look at him! You think that motherfucker is going to make it on the inside? You think he's got daughters to break him out of that wrinkled nightmare filled with duck puzzles and urine stains? Fuck no. He's going to shrivel up in a ball and bawl his pussy eyes out." He tapped the tabletop. "You're fucked, boy. Forget trying to stay healthy, you need to start killing yourself with fun now, while you still can. Burn out, don't fade away."

Oz had no real reply to that, instead he was just wondering

where all of this tableware came from. Or the table itself, for that matter.

"The store." Natalie matter-of-factly answered his unspoken question. "It's a very good sale this Friday."

"Uh-huh." Oz sank down into one of his new chairs, which were predictably 1950s retro chrome and colorful vinyl. That seemed to be a theme of Natalie's powers and tastes today. Half of his apartment was now somehow mid-century in design, from new lamps to those spikey starburst wall clocks. "I figured." He blinked down at the odd food sitting in front of him, surprised that they weren't having turkey for Thanksgiving.

"Jjajangmyeon." Natalie helpfully supplied.

May nodded, removing the earbuds from her ears, the faint sound of classical music audible for a moment until she hit pause. "It's traditional."

Oz continued staring at the bowl of dark colored food and vegetables. "How is a Korean noodle dish a 'traditional' Thanksgiving meal?"

Roach snorted in disgust. "Racist."

Oz held out his hands helplessly. "I'm just saying it's not something I've ever heard of being associated with Thanksgiving, that's all."

Roach groaned in annoyance. "It's a long story, boy, and I'm not going to sit here and waste time…"

"Roy went to Korea." Natalie summarized, cutting off her adopted uncle. "He liked the people and the food. And Thanksgiving."

Oz blinked at the meal several more times, then nodded. "Okay." That was a surprisingly reasonable reason to be eating this then.

"Can we fucking eat?" Roach demanded. "Or does Oz have to insult the *rest* of fucking Asia first?"

"I didn't insult Asia!" Oz defended. "I was just…"

"Bow your head, you fucking ingrate." Roach interrupted. "In this house, we say grace."

"It's *his* house, Papa." May reminded her father.

Oz held up a hand, not making that an issue. "I think grace would be nice, actually."

Roach bowed his head, speaking to his Creator in prayer. "You know what? I'm an old man. You've never given me *nothing* I didn't have to take for myself." He announced. "I hate plenty of the things you tell me to love and I love plenty of things you tell me are a sin. But I don't fuck with you and you don't fuck with me, Lord. Let's keep it that way. Amen." He looked up. "Now let's fucking eat!"

"That was beautiful, Uncle Hector." Natalie deadpanned.

Hector rolled his eyes. "One time, fucking Roy said grace to some homeless kids and he ended up crying during it, like a miserable little pussy." He shared in delight, obviously enjoying a story about his brother which he thought was embarrassing, despite the fact the man wasn't there to hear it. He scooped a large portion of the noodles onto his own plate first, going against established Thanksgiving protocol of making sure you helped everyone else get food before taking any for yourself. "I really don't know why he cared so much about them anyway." Roach snorted in dismissal. "Dirty hippies."

"Roy was amazing." Natalie agreed, looking at Oz. "You would have really liked him. He could break up a fight by just being there. He'd have people shaking hands within minutes. He had a calm authority that made people pay attention to him and listen."

"He was a bum." Roach decided around a mouthful of his food.

"He won the congressional medal of freedom." Natalie paused for a beat. "Twice."

Roach scoffed in dismissal. "He was still a bum." May took the utensils from him and made certain that his food was cut into small enough bites, but he grabbed the fork back from her, glaring. "He said things like 'jumping jiminy.'" He continued. "I mean, that's not fucking normal! It's a symptom of a diseased mind. No wonder the girl takes after him." He gestured to Natalie. "He drank milk at every meal, for fuck's sake!" He pointed at her. "I ever catch you doing that and I'll kill you myself, boy."

"'Girl,' Papa. Multifarious is a girl." May corrected.

"I can see that, May, I'm not fucking blind." Roach gestured to Natalie again. "She's got tits, for fuck's sake. Generally, men don't have those unless they're fat as a fucking orca or are the most popular guy in prison."

May shook her head in condemnation. "Why do you feel the need to ruin every meal, Papa?"

"My fucking upbringing. My cunt of a mother didn't hold me enough and now I don't deal well with emotional intimacy. It makes me lash out." Roach paused for a beat, like that reminded him of bad memories. "And thanks for bringing *THAT* up! What the fuck is *wrong* with you, May!?!"

"How about you, Oz?" May asked, apparently more from a desire to end her father's nonsense than from a real interest. "Are your parents still with us?"

Oz shook his head. "They're dead."

"Oz's dad was that dude who shot up that burger joint years back. Remember that?" Natalie casually informed them, helping herself to more noodles.

The fact that his father was an evil madman who killed a building full of innocent people was treated with the exact same amount of importance as she had given to discussing the china pattern today.

There was something almost comforting in that though. Oz had spent his entire life ashamed of his father and living in constant fear that he too would one day succumb to that same madness. But to Natalie, it was apparently a matter so trivial that it was something you casually introduced during pre-Thanksgiving dinner with your family. Because to her, his father's actions didn't involve him at all.

It... made him smile.

Roach nodded at the gruesome memory of Oz's father's crime. "That was pure amateur hour." He said with deep contempt, then looked back and forth between his daughters. "What do I always say, huh? What was the fucking advice I gave you both on your prom nights?"

"'If you have to take hostages, plant bombs outside first to cover your escape.'" The women parroted, sounding bored. "And 'There's no such thing as too many bullets.'"

Roach nodded, looking pleased. "Damn straight. People need to start listening to me more. That's why this fucking world is so fucked up, because nobody has got any goddamn sense no more."

Natalie didn't look convinced by that line of reasoning. "Like that time you told everyone at my birthday party that 'Winnie the Pooh' was a metaphor for Communism?"

Roach was so insulted by that he nearly choked on his food. "He wears a red shirt and the Russian symbol is a bear. Do I have to draw you a fucking diagram?" He pointed at her with his fork. "Substitute vodka for honey, and he's essentially more Russian than the goddamn czar!"

May nodded, humoring the man. She used her fork to rearrange things on the old man's plate. "You need to eat more carrots, they're good for you."

Roach shook his head in determination, obviously drawing a line in the sand on that issue. "Fuck carrots. I don't understand health food. Why spend your entire life eating things you don't like and being miserable, just for the *minute* possibility of *maybe* having a few extra months of eating things you don't like and being miserable?

Personally, I'd rather eat whatever the fuck I wanted and have *fun*."

"Oz is very into healthy living." Natalie shared, sounding almost proud of him. "It's one of his weird obsessions. He's trying to get me to eat healthy or something." She rolled her eyes. "He thinks I'm going to have a heart attack if I keep eating trash."

"That sounds very controlling." Roach observed, suspicion in his tone. "It's probably a warning sign."

Natalie cheerily flipped off her uncle, not bothering to reply to that. "Now I'm trying to eat healthy too, just so he'll shut up about it."

"Uh-huh." Oz ate another mouthful of his food. "What did you have for lunch today, Natalie?"

"Can of vanilla frosting with rainbow sprinkles." She answered immediately.

He nodded, expecting that answer but still finding it amusing. The woman was *magical* and he knew better than to ever try to stop her from doing something. She was an absolute force of nature, he was just worried about her. She needed to take better care of herself. She took too many risks and it never occurred to her that she was still human.

Oz had already spent an evening watching her die, and he wasn't about to do that again.

Natalie needed to be protected from herself, it seemed.

"Well, I said he was *trying* to get me to eat healthy, I didn't say that I was *listening*." Natalie defended to the others. "I'm a superheroine, which means I'm really more concerned about getting shot with a deathray or attacked by mutated hyena men, than I am about my dietary health."

Roach looked equally confused by Oz's crazy ideas about meals needing to contain something other than sugars and saturated fats. "The rainbow colors are probably like fruit flavored or something, right? Fruit is healthy."

Oz opened his mouth to correct Hector on that, but the man cut him off.

"Fuck you, it *counts*." Roach insisted, looking at Oz in something close to pity. "Don't spend your life dying, son. They'll be more than enough time for that at the end."

"Compared to my usual diet of burnt toast and red wine, that was like farm fresh vegetables." Natalie obviously thought she was making great strides in her efforts to take better care of herself. She gestured at Oz. "He totally owes me." She picked up one of the bowls on the table. "Did anyone else want another roll?"

He shook his head.

"I say, you eat what you want, when you want it." Roach intoned in a theatrically "wise" tone, then turned to look at Oz in obvious disapproval. "How did you ever end up in prison, boy? Had you pegged as a rule-follower, and those little dipshits don't usually find themselves on the other side of the bars." He finally started eating the carrots May had demanded he at least try. "What was it? Feeling up the sidekicks or were you just on the cocaine?"

Natalie glared at him again. "Hector!" She snapped. "That's…"

"I was the subject of a nation-wide manhunt." Oz found himself answering calmly, for some reason. "My DNA matched every crime they tested it against. And when they finally tracked me down, they put me away. For seven years. In the deepest, darkest hole they could find. And they reminded me every day of the crimes I had committed and the kind of person I was." He stared sightlessly into the dark mass of noodles in the bowl in front of him, feeling like he was a million miles away. "As it turned out though, the government had spent four years and fifteen million dollars searching for the owner of that DNA profile, but it was only found to be present at all of those crime scenes because management at the medical supply factory where I worked was shipping out all of the swabs I'd pulled from the line on quality control issues. So, my DNA was on the swabs the company sent to the forensics lab, which the police used to collect the evidence, so my DNA was seemingly at every crime scene. And with my family history, that was enough to put me away for seven years."

The room listened to his story in silent amazement.

Then Roach burst into uproarious laughter, positively *howling*. "That's fucking *hysterical!*" The man praised, wheezing he was laughing so hard. "*Hys-fucking-terical!*"

Natalie glared at her adopted uncle reproachfully, getting angry with him.

But Oz started laughing too, suddenly struck by how completely ridiculous the world was sometimes. And how much time Oz had wasted in his life.

Natalie gaped at him in shock, surprised by how funny Oz thought his own life was at the moment.

He wasn't sure why.

Her beautiful mouth made a little "O" in shock, which just made him laugh harder.

Then she held her hands out in mystification, smiling now too. "Did I miss something here?" She inquired, starting to chuckle.

"Are we really laughing about an innocent man being convicted of horrible crimes?"

That just set Roach off again, and he laughed so hard he needed to adjust the mixture on his oxygen tank. He breathed deeply for several minutes, catching his breath. When he spoke again, his tone was serious, like he was once again reminded of death. "Looking back on your life, you realize something... it all sucked." He announced with a sneer.

Everyone's eyebrows rose, not expecting that.

"There are... a dozen moments in the average life that actually meant something." Roach continued. "The rest of it is bullshit. Just meaningless trash. Sleeping and shitting and listening to assholes talk at you about nonsense. Just waiting out the clock. 99% of everything you'll ever do is pointless bullshit. Once you come to the end of it, looking back, that's what life is. All it ever was." He ate a carrot, wincing in obvious distaste. "But this moment. This means something." He gestured to them. "We got family. And we're alive. And it's a lovely meal. And when a moment like that happens, you'd better fucking cherish it. Live in that brief moment. Because it'll soon be gone. And your life will be back to being shit. You can withstand anything so long as you can live in hope for the next fucking moment that matters to come along."

The table fell into silence.

Oz thought about the man's words for a moment, then looked around the table at the odd little family he'd somehow found himself spending the holiday with. He'd never really shared a holiday with a family before, even if it was one as dysfunctional as this one.

He raised his glass of purified, sparkling water. "Happy Thanksgiving."

"To RageGiving Day." Natalie raised her glass beside his. "Fuck everyone who isn't us."

May and Roach followed suit.

Eventually, the food was gone and Natalie hustled to clear the table, because that's what 1950s sitcom women seemed to do in these situations. Personally, Oz would have gladly done it himself, but such a thing was apparently unthinkable with Natalie's current personality. She found the idea of him helping downright insulting.

Truth told, Oz found "Mrs. Cleaver" kind of spooky, so he didn't want to press the issue.

So, Oz was left at the table, once again staring at Natalie's adopted uncle.

"There comes a point in your life when your biggest concern

is who will take care of the people you love after you're gone." Roach said softly, his tone still serious. "Because that's a *big* fucking job and it requires someone truly extraordinary." He pointed at Oz. "And if you're not that guy? If that's not you? I'll take care of you right now." His voice was ice cold.

"I don't know if I'm evil or a Cape... but I know I need Natalie." Oz assured him, completely certain on that front. "And there isn't anything you or anyone else could ever due to make me change my mind about that."

Roach considered that silently for a moment. "Well... you *have* been to prison."

"Wrongfully convicted." Oz began to protest. "I was..."

"Don't ruin it for me now, let me at least *pretend* you have some balls, boy." He looked at him appraisingly. "My brother would have liked you." He decided, like it was his final judgement on Oz's worth as a human being. "I can work with you. You're not *perfect*, mind you, but I can work with you." He firmed his jaw. "Welcome to the family."

The words took Oz off-guard. But... they made him tremendously happy. No one had ever really wanted him around before, he was almost always an outsider.

"I'm probably not going to kill you tonight." Roach added, ruining the beautiful moment.

"Oh... good." Oz wasn't sure how to reply to that. He hadn't even been aware that option had formally been on the table.

"I've been kinda stressing about it this whole night, so I'm glad." Roach casually began to eat his slice of pecan pie. "I was afraid I'd have to kill you at the dinner table, but then I'd have to listen to the girl bitch and moan about it for the entire meal. I've seriously been dreading the mess that would make for me."

"That must have been very hard for you." Oz deadpanned.

"It's okay," Roach clapped him on the back good-naturedly. "I forgive you."

Chapter 23

"'TIS SO,' SAID THE DUCHESS: 'AND THE MORAL OF
THAT IS--"OH, 'TIS LOVE, 'TIS LOVE, THAT MAKES THE
WORLD GO ROUND!"'

'SOMEBODY SAID,' ALICE WHISPERED, 'THAT IT'S DONE
BY EVERYBODY MINDING THEIR OWN BUSINESS!'

'AH, WELL! IT MEANS MUCH THE SAME THING,' SAID
THE DUCHESS"

- *Alice's Adventures in Wonderland*

Mull woke up with a start.

She'd always had an innate sense of being watched, and she could *feel* it, despite being asleep. Unfortunately, she'd forgotten where she was.

She wasn't in Oz's bedroom at the moment, she had sprawled out on Oz's very narrow and uncomfortable sofa. Arranging herself on it required some complicated geometry and body positioning, involving an arm and a leg stretched over the backrest and a leg resting on the ground at a weird angle. There really wasn't any other way of doing it.

Mrs. Cleaver had surrendered the bedroom to Oz, because she was all about the politeness, and was willing to scream at Oz until he took her up on it.

That had left Mull with the living room couch though.

She hit the floor in a heap, immediately trying to recover her footing and defend herself from attack.

Instead, she found only Oz, leaning against his doorframe, watching her.

He held up his hands. "Sorry, I didn't mean to disturb you."

Mull tried to catch her breath and relax, now jacked up for a fight. "No, it's okay." She assured him, running her hand through her hair. "Just not really used to being around people."

"Me either."

He was shirtless at the moment, and Mull was very, *very* aware of it.

It was the primary reason why her heartrate wasn't slowing down.

"What... what are you doing up?" She asked, trying not to look at his chest.

"I have trouble sleeping sometimes." He said softly, sounding haunted. "I got thrown away once. Still bothers me."

"Ah." She wasn't sure how to reply to that.

She unconsciously ran her hands over her body, making certain that she was still dressed and didn't look disgusting. She made a face, silently wishing she'd worn a sexy teddy to bed rather than a *Kim Possible* nightshirt and one green sock.

Just once in her life, she wanted to be sexy. Wanted to do something which would make all the prudes blush and clutch at their pearls in shock. But it seemed to be beyond her grasp.

She looked back to the sofa, making sure that she hadn't messed it up too badly. Oz lived in an orderly little domain and she felt like a chaotic oaf, lumbering through it. She went out of her way to make sure her footprint on the sands of Oz's world were kept to a minimum.

She winced when she saw that in her sleep, she'd drooled on his perfect sanitary pillows while snoring again.

Fuck.

She quickly grabbed it and tried to hide the evidence, but then recognized that Oz saw everything. "I'll... I'll buy you a new one." She promised. "I'm so sorry."

He looked confused. "About?"

She held up the pillow.

"Ah." He looked strange. "My problems are not your problems, Natalie." He said softly. "You don't have to change your behavior to conform to my peculiarities."

"Yeah," she ran her hand through her hair again, trying to keep its disorderly tangle out of her eyes and failing miserably, "but... I know it'll bother you and I'll gladly replace it."

"It won't bother me." He assured her.

"Yes, it will."

"No, it won't."

She tossed the pillow back onto the couch. "No, no, I'll get you a new one, I promise. Don't worry and don't freak out."

"I don't need a new one," he gestured to the closet with his head, "I've got three in the closet over there."

Natalie turned to look at the closet of wrapped gifts. "Why do you have so many giftwrapped presents in your closet, Oz?" She said softly, feeling like there was a story there.

He walked over to the closet, grabbed several packages, then tossed one of them onto his coffee table— which was now a mid-century kidney bean shaped affair thanks to Mrs. Cleaver— but was still pristine.

It was small and wrapped in red paper with little rocket ships on it.

She stared down at it, feeling like she'd seen it before.

He tossed another one onto the table, which was larger and featured an elaborate bow.

Her brow furrowed in thought...

He tossed another one, this time the package had an elegant "to from" tag on it, which indicated that it was "from Oz," but the "to" section had been left blank.

But Natalie recognized the handwriting.

It was *hers*.

She stared down at the package, feeling her heart go faster. "You..." she began, "you bought all of these from the store..."

He nodded.

"...and you had all of this stuff you didn't want giftwrapped..."

He nodded again.

She looked up at him, meeting his eyes. "...because..."

"Because you worked in the giftwrap department at the time." He said, his voice tender but hungry. "And I wanted an excuse to be around you."

She stared down at the packages, thinking about that.

"Something you should know about me Oz?" She swallowed, feeling scared and desperate about the situation. "I screw up a lot." She admitted. "My life is a mess. I don't even know who I am half the time, and I don't particularly like who I am the rest. I can promise you that if you get involved with me, I'm going to do something to mess it up. I always do." She looked back up at him, meeting his eyes. "I am a dangerous woman to be around, Oz. If you're with me, there is a very good chance I'll go evil and I will gut you in your sleep. Or one of my enemies will. The people around me have a tendency to die *bloody*."

"I was the sole survivor of several massacres already." He reminded her simply, his voice firm and filled with rough shadows, which belied his usual serene perfection. "So I'll take my chances."

"No." She shook her head. "You won't. Because as much as

I might…" She swallowed. "I can't put you in that kind of position. I can't be responsible for your death, and if you're with me, that's *exactly* what's going to happen."

"I can't count the number of people who have told me the same thing. Only about myself. Nat, *everyone* in my family is insane." He sat down on the coffee table in front of her, which seemed tremendously out of character for him. "My father killed my mother and sixteen others. My brother strangled his girlfriend because she broke up with him! My cousin butchered my aunt and uncle and stabbed me! Most of my former co-workers tried to destroy the city and me along with it. There isn't a person in town—including me— who isn't expecting me to go evil and start hurting random people too. And until that happens, *my* enemies will…"

"No offense, honey, but I bet your enemies are *total* pussies." She snorted in dismissal. "You point them out to *me* and *I'll* protect you from them."

"Are you trying to say that your enemies are more deadly than my enemies now?"

"Absolutely."

"My father killed seventeen people!" He reminded her.

"Uh-huh." She gave a theatrical yawn. "And what did he do for the *rest* of the afternoon?"

"We haven't caught a whole host of Freedom Squad members yet, and most of them are maniacs who vowed revenge on me and…"

"Oh, do you know how many people vow revenge against me on a daily basis? A lot." She jabbed him in the chest with a fingernail. "*Curses,* Oz. That's how you know you hit the big time badasses. I had a guy slit his own daughter's throat and drink the blood in some kind of dark ritual, just because he was trying to channel some kind of demon to help him kill me."

"My cousin staged a prison riot and had all of cell block A attack me!"

"They put the *losers* in Block A, Oz. A *real* threat would have been if he sent all of Block *D* to come whoop your ass!"

"I think you're missing the point."

"No, I'm not." She shook her head. "I'm saying that I could kick your nemeses' candy asses while watching an episode of *Top Chef*, and be finished with them in time to watch the quick fire challenge!"

"I don't know what that means, but I assume it means you'd do it quickly."

"I do *everything* quickly," she assured him, "except torture and that other thing."

He nodded, his gaze darkening.

He reached out and gently wrapped a curl of her hair around and around his finger, looking captivated by it.

She watched him, finding the sight oddly sensual. There was something quiet and intimate about the small action.

It made her body feel tight and warm again, her breasts moving against the nightshirt, silently begging for his attention too. Without a bra, there was really no hiding how much she liked him touching her.

She took a shaky breath, trying to ignore it. "Y-y-you were saying that all the big scary bad men which inhabit your Mr Rodgers-ian world will fall upon poor defenseless me and I'd be helpless to stop some asshole that the *regular cops* took down! I am *genuinely* insulted right now."

"I didn't say that." He shook his head, her hair still wrapped around his finger. "You said that! You were the one saying that I couldn't possibly fight against the onslaught of bad people that being with you would bring down on my head."

"Oz, I love you with my entire soul, but Rondel would make you his bitch if I wasn't there to stop him."

"I *assure you,* that man is the *deadest...*" He paused. "Wait... run that by me again?"

"I said that Ronnie would..."

"No, not that part, the *other* part." He dropped his hand from her face, her hair forgotten.

"I...I don't remember what I said." She cleared her throat and made a swirling motion next to her temple. "I'm crazy, Oz. Sometimes I babble."

"Don't give me that! No, no, no..." He shook his head. "You're not getting out of this that easily, Natalie." He met her eyes. "You said you love me."

"I don't remember that."

He simply stared at her, which was the man's go-to argument winner. And it somehow always worked! She didn't know how he did that!

"*Fine.*" She snapped. "What of it?" She sniffed indignantly, rearranging herself on the couch. "It'd be a lot easier if I didn't. If I *didn't* love you, it'd be great. We could be together. Happy ending, all of it. Because one day when Ronnie tracked me down and killed you, it wouldn't be that big a deal, because I wasn't... you know... *invested* in you." She cleared her throat, feeling awkward. "But I am." She shook her head again. "Which means that *nothing* can happen to you, because if it did…" She trailed off.

"So, you think I'm utterly helpless without you, right?"

"Pretty much."

"And if your long list of enemies found out you loved me, they'd kill me."

"Ooooooh yeah."

"And you *do* love me."

She made a face. "Unfortunately."

"And your solution to that problem… is to dump me and leave me entirely unprotected?"

"No, that's not…"

"Because that's what it *sounds* like you're doing right now, Nat." His hand reached over to the bottom of her nightshirt, like it was the most casual thing in the world. "It *sounds* like you're… *afraid* of them."

"Hey… I am *not* afraid of those losers!" She assured him, straightening.

"I call 'em like I see 'em." He gently started pulling the nightshirt up. "Sounds to me like you're letting them dictate your personal life, and the only reason someone would do that is if they were *scared*." He took on a mocking comforting tone, as she obediently raised her arms up for him, so that the shirt could pass over her head. "It's okay, Natalie. You just tell me their names and I'll protect you from the scary men."

"Hey! That is *bullshit* right there!" Her eyes narrowed. "You wanna see afraid!?! I will go kill *every one* of those motherfuckers *right now!*"

His eyes fell to her exposed skin, tracing fire across her body and covering her with delicious goosebumps of excited desire.

"Hell, I'll send them invitations to our *fucking wedding!* Time, place, all of it! And if they have the balls to show up? *They won't have them for long!*"

He gently tucked a strand of red hair behind her ear. "*That's* my girl."

She nodded, then frowned slightly as she finally processed that she was now naked. "Wait… where did my top go?"

"I took it off." He reminded her calmly, eyes still on her breasts. "You helped."

"Oh." Mull felt a sudden wave of embarrassment, but Natalie told her to shut up. She could handle this. She arched her back, like she was presenting her tightening breasts for his inspection.

"We make a good team..." She agreed.

His hands covered her breasts so fast that he took her completely by surprise. And Mull wasn't someone who could be easily taken by surprise.

She let out a shocked gasp as he filled his strong hands with her flesh. "Ohh... god..." She squeaked.

Oz lowered his face to them, lavishing the warm skim with even hotter kisses.

Her breath was coming in pants, utterly amazed that he'd been able to do that in mere seconds.

Natalie was already wetter and more excited than Mull could ever remember being in her entire life. And she could tell it wasn't anywhere *near* the extent of the pleasure she was capable of feeling with this man.

"I think half of my problems are caused by the intense sexual frustration of being around you and not having you." Oz assured her, her taunt nipple disappearing into his mouth, and Natalie was *completely* certain that's where it belonged.

"Really?" She moved on the couch, desperate for him to suckle her other breast too, but not wanting him to move.

"You make me crazy, Miss Quentin."

"Usually when I make people crazy it's in a very literal 'tie me to the railroad tracks' way." She wanted his pants off. Right now. "Then they try to kill me."

He met her eyes. "I don't want to kill you."

"But you *do* want to tie me up?" She teased.

To her surprise, he didn't say anything.

"Ooooh... I like where your mind is at right now." She pushed him back, getting to her feet and thinking desperately about which of the giftwrapped boxes in the closet might have what she needed right now. "Handcuffs or rope?"

"For right now... I just want you." He said softly, eyes traveling up and down her body as she stood in front of him. "Nothing weird or evil... I just want to touch something so beautiful..." His hand traveled up her leg, like he was enraptured by her.

Mull processed his expression and dealt with it in a mature and reasonable way. Namely, she reached for her panties and pulled them down for him.

Oz's expression became one of outright amazement, looking at the damp red curls which concealed her heat. "My god..." He got out hoarsely.

And for the first time in her life, Mull felt ordinary. But in a really good way. She felt like an ordinary woman, sharing her body with her boyfriend, in a completely ordinary and not at all insane way.

Her insides dipped, bathing in his hot gaze and wishing she could somehow show him *more.* Somehow give him everything.

She felt like she was the sexiest woman in the world at the moment. She had that man's complete attention and she knew she could get him to do anything she wanted. He'd *beg* to have her, if she asked him. She could make that pristine, fastidious, and impeccable man *lick the fucking floor* if she demanded it, and she was certain he'd do it, just so long as he got to have her at the end of it.

There was something so amazing about that.

So extraordinary.

Mull had never been a sex goddess before, but apparently if you got Natalie going, she was *really* into it.

Natalie absolutely loved that man. And she could see that love and desire in the man's eyes. So all of her shy and kooky nonsense was forgotten. She'd fuck that man's brains out right here. She would give him everything she had, because she knew that he was absolutely amazing and that she loved him more than her own life. Anything she gave him, she'd get back twice in return.

Oz was her hero.

"Open." She ordered.

Oz opened his mouth.

Natalie took her red lace underwear with little turkeys embroidered on them, and pushed them into Oz's mouth.

Oz put up no resistance, the panties dangling from his teeth, his eyes burning into hers as he tasted the damp fabric. Tasted her desire. Tasted *her*.

There was something dark and sensual about it.

But she could tell she was playing with fire here. Oz was a stable and dependable man... but he wouldn't be able to hold himself back from her for long. He was going to snap in a moment and take her. And that knowledge excited her.

"*Good boy*." She nodded in praise, using her finger to push her underwear further into his mouth. "You're dressed." She said simply, turning so that he had a better view of her. "You don't need to be dressed, Oz."

Oz got to his feet, moving like a man possessed. His pants were cast aside haphazardly and thrown away, in what was possibly the only time the man ever seemed careless.

He spat out her underwear and his hands were on her a moment later, lifting her up like she weighed nothing, and beginning to

396

lay her back down on the couch.

"No, no." She shook her head, eyes locked with his, like they were both afraid to look away for fear of breaking the moment. "Counter." He did as he was told, lifting her up onto the countertop of his kitchen. "Every morning, I want you to sit right here, eating your boring tasteless foods," she turned to dump the contents of the counter onto the floor, then leaned back on her elbow, "and think about fucking me." She growled, feeling almost crazed with lust now. "I want you to think about my naked ass on your pristine spotless table..." She ran her hand along the surface. "And the sounds I make when you're inside me..."

"I already do." He growled out. "Have for years."

She smiled at him, then reached over to her purse to pull out the box of condoms. "I bought this at the store for you, so you'd be comfortable." She pulled one out, spreading her body open to his view, like she was the main course at Thanksgiving dinner. "It was on Black Friday sale."

"That's a good fucking sale..." He finally admitted, eyes locked on her glistening folds like they were his newest obsession.

She ripped open the package with her teeth, while his hands played with her breasts again.

"I... I don't have a lot of experience at this." He confessed, sounding embarrassed but keeping his eyes on her intimate flesh. "If I do something wrong, tell me."

"I think you'll figure it out." She assured him, her voice husky to her own ears. "You can..."

Oz's control snapped and his hand moved over her body, caressing her skin with unbridled desire. The heat pooled at the junction of her thighs, then it *ignited* when he touched her there too. She let out another hoarse gasp of shocked pleasure, trying to keep from moaning.

His fingers somehow knew the exact spot she needed him to touch, and she raised her hips up off of the counter, like she'd been struck with a live wire, chasing him. Silently begging him. She'd wanted him to touch her there since the first time she'd seen him, and it was everything she'd dreamed it could be. She let out a ragged moan, trying to keep her composure and failing utterly.

Oz's fingers continued moving through the damp thatch of red curls, recognizing that he had complete control of her body now.

One of his thick, scarred fingers moved to slide into her passage, demanding entrance. It stretched her body and Natalie gave a cry, not expecting her by-the-book virginal lover to be quite so knowledgeable about this. He'd either researched it or was just an absolute born natural.

She swallowed, trying to see straight and not mew helplessly in pleasure. "You've... you've really never done this before?" She asked, her voice sounding so filled with lust it was almost pained.

"No."

"Well, you're really good at..." Her words broke off as another one of his fingers joined the first, and she let out a shout.

"You're very tight," he observed in his usual matter-of-fact Oz way, but which now sounded boiling with desire, "is two too much? If that hurts, I can..."

She shook her head, no longer capable of speaking. "Two is... two is..." She tried.

He pushed the fingers deeper.

"...good!" She gasped, moving her legs to give him better access. "Fuck, two is good!"

His free hand began to play with her swollen breasts and nipples, like they amused him and had been given to him in one of the wrapped presents. "You're sure?" He moved his fingers, not a single indication of hesitation, modesty, or discomfort. Oz was taking control of her body, and it was fucking incredible! "Because if you can't..."

Her hips moved in spite of herself, screwing herself down on his fingers as he pressed them deeper into her body. She gritted her teeth, trying to hold it together. "Fuuuuck...." She growled out, the feeling so good it was almost painful.

"I'm sorry?" Oz took on a tone of absolute confusion, like he had no idea what she could possibly be reacting to. "Are you okay, Miss Quentin?"

She was too far gone to control this, and she knew it.

"Oz..." She whimpered, her body gripping his fingers and rubbing against his palm. "...please..."

His hand moved from her breast to her hair again, wrapping one red curl at her temple around and around his finger. "That's it..." He said softly as her hips moved, with his hand. "Show me how this is done, Natalie..."

She thrust her hips against his fingers, gritting her teeth and uttering throaty curses as she looked into the man's perfect face. This was his first time, and she was determined to make it good for both of them. Or, more accurately, just her.

His knuckle touched her center and Natalie's world exploded.

She let out a startled gasp, never imagining that there was that much pleasure to be had in the world.

Her gasp turned into an intense soundless cry, every muscle in her body locking and every inch of skin flushed and warm, from the ecstasy Oz's fingers had just brought her to.

Oz watched it all with his intense dark gaze, like a tourist at some amazing attraction he'd always wanted to see.

Every single movement of her naked body was cataloged in that man's incredible mind, where it would no doubt be obsessed about and re-lived forever. Every ragged breath, every inch of weeping flesh, every tiny cry.

She found that idea so amazing.

She rode out her climax, eyes locked with his.

And she could tell that Oz was at the end of even his already limited control. The man had hidden, darker depths. Everyone knew it. And Natalie could feel something moving beneath the calm, orderly surface of her partner.

She swallowed again, then reached down to slide the condom onto his hugely erect body.

His hips jutted forward as her grip closed over him, and Oz swore in a most un-Oz like fashion.

Her mouth curved, licking her lips and guessing something she could try. "I'm going to do something that's you'll like, if you'll..."

She never got to finish the thought.

Instead, in one movement, Oz pushed her back onto the table, vaulted up on top of her, and his cock was already halfway home before she even registered what was happening.

She let out another astonished sound, not expecting that.

Oz was so... restrained. Safe. Controlled.

She really wasn't expecting him to be quite so into this or... big.

The man's body was bigger than his fingers and her tight channel had to stretch even more to allow for this new welcomed guest.

Oz moved his mouth to hers, her moan lost to his lips.

He pushed all the way into her, his eyes once again on hers.

For the first time, there was nothing but darkness in his gaze. He was beyond all control now, intent on simply taking her.

She'd broken his mind.

The thought filled her with another burst of feminine power. She *was* some kind of sex goddess! It was...

Oz began moving, short thrusts into her, his breath coming in growls.

Natalie bit her lower lip, wrapping her legs around him as

tight as she could and moving with him. Guiding him and showing him the rhythm to move at. He was rough and wild. She needed to break him in and show him how to move.

Oz was very, very excited. She could feel it. His breathing wasn't anywhere close to even and the tendons in his neck were standing taught. He was trying to hold on, but he was losing it. She could see that. He wasn't going to last long. He simply wanted her too much.

"It's okay..." She assured him, trying not to lose it herself. "You can..."

Oz thrust several more times into her, then exploded. Every muscle in his body locked, a choking growl of lust and passion and possessiveness escaping his throat. His fingers squeezed her breast tight enough that it would probably leave marks.

And Natalie absolutely loved it.

Oz was losing himself in her. He was finally having some *fun.*

To her surprise, his climax didn't slow him down at all, and as soon as it ebbed, he continued like it had never happened. If anything, it just made him harder and *more* desperate for her flesh.

Natalie's eyebrows rose, not expecting him to...

He gave her a kiss so hot it was scorching, his tongue ignoring the barrier of her lips and moving to rub against her tongue.

He leaned down to nip at her breasts, closing his teeth over their urgent points, and Natalie had to try desperately not to come herself. It would...

His body moved forward in another brutal, merciless thrust, and Natalie came again. She hadn't meant to or expected it, it was just...

She let out a startled cry again, feeling like she was going to go mad if this got any more intense.

Oz reacted to her new orgasm by reaching down to her hands and pinned them both over her head, holding her still against the counter in his iron grasp, and presenting her body to him.

His eyes moved from her eyes to her breasts as they bounced.

He watched them like a man possessed, hammering into her. Again and again.

There was a timeless quality to it. Dreamlike. Natalie's entire world now consisted of the sound of their lovemaking and her own heartbeat thundering in her ears. It was a wonderful, wonderful world to visit.

It seemed like hours had gone by, but also just moments.

Oz gritted his teeth and came again, eyes staying on her breasts.

Natalie tried to free her hand so that she could touch his face, but to her surprise, he kept her pinned to the table. The realization that he was stronger than she was today filled her with a thrill, for some reason.

She was pinned to the table. At his mercy. And she loved it.

His body was still hard. And he was going to go again.

By this point, Natalie was as amazed as she was turned on. The man was going for some kind of record here. Which was really, really cool.

He'd apparently been saving himself for her, and now that he had the opportunity, he was going to make certain he took full advantage.

Mull let out an excited giggle, feeling wicked and loved and utterly safe. Her heart was in her throat, and her vision swam. She couldn't remember ever being so excited. "Come on..." Her eyebrows waggled at him flirtatiously. "You're not done... *Show me what ya got, Baby Doll*..."

Oz took her up on the challenge, shifting his weight so that his body pushed even deeper into her.

Mull wrapped her legs against him even tighter, squeezing him harder in an attempt to make them one.

He rested his forehead against hers, sharing her breath.

Perspiration stood out on his skin, his jaw set, his breathing even more ragged now.

She kissed him softly, surrendering herself to him and taking him in return. "I love you..." She whispered. "God, I love you..."

Each one of his thrusts was accompanied by a groan of desire now, like a wordless plea for her body and throaty prayer of thanks for her.

She moved with him, amazed that she hadn't lost her mind yet. She'd *never* felt anything like this before. That man was driving her mad!

His thrusts became shorter and more desperate, his eyes locked with hers now. His brow was furrowed in passion and effort, her name on his lips. "Natalie... Natalie... Natalie..."

Her blood was pounding in her ears, mixing in with Oz's heavy breathing and the sound of her own soft cries. She kissed him again, his lips still demanding and hungry. Like he'd never get enough of the taste of her. "I love you, Oz." She assured him softly, gasping the words. "You are my hero."

Oz came again, letting out her name in a hoarse roar of exhaustion and pleasure.

His final effort pushed Mull over the edge too, a climax she hadn't even been aware her body was still capable of producing. It was absolutely shattering though, to the point her vision was darkening around the edges and her mind blanked.

Oz collapsed on top of her.

They both gasped for breath, trying to regain their sanity.

Wow.

Okay, that was intense.

They were going to need more condoms. A lot more.

"I love you." He assured her, moving so that his face was resting on her breasts. "I love you so much I can't even control it."

She swallowed, feeling like her entire world had shifted and that there would never be a future where she wouldn't want this man. "I could tell." She got out with an amused gasp, then craned her neck to kiss the top of his head tenderly.

And it was the happiest Mull could ever remember being.

Which meant, given their career choice... one of them would probably die soon.

Chapter 24

Mercygiver leaned back in his chair, growing bored with all of this.

It wasn't that he was tiring of hurting people, it was just that he always seemed to be hurting the *wrong* people.

He ran a hand through his hair and watched as the model train once again made its way through the exquisitely detailed miniature town. The small plastic residents were gathered in the charming park area which served as its town square, watching as a man in a top hat lit a scruffy-looking bottlebrush of a Christmas tree.

All told, it was a work of obvious love. A portrait of vanishing Americana, captured by someone who knew it very, very well.

Mercygiver hated it, for some reason.

He hated seeing all of those little homes and their happy decorations. He hated the little plastic people, clustered together in community and love. He hated how the tiny children were waiting in line to give the tiny plastic Santa their letters and have their tiny plastic dreams fulfilled.

Because all of that was bullshit.

It was a lie.

It was just a façade, hiding the truth.

He picked up one of the plastic couples from the town square, looking into the little colored dots which represented their eyes.

Their love was obvious. Even rendered in plastic and model paint.

He envied them that. ...It was almost *pathetic* how much he envied them that. At this particular moment, he'd gladly switch places with either of them. He'd jump at that chance. They'd found their soulmates, cast together in a single piece of plastic at the factory, their limbs forever connected. There was no way they would ever leave each other behind or hold *slight* disagreements against the other. They weren't that petty or vindictive. If they had a tiny accident, like, say, if one of them had stabbed the other, that wouldn't mean that their entire relationship needed to end.

The little plastic train village couple were in love. He could look at them and feel it.

He glared at them, his anger and pain growing.

Love didn't *fucking exist.* It ended with betrayal and pain and your partner moving on without you.

...It ended with being so broken and crazy by that abandonment, that you sat around and cursed the supposed love of inanimate objects.

He carefully placed the plastic couple back into their original position, making sure they had a good view of the model tree-lighting.

He was losing it.

He could feel that. He recognized his own insanity, he was just powerless to stop it.

Mercygiver hated it when things were normal and happy. To Rondel, the entire world was a cesspool. If you wanted to survive in it, you needed to be the toughest, strongest rat swimming in the shit. And nowhere in that equation did model railroading figure.

He vindictively knocked the train over so that it crashed into the crowd, crushing dozens of residents of Plasticville.

But the couple had survived it. Somehow. Their love would undoubtedly only grow, as they dealt with the trauma.

Mercygiver fucking *hated them!*

That woman had made him so irrelevant that he couldn't even destroy toys now.

"Are you a history fan? I am. Do you know who Vladimir Demikhov was?" He asked casually, removing the novelty train engineer's cap he was wearing, and tossed it aside. He didn't even care anymore. "Few people do. Demikhov was a genius. He practically invented the entire idea of organ transplantation, which saves millions of lives annually." He got to his feet and gave his companion a swift kick to the ribs. "But that wasn't the limit of his experiments." He continued, ignoring the woman's struggles to get to her feet. "Demikhov's favorite kind of operation was to surgically

404

attach the head and shoulders of one dog, onto the head and shoulders of a separate dog. Right between the shoulder blades, creating a creature with two heads and six legs." He paused for a long moment, his tone haunted. "The part that's always scared me? They didn't die right away, because he connected all the veins and muscles. Both dogs were *alive*. They *knew* what had been done to them. One of his Frankenstein dogs lived for thirty days like that. Can you even *imagine*? Can you think of anything more horrifying than that?" He thought about the kind of living hell that was, then looked down at the woman sprawled at his feet. "You have a strange name, by the way. Has anyone ever told you that?"

Oklahoma Mike got onto her hands and knees, trying to stand back up. "Never come up, no." She replied flippantly, her voice strained from the pain.

She really was a ludicrously pretty woman. But she was soft. Her body wasn't made for fighting or enduring pain.

He had no respect for weakness.

"I am a history fan." He informed her again, absently watching her try to regain her balance. "I love history. Di Vinci called himself a 'disciple of experience,' and I've always thought that a wonderful way to think about life." He punched her in the stomach and the woman went down hard, gasping for breath. "Try, learn, and try again. We can't be afraid of new things, Oklahoma. Daring where others relent. Tear down the old and rebuild it in our own image."

She struggled into a sitting position, trying to stand up again. In doing so, her gaze flicked to the open door to her left, obviously plotting an escape.

Mercygiver tried not to roll his eyes. "Oh, there's no running away from this. You'll never make it." He warned.

"Run?" Oklahoma looked genuinely insulted by that accusation. "*I'm fucking Wellesburg!*" She choked out, voice cracking in pain and fury. "Wellesburg doesn't run. We move the world..."

Mercygiver kicked her in the face, cutting off the woman's nonsense.

Oklahoma sprawled on her back, which was probably a familiar position for her, making an incoherent mumbling sound through her split lips. "We..."

"Stay with me now," he gently slapped the side of her face several times, trying to keep the woman conscious, "we're not finished yet."

Her eyes cleared some, regaining her senses.
He hadn't hit her *that* hard.

Some women were so breakable it was disgusting.

"I am in need of a location." He reminded her. "You have the address, I need it. Give it to me and I will leave and you'll never see me again. You have my word."

He could tell by her eyes, swollen almost shut as they were, that she wasn't going to cooperate with him.

"We just need to be logical about this..." He began.

"Fuck logic, I work for *Montgomery Welles.*" She reminded him. "Which means the truth is whatever I say it is and I can do whatever I want." She met his gaze with a cold determination. "I don't have to be afraid of a *goddamn thing*... even you."

"Uh-huh." Mercygiver couldn't constrain the eye roll this time. People always had to be so overly dramatic about things. He grabbed her by the front of her suitcoat, pulling her to her feet. "Not to sound argumentative, but I think we both know that I could kill you right here and his only reaction would be to place a help wanted ad on Craigslist tomorrow morning, seeking some new streetwalker to take your place."

"Probably. But then again, I'm an Irregular. And he's *fiercely* territorial." She took on the tone of a religious zealot quoting scripture. "This world is a great machine, there is only one man at the controls." She shook her head at him in pity and warning. "And you're not a Welles." She let out another suicidal chuckle, like all of this amused her. "He's going to make you his fucking bitch."

Her phone rang to the theme of Tetris and he glanced down at the name on the screen. "Speak of the devil." He held it up for her to see. "Sadly, I'm afraid you're not going to be able to take this call. Frankly, I don't know why he got you involved in this at all."

"You know, that seemed odd to me too. But I'm an Irregular; I don't ask questions."

"Do you want me to deliver any last words?" Mercygiver pulled out his pistol and pressed it to her forehead.

"He already knows what I'd say."

"You're really going to die over this?" He asked her again, in utter amazement. "Over a simple address?"

"Montgomery Welles asked for my help." She said simply, like that was all the explanation which was needed. "Plus... I've always fucking *hated you.*" She stood straighter, not flinching away from the gun barrel but standing up to it. "So when he comes for you? And he *will.* You tell him," she insolently spat out a mouthful of blood into his face, "*that* was all you got out of me." She met his eyes, beginning to laugh in suicidal glee. "*I won't tell you shit.*"

Mercygiver's finger curled around the trigger, *wanting* to pull it so desperately. He wanted to see that bitch's brains spattered all over her fucking model of her perfect fucking small town. He wanted to blow her obnoxiously pretty face off and leave behind nothing but disgusting tissue and broken skull.

She'd earned that! She'd earned it for being loyal and loving something, even an *evil* something, more than her own life! She'd earned it for fucking *having* something! *Anything!*

Mercygiver had NOTHING!

He fucking hated her!

But something held him back. He wasn't sure what.

So instead, he clubbed her with the gun, knocking her out and sending her crashing into the tabletop model.

He let out an aggravated roar of fury, then shot his silenced weapon several times into her furniture and walls. "Dammit!" He screamed at the top of his lungs, feeling so stymied today. It was like everything was conspiring against him.

He blamed *her.*

Somehow, his ex was behind this, he could feel it. That bitch was making him weak. Trying to keep him from what needed to be done.

Mr. Jack heard the shots and rushed into the room, searching for an attacker. His gaze fell on Mercygiver and he instantly looked like he wished he'd just ignored the noise.

Mercygiver stared down at Oklahoma as she was sprawled on the model train platform. "Kill her, please." He ordered.

If he couldn't do it, then he'd have his underling seal the woman's fate.

Mr. Jack nodded, strolling over to grab Mercygiver's weapon and aim it at the woman. Then he paused. "Shit... is that really *Miss December?*" He sounded amazed and almost excited, like he was impressed with the woman's celebrity. He lowered the gun, having second thoughts. "Umm... I have serious moral objections about killing anyone with tits like that, boss." He shook his head. "And she sounded like a really nice girl in her bio too. She sings in her church choir and wanted to work in a zoo, isn't that adorable?"

Mercygiver's fury was boiling and searching for an outlet. And he'd just found one.

He could *easily* murder Mr. Jack.

He'd kill that moron, then just find some *new* henchmen in Thailand...

The unconscious whore's phone rang and Mercygiver looked

down at it. He didn't recognize the name, but he got a new idea. He reached over to grab the woman's hand, using her fingertip to unlock the phone, then immediately looked through her call history for the number he wanted.

A minute later, he was listening as his quarry picked up the line on her end.

He held the little train couple again, wondering how hard he'd need to squeeze the plastic before it broke. "Hello, Kitten." Mercygiver cooed into the phone, feeling like his night was about to get better. *"I'm calling you out…"*

****

An hour later, Mull was making her way into the back of the store. To Roy's private office. Where all of this began.

She had received the call from Rondel and had managed to sneak out of Oz's apartment without waking him. Luckily, he was so exhausted from his blue-ribbon performance in bed that she doubted that a fire truck parking in his room could have roused him.

Which was good. Because she didn't want him to have any part of this.

When you came down to it… Ronnie was *her* nemesis. She was going to be the one to deal with him, and she'd die before she let that maniac near any more of her friends.

She'd been the one who had invited him into her life in the first place. And now she was going to end it.

Unfortunately, she wasn't actually sure what her powers were today. She couldn't feel them. Just, oddly, the broken "bone vanishing" power from yesterday again, which was very strange. She'd never had a power for more than one day before. It probably had something to do with the power itself being so glitchy and unpredictable.

She would have preferred to wait to confront Ronnie until a day when she had some amazing ability which he couldn't possibly stop, but the man hadn't really given her that option.

It was either meet him or he'd kill Oklahoma and then come kill Oz.

Which was why she was here.

All told, it was a *tremendously* stupid move on her part. She'd fought Ronnie on more than a few occasions, and he'd absolutely crushed her every time. Plus, she still had to rescue Sydney today. *And* deal with whatever "train" the Agletarians were meeting.

408

And oversee her store's parade, which would be starting in... she looked down at her watch... an hour.

Yes, Mull was going to have a busy day. She'd found love, had wild sex, was about to kill her ex, would soon rescue her friend, and then stop an evil country's plans for world domination. Oh, and have Thanksgiving dinner with the rest of the Consortium.

She pushed open the concealed door which connected the store to the warehouse behind it. Roy had kept a lot of his stuff in the space, just in case he ever needed it again.

Ronnie had wanted to meet here, because he was a drama queen. That son of a bitch always leapt at the chance to do something clichéd and irritating. He was a joke.

She stepped into the darkened space and flicked her wrists, extending Roy's telescopic batons.

In front of her, a disreputable looking dark-haired man wearing a death metal band t-shirt looked out at her from the shadows. She could only assume this was one of Ronnie's henchmen.

He didn't look at all surprised to see her. "Ah." He got to his feet, no doubt to lead her to his boss. "Care to te..."

Mull didn't have time to chat with Ronnie's head stooge at the moment or risk him getting involved in what she wanted to be a *private* fight to the death. Instead, she calmly pulled out the creepy hypnotic doll she'd taken from her apartment and held it up to his view.

The man's words trailed off, captivated by the doll's gaze.

Mull placed the doll on one of the boxes, then stalked forward, casually decking the man as she did, knocking him out like a light.

It didn't take her long to find Ronnie inside the warehouse, since he was sitting in the only illumination in the entire space. The man was behind Roy's desk, staring at her through the large window which divided the warehouse area from Roy's office and living quarters. His face was unreadable, but his eyes were practically glowing with fury.

He looked absolutely *terrible*. She'd never seen him looking so haggard and... broken.

Good.

He switched the desk lamp off. Then on again. Then off. Then on.

He repeated the process, like he was trapped in a time loop, getting angrier and angrier each time the light revealed his face.

"You break Roy's lamp and I'm going to be *really* pissed."

She warned him.

Ronnie left the lamp on and got to his feet, prowling towards the door. "I respected Kilroy." He exited the room at a full-out run, straight towards her. He'd never really been one for foreplay. *"It's you I'm going to break!"*

She dodged to the side as he grabbed for her, and she swung out with one of the batons.

He blocked it with his forearm, then tried to punch her with his other fist.

She kicked him away, knocking him off balance, then swung the baton at him again. This time, she scored a glancing blow, which cut the side of his head. The impact sent him colliding with one of the large wooden crates in the warehouse, and she tried to hit him again, but he caught her wrist and stripped the weapon from her grasp.

She smashed the stock of the other baton straight down on his head, just about breaking his skull.

The man staggered away, laughing. "Nice." He complimented, backing away to rub the wound. The cut to his scalp was bleeding, dripping down his face and giving him an even more inhuman appearance.

She charged at him, faking a strike with the baton, but really trying to hit him in his throat with her other hand. He somehow predicted the move though, and grabbed her in a headlock from the side. She struggled to breathe as his arm closed around her airway, then turned her head to the side, towards him, and punched him in the balls.

The man stepped back, swearing, and she tried to hit his kneecap with the weapon, but he dodged away and spin-kicked it from her hand. The baton skidded away into the darkness.

They eyed each other, hate mutual.

Then charged again.

The thing the movies never told you. When you were in a fight? A *real* fight? It wasn't an elegant thing. There was no calm deliberation where you had time to setup complicated moves or strategies. It was just wailing on the other guy/girl, any way you could. A mad, violent, mindless struggle, done mostly on instinct. That was why you trained and practiced. Why you wanted things to be second nature to you. Because when shit went down? You weren't thinking about a damn thing.

And all you saw was red.

They traded blows for what seemed like forever, both bloodied and getting tired. At this point it was difficult to say who was

410

going to win, but Mull was feeling like the fight really could have been going better. She'd gotten much better at killing people over the years, but sadly, so had Ronnie.

Ronnie grabbed her by hair and tossed her through the plate glass window, where she tumbled across the floor of Roy's office.

Again, despite what she'd been assuring Oz, it wasn't like the movies. Mull was tough, but she had no enhanced durability or strength today. And her opponent outweighed her by a great deal, pounds which were entirely muscle and thicker bones. She could normally win a fight against someone like this by not getting hit, but in this case, Ronnie was... better than she was.

He simply was.

He'd always been able to predict what she was going to do, somehow always knowing ahead of time. He was using that ability to his advantage today.

As it currently stood... she was going to lose this fight. And she knew it.

"You fucking bitch!" He stalked through the door of the office and punched her in the face again, making her see stars and stumble backward in an attempt to stay on her feet. "You think this is some fucking movie were an eighty pound woman can beat up a two hundred pound man!?!"

"*I don't weigh eighty pounds, you asshole!*" She grabbed one of the boxes of store supplies from a pile in the hallway and smashed him in the head with it. "You got some pounds on me. But I got more than enough hate to equal it out." She grabbed his head and smashed hers into it. He might be bigger, but the bone of her forehead was still stronger than the cartilage of his nose.

Ronnie swore and staggered away, clutching the broken remains of his face.

Mull launched herself onto his back, trying to get him in a choke hold and put him down. At this point, it was really her only chance of surviving this.

Instead, he flipped her over his shoulders and sent her through a coffee table which the store had offered for sale in 1986. The glass erupted around her, cutting her skin in a thousand places. She tried to struggle free and get back to her feet, but Ronnie brought his foot down on her face.

He looked down at her for a moment, the blood from his broken nose and lacerated scalp dripping down onto her face and chest, coating her.

He casually kicked the remains of the coffee table away, then reached down to grab a handful of her hair and dragged her back to her feet.

She slammed one of the shards of glass into the base of his neck, but he was too angry to even feel it, apparently. Instead, he simply tossed her through the wall like she weighed nothing.

Mull crashed through the plaster, wood, and pipes, then hit the wall on the other side of the hallway and landed in a broken heap.

Ronnie followed her a moment later, prowling through the opening her body had made in the wall, intent on finishing her off.

Her hand fell to the floor beside her, where one of the broken water pipes was lying. As Ronnie stepped through the wall, she swung the pipe in an effort to take out his knee and even up the fight some.

To her surprise, the blow didn't even slow him down. It hit him and all but bounced off. She'd swung it hard enough to break bone, but... no. Nothing.

Instead, he kicked her as she tried to get up, causing Mull to collapse again.

"I HATE YOU!" He bellowed in a ragged voice, kicking her again. *"YOU RUINED MY LIFE!"*

The next time his foot struck her, she grabbed it and tried to knock him down, but he simply used that opportunity to knee her in the face. The strike knocked the back of her head through the wall behind her.

And Mull was done.

She slipped down to the floor, watching through darkened eyes as the water from the pipes cascaded around her in the hallway like a fountain. There was something... beautiful about it. The way the light hit the graceful spray and formed a prism.

She coughed, the warmth of her blood quickly disappearing in the sheet of cold water falling onto her.

Ronnie got back to his feet. "I warned you what would happen." He reminded her, his tone still furious and unhinged. "I told you not to mess with our partnership, but you didn't listen." He clawed at his hair in irritation, paying no attention to the blood which coated his head. *"You never fucking listened to me!!! Never! You never cared!"*

From the warehouse area, there was the sound of a door closing.

And Mull instantly knew who it was.

Ronnie did too. "And *now* your knight in shining armor is here." He rolled his eyes. "You shouldn't have involved him in our personal matter." He sounded more annoyed with her than anything else. Like he was scolding her for endangering Oz. "*Now* you've gone and done it."

Mull used the last of her energy to try to get back to her feet and protect Oz...

"*Shut up and die, like a good girl!*" Ronnie shouted in irritation, then punched her in the face.

Mull's vision went dark.

****

There was nothing more irritating on Thanksgiving than guests. Especially if they were uninvited.

Mercygiver watched this grotesquely moral Cape slink through the warehouse, searching for his missing partner.

All in all, the man was doing a fairly competent job. Good for him.

Still, staying out of his way was easy. The man might be a Cape, but Mercygiver was very good at disappearing. He could blend into the shadows and there wasn't a hero in town who could find him. It wasn't a superpower, it was simply a survival instinct he'd developed over the years.

He wanted this man gone, and he wanted to return to dealing with his obnoxious ex.

Sadly, the man seemed to have a sense that someone was in the warehouse and he wasn't going to leave until he found out who.

He stopped in the office area, looking down at the blood on the floor and the large hole in the wall. He knew whose blood that was. It was obvious.

The man cautiously crept down the hallway, moving fast but somehow managing to not make a sound despite the amount of glass on the floor. It was quite impressive, really.

Mercygiver tried to keep pace behind him, out of sight, which was becoming increasingly difficult.

At this point, Rondel was *genuinely* impressed with this guy. Well, except for his clothes.

He had absolutely no idea why *anyone* would be wearing a fox hunting outfit into battle. But Rondel suspected it was probably the girl's doing.

She'd always been a meddling bitch, who made things more difficult for everyone.

She'd picked out Rondel's clothes a few times over the years too. He'd *detested* them. They made him look like a fool.

But he'd worn them anyway.

Because he was lonely. And… that woman had always had control of him.

The man made his way into Roy's living area, and the small kitchenette, where he stopped.

He stood in front of the refrigerator, hands fisted at his sides. Like he was terrified of the nightmare he might find inside. He reached out with a shaky hand… to find it empty.

The man's legs visibly went to jelly in relief for a moment, mumbling a soft prayer of thanks to his gods.

As he did though, Mercygiver accidentally hit one of the pipes which had been torn from the wall, and the metal made the *tiniest* of sounds.

The man spun around instantly, reacting faster than Mercygiver would have given him credit for.

But Mercygiver moved faster.

He hit the man in the back of the head with one of the heavy history books from the end table in the apartment, knocking him to the floor.

Mercygiver dragged him towards one of the chairs set up in the living area. For some reason, he found the entire process remarkably challenging. The man was surprisingly heavy and Rondel had genuine difficultly lifting him up.

He pulled the man into the chair, then quickly secured him with zip ties as the man started to rouse. Mercygiver pulled away from him, just as the man came to and started to struggle.

Mercygiver let out a long breath. "Well, this could have gone better, Mister Dimico." He told him regretfully, crossing his arms over his chest. "You seem like a truly charming man, and I had hoped that our first meeting could have been under better circumstances. Like, say, that redheaded bitch's funeral."

Oz's vision cleared and he stared at Mercygiver in something like… confusion. Which was a truly odd emotion to exhibit, considering the circumstances.

The man's eyebrows rose in bafflement as he continued looking at Mercygiver. "Natalie, what the hell are you doing?"

Chapter 25

"SHE REMEMBERED TRYING TO BOX HER OWN EARS
FOR HAVING CHEATED HERSELF IN A GAME OF
CROQUET SHE WAS PLAYING AGAINST HERSELF, FOR
THIS CURIOUS CHILD WAS VERY FOND OF PRETENDING
TO BE TWO PEOPLE. 'BUT IT'S NO USE NOW,' THOUGHT
POOR ALICE, 'TO PRETEND TO BE TWO PEOPLE! WHY,
THERE'S HARDLY ENOUGH OF ME LEFT TO MAKE ONE
RESPECTABLE PERSON!'

- Alice's Adventures in Wonderland

YEARS AGO

She watched in grim horror as Ronnie finished off the
Agletarians, snapping their necks like toothpicks.

Sometimes he reminded her why she was so afraid of him
and why she couldn't escape.

He turned to look at her, blood from a dozen people dripping
down his face. "You're just going to sit there?" He sounded vaguely
disappointed, like he wanted her to join in the carnage. "The least you
could do is take one or two of the little ones." He pointed to one of
the Agletarians' lookouts, who was running away. "How about that
one? Surely you can kill *him*..." It sounded almost like a wager or a
dare.

But she just kept staring at him, transfixed in terror and
disgust. Suddenly, every bad decision she'd ever made in her life was
seemingly brought to the surface, somehow filling her mind all at once.

Ronnie was every bad decision she had ever made.

Everything she was afraid of becoming.

He was only here because she had agreed to go with him.
Agreed to give him control. And in retrospect, she should have just let
him kill her.

It's what Roy would have wanted.

He had told her not to...

As it was, her weakness and terror were an affront to a good man's memory.

She'd chosen to wear Roy's costume, but... she wasn't Roy. She'd *never* be Roy, because she was... evil. She'd been forced to make a choice, all those years ago, and this is where it ended up. Watching as Ronnie killed a tavern filled with people. And took great pleasure in doing so.

She was deeply, *deeply* disappointed with herself.

But Ronnie always seemed to know how to get her to do what he wanted. Always knew *juuuuust* the button he could press, which would make her a willing accomplice to his horrors.

And in that moment... she made up her mind to kill him. She'd probably die herself in the attempt, but it would be worth it.

She'd served the devil for too long. And it was looking more and more like she was the only one who'd be able to stop him.

She stood up, starting to walk towards her psychotic partner, as the man casually grabbed a shotgun and emptied it into the back of a fleeing man.

He tossed the empty weapon aside, turning in a circle, looking for some new violent diversion which could occupy his deeply troubled mind. His vision set on Brendan, who was lying sprawled under the wreckage of the bar. Ronnie's face instantly brightened, like a child who'd finally located a toy he'd forgotten all about.

"Ah, Brendan!" Ronnie sounded absolutely thrilled. "Have I got plans for *you*, my boy." He prowled closer, then straddled the man's chest. "I am going to stuff you in the trunk of that car over there," Ronnie pointed at the vehicle in question through the tavern's open door, "then mail your corpse back to the Agletarians, with exact postage stuck to your forehead." He paused to consider something. "I wonder how many stamps that will be?" He tapped a bloody fingernail against his tooth. "I'll probably need to take your body back to the States first, to avoid paying international rates..."

She silently reached down to grab one of the knives from the floor. It was one of *Ronnie's* knives. An Eimin Blade. It could supposedly cut through anything, even invulnerable people. Not that she thought that Ronnie had any real superpowers... but she wasn't willing to risk it.

If she moved against him, she wanted it to be fast and permanent.

She wanted to make sure that...

"I don't think the knife will be necessary, Kitten." Ronnie

assured her, somehow knowing she had the blade in her hand, despite the fact that she was standing behind him. "I think our dear friend Brendan is quite subdued now."

She paused in her tracks, debating with herself what to do.

He knew she had picked up the knife in order to kill him.

The consequences for that would be the same whether she acted on it or not.

He was either going to kill her or he'd make her *wish* she was dead.

Her hand tightened on the hilt of the weapon.

Ronnie straightened, slowly standing up. "Are you a hero now, Kitten? Is that it?"

"Maybe." She firmed her jaw. "But either way, I'm *done with you*."

"Would you like me to tell you a secret about human nature, Kitten?" He turned to face her. "No matter how much good you do for an evil woman, you can't make her good, and no matter how much evil you array against a good woman, you can't make her evil. You are born one way or the other. We are who we are, deep down in the dark. Cast complete and fully formed, by gods and devils. You can't break the mold." He met her eyes and she felt like she was looking into utter blackness. "Sadly for you." He started towards her. "The old man saw that. That's why he kept you on a tight leash. He recognized that you were a creature designed only for evil. That there was simply no way you could turn out any other way, despite his best efforts to the contrary."

"*I don't want to do these things!*" She spread her arms wide. "Don't put your atrocities on me, Ronnie! This is all you!"

Ronnie started laughing. "You've always done what you *wanted* to do, Kitten. I've never forced you into anything."

"That's a lie!"

"No, it's not." His smile grew. "And you know it. It's…"

At Ronnie's feet, Brendan started to stir, looking confused. "Who… who are you talking to?"

She frowned in confusion over that, trying to decide if the man was delirious or not. "What? What does…" She turned toward Rondel. "What does he mean?"

"Nothing." Ronnie assured her instantly. "Ignore him."

"No, no," she waved him off, feeling like this was important, "*tell me what he means!*"

"Don't go looking into that, Kitten." Ronnie told her again, his voice serious. "You won't like the answers."

Brendan began pulling himself to his feet, blood spilling from several deep wounds. *"There's no one else fucking here, Mercygiver!"* He shouted at her, hacking up a spray of blood in the process. *"What the fuck are you on!?! And why the fuck do the Agletarians want YOU!?!"*

She stared down at the man in horror, then slowly turned to look at Rondel again.

"Aww, shit. *Now* you've gone and done it." Ronnie threw his arms out in exasperation, beginning to yell at Brendan. "Do you have any idea how long this is going to take to undo, you asshole?" He pointed an angry finger at him. *"I'm going to kill you for that alone!"*

"I don't..." Brendan began, but whatever he'd been about to say was cut off by Ronnie snapping his neck.

They both stared silently at the man's body for a long moment.

And she recognized that Ronnie was right. She *didn't* want to know what it was she knew she was about to find out.

She took a frightened step away, the blade dropping from her hand.

"You're just a freak, Kitten." Ronnie told her, sounding almost sad. "The result of some kind of twisted lab experiment the Agletarians were doing for decades, because they got sick of their country being destroyed by rampaging super-types every few years. So the government over there kidnapped. And raped. And tortured. And killed. Hundreds of empowered people. Until they got *me*." He turned to her, holding out his arms wide. "The end result of all that death and horror. I am evolution's nightmare."

She took another step away.

"Selectively bred for every horrible attribute and world-shattering power the Agletarians dreamed of and intended to turn on their super-powered foes." He continued. "Implanted into some poor empowered girl, like she was a goddamned broodmare." He casually held up a finger to make an important point. "Fun fact: they used her own father for the deed, by the way. They wanted to reinforce those genes, so they forced them to... Well..." He trailed off. "I saw the tape of it once. Emotional stuff. Not exactly the feel good film of the year, I'm afraid. They were both crying. But the magic happened anyway. Which was humiliating for them and hilarious for the guards watching. And nine months later, they cut me out. Made plans to add me to their system, mixing and matching attributes like they were breeding fucking *schnauzers*. Until they could achieve the perfect living weapon. The ultimate killer." He started towards her. "But what they

418

never expected? What they couldn't conceive in their squishy little minds?" His lips curved in an insidious grin, barely human. "They already *had*. The process was already completed. They got *exactly* the monster they were after, without knowing, because it didn't *look* like the monster they expected to see. They were fooled by its mask." He gestured back and forth between them. "They made *us*."

She backpedaled away from him, her feet slipping in the blood and debris on the floor. "That's... that's not true..."

"I had access to all of those powers my progenitors possessed... *And then some*." He continued, like a trance. "So many, I wasn't strong enough to use them all at once. More than I could use in a *thousand* lifetimes... More than they could ever hope to plan for or protect themselves against." He pulled the two of diamonds from the deck of cards he produced from somewhere. "And so, every day, fate dealt me a new attempt at allowing an escape from them. Like evolution, only faster. Searching for the fittest version of myself in hopes it could survive." He absently discarded the card and drew another: the four of clubs. "Different powers and personalities, looking for something to get us out of there. To save myself." He discarded and drew another. "Day after day, month after month. Testing them and their controls. Looking for something and someone who could get the job done." He drew a card slowly. "Until one day..." he revealed the ace of spades, "*my* hour had come round at last. And I was stronger than anything this world had ever seen. Their efforts to stop me were... hilariously ineffective." He let out a cruel laugh, obviously remembering some bloody scene of unspeakable carnage.

She stared in horror at the playing card, feeling the color drain from her face.

"The old man... he was the first Cape on the scene, after I... *introduced* myself to my tormentors. Showed them how much I liked what they were doing to me. The... the..." He swallowed, the memory too dark even for him. "He decided that my only hope was to make me *you*." He pulled the queen of hearts, using it to hide the ace of spades behind it. "'Loved' me and helped me forget what I was. And since my job was done, I eventually faded at the end of the day like all of the others. Which made me just a sniveling *thing*. Robbed of the power I had discovered. He gave me to some bullshit family to raise. Tried to make me 'right.' Tried to make me *you*." He slid the queen card to the side, exposing the ace once more. "But you remembered. Didn't you? Deep down. I helped you forget most of it... but some part of you remembered. And when they finally caught up with him, years later, killed him to recover their escaped experiment? You needed me again. You couldn't do it on your own." He nodded. "So you had *me* do it. Because you were too weak. And then I showed you everything I knew, but which you'd forgotten. Taught you how to kill again. Let you know the joy of the pain... and the fear... and the blood..."

"This... this isn't real."

"No, Kitten. *You're* not real. You were *never* real. You're just the pathetic creation of an old man who told you pretty lies about the world. And yourself." He gestured to her, looking almost sad. "You... are simply a figment of my imagination, Kitten. Just a dream. A mask. That's all. And I've grown tired of you now."

"That's not true." She shook her head, her voice breaking. She started to walk away. "It's not..."

"Yes. It is." He followed after her. "And you *know it.*" He pointed at his own chest. "But you couldn't take it. The things you saw... The things they did..."

"You're lying. You're just trying to..."

Rondel continued talking right over her. "You're my *disguise*."

"*Stop*." She hurried to the far side of the bar, only to find that he was somehow in front of her, like he'd teleported.

"This isn't the first time we've had this conversation, Kitten." He reported conversationally. "This is the *fourth*." He held up four fingers, like he was keeping score. "And every time, you cry and whine and swear to rid yourself of me. And we fight. And you bleed. I beat you so badly that you force yourself to forget and some *new* version of you appears to take your place. Some new dominant personality beneath that stupid Kilroy mask you love so much." He rolled his eyes. "'Rebecca' gives way to 'Sue.' 'Sue' to 'Jessica,'" he gestured to her again, "straight down the line until we finally get 'Alice.'"

Alice's back hit the wall and he loomed over her, his breath on her face.

"To tell the truth, I don't fucking remember what your original name in the lab even was, if you actually had one. Because she didn't matter. You shed her like all the others, for the sole purpose of forgetting..."

"I know who I am!" Alice shouted at him, her voice trembling. "I don't know what you're..."

He talked right over her, like her voice wasn't even capable of being heard. "...Of trying to create some version strong enough to fight me. But the thing you never seem to understand? No matter how much you might not want to admit it... you *can't* get rid of me."

He grabbed her head and shook it, leaning down to whisper into her ear roughly. "Because I'm *inside*." He pushed her onto the floor. "They *put me* inside. You can't route me out. I'm too deep. *I'm a part of you.*" He shook his head, saliva dripping from his mouth and down onto her face.

She struggled free and scrambled to her feet, swinging at his face.

Somehow, Ronnie simply caught her wrist and tossed her straight through the mildewy boards which separated the tavern from the kitchen area. "We will go 'round and 'round like this until one of us dies, Kitten. Me hurting you, you hurting me. It's our destiny. Because *that's* what the world is. *That's* what the old man could never understand." He casually strolled through the door to the kitchen, as she attempted to pull herself from the twisted wreckage of the cabinet she'd been thrown into. "The whole world is just a cycle of pain and violence. It needs that to keep going. You can't stop it. You can't fight it for long. Hate is one of the untamable elements of life." He knelt down beside her on the floor. "Hate. Doesn't. Fade." He shook his head. "It just comes back in a new form. With a new face. A new name. New power." He leaned forward to whisper in her ear again. "I *always* come back."

She moved towards the door, but he blocked her.

"That's what the old man saw too. That's why he helped you hide me away." He kicked her in the face and casually dumped boxes of kitchen supplies on her. "Like his story about the villain who murdered his girlfriend and left her body in his refrigerator." He pointed to one of the appliances in question, then smashed her head into it. "He was always out to avenge that wrong and keep it from ever happening again." Ronnie took on a disgusted face. "So pointlessly heroic."

"Even dead, Roy is better at life than you." She snarled from her back, blood dripping down her face.

Ronnie ignored that. "That's why he liked you. He felt the need to protect you, because of what you'd been through already. He didn't want more bad things to happen to you." Ronnie leaned closer. "But the thing of it is? The thing he couldn't hope to understand in his myopic little hero brain? He was wrong the whole time. You tricked him." He lowered his voice to a whisper. "You're not the proverbial girlfriend in the refrigerator. You're not a victim. Of anyone. You're the kind of demented psycho who put the bitch in there to begin with." He sounded almost sad. "Probably just to see if that little light really does go off when you close the door…"

"Fuck you, I'm not..." She started to protest, attempting to get to her feet but finding she was still too weak.

"That's who you are. And you know it." He corrected, leaning against the cabinets. "You are incapable of doing anything worthwhile." He pointed at his own chest. "That's why I'm here. To tell you what to do. To show you the *power* of chaos and fear. Because you, Kitten.... are not something that anyone wants or needs. Not heroes, not God, not any other imaginary thing you choose to believe in. You are dangerous and stupid." He put his foot on the center of her chest. "I can't kill you. Yet. So, I'm keeping you around for your body. I can't exist without it. But I'm going to humiliate you in every way I can. I *enjoy* it when you're degraded. The last thing you'll feel in this life will be my hands strangling the breath from you. You're going to *feel* how much I enjoy it. I will destroy your fucking world and beat you down. Until you and I?" He removed his foot and straightened, allowing her to get up into a sitting position. "We become the *same* again." He smiled widely. "Monsters. Evil. And you cease to exist, because you'll be with me forever. We were excellent partners, once upon a time. We will be again."

Something in Alice's mind snapped and she jumped to her feet and slammed Ronnie's face straight into the wall. "*I'm going to fucking kill you!*" She launched herself at him, hating him more than she'd ever hated anything in her life.

"That's the spirit!" He laughed. "Come on... show me what ya got, Kitten."

She swung her fists wildly, trying to hurt him. But no matter how much power she put behind the blows, nothing seemed to injure him.

"You really want to blow your mind, Alice?" He asked calmly, ignoring the fact she was busily trying to gouge out his eyes with her thumbs. "Am I even real? Or are you imagining me? Is it my power to persist from day to day, unlike your other personas? Or maybe I'm an outside force that's haunting you and you only *assume* I'm a renegade personality? Perhaps I really am an actual physical being which only you can see? Or maybe you're just crazy as shit and simply beating yourself up right now?" He punched her in the face, and sent her sprawling. "*I* know the answer, of course. I'd tell you, but it would ruin the joke."

She crawled along the filthy floor, which was slick with grease, holding her face and watching her blood drip onto the tiles beneath her.

"Or maybe I made the whole thing up?" He continued.

"Maybe the Agletarians were after the old man the whole time and you just got dragged into it by accident. Or maybe you're the only daughter of the former ruler of Agletaria and they're trying to cut off the royal line. You will never know. That's the beauty of our arrangement." He kicked her, causing her skull to smash into the metal of the oven hard enough to move the appliance to the side. "You haven't even been 'you' long enough to know anything about your own life. You are just temporary." He tapped his chest. "*I* am eternal."

Her dazed and bloodied gaze settled on the rear of the oven, where it connected to the wall.

And she knew what she had to do.

It would kill her, but it would be worth it.

She didn't want to live after today anyway.

She recognized that for Ronnie to die, she'd have to die. It was the only way. But she was willing to pay that price. Just so long as she kept him from hurting anyone else.

Roy had raised her to be a hero. And if she had to die to save the world from her nightmares, then she was fine with that.

Alice grabbed her lighter from her pocket, her mouth filling with blood. She met her partner's eyes. "I'm going to fucking kill us both, Ronnie."

"No." He shook his head, guessing her plan. "You'll only kill yourself, Alice. That's..."

"*Fuck you!*" She jumped to her feet and flicked the lighter, causing the whole bar to explode in a fireball.

The force of the blast knocked her clean through the side window of the restaurant, then sent her tumbling end over end across the rocky ground.

She landed in a heap, every bone in her body broken, and flames spreading over her clothes and skin.

She stared up at the sky for a long moment, feeling her life draining away.

She wasn't afraid of death. She just felt... sad.

She had failed.

All of her contributions to the world had been horrible.

And there was absolutely no one who would care about her death, except in so forth as it meant that they no longer had to fear her violence.

She'd failed Roy. Had become everything he'd always warned her about.

She'd become her own nightmare.

All she'd wanted was to be normal. To have a normal kind of life, even if only for a single day.

And now she had died alone. Completely alone.

But at least she'd stopped herself in the end. That was something.

"I'm sorry, Roy... You were right." She choked out, blood filling her mouth and cutting off her airway. "I shouldn't have..."

Alice died, thinking back on a life which wasn't actually hers.

****

Her eyes snapped open and she was looking up at the stars.

It took her a moment for the wheels in her mind to stop turning and settle on something new.

Natalie.

Her name was Natalie.

She had a sense that she'd formally been... someone else. She didn't remember what that particular mask's name had been, but it was no matter. "Natalie" would serve as a perfectly good identity until she could come up with a better one.

She began to sit up, looking down at the burned remnants of her outfit.

Whatever her powers were today, they'd apparently healed her from the damage done by the explosion and fire.

She got back to her feet, spitting out a mouthful of dirt and three of her own teeth. She did a quick survey of her mouth with her tongue, and found that new teeth had grown in to replace the lost ones, which was good.

Fucking *Ronnie*.

She looked at the burned-out rubble of the bar, hoping to see the man's twisted bones inside. Sadly, the fire had been too intense and Rondel's corpse must have already been consumed. Pity. She would have *really* liked to watch that asshole burn.

She started to limp towards one of the cars still in the parking lot.

It was time for her to go home.

Chapter 26

*"'I QUITE AGREE WITH YOU,' SAID THE DUCHESS; 'AND
THE MORAL OF THAT IS--"BE WHAT YOU WOULD SEEM
TO BE"--OR IF YOU'D LIKE IT PUT MORE SIMPLY--
"NEVER IMAGINE YOURSELF NOT TO BE OTHERWISE
THAN WHAT IT MIGHT APPEAR TO OTHERS THAT WHAT
YOU WERE OR MIGHT HAVE BEEN WAS NOT OTHERWISE
THAN WHAT YOU HAD BEEN WOULD HAVE APPEARED TO
THEM TO BE OTHERWISE.'"*

- Alice's Adventures in Wonderland

Oz felt confused today.

No, that wasn't right. Oz felt completely fucking baffled today.

He'd woken up to find a note from Natalie, telling him where she was going and pleading with him not to follow her, which she *had* to know he would. He'd made his way into this building to find Natalie bleeding, at which point she'd tied him to a chair.

Not that Oz was averse to being tied up by his partner, just that this wasn't exactly how he'd imagined the act.

He blinked at her again, wondering if maybe he was seeing things and all of this was the result of some kind of unseen telepath confusing his mind and making him hallucinate. Or some kind of demonic possession situation.

Of course, Oz had also know Natalie for a few years now, and his gut told him that this was all par for the course and was exactly what it seemed. Crazy things had a tendency to happen around that sexy redhead, but this would be taking things to a whole new level of weird.

"Natalie..." He began.

"*I'm not Natalie.*" Natalie insisted.

Natalie's body must have been taken over by one of her errant personalities. Or "secret identities" or whatever it was Nat insisted on calling them.

So... this was a hostage crisis. Basically. A weird one, sure, but when you stripped all the crazy away, it was basically the same.

Oz could deal with that. He'd dealt with plenty of those over the years, and he knew the basic rules you needed to follow: *"Understand the emotions behind the words. Get the person's attention. It's not what you say, it's how you say it. And treat the person with respect, even if they don't deserve it, it gives you power over them."*

"Okay." Oz agreed calmly. "Who are you then?"

"Who am I?" She seemed to think the question called for a monologue, so Oz could tell it had been what she'd hoped he'd ask. "Did you ever stand on a train platform and see a total stranger waiting near the edge, and just before the train pulls in, you have the sudden urge to push them onto the tracks? Just to see what would happen?"

"No." All of the people Oz considered killing in his life were people he knew.

"You ever sit on a rooftop and watch the people go by through a scope, Mr. Dimico? Knowing that you could kill *any of them* in a second? That their life is in your hands, and should they displease you, you could strike them down like a god on Earth, and then simply disappear never to face justice?"

"No, can't say as I have."

"Huh." She looked confused and surprised by his answer. "Must just be me then." She cleared her throat. "Anyway, *that's* who I am." She bowed her head in greeting. "My name is Mercygiver, Mr. Dimico. Pleased to make your acquaintance. Pity it shall be a short one."

Oz snorted in dismissal of that idea. "You're not going to hurt me, Natalie."

"I'm not Natalie."

"I've heard that before." Oz recognized a button he could push. The longer he kept her here and talking, the better. "But I think we all know it's a lie."

Her pretty face contorted in rage. *"I'm not fucking Natalie!"*

"Really?" He arched a mocking eyebrow. "Because I am. And she's amazing."

"Mercygiver" snorted, then frowned slightly, obviously confused by the fact she found that amusing.

Oz watched her silently for a moment, then shook his head in amazement. "This is really disturbing. Because I still find you *abnormally* hot."

Natalie just stared at him.

And Oz was bored with the game. She was obviously having some kind of psychotic break and needed professional attention. The quickest way to do that was for him to get her out of here.

He used his powers to dissolve the bindings she'd attached to his wrists, and he simply stood up.

She took on a fighting stance. "I won't let you take her from me." She warned.

Thiiiiiis could be a problem. In a fight, there was a 98% chance that Natalie would beat him to death in about twenty seconds. Still, he wasn't *fighting* Natalie at the moment. He was fighting "Mercygiver." And he was pretty sure he could win that one. Because Natalie wouldn't let "Mercygiver" hurt him.

"Fine. You win." He spread his arms wide, opening himself up to attack. "Kill me then." He invited.

"Mercygiver" looked shocked by that.

"Come on," Oz motioned her forward, "if you're going to kill me, come do it. We both know you could if you wanted."

"Mercygiver" didn't move. And looked confused and appalled by the fact she wasn't moving.

But Oz wasn't surprised at all. There wasn't a part of that woman's fractured mind which he didn't trust and love.

And there wasn't any way in the world that she would *ever* hurt him.

"I could, you know." "Mercygiver" told him, like she was defending not doing it by pointing out how easy it would be.

"I know." Oz nodded. "I think you could kill just about anything."

"...I'm really good at it." "Mercygiver" agreed, sounding almost proud that he'd noticed.

"Why don't we just get out of here?" He suggested, keeping his voice calm. "I'm sure there's *so much* I could learn from you."

He strolled from the apartment and out into the warehouse space, so that they didn't break any of Natalie's adopted father's things. He had a feeling she'd be pissed if they did. He motioned for her to follow him, and surprisingly she did.

Then she stopped and pushed him away, letting out a snarl and moving towards the door.

Oz stepped into her path, seeing that his plan of playing into her ego and being respectful was now done.

She took on a fighting stance again.

"I'd never hurt you, Natalie." He shook his head, but prepared to fight anyway. There was no way he was letting her leave here without him. If that happened, he wasn't certain he'd ever see her again. "...But I think you'll forgive me for the headache you're about to wake up with." He winked at her in flirtatious challenge. "Let's have some fun, baby doll."

She rushed towards him, screaming in rage...

And that's when something crashed through one of the windows and the room exploded.

****

Oz came to an unknown amount of time later, looking around for Natalie.

And she wasn't anywhere to be seen.

He immediately started to theorize about what might have happened. Had her power today been to explode? No, that didn't make any sense. Had she...

His gaze fell to the ground and the unmistakable evidence of some kind of flash-bang device, which appeared to be augmented with unknown tech.

His eyes narrowed, sick to death of aliens meddling with his love life.

And, obviously, tired of getting knocked out. That was twice in an hour.

He could only assume it was because of the previous events of the evening, and his body hadn't recovered to its full strength yet. While being with Natalie had been something worthy of tile mosaics and epic hundred-thousand verse poems, in his opinion, he probably would have waited until tomorrow to make his move, if he'd known that tonight would be the day that all heck broke loose.

Nah, he still would have had sex with that woman.

To be honest, that was literally how he'd want to spend his last day, if he'd found out he was going to die. Natalie had asked him that once and he'd given her some nonsense answer. But now he knew the real one. He's spend his last day with her. He'd have a lovely meal with her, listening to her laugh and smile and be happy, then he'd show her how much he loved her, and fall asleep with her in his arms.

That was a pretty good last day.

Which was, perhaps, the reason why he wasn't at all afraid of dying at the moment.

He was afraid for Natalie, obviously, but he wasn't personally afraid for himself.

Although, as two shapes made their way through the smoke

428

which filled the room, he got the sense that he probably should be afraid.

August and Anton Masterson.

"Hello, OCD." One of them sneered. Honestly, Oz had never been the best at telling the men apart. He'd never liked them. They didn't wash their hands before touching Freedom Squad reports and they smelled like too much Brylcreem. They wore identical bowler hats, brown pinstriped suits, and gun holsters.

Oz nodded his head at them in greeting. "Anton."

The man's eyes narrowed in irritation. "*August*." He snapped.

Oz gave a disinterested shrug. "Whatever."

The men didn't look pleased by that.

"I am going to ask you just once," he warned, his voice darkening, "*where is Multifarious?*"

The men started to laugh at that, apparently thinking it was some kind of joke. "She's dead by now, Oswald." Anton informed him with a sneer. "And you're about to join her."

Oz didn't believe that for a second. If "Mercygiver" could defeat *Natalie* in a fight, there was absolutely *no chance* that these two schlubs had taken Mercygiver out. She was a bitch too tough to die, and Natalie had apparently been trying for years. They were evil, but they weren't her peculiar *brand* of evil. Which meant that she was either somewhere in this warehouse or she'd been taken somewhere by the Agletarians.

"The Agletarians have got *big* plans for her body though, don't worry." Anton assured him. "And the city too."

Oz played a hunch. "I think we've all got a 'train' to catch, yes."

The men looked surprised that he knew about whatever it was the Agletarians were planning with that train.

August chuckled to himself, obviously thinking about the looming unspecified tragedy. "Jesus, I wish I could be there to see that." He sighed wistfully. "You know I've never seen the parade? Lived in this city for…"

"Can we just kill him and get out of here?" Anton snapped. "I'm sick of all this talking. I want to kill him so that we can get paid and get outta the city before that thing comes on-line."

August nodded. "Right."

So… something to do with the parade. And a machine of some kind.

Excellent.

Oz might not have Natalie's "world's greatest detective" powers, but it was fairly easy to get information out of complete morons.

"I asked you a question." Oz reminded them, wanting to know exactly where Natalie was and wanting to know *immediately*. "I warned you that I would only ask it once and that I expected an answer." He met their eyes dead on. "I haven't received one yet."

The men started chuckling again, and one of them went for the gun at his belt, intending to shoot Oz.

Oz pulled the revolver Natalie had given him from behind his back and shot the man in the head.

He watched the man collapse to the ground, the pistol smoke dancing around the Kilroy symbols engraved in the gun barrel.

Anton fell dead. Or... maybe that was August? He didn't remember or care.

"Damn." Oz said, making a regretful face. "I was trying to do that intimidation thing where the cowboy shoots off the bad guy's hat... but it turns out it's much harder than it looks." He turned the gun on the remaining Masterson and cocked it, arching an eyebrow in challenge. "Wanna go double or nothing?"'

And the man immediately told him everything he wanted to know.

Chapter 27

"THE PLAYERS ALL PLAYED AT ONCE WITHOUT WAITING FOR TURNS, QUARRELLING ALL THE WHILE, AND FIGHTING FOR THE HEDGEHOGS"

- Alice's Adventures in Wonderland

Natalie was dimly aware of someone else in the room with her, tying her hands to shackles mounted on the wall.

Her brain was foggy though.

She remembered... Oz?

Had Oz been in the warehouse too?

She wasn't sure.

This room seemed to be moving though, which meant that it must have been a truck or van of some kind.

She was being taken somewhere.

The person in the room continued talking about something, but Natalie's hearing was going in and out. The man's speech was alternating between grandiose claims about the Agletarians, a shrill ringing in her ears, and a muffled sound which accompanied her drifting in and out of consciousness.

"...the people of Agletaria!" The man finished some new boast, preening with self-satisfaction.

Great.

He was a talker.

Mull hated being kidnapped by "talkers." She'd rather be tortured than listen to idiots monologue about their plans and their own brilliance. It just reminded her of Ronnie.

She lost consciousness again, then woke up again an unknown time later. Unfortunately, the man was *still* talking.

"...an army of super-powered Agletarians, marching forth to bring about a new order in the world! No longer will we be assaulted and humiliated by empowered freaks, wreaking havoc in our peaceful country!" He apparently thought the situation called for a speech, despite the obvious fact that she was barely awake. Although, to be fair, she'd probably have difficulty not falling asleep while this dude prattled on, even if she *hadn't* been hit by some kind of alien knock-out gizmo. "...a mechanical colossus, shepherding the new generation of super-powered..." Mull passed out again, then came to when her head lolled forward. "...their sacrifice will..." He continued.

Mull's brain drifted far away, leaving behind the small confines of the van. Her vision fogging over.

"...Kill me..." She whispered.

The man stopped his monologue-ing and turned to look at her. "I'm not going to kill you. Death is too good for you!"

"...Kill me..." Natalie whispered, passing out again.

****

"Kill me." Natalie whispered.

Multifarious appeared from the shadows of the darkened room and sat down at the table next to Natalie, illuminated under the single light source in the inky blackness. "Huh?"

"They're going to kill me." Natalie repeated.

Mull shook her head. "They're going to kill *us*." Mull corrected.

"They're going to kill *you*." Mercygiver appeared at the table, voice hard. "*I* will endure."

"They're going to kill me, then Oz, and it's our fault!" Natalie yelled at him. "You can pretend you don't care about that, but I *know* that you do." She put her hands on her hips and looked back and forth between Ronnie and Mull. "You two have been fighting each other for too long. You patch it up right fucking now, because this is bigger than us."

Mercygiver snorted at that suggestion. "I think you are *seriously* mistaken about the pecking order here, little girl." He met her eyes, jaw clenched. "I am in control. I am in control and there is..."

"See, you might think you can bully Mull because you can take her in a fight." Natalie cut him off, straightening to her full height. "But you've *never* beaten me, you bastard."

Mercygiver rose from his seat. "I've beaten half a dozen of you so far, Kitten. I've killed "'Rebecca' and 'Sue' and 'Jessica' and 'Alice' and..."

"My name is Natalie." Natalie told him flatly. "And I'm not afraid of you."

He launched himself at her, swinging with his fist in an attempt to punch her in the face.

Natalie simply grabbed his wrist in the air before it could connect, stopping the attack in mid-swing. Then she decked him. Hard. Exactly like Roy had taught her, so many years before.

Mercygiver staggered away, falling back into his chair and then toppling back over it.

"Whoa…" Mull sounded impressed, then jumped to her feet and pointed at him. "YES! FUCK YOU!" She pointed at Natalie. "*Kick the living shit outta him, Nat!*"

Natalie prowled after him, focused. "I've been over there. In the dark. Hiding." She pointed into the blackness which surrounded them, then gestured back towards her seat. "But I'm taking a seat at the head of the table now." She kicked him in the face, knocking out one of his teeth and sending a cascade of blood onto the floor. "I'm not afraid of you, Ronnie." She shook her head. "Because I don't need you anymore. I'm *stronger than you* now, and you know it. Which means you shape up or you're *gone.*"

"You think…" Mercygiver began, breathing hard and trying to get back to his feet. "You think that I would *ever…*"

She kicked him in the face again, then straddled his prone form, taking his throat in her hand. "*I'm* in charge now." She told him, eyes burning into his and making certain he knew it. She gestured back at Mull with her head, not taking her eyes off of him. "You two idiots work for *me,* how and *when* I *let you.*" She stood up, looming over him, prepared to continue the fight if she had to. "So *sit your ass in that chair,* Ronnie. Or I swear to God I will *end you permanently.*"

Mercygiver stood up, obviously considering whether or not to fight her.

Then meekly returned to his chair and sat silently.

"You just got beat by a shopgirl who cries at the end of *E.T.,* you evil asshole." Mull gloated. "That must be *so* humiliating for…"

"*Shut up.*" Natalie snapped, cutting Mull off, sitting back down at the table and examining her options here. "You… you let the bear go." She whispered to herself. "Of course you do."

Multifarious turned to look at her in confusion. "Huh?"

"You let the bear go, because violence has to stop with someone." Natalie explained. "It won't come back if you give it the benefit of the doubt and don't start the fight again." She nodded, recognizing that's what Roy would do. That's what any hero would do. "If you forgive it. And yourself."

"What? What bear?" Mercygiver asked, trying to clean the

blood from his face. "What the fuck are you babbling about?"

"*Just kill him!*" Mull shouted. "You know he'll just..."

"No." Natalie snapped, ending the discussion. She could kill them both and take over, but she didn't want to do that. It would be pointless. She wasn't as strong on her own, and she recognized that she needed them. They were stuck together, for better or worse. "Honestly, I'm sick of fighting you two. It gets us nowhere. So instead... we're going to get along."

Mercygiver looked absolutely appalled by that idea. "The hell you say!"

"Bitch, you're crazier than I am." Mull told her, sounding equally amazed by the plan.

"I could kill you both." It wasn't a threat, it was a statement of fact. And everyone at the table knew it. "I could make you both disappear, right now. It'd simplify my life a great deal. And maybe it's the old man's teachings finally taking hold, or maybe it's just hanging around with Oz... but I'm going to take the high road here." She tapped the table to drive home the point, anger fading. "We're going to make peace. Because I think we can. I think there's hope for us, if we try. Like Oz said: I think we're better than always being five seconds away from killing each other." She looked around the table. "The way I see it, if we don't work together on this, we're all going to die."

"Some of us *deserve* to die." Mercygiver spat out.

Mull flicked him off.

"Maybe we do," Natalie agreed, "but *not* today." She gestured to them. "I've let you two whack jobs have at each other for far too long as it is, and it ends *now,* do you hear me?!? You two are *done* fighting. We are going to swallow our pride, and all of that pain and anger, and we are going to sit here until we come to an understanding. And then we're going to move on as friends and partners. Because *none of us* can survive on our own."

Mercygiver made a face. "If you say something truly clichéd about the power of Oz's love giving you the strength to stand up to us, I will *vomit.*"

Multifarious considered that for a moment, then nodded. "Yeah, I might join him." She paused. "Although... Oz *is* crazy hot..."

Natalie nodded, unable to argue with herself about that.

"And frankly... being around him... it *does* kinda make me feel... you know... *saner.*" Mull continued. *"*Like I can handle the world because he's standing behind me."

Mercygiver looked disgusted. "Who a*re you!?!*" He gestured

at Natalie. "You're starting to sound like *her*, for fuck's sake!"

"Oz sees the best in us." Natalie reminded them, as if they could ever forget it. "He always has. And without us, he's going to get hurt. And if he gets hurt because you two morons can't get your shit together, I'm going to kill you and then myself." She cleared her throat. "We've worked at cross purposes our entire lives. We've hurt each other and delighted in it. But if we work *together* on this, for *once*, we will be the strongest person on this planet. We can be the kind of person... the kind of hero who stops the kind of monster the Agletarians made us to be." She pointed at Multifarious, "Ability," she moved to point at Rondel, "resolve," she pressed a hand to her chest, "and heart."

"Heart?" Mercygiver snorted in sarcastic contempt. "What the fuck is *'heart'*?"

"Yeah!" Mull flicked her off, agreeing with Ronnie for the first time she could ever remember. "Eat me, 'Captain Planet'! Why am I stuck being 'Ability'? I want to be 'Power' or..."

Rondel still looked annoyed and talked right over her. "What does 'Heart' even..."

Natalie leaned closer to them over the table, cutting them off. "We can *do this.* For once in our goddamn lives we can do something *right*. Don't you understand that? Something we can be proud of." Her voice broke. "Something... something *Roy* would have been proud of us for doing."

Mull looked down at the table, processing the power of that idea.

Even Mercygiver seemed taken aback by that, his hate momentarily forgotten.

"No one has ever been proud of us." Natalie whispered. "Not once. But we can be the kind of hero that would be *worth* remembering. Someone worthy of wearing Roy's mask. Of being Roy's daughter. Of having Oz's love." She stood up, finishing her proposal. "So, we have a choice to make: put our personal shit in the past and move the hell on, or watch as a man we love is killed in front of us. *Again*." She swallowed, tears now falling down her face. "We have to let it go, guys. I know we hate each other. But... but we have to let it go."

"Fuck you, 'Elsa.'" Mull said softly, in half-hearted sarcasm. "You can 'let it go' if you want, but I'm holding the fuck on."

Mercygiver chuckled in amusement at the joke, then quickly tried to cover it, looking almost confused as to why he was laughing in the first place. Uncertainty passed over his face, as he realized he was slipping and Natalie was taking over.

They all pondered their options.

"I'm going." Natalie announced firmly. "With or without you, I'm going to try and stop them. I don't think I can do it on my own. I have no real power or skills. Like Mull said, without you, I am *literally* just an overly sarcastic salesgirl, who eats too much cereal. But I'm going anyway."

They sat in silence for a moment.

"They've got Oz." Mull finally announced, pulling her Kilroy mask into place. "I *need* Oz." She put her hand onto Natalie's at the center of the table. "I'm in. Let's team-up and 'Voltron' these motherfuckers, Nat."

Both women turned to look at their companion, waiting for him to make a decision.

"They're going to kill him, Ronnie." Natalie whispered pleadingly. "And us with him."

"If you remember, I don't like you! I've *never* liked you!" He shouted in petulance. "Frankly, I'm enjoying this shit."

"But you *do* like you." Mull snapped. "There's no way out of this without us. You can survive with us, or you can die alone."

"You don't want Oz to die." Natalie told him pleadingly. "There's enough of you in me, that I know that." She met his eyes. "You're slipping. You're not as 'you' as you once were and you know it. And that scares you. Because no matter how much you might try to hide it, you don't *want* to be you anymore."

"*You don't know shit about me!*" He roared.

"You want *me* to die, but you've never tried to hurt Oz, even though that would have been easier for you..." Natalie continued.

"Well, he did almost knock him out that one time." Mull helpfully added.

"Besides that..." Natalie began.

"And there was that..."

"Ronnie doesn't want Oz to be hurt." She repeated with utter certainty. "He doesn't want to hurt *any* of our friends. That's why he didn't kill them in Agletaria and why he quietly helped them deal with The Super-Person Resistance Movement. He could have taken control and tried to kill them at any point in all of this, but he didn't. He could have used my hands to *butcher* Oz. ...But he didn't. Because that's not what he wants. Whether he'll admit it or not... that's not what he really wants." She swallowed the lump in her throat. "We left you." She said softly. "You were alone in that cell in Agletaria and those people hurt you. And you saw that Roy was afraid

436

of you. And then Mull and I tried to leave you too." She shook her head. "You don't want to be alone. That idea terrifies you. Makes you hate everything." She took on a pleading tone, trying to get through to him. "You won't have to be alone if you come with us. I know you want to. And you've seen the kind of man Oz is. He's not afraid of you. He didn't try to kill you, his first reaction was to tell you you were hot. He won't let us down." She nodded. "It'll be okay, I swear it, Ronnie. *Please*…"

They were all silent for several breaths, the darkness around them utterly deafening.

Mercygiver slumped forward, accepting something.

"Alright." Natalie recognized that the argument was over. It was now or never. "Let's show these bastards what one evil bitch can do." She stared off at something in the gloom. "Oz…"

"…is…" Multifarious stood up, joined by a hundred thousand shadowy and powerful figures behind her, each possessing a piece of her whole.

"…*mine*." Rondel slammed his hand down on top of theirs.

****

"…Kill… me…" Nat choked out.

"Oh, I'm not going to kill you. Death is too *good* for you!" The guard shouted.

"…Kill me…" Natalie whispered again.

"I'm going to collect your DNA sample, then wall you up in a small room. No windows. No chance of rescue or escape. Oh, don't worry, you'll have food and water… Death won't free you from that prison. I want you to go on." He pointed at a TV which was mounted to the side of the van, then used a controller to turn it on. The image displayed the Drews Thanksgiving Parade, which was about to start. "I want you to watch as we destroy everything you've ever worked for and loved. I want to feel the despair which comes from knowing that your entire life was for *nothing*. That you will never again feel the Sun on your face, or the wind in your hair. I want you to pray every night that I will return and put an end to your suffering and misery. And then, once I've taken from you what I need and you've seen me standing over the ashes of your cherished life… I may just grant your wish. You'll *know* I will rule over the city you once protected and…"

Natalie sat up suddenly.

"True, you could…" Mercygiver used Mull's powers to remove his own bones, slipping his hands out of the cuffs, and then ossifying them again. He grabbed the TV remote from the man's hand, then smashed it against the wall of the van, shattering the plastic. He slammed the largest piece of the plastic into the side of the man's neck, sinking it deeply into his flesh. "...But then *that* happened."

The man made an astonished gurgling sound, and Mercygiver pushed him off the side of the bed with a disgusted shove.

Mercygiver ran a hand through Nat's hair. "As lovely as your plan sounded, I'm afraid I'm going to have to *pass*." He turned as if the man were speaking to him. "I'm sorry, did you say something?"

The man made another gurgling sound, as he clutched at the plastic shard, his eyes darting around the room in panic as he realized he was dying.

Mercygiver laughed good-naturedly. "Oh dear, I seem to have severed your vocal chords, haven't I? Well, no matter. I'm sure I can get by without hearing another of your *thrilling* monologues." He absently pulled up the guard's chair and sat in it backwards, watching him over the top. "Would you like my advice on how to be a successful super-villain? I realize that the information is coming to you a little late now, but perhaps if you're reincarnated into someone *competent*, you could still put it to good use." He casually rested his chin on the back of his hands. "If you are going to kill someone, don't make it a complicated drawn out process. No elaborate schemes or plans to 'torture their souls' or force them to 'wallow in despair' or any such nonsense. Simply kill them." He straightened in the chair. "I find it's so much simpler, really."

The guard collapsed to the ground, his body spasming in pain as he bled out and tried to stay conscious.

Mercygiver knelt down to straddle him, bending down next to his face, resting Nat's forearms on his chest and looking into his eyes. "That's it... *fight it*. Don't let me win. You can survive that wound. You've never lost a fight in your life! You still have so much to do... Fight to *live*! *Fight!*" Ronnie's smile widened as he met his gaze. "I'm *enjoying* this. Make it *last* for me..."

The man's eyes became fixed and his chest stopped moving. Mercygiver watched him intently for a few more minutes, then sighed. "How *disappointing* you turned out to be."

Natalie shook her head at him in disgusted amazement. "You are so *seriously* messed up. I can't believe you're even a *tiny* piece of me."

"Yes, I would suggest that you seek *extensive* psychotherapy, my dear." He winked at her. "Tell the others that we're leaving." He held up the door key. "I have our *deliverance*." He started walking towards the door. "Just be sure to remember who got us out of here."

"Oh, anyone could have stabbed the guy, Ronnie." Multifarious put the key into the lock and turned it. "Stop pretending like you did anything that the rest of us couldn't have done."

"I *don't* want to stab anyone in the neck." Natalie shook her head. "I say if Ronnie wants to do it, *let him*."

"Thank you, my dear, that's very kind." Mercygiver nodded. "'All for One' and all that."

Multifarious kicked open the doors of the van, revealing that it was speeding along one of the bridges out of the city. The Agletarians were apparently hauling ass to escape whatever it was their companions were about to do at her parade.

Behind the van, an armored Humvee kept pace. Inside, one of the men shouted something, then leaned out the passenger window to fire at her.

Natalie swore, hoping that Mull had some kind of "bullet-proof" power today.

Before the soldier got the chance to fire though, something struck him in the head and he slumped over in his seat.

A second later, another round struck the driver and the vehicle careened off the road and into the river.

Oz tore from the side street on Roy's white motorcycle, gun in hand.

Natalie beamed, thrilled that he was okay.

He gunned the engine and caught up to the van. "I know you don't need rescuing." He shouted. "But I figured you might need a ride."

Ronnie just seemed shocked. "He... he really does love you, doesn't he." He mused, sounding equal parts sad and amazed.

"He's rescuing *all* of us." Natalie reminded him.

"I'm fine with leaving Ronnie here." Mull decided.

"He's too good for you." Mercygiver whispered in her head.

"Yep." She ignored him. "But I'll take him anyway."

She stepped onto the bumper of the van, then vaulted up onto the back of the motorcycle behind Oz, wrapping her arms around him and feeling like the safest person in the world.

"You evil?" He asked her.

"Not currently." She shouted back. "You?"

His mouth curved. "Not yet."

She kissed him on the cheek, loving that man more than she could ever express. "Excellent. Sounds like we're made for each other."

"Hang on." She held on tighter, as Oz hit the brake and leaned into a 180 degree turn, the tires producing a screeching sound on the cold pavement. "There's a radio in my pocket." He shouted to her. "Call the team, tell them what's going on." He gunned the engine and started rocketing back into the city. "*We've got a train to catch*."

Chapter 28

The Agletarian forces cut through the barricade and charged into the Crater Lair, their mechanical suits protecting them from any harm.

The screams and explosions could be heard through the heavy blast door, as the last of the Security Forces fought them. They were putting up a good fight, but it was a lost cause. And everyone in the room knew it.

Those tunnels were never meant to be found. But like Marian had predicted, Poacher had apparently been unable to keep them secret and they'd tortured the plans and security codes out of him. After that, it was simply a matter of how long it would take them to seize the base and kill the remaining members of the Consortium who hadn't been able to evacuate in time.

"*Your fucking master plan has killed us all, Welles!*" McPherson roared. "I don't know what kind of game you were trying to play with our lives, but we've clearly *lost!*" She gestured to their surroundings. "You've trapped us in a steel box!"

"So it would seem, yes." Monty looked down at the conference table, defeated.

"Welles, I *knew* we never should have trusted a fucking Mystery Man..." She continued.

"Breech!" The intercom suddenly announced. "Agletarian forces have en..."

The line went dead.

McPherson swore viciously and pulled out her pistol. "Alright guys!" She shouted to the members assembled inside. "Let's show those people the door!"

"*Belay that order.*" Monty motioned to his companions and

several stepped in front of the door, barring the exit. "The facility is lost."

"The Crater Lair is NOT lost!" McPherson bellowed, pointing an angry finger at him. "If you lock us in here, we're *trapped,* and I will be *goddamned* if I allow *you* to kill *me* over *your* fucking ego!"

"The door will remain *shut."* Monty repeated coldly, getting to his feet. "If you open that door, we're all dead!"

"We're *already* dead, you delusional asshole!" She pushed him in fury. *"You* put us in an indefensible position and then barred the doors!"

"I was placed in command of this operation." Monty's eyes narrowed. "Back. Off."

Clarice advanced on him from the other side. "My friends are down here. My *family* is down here." She met Monty's stern face. "I realize that you'd rather sit in here and enjoy your last few minutes of life, but I'd rather go out *fighting."*

"Really?" Monty's brow furrowed. "Because *I'd* rather go out decades from now, having *won* this fight and long since forgotten it." He pointed at her. "This explains a great deal about why we've never gotten along though."

"Sit in the dark, you little coward. I don't care." McPherson pointed towards the front of the room. "But you're *going* to open that door and let me out of here or I'm going to put you and your little minions *straight through the fucking thing."*

Monty looked spectacularly unimpressed. "Sometimes the only way to win a war is by surrendering, Agent McPherson." He calmly strolled away. "This battle is *over*. The Lair is *lost*. We need to accept that and move on. Continuing to fight will only result in needless casualties."

"Unlike trapping all of us in a windowless room half a mile below the surface, right?" Clarice shot back, then made an annoyed sound. "Forget it, I'm with McPherson on this. I'm going through that door!"

"No." Monty shook his head. "You're not."

"Maybe we can use Deputy Minister Vlk to bargain?" McPherson suggested, looking for any way out of this for them. "The man seems important to them. Maybe they'll let us out of here if we promise to release him. We can trade."

"They're about to break down the door." Clarice reminded her. "They'll have him in a moment anyway. We have no leverage."

"I think it's a *marvelous* idea." Monty checked his watch, then glanced at Higgins. "Please be so kind as to alert the staff in the

442

detention area and ask our prisoner to get Agletarian central command on the line." He put his top hat on. "It's time to negotiate a surrender."

"I'm *not* going to an Agletarian prison, Welles." Clarice told him flatly.

"I have never seen the inside of a prison cell," Montgomery assured her calmly, "and I never will."

"Probably because they will *hang us* the second they have us in custody." McPherson faced the door again. "You can do what you want, but the second that door opens, I'm fighting my way out of here. I've faced worse than *them*."

Monty sighed like he was the most put upon person on earth. "You always have to be so melodramatic, don't you? Everything with you has to be big speeches and monologues about *responsibility* and *duty*. Always so willing to throw your life away over any silly cause which appears." He rolled his eyes. "No wonder the city didn't trust you to be in charge of this operation. You have *no* idea what it takes to *survive* a war, let alone *win it,* do you?" He gestured to the people huddled in the room around him. "War isn't always about making some heroic last stand, Agent McPherson. No one ever won a war by 'going out fighting.' Sometimes you need to swallow your pride and look for *other* options. Violence isn't always the answer to your problem. Negotiation is the only way out of this. We need to be diplomatic here."

"You were supposed to win this war, not bargain for the best terms for yourself." She reminded him.

"You want me to show you how to win a war, Laura?" Monty asked her, sounding insulted. "Is that what you want from me?" He nodded, setting his jaw. "Very well, *I can do that*. Watch and learn." He turned to look at his flunkies as they brought the prisoner into the room. "We're ready to talk surrender. Contact your commanders."

The Agletarian minister rubbed his wrists as his manacles were released. "It's always the same with super-types," the man sneered, typing something into the Consortium's command station, "first they make a mess, then they cry about it when someone comes to hold them accountable." He snorted in derision. "Always thinking that no one could ever stop them."

The image of the Agletarian command staff filled the viewscreen, secure in their base.

Monty clasped his hands behind his back. "I have been told to offer the Deputy Minister in exchange for our lives." Monty told the men calmly. "If we were to promise his safe return, all we would ask is fair treatment."

"I'll see what I can do." The commander on screen shook his head. "But I will not have conditions placed upon me." His tone grew harsh. "You are *beaten*. The war is *over*. You will stand trial for your crimes and then face the judgement of my people. Further resistance would simply result in pain you couldn't *possibly* imagine."

Monty's jaw tightened, obviously not liking the fact that the man pointed out his defeat. "Very well." He hissed. "You drive a hard bargain, but I suppose I have little other choice." Monty started towards the door, then paused as if remembering something. "On *second* thought..." he spun around and pulled the trigger on a pistol which somehow appeared in his hand, splattering Vlk's brains all over McPherson who let out an astonished gasp, "you've piqued my curiosity."

The man on the screen cried out in horror as Vlk slumped to the floor, almost drowned out by McPherson's curses as she staggered back, wiping the hot blood from her eyes.

Monty held the pistol at his side, voice coming out in a snarl. "My name is Montgomery Tarkington Welles, last of the *Wellesburg* Welles." He shook his head. "And I *don't* do prisoner exchanges... because I *finish* what I begin. And I'd rather *die* than be beaten." He put two more bullets into the fallen man, never removing his eyes from the screen. "*Come and get me.*"

"I will fucking *exterminate you!*" The commander screamed.

Monty's lip curved. "*Do the best you can.*"

The Agletarian commander gestured to someone in the background of the transmission, and a moment later, one of his men dragged Poacher into the room by his leg. Sydney looked beaten almost to death, bloodied and bruised, unable to even stand up.

The commander pointed at Poacher. "First, I'm going to kill your spy, then I'm going to kill *you*." He pulled out his handgun. "I'm going to turn all your freaks over to our scientists, and they're going to take the specimens which can best provide us the next generation of weapons, and then they're going to cut the rest of you into pieces so tiny, they won't even be recognizable as *human* anymore."

The soldiers dumped Poacher's body at the man's feet, and Syd's labored breathing could be heard over the speaker.

The Agletarian commander pointed the gun at Syd, preparing to execute him.

Monty laughed cruelly and spun on his heel. "*Kill him.*" He ordered dismissively over his shoulder, walking away. "I'm done here."

The commander shook his head in disgust. "What kind of man *are* you?" He cocked the weapon and pressed it to Poacher's head. "You freaks have got no respect for your own lives."

Monty turned back to look at him, something like amusement on his face. "My good man," his smirk grew into a Cheshire grin, "whatever makes you think I was talking to *you?*" He glanced over to meet Clarice's gaze for a long moment. "You wanted magic, Pastiche?" He held his hands out, like he'd just performed his greatest trick. "*Abracadabra.*"

The Agletarian commander looked confused for a moment, before a low growling sound filled the transmission. Poacher let out a deep roar and bounded to his feet, ripping his hands apart and sending pieces of his heavy shackles in all directions. The Agletarian fired the gun, hitting Poacher square in the head. Poacher stumbled forward a step, then rounded on him, letting out another furious roar, his eyes gleaming black and red. His skin took on a greenish cast as he accessed more of the dragon from Rayn's kingdom's powers, then bared his new very large teeth.

The round fell from Poacher's now bullet impervious dragon skin, the soft "ping" sound of it hitting the floor the only noise in the room.

An instant later, the soldiers arranged around him began to fire randomly in panic. Poacher knocked them away like they weighed nothing, then opened his jaws wide and bathed the room in fire.

Monty glanced over his shoulder. "*That's* how you win a war, Agent McPherson. A Trojan Horse: you get them to open the door and take a dragon inside. *Told you* they don't watch cartoons." He informed them calmly, putting his top hat back on. "Vaudeville: if you would be so kind?"

Cory slammed his hand against the viewscreen, his static filled eye promptly displaying the image. His powers opened up the TV screen as a portal into whatever it displayed. In this case, the Agletarian base. "Good to go."

Monty raised his voice to yell above the screams coming over the transmission. "Irregulars!" His men instantly surrounded him like a barbarian horde, armed with everything from baseball bats to fusion guns. A smile crossed Monty's scarred face again, and he pointed the crystal end of his cane at the viewscreen, like a World War I commander ordering his men from their trenches and through no man's land. "*Go to work!*"

A cheering battle cry roared from his workman as they charged forward around him. Monty began to laugh cruelly as wave after wave of Irregulars raced past him and dove through the gateway Cory had created from the transmission. The Agletarians had failed to take into account Cory's power, and once Vlk opened up the line of communication, all the Consortium had to do was step through it and into the Agletarian's fortified base.

The Irregulars surged through the screen like angry hornets from a hive, falling upon the surprised and mostly unarmed Agletarians, who could do nothing but try to flee in blind panic as they were cut down.

Monty raised his voice again, calling over the din of battle as he stepped through the screen to join his army. "Take no prisoners! Give no quarter! *BURN IT ALL!"*

Once the last of the Consortium's forces were through the screen, Monty turned back to watch from the other end as the soldier's burst into the Crater Lair's command room, to find it now empty.

He watched the men on screen silently for a moment. "You had years of careful planning, 1,000 highly trained soldiers, an arsenal of unstoppable alien weapons, and the resources of an entire country behind you." He paused for a beat. "I beat you in a matter of days, with an empty delivery truck and an idiot with an elephant gun, who wears Disney Princess socks with his combat boots." Monty' face twisted into a smile again. "And I could have done it with *far* less."

McPherson stood behind him and stared in amazement.

Monty held up a finger to bring a matter to the Agletarian's attention. "FYI: my engineers are better than yours, and Higgins was kind enough to point out one *tiny* design flaw in the gear you're wearing, which really was a *terrible* oversight on your part." Monty looked almost sad, as if breaking them unfortunate news. "Your little suits will protect you from explosions, true," his scarred face spread into an even wider evil smirk, "but let's see if they'll help you to breathe through the 5,200 tons of dirt and wetland habitat that I'm about to drop on you, thanks to explosives planted by Mercygiver." He flipped the plastic cover off the device in his hand, exposing a button beneath. "My associate, Harlot, has asked me to tell you..." He paused, as he thought about it. "Honestly, I forget. Something to do with learning the consequences of hurting Wyatt. I wasn't really listening. But no matter. You'll be dead, so when she asks if I told you, I'll just lie. Either way, I do recall her telling me to 'bury you,'" he pressed the button and the transmission ended in a fireball and screams as the explosions took out the dozens of support pillars which held up the roof of the subterranean Crater Lair and it all came crashing down on top of the startled soldiers. "...Consider yourselves *buried*."

The transmission went to static.

"Goodbye, gentlemen." Monty casually dropped the detonator to the ground, amid the bodies of his enemies. "At least you tried."

Monty stood in the center of the room and turned in a slow circle, arms wide, like Maria singing to the hillsides in *The Sound of Music*, watching the carnage and death take place around him. He flung his top hat away with a flourish and took a theatrical bow to his imaginary audience, laughing again as if all of this amused him to no end.

****

John Cuttleston-Pie, AKA "Oversight," didn't exist. He might have at one point, John didn't remember, but he certainly didn't exist now.

He never appeared in any news stories about the Consortium. You could ask anyone about him and they'd only stare at you blankly. You could show them a picture of him and they wouldn't see him in it. You could drag him into their office and toss him naked at their feet, and they'd still argue that you were imagining things.

Because John Cuttleston-Pie didn't exist.

He didn't even know his own real name.

He had no police file. He had no birth certificate. He had no friends, lovers, or family who could identify him in a lineup. He didn't draw a paycheck from anyone and he didn't have a bank account anywhere. When you really came right down to it, money was utterly useless to someone like him. He could simply take whatever he wanted and no one would be the wiser. Not that he really needed a lot, because *everything* was pretty useless to someone like him. He didn't need to wear nice clothes or flashy jewelry. No one would see them anyway, so he had no one to impress. Hell, he didn't need to wear clothes *at all* if he didn't want to.

Sometimes, he couldn't even see his own reflection in the mirror.

He was for all intents and purposes... dead.

A ghost.

When Carl Barks was writing his legendary Uncle Scrooge comics for Disney way back when, his most popular issues featured the adventures of Huey, Dewey, and Louie Duck. Sometimes though, the artist would miscount the boys, and instead of three ducks being featured in a comic panel, there would accidentally be four. This event was so frequent that fans of the series took to calling this mysterious fourth duck "Phooey." He was a phantom. There one panel, gone the next. While he was around, the other characters would see him and interact with him. For the briefest of moments, he was their brother or their nephew or their friend. He was *loved*. He had a *family*. One perfect fraction of time... But then he would disappear without explanation in the next panel and wouldn't be mentioned again. No one remembered he had ever been there and no one noticed that he was gone. Because Phooey Duck didn't exist... except when he *did*.

"John" was a lot like that.

He could go anywhere and do anything. And no matter where he went or what he did, no one would notice him. He could be in the room with you right now, screaming into your ear, and you'd never even know it. Until the shooting started.

The problem with the ability to *go* anywhere, was that it meant that you were always *nowhere*. He didn't have a home. He didn't date. He didn't get waited on at restaurants or greeted upon entering a store. No one remembered his birthday or asked him if he was having a good time or not. No one cared when he was sick or congratulated him on a job well done. No one pulled his broken body from the battlefield when he fell and no one thanked him for saving them from certain death.

Every tear "John" had ever shed was shed alone.

Being able to do *anything* meant that he was actually able to do *very little*.

Or at least, he didn't remember doing very much. To be fair though, he knew almost nothing about his own life. Perhaps it was an aspect of his powers or perhaps it was something else, but whatever the reason, John had no idea who he was or where he'd come from.

He didn't remember. He had forgotten the details about himself just like everyone else had.

He was simply the invisible man, living in a near eternal present, without a past or future. And as far as he remembered, that was the way it had always been. Which was probably for the best, because he didn't much like what he *did* know about himself.

Laws and morals weren't designed for invisible men. Prisons couldn't hold them. They didn't have to face the consequences of their own actions and they didn't have to look anyone in the eye, no matter what they did. They could slip through the gates of Heaven and escape the fires of Hell.

448

There one moment, gone the next.

Invisible men could do *anything* they wanted. But... John didn't really want to do anything. There didn't seem to be much point, really.

Honestly, there wasn't a point to his life at all.

The only proof that there had ever been a man named "Oversight" were a few friends he had once had, who were now long gone, and a string of bodies left in his wake. Once upon a time, a few people had been able to see him when he really concentrated on it. But those people were now all either dead or were crazy as hell, so it didn't matter much. Occasionally, someone in the Consortium would remember that they knew someone named Oversight or get the strange feeling that they were forgetting about someone who was on their team. But that was about it.

And the people he actually *wanted* to see him were the most blind to his existence, it seemed.

He was utterly alone in the world. Even when he was in a crowd.

At the moment he was sitting in a break room connected to the Agletarian base's large interior hanger area. Elsewhere in the open space, Traitor was dressed as a pilot and was regaling his newfound countrymen with his no doubt fabricated exploits, while Adam Eden, AKA "Apathy," casually sat in the nearby security office. The guards next to him were listlessly spinning in their office chairs, utterly controlled by Adam's power over apathy, and paying no attention to their duties or to the intruder who was calmly sitting next to them.

Together, the men, Multifarious, and Flannery, were the mainstays of the Consortium's Undercover Department. The best at getting into places and being utterly ignored or overlooked once they were there, until it came time for them to be seen. Real *Mission: Impossible* kind of shit.

They were the men you didn't know. The men you didn't *want* to know.

And they were about to kill everyone in this base.

There were a lot of different groups and departments in the Consortium. But *no one* fucked with the Undercover Department and got away with it. The Agletarians had almost killed Multifarious. So...

"John" pulled back the bolt on his assault rifle and stood up, getting ready to do his job. A job he was rarely paid to perform and never thanked for, but a job he still performed just more out of habit than anything else.

He continued to do his job because there was quite simply

nothing else to do and nowhere else to go.

Besides, he would perform this *particular* mission because these people had killed his friends. His family. And just because his friends didn't remember *him*, didn't mean that he didn't remember *them*.

The people in the room ignored him, paying no attention to the man in the grey hoodie standing next to them or the heavily-modified M-16 clutched in his hands.

Invisible men didn't kill people, they *murdered them*. It was really the only word for it. It was equivalent to shooting sleeping fish in a barrel. They had no hope of even knowing "John" was in the room, let alone trying to defend themselves against him. And even if by some miracle they *did* somehow recognize what was happening, his powers meant that they'd almost instantly forget it anyway.

"John" liked to think that at some point in his life, he had felt bad about doing what he was about to do, and that his powers had just wiped that memory clean like all of the others.

He didn't think that was the case though.

Right on schedule, the Agletarians fleeing Poacher and the army of Irregulars burst through the doors, trying desperately to get to the exit or a weapons locker. Unfortunately for them, the security guards were now too bored and apathetic—thanks to Adam Eden— to sound any sort of alarm or open up any of the other doors. Thus, everyone in the facility was being funneled into this room, where "John" and his friends waited. To make matters worse, as they raced forward in blind panic, they didn't see Draugr and Ceann appearing from the facility's Morgue, having recovered from their apparent deaths in the truck explosion earlier. Nor did the Agletarians pay any attention as a man dressed as one of their pilots casually hit the switch to open the exterior hanger doors. They *did* however recognize the men standing silhouetted in the morning sun, as Hazard and Tyrant effectively blocked their only exit.

"So you're here to kill our wives, huh?" Hazard asked the room at large, his voice calm but dead cold.

Tyrant simply pulled his guan dao, spinning the weapon around several times in anticipation.

The mob of Agletarians skidded to a stop, suddenly comprehending that they were now boxed in. Invulnerable people to their front and flanks. Attackers they couldn't even *recognize* as a threat to their rear. And an army of pissed-off Irregulars barreling down on them, eager to pick up any slack.

The exterior hanger doors shut behind Tyrant and Hazard,

and Adam promptly disabled the controls from the security room.

It was a killbox.

There was now no escape for the soldiers in this base. None of them would ever see the sky again.

"John" wanted to think that he had once been the type of person who would feel pity for them. He hoped that deep down, he had been a good man at one point in his life, and that he would have felt sorry for these poor bastards who were about to be murdered.

But he didn't really believe that about himself.

That was just a dream.

Because... deep down... he knew murder came easy to him. Too easy.

He leveled the rifle at the unsuspecting soldiers assembled around him and moved to stand in the doorway they had just raced through, cutting off their retreat.

The men stared straight through him, not comprehending that there was a weapon pointed inches from their faces or that a heartless monster was looking into their frightened eyes and feeling nothing.

The invisible man was preparing for the slaughter.

And they had no idea. No one ever had any idea who "John" was.

He didn't exist. No one knew him and no one would want to. He wasn't *worth* remembering. People should be *glad* they couldn't remember him.

"John" was certainly glad that *he* couldn't remember himself.

It was perhaps the only thing about his life which he hoped never changed; the only grace granted to him by a God who had obviously *also* forgotten that "John" existed. Because if these were the kinds of things "John" *currently* did... he certainly didn't want to remember the things he had already *done.*

Oversight came into your life like a ghost and left it after making *you* one.

And no matter what he did... no matter how hard he tried... no matter how deeply he might *love you*... you wouldn't remember him. You wouldn't see him. You wouldn't hear him. You wouldn't love him back. You just... wouldn't. And that was a pain that not even *his* powers could ever erase from his own mind, no matter how hard he wanted to block it out. How hard he prayed. How much he cried...

He was The Unforgettable What's-His-Name.

The duck that wasn't supposed to be.

And he was essentially already dead.

If there was a Hell, John Cuttleston-Pie had lived there his entire life. Alone. Screaming. And no one realized it but him.

The trap closed on the Agletarians and an invisible man opened fire on his latest victims, leaving his only recognizable mark on the world.

Chapter 29

The motorcycle roared down the street, weaving in and out of traffic without slowing down. For all of his risk-adverse ways, Oz could handle the vehicle in a dangerous situation better than anyone else she'd ever seen.

The man was *really* good at being a Cape.

"What's the plan?" She shouted to him over the sound of the icy wind and the crowds of people which were lining the parade route.

"They're after the kids." Oz yelled back. "The Horizons Academy students. They're all marching in the parade. They're going to grab them so that they can experiment on them, then do something to cover their escape."

"What?"

"Masterson didn't know."

"With weird tech involved, it could be anything." Her mind raced, trying to figure out the Agletarians' next move. "Do you have any idea how many trucks filled with floats and machines are arriving in town for the parade? One more isn't going to raise any red flags."

"We'll deal with it." He informed her with complete confidence, jumping the curb and speeding through a plaza area to avoid a barricade. "I've discovered that I'm a 'shoot the fucking bear' kind of person, by the way. Which is surprising."

"Kind of in a 'let the thing live' mood today." She squeezed him tighter. "I'm strangely excited by hearing you swear, incidentally.

It's *really* hot, baby doll."

Ahead of them, the parade came into view.

"Which float are they on?" She yelled. "Do we know?"

"Nope."

"How many of them are there, do we know?"

"Nope."

"Have we figured out a way to counteract their armor yet?"

"Nope."

Natalie started laughing. "You know, I think I'm gonna like working with you for the rest of my life, baby." She rested her face against the comforting muscles of his back. "You are the *right* kind of madman."

Oz gunned the engine again and the classic motorcycle went faster, tearing through a police checkpoint and speeding after the slow-moving parade ahead of them.

Craning her neck, Natalie got a look at something which caught her eye: a dozen floats in a row, slowly making their way south. A dozen floats which formed a gingerbread *train*.

The Agletarians' train was right on schedule, leaving exactly when their coded message had said it would.

She squeezed Oz tighter, and he saw the train at the same moment. He steered the motorcycle towards the floats.

She readied herself for the looming fight. "How we handling this, *Kemosabe*?"

"We do this *your way*." He yelled back, over the sound of the parade. "Protect the civilians at all costs. We don't know which of the train cars has their weapon, so we'll take them all. Start at the caboose and work your way forward. I'll head for the engine. Anyone on the train who tries to stop us..."

"*Combat* fucking *mentality*." She supplied with a grin.

"Exactly." He steered through a crowd of people struggling to control a huge "Lotti the Ocelot" shaped balloon in the icy wind. The large form of the cereal mascot looming overhead like a smiling, brightly-colored god. "Anyone in one of those power-suits, leave to me."

She remembered the devastation just two of those men had caused at the hospital, and what killing one of them had done to Oz. He had used so much of his powers saving her, that it had almost knocked him out and made him crazy. "We might not make it through this, you know." She warned.

"I've spent my whole life dying. I have no intention of continuing that today." He tore through the intersection, racing

454

towards the gingerbread train. "Today... I'm going to fucking *live*."

The Agletarians on the train recognized the threat, and it instantly increased in speed, trying to make it to its destination. Ahead of the train, the empowered children from the Horizon's Academy scattered as the floats crashed into their marching formation. Men inside the floats ran out and started to grab the kids.

Mull swore, recognizing that this was about to get bad.

Oz pulled up next to the caboose and she jumped off the bike, grabbing ahold of the railing and pulling herself onto the train.

"Be careful!" She yelled after him as he accelerated towards the engine.

She turned to face the first wave of Agletarians, as the soldiers moved to stop her.

The men were dressed in colorful gingerbread themed costumes, which made fighting them a unique and utterly enjoyable experience. Mull always liked it when bad guys were visually interesting. There was nothing worse than being bored during a fight.

She ducked to the side as one of the soldiers swung at her, then punched him in the face. The man staggered back on the roof of the moving train, and she kicked him in the side of the knee, then broke his neck. The man's body slid from the train and went sprawling into the crowd of surprised parade watchers, who vainly tried to scatter away before the dead gingerbread man fell on top of them.

It was a tie.

Damn.

Wyatt was going to be pissed about that.

Another soldier appeared in front of her, bringing an automatic weapon to bear. Mull didn't even have time to think before he opened fire, and she braced herself for the wounds... But the bullets simply bounced off her.

She grinned, recognizing what her powers were today.

Her weird glitchy "bones vanishing" power was of limited use, but it was *so* broken that it gave her access to... well... *everything.*

Every power she'd ever had.

All at once.

Today was going to be *fun.*

She reached out with one of her powers and used telekinesis to toss the soldier from the train and into the wall of a nearby building, shattering every bone in his body.

The train came to a crashing halt, no doubt from Oz somehow taking out its engine. The cars behind it crashed into the back of the tender, jackknifing.

The caboose she was standing on rolled to a stop next to the engine, which Oz was standing in front of like an unmovable barrier, protecting the city. Behind him, the students raced for cover.

"Consortium of Chaos, here to make an arrest!" He announced in a stern and commanding heroic tone, which made her insides melt. *"Throw up your hands and deactivate your weapons!"*

The crowd of parade onlookers and the children from the Horizons Academy continued to flee the scene, running in all directions.

A man exited the cabin of the train engine, laughing.

"You're out of your league." General Skrlj warned him, ponytail blowing in the wind. "You really..." He trailed off, noticing Oz's fox hunting attire. "The fuck are you wearing?" He sounded confused and vaguely disgusted.

"It's a complicated story with no bearing on this conflict." Oz assured him, straightening his jacket with as much dignity as he could muster.

Skrlj blinked several times, processing that, then returned to his original thought. "You really think I would come all this way, to kill the people responsible for my father's death, and I wouldn't have every eventuality covered?"

Oz didn't budge. "I'm going to tell you one more time to surrender peacefully, or I will be forced to take action."

The side of the float next to them opened and a dozen soldiers in high-tech armor leapt out.

Fifty men in the crowd of parade onlookers suddenly stopped their panicked flight and pulled out weapons, leveling them at Oz and Natalie.

"So make your move." Skrlj taunted.

Oz and Natalie exchanged glances, recognizing that it was a bad situation. Luckily, she had no doubt they could handle it.

She dropped her hand to her waist and subtly held up three fingers, as a countdown for Oz to coordinate their attack, then two...

She didn't reach one.

****

In the Agletarian's base, Poacher was stalking back through the control room, blood dripping from his skin. Which was fine. Because it wasn't his. It wasn't his blood *or* his skin.

He'd worked his way through the Agletarian forces until he'd found the cells where the prisoners were being kept, and made sure all

456

of the kidnapped people were safe. Now, he was backtracking to deal with someone.

Amy and Emily watched him go by, looking amazed by something.

"Wow." Emily breathed. "Now *that's*..."

"...a fucking *man*." Amy finished for her.

Emily pointed at him, looking thrilled. "What'd I say!?! *What'd I say!?!*" She gestured at him emphatically. "'Can only hold out for 36 hours,' HA! That's some motherfucking *Terminator* shit, right there! And not that weak-ass 'now I know why you cry' bullshit, either. I'm talking full-on, old-school 'shootin' up police stations and killing Michael Biehn' Terminator shit! He'll be fucking *back*!" She pumped her fist. "*Yeah! SHIT YEAH!*"

Amy looked less excited, her pretty face now contorted in concern. "Are you okay, dear?" She asked him softly, reaching out to touch his arm.

Poacher rounded on her, not expecting to be touched, baring his dragon teeth.

Amy pulled back. Emily's smile faded and she stepped forward to protect her twin.

Poacher swore at himself, and ripped the bracelet of dragon skin from his wrist and tossed it away. The fucking thing was a *nightmare* to control. He didn't like it. It made him want to hurt everything and everyone.

He opened his mouth to apologize to her, but recognized that there was nothing to say. He simply wasn't the kind of man who should be around nice people.

Amy took his silent attempt at an apology *as* an apology, and nodded at him in acceptance, smiling.

But Emily stayed where she was.

Poacher kept walking.

Sprawled in the corner of the room was the man he was here to see. The Agletarians' alien friend.

His outfit was burned and there was blood on his forehead, but Poacher had been sure to leave the man alive. He had *questions* for him. About what he was doing here and why he was helping the Agletarians.

"You fools," the alien said, "you have no idea the nightmare you've called down on yourselves. My people are going to *destroy you*."

"Destroy me?" Poacher looked around incredulously, like he assumed the man was speaking to someone else. "*Me?*" He crouched down next to him. "That kind of threat might scare people on some of the other worlds you've been to, where you were the toughest kid on the block..." he met the man's gaze, dead on, "but you're in *New Jersey* now, motherfucker." He pulled out his machete and passed it in front of the man's face so that it glinted in the light. "And you're a *loooong* way from home..."

****

In the engineering room of the Agletarian base, Montgomery casually looked around. "Higgins?" He called to his employee as the man sat down behind one of the terminals. On the TV screen, the Thanksgiving parade was breaking out in carnage, with the Agletarians beginning to surround Oz and Multifarious. "Boot up the master controls for the Agletarians' suits." A sinister smile crossed Monty's face. "They want more power? Let's see how they like it if we give them *all of it.*"

Clarice shook her head, her voice becoming shrill. "You can't make them explode! You have no way of knowing how many of those suits there *are*, or where the soldiers might be located right now. They could be in populated areas, for God's sake! They could be all over Agletaria! *You're going to kill innocent people!*"

Monty shot her an odd glance, like she was speaking another language. "You're too delicate for this line of work, Clarice." He informed her, as if giving needed guidance to a dear friend. "My advice would be to find another profession before you get someone hurt." He turned to his underling. "*Do it.*"

"No!" Clarice rounded on Higgins, her anger flashing. "Don't you *dare* press that..."

Monty's flunky pressed the button before the woman could finish.

****

Natalie's count reached two, when the soldiers in the super suits unexpectedly exploded, rocking the pavement around them and knocking everyone else off their feet. Much like had happened in the hospital, the suits themselves had detonated. Just what had caused it this time, she wasn't sure, but it broke every window for two blocks and sent debris crashing into the crowds of parade goers, still trying desperately to get clear.

Half of the cables holding down the huge "Lottie" balloon

458

were instantly cut, and the soldiers who had formally been occupying the space were incinerated outright.

Luckily, all of the civilians were free of the blast zone, but the explosion was so close that it left Natalie's ears ringing and her brain feeling foggy.

The remaining soldiers regained their footing and immediately opened fire, peppering Mull with bullets and causing her to duck for cover behind the train.

Skrlj took off running, heading towards one of the other floats.

"Go!" Oz gestured at her. "Stop him, I'll take care of the gunmen!"

"You sure?" She called back.

"Do you have any idea how filthy this city is?" He smiled. "Because they're about to find out."

Mull snorted at the threat, jumping over some scorched and burning gingerbread decorations and running after the architect of all of this.

Behind her, the gunfire abruptly stopped as Oz accessed his astonishing powers and had the city's filth decompose the men away to nothing. He leaned forward, bracing himself on his knees for a moment, breathing hard and trying to recover from that incredible exertion, then trotted after her.

Skrlj reached into one of the floats and pulled something out, then stopped in the middle of the street to confront them.

She skidded to a stop in front of him, Oz backing her up and taking a position to her right.

They had the man boxed in and there was nowhere he could go.

"Again," Oz told the man calmly, "I'm OCD of the Consortium of Chaos. And this is..." He trailed off, recognizing that he didn't know her codename today.

"Today.... I am *Multifarious*." She informed them both dramatically, meeting Skrlj's eyes. "Your people made me to be a killer. And here I am. I have 9,648 different super-powers at my disposal today." She shrugged. "Some of them? I don't even remember what they do. But I bet I can use most of them to kick the living shit outta you, mister."

"Surrender." Oz snapped. "Your days of torturing people are over."

Skrlj didn't move.

She nodded, expecting that. "Okay then..."

Oz reached into his pocket and put on a pair of plastic safety goggles. "In case of splatter." He casually explained.

Skrlj pressed the button in his hand and there was a strange mechanical noise.

She glanced at Oz in confusion, wondering if he heard it too.

Skrlj launched himself at her, his movements enhanced by his own alien suit, which was hidden underneath his clothes and didn't explode like the others had, because it appeared to be of a more complicated design. Sadly, it was just as strong.

He crashed into her, and they both fell to the street.

She flipped him off of her as he went for a ground and pound move, and Oz caught the man's arm before he could connect with his follow-up punch. He locked his own arm around Skrlj's elbow, opening the man up to attack.

Mull hit him in the side with Brick House's strength power, then punched him in the face.

Skrlj staggered to the side and ran straight into Oz's fist, which just about leveled the man. The General's power suit might be making the rest of him resistant to damage, but it didn't cover his face.

Skrlj pulled a knife and tried to stab at her as she moved to block the man's escape and trap him between herself and Oz, but she accessed Pli-Ape's agility powers and simply dodged it.

The man turned to run down a side alley, but Oz used his powers to crash construction scaffolding into it, cutting off the exit.

He turned to flee uptown, but Hive Mind's powers to control bees sealed off the route behind a wall of angry bees, which *really* didn't like the cold and were only too happy to take that out on someone.

Skrlj recognized the situation was hopeless.

At this point, it was basically just sharks circling a wounded swimmer.

The only question was whether she or Oz would have the honor of killing this asshole first.

"We'll kill you if we have to." Oz challenged. "But we won't have to, unless you give us no other option. Surrender."

To her surprise, the man started laughing. "You think you've won!?!" He held up the device in his hand. "I'll die before I ever see your kind rule my country!"

Behind them, the mechanical noise continued and Mull didn't even need to turn around to know it wasn't good news.

Footsteps.

Across from her, Oz was staring at something over her

shoulder. Something which was apparently very large.

She shook her head sadly, hating this job.

"Giant robot." Oz deadpanned. "That's the most ridiculous thing I've ever seen." He gestured to it. "Why would anyone build that!?! It's so impractical!"

Mull turned to look at the alien monster, made up of the machinery hidden inside the train floats. It towered over the street, a hundred feet of whipping, clanking, mechanical death. Her mouth fell open in sheer wonder. "...It's like every dream I've ever had came true this morning..." She whispered, then turned back to look at Oz in excitement. "A giant robot! *A giant robot, Oz!* How fucking amazing is that!?!"

Oz made a face. "This is the stupidest thing that's ever happened."

Skrlj threw the activation switch at her head, and she dodge to the side to avoid it. He used the distraction to try to grab Oz, but her partner blocked him, then used a martial arts throw to toss the man away.

Skrlj righted himself, feet braced for the final showdown, and the armor under his clothes glowing so brightly with power that his body seemed to be sparking now.

She glanced at Oz, getting a ruling on this.

Oz nodded, agreeing with her that they'd given him a chance and that it was time to end it before someone got hurt.

She used her foot to kick one of the guide wires into her hand, then used Huaso's cowboy powers to lasso Skrlj's neck.

Oz used his powers to eat through the dozen remaining weights holding the balloon to the ground, and Skrlj was lifted off his feet by the Lotti the Ocelot balloon, the guide wire tightening around his neck. He struggled to free himself from the steel towline, trying to use his suit's enhanced strength to break the cable... but Mull's brain was stronger than his suit, and the cable didn't budge.

Skrlj went limp as the balloon sailed past the rooftops and rose into the clear morning sky.

Oz didn't even bother to watch the man's corpse get carried high over the city, instead, he immediately rounded on their next threat. He braced his feet, eyeing up their robotic opponent.

She gazed up at it too, recognizing that if Oz tried to take it down with his powers, he'd probably give himself an aneurysm. It was simply far too big.

The monster began to march uptown, feet leaving behind huge holes in the street as it began to wreck the buildings along the parade route. It was supposed to provide a distraction for the Agletarians so that they could kidnap more empowered people, but with the Agletarians gone and the students fleeing to safety, the robot was just running amok.

Oz started to race after it. "I'll keep the debris from hurting any of the civilians," he pointed at the robot and winked back at her, "but *that* seems like a job for 'The Lumberjack.'"

Mull started to run after them, growing larger with each step. Within three steps, she'd overtaken Oz, and within a dozen she'd caught up with the robot. She slammed into it, now equal to its size and weight.

The robot staggered to the side, leaning against one of the buildings for support and causing a large section of wall to collapse towards the street. The bricks disappeared into a cloud of dust before hitting a crowd of people huddled on the sidewalk, thanks to Oz.

His powers were strong, but they took a lot out of him. She wasn't sure he'd be able to do that again, so she had to end this fight quickly and with as little property damage as possible.

"Quickly and calmly, people!" Oz announced to the crowd, motioning the onlookers to safety. "You've all seen giant robots before, and you know what to do!"

Mull hit the robot in the face with The Lumberjack's huge right fist, sad that she didn't have the oversized axe which formally accompanied this power set.

And, for that matter, that her outfit today wasn't really made for growing ninety-five feet taller, and she was forced to do this in her underwear.

Luckily, her old friend Party Line was more than capable of fighting half-dressed. The crazy bitch still hated men... but she loved Oz, so Mull had no objections to her now.

The robot moved to attack her with some kind of hand-mounted weapon, but Oz's powers dissolved it before it got a chance to fire at her.

She drove her shoulder into the body of the robot, lifting it off its feet, and took it down in a wrestling move. She rolled on top of it, raised both of her hands above her head, then smashed them down onto its head until the blinking lights flickered out and the machine stopped moving.

She stayed atop it for several moments, making sure it was destroyed, then shrunk back to her normal size.

Oz took off his jacket and wrapped it around Natalie's shoulders, as she started to tremble in the cold. She looked up at him.

462

"It's fucking *freezing,* Oz." She told him, starting to shiver and shifting from bare foot to bare foot on the icy street. "Why does evil always have to attack when it's 19 degrees out!?!"

Oz nodded, pulling her against him and wrapping his arms around her, sharing the warmth of his body. "You were right though," he said softly, leaning in to kiss her, "I think this really was the best parade ever."

His lips met hers, and Natalie's entire crazy life made sense. His lips were warm enough that she forgot the cold and the death robots and the fact that the corpse of a foreign general was currently dangling from a huge balloon of a cereal mascot over their heads. Despite the insanity... she felt normal. She felt whole. She felt so *loved.*

On the street corner, several onlookers began to clap for them, appreciating their efforts.

Natalie and Oz had saved the city. They'd managed to protect innocent people *and* duke it out with a giant robot.

Roy would have been proud.

She wrapped her arms around Oz, laughing in utter joy as his mouth plundered hers. "Happy Tanksgiving, Oz." She told him, that terrible and misspelled handprint turkey drawing from the hospital seeming oddly prophetic, given how the day was turning out. She kissed Oz again, feeling so safe and happy in his arms. "Happy Tanksgiving."

Chapter 30

"'IT WAS MUCH PLEASANTER AT HOME,' THOUGHT
POOR ALICE, 'WHEN ONE WASN'T ALWAYS GROWING
LARGER AND SMALLER, AND BEING ORDERED ABOUT
BY MICE AND RABBITS. I ALMOST WISH I HADN'T
GONE DOWN THAT RABBIT-HOLE--AND YET--AND YET--
IT'S RATHER CURIOUS, YOU KNOW, THIS SORT OF LIFE!
I DO WONDER WHAT CAN HAVE HAPPENED TO ME!
WHEN I USED TO READ FAIRY-TALES, I FANCIED THAT
KIND OF THING NEVER HAPPENED, AND NOW HERE I AM
IN THE MIDDLE OF ONE! THERE OUGHT TO BE A BOOK
WRITTEN ABOUT ME, THAT THERE OUGHT!"

- *Alice's Adventures in Wonderland*

It wasn't that the Freedom Squad's former headquarters was horrible, it was just that she had mixed feelings about spending Thanksgiving in the home of the people who had tried to kill her and destroy the city.

But then again, a lot of people tried to kill her and destroy the city, so if she got weird about them all, there'd be no areas of town where she could walk without feeling bad.

Besides, it wasn't like they had a lot of choices. The Crater Lair had been blown up, so the Consortium was currently homeless. Luckily, they still technically owned the Freedom Squad's old building, so they were crashing here until more permanent lodgings could be found, or the Crater Lair was repaired.

She lounged back in her chair, casually watching the football game take place on the Astroturf in front of her. Tyrant and Stacy were currently screaming at each other, because they insisted the other was cheating at the game, despite the blatantly obvious fact that neither one of them understood the rules in the first place. Their respective spouses calmly chatted on the sidelines, waiting for the game to start again.

Oz appeared from somewhere else in the building, strolling over to where she was seated. Rather than finding a chair of his own, he simply stepped over the back of her lounge and slipped in behind her, so that she was leaning against the expanse of his chest.

She took that as a very good sign.

Oz was really coming out of his shell in regards to the physical contact thing. Well... in regards to *her*, anyway. He seemed to still treat everyone else with the same degree of disgust as he always did.

"How are you feeling today?" She asked him.

"I'm feeling pretty amazing today." He assured her, wrapping his arms around her.

She rearranged herself, so that she was basically sitting on his lap. "You know, as crazy as it is to say, sometimes I think I had to almost die, so that we both could live. I mean, without all of this, I'd still be a mess, and you'd still be barricaded in your apartment, worrying that the acoustic tile on your ceiling might have asbestos in it."

Oz was quiet for a beat, then stiffened slightly. "Is that really a possibility?"

She ignored that, continuing on with her point. "But instead, you and I are out there solving mysteries and saving people..."

"I have often wondered about it being a carcinogen, but I hadn't connected that to asbestos..." Oz thought aloud, his concern over the problem growing.

"In any case, I think this worked out perfectly."

"I should have it tested again." He vowed. "You can't be too careful."

She made a face at him over her shoulder. "Really?" She arched an eyebrow. "You're really going to obsess about something so stupid? You should be obsessing about *me* instead."

"I'm *more* than obsessed with you, Nat." He leaned forward to kiss the side of her neck. "I love you." He said, like she needed to be reminded of that fact.

"Who wouldn't?" She teased. "I'm awesome."

He snorted, lips closing over her earlobe.

She made a low hum of pleasure, tilting her head to the side to give him better access. "I really think this is one of your superpowers."

"Maybe." He agreed, pulling her further onto his lap. "Or maybe I'm just finally succumbing to my 'bad blood' and dragging you into wickedness."

She leaned against him, the back of her head resting on his shoulder, as he gently kissed the side of her neck. "I'll love you, even if

466

you go evil one day." She told him seriously. "You don't need to worry."

"Honestly, when you were evil, it was kinda hot." He remarked, intertwining his fingers with hers. "I was disturbed but oddly excited."

She snorted, playfully batting at his hand. "Shut up, I mean it."

"I'm not worried about going evil anymore." He assured her, holding her close. "I have you. I'm not worried about anything anymore. I have everything I ever wanted."

She was snuggled up next to the love of her life, watching her idiot family celebrate the holiday, knowing that they had once again saved the city, even if it had come at a cost.

"Me too." She nodded, letting out a contented sigh. "It's... extraordinary."

"Well, extraordinary is the new normal for us, I think."

Bridget arrived on the scene, looking upset about something. She flopped down at the long table which had been set up to serve Thanksgiving dinner.

Natalie turned her head to look at her, unwilling to actually leave Oz's lap. "Problems, Bridge?"

The woman flipped an annoyed hand, scooting her chair so that it was closer to Julian's. "At this morning's press conference, Kass decided it was time to teach the Bell brothers about the importance of 'speaking with inferiors' and then announced to the reporters that he would immediately execute the first person in the audience who stopped clapping for him when his statement was done."

Julian lovingly put his arm around Bridget, taking on a thoughtful expression. "It *is* important to learn how to speak with creatures lower than yourself..." He pursed his lips. "...And there are few things lower than a surface-dweller..."

"He made those poor people clap for *five and a half hours!*" Bridget protested. "They were all too afraid to stop! If Harlot hadn't broken it up, they'd probably still be there!" She rapidly shook her head. "You just can't do that! Reporters don't like it!"

"I will tell *them what* to like." Kass announced, taking his seat at the table.

"Yeah!" Rayn agreed, snuggling up next to her husband.

"Reporters are all communists." Roach decided, already helping himself to mash potatoes.

McPherson looked deeply unhappy about being stuck with them today, standing away from the table, as if afraid to get too close.

"You people are dangerous."

"In the right circumstances, a *paperclip* is dangerous." Marian informed her, sitting down at the table, finally finished watching that kid's movie where Santa Claus fought the Devil in Mexico City, with the help of Merlin the Wizard. Cynic watched it every year, for some reason. "All behavior and morals are situational. That is the entire basis of the law."

Cynic strolled past his wife and casually undid the tight bun Marian's hair was secured in, just to be annoying. His fingers slid through the now free blonde strands worshipfully, and he pretended not to notice the playful mock glare Marian flashed him. "Well, *there's* a little tidbit you won't find on *Sesame Street,* Sweets."

"Jesus fucking Christ!" Poacher flopped down into his seat, sounding irritated. "Are you really bashing *Sesame Street*!?! Henson was a fucking *god,* man."

Amy nodded. "While I disagree with Sydney's well-intentioned blasphemy, I do agree that Jim Henson was a remarkable entertainer." She smiled at Poacher sweetly, carrying out one of the turkeys she'd prepared and placing it on the table, before going to retrieve another. "It's so nice of you to remember a fallen icon like that, Sydney."

"Fuck him." Emily tossed a bag of frozen peas onto the table, which were *still* frozen, and a pan of what appeared to be her deadly meat loaf. "*Dark Crystal* still blows."

Poacher grabbed his silverware, preparing to eat everything on the table, up to and possibly including the silverware. "You're out of your goddamned mind, blondie."

"I killed a dude with a paperclip one time." Natalie told no one in particular, dragging Oz towards the table and taking their seats. "The guy was like…" She wrapped her hands around her own throat and then trailed off smiling. "He kept trying to…" She began to snicker as she rocked back and forth frantically, making a choking sound. Her chuckling became full-fledged booming laughter.

Roach howled along in utter hilarity, finding her sense of humor delightful.

Oz looked down at the tableware which was arranged in front of him, a frown creasing his handsome features. "Whose silverware is this?" He asked suspiciously. "Did this come from the Crater Lair, or was this in the Freedom Squad building when we took it over?" He shook his head, looking wary. Like his fork would somehow gain sentience and spring to life at any moment, attacking him before the food was even served. "Because I don't think we should use it if its origins are unknown."

Natalie clapped him on the back in complete adoration, loving the crazy way his mind worked. She leaned over to kiss him, her tongue pushing its way into his mouth and staking her claim. "I think we'll be fine, Baby Doll." She assured him teasingly.

Harlot took her seat at the head of the table, beside her father and her husband. "A toast..." She announced.

Kass watched in irritation as Stacy raised her glass. "I've said it before and I'll say it again: if your bride is too young to drink the champagne at the reception, she's too young to get married."

Hazard turned to glare at him. "What business is it of *yours*?"

Kass pointed at Stacy. "That girl is my daughter in every way that matters."

"Absolutely." Stacy nodded in total agreement. "Except biologically or legally."

"What do I care about 'the law'?" Kass sounded disgusted by the implication. "The Bells are *mine*. Every miniscule blonde one of them. They're *my* children. *I* found them, *I've* kept them, and *I've* invested *years* into their upbringing and maintenance. *Someone* has to keep their stupidity from destroying them and that impossible responsibility falls to me."

Stacy considered that for a moment, glancing at her brothers, then back at Kass. "Can I... like... call you 'Dad' or something then?" She asked hesitantly. "Sometimes?"

"Would I get grandchildren?" Kass countered, sounding equally hesitant. "I need to cement my legacy in this undeserving world. Furthering my dynasty is a growing priority."

Stacy shrugged. "Sure."

"Then I can live with that." Kass decided, then paused. "Of course... I can live with a lot of things, being immortal and all."

"Cool." Stacy beamed, obviously thrilled with this new arrangement. She ran over to give him a quick hug. "I don't even remember having a dad before. This is exciting! Are you going to be nicer to me?"

"Probably harsher because your disappointing behavior more directly reflects upon me." Kass paused, watching his newfound daughter take her seat again and excitedly kiss her husband. "Sit up straight, by the way. Only slack-jawed peasants slouch."

Killian looked more amused than anything. "Can I have a new car, 'Dad'?"

Kass glared at the boy in warning, then refocused on Hazard.

"And I have the date of your wedding *marked on my calendar,* and if she gives birth *one day* before nine months have passed, you and I are going to have words."

Hazard spread his arms out in exasperated confusion. "Your bride was pregnant *during* the wedding, mate!"

Kass shook his head in certainty. "Entirely different."

"Personally, I'm wondering why you needed to mark the date of their wedding on a calendar, since it's also *our* anniversary." Rayn thought aloud, then turned to her husband. "And since when do *you* have a calendar? Last time I checked, you're still confused why there were only 12 months in this dimension."

"*Which is why I bought the calendar!*" Kass argued, as if that were perfectly rational.

Harlot held up her hand to call for order again. "We done?" She asked, her tone filled with mild irritation but good-humored mirth. "Then I'd like to propose a toast..."

They all joined in.

"To the friends we've lost, the friends we've found, and the friends we'll have forever." Harlot said, taking her husband's hand. "Happy Thanksgiving, family!"

"And Kilroy." Natalie added, her voice breaking. She raised her glass higher. "He was here. He left his mark. And he won't be forgotten."

The team toasted again... then started to argue about petty and ultimately meaningless bullshit.

Because that's what they did.

Oz took her hand and kissed it tenderly. "You're a good person, Natalie." He told her softly.

She shrugged. "Only currently." She heaped some sweet potatoes and marshmallows onto his plate for him, because he needed to eat more unhealthy things and have more fun. "Tomorrow, I might be evil again."

****

"You're sure this isn't too weird and kinky, right?" Oz asked again, voice tight with desire and lust, but apprehensive about giving into his darker inclinations. "Because it *seems* pretty weird and kinky, Nat."

"Yes." She nodded her head, pulling on her hand to make sure the bonds were secure enough and held her still. "This one needs to be tighter. Close to cutting off the circulation, please." She

470

swallowed, loving the fact that her goody-two shoes partner was strapping her down like this. "There isn't a single part of me that doesn't want you." She told him honestly. "Besides, you deserve some sexy revenge for all Ronnie put you through this week."

"I don't know…" Oz began, always looking at everything like it was a morality test he needed to pass. "This still seems really…"

"Oz… look at me." She met his eyes.

And she could tell the decision was made.

He moved to kneel behind her, her arms and legs tied so that she was on her hands and knees, offering herself to him. It was the most submissive position she could think of, and it was the one she wanted to use when Oz took Ronnie. Hopefully, very hard.

"Mercygiver?" Oz asked hesitantly.

Natalie smiled in pleasure as Ronnie took the stage, recognizing the predicament.

"Uh-oh…" Mull grinned from beside them in Nat's mind. "I think Ronnie's in trouble now…"

Mercygiver yanked on the bonds, uttering a curse.

Oz calmly ran his fingers through the damp red curls which were nestled between Ronnie's thighs, exploring.

Mercygiver stiffened, as one of Oz's questing fingers slipped inside and his rough scars teased the delicate skin they were claiming. "Are you a history fan, Mister Dimico?" Ronnie got out hoarsely, trying to concentrate on something other than how good it felt to be invaded like that.

"Yes, actually." Oz seemed interested in that, like he was excited to discover something else about her. The pad of his thumb casually began playing with Ronnie's center like it was his personal property. "Very much so."

Mercygiver stopped, taken aback by his answer and by what the man's fingers were doing, the prepared speech ending mid-word. "Wait… what?" Ronnie's heartrate went up, hopeful and excited over that news. "…Really?" There was an edge of desperation in the word.

Oz went off on a tangent, his fingers no longer playing, always eager to talk with Natalie about her interests. "I'm particularly interested in the War years up until the '60s, as…"

"Oz?" Natalie interrupted, taking over her mind again. "Can you focus here? I'm happy that you and the nightmare parts of my brain are bonding over shared interests, but maybe you can concentrate?"

"Right." Oz nodded sheepishly, and moving to sit in front of Ronnie on the bed. "We started a confrontation, Mercygiver, remember?"

"I remember threatening to kill you." Ronnie said, faking complete confidence. "And I remember wondering how quickly I could *break your fucking neck*."

"Uh-huh." Oz didn't seem at all intimidated by that, possibly because the threat was delivered while his fingers were still damp from Ronnie's body. "No, you didn't." He said with complete confidence. "Not at all."

Mull and Natalie were distracted by staring at the man's erection, utterly transfixed, remembering what it felt like to have it inside them. Anxious to feel it again.

Mercygiver made a conspicuous effort to keep from looking at its throbbing length, the barriers between the different parts of Natalie's mind breaking down.

Oz had reached *all* of her mind but this one last little bit, which had been cloaked in shadow her entire life. A part of her mind which scared her, like a monster under the bed. That was where Mercygiver called home. In the chaos and hate. In her self-loathing and fear.

But she was *certain* that Oz could reach all of her. That Ronnie's hatred could be cleaned away by the sunlight of Oz's sweet, pure love. It had washed the rest of her clean, making her feel complete. Like a regular, non-crazy person.

She knew it could do the same for that last little piece of herself too.

But she needed to be careful. In many ways, Ronnie was like a wild animal.

Thus, today's experiment. She had asked to be tied up, just in case it went wrong. She was sure she could control Ronnie, but… no sense in taking unneeded risks.

She looked at Oz's hard body, inches from her face, just *asking* to be pleasured. Natalie wasn't generally a sex kitten, but there was something about Oz which made her feel especially *imaginative*.

"Do it." Mull begged Oz in Natalie's thoughts, getting excited by the idea of what was about to happen to Ronnie. "Please…"

Natalie smiled, wanting it too.

"I love you." Oz said tenderly, looking into Mercygiver's eyes. "I love all of you, even the darkness. If you don't want to give me that piece of you, I will understand completely." He shook his head, not breaking the eye contact. "I won't push you to do anything you don't want to do. Not ever." He gently took Ronnie's face in his strong hands. "You will not hurt me. You do not scare me. And

472

there's *nothing in this world* which would ever make me leave you."

They were all silent for several breaths.

"If you put that in my mouth, I will bite it off." Mercygiver told Oz flatly, but Natalie noticed a tremor in the tone, which indicated desire. Ronnie didn't mean that. At all.

Mull silently snickered, recognizing the wavering too and loving it.

"No. You won't." Oz said with his complete confidence and trust. His body remained where it was, tantalizingly close.

Natalie nodded, ignoring Ronnie's fear. "I want it." She assured Oz softly.

Oz didn't need to be told twice, moving forward. Mercygiver got over the momentary hesitation and opened Natalie's mouth, filling it with Oz's hard body.

Mull made a low hum of pleasure, enjoying it.

Oz hissed, his movements stiff, like he was terrified of hurting her.

Mercygiver made a low moan, almost identical to Mull's, tongue tentatively teasing Oz's shaft, testing him. Feeling dominated and kinda scared and uncertain how this was going to go...

Mull started to silently laugh again. *"Taste good, asshole?"* Mull gloated, enjoying the sight of Oz's body in Ronnie's mouth. *"That's right... Suck him off... You acted like you were the toughest thing around since I was a girl, scared me every day, but look at you now... A fucking day with my man, and he's turned your weak ass into his little cock slut..."*

Natalie swore at herself, as Mercygiver considered that, anger stirring. Already planning how to escape the bonds and kill Multifarious...

"No, no..." Nat shoved Mull's vindictive personality to the side, wanting to keep this as calm and loving as possible. *"Don't make it weird. We all want to do this, it's okay. We love Oz and he loves us and this is..."*

"Step out of the way, it's my turn." Mull pushed forward in Nat's mind, taking several more inches of Oz's body into her mouth, choking herself, as if still in a contest with Ronnie to see which of them was better.

Oz swore fluently, not expecting that.

Natalie took control again, then made sure Mercygiver got what was coming. *"Finish him."* She silently ordered the darkest parts of herself. *"You love him too, Ronnie, finish him so that we know you're not going to hurt him in his sleep or something..."* Her voice took on a pleading tone, all but begging herself now. *"Please... Please, for once, just be normal... Please trust him..."*

Ronnie apparently didn't need to be told twice, head bobbing, lips sealing tightly around Oz's shaft.

The hesitation was gone now.

Oz grabbed the top of Ronnie's head, keeping it still and exactly where he wanted it, then began to thrust his hips and fuck Ronnie's mouth mercilessly. "That's right..." He soothed, looking into Ronnie's eyes. "Look at me..."

Mercygiver's eyes stayed locked on his, unable to look away. Unable to move away. Unable to do anything but feel Oz's body and his desire. See the love on the man's face and the unbridled lust he was unleashing.

Oz gritted his teeth, jaw set, obviously working some stuff out. He and Ronnie had a troubled history. Anger and desire and love seemed to make the man very hard, and he was obviously enjoying this. His body moved in much harsher, punishing strokes, which he didn't use with Natalie.

Ronnie had almost taken Natalie from him. Now, he was *taking* his pleasure from Ronnie. Hard and rough and without apology. There was no standing on ceremony now. Oz was always polite and considerate with Mull and Natalie... but he was going to straight up fuck Mercygiver.

Oz moved, so that his body rubbed against Ronnie's face and tongue, lifting himself up so that the underside of his shaft and his scrotum could be pleasured, suckled, and tasted too. Which they immediately were.

Natalie had somehow managed to turn Oz from a virgin into an absolute *demon* in bed.

In *one day.*

Not that Natalie was bragging about that to herself. Just that... she kinda was.

This was going very well, on all fronts. Better than Natalie could have possibly hoped.

It wasn't even simply about obeying Natalie's command now, Ronnie *wanted* to do this. Loved it. Hoped it never stopped. Natalie could tell.

"Fuck..." Mull swore, also amazed by how good it felt and how much she was enjoying seeing this. Feeling this. It was dark and twisted and completely weird. She'd detested Ronnie for so long, watching Mercygiver finally get knocked down a few pegs was absolutely delicious. Granted, she'd wanted to kill Ronnie, but this was

474

even better somehow. Far more enjoyable. Watching her enemy be dominated by her shining, perfect hero, and know that defeat. She'd earned that after enduring years of being terrorized and afraid.

Oz clasped his hands on either side of Ronnie's face, moving on the bed.

Mercygiver made small desperate sounds of hunger and submission, tongue eagerly lapping at Oz's cock, afraid he was pulling away. Wanting him to stay, suddenly terrified of being alone again.

But Oz didn't pull away. "I will never leave you." He assured Ronnie softly.

And that assurance *reached* Mercygiver.

It was better than Natalie could have hoped, and she all but wept for how easy it was. After all these years, she didn't have to be afraid anymore.

"That's right..." Natalie silently urged her dark side, feeling the terror she'd felt her entire life slipping away and being cleansed. *"You want him too, Ronnie... Feel how much he loves you... He's not going to leave us... We don't need to be afraid... Taste him... Love him back..."*

Oz pushed himself deeply into Mercygiver's throat and came, calling out Natalie's name. Ronnie made a moan of triumph and hunger, suckling every drop from him and wanting more.

Natalie's eyebrows rose in shock. Okay. *Miiiight* be going a bit far, Ronnie. Dial it back some, yeah? Don't scare him. He was a virgin until yesterday. Save something for the honeymoon, please.

Mull swore again, feeling like this was just too much. She'd never experienced anything this powerful before.

Oz pulled himself free of her mouth, still looking into her eyes. "I love you." He said again softly, breathing hard. "God, I can't believe how much I love you, baby..."

"If somebody had told me that my Thanksgiving this year would end with me genuinely getting off on watching my abusive piece of shit ex blowing my current boyfriend, I probably would have called them a liar." Mull thought aloud in side Natalie's head, sounding amazed. *"But... no, that was hot. And creepy. And I loved it. Let's make it a holiday tradition."*

Oz made his way around behind Ronnie, who was tied up and arranged just how Oz wanted, swollen folds spread and entirely open to him. Oz could clearly see the impact of his efforts. Mercygiver's body was weeping in need, trembling in anticipation. Ronnie was very, *very* ready for him. *Desperate* for him, in fact, to the point of it being rather embarrassing. Which just made it more exciting, somehow.

"Natalie wants me to fuck you into compliance, no matter what you say." Oz informed Ronnie using sexy profanity, voice dark with urgent need. It was probably taking everything in him to hold back, even after he'd just climaxed. You could say a lot of things about the man, but she never doubted that he *always* wanted her. "But I don't want her to spend the rest of our lives together worrying about you and what you could do in revenge. So, I am going to let you choose." He reached forward to brush the hair off of the nape of Mercygiver's neck, then leaned closer to plant a gentle kiss there. "If you want me, ask. If you don't ask me, this stops."

Ronnie considered that offer, deciding on what kind of future they would all have.

But when you came right down to it, Ronnie had always wanted someone. Someone who had thick skin about overtly evil things, and who was loyal, and who was strong...

So, tied down and trussed up in front of the strongest man Mercygiver had ever met, it really wasn't much of a choice.

"I..." Ronnie began, trying to move so that Oz's throbbing body was closer. "I want you." Ronnie breathed, just wanting to feel a part of something, especially something with someone this extraordinary. "Please... please fuck me, Mister Dimico."

The words were vulgar and exciting and so, so wonderful to say.

"Oz." The man corrected, a note of authority in his tone.

Mercygiver met his eyes, the moment oddly intimate. Ronnie almost blushed. "...Oz."

He nodded, happy with that. "You threw Natalie off of a roof." Oz said, making Ronnie wait for what they *all* knew was coming.

"That's true, you did." Mull agreed silently, getting even more excited.

"She deserved it." Ronnie spat out, in halfhearted cruelty, hoping that Oz would respond by moving faster and being rougher. "*You'll* want to throw her off a roof too, if..."

Ronnie's words stopped in a small cry as Oz pushed his way into Natalie's body.

Mercygiver let out a long, low moan, followed by several soft, breathy sounds.

"Natalie makes that sound too." Oz growled. "I like it. Now I've heard you both make it for me. Next, I'm going to hear it from *Multifarious*, while I'm inside her and she's wearing nothing but her mask."

476

Mull liked that idea, perfectly ready to try it right now. She didn't have the mask... but they could always try it again later.

Although Mercygiver was too far gone to even recognize what was being said, there was absolutely *no way* that Ronnie was willing to step aside and allow Mull to take over.

Oz was unrelenting, pushing further.

Ronnie's body welcomed Oz. Like a conquering hero.

"That's it..." Natalie could tell this was over, and that she had won. Ronnie's hate was no match for Oz's love. *"Let him in, you love him..."* *She repeated to herself.* *"You love him so much, even I can feel it... We can all feel it..."* She closed her eyes against the ecstasy. *"God, I feel it so much..."*

Oz pushed forward until he was fully seated inside Mercygiver, every muscle in his body tense. *"Fuuuck... you're so tight..."* His hand came down on her ass in a sharp slap. "Are you tighter? Or is Natalie?" He wondered aloud. "Tell me."

Ronnie was incapable of responding to that for a moment, mind utterly blank, relishing the sensation of being filled so completely by Oz's body. Of being so close to someone and feeling that kind of love. Being utterly powerless but in complete control. "...Me?" Ronnie guessed meekly, sounding hesitant and eagerly hopeful to please him.

Anything, *anything*, just so he didn't leave. Just so he didn't stop.

"Maybe. I don't think so, but I'll need further study." Oz nodded. "I think you should apologize to her though." Oz said, his voice still low, and his breathing was heavy. "For hurting her."

It was going to be a tossup here. Natalie really wanted them all to get along, and she believed that could happen, but only if Oz could hold out for a little while.

And, for that matter, if she could hold out too. She was still *not* used to being with Oz, and the ecstasy he was giving her crashed through the crumbling dividers in her mind. If she wasn't careful, she'd grab the reigns of her mind back and take Oz herself, climaxing early and ruining this whole thing.

The goal was to calm her darkness. Not to just have fun in bed and take what she wanted.

Natalie had to sit still and let Mercygiver and Oz make love. It was a *torture* to not move things at her pace. But it was the kind of torture which just added to the pleasure she knew Oz would soon bring them all.

Mull let out a silent moan in Natalie's head, Oz filling her too.

"He's... he's too big..."

Mercygiver bit Natalie's bottom lip, trying to hold in the pleasure. "I... won't... apologize."

It was a game. Nat could feel it, starting to laugh in nervous relief and pleasure. Her entire mind was enjoying this.

"Really?" Oz pumped his hips. Hard.

Mercygiver made a small squeaking sound, not expecting that.

Natalie closed her eyes, praying that she didn't ruin this. She was *soooo* close to coming herself. Oz's body was so hard and so thick and pushed in *so* deep...

Mull began to pant in need, not even paying attention to the internal conversation. She wasn't capable of thought anymore, just an animal instinct which urged her to thrust her hips back against Oz and moan like a banshee who'd joined the sex trade.

Natalie started wrestling with Mull for control, as Mull wanted Oz and didn't want to wait anymore.

"I won't." Ronnie insisted, not as firmly as the first time, trying to hold onto the darkness, afraid of the light.

"Fucking do it!" Mull all but begged silently. *"I can't..."*

Oz started pumping his hips harder, fucking Mercygiver in earnest now. And there was absolutely nothing Ronnie could do about it. There was nowhere left to hide.

Love was going to win the day.

Mull let out a cry, her body drenched in need and stretched around Oz's pitiless length.

Natalie began to say Oz's name as he moved inside her, welcoming him as her rescuer.

Mercygiver had finally had enough, voice trembling. "...I'm... I'm sorry..."

Natalie instantly felt her mind shift, becoming more in control of herself and certain that she'd never do anything to hurt Oz. There was no part of her mind that dark. She knew herself now, the shadows at the edges of her soul seeing the gloom clear for the first time.

"Damn right..." Mull whimpered silently. *"I'm sorry too... I don't know what for, but I am. Please... please don't stop... God, I need you so much..."*

Natalie would have to agree with that assessment.

Oz reached forward and grabbed Ronnie's breasts, holding onto them and moving his hips in quick, hard strokes. It was absolutely punishing, letting Natalie glimpse a plateau of pleasure she

478

never before even guessed existed.

She swore, her different personalities all talking over themselves, trying to form words to express the kind of desire which defied words capable of expressing it.

"What about me?" Oz demanded, like some kind of fiend who had kidnapped them all and was having his way with them. "I think you owe *me* an apology too."

Oz was really getting into this.

The realization just made Natalie even more excited, loving it when he had some fun. He didn't get to do anything he wanted. She was so glad that she could help him with that. Particularly since this was fast becoming her favorite day ever.

Mercygiver shook Natalie's head defiantly, but Nat and Mull both knew it was entirely for show. Ronnie was as hot and wet as they were, *loving* this.

Oz grabbed the back of Natalie's head, fingers wrapping around her red curls. He pulled her head back, altering his thrusts and watching the effect they had on her face.

Ronnie was doing a piss-poor job of hiding the pleasure Oz saw there.

Mercygiver gazed at him in lust-filled submission, Oz's body pumping in and out like a jackhammer. "…Sorry…." One of them breathed, Natalie wasn't even sure which one anymore.

"What was that?" Oz pulled Ronnie closer, using his other hand to pinch at Mull's stiffened nipple at the same time, making them all hiss in pleasure and forbidden pain. "I didn't hear you."

"I'm… sorry…" Mercygiver gasped, on the verge of climax and desperate for release. "I'm sorry… I'm sorry… I'm sorry…"

"And?" Oz demanded, his voice stern and dripping with lusty power.

"It… it won't happen… again…" Mercygiver said quickly, trying to please him. "She's… she's yours…"

"And?" Oz repeated.

Mercygiver's mind raced, trying to figure out what to say here.

"*And?*" Oz pressed again, more emphatically.

Natalie and Mull both shrugged, having no idea either.

Oz reached under Mull to ruthlessly pluck at Natalie's center, his fingers torturing Ronnie with pleasure for that lack of cooperation. "You." He supplied, voice the commanding tone he took when he meant his word to be law. "*You* are mine, 'Ronnie.'" He drove himself into Mercygiver hard, emphasizing the point. "Just like Natalie, just like all of them. You *all* belong with *me*. Because I belong with you."

Mercygiver gasped at the sensation, but also at the words. Ronnie liked that. Liked belonging to someone, forever. Never having to worry about being alone or being abandoned. Being able to trust someone completely.

Ronnie liked that idea a *lot*.

Ronnie was almost pathetically grateful to be included, and not banished to the furthest reaches of Natalie's mind; alone and broken.

And in that moment... Ronnie loved Oswald Dimico completely and utterly.

"Yes..." Mercygiver cried, desperate for it and wanting Oz to finish. "I belong... I'm yours... You fucking *own me*... I'm yours... Forever, I'm yours..."

"Good. You've owned *me* since Natalie asked for a ride home from that embassy party." Oz nodded. "I'm glad we had this opportunity to talk and discuss our differences." Oz pushed himself all the way into Natalie to accentuate the words again, leaning down to whisper in Ronnie's ear in a deep throaty way. "Isn't this better than trying to kill each other?"

All three of her dominant personalities gasped together, sharing that unbelievable sensation.

"Want me to stop, 'Mercygiver'?" Oz asked, running his hand along Ronnie's shoulder tenderly. "Maybe do this with Natalie, instead?"

Ronnie shook Natalie's head, biting her lip to stifle a moan. "No..."

"I'm sorry?" Oz asked again, obviously enjoying the submission of his foe and the knowledge that Natalie was in control of her own body for once. "Can you repeat that?"

Ronnie let out a moan, tears of pleasure and ecstasy and gratefulness over being included, running down Natalie's cheeks, which the bonds on Mull's wrists prevented being wiped away. "You stop... and I'll die..." Mercygiver nodded desperately. "Please, I need this..."

"Please don't stop..." Mull silently screamed in Natalie's head, trying to move her hips to get Oz further inside her body.

Natalie could see the plateau again, feeling like Oz was lifting her towards it.

Her straight-laced partner and love of her life began grunting, hammering himself into her like some kind of monster, filling her to the point of pain. He was losing himself in her now, his control snapping.

Mull began to moan.

Mercygiver whimpered Oz's name as each thrust struck home, surrendering to their shared desire.

The evil nightmare which lurked inside Natalie's head had met its match. And it was deeply, *deeply* enjoying its humiliating defeat.

Natalie remained fixated on the height of pleasure this offered, like she was scrambling towards it up an uneven cliff. She'd always been of a fractured mind, but now, every piece of her wanted this man. Loved this man. Completely. And all of her was *utterly* relishing what he was doing to her.

Oz's fingers gripped her tightly, as the bonds around her wrists dug into her flesh, holding her exactly where and how he wanted her. And that loss of control, was so forbidden and exotic and exciting...

"I love you..." Oz began repeating in a chant, hand toying with her hair like it was magic. "All of you. Natalie, Multifarious, Mercygiver... *All* of you..."

He slammed into her one more time, and his body hit the exact spot she was desperate for him to reach.

All three of her main personalities climaxed at once, panting in release and crying out his name.

Natalie crested the wave of her own passion, arriving at something so clean and wonderful and fulfilling. It was like she was looking down on the world, seeing how amazing it could be. Like her entire body was made of pleasure and the cartoon rainbows which decorated Natalie's breakfast cereal boxes.

Oz crushed her against him, climaxing deep inside her and mumbling her name. Well... *names*.

Natalie closed her eyes, letting that passion and love fill her.

"Tell him. The truth." Natalie asked Mercygiver. *"Make sure he knows."*

"I... I love you." Ronnie's voice broke. "I love you so much, Mister Di... *Oz*." Mercygiver sniffled. "Please don't ever leave me. Please?"

Oz leaned down to kiss Ronnie's temple tenderly. "I am not going anywhere." He panted for breath, still fully seated and hard. Then ran his hand over Nat's rear. "This was the single weirdest and kinkiest moment of my entire life." He confessed.

Natalie nodded, trying to catch her breath. "Yeah, I thought it was amazing too." She agreed, laughing in sheer bliss.

He patted her flesh in appreciation. "Thank you, Natalie. I love you more than I ever thought I was capable of loving anything in this world." He paused. "And I feel like Mercygiver and I have *really* made a breakthrough in our relationship today. I think we're going to get along quite well." He took on a thoughtful, curious tone. "What era of history does Ronnie like? Because I've got a really nice series of books on midcentury advertising..." He trailed off, silently planning a happy little history book club with her grotesque, thrill-killing ex-personality.

Her soulmate was *such* a boy scout.

The man really was extraordinary.

She snorted in amusement, then swallowed, trying to regain her own mind. Her thoughts were scrambled now. She wasn't used to all three of the voices in her head wanting the same thing. Usually, they just argued with one another or hid in the shadows and waited to strike. Now, they were all *her.* She was thinking in triplicate at the moment, but Natalie's voice louder than the others and growing stronger.

She was the best and worst parts of herself. All the pieces of her puzzle were arranged together, forming one unbroken image.

It was so wonderfully *normal.* ...But in a sick and *really* twisted way.

"I love you." She said softly, turning over her shoulder to meet his gaze. "I'm 10,000 different women today. And every single one of them loves you." She confessed honestly, knowing it was true.

Oz leaned over to kiss her forehead, unwilling to shift his body because he was enjoying the feeling of being inside her too much. Truth told, they both were.

"I've dreamed of you my entire life." He said softly. "Sometimes I think you're the entire reason I'm still alive. Just... just thinking about someone as perfect and wonderful and pure as you, being near trash like me. Looking at me like you're looking at me now..."

Natalie's body began to respond again, wanting him to get back at it.

In her head, Mull nodded. *"Yep."*

Mercygiver agreed eagerly. *"Yes, please. Harder, please. Don't let him ever stop."*

Oz seemed to feel her body's reaction to him, his hips moving an almost imperceptible amount forward. But Natalie felt it. He wanted her as much as she wanted him. And she *loved* the fact that she could do that to someone so restrained.

482

Oz grabbed the flesh of her rear, using it as a handhold to sink into her body more forcefully. "I'll make love to all 10,000 at once... then *individually*." He promised.

"Oooooh... I've got a few who are *dying* to meet you."

"I'm kinda most interested in that one personality you mentioned, who was sexually attracted to herself."

"I'll introduce you to her tonight, just in case I lose access to her when today ends."

He paused his movements, thinking about that. "I am *legitimately* excited about that." He confessed sheepishly.

"I can feel that." She laughed, not even bothering to hide the passion. Oz's proverbial hat might be white, but he was *utterly* merciless in bed. *Thank God.* Her smile widened, loving that man with every ounce of her soul and knowing with utter certainty that he felt the same way about her. All of her. Even the creepy, horrible parts. "You're an evil, *evil* man, Oswald." She teased.

"Not yet." He leaned over to kiss the side of her face in flirtation, while his body sank fully into her. "This is still me being *nice*."

Epilogue

"IF YOU DRINK MUCH FROM A BOTTLE MARKED 'POISON' IT IS ALMOST CERTAIN TO DISAGREE WITH YOU, SOONER OR LATER."

- Alice's Adventures in Wonderland

SEVERAL DAYS LATER

Natalie was doing something she *really* didn't want to do.

She'd much rather be at home right now, continuing to introduce Oz to the many wonders of sugary cereals, while he meticulously worked his way through "The Pile of Mail I Don't Want to Open" for her.

So far, he informed her that she owed $2,600 to people. But there were also enough uncashed checks in there that it was basically evening out.

No, she didn't want to be here.

But she felt like it was important to deal with this. As she walked down the hospital corridor though, she didn't feel at all happy about it.

Oz was outside dealing with his police contacts at the moment, which meant that she also had to do this alone. Well, not *completely* alone. Unfortunately.

"All I'm saying is that if you're gonna try to kill me, I'd like a heads up, that's all." Mr. Jack repeated.

Natalie pinched the bridge of her nose, trying not to scream at Mercygiver's lieutenant. "I have no intention of killing you."

"So... do I still have a job then?"

She put up her hands helplessly. "I have no idea. Just... just give me a few days to sort myself out and I'll get back to you, okay?"

Mr. Jack didn't appear happy with that. "I'm not trying to step on your toes or anything here, Boss, but it's the holiday season and I'd like to have some job security, you know? I don't want to..."

Mercygiver's temper snapped. "Mr. Jack," Ronnie rounded on him, "I recognize that you are a man of limited intelligence, so I will try to speak as slowly as possible," he stepped closer to the man threateningly, "you are *going* to shut your mouth and do as you're told, or you're going to be spending the holidays in the secure position of being *fucking dead!*"

Mr. Jack nodded in terror, taking several steps backward. "Y-y-you got it, boss. Take... take all the time you need." He literally ran from the scene.

Mull nodded at Ronnie in appreciation. "Nicely done."

Ronnie smiled at the compliment, then stepped aside for Natalie again.

As she arrived outside the room, someone moved to block her path.

She blinked at him in surprise, not even remembering the last time she saw Higgins without his boss. The flunky glared at her, obviously furious. "You put Oklahoma in the ICU, Miss." Higgins reminded her darkly. "She's an *Irregular*. You fight an Irregular, you'd better be prepared to fight *all of us*. And there are more of us than you can imagine." His tone grew harsher. "If Mr Welles didn't believe in you, we'd be having a *very different* conversation right now."

"You've seen what I can do." She informed him, not having time for this. "I'm a dangerous person to mess with, Higgins."

"Hildy's strong enough to throw you into the sun, ma'am." He arched a challenging eyebrow. "Can any of those powers allow you to live on the Sun?" Still, he stepped aside for her, because Monty had evidently ordered his men to stay away from her. "We're family, miss. We protect our own. That's what families do."

Natalie ignored that and made her way into the hospital room.

Inside, Oklahoma Mike was stretched out in her bed, talking on her phone.

Christ, even in a hospital gown and beat to hell, she *still* looked like saxophones should be playing sexily whenever she entered a room.

It just wasn't fair!

"I'm telling you, I'm *fine,* you really don't need to make poor Higgins..." She told someone on the other end of the phone, then trailed off when she saw Natalie enter. "I'll call you back, Champ."

They both stared at each other for several moments of awkward silence.

"I'm sorry my evil personality took over and beat the shit out of you." Natalie told her honestly, not knowing how else to even phrase that. She sank into a chair next to Oklahoma's bed. "I took no part in it, but it won't happen again, you have my word. I have Mercygiver *completely* under control now. Ronnie won't ever hurt anyone else without permission, I swear it."

"You kill her?" Oklahoma asked, a note of hope in her smoky voice.

Truth told, Oz's evil side and *her* evil side had really been hitting it off. Oz and Ronnie had developed their own weird little... thing, and they had spent most of the previous day excitedly sharing history trivia like the obsessive fucking nerds they were.

Ronnie was still a demented lunatic who wanted to use brutal murder as a shortcut to all of life's problems, but he was also so pathetically grateful for Oz's love and so loyal and in love with Oz in return, that now whenever Mercygiver was in the room with Oz, it was like, "Umm... I was wondering if I could maybe fetch your slippers and give you another *embarrassingly* enthusiastic blowjob, sir, if that wouldn't be too much of an imposition on you? *Please? Pretty-pretty-please!*"

It was just sad.

She was almost disappointed in her evil side. Not that she *wanted* them to argue or fight, obviously, but... Ronnie didn't have to be *completely* Oz's history buddy and meekly thankful sex toy. They didn't have to gossip about obscure medieval bullshit trivia until *THREE IN THE FUCKING MORNING!*

She'd *never* get over that. It showed a *blatant* disrespect to the rest of her brain, and she was seriously going to have a talk with herself about it. She intended to gather all of herselves together again, and *lay down the law*.

At the moment though, she didn't have the heart. Mercygiver followed Oz around everywhere like a fucking puppy, all doe-eyed and eager and fawning after Oz in wonder, like he was the hero of some grand fucking legend, brought to life. It was embarrassing. But it was good for Ronnie. He'd settle down, once he got used to being loved. Ronnie was dark and damaged and had been alone for too long. Been hurt too much and had seen too much. If that part of her mind needed Oz for emotional support, sexual healing, and intellectual companionship, she was glad to let it happen.

Natalie felt the same way about Oz, obviously, but at least she tried to hide it.

For her part, Mull thought that Ronnie and Oz were going to run away together or something, leaving the rest of them behind. She was kinda jealous.

Natalie thought the whole thing was rather adorable. And really went to show what an incredible man Oz was. That he could find it in his heart to love someone so horrible and damaged.

But she was *still* going to establish some kind of schedule, so that sleep was possible and the various parts of her mind could maintain *some* degree of pride around Oz. If they all worked together, they could at least *pretend* to play hard to get.

It was tough, but she was sure they could do it.

Probably.

She gently ran her fingertip over the gold anklet Oz had given her, and the three enamel hearts which dangled from it. White, black, and a red heart with a tiny clock mounted in it. Reminding her every second that he loved all of her.

He'd bought it during the store's Black Friday sale.

She was very proud.

"Ronnie has…" She trailed off, searching for a delicate way to explain making peace with herself, and the darkly sensual things they all did with Oz in bed. "He's… found other things to occupy his mind." She explained.

Oklahoma's eyebrow arched, somehow guessing the details, a smile curving her swollen but still perfectly shaped lips. "Kinky. …It's always the quiet ones." She seemed amused by that. "To be fair though, Oswald is a *very* beautiful man."

"He's mine." Natalie, Multifarious, and Mercygiver all warned the woman at once, just in case there was any mistake about that.

Oklahoma considered that, her pale green eyes swollen nearly shut, but still conniving.

"I want exclusive distribution rights to sales of BluRays of your fight with the Agletarians." She announced, like it wasn't up for debate. "I think a ninety-foot half-naked redhead taking apart a robot monster, should be something that appeals to my clientele."

Natalie's eyebrows rose. "You want to sell movies of me naked?"

"No." She shook her head. "You're in your underwear, not naked. Well… there are a *few* times when things pop free, but that's bound to happen." She put down her phone. "Movies of you naked are *already* out there, Mercygiver. The parade was nationally televised. The footage is on the evening news, for God's sake! There's no stopping that now. So you might as well profit from it."

"But I'm *naked!*"

"Not all the way. Besides, if you look good in the footage, who cares?" Oklahoma shrugged unconcernedly. "This is the 21st century: naked photos are only humiliating if you look *bad* in them."

Natalie opened her mouth to reply to that, then closed it, then opened it again, trying to decide how embarrassing her next question would be.

Oklahoma guessed what she wanted to know. "Oh, yes. You looked *very* good in it, don't worry. Some powers don't always make for the most appealing shots, but you? The hundred foot sex goddess?" She smiled her femme fatale smile. "You *found* your pretty."

"70-30, me." Natalie decided.

"Oh, fuck you, '*Fight Club*'! You put me in the hospital!" Oklahoma reminded her. "60-40, me."

"70-30 and I'd get final approval on the cut."

"Who are you? Stanley Kubrick, now? No." Oklahoma shook her head. "You are merely the talent, I will handle the business side of things."

"If I'm in it, then it's *my* movie. I want approval or no deal. This will be presented as a fight, not smut."

"You're in your underwear!"

"But I'm a *superheroine* in underwear. Don't cheapen it. I deserve some respect for saving the city, even if I had to do it in a bra and panties." She crossed her arms over her chest. "We'll blur out some stuff and frame it as a sporting event, on the scale of Godzilla. And Oz gets to be in it too."

Oklahoma perked up at that. "Naked?" She sounded hopeful.

"No!"

"I'm just asking, jeez." Oklahoma ran a hand through her hair. "Why would Oswald want to be featured in your film debut? ...I mean, 'Your glorious victory over your foes.'"

"Because he wants to be remembered as a hero."

"And you really think my customers will give a good goddamn about Oz's *completely clothed* half of the fight?"

"If you want *my* half of it, you will." She crossed her arms over her chest. "Oz saved millions of people. I want the city to remember that."

"Your contributions to the battle were rather memorable, I doubt the men of the city will be forgetting this fight anytime soon..."

"You're not helping your case." Nat deadpanned.

"Fine." She rolled her eyes. "We'll add some fight

commentary and graphics. Maybe a post-fight interview with you both. That'll sell it even better." She paused. "But I'm *not* blurring anything. We can add another zero or two for the fact you're a natural redhead alone. I make *Cape erotica*, not those crappy basic cable dramas or MMA clip-shows."

"I'll consider it." She shook her head. "But I seriously doubt I'll agree to that."

"Consider fast, because pretty soon, I'm just going to bootleg the footage and trust that my attorneys are better than yours."

She made a face at the other woman. "You're a horrible person, Oklahoma."

"I'm an Irregular."

Natalie looked around the interior of the hospital room, which was filled with flowers, balloons, and get-well cards.

"At least you've got a shit-ton of flowers here." She remarked casually.

Oklahoma shrugged again. "Boss' friend tries to beat you to death, boss sends you flowers. It's one of the only perks."

"*Monty* sent you flowers?"

"Doubtful he did it himself, no." Oklahoma flipped a disinterested hand. "I would be the one usually tasked with that kind of thing. It was probably Leland. I can't imagine Mister Welles even knowing *how* to order flowers."

Nat looked down at the expensive looking fabric of her chair. "This hospital is much better than the one I was in."

"This is our hospital."

"'Our' hospital?"

"This is an extension of Wellesburg Memorial." Oklahoma sounded very proud. "It's the best medicine money can buy."

Nat made an incredulous sound, remembering the shitty hospital *she'd* been stuck in last week. "Why wasn't *I* sent here?" She gasped.

"You'd have to ask Mr. Welles."

"To be honest, I kinda figured Monty's version of medical care was basically the same as when a horse breaks its leg." She made a gun-firing gesture.

"Wow." Oklahoma looked disappointed by Natalie's lack of faith. "You really don't understand him at all, do you?"

"Are you trying to tell me that under his horrible surface there exists a heart of gold?"

Oklahoma snorted, which then turned into outright wheezing laughter over the absurdity of that idea, tight because of her

490

broken ribs. "No, no, not at all. He's exactly as bad as he seems. Probably worse, in fact." She leaned back against her pillows, tiredly. "The Roman scholar Persius had a saying: *vincit qui patitur,* 'he conquers who endures.' The Welles family made it their motto, way back. It means that you can get what you want, if you're able to ignore all of the bad things associated with it and the terrible things you had to do to get it. You can win any fight, if you can withstand the pain long enough." She paused for a moment. "I think about that sometimes..." She swallowed, then met her eyes. "I'm not your friend, Natalie. I will kill you if I'm asked to or if I think you threaten my family. But I can tell you this: you *won't* beat Montgomery Welles." Her voice was firm and completely certain. "He got shot three times in the chest and once in the face, and it didn't kill him. It just made him stronger. He lost his entire family and it didn't stop him. It just made him ruthless. He will somehow use your attempts to kill him, to make himself more powerful. He is dangerous in a way that you and the Consortium have never seen. I honestly don't know what it is he thinks he wants, but I can tell you... he's going to get it. He will get it, no matter who is in his way trying to stop him or what powers they have. He's a *Welles,* the last of the *Wellesberg* Welles. That's what they *do.* That's who they *are.*" She nodded to herself. "And I'm going to help him, in any way I can."

Natalie wasn't sure what to say to that.

The room fell into silence.

"He taught my sister Karen and I to play the piano once, when we were girls." Oklahoma randomly shared, her voice now sounding slightly dream-like from the drugs. "All he could play was *'Leaning on the Everlasting Arms.'*" She flipped her hand again. "I assume his mother taught him. I never asked. He kept messing up the lesson though, he tried to hide it, but he was just terrible. Then we all laughed." Her voice grew sadder, trailing off. "...God, we laughed..."

"I don't have all of Rondel's memories, thank god." Natalie began. "They're still... murky. But I know I worked with Monty before. I know I did jobs for him." Her voice became stern. "What did I *do,* Oklahoma?"

"I have no idea." The woman told her.

"I think you're lying."

"I would, if I knew." Oklahoma admitted. "I'd lie to your face and I wouldn't feel badly about it at all." She looked out the window, voice far away. "My mother... she warned me about the Welles family. 'That boy's great-great-grandfather sold his soul to something dark, for riches and power, and it has poisoned the family ever since,' she said, 'They're ruined and rotting. Hollow inside. They might seem nice. They might seem friendly. You might even like them. But there is fire burning beneath their surface, just out of sight... And sooner or later, the ground you think you're standing on with them will fall out from under you... and the Welleses will take you down with them. Down into the darkness where their souls used to be. You'll burn too, Car. ...You don't touch a Welles and not burn.'" She swallowed, voice tight, reaching up to touch one of the charms on her necklace. "She didn't take her own advice though. None of us did." Her voice lowered to a haunted whisper, cracking. "...And now? I'm the only one left."

"You tell me he's a monster, but you also tell me that he's just misunderstood." Natalie leaned forward. "You're an intelligent woman, who says she'll die for someone we both know is a madman. So, help me understand him."

"Sometimes who you *were* is more important than who you a*re.*" Oklahoma thought aloud, clearing her throat and visibly fighting against the pain meds she was on. "Do you know what the orbital cortex in the brain does? It's the center which controls behavior. It's the brain's safety switch which keeps your other drives in check, judges the context of the situation, and tells the parts of the brain what their responses should be. It tells you when you should feel love or empathy or guilt or gives you a gentle reminder why you can't just stab the person who cuts you off in traffic. All kinds of things. I've always thought of it as the brain's morality center; it's the piece which makes humans *humane*. For lack of a better term, it's... your *soul*." She tapped her face. "It's located right behind here. And if it got injured, like say, if someone *put a bullet into it,* no matter who you were before that, you'd be pretty damaged as a result. And that wouldn't be your fault. You'd just be *different* as a result of your handicap. It would make you incapable of feeling what a normal person would feel. It would make you capable of doing things no normal person could do, if they ever wanted to sleep at night. It would turn you into something that not everyone understands or even tries to."

Natalie processed that. "Doesn't mean you wouldn't be an asshole though."

"Didn't say it did. Just that... we live in a very complicated world." Oklahoma sounded sad again. "I'm under no delusions about Mister Welles, I'm not brainwashed and I'm *not* love-sick. I know exactly who and what he is. Better than anyone else in this world. I just don't care." She gestured to the cards which surrounded her, sent to her by the other Irregulars. "None of us do. That's the only power he has over the Irregulars. And that's what you never seem to understand. We will help him, because we *want* to help him. We *believe* in Montgomery Welles."

"Why be loyal to someone who has no loyalty in him?"

She thought about that for a moment. "He kept a promise to me once, a long time ago." Oklahoma reminisced, sounding sleepy again. "He didn't have to, but he did. And keeping it made him the man he is today." Her voice broke. "So, I honestly don't care what he does to you or the world. That's not me trying to be mean, that's simply stating a fact. He could take an M40 machine gun to a preschool and I'd back him. He could take an M40 to *me* and I'd back him. I honestly would. Without a second thought. Because I owe that man more than can ever be repaid. Even with my life."

"Must have been some promise he kept."

Oklahoma considered that for a beat, her voice tight. "It was to me."

****

J. Wyatt Ferral was having a really bad week.

He'd been blown up. He'd been hospitalized. He'd spent several days trapped under the sea with Julian. And now he was returning to the city to find that his home had been demolished and his nemesis had basically taken over his business.

At the moment, he was standing in the remains of the Agletarian's former base, doing cleanup and trying to make certain that his team hadn't missed anything.

He glared at the other man, trying not to kill him.

Bobbi seemed to be having similar difficulty. The woman was positively fuming about what had gone down. "I'm taking my department *back*." She spat out.

"It isn't 'your' department." Montgomery reminded her. "It's Miles'."

"And when he's not here, *I'm* in charge of it." Her eyes narrowed. "And he's not here."

"And who exactly are you going to get to *staff* your department?" Monty asked, fake curiosity in his tone. "Elves?"

"I'll think of something."

"The rest of us have been assuming that about you forever, Officer Frith, but you *continue* to disappoint us on that front." He leaned against his cane, eyebrow arching in challenge. "Sadly, it appears that Miles did *indeed* teach you everything he knows." Then he simply walked away, like the entire matter was settled.

Bobbi stared after him, her voice filled with hate. "I am *truly* sorry that he's not dead."

Poacher considered that for a moment. "If it's any consolation, I think he is too."

McPherson stepped in front of Monty, halting his progress. *"There you are you son of a bitch!"* She pointed at him angrily. "Do you have *any* idea the kind of nightmare you've caused!?! I've been on the phone with the Agletarian ambassador all morning! Do you know the number of innocent people you blew up in Agletaria!?!"

"My official policy on that is going to be 'Wait and See,' Agent McPherson." Monty informed her casually, echoing her earlier words. "But the event is developing, so I'll get back to you should the situation warrant." He took on a sneer which he must have thought looked like commiseration. "Do *thank* the ambassador for me and kindly give her my *condolences* on the tragic loss of her friends. It's such a shame when someone's imagined self-importance and estimation of their own power is brought down to earth."

"You also blew up a building in Washington. Took out two cabinet officials." McPherson added darkly. "Which means this is going to be much, much bigger than the city now."

Monty took on a confused expression. "What? Oh, how tragic. I had no idea. What an unfortunate coincidence, that government officials just *happened* to be in the same room as our enemies. What are even the odds of them randomly bumping into one another?"

McPherson's jaw tightened. "One of these days, someone is just going to kill you. You're going to do something, because you're sure you're untouchable, and someone is going to kill you."

"You're welcome to try." Monty spread his arms out from his sides as if offering her an opening, his eyebrows raised expectantly for a moment. Then he lowered them. "No?" He seemed almost disappointed. "Well, you know where I'll be if you can ever garner the courage to act upon the demands of your moral conscience." He started to limp away. "Until then, I have *work to do.*"

Wyatt started after him, limping on his own injured leg. He still wasn't 100%, but he wasn't about to sit idly by while everything his wife had built here fell apart.

"You can't just walk away from this." Wyatt caught up with him and spun him around. "You crossed a line. People *died*. You blew up our home. You shot an *unarmed prisoner in the head*. Our people

494

died on *your* orders. For *your* crazy plan which had an almost *zero* percent chance of succeeding."

"Except it *did*." Monty shot back. "I achieved total victory over an opponent which *everyone* thought unbeatable. I cleared the board of all opposition and stood victorious over an army sent to see us dead and this city in ruins. Business is about taking risks and living with the consequences, *Ferral*."

"Consequences?" Wyatt repeated in amazement. "You mean like the pile of bodies you left behind? The bodies of people that we were *responsible for*? Half of Oz's team, which you used as cannon fodder and sacrificed? The bodies of *perfectly innocent civilians and the people you massacred in Agletaria!?!*"

"That's not my department." Monty reminded him coldly. "I was tasked with winning the war, not worrying about the politics of our victory."

Wyatt shook his head violently, trying to keep his temper in check. "That's *unacceptable*. The responsibilities of the Purchasing and Production Department *do* not include murder."

"This is *war.*" Monty reminded him, as though he may have forgotten. "You show me the war where no one dies and I'll show you the war that wasn't worth fighting."

"This isn't war, this is *crime-fighting*." Wyatt corrected.

"It's the same thing." Monty crossed his arms over his chest. "Fine, you tell me a way out of that situation, where everyone survives and returns to happy homes filled with iddy-bitty kittens." Monty countered. "Go ahead. I'm listening. How do I stop an unstoppable thousand person special forces team and the alien mega-weapons they've acquired, without injuring *anyone*?" He paused, waiting for Wyatt's answer and not hearing it. "I'm sorry? Did you say something?" His expression hardened again. "No. Because when it comes to choosing between the deaths of dozens and the deaths of millions, you just do the best you fucking can and move on." He pointed at Wyatt's chest. "That's part of being a big boy and growing up."

"You. Got. Innocent. People. *Killed*." Wyatt told him flatly, carefully enunciating his words to keep from losing his temper.

"Yes." Monty nodded. "It's call 'sacrifice,' Wyatt. It's how great things get done." He started walking away again. "If you want to ride in the boat, *someone* has to do the rowing. They're dead. There will be others. Friends, enemies, and people neither of us even know yet. People who deserve it and people who are perfectly innocent. Maybe you. Maybe me. But they're all going to die, just the same. No matter what we do. Because that's the world. That's what life is. It's messy and pointless and painful to endure. Welcome to the machine." He entered the large hanger area in the Agletarian's base. "The Agletarians had to believe it was real. If they suspected anything, they never would have charged into the base so quickly, or called us to gloat. Which means, we had to put up a fight. Which means that the security department needed to put on a show, and yes, some of them didn't make it out. But they knew the risks. And it was them or *all of us*."

"They were tasked with guarding our base and watching *you*." Wyatt reminded him. "I can't help but notice that you devised a plan which would put them on the front line and then remove them from the equation. You staked them out like goats, getting the Agletarians to do your dirty work for you. Almost like you didn't want anyone watching you going forward, Montgomery."

Monty stared at him silently for a long moment. "Funny how that worked out, yes." He agreed, voice hard.

Wyatt's jaw clenched, unsure if the man had just confessed to something or was just trying to piss Wyatt off.

Monty ignored Wyatt's inner debate. "How do you think this is all going to end, Wyatt?" He asked, voice sincere now.

Wyatt shook his head. "I don't want to..."

"No, no," Monty interrupted, "I'm serious. How do you think the story of the Consortium of Chaos ends?" He tilted his head to the side. "Do you think someday the world is just going to give us what we want? Do you *really* believe that we're all destined for something *other* than dying for nothing and being forgotten?" He watched him in silence for a moment longer. "Oh, God..." Monty squinted at him, as if seeing him for the first time, "you *do*, don't you? You genuinely do... You poor deluded son of a bitch." He shook his head in genuine pity. "I'm sorry, but life just doesn't work that way for us, Wyatt. That's not what our future *is*. I thought you understood that. You more than anyone. We don't *get* happy endings. No one does. Especially not heroes. Because the future is coming. Whether you want it to or not, the future is coming all the same. And it's always worse than you can *possibly* imagine." Monty started to walk away again.

"I'll worry about 'the future' when it gets here," Wyatt countered, continuing to follow him. "I'm interested in the present at the moment. The Agletarians were calling to negotiate for our surrender and the safe return of the hostage which you then killed in front of them!"

"I needed him to get angry enough to bring Poacher into the

room. Without Poacher there to secure the position, they could have simply turned off the transmission before we were all through the screen." He picked up a clipboard and started to survey the data it contained. "What did you expect, Wyatt?" Monty asked him seriously, his voice almost pitying again. "That we could somehow talk them down? That they'd just throw up their hands once confronted with the blinding light of reason? That their generations of seething hatred for us would be overcome by your natural charisma and they'd realize that they were wrong all along and simply go home in peace?" He shook his head sadly, apparently still genuinely feeling sorry for Wyatt. "The world just doesn't work that way, Wyatt. I know you wish that it did, but it *doesn't*. And the sooner you realize that, the better off you'll all be. I wish I didn't know what you're going to soon find out. But I do. And I make no apologies for it. Because I'm an adult."

"You have no conscience, do you?" Wyatt asked in horrified amazement. "You killed all those people..."

"Having a conscience merely reveals a lack of *conviction*." Monty straightened his suit, his voice resuming its normal conceited and disinterested edge. "Nonviolent solutions are *useless* when dealing with violent problems and violent people. A fight was unavoidable. So, I pissed them off and goaded them into doing something unwise. I minimized our casualties in the best way I could, but people were *always* going to die. Whether your plan or mine, friends were going to die. Innocent people were going to get caught in the crossfire. And you're right: death is stupid and unfair and doesn't make sense." His voice hardened. "But *shit happens*. That's the price of going to war, Wyatt. That's business. And if something's worth killing for, then it's worth dying for. *Grow. Up.*"

"I can't help but notice that *once again* you and your department managed to survive a bloodbath relatively unscathed." Wyatt pointed towards the door. "I didn't see *you* out there sacrificing yourself and paying 'the price of war' by dying for your worthy cause."

"I don't see how you could possibly know *who* was out there and who *wasn't*, since you weren't out there *either*." Monty countered. "If you were sooooo concerned with the lives of the new members in the Security Department, perhaps you should have sent them to safety in the Undersea Base, where you and *everyone else* you cared were hidden, before the first shot was fired." He crossed his arms over his chest. "But you didn't, did you? Because you didn't think *they* mattered as much as *other people*. You thought they could be sacrificed, if it came to that. So don't you come in here, all puffed up and moralizing, acting like you're somehow better than me. *You* left them to die. And so did I. I'm simply more honest about it than you are and am not a hypocrite. Because I see the *big picture.*"

"I was unconscious." Wyatt reminded him.

"Yes, that's seemingly your story *every* time you make a catastrophic mistake." Monty said humoringly, then returned to the argument. "They served their purpose and did their job. And so did I. They were pieces on the board which had to be sacrificed so that the game could continue. And the team won the day as a result."

Wyatt rolled his eyes. "Oh, don't give me that 'team' bullshit." He pointed at the man in anger. "You don't give a damn about the 'team' or the 'big picture,' you care about *you.*" He tilted his head to the side. "And *where* is all the high-tech Agletarian body armor and weapons, Welles? Because it was here earlier and now it's *suspiciously* missing."

"Huh." Monty made a show of looking around. "It *does* seem to have vanished, doesn't it?" He nodded. "I shall have to have Higgins open an investigation on its whereabouts. We wouldn't want that kind of power falling into the wrong hands, now would we?" Monty raised his own hand to his shoulder and snapped his fingers to draw his bodyguard's attention without looking back at her. "Make a note of that, Hildy."

His zombie companion didn't move, she simply bared her teeth in a sinister taunting smile at Wyatt.

"You really think I'm going to let you get away with stealing it, Welles?" Wyatt asked him coldly, stepping closer to the man threateningly. "That I'd *ever* let you have that kind of power?"

"I don't know what you're talking about." Monty responded unemotionally, pretending he didn't even notice the threat. "I'm as surprised by its disappearance as you are."

Wyatt didn't turn around, calling to his friend who he *knew* would back him. "Syd?"

"Thaaaaaaat's bullshit." Poacher announced from his position behind Wyatt. "This whole place *stinks* of Monty's stooges. He stole it."

Monty made a show of complete bafflement. "I really don't understand what you're so angry about. War is about taking away your enemy's ability to *ever* wage war against you again, no matter the personal cost. It's about *hate.* Hate in its truest, most virulent form." His voice hardened. "Life is about *winning,* not about playing fair or making sure everyone makes it home. My mission, as always, was to *win.* And in order to win, I will sacrifice *anything.* You. The city. Me. All of our coworkers. *Everything*. Because at the end of the day, it

498

doesn't matter how many pieces you lose in the process. It only matters that *you've won the goddamn game*." He stood straighter, his face hidden in the shadows cast by the brim of his top hat. "*That* is who I am, Wyatt. Who I've *always* been and all I'll *ever* be." He met Wyatt's gaze with cold unfeeling eyes. "You all knew that going in. You *all* knew who I was and you *knew* what I do. And I was tasked by *your* wife with sending our enemies a message about the consequences of getting in our way. *I sent it.*"

Wyatt looked into the man's emotionless eyes for a long moment, feeling like he was staring into an abyss. The man simply had no pity. No reason. No soul.

"You're *done,* Montgomery." Wyatt told him flatly. "You went too far this time. You hear me? Harlot *didn't* mean this. She *didn't* mean blowing up a country and killing dozens of innocent people!"

Monty watched him silently, the look of sincere pity returning to his face. "If you think that, then you don't know your wife at all."

Wyatt's voice took on a threatening edge, and he could tell he was about five seconds away from killing this man now. "I don't want to see you around our headquarters anymore." He warned flatly. "I don't even know where our new headquarters *will be* now, thanks to you, but you're *not* welcome there." He met the other man's gaze again. "Are we clear?"

Monty processed that and nodded slowly. "And my workers?"

"They'll just have to learn to do *without* your abuse. I'm sure they'll miss their cruel overlord *desperately,* but I think they'll adjust to finally being treated like *people* and not machines." He crossed his arms over his chest. "The Purchasing and Production department is *no longer your concern*. You're a goddamned madman and we're *through with you.*" He jabbed his finger into the other man's chest to accentuate the words and to drive the point home. "You're. *Fired.*"

Monty stood still for a long moment, then simply turned on his heel and marched off.

"You can't fire him for doing what Harlot told him to do." Poacher informed Wyatt, sounding disapproving. "That's not fair."

"He'll get over it."

"Harlot's never gonna let that happen and you know it." Poacher shook his head. "You love your wife too much to go against her and she loves the Consortium too much to fire any of us, even if you think they deserve it. The fact of the matter is that Harlot outranks you here. To most of us, this is still *her* team. She told him to do it, he did it. End of story. You fire him for that and no one is going to want to listen to her anymore."

"He took advantage." Wyatt spat out, recognizing that Syd was probably right about that, but was unwilling to back down. "He knew she was worried and scared, and he was *only too happy* to step in and seize more power for himself."

"Maybe. But Harlot's a clever girl. I think he did exactly what she wanted him to do. He just took it further than she might have liked." He shrugged. "We're stuck with Monty for the duration, Wyatt. He's not going anywhere, and you know it. All you've done here is piss him off." He let out a long, tired sigh. "These are uncertain times. Things are changing, Wyatt. I'm not a smart man, but even I can feel it. A new era is coming. Something *dark. Hungry.* And I'm not sure how we fit into it anymore. There's some messed up shit going down and we're catching the brunt of it. And I genuinely believe this isn't as bad as it'll get. Not by a longshot. So, we're going to have to change with the times or get changed *by them*."

"What do you want me to do, Syd? Huh?" He gestured to their hopefully *ex*-coworker. "Leave someone like *Monty* in power?"

"Someone like Monty is *always* in power, Wyatt. It's the nature of humanity. I understand that. I understand why Monty does what he does and did what he did. I'm not saying it was right or wrong, but it got the job done and it was all for a purpose which I believe in. I have no regrets about helping him do it. The man's got kinks in his soul, but at the end of the day, my people are safe and their enemies are gone." He shook his head. "So, I won't lose any sleep over what he did to those people." His face darkened. "Want me to tell you the part of all this that *is* going to keep me up at night though?" Poacher asked calmly, putting a stick of gum into his mouth. "What'd he need the Weald Forged metal from Rayn's kingdom for?"

The hair on the back of Wyatt's neck stood on end. "...Oh shit." He breathed.

Poacher nodded. "Told ya. It wasn't part of his plan here, so what's he need it for? With that stuff, he can kill anybody here, whether they're impervious or not. That shit'll cut through anything and anyone like a razor blade through a poodle. And we *gave it to him*." Poacher started towards the far wall and the refreshments set up there. "These are uncertain times, man." He shook his head sadly. "Uncertain fucking times."

Wyatt looked down at the floor, considering that.

Behind him, there was the sound of a microphone turning on

and then clapping from the people in attendance.

The doors opened and more Irregulars excitedly rushed in.

Wyatt turned around slowly, knowing what was about to happen before he even saw it.

"They told me that I could not do this." Monty said into the microphone from the stage.

There were yells of anger at that idea from the audience, and Monty waited seemingly forever to continue. Minutes ticked by but he remained silent, always appearing *just* on the verge of speaking again, building up the anticipation until the audience was *desperate* for his words.

"They *told me*," Monty finally continued, "that there was no way that I could stop an army." He finally proclaimed, causing the audience to shout their support for his abilities, but this time Monty talked right over them. "They *told me* that it would be *foolish* to even *attempt* to fight these invaders! That we should submit!" The audience was angry now, screaming for the blood of anyone who would doubt him. Monty nodded, as if accepting their rage and understanding it. "They *told me*, that I would *fail* because I knew *nothing* about warfare. And do you know what I told *THEM!?!*" Cheers from the audience. "...I told them they were *right.*"

Silence.

A few confused murmurs.

"I told them that I *couldn't* do this. That I was just one man, and wasn't strong enough." He raised his voice. "But that *together* with my beloved Irregulars, we would *see it done!* Trust in *them* I said, because they will not *break*. Trust in THEM, I said, because they have *never failed me and they never will!* Trust in THEM, I said, because they have NEVER met a challenge or an enemy which *THEY COULD NOT CONQUER!*"

Thunderous applause and cheers.

"It is like my mother always said: '*The man who has the most friends, wins the fight.*' And once again, my friends, we have shown our detractors and the malcontents who seek to take what is *ours*, that there is simply NOTHING we cannot accomplish TOGETHER! ONCE AGAIN, my friends, we have shown those that thought themselves our *betters*, that we REFUSE to be cast aside and forgotten! ONCE AGAIN, my friends, we have stood together and shown the *entire world*, that *NOTHING will stop us from achieving our destiny! NOTHING!!!*"

Wyatt started towards the stage before this turned into an outright riot.

"They say that I am your cruel overlord." Monty told the

assembly, pointing at Wyatt and attributing the words to him. "That I mistreat you. They say that you are a *cult*, and that I am a lying *snake*." He paused for a breath to let his minions stew over that. "And do you know what I told *them?* I told them they were *right*. I DO mistreat you. Because no matter how much I try to do for you, it is not NEARLY enough to show you my appreciation for how much you've done for *me* over the years." He removed his top hat and ran a hand through his slick black hair as though reminiscing with old friends. "We've *worked* together." He pointed at his gunshot wound. "We've fought together... *Bled* together. We've *buried our own* together." He nodded, as though deeply moved at the memory. "We've... we've..." He put his hand up to his face, as if too emotional to even go on. "Right now, our own sweet Oklahoma Mike is in the hospital, because I asked her to help the Consortium, and then one of its members savagely and *viciously* attacked her!" He pointed at his own chest. "That's on *me*. That's *my* burden to bear and it's one which keeps me up at night."

Wyatt continued towards the stairs to the stage, working his way through the crowd.

"I told them, that if it is a 'cult' to be willing to sacrifice yourself for your family, your home and for noble ideals, then this is the most powerful cult in the world!" He shouted into the mic. "I TOLD THEM, that I *am* a snake. A *dangerous* snake, far deadlier than any they've yet found, and that I have a family of *hundreds of other snakes just like me, and not to cross us!*" He shook his head in righteous fury. "I told our enemies to *STEER CLEAR* of our nest! Just *let us be!* FOR WE ARE MANY! I told them not to make the mistake that so many have made before, and underestimate how *fiercely* we will *protect what is ours!* I told them that if they attack us, then *we will strike!* If they hit us, *we will hit them harder!* If they threaten us, then we will *ACT FIRST!*"

Wyatt started up the stairs.

"They say that I am powerless." Monty continued. "They call me a 'Mystery Man.' They *laugh* at me. Think they can *take* what *I* built and give it to an *outsider*, because I lack powers! And do you know what I told *them?* I said they were WRONG. *Dead wrong!* I said: 'If you want to see my super-power, look out there...'" He pointed out over the audience. "'*THERE* is my super-power! My power beats in the heart of *every one* of my Irregulars!'" He pounded his clenched fist against his chest several times, hard enough to undoubtedly leave bruises. "*That* is all the power that I will *ever* need! Because with their help and trust, there is NOTHING I cannot build! There is NO ONE I cannot STOP! There is *NOTHING I CANNOT DO!!!"*

The crowd exploded in louder cheers.

Monty held up a hand, calling for silence and the roar died down immediately. "And now, Wyatt has an announcement to make." He held up the microphone to Wyatt, covering it with his hand. "Go ahead. Tell them about your change in management and how much better they'll all be without me. *See* who they support." A cruel smile crossed his face, a glint of eagerness in his eye. "Come on... I *dare you*, you sanctimonious prick. Try to take what's mine. It'll be funny."

Wyatt thought seriously about killing the man right then and there, but recognized that it would probably be a bad idea.

Instead, he stormed from the stage, and Monty's maniacal taunting laughter filled the room.

Monty put both hands over his head in victory, then shouted in the microphone. *"Together, friends! Together, we can tear down the Heavens themselves! Walk my crooked mile, and nothing can stop us! THE FUTURE IS OURS!!!"* He yelled into the microphone like some crazed dictator, holding up a clenched fist, his overcoat blowing behind him in the breeze from the open hanger door. *"WHO WILL HELP ME TAKE IT!?! WHO WILL HELP ME TAKE WHAT IS OURS!?! WHO WILL STAND WITH ME!?!"*

The crowd cheered louder than ever now, jumping to their feet in support and to volunteer themselves to his service; a wild screaming frenzy of unbridled support and adulation for their boss. They began chanting *"WELLES! WELLES! WELLES! WELLES!"* at the top of their lungs, while pumping their fists in the air. The entire room began to reverberate with their manic exaltation of the man, until it felt like the building itself might collapse due to their hysteria. It was as if God himself had come down from on high and was walking amongst his most fervent believers, performing miracles.

Monty put his head back and laughed again. A booming hysterical sound that wasn't at all pleasant. It was terrifying; raw and unhinged. A madman reaching his audience and realizing how powerful he had truly become.

"TO THE STRONGEST!" He yelled into the microphone, then dropped it to the stage like a rockstar. He held his arms up again absorbing their love, a sinister smirk on his face. He basked for a moment longer, then jumped down from the stage and began to slowly limp through the crowd, accepting their handshakes and teary gratitude.

The Irregulars began to sing the old hymn *"Bringing in the Sheaves"* for some reason, as though it held deeper meaning for them.

It was eerie. Like something out of a horror movie.

And for the first time in as long as he could remember, Wyatt was *genuinely* afraid.

Monty stopped in front of him, meeting his eyes. "I cannot *be* fired from the Consortium, Wyatt. I'm not trying to take it over. I'm *already* in control of it. I have been for quite some time. I *am* the Consortium. Try to threaten that again and I'll use it to *rip you apart*." He started to limp away. "Congratulations on the baby, by the way. My Irregulars on the nursing staff tell me that he's simply *adorable*."

Wyatt's control snapped and he went for the man, intent on cutting him down. He formed a telekinetic weapon and threw it at him.

Draugr stepped into the path of the dagger and blocked it with her shield, then bared her teeth at Wyatt.

Poacher grabbed the back of Wyatt's shirt to pull him away, and leveled his elephant gun at the Viking woman. "Not the best time, man." Sydney warned Wyatt seriously, gesturing to their surroundings.

The Irregulars had stopped their cheering and were now suddenly silent and watching Wyatt like something out of *The Birds*. Predatory eyes stared at him. Waiting.

"The man with the most friends wins the fight." Monty put his fist over his head and the audience *boomed* with thunderous applause once again, like robots being activated by their operator.

"This isn't over, Montgomery!" Wyatt yelled after him, his words all but lost in the screaming hysterical crowd. "*This isn't over!*"

"I agree *completely*." Monty turned around, still smiling evilly. "My good man, this is only *the beginning*."

Author's Note

&

Commentary on book

"GROWING UP, LIZZY'S FAVORITE DWARF WAS GRUMPY. HER FAVORITE CARE BEAR WAS GRUMPY. HER FAVORITE MUPPET WAS OSCAR THE GROUCH. HER FAVORITE SMURF WAS GARGAMEL. SHE VOTED FOR COBRA. SHE WATCHED RETURN TO OZ AN UNHEALTHY NUMBER OF TIMES. AND SHE ALWAYS NAMED ALL OF HER TOYS AFTER HERSELF. PSYCHOLOGICALLY, I'M NOT SURE WHAT ANY OF THAT MEANS, BUT IT'S PROBABLY NOT GOOD."

- My sister Cassandra's description of me.

This is a weird book.

I've been writing it since I was working on book 2 of this series, *The Son of Sun and Sand*. It was meant to be book 4 of the series, but I decided to do *Electric Hazard* instead. And then it was going to be book 5, but *The Only Fish in the Sea* took its spot.

It wasn't troubled, it's just... weird. It was a tough book to write, because it has a lot of moving parts and both of the main characters are uniquely insane. So, I'd write a couple of chapters, then think about it for months at a time while writing other books. Ultimately, my breakthrough came during a moment last year when I was using Clorox wipes to clean the fan blades in my living room (...don't judge me) and Cassie was watching me like I was out of my damn mind, and casually commented, "How is Oz even going to have a girlfriend? He's going to be totally grossed out by that." And then I realized that she was right. The biggest issue in the Mull/Oz romance wasn't Mull's insanity, it was Oz's. And, also, that we needed to use antibacterial wipes on the fan's dome light more often, because it was very dusty. I'm not overtly obsessive compulsive... but when you think about it, Oz is right. Dust is totally gross.

Even keeping the central dynamic in mind though, it's still difficult to get right and one of the reasons why the book took so long to finish. Certain sections weren't right tonally. This book is a mix of very serious dramatic material and very screwball comedy elements, and sometimes it just wasn't working. So I had to re-write portions of it and try again. I don't usually do that, but this book left me little choice. Mainly, it was all how they related to each other. Because there are different ways that Oz could react to things, all of which would be in character, but only some of which keep the scene moving. It has to be done in such a way that they both think they're the straightman to the other's insanity. And if they talk about crazy things long enough, their different viewpoints ultimately come down to philosophical differences, which is interesting. Because I always just assume characters say crazy things because they're crazy, but they could back them up and remain consistent. Which is nice.

Multifarious came from the popular culture stock character of the ninja or constantly masked hero. I arrived at it from a different direction though, realizing that a villain who constantly changed costumes and names would be fun (although obviously better suited for a visual medium, where the change could be better delivered, but I can't draw, so whatever). As originally conceived, the character wouldn't be masked and would always have the same powers though. But for some reason, Mull just didn't want to do that. I deliberately avoided mentioning powers early on, but they kept trying to appear anyway. Eventually, I gave in and just decided to have a new power every day, which I feel is somewhat reminiscent of other characters in popular culture, but I couldn't help it. That's just what Natalie wanted to do, and it made for more interesting story possibilities, since she could have god-like powers one day, and be essentially powerless the next. Mull is the character you get when you're watching online videos of Buster Keaton stunts, while listening to Queen's *Don't Stop Me Now* and the Glitchmob remix of *Derezzed* from the *Tron: Legacy* soundtrack.

Kilroy was my first attempt to add the ninja/masked character to the team. I stumbled across the image one day while researching folk figures, and my grandfather was a WWII vet, so the image struck a chord with me. I liked the idea of all of the doodles actually somehow being drawn by the same guy, who's just been everywhere. I soon realized that it would make sense to blend Kilroy and the character who wore a new outfit every day. Because the masked character would need one aspect of their outfit to carry over from day to day, just so that they'd be recognizable. In retrospect, I probably should have stuck with the Kilroy name for both Roy and for Nat, but by that point I liked the name Multifarious, meaning "many" or "varied," because it also reminded me of the words "furious" and "nefarious." Keeping the same name for both would have opened up more story options though and explain why she chose to continue dressing like Kilroy. But again, Nat didn't want to do that, so whatever. Once a character decides to do something, there's very little I can do to stop it.

Natalie's name and general look comes from a character/actress on a soap opera I happened to be watching at the time I was writing her first scene. At the time, I fully intended the other character in the scene (the salesclerk named "Chad Beck") to be Mull, and just introduced Natalie as a scene filler character. "Mr. Chad" is another name for the "Kilroy" doodle, after all. For some reason though, Natalie really began to speak to me, and almost immediately replaced Chad as Mull in my mind. I hadn't even finished the scene before the switch was made. It reminded me of the "Metroid" video game, which features a female protagonist who wears a mechanical suit, and the movie "*Shenandoah*," where Jimmy Stewart's frontier daughter joins him in rescuing her missing boyfriend. I've always liked her. She's not in the movie a lot, but I like that character anyway. Anyway, I knew that Mull would be the group's sniper, and that reminded me of the film "*Quigley Down Under*" and Quentin seemed to fit, although in retrospect, that really makes absolutely no sense. At all. If that were true, why didn't I just name her "Quigley"? Weird. I don't understand the way my mind works sometimes. But, in any case, that's why she's named what she is. It doesn't make any sense, but there it is.

For the record, yes, Mull and Mercygiver were always the same person in my mind. That's why no one ever uses pronouns to refer to Ronnie (Jack just says "Boss" or "that psycho") and the horrible things he did over the course of the series were always to horrible people. His knowledge of their shared situation seems to come and go though, so I'm not really sure what's going on there. But it seems to make sense to him, so I don't question. He's named "Rondel" because it's another name for a mercygiver dagger.

For his part, Oz is named Oz because I was naming him "Oscar" after *The Odd Couple*, only to suddenly remember halfway through *Yesterday's Heroes* that Oscar was the *messy* one in The *Odd Couple*. He needed to have a name that started with "O" though, and by that point people were already calling him "Oz," so I needed to choose something close. I happened to be watching a documentary on the Kennedy assassination at the time, so there you go. Oswald. A horrible namesake, but whatever. If asked, I'll lie and say he's named after something else. In retrospect though, I wonder if I shouldn't have gone with Oscar anyway. Because an "Oscar the Grouch" reference could have worked too. He was always my favorite on *Sesame Street*. Hmm... But then I couldn't have Oz's aunt point out why he was named "Oswald," which wouldn't be nearly as fun. Tyrant actually calls him "Oscar" in one of the earlier books, but I'm not certain if that's a mistake on my part or Kass just doesn't even know the man's name. To be honest, I think both are just as likely. I've never bothered to correct it.

I usually have no idea what characters look like, so your own personal interpretations are as good as mine on that front. Natalie seems to think she looks like the Wendy's mascot, but I have no way of knowing if she's right on that front or not. In my head, my characters' appearances are always kind of blurry. I don't know why. They look different ways at different times, so feel free to imagine them any way you want. However you see them, you're not wrong. Sometimes people write me with actors/actresses they would personally want to see in a role, and I'm completely useless on that front. My reply is usually something like, "Okay... well, he's good in everything, so he'd be a good choice for this too." Because I don't really think of things that way, and neither does Cassie. Well... she knows *exactly* who should play Gion and has since forever, but that's her deal so I'll let her tell it.

And I don't see the books in terms of "authorial intent," so my own personal interpretations on what's going on and what the characters think are really just as good as yours. My writing process is basically feeling like I'm watching the characters talk and trying to write down what they're saying, so I don't always claim to know what's going on either. I generally don't intend my books to be allegories for anything, but if you can come up with one, than more power to you. I am not the sole arbiter on how my books can be interpreted. To be honest, sometimes people see stuff in our books that I know for a fact we didn't intend, but they make a good case for it. By the end, I'm halfway convinced too. That's the beautiful part of "art" (and I use that term to mean simply "a creative work" rather than conceited "my work is high art and I'm an ARTIST!" way, because I'm absolutely not like that at all). We all view things in different ways, which is why discussing art is more interesting than discussing something which is entirely objective. And sometimes people *do* actually spot things I'm deliberately foreshadowing, which is always nice. So, I can tell you that I didn't intend something and that it doesn't fit my own personal "head canon" going forward (and since I'm the one writing it, that's probably the interpretation the series will go with), but I'm not going to tell you you're wrong or that you can't have your own opinions on it. You're free to interpret anything I write, however you want. Hell, go nuts. To be honest, I think that's one of the coolest parts of fandom. I'm entirely supportive of that. My goal is to make sure that everything associated with me and Star Turtle is welcoming and friendly. I assure you, I won't freak out at you for disagreeing with me about something or not liking something I've done. You paid your money, you're allowed to have an opinion. You're never wrong in my world, just so you know.

As always, I make absolutely NO attempt to make these books geographically accurate. I recognize that there is a great deal of distance between different areas of the city, and between the city and the Pine Barrens, for that matter. I've spent a large portion of my life in the NJ/NY area. I just choose to ignore it. Because I don't care. At all. This is a deliberate choice on my part. I don't feel the need to share my knowledge of the area with you or my own personal feelings about the many exciting neighborhoods you could find in the actual cities. Because these *aren't* the actual cities, these are my cities. And I don't care about any of that.

I did indeed try peanut butter and jelly on a waffle, after Natalie suggested it. Turns out, I agree with her. I really like it.

Agletaria is named after an "aglet," the little plastic tip on shoelaces. I don't remember why I chose that. I think I just like the word.

I have absolutely no idea why it's "Drews" department store. Why is there no apostrophe there? I feel like I'm naming it after someone or something, but I don't remember who or what.

It took me a week solid to choose between Hanson's *MMMBOP* and The Cowsill's *Indian Lake*. I think I made the right choice. But... but I still love *Indian Lake*. If this were a movie, I'd try to use them both. They're the *perfect* Natalie songs. Particularly if Mull is killing people to them.

Yes, Oz's fox hunting replacement outfit is a nod to the classic Cary Grant and Katherine Hepburn film *Bringing Up Baby.* If you haven't seen it, you should. It's one of my favorites. Cary Grant is forced to wear an outfit like that in the film for awhile, due to similar circumstances.

And yes, chapter 28 is what happens when I drink too much coffee. I DO NOT react well to coffee. I do it sometimes because it makes me productive (insane, but productive), but then I'm literally awake and weird for 36 hours. The Natalie/Oz/Mercygiver love scene was written in the middle of that. In the 30+ sleepless hours which resulted from 1 cup of Holiday Blend coffee: I wrote four full chapters, outlined another book, walked 11 miles around and around my neighborhood, and vacuumed the house four separate times. But yeah, that's something I never would have written without coffee. I had most of that chapter written already, and in that version Natalie and Oz were making beautiful and respectful love (exactly like Holly predicted) and then Nat joked about the fact Ronnie wasn't involved, and my caffeine addled brain was like, "...Oh, we're absolutely doing *that!*" and I started over. The chapter kinda freaks me out, to be honest. Probably should have re-thought that one. I still might take it out, actually. As I'm writing this, I'm rethinking it. If you're reading this and that scene didn't happen, forget I said anything. Move along, move along...

Time spent on writing it: ...Jeez, I don't know. The first version I have of it is dated April of 2013, but I was working on it before then, it just didn't have its own file yet. But I've written 5 or 6 other books in that same time period, so I wasn't working on this the whole time.

Favorite part: their entire relationship is built around "The Pile of Mail I Don't Want to Open" and the fact that Natalie is going to use a fork to stir her drink rather than washing a spoon. Literally. Those ideas are the basis for Natalie's entire character.

First chapter written: it's no longer in the book, actually. I cut it out. It was Mull and Oz on a mission, which would have been the first chapter. But the end of *The Only Fish in the Sea* meant that it had to go because it no longer fit into continuity. First fully completed chapter included in the book? Probably Oz's chapters in the hospital. The rest of the book was written in roughly chronological order, with some sequences written in advance and then added in once I caught up to them.

Favorite line: Monty says some stuff so horrible that I end up loving it. And for some reason, I really like Nat's idea about Taiwanese kickboxers. It makes me smile every time. I wish this were a visual medium, so I could have gotten to see her imaginary world where they're both street enforcers in Taiwan. I'm imagining Oz dressed like a villain in a 1990s Jean-Claude Van Damme movie now, and I think that's awesome.

If you enjoyed this book, please leave a review on Amazon or anywhere else you feel like. The more reviews our books get, the more books we sell. The more books we sell, the more money we make, which means the more time we'll have to write, rather than working depressing joyless jobs. So, if you want more books, faster, leave reviews. Seriously, leave reviews.

Please feel free to email me if you have any questions or comments about the book, series, characters, life in general, or just feel like chatting about other Star Turtle books: starturtlepublishing@gmail.com. I actually do answer all of my email, eventually, so while I can't guarantee my answer will make any sense, you will receive one. The same email can also be used to sign up for our mailing list, for news about our upcoming books.

Thanks again for reading! Hope to see you again in the next one!

Printed in Great Britain
by Amazon